Bridget Wood is the daughter of an Irish actor and after a convent education worked in newspapers and the legal profession. She now lives and writes in Staffordshire.

SORCERESS is her fourth fantasy, an eerie and disturbing fusion of Christian and pagan mythology.

Also by Bridget Wood

Wolfking
The Lost Prince
Rebel Angel

Sorceress

Bridget Wood

First published in 1994
by HEADLINE BOOK PUBLISHING

First published in paperback in 1994
by HEADLINE BOOK PUBLISHING

A HEADLINE FEATURE paperback

10 9 8 7 6 5 4 3 2 1

ISBN 0 7472 4490 1

Typeset by Keyboard Services, Luton

Printed and bound in Great Britain by
Cox & Wyman Ltd, Reading, Berks

HEADLINE BOOK PUBLISHING
A division of Hodder Headline PLC
338 Euston Road
London NW1 3BH

Sorceress

Chapter One

Theodora had stolen downstairs soon after the banquet began, and had gone quietly along the passages that led to Great-grandfather's Chamber of the Sorcery Looms.

She would quite have liked to be present at the banquet, but probably it would be boring, with everyone falling out and some people falling asleep. Father would glumly count up how much wine was being consumed, and Mother would count the silver after the Mugains had left the table, and everybody else would count Rumour's newest tally of gowns. Rumour, who was Theo's cousin, was supposed to be reckless and extravagant, and also something called 'wanton', which sounded bad but fun; people like Herself of Mugain and Great-aunt Fuamnach murmured things about Rumour behind their hands which Theo was not supposed to hear, on account of being only six and a half. But Theo liked Rumour best of all the Amaranths. She liked the way that Rumour smiled as if she found people amusing and life great fun, and she liked the way Rumour told marvellous stories, and the way she wore dazzling silk gowns and unexpected headdresses. Theo suspected that Rumour did it just because people expected it. 'My dear, I have a reputation to keep up,' Rumour might have said, winking at Theo on the side no one could see.

To get to the Chamber of the Looms you had to go along dark and rather gusty corridors. They were dark because Mother said she was not going to spend good money on lighting the passages, especially since no one but Nechtan ever used them. Theodora was strictly forbidden to use the passages on her own; Mother had thinned her lips in the way she did when she was displeased, and had said, 'Spies and renegades from *you know where*.' Father had looked solemn and said, 'You never knew what you might

1

find prowling about', and Theodora was please not to go there by herself.

'You know where' meant the Dark Ireland, Theo knew that. It was very important – well, it was vital really – that you did not let any of the creatures from the evil bad Dark Ireland get in to the Palace.

But Great-grandfather Nechtan had spun all kinds of good strong enchantments to keep the Dark Ireland out, and so long as you were very quiet and so long as you were very stealthy, you could go along the passages and reach the Looms Chamber and be perfectly safe.

She would be perfectly safe now. She had taken a candle in a silver bracket, because of the darkness. As she went along, it flickered in the horrid, whispery winds and threw huge shadows on the walls. She did not mind the shadows, or not very much, because she had seen them before. They were roaming enchantments; spells that had somehow slid away from the Looms. They were nearly always friendly, and they would talk to Theodora in the Ancient Language of Cadence, which was the magical tongue of sorcery. Hardly anybody could speak in Cadence these days because it had been lost to the Amaranths during the terrible Wars, but Theodora could follow it a little, because Great-grandfather sometimes lapsed into it when he was angry or excited, and Theo had listened without him being aware of it, and also she had picked up a bit from the enchantments. Sometimes the enchantments were lost and confused, and had to be shown the way back to the Looms and put with their friends.

The shadow tonight was not very friendly-looking. It was following her, tiptoeing along after her, holding up huge, grotesque hands that looked as if they were poised to catch her up.

Theo took a deep breath and walked a bit faster. Probably it was nothing to worry about. Probably it was simply one of the horrid dark enchantments that Great-grandfather had spun for the High King and the Court to help keep out the necromancers of the Dark Ireland and the Human-greedy Fomoire.

Theodora knew all about the Fomoire and the Dark Ireland, because Great-grandfather had often talked to her about it:

2

sometimes chuckling to himself as he stirred something that was bubbling over a fire, or measuring a skein of thread that would be woven into a spell; but sometimes looking very solemn indeed. Theodora would curl up in the chimney-corner of the workroom, which was the best place in all Ireland, and listen, her cheeks flushed from the fire, her eyes shining, watching the tall, robed figure that moved between the Looms and in and out of the rows of vellum-bound books that were the famous *Amaranth Chronicles*.

'The Dark Ireland,' said Great-grandfather, fixing Theodora with his long brilliant Amaranth eyes, and gesturing with his slender white Amaranth hands, 'is fearsome and evil and malevolent, Theodora, and when you are old enough you will take the Solemn Vow to keep it from the true Ireland at all costs.'

Theodora would take the Vow when she was eighteen, which was what all Amaranths did, but she would not take it in the Language of Cadence, because of it having been lost, which was rather a pity.

'*Has* it been lost?' said Great-grandfather, his expression suddenly amused. 'Has it indeed been lost? Well, they may think so if they wish. You and I know better, little one.'

And then, just as Theodora would have liked to know more about the Lost Language of Sorcery, and why it had been lost and who had lost it and how, Great-grandfather would be off again, telling Theo all the stories. He would tell about the terrible wicked Dark Lords, who had come rampaging out of the Dark Realm in the past, and who had tried to take Ireland for their own. He would tell about the defeat of the Fomoire, and also about the truly dreadful Fisher King, who had been driven back by the Amaranths themselves at the very end of the Wars, but whose dying curse had been that he would one day return, and that his spawn would destroy their House for ever.

'But he was defeated,' said Great-grandfather, frowning. 'The Fisher King was defeated,' he said, and Theo looked up because it had sounded as if Great-grandfather was talking to himself for a moment, and in that same moment there had been something in his voice that had been unsure.

'They were all defeated,' said Nechtan a little louder, and Theo remained silent, because she knew that even though the

3

Fomoire and the Fisher King had been vanquished, there were others who had not.

Nechtan said, very softly, 'They were all defeated save for two,' and Theo inched nearer to the fire and whispered the words that came next.

'*They were all defeated save the Lord of Chaos and his Lady . . .*'

It was important not to think too much now about how Great-grandfather had enjoyed weaving his enchantments, and thinking up new ways of keeping the creatures of the Dark Ireland at bay for the High King. Great-grandfather was dying upstairs – Mother had been annoyed, and had compressed her lips all over again, and said, 'Dying, and without the slightest *warning*!' – and all of the family had gathered to find out who Great-grandfather's successor would be.

It was important not to think about the Dark Lords as well, especially when you were stealing along to the Chamber of the Looms, where you were not supposed to be in the first place, and when everyone else in the Porphyry Palace was upstairs in the marble hall, feeding and drinking and trying to decipher the ancient Ritual of Succession. Theodora would not think about it. She especially would not think about the Fomoire and their caves where they kept Humans, and fattened them for their skins.

She scurried down the last bit of passage and through the Silver Door.

Behind her, the shadow loped its grotesque way forward.

The great Sorcery Chamber of the Silver Looms, where the dying Nechtan had woven his strong magic, hummed with nascent bewitchments and shimmered with glinting rainbow iridescence. Theodora felt the warmth and the scents and the enchantment-laden shadows close about her, and it was familiar and comforting and safe after the horrid gusty passages with the lurking shadows.

There were the warm scents of ancient magic and frequently spun bewitchments, and just beneath the surface was the faint ebbing and flowing of something dark and secretive.

Theo stood for a long time just inside the door, waiting for her eyes to adjust. There was a soft spill of radiance from the Looms, and from the tumbling raw magic that lay all anyhow at

4

the feet of the giant Looms, waiting to be formed into spells. The unhewn spells gleamed as Theo moved cautiously nearer; they sent spears of rainbow light across the floor, so that there were harlequin patterns at the Chamber centre, crimson and purple and pink. It was very quiet now, and Theo could hear the live magic stirring.

The live magic stirring . . .

There was a moment when everything was normal and familiar and friendly, and then – she was not sure how it happened – there was another moment when nothing was normal and everything was sinister and creeping and threatening. Theo, her skin prickling with sudden apprehension, stretched her every instinct to its fullest point.

There is something evil *in here* . . .

The Silver Door swung shut behind her with a satisfied little click, and Theo turned. In the same moment, the shadows clotted and coalesced and slithered nearer, making a black creeping river between her and the door.

There is something in here and I am shut in with it . . .

The Looms towered above her, black and silver and ivory, their feet embedded in the ground, but their heads and arms seeming to reach out to the source of their power. If you looked at them through half-closed eyes, you could nearly imagine that they were massive giants, with great legs buried in the floor, and immense shoulders and arms reaching up, their blank faces turned to the skies, far beyond the Porphyry Palace, far into some infinity.

Theo could hear the power in them; she could see it and she could feel it. A dull thrumming on the air. And there was gentle sly movement everywhere, the occasional darting of a silver thread, or the pouring of a skein of brilliant crimson across the floor. Magic is alive, Great-grandfather had said. It is alive, just as we are alive, so you cannot expect it to stay exactly where it is put.

But it was not raw magic, it was not uncut sorcery that was slithering at the core of the shadows.

Theo knew the soft rustlings that enchantments made before they were formed and moulded and shaped. She knew about the gentle whisperings and about the sudden silken movements, and about the silvery scurryings and the darting lights, and the glancing notes of sweet music that touched the air and then vanished.

The sounds she was hearing now were none of these things. Theodora stood very still and tried to see into the deep shadows and tried to hear the sounds coming from the far end of the Chamber.

Scratching sounds. *Cold* sounds. Sounds that made you think of words like claws and that made you think of things like slithery tails and inward-slanting red eyes. And something else . . . Something that was scaly and leathery and that might be finned as well; something that might have webbed hands and feet, and horrid lidless eyes; something that would come loping out of the dark on its great long legs with reaching, clutching hands that would wind about your neck and cover your eyes, so that you could not see what was going to happen to you . . .

Every one of the stories told by Nechtan tumbled through Theo's mind. The Dark Lords and the Fomoire, forever trying to find a way into the real Ireland, forever covetous of the Porphyry Palace itself . . . The Lord of Chaos and his terrible henchmen who were called Murder and Anarchy and Misrule. It might even be the Fisher King, the huge repulsive piscine creature, who had squirmed out of his dank ocean palace nearly a century earlier, and who had been vanquished, but who had vowed with his dying breath to return:

'*My spawn will return to destroy those who have vanquished me . . .*'

Supposing the Fisher King had found a way to return . . . ?

Theodora drew in a deep breath, and in the same moment a soft, slimy, *cold* voice close by, said, 'Come over here, little girl.'

The banquet that had cost so much was very nearly disintegrating into chaos.

Cerball, who had given up trying to compute the exact cost of it all, had tried to persuade everyone to go along up to the dying Nechtan's bedchamber before they began the ancient Succession Ritual. Visiting the Head of the Amaranths for the last time was something they all ought to do, said Cerball, tucking his chins firmly into his neck, and trying not to see Himself of Mugain helping himself and his immediate neighbours to yet another flagon of Cerball's best tawnyfire wine. But when it

6

came to it, visiting a dying sorcerer was not something anyone was very enthusiastic about. Laigne, Cerball's wife, had said at once that Echbel could not go because he was far too sensitive to watch anyone dying, and Great-aunt Fuamnach gave this her unexpected support, because dying was something people ought to do quietly and as inconspicuously as possible.

'We'll have the procession to the Cadence Tower,' said the Mugain of Moire who could not be doing with deathchamber rituals. 'We'll go along altogether, and Cerball and I will pronounce the Ritual. As Elders,' he said, in case anyone should have forgotten this. 'And then,' said the Mugain, firmly, 'we'll all come back up here for a drop of mulled wine.'

This necessitated everyone getting up from the table, which took rather a long time because the Mugain had to find the five-branched torch, and then Rumour had to be prised away from the bevy of young sorcerers who had gathered admiringly about her, and several cousins were found to have gone off exploring the palace, so that they had to be rounded up. And then, just as they were all set to start out, Cerball dropped the Ritual, and everyone had to crawl under the table to retrieve it, and it was finally discovered with somebody's soup splashes on it, so that it had to be sponged off, and it all took time. It was not at all in keeping with something as solemn and ancient as a Succession Ritual to splash it with soup, and it was none of it in keeping with the dignity that should attend the dying of the Head of the Royal Sorcerers. Laigne, who liked to think she was a firm but fair-minded mother, was very glad to think that Theodora was too young to be present at the banquet, while as for that hussy Rumour, Laigne told Cerball that the wanton creature would enter the Porphyry Palace again only under the most extreme of necessities, and probably only over Laigne's dead body.

'I would not soil my best slippers with the dust of the place, if you want the truth,' said Rumour, who had actually had the effrontery to present herself in one of her scarlet silk gowns with swirling tongues woven into it and precious little top to it. She smiled in a catlike fashion through her long green eyelashes and twitched the silken skirts of the indecorous gown about her ankles, sending out several hissing sounds as she did so, causing several people to back away in alarm because Rumour had the nasty way of summoning the Whisperers when you least

7

expected it. The Whisperers, who had served Rumour ever since anyone could remember, were nasty, ten-inch-high dwarfs, with grinning faces and huge, flapping ears, who scurried under people's feet and told terrible stories behind their hands, and who went by names like Slander and Scurrilousness and Lies. Rumour could summon them with mischievous facility and, as Cerball said, they were always extraordinarily ugly and inflicted quite the nastiest of barbs in people's minds. You did not really want to hear one of Rumour's dwarfs scurrying about, telling the entire Amaranthine clan that your wife had spent all your money, or that your best friend was bedding down with your youngest daughter, or that you yourself were inches from a debtors' prison.

It was the kind of thing that Rumour was good at. 'Well, she has plenty of practice,' said Great-aunt Fuamnach, crossly. 'Doesn't she bring those nasty creatures everywhere she goes?'

'As guards, dearest Great-aunt,' said Rumour, who had indeed summoned the Whisperers, and had sent half a dozen Gossips dancing about the floor, with the solemn purpose of informing the company that the Mugain was the next best thing to impotent, and that Herself was seeking consolation with grooms and gardeners, and the occasional vegetable marrow.

'I am bereft and alone in the world,' said Rumour, promptly deriving as much enjoyment out of the situation as was possible. She clasped green-tipped hands which matched her eyelashes to her breast. 'I am alone and unprotected, and my poor loyal Whisperers are my only armour against a cruel world.'

Laigne started to say that Rumour had always been a shocking liar, when Rumour suddenly turned and fixed her eyes on the door, and said, in a voice sharpened with interest, 'My dear cousins, it seems we have an uninvited guest at the feast.'

Framed in the doorway at the far end of the great banqueting hall was the cowled figure of a black-robed monk.

Andrew had approached the gleaming Palace of the Amaranth Sorcerers with extreme caution. He was not especially awed by it because he had seen several such places in England. His own monastery was a huge sprawling stone building; once, he thought, the stronghold of some long-dead Saxon chieftain, which St Augustine's followers had found decayed and almost derelict, and had had renewed and rebuilt. He was accustomed to the English castles and fortresses, and he was beginning to be accustomed to the Irish ones.

Because he dared leave no place unexplored if he was to fulfil the strange mission laid on him by Brother Stephen, he must go up to the doors of every towering fortress, every dark stronghold in Ireland's wild, pagan land. He must knock on the gates of the palaces and the mansions and the castles and request admittance. And, once inside, once accepted as a guest, he must question and search and listen.

But he had not bargained for pagan Ireland being so beautiful and so darkly seductive. More than once the thought that it would be a pity to lose the myth-soaked religions and the time-crusted rituals flickered dangerously on his mind. But he had been warned about this, and he was here not to convert but to fulfil a quest; he had been chosen above all the others to capture the traitor.

The traitor. The renegade. The wild, rebellious Monk who had broken free of the cloistered monastic world.

Andrew knew a little of the creature's history, for when he had entered the Order, young and idealistic and fervent, the story was already a dark legend, a warp in the gentle aqua-tints of the monks' short history.

The legend had begun quietly; where does a legend begin anyway? thought Andrew. At first there had been only strands and fragments: whispers of greed and lust. But the mission monks, doggedly preaching their message of love and light across Ireland, faithfully sending back word of their progress, had been at one in their accounts. The Monk was somewhere in Ireland; he was serving the pagan gods. Darker, wilder tales had shaled on with the years. Blood-hungers and human sacrifices. The sinister bartering of souls.

Brother Stephen had feared that the tales would harm their cause. Perhaps they would kill the burgeoning shoots of Christianity before they had time to unfurl, withering them like frost touching too-early crocuses. Christianity would be doomed before it had even rooted, and Ireland's conversion would be lost. It could not be allowed to happen.

One of their number must somehow follow the trail of greed and lust that the Monk had strewn across Ireland. It would be

9

difficult and it might be dangerous, for pagan Ireland was steeped in ancient beliefs, and although they knew paganism to be wrong, it did not stop it from being tempting. Whoever was chosen for the mission might find not only his body imperilled, but also his soul . . .

The mission would be hard because the Monk's name had been erased from the monastery's memory. Brother Stephen's predecessor, taking his lead from the harsh, unyielding anchorites, had decreed it. The creature's very existence must be struck from their records. It must be as if he had never existed.

It would make the quest doubly difficult, said Stephen, his old shrewd eyes on Andrew. But it would not be impossible. And if pagan Ireland was to be converted, it was their responsibility to find the one who was damaging their cause.

The creature whose real name was lost, but who was known throughout the land as the Black Monk of Torach.

Chapter Two

The Amaranths had never, so far as they could remember, welcomed a monk into their midst before.

The Porphyry Palace had always been known for its lavish and unquestioning hospitality, of course; Nechtan had been firm about this, because it was a great Amaranth tradition that no creature – Human, Beast or otherwise – was ever turned from the doors. He had said it behoved all sorcerers – well, all Men – to open their doors to pilgrims and travellers, and to listen to the stories of their travels. It broadened the mind, said Nechtan, who liked to hear about other ways of life, and had even entertained druids and would not listen to the people who said darkly that druidism was beginning to incorporate some rather odd customs, and was it true that the druids were reviving the practice of Human Sacrifice for Beltane?

The young monk who had come to the great western gate was quiet and extremely courteous, and rather self-effacing.

Questioned by Cerball and the Mugain, who said the procession and the Ritual could wait another few minutes, he explained that he was travelling alone, and that he was what was called a 'mission monk', which meant he had to travel as widely as possible to teach people about his religion. He said this rather with an air of watching closely to see how it would be received. Probably he had encountered some hostile receptions on his travels, because not everybody was favourably inclined towards monks, who were apt to lean dourly towards such things as fasting and silence, and even – it was rumoured – celibacy.

But Cerball and the Mugain were interested in Andrew; they had heard of monks, but never met one. The Mugain said this method of telling about the new Eastern religion was called 'preaching', and although they mightn't want to embrace the queer, stark practices of Christianity – well, they did not want to

11

embrace them at all – it did not prevent them from being courteous.

Also, said the Mugain craftily, hadn't the High King himself held a meeting with several monks, and wasn't that sufficient to see which way the tide of belief was turning? You went with the prevailing wind, said the Mugain, and neglected to refer to the fact that the meeting had in fact taken place on the Plain of the Fal, where the wily High King had known he would have Ireland's old tested forces at his back just in case the new beliefs might be a touch necromantic. The Plain of the Fal was so imbued with Ireland's own tried and trusted magic, that any new and dubious sorcery the monks might be planning on smuggling in would not stand a chance.

And so Andrew was given a place at table, and served food and wine. He was an easy and easily pleased guest; he ate sparingly but politely, praising the baked carp and asking only that his wine should be diluted with a little water. He listened to their discourse with what Herself of Mugain said was plainly a genuine interest, and did not seem to feel it necessary to *preach*, although several people noticed with interest that he traced some kind of symbol on the breast of his robe before eating and murmured a few soft words of some kind of brief ritual.

The sorcerers allowed themselves to be assembled into line for the ceremonial procession. The Succession Ritual had to be invoked over the legendary Well of Segais, which nobody present had seen, on account of it being a very long time indeed since the Ritual had last been chanted. Great-aunt Fuamnach said it was five hundred years, but nobody believed this because not even Nechtan could live that long.

The Well of Segais was situated in the bowels of the dark, legend-haunted Cadence Tower, the grim and sinister *Tur Baibeil* that Nechtan had raised from a mixture of Amaranth sorcery and ordinary prosaic Human building many decades earlier. The Well was so deep it was said to stretch down to the fabled underwater Cities of the *sidh*, and might even come out in the terrible core of the Black Ireland itself, but this was another of the legends that might very well turn out not to be true.

But to discover Nechtan's true successor, they would have to enter the Tower itself, they would have to open up the huge, jagged portcullis that had been sealed for almost a century.

No one had dared approach the Cadence Tower since the dark and evil Fomoire had come pouring and dancing out of it, singing their terrible Hunting Song, capturing Humans and flaying their skins.

Nobody knew what might live at the Tower's centre.

Standing in the Sorcery Chamber, with the evil whispery thing watching her from the shadows, was quite the worst moment Theodora had ever known. It was the nastiest thing that had ever happened to her in her entire six years and a bit.

Whatever had crept after her was something that was very bad indeed. It might be something that had got in from the Dark Ireland and been hiding in the passages, waiting for her. It might even have been waiting for somebody to come along and open the Silver Door so it could get at the Looms. Theo was very frightened indeed, but it was important not to show it, and it was important to think what was best to do.

It was clearly impossible to cross the black puddly shadows to reach the door. The shadows were being cast by the creature: long, distorted blacknesses; and so Theo knew it was standing quite near to her.

What I had better do, said Theodora to herself, is to stay here, and try to find out what it wants. It was comforting to glance up at the Silver Looms, and see the faint gleam of life and remember how Great-grandfather had said that the Looms never truly slept. They're awake, said Theodora, firmly. They're awake, and I think that if I tried very hard indeed, I could make them spin, and banish the something for good.

This was a cheering thought; Theodora held on to it very firmly and remembered, quite suddenly, that Great-grandfather had said that she would find spinning the Looms quite extraordinarily easy. He had said it with one of his mischievous chuckles, as if it was something that might not please people. But Theo held on to Great-grandfather's chuckle now, and she held on to his belief that she could work the Looms.

She moved into the centre of the Chamber so that the light would fall directly on her and the *something* would see that she was perfectly at home here. There was the scuttling sound again, and Theodora caught the flash of movement. Had she? Yes, something dark and crouching. It was watching her.

13

'Of course I am watching you,' said the voice, and Theo shuddered because it was a dreadfully cold, horridly slimy voice. It made you think of ancient sluggish rivers with silted beds, and of dank under-sea palaces where water-light rippled greenly on the cold, mouldering walls . . .

Theodora said, quite loudly, 'Who are you?' and at once there was an evil, bubbling chuckle.

But when the voice spoke again it only said, 'A creature from another world who seeks its freedom from a terrible bewitchment.' The shadows moved again, and quite suddenly the voice was much nearer. 'You look like a little girl who might help me,' said the creature, and this time Theo caught a glimpse of a great dark shape with a bulging forehead and pale glittery eyes and elongated arms and legs that ended in webbed fingers and toes.

Something that might once have dwelled in green ocean palaces with the cold ocean forever lapping against the walls . . .

'If I am to help you,' said Theo, carefully, because it would be as well to be a bit cunning about this; 'if I am to help you, I should need first to know who you are.'

A pause. Then, 'In the place where I have lived, I am called the Gristlen,' said the slurry, bubbly voice.

'Yes?'

'If I had another name, I have forgotten it,' said the voice, but there was a slithery slyness in its tone.

'But what are you?' said Theodora, peering into the shadows, not really wanting to see a creature called a Gristlen, but thinking it might be better to see it than imagine what it looked like.

There was a pause, as if the Gristlen was considering its answer. Then, 'I am a cursed creature,' it said, and there was another movement, as if it might be moving closer. 'But I have dwelled in many places. I have sucked dry many places,' it said with sudden relish. And then, 'But I was cursed by the Dark Lords,' said the Gristlen, 'and so I wear the carapace of their punishment.' It stopped and appeared to wait for her response.

'How did you get here?' said Theo, and the Gristlen chuckled with a thick, wet-liquid chuckle.

'Through the Gateway,' it said gloatingly. 'Through the Gateway between your world and the Dark Ireland.'

'The Gateways are closed,' said Theo firmly. 'They were closed when the Sorcery Wars ended. We fought in the Sorcery Wars,'

14

she said loudly, so that the Gristlen-thing would know it was not dealing with what Great-grandfather called, 'No-account magicians'. 'We fought and we won.'

The Gristlen chuckled its horrid, slurry chuckle again. It said, 'I know of the Sorcery Wars, little girl. I fought in them, also.' And half to itself, it said, 'And lost so much.'

'Did you fight on the side of the Lord of Chaos?' whispered Theo. 'In his Armies?' and at once the Gristlen gave another dreadful, bubbly laugh.

'Chaos is a weakling and a charlatan,' it said. 'He permits his lusts to cloud his true powers.' The shadows moved again. 'I was greater by far than Chaos,' said the Gristlen, and there was a quite dreadful note of pride in its voice. 'I had my own Armies.'

'Well, where are they now?' said Theo, knowing this sounded impolite, but thinking you could not let horrid whispery Gristlen-things get the better of you. 'What happened to them?' she said.

'They will come back to me,' said the Gristlen. 'Once I have sloughed off the carapace cast about me by the Dark Lords, my people will return to me.' A pair of huge-knuckled hands, covered in tough dark hide, reached from the shadowy corner. 'And you look like a little girl who could help me to do that,' it said, and now there was a soft, persuasive note in its voice. Theo shuddered and backed away to the far wall. Could she reach the Looms? She was standing almost directly beneath them, and she thought that if she stood on her tippiest tiptoe she might reach up.

'What would I have to do?' she said, keeping one eye on the hidden figure, and trying to assess how far up she would have to reach to the Loom.

The Gristlen chuckled thickly and, without warning, it reared up out of the darkness, a giantish figure with great, clutching hands and pale, bulging eyes and a flat, snouted face that loomed up at her, impossibly close.

And it is covered with a hide, thought Theo, shrinking back in horror. Whatever its true self is or was, it has been given a thick dark skin like old cracked leather. The carapace of a curse . . . This is the worst thing that has ever happened to me, thought Theo, trying not to panic.

There was a lingering stench to it as well, something that made you think of tainted meat and badly cured animal skins.

Dreadful! But Theo kept her eyes on the Gristlen, and said again, 'What would I have to do?'

The Gristlen chuckled and wrapped its long, fibrousy arms about its repulsive body. 'Come into my embrace,' it said, and there was a high-pitched whine to it now. 'Come into my embrace and help me to tear off the accursed Gristlen skin and emerge as my true self again.' It loped forward, no longer as giantish as it had first seemed, but moving in a crouching, hunchbacked way, brushing the floor as it came with one hand, leering and grinning with its flat, slash-like mouth.

'The warm embrace of a Human,' it said again, and quite suddenly it was not only frightening, it was pitiful and grotesque and there was a heart-wrenching sadness about it. The blurring lights of the chamber fell across it, and it held out its repulsive hands mutely, its eyes resting on Theo beseechingly.

'Help me . . .' it said. 'Free me of the ugliness.' Its bulging, glittering eyes were filled with entreaty, and Theo shuddered and reached up to the great Sorcery Looms.

The instant the cool soft silver brushed her fingers, something that crackled and spat ran down her arms. But it was a stinging, sizzling something, sharp and brilliant and exhilarating. A bolt of rainbow light poured into the chamber from above as abruptly as if a huge trapdoor into the sky had been opened, and whiplashed about the Gristlen's thick body, flinging it back against the far wall. There was a sickening wet crunch as the creature fell and the light dissolved and ran into nothing.

The Gristlen lay half against the wall, shaking its head and looking up in bewilderment.

'You hurt me . . . You hurt me when I wanted only your help . . .'

The cringing puzzlement in its voice was unbearable. Theo choked back a sob, but kept her fingers curled firmly about the thin cool silver of the immense Loom above her.

'Only to lose the ugliness,' whimpered the Gristlen, rocking itself back and forth, shaking its head from side to side. 'It was only so that I could slough off the accursed carapace. A Human embrace . . .' It began to crawl across the floor towards Theo again, dragging itself by its great, disproportionate hands. 'Pretty little thing,' it said. 'Pretty little thing has such beauty to spare . . .'

Theo gasped and, without thinking, shot across the room, tumbling headlong through the Silver Door and slamming it shut behind her.

Andrew had stayed behind in the banqueting hall when the Amaranths left for their procession to the depths of the Porphyry Palace, because it had seemed a secret, rather closed Ritual that they were about to perform. His Order knew about secrecy and it knew about rituals, and Andrew, listening to his hosts, had found himself comparing the monks' own daily hours of prayer to this strange Succession Rite the Amaranths were preparing to chant.

Cerball had unrolled the Succession Ritual carefully and spread it on the table for everyone to see. Andrew had been interested; he thought that the thick, lovely parchment with its thin gold veining and the tiny winking lights had much in common with the painstakingly copied liturgical works of his Order's Scriptorium.

When the Mugain told how the early Amaranth Scholars would have set their apprentices to the copying and the embellishing of the parchment, Andrew had said, 'We, also, have our skilled workers who spend much time in similar work,' and a faintly eerie breath of familiarity touched him.

He found the Amaranths with their long slender hands and their exotic looks unexpectedly attractive. They had narrow, brilliant eyes that seemed to see a little more than ordinary people's, and pale luminous skins and glossy dark hair. And charm, thought Andrew, seeing their quick, unemphatic way of speaking, but seeing as well that they had a way of tilting their heads to listen, as if they might be able to hear the things left unsaid. They have charm and something faintly foreign and something strongly unHuman. Something that made you think they would be strong friends but dangerous enemies, and something that made you think you would do well to guard your thoughts in their company.

When they left the banqueting hall, their faces intent, their eyes filled with deep inner concentration, Andrew had, half guiltily, moved to great double doors that led out of the banqueting chamber and stood in one of the deep window embrasures looking out.

He saw the sorcerers set out, falling naturally and easily into line, the burning torches they carried flickering in the night wind. They had donned plain dark robes with deep concealing hoods and, as they crossed the courtyard, the pure sweet singing of the light-filled Descant they chanted came clearly to Andrew's ears. Recognition prickled his skin again, and for a brief, aching moment he was in England again, with the great bronze mouth of the sonorous monastic bell chiming through the cloisters, and the monks walking in solemn procession to Vespers. Listening to the Amaranths, he heard not the ebb and flow of sorcerous ritual, but the monks' plainsong, the lovely and simple music they had adapted from the Italian Ambrosian Chant and that they sung on festal occasions.

I do not believe any of this, thought Andrew, watching the procession. I do not believe that there are sorcerers and people who can spin magic, and who have at their beck unseen powers and unguessed-at forces. I certainly do not believe in creatures who are not altogether Human. These are simply heathenish people who follow ancient beliefs, perhaps a branch of some little-known race from somewhere. The east, could it be? Yes, that would explain the narrow eyes, the exotic charm. And there were many people throughout the world who followed ancient, apparently meaningless rituals. There were stranger methods of selecting the successor to a Royal Throne.

And it would be a pity to destroy all of this . . . The thought slid unbidden into his mind, and he felt the pull of this dark, seductive world that lay deep in Ireland's heart.

A pity to destroy it . . . A pity to subject these people to persuasions and the arguments that would disturb the foundations of their ancient magical stronghold. It was a tiny, treacherous whisper. *A pity to lose the ancient Amaranth enchantments* . . .

But I do not believe in magic, said Andrew firmly, and I have surely learned, by now, to turn my back on temptation. That is why I was chosen for this mission. Brother Stephen believed I could resist temptation. He trusted me.

He turned back to the banqueting table, thinking he would permit himself a half-glass more of wine, when the great double doors at the far end were pushed open. A child, her eyes huge with fear, her face white with panic, stood there.

* * *

18

Theo had run as fast as she could through the dark narrow passages that wound upwards from the Sorcery Chambers. She had found her way to the banqueting hall – not really thinking where she was going, but knowing the banqueting hall was where everyone would be. They would all be eating and drinking and saying wasn't it a terrible thing to think of Nechtan, may the gods preserve him, away upstairs dying, and was there any more wine to be had?

Mama would exclaim and draw her lips tightly together in disapproval at Theo's interrupting it all, but Theo would not mind this because of escaping from the Gristlen. And once she had explained to them about the Gristlen, hiding below in the Sorcery Chambers, it would be all right. Father and Uncle Mugain would push back their chairs and say they would deal with it at once, and Great-aunt Fuamnach would rap her hazel stick sharply on the ground and say, My word, how dared such a creature come into the Palace and threaten Theo? What would Rumour do? But Rumour would probably call down one of her dazzling extravagant enchantments and frizzle the Gristlen where it stood while everybody else was talking about what to do.

It was disconcerting to find that they had already set off for the Cadence Tower, and to discover that there was only the unknown guest left behind. Theo had never encountered a monk, although she had heard Great-grandfather and Uncle Mugain talk about them. They were good people, monks. They were strict and silent, but they were good.

Andrew was reassuring and surprisingly easy to talk to. He made her sit down next to him, and gave her a glass of water with a tiny sip of wine in, which she was not normally allowed to have, but which Andrew said would be reviving. Theo sipped it warily, and after a while managed to tell him about the Gristlen-creature, ugly and terrible but so pitiable you could not bear it, and about how it was trying to get rid of its terrible carapace.

'Only it has to be embraced by a Human to be its own true self again,' said Theo, in a small, rather trembly voice, because this had been almost the worst part of all, and the only bit worse still had been the puzzled way it had looked at her when she had sent it hurtling across the Chamber.

Andrew turned out to be the kind of nice person who listened to you – really listened; not pretend, polite listening – and Theo

19

began to feel better, because there was something reassuring about people who did that. Rumour always listened properly as well, which was one of the reasons Theo liked her.

She was not crying, although her voice was still a bit trembly. But the wine was warming, just as Andrew had said it would be. Theo began to feel a bit more hopeful.

Andrew was looking thoughtful. After a moment he said, in an expressionless voice, 'Did the ... creature touch you at all, Theodora?' He had a nice way of saying her name, not shortening it as most people did, but saying it courteously and carefully, as if he thought the correct pronouncing of people's names was important. 'Did it reach you at all?' he said, and Theo explained about managing to reach up to the Looms and send a bolt of light to smash the horrid Gristlen against the wall so that it was dazed and bewildered.

'You did that?' Andrew had only been amongst the Amaranths for a few hours, but he already understood that the powering of the immense Sorcery Looms was regarded as a massive undertaking. Something requiring enormous power and control. Had this child really been able to manipulate them, even for those vital few minutes?

'It was only a very little bit of power.' Theo did not want Andrew to think she was boasting. 'And the Gristlen won't be dead.' Evil creatures did not die very easily, they lived for hundreds and hundreds of years, longer even than sorcerers. 'It will still be there,' said Theo, looking down at the wine glass and biting her lip.

Andrew stood up, holding out his hand. 'I think,' he said, 'that we must go in search of your people, Theodora,' and saw her eyes fly upwards in mingled fear and alarm.

'But they're in the Tower. It's the Succession Ritual because of Great-grandfather dying.'

'Yes?'

'It's a bit forbidden to go in the Tower,' said Theo uncertainly. 'I don't think I could.'

'Not if I came with you?' Andrew had not planned to say this, he had not planned to be drawn into any of this. Because I don't believe any of it! he cried silently.

But Theo said at once, 'Oh yes, that would make it all right.' And slid off her chair and held out her hand to him.

Chapter Three

As they walked through the Palace, Andrew talked to Theodora, reassuring her and trying to calm her. He asked her about the Palace, which he said he found beautiful and unusual, and he listened with interest to what she said.

He did not refer specifically to the Gristlen, but he said in an ordinary, unworried voice that there were a great many things in the world that were evil and wicked; Theo should not be too frightened because there was Somebody who watched over good people always and especially over children. It did not matter that you did not know about the Somebody, because He would always be there for you.

'A king?' said Theodora hopefully. 'A great warrior who comes storming and galloping in to kill everyone?'

But Andrew said, No, the Person was not precisely a warrior or a king, but somebody who had lived a very long time ago and done a great many good things, and who still lived in people's hearts and who looked down from Heaven, which was where Andrew's own people believed you went after you died. He had been gentle and immensely good and more powerful than anything in the whole world, this Person. He loved everybody, but He especially loved children, said Andrew, his eyes serious and his expression intent. He loved them all and after He died, He had made a special place for all children in Heaven.

This was very interesting indeed, and Theo would have liked to hear more, because the notion of a Somebody who looked down on you and guarded you from evil creatures was quite the most reassuring thing ever. Andrew said they would talk about it properly later on, but for now they had to go across to the Cadence Tower; it was a good thing they had thought to bring one of the branched candlesticks from the banqueting hall, because it meant they could see their way quite easily.

The ill-starred Cadence Tower, Nechtan's infamous dark *Tur Baibeil*, was wreathed in scudding clouds and shrouded in darkness.

Theo knew the legend; she knew how Great-grandfather had created it out of sorcery that was whispered to have been just a little bit dark, twisting into it fearsomely strong incantations, and raising it higher and higher, so that it would reach the unseen lands beyond the skies, or the fabled Cities of the dead. It was when the Tower had reached its highest point that the Cadence itself had been lost; sliding beyond their grasp, so that they could no longer call upon the marvellous, mystical Sorcerous Tongue, the silver-tipped, convoluted Language of Magic bequeathed to them by the *sidh* centuries earlier. People like Uncle Mugain said sadly that Nechan had overreached and underestimated; in creating the *Tur Baibeil*, he had unwittingly opened up one of the fearsome dark Gateways into the necromancers' realm. The rescinding of the Cadence and the abrupt descent to a single language, had been the punishment.

It was through the Tower that the fearsome Human-hungry Fomoire had last come into Ireland, pouring up from the subterranean depths of the Dark Realm. They had come prowling and creeping out from the black-mouthed caves in the bowels of the earth; up through the ancient Well of Segais, and through the tunnels and the dark catacombs that twisted beneath the Tower's foundations. It had all happened a long time before Theo had been born, but nobody would ever forget it. Everyone who had ever heard the Fomoire's grisly Hunting Song, and seen their terrible whirling dancing as they circled their victims, said it had heralded the beginning of Ireland's dark age.

But of course, the Fomoire had long since been driven back and the Gateway to the Dark Ireland was sealed for ever.

The Tower was directly ahead, and Theo's hand tightened in Andrew's, because this was not as exciting as she had always thought it would be.

At the centre of the great rearing bulk was the portcullis, the massive iron grille that sealed the Tower. At the height of the Sorcery Wars, the Fomoire had held the Tower for their own, operating the portcullis with screeching glee, causing it to rise and fall so that they could drag their struggling victims beneath the spikes and take them down into their caves.

The portcullis had been raised, and Andrew, looking up at the jagged iron teeth, half sunk into the stonework, thought: well, at least the Amaranths got this far. At least we are going in the right direction. And then: has my quarry been this way? he thought, suddenly. Would he have been tempted by the shining Amaranth Palace as I was tempted by it, and would he have been drawn by the strange darkness of this Tower? As they approached the dark, yawning maw of the entrance, a tiny sour wind scudded across the night skies, huffing dry, rank breath into their faces; and Andrew shivered, and drew the thin woollen habit more closely about him.

From the ground it was impossible to see the Tower's zenith, and Andrew wondered, a trifle cynically, if this had added to its dark legend. It seemed to lean away from you, so that the closer you got it, the harder it was to see where it ended and where it began. He thought its very construction would have made it a place that would easily become the core of legends and myths and creeping folklores.

Dry stale air gusted outwards from the entrance, as if an ancient, long-sealed tomb had been forced open, and dribbling blackness spilled across the cobblestones at their feet.

Theo stood very still and looked at it because, although she had known what to expect, it was still disconcerting to see the dark and sinister *Tur Baibeil*, once the lair of the Fomoire, unsealed after centuries of disuse.

It was like stepping into a black, fetid tunnel. As their eyes adjusted, they saw that just inside the portcullis was a small, round room, with two tiny, slitlike windows high up. Thin moonlight seeped in, silvering the walls, showing the yawning well of the Sable Stairway, the remarkable structure of ebony and jet that Nechtan had believed reached down into the bowels of the earth until it came out in the heart of the Dark Realm itself.

'That is surely where your people are,' said Andrew, indicating the Stair. 'That is where they would go.'

'Yes. Down to the Well of Segais.' Theo was staring at the stairwell. 'It will be a very long way down,' she said, softly.

It was smaller inside than they had expected, and it was dark

23

and musty. Andrew held the branched candlestick up and fantastical cavorting shadows leapt, making Theodora shiver. Above their heads was a black infinity, stretching up and up.

They moved towards the Stair, hand in hand, the candles burning with a thin, dry, blue flame. The footprints of the Amaranths lay in the dust at their feet, ordinary prints of boots and shoes, and Rumour's extravagant high-heeled slippers.

Theo had explained about not interrupting the Succession Ritual if it had begun. They would have to stand on the edges and be mouse-quiet until it was over. Andrew had nodded seriously and had said he understood about rituals and about how you had to treat them with respect. It was a question of politeness towards whoever you addressed the ritual to. His own people called it 'praying', he said, and not one of them would have dreamed of breaking in on somebody who was praying. It would be like interrupting a private conversation.

The steps of the ancient black Stairway curved steeply and sharply, and the flickering candles threw shadows on to the walls, weird and leaping and grotesque. Andrew felt a cold prickle of fear against his spine, because just for an instant it had seemed as if the shadows were not the shadows of himself and Theodora, but of something else . . . Something that had long, fibrousy arms and huge-knuckled hands and that was creeping stealthily after them; something that was dark and ugly and that wore a fearsome carapace that hid its true self . . . The light flickered again, and Andrew caught the fleeting shape of a creature crouching on the stair above them, huddled into the shadows. There was the brief impression of a snouted face with pale staring eyes that glittered cunningly and malevolently . . . Theodora's Gristlen? Had she seen it? Did *I* see it? But Theodora was going on down the Stair, treading carefully, one hand touching the wall for balance, and her small face was intent on the perilous descent. Perhaps it was only a shadow, thought Andrew, following her.

The Cavern of the Segais Well was smaller and darker than the Amaranths had expected.

They had descended warily, chanting the Cantor of Starlight as they went, Rumour leading them, her voice husky and rather like a young boy's. The younger sorcerers, led by Echbel, had started the secondary chant, the Descant of Sunrise, and the patterns had

24

mingled and blended, driving back the dark shadows.

Rumour, accustomed to her own small, beautiful Castle, found the Cavern almost unbearably dank and oppressive. The roof was low and crusted with mould, and in the corners were pale, blind growths, fungal things that had sprung up in the dank, cold atmosphere. There was the suffocating feeling of the great dark Tower above their heads, and from somewhere beneath them was the sound of water dripping against stone. Rumour remembered that the entrance to the underwater City of the *sidh* was believed to be beyond the Segais Well.

As they stood at the foot of the Sable Stair, Rumour looked at the others, waiting for someone to make the first move, and then with a shrug, stepped forward, lifting her hands above her head, the palms upwards. At once she was engulfed in light, cascading rainbow colours, pouring harlequin brilliance that sent shards of iridescence into the shadows, and then solidified into a swirling, silken cloak that fell about her ankles with a sensual whisper.

'Eye-catching,' said Great-aunt Fuamnach, tartly. 'How like Rumour to produce something so *exaggerated*.'

But Bodb Decht said it was actually rather a useful thing for Rumour to have done, and Great-aunt Fuamnach snorted because it was as she had always said: Rumour had no sense of occasion and the Rainbow Cloak was simply a piece of exhibitionism.

Laigne said, rather haltingly, 'It's very dark down here . . .' And then in a different, sharper tone, 'Echbel, your heavier cloak would have been—'

'It's musty as well as dark,' said Cerball hastily. 'But we'll wedge the torches into the wall-brackets for extra light.'

Great-aunt Fuamnach dug her hazel walking stick into the ground and was looking round disapprovingly. 'It's damp and neglected,' she said, frowning. 'My word, Cerball, this is not at all what I expected.'

'It's perfectly ruinous on silk slippers,' said Rumour. 'My dears, if I had suspected it would be as damp as this, I would have worn fur. Next to my skin,' she added with a suggestive purr, and was glared at.

She barely noticed the glares; she had spoken more or less automatically, simply because they would be expecting her to be vain and flippant. She looked back at the Stair. Was that a shadow, crouching just round the curve? She murmured an incantation of light and the Rainbow Cloak glowed a little more strongly.

The Well was at the centre of the Cavern, embedded deeply into the floor, a gaping black abyss. There was a narrow brick parapet, crumbling with age in places, and from the depths came a faint mustiness. It was much smaller than they had expected, barely eight feet across, and the brick parapet was stained and blackened. Rumour saw that there was an iron ladder clamped to the inside of the Well, rusting and ancient, but looking sound enough. So it would be possible to climb down inside it, would it? Could I do that? thought Rumour. If I had to, could I set foot to that rusting ladder, and go down and down into the darkness? Did the Well truly lead to the hinterlands of fabled Tiarna, the magical under-sea realm of the *sidh*, or was that only another of the jumbled myths about this place? She leaned forward, and just for a moment there was not the tomblike stench and the impenetrable darkness, but something that ruffled the air with sweetness . . . On the rim of vision, she caught a flash of vivid turquoise at the darkness's heart: the glint of iridescent wings, the sinuous bodies of eerie sea creatures with not the smallest drop of Human blood in them . . . She shook her head impatiently to clear the images, and as she did so, Cerball wedged the last of the torches into the ancient brackets. Light flared up, casting the Well into sharp relief, and Rumour turned back sharply.

'Everyone. Look.' She held out a pointing finger.

'What is it?' said several voices anxiously.

In the ancient dust surrounding the Well were tiny footprints, dozens upon dozens of them, light and swift and darting, as if the owners had traced circles inside circles inside circles . . . As if they had not walked but leapt and cavorted. Exactly as if creatures had come swarming up out of the Well's black depths into the Tower. Exactly as if they had been dancing as they came.

In the same moment, they caught the whisper of sound from the Well and the breath of a chuckle. And then, fainter than the faintest of winds, as insubstantial as the frozen fingers of trees tapping against a window, the sound of voices singing.

'O, give us skins for dancing in,
Pelts of Human silken skin.

> Give us hides with Humanish veils
> Fleeces with rinds of pale thin shale.'

The Hunting Song of the Fomoire.

'It's an echo,' said the Mugain, a bit uncertainly. 'That's all it is, an echo.'

'Yes, of course.'

'Echbel ought to go back to the Palace—'

'Oh, there's nothing to worry about,' said Cerball, hastily.

'No, echoes can't hurt anyone . . .'

'And we know that echoes linger for – well, for quite a long time.'

Rumour said impatiently, 'But all echoes were once attached to something, and it is the *something* we have to be wary of.' She moved around the Well cautiously. 'Cerball, you had better lose no time in pronouncing the Ritual.'

Laigne opened her mouth to say that Rumour had no right to be ordering people about like this, and Cerball had just begun to unroll the parchment, when the light shifted suddenly and became suffused with crimson.

Pouring upwards from the Well of Segais, there erupted baleful magenta light with, deep in it, dancing, whirling figures.

The Fomoire.

They danced as they came, whirling and leaping, the malevolent glow streaming about their bodies like a crimson mantle.

To begin with they were insubstantial; black silhouettes, paper cut-outs limned sharply against the red glow; dancing and prancing, casting weird, fearsome shadows against the crimson-lit Stair. But as they came pouring out of the Well, they seemed to solidify, and the Amaranths felt the terrible evil of the Dark Ireland surging and gushing about them.

Cerball and the Mugain began to form a circle, frantically gesturing to the others to link hands, and the Mugain's voice was raised in a Banishment Chant, joined, after only seconds, by several others. Rumour held up her hands to summon power, and felt, with the purest horror she had ever known, the power slither out of her grasp.

'It's the darkness!' shouted Bodb Decht, seeing her. 'The

Fomoire are blanketing everything with darkness!'

A noxious, pulsating menace was filling the Cave, and the voices of Cerball and the Mugain with Bodb Decht rose strongly in the Banishment Ritual. Several of the sorcerers were forming spears of light and hurling them at the Stair, and the Cave was becoming filled with sizzling, white-hot shards that pierced the malevolent crimson glow, and then splintered.

The Fomoire were leaping and whirling into the Cavern, and Rumour thought there were not so very many of them: perhaps there were fifty. But they moved so quickly, and they danced so wildly and so frenziedly, that it was impossible to count.

They whirled and spun, and caught one another's hands and circled and pranced, and their shadows fell across the Tower walls eerily and fantastically. Several of them were astride snarling black creatures that reared and bucked, and tossed gleaming black heads with inward-slanting red eyes.

'They are riding the NightMare Stallions,' said the Mugain, in a voice of sudden awe.

The terrible legendary Fomoire, the hungry Dark Spirits who carried Humans off to their dungeons and flayed them alive . . . the Servants of the necromancers, breaking the bounds of their Realm, riding the NightMare Stallions into the heart of Ireland again . . .

'The Gateway is open again!' cried the Mugain. 'Dagda preserve us all, the Gateway is unsealing!'

'Then do something!' shrieked Laigne. 'Somebody do something!'

But the Fomoire were in the Cave with them, they were spilling into the Cavern, and they were marching round and round the walls, and the Amaranths could see that more were following them, pouring up from the Well, dancing and whirling as they came.

They sang as they danced; eerie, rhythmic chanting that set Rumour's teeth on edge, and that ran slyly in and out of the Cavern's crevices.

> 'Give me a skin for dancing in;
> And a pelt with a trim of silken sin.
> Give me a hide with a Humanish veil
> And a fleece with a rind of pale thin shale.

Give me a hide to climb inside
A murderer's cloak or a child-eater's fleece.
Give me a skin of Humanish thin,
A husk to hide my true self in.'

The crimson glow fell across the cave, and the distorted shadows leapt and danced wildly.

'Do something!' screamed Laigne again. 'Cerball! Mugain! There must be something we can do!'

Rumour strode to the centre of the Cavern, her skirts swishing angrily, and lifted her arms high above her head, the silken sleeves of the Rainbow Cloak sliding back. She pronounced the first lines of the awesome *Draiocht Tine*, the great Fire Enchantment, and at once the sorcerers fell back, because the *Draiocht Tine* was a fearsomely powerful Enchantment; it required immense power and supreme confidence, and was believed to reach the Temple of the Dagda himself. Several people glanced with unwilling respect at Rumour.

As the last lines of the Enchantment died away, the air began to sizzle and forked lightning tore across the Cavern and buried itself in the sides of the Tower. Cascades of sparks shot high in the air and several of the NightMare Stallions reared up, flinging their riders to the ground.

Rumour, the Rainbow Cloak swishing about her slender figure, grinned in purest triumph because, despite the danger, and despite the terrible creatures pouring down upon them, it was the most marvellously satisfying thing in the world to pronounce a genuinely powerful spell and see it take substance in front of you.

And for a moment, it seemed as if Rumour's spell had worked. A shriek of pain and fury went up from the Fomoire; the NightMare Stallions reared and bucked, and their inward-slanting eyes glinted.

'The *Draiocht Tine* has never yet failed!' cried Rumour, turning to regard them with malicious triumph. 'All you need is confidence, my dears, that is all you need! We are opening the Temple of the Gods! Prepare to meet the Dagda!'

'But the Fomoire are still coming!' cried the Mugain, pointing. 'They are still coming! Rumour, the Ritual, the Ritual!

Pronounce it again!' And even as he spoke, the Fomoire were remounting the NightMare Steeds, and were re-forming. The chill, grisly song filled the Cavern once more.

'Give me a skin of Humanish thin
A husk to hide my evil in . . .'

'Stop them!' cried Herself of Mugain. 'At any minute they will be upon us, and we shall all be carried down into the Dark Realm!'

Rumour was staring at the grinning, evil creatures in frustration and fury. 'I cannot pronounce the Ritual again!' she cried. 'Foolish creatures, no one can call upon the gods more than once in a single night! *You* try something!' said Rumour.

'Give me a hide to climb inside,
A murderer's cloak or a child-eater's fleece.
Give me a skin for murdering in
A husk to hide my darkness in.'

'Then back!' cried Cerball. 'Everyone! Back up the Stair and out to the Palace! Re-Seal the Tower!'

'Run away? Never! See here, Cerball—'

'Listen, it's the only way—'

But, even as the words formed, even as the Amaranths tried to reassemble, a shadow fell across the Stair's foot. They turned sharply and Andrew, with Theodora clasped tightly in his arms, half fell into the Cavern.

Behind Andrew came a fearsome creature, a hunched-over shape with a grotesque, snouted face, darting, lidless eyes and a thick, scaly hide.

The Gristlen stood at the entrance to the Stair, hugging itself with its huge, disproportionate hands, and peering hungrily at the Amaranths from its pale glittering eyes.

'Prettinesses everywhere for me to take,' it said, and threw back its dreadful head and laughed.

Chapter Four

Andrew was holding Theodora very tightly, surprised by the sudden feeling of fierce protectiveness. She had been trembling with fear ever since the Gristlen had come prowling out of the shadows and had run down the Sable Stair after them, and he tightened his hold, aware of the light, frail bones and the silky spill of dark hair, wanting to carry her to safety, knowing it to be impossible.

The sight in the Cavern assaulted his senses like a blow. He stood blinking in the pulsating crimson light from the Fomoire, feeling the thick clotted evil that surged and eddied everywhere. There was a moment when he thought, 'Hell has opened and is spewing out into the world,' and when he thought that, after all, his Leader had been wrong; Hell was not something that waited for sinners after death – it was here, now, its gates were yawning, and it was spilling its evil into the world. He stared at the leaping, grinning Fomoire and saw that this, then, was the old Ireland, the Ireland Brother Stephen had warned him against. This was the Ireland that was steeped in paganism and in magic and wreathed in enchantment and necromancy. This is the Ireland that beckoned to the Black Monk, thought Andrew. And this is something that cannot be fought with prayer or fasting...

The Fomoire had driven the Amaranths to the far end of the Cavern, and at least two dozen of the repulsive, grinning things were guarding them. A nauseating stench came from the creatures, a stench composed of badly cured meat and earth, and of old blood and raw agony.

Before us are the Fomoire, and behind us is the Gristlen. Andrew shot it a covert glance and saw that it was half crouching, half sitting on the Sable Stair, hugging its elongated legs in evil glee as it watched the Fomoire.

How sentient was it? How powerful? It looked stupid. I believe I would rather challenge that than the Fomoire, thought Andrew.

The torches that Cerball had thrust into the brackets were burning more strongly now and, as they flared up, Andrew turned back. For the first time he saw the Fomoire properly.

At exactly the same moment, Theo said in a small, frightened voice, 'Andrew. They are wearing skins. They are hiding inside Human skins.'

At once there was a slithering, chuckling sound from the Fomoire.

> 'O but give us skins for murdering in,
> And give us pelts of silken sin.
> Hides of evil to conceal ourselves in,
> And then you shall see us, puny Humanish one.'

Human skins. Andrew felt the sick horror of it wash over him.

The skins were not slung about the creatures' waists, or even worn like cloaks or hooded robes, as Andrew had heard of other pagans doing. They had each taken a whole Human skin, which had been slit open down the front, neatly and cleanly. They had spread the skin flat on the ground.

And then they had climbed inside.

Andrew thought he had never seen anything so extremely sinister as these nearly concealed creatures who peered slyly from inside their Human carapaces. The Human heads lolled on the dead necks; the features were blank and staring, but even so, there was a travesty of life; the legs walked and the arms jerked, and you felt that at any minute the empty, dead eyes might open and turn to look.

But the walk was a horrid jerking walk, as if strings were being pulled from somewhere unseen, and as the heads fell forward, the jaws were slack, with the mouths open and tongues falling out.

They were the most sinister creatures Andrew had ever seen.

But most sinister of all was the way in which the slits which the Fomoire had used to climb inside were not quite closed. They gaped raggedly open and, through the gaps, the evil sly eyes of the Fomoire could be seen, peering out. It was rather as if something wicked and alien had hidden itself behind heavy curtains and was looking out through a chink.

I wonder what they are really like, thought Andrew, and as if the Fomoire had heard his thoughts, they began to chant again.

> 'Give us skins of Humanish thin,
> Hides of evil to conceal ourselves in.
> A fleece with a rind of pale thin shale,
> A murderer's cloak, a child-eater's veil.'

At the foot of the stair, the Gristlen chuckled and mumbled to itself, and Andrew looked back at it.

'Won't take the prettiness,' it was saying, in its gloating bubbly voice. 'It won't be allowed. The prettiness is mine. The prettiness is to save *me*. I *chose* it for myself.' Its eyes swivelled round to Theodora, and it rubbed its hard horny hands together with a dry leathery sound that set Andrew's teeth on edge. He tightened his hold on Theo, feeling again that fierce surge of protectiveness.

The Amaranths were recovering; several of the younger ones had banded together to charge the Fomoire, and the Mugain and Cerball began a Chant which several of the others took up.

Rumour and Great-aunt Fuamnach were drawing a circle using the hazel wand, and Rumour was standing with her arms outstretched again, calling down ribbons of rainbow light. But even as the light reached the ground, the Fomoire sent black glinting shards to splinter it, and the nearest of the creatures chuckled slyly, and reached out a hand from inside its Human skin.

Andrew heard Laigne scream and saw her dart forward, and in the same moment, several of the Fomoire pounced on Echbel and dragged him, struggling and flailing, across the floor to the Stair.

'The cages! This one for the cages!' they screeched, and Laigne screamed again, a terrible frantic sound, and clawed at the restraining hands of the Amaranths who were holding her back.

'My boy! Echbel . . . Save him! Kill the evil filth!'

Cerball had moved at once, but the NightMare Stallions rode at him, rearing up on their hind legs, forming a guard, and striking him with their hoofs, so that he fell to the ground. The sorcerers backed away, looking to one another for guidance, and although there was not quite panic in their eyes, there was something very near it.

Theodora was aware of a strength and a comfort from Andrew, but she was very frightened. She was trying very hard to think what Great-grandfather would have done, although it was the hardest thing she had ever had to do, what with people screaming, and Echbel being dragged across the floor by several Fomoire, and what with Mamma crying and begging them to do something, anything, only save him. And chuckling and gobbling to itself on the Stair was the Gristlen. Theo sent it a sideways look, and sensed, as Andrew had not been able to sense, that the Gristlen possessed far more power and far more necromantic strength than the Fomoire. The Fomoire were hungry for Humans and they were wicked and sly, but the Gristlen was soaked in ancient evil and it was intelligent evil.

Great-grandfather would have known what to do. He would have saved Echbel and he would have vanquished the Gristlen. *But I don't know what to do!* cried Theodora silently.

She looked up at Andrew, her eyes filled with anguish. 'I don't know what to do.'

Andrew, his eyes on the struggling Echbel, his own mind searching frantically for a means of escape, said, 'Theodora, there is nothing you can do,' and Theodora said, impatiently:

'Yes, there ought to be *something*. Great-grandfather would say that I ought to be able to do something . . . He would *expect* me to do something.'

'What?'

'There ought to be a spell – something in Cadence . . . Only I can't think of one!' cried Theodora, torn between tears and anger. 'I ought to be able to think of something, but I can't!'

The Fomoire were dragging the screaming Echbel towards the Well, chuckling and prodding him, reaching out with hard, bony fingers, prodding and probing and fingering. 'But preserve his skin!' they cried. 'No marks, no scars, no punctures!'

'Preserve his skin for the wearing!' shouted several more, leaping high into the air, the crimson fireglow falling eerily across them. The skins gaped wider now, and the Amaranths could see the wizened shapes of the Fomoire more clearly through the slits.

Theodora was staring at the Fomoire, and Andrew saw that she was still struggling to think of a spell, something the dying Amaranth Ruler would have known and invoked. He had just time to think all over again that this was a remarkable child, and he remembered how she had said that Nechtan would have expected her to know what to do, when the Fomoire began circling the Cavern again, pouncing and darting, and jabbing their tiny claws at the Amaranths.

'Your puny spells will be useless!' they cried in their gobbling voices. 'We have the ancient dark blood in us and our powers are greater than yours! We have your little brother, and we shall take him back to our caves, and we shall *enjoy* him!' They rubbed their hands gleefully together, leaping into the air, so that the dead heads of their Human garb rolled wildly.

'Skins of Humanish thin!' cried the Fomoire.

'Cloaks of pale thin shale!'

'To the cages with him!'

'He is our reward for opening up the Gateway!'

Laigne, moaning, half lying at the centre of the Amaranths, with Herself of Mugain and Great-aunt Fuamnach supporting her, said in a terrified voice, 'What will they do to him? What will happen?' and at once the Fomoire turned, chuckling and leaping towards her.

'We shall take him down to the black-mouthed caves.'

'The caves that guard the entrance to the Dark Realm.'

'Down below below—'

'We shall lock him away in our cages.'

'And while he is there, we shall anoint his skin with balms and unguents and with the fat of murderers' brains.'

'We shall bathe him thrice daily in the blood of unborn babes.'

'Why?' screamed Laigne, pushing away Great-aunt Fuamnach and trying to fight off the grinning, skin-clad creatures. 'Oh why?'

'To soften his skin, of course,' cried the Fomoire.

'To make it silken soft and Humanish thin.'

'And when it is soft and when it is thin, then we shall flay him of his Humanish veil.'

'And then we shall wear it!'

'Do something!' screeched Laigne, turning to the others imploringly. 'Save him!'

The Mugain was facing the Fomoire truculently. 'Why are you here?' he cried, and the Fomoire grinned and gibbered at him.

'To take captives. To harvest the skins of Humans.' There was a dry, leather-on-bone chuckle. 'To fill the cages of our caves.'

'To carpet the way for the Lord of Chaos,' they cried, in sudden, disconcerting unison. And then, without warning, they turned to regard Theodora with their glinting sly eyes.

'To steal away the Amaranth Princess,' cried the Fomoire, and as the words formed, four of them leapt on Theodora and tore her from Andrew's arms.

As Theo screamed, the Gristlen leapt to its feet, its face contorted with fury.

'Mine!' it shrieked. 'That one is mine!' It was almost dancing in fury, and for a moment Andrew thought it would fall on the Fomoire and tear Theodora from them.

But in the same instant, light blazed from the Well, and Andrew and the Amaranths fell back, dazzled. Andrew threw up his hands to shield his eyes from the vivid, hurting brilliance, and as he did so there was the dull, rumbling sound of something being rolled back; and so vast was it that Andrew's senses spun. It is the stone from the sepulchre, he thought wildly. They are rolling back the boulder and opening up the tomb . . .

But it is not a tomb, it is a Gateway: The Gateway to the Black Realm, the entrance to the Dark Ireland . . . That is what they said might happen, that is what they feared . . . But this is not happening, thought Andrew. I won't believe this is happening.

When the sick dazzle faded, he saw that, silhouetted against the fiery crimson, was a darkly gleaming figure, armoured in ebony and jet, and he knew that his senses had not entirely played him false.

Through the visor of the figure's helmet glittered long, evil eyes, devoid of humanity and warmth, and beneath the gleaming black steel was a cruel, beautifully modelled mouth.

The Lord of Chaos.

The Amaranths and the Fomoire fell back at once, awe-stricken terror in every face. Andrew was half aware that the Gristlen had cowered back in its corner, snarling, but he had no eyes for the Gristlen; he could look only at the dark figure limned against the light. Ice closed about his heart and he thought: evil! This is the most evil creature ever beheld.

He stared at the Lord of Chaos, and confused memories of Brother Stephen's earnest teachings tumbled through his mind.

Not Satan, who tempted sinners to his wicked and sensual ways . . . Not Lucifer either; Lucifer who had been bright as the morning, radiant and seductive . . .

But something closely akin.

The Lord of Chaos, who would ride at Satan's right hand when the powers of Hell were unleashed into the world . . . Who would beckon with that cold and beautiful allure to Mankind . . . Had Andrew's quarry encountered this one? Had the Black Monk been here, and was it this strange and terrible lure that had ensnared him? And could I find it in me to blame him if it had? thought Andrew, caught in helpless fascination.

The inward-slanting eyes looked across at him, and Andrew felt his limbs weaken. A terrible numbness gripped him and the surface of his mind was stirred by a ripple of cold, malevolent amusement.

Puny Human to think you could challenge me.

The Fomoire were bowing before the Lord of Chaos, cringing and subservient, holding out their wizened hands here and there, throwing back the concealing skins, so that their tiny bald heads were visible and their wrinkled, ancient-crone faces gleamed.

Several of them tore off the skins completely and spread them on the floor before the figure in the doorway, making a carpet for him to walk across. Andrew saw, without really registering, that they were small and goblin-like beneath.

As the Lord of Chaos moved slowly forward into the Cavern, the Fomoire prostrated themselves on the ground, and in their chuckling, sly voices, began to chant, softly at first, and then more loudly.

'Carpet the world in Human misery,
Strew thick the harvest of the creatures of night.
Lay down the gleanings of the soul-eaters
Kill the veil of the world of light.'

The Lord of Chaos moved soundlessly across the Cave and stood directly in front of Theodora, still helpless in the Fomoire's grip. His arms were crossed on his breast and his eyes glowed with hungry fervour.

Andrew looked frantically about him for something to create a diversion, and saw for the first time that, directly behind Chaos, an immense, blood-red chariot had formed, with great stone millwheels to draw it. At the helm were his three henchmen: Murder, Anarchy and Misrule.

Dismay closed about him, for he saw that, although they were less awesome than their Lord, they were terrible and immensely powerful.

In the prow of the chariot stood Murder, and Andrew received the impression of twisting dark shadows and a swirling black silk cloak, the hem draggled with blood. Behind him was a crimson, snarling, masked creature that must be Anarchy; and with Anarchy was Misrule, again masked, but this time by a sly, grinning carving of gold. But after the first glance, Andrew's eyes went back to Chaos.

Chaos, the Dark Lord of the sinister Black Realm, treading across the carpet of Human skins laid for him by the Fomoire, his eyes glowing like coals.

This is evil, real and pulsating, and *seductive*. It is not the absurd red-eyed demon-figure of punishment that some of my Brothers try to instil into the minds of peasants and pagans; it is not the scaly, horned and tailed beast that some monks describe to force Christian conversion by fear.

This is pure, malevolent, *intelligent* evil.

Chaos accorded Andrew and the Amaranths barely a look. His eyes were still fixed on Theodora; they were burning and smouldering, and as he approached her the Fomoire fell back.

Chaos half turned and signalled to the three creatures waiting in the chariot, and Murder moved forward at once, his cloak swirling evilly and emitting a faint, noisome stench of stale blood. He scooped Theodora up in his arms and flung her into

38

the great millwheeled chariot, and Anarchy and Misrule both let out screeches of malignant laughter; Misrule flung snaking silver chains about her wrists.

The Gristlen howled in fury and loped across the Cavern until it was standing before the immense chariot. It raised its fists in rage, and its eyes glittered with malevolence.

'Mine!' it screamed. 'The prettiness was mine, to break the curse of the Dark Lords!'

Chaos turned to regard it, and as his eyes fell on the grotesque thing, he smiled with such cruelty that Andrew shuddered.

'A Gristlen,' he said, very softly. 'A warped, exiled thing bearing the carapace of the necromancers' anger.' He studied it, and the Gristlen cowered. But Andrew saw Rumour make an abrupt movement, and glanced across at her in surprise. Rumour was watching the Gristlen very intently, and Andrew saw wariness in her expression. Did Rumour then believe the Gristlen to be an enemy to reckon with?

The Gristlen had thrown up its horny hands as if to hide its face from Chaos's burning stare, but although it spoke in a cringing whine, the pale eyes peered slyly through its fingers.

'You have taken the prettiness, Master,' it said, and Andrew heard, for the first time, an underlying lick of arrogance in its voice and a cold, cruel anger. It said, 'You have taken the one who could have dissolved the curse. Cruel, Master,' said the Gristlen, and it crouched on the floor, wrapping its long arms about itself and rocking to and fro, keening softly.

Chaos walked round the Gristlen, his eyes never leaving it. 'So you are one of the escaped creatures who walks the world dragging its curse,' he said. 'You are one of the outcast things who must find a willing female who will endure your foul embrace. Yes, I have heard of your kind, Gristlen. Perhaps I have even condemned transgressors of my own laws to such a fate.'

For a second, the Gristlen eyed Chaos levelly, and there was such hatred in its mien that Andrew thought: is that what happened to the loathsome thing? Was it one of Chaos's people, and did it somehow offend his laws so that he pronounced a curse over it?

But the Gristlen looked away. It said, half to itself, 'Prettinesses, all of them,' and leered and twisted its hands together, darting sly glances at Theodora from the corners of its eyes. 'And you have taken the best.'

'Because she is the Amaranth heir,' said Chaos, and Andrew drew in a sharp breath and thought: of course! Of course it would have been Theodora whom the Ritual would have named! He looked across the Cavern and for a moment his eyes met Rumour's, and he saw understanding in her expression. Rumour of them all had seen Theodora's remarkable power. Rumour had known, just as Nechtan had known: 'Great-grandfather would expect me to do something,' Theo had said.

Chaos turned away from the Gristlen, as if deeming it of no interest. He looked at Theodora, still held in the chariot by the sinister cloaked figure of Murder, and his lips stretched in the thin, cruel smile again.

'A great prize,' he said. 'A brilliant mind already lit by the Sacred Flame of the Amaranths.' He moved nearer. 'It will be an intriguing challenge to reverse the Flame, my dear, and to see if we can coax it to burn in a dark mould. I have some skill in these things. Within the Castle of Infinity, you will meet creatures of blood so mixed that only necromancy could have created them.' He struck his breast. 'Only *I* could have created them!' he said. 'My life's work! And if I can reverse the Amaranth Flame of the Dawn Sorcerers, it will be my finest achievement! I shall rule unchallenged!'

Andrew felt a ripple of horror go through the Amaranths, but only Rumour moved. Rumour swished forward, her silken skirts brushing the ground, and stood before Chaos, her chin tilted defiantly, a reckless light in her eyes.

'Take me instead!' she cried, and Andrew saw the Amaranths stare at her.

Chaos studied Rumour. 'You are very tempting, my dear,' he said at last. 'I am honoured.'

'But – you refuse? You prefer the child? Then you are indeed warped,' said Rumour, contemptuously.

Chaos looked at her very intently, and Rumour held his gaze. And then he smiled, and it was a dazzling, darkly beautiful smile filled with unexpected intimacy, as if he recognised that, next to Theodora, Rumour was the strongest of the Amaranths, and as if he was sharing the knowledge with her and acknowledging her strength.

For Rumour there was a brief, terrible moment when her senses stirred and Chaos's dark glowing eyes awoke a dreadful response. Desire sliced through her from breast to womb, and she tore her gaze from him and looked down at the ground.

He said, very softly, 'Let us say that for the moment I prefer the child. But we shall meet again, Lady, and I shall remind you of your offer to me.'

He turned back to Theodora, who was struggling against the silver chains in the chariot. 'The Amaranth heir,' he said again, and his voice was silky with satisfaction. 'Many will fight me for you, Princess, but they shall not take you from me.' He looked across at the Amaranths, and fervour blazed in his eyes. 'I shall keep this one,' he said. 'You may send your puny Armies against me; you may revive the ridiculous Sorcery Wars in which you all fought so uselessly and so profitlessly, but I shall keep her.'

'There will be others of your world who will want her,' said Rumour, and Chaos nodded.

'Oh yes, Lady,' he said. 'Oh yes, they will all covet her. But I shall never give her up, not if I have to plunge the Dark Ireland into internal War. Not if there is necromantic Civil War in the Black Realm for decades ahead. I shall turn the Amaranth Flame, the accursed Sacred Flame of your House, into the ebony fire of necromancy. It may take many years, but I shall do it. Your Princess will eventually sit at my right hand and rule the Black Domain with me.'

Without warning, he looked back at Rumour, and now the smile was warm and gentle. 'We shall certainly meet again, Lady,' he said. 'And I look forward to it, for you will be a worthy foe and a stimulating lover.'

He sketched a brief bow, and turned back to the chariot, gesturing imperiously to his henchmen. At once, Murder took up the chariot's reins, his cloak hissing and swirling, Anarchy beside him. Misrule leapt on to the seat, the sly golden mask glinting evilly, and the Lord of Chaos stepped into the chariot. He lifted a slender white hand again, and the chariot turned, the great millwheels striking sparks of fire.

The Gristlen leapt forward, but the chariot was becoming bathed in dazzling light and the heels of the Fomoire were already vanishing over the edge of the Well.

The Gristlen's roar of frustration and fury split the Cave, and reverberated off the ancient walls. It reared up from its hunched, cringing stance to its full height – eight feet at least! thought the horrified Andrew – and its clenched fists were raised above its head as it bellowed its black rage. As the great chariot was swallowed by the gaping darkness of the Well, the Gristlen gave another of its terrible cries and, grasping the edges of the iron ladder, flung itself over the parapet and began to descend into the yawning maw.

There was the sound of its leathery skin rasping against the old dry bricks, and of stones being dislodged. But everyone in the Cavern heard the Gristlen's feet smacking against the iron rungs as it descended, the sound gradually fading.

The deep thunderous roll of something being rolled back into place filled the Cavern again, and Andrew thought: the stone is being rolled back into place. The Doorway is closed.

But the Lord of Chaos had carried the Amaranth Princess and her brother into the heart of the Dark Realm of the necromancers.

And the Gristlen had gone after them.

Chapter Five

The sentinel *sidh* had long since ceased to bother much about the patrolling of the southern ramparts of the Elven King's undersea City of Tiarna and the Palace of Nimfeach. It would have been a different matter if there had been any danger of anyone actually stealing up to the gates, of course, but everyone knew there was not the smallest possibility of this happening, because it never had happened, not even in the memories of the oldest *sidh* of them all.

The southern gate was not very vulnerable at all. It was not as if it was the eastern boundary, where the fabric between the True Ireland and the Dark Realm had become threadbare, so that it was occasionally possible to glimpse the black citadels of the necromancers, and the Crimson Lakes, and the NightFields with their sinister red harvests. One of the most venturesome of the *sidh*, who was called Inse, said he had once actually caught sight of the Lord of Chaos himself, riding out into his realm, with his fearsome servants, Murder, Anarchy and Misrule, in train behind him. But Inse was known to be rather over-imaginative, and this had never actually been proven.

The gates on the southern side of Tiarna were pale and studded with ivory and opal and pearl; they glinted coldly and occasionally threw out slender, white-hot spears of heat. The older *sidh* told how there was a spell composed of fire and ice in them, which Aillen mac Midha had commissioned from the sorcerers when the *sidh* had wrested the City from the *nimfeach*, the long-ago water-nymphs of Ireland. The Fire and Ice Enchantment was generally thought to be a very good deterrent to prowling Humans who might try to sneak into Tiarna, and penetrate Aillen mac Midha's Silver Cavern. Humans did not like fire any more than they liked ice. The *sidh* did not like fire

43

either, which was another good reason to avoid sentry duty at these particular gates. And while the *sidh* were all for welcoming Humans who could be pounced on and drained of Humanish senses (which was useful) and sometimes drained of Humanish seed as well (which was fun), Tiarna and her Water Caves were not intended for the prying eyes and clumsy, skin-covered, muscle-laced hands of Humans.

In fact none of the *sidh* had ever heard of any creature at all trying to get in, never mind Humans. This was another reason why sentinelling the southern boundary was the most tedious of all the sentinel duties. But it had to be done because you could not leave a single section of your boundaries unprotected, anyone knew that. Even the Humans knew it.

The *sidh* went out into the Humanish world and took whatever victims they could get, but that was within the rules. The Humans understood about it. They did not like it; most Humans fought quite hard to evade the *sidh*'s sinuous arms and serpentine embraces, and it was usually the ones who fought hardest whose souls and whose senses provided the best elixirs for the *sidh*'s music.

The four *sidh* on the southern ramparts were finding it very dull and extremely boring tonight. They had whiled away quite a good long time by recounting to one another the tremendous epic adventures of the High King, Aillen mac Midha, with especial attention to the remarkable time when he had clothed himself in the semblance of a Human and walked in the world of Men. This was always a good story; the grand old ballad, 'Humanish Elven', could be sung, and the echoes chased and caught and rewoven into the music. The *sidh* enjoyed darting about the tunnels in pursuit of echoes, and catching them and pouring them back into the music. And nobody ever grew tired of shuddering at the gruesomeness of the Ritual which Aillen mac Midha had had to submit to make himself visible to the Humans. This was a Ritual which was kept safely in the deepest and dimmest of all the crystal pools in Tiarna's cool, water-lit library, down among the Scrolls of Language and the silver-bound Sacred Enchantments which the *sidh* had stolen from the long-ago Fisher King.

So far as any of them knew, the Ritual had only ever once been taken out and invoked. It was something that was so dangerous and so complex that it could only be contemplated in times of the severest danger, when either Tara, the Bright Palace, was threatened, and the *sidh* honour-bound to come to her aid, or when Tiarna herself was under siege.

It was a gruesome Ritual, the acquiring of Humanish form. It was generally believed that the skins of Humans were cold and leathery, and Inse had heard from the High King's son, the Crown Prince Maelduin, that the skins made you feel heavy and sluggish. You felt muscles grating and bones crunching inside your skin, said Maelduin, with one of his slanting grins and one of his sudden, whiplash bounds upwards. Maelduin could sit absolutely motionless, drinking in the wisdom of the High King and the Elders; he could melt into the shimmering walls of the Silver Cavern itself if the mood took him, and the elder *sidh* would nod and smile and say that, after all, the Prince was absorbing the wisdom of his ancestors.

And then, without warning, something would spark his attention, and he would bound forward with one of his sudden pouring movements, and he would call his particular friends to his side, and light would stream over him like a shining cloak, and he would eye the others with his mischievous, brilliant eyes, and say: wasn't it time they had a raid on the Humanish world, and stole a few Humanish senses? Wasn't it time they drained the loins of some poor wretch of a Man of his thin, colourless seed? And he would be off, before the others had gathered their wits, darting through the tunnels with the rippling water-light, streaking up and up into the world of Men, sometimes taking them out through the ancient Well of Segais, sometimes taking one of the other routes, so that they might surface on the shores of Ireland's beautiful, sun-drenched west coast, where the entire sea could look as if it was on fire, and where the gulls swooped and dived at the *sidh*, and the *sidh* laughed and flew up at them, arrows of pure, turquoise light, with Maelduin at their head, leading them, laughing, and hurling bolts of pure, cool music into the air. Or they would come out at the heart of the Wolfwood, where you could slice through the layers of enchantment, and where you could cup in your hands the slanting rainbow mists of twilight, and where Maelduin would sometimes curl up on a grassy tussock and pour the *sidh*'s music into the deepening dusk, simply for the pleasure of seeing the

45

woodland world come alive, and the creatures of the Wolfwood come dancing and obedient to his call.

All of which, said the older *sidh*, was actually very wasteful. The *sidh*'s music was not something you should squander on reckless fights with seagulls or the luring of frivolous squirrels.

If Maelduin had been on sentry duty at the south gate tonight, it would not have been in the least boring. He might have started up a Chaunt which might have summoned a few minor spells, with whom they could have held a contest of some kind. Or he might have taken a Lure from the oaken chest when the High King was not looking, and played it (Lures were nearly always composed of music, of course), just to see what kind of creatures would come in answer. Or he might dive into one of the crystal lakes in his father's Palace, and come up streaming with silver droplets, the crystal water clinging to him like hoar frost, holding a Beguilement which he would unroll at their feet, so that they could hear one of the many hundreds of tales about the City of Tiarna and the Palace of Nimfeach, or about the long-ago battles between the *sidh* and the *nimfeach* people who were ruled by the cold, merciless Fisher King.

And then one of them, who was nearest the tunnel entrance, suddenly said, 'There's a shadow on the wall.'

The shadow was elongated and black, and very furtive indeed. The *sidh* were at once alert, becoming silent, nearly invisible wisps of blue-green smoke, only their long narrow eyes glinting in the dimness, only a faint iridescent shimmer betraying their presence.

The shadow was creeping nearer. It was a rather horrid loping shadow, as if its owner might be bending over, or as if it might be continuously looking back over its shoulder furtively, in case it was being followed.

The four *sidh* moved silently, banding together, melting into one for strength. This did not sound like a Human, but Humans were clever and cunning sometimes. It might be a subtle trap to decoy the guards away, so that Armies of Humans could pour down and overcome Aillen mac Midha's kingdom. Strong sorcery, properly woven and authoritatively used, had been known to weaken the *sidh*'s powers. It had certainly been known to quench their music, and the *sidh* were very nearly powerless without their music.

The thought passed swiftly between them: *this is no Human, but is it a creature we can use? Can we take its senses and its soul?*

The dark shadow was with them now, and they could smell that it was not anything Human.

A Creature of Deep Dark Enchantment . . .

And then the creature said, in a thick and clotted voice, 'Good *sidh*folk, I am come to offer you the greatest prize in all Ireland.' And, as the four *sidh* waited, not moving, not doing anything, the creature said, 'If you will allow me into your City of Tiarna, and give me audience with the Elven King in his Silver Cavern at Nimfeach's heart, I will show you the way to take, for your own, the entire Amaranthine race.'

Chapter Six

Cold, pure light poured into the Silver Cavern of the Elven King.

The four sentry *sidh* had snaked ropes about the dark intruder who had come stealing and sniffing down the watery tunnels into Tiarna; they had bound it with the silken cords spun in the underwater Seirician Caves and then they had drawn it through the pearl and opal-studded City gates, into the walled City and on through the Silvery Caverns to the Palace of Nimfeach.

Aillen mac Midha was seated on the immense carved Throne of the *Nimfeach*. The Prince, Maelduin, was at his right, for Maelduin would certainly not miss the chance of seeing the prisoner who had tried to infiltrate Tiarna. He might disrupt the Court if he was feeling particularly mischievous, but he was just as likely to listen, and perhaps even proffer some useful suggestions.

Aillen mac Midha had clothed himself in the half-garb of Human form which he assumed for these occasions. It was easier and swifter than the terrible Humanish Ritual; it gave him the semblance of Humanish form and it enabled him to converse with the prisoner in the clumsy, imprecise Humanish speech, assuming that the creature could use Humanish speech . . .

He was seated cross-legged at the centre of the great Throne of the *Nimfeach*, stolen from the Fisher King so many centuries ago, and although he had the silhouette of a Human, he would never have walked unnoticed in the Humanish world. There was a cool opalescence about him, and although his features were faintly Humanish, his eyes were huge and opaque. Several of the *sidh* thought that, like this, in this not-quite-Humanish, not-quite-*sidh* form, the Elven King was rather sinister. Inse thought it was because you were reminded that His Majesty had the ancient ability to alter his shape, and that there had always

48

been something sinister about creatures who could do that.

The creature caught at the south gate of Tiarna was not especially sinister. It was ugly and repulsive, but nobody was regarding it as sinister. The sentries had pushed it forward until it was standing before the Elven King's throne. Light fell across it, soft rippling waterlight, casting its features and its body into cruel relief. The *sidh* who had caught it saw and felt for the first time that it was indeed a creature under a deep and terrible enchantment, and shuddered.

Aillen mac Midha did not move, but Maelduin, curled smokily at his right hand, felt a sudden alertness from him, and knew that his father believed that standing before them was a being that trailed with it the malignant cloak of necromancy, and that carried across its repulsive shoulders the terrible burden of a dark curse.

He thought: *this creature has come from the Dark Realm, and therefore will have brought its aura of evil with it . . . It will have dragged its creeping stench of corruption into Tiarna, into our beautiful fragile world that we have so long guarded and that we have fought to bastion against the Dark Realm, and the clumsy brutalities of the Humanish . . .*

The prisoner was taller than most Men would be, although it was not giantish; it was Humanish in shape with the arms and legs of Men. The joints were swollen and fibrous-looking, and it had enormous feet, with the toes webbed, and long-fingered, huge-knuckled hands. Its shoulders were hunched and its back was bent and lumpish and, when it moved, it did so in a lurching, loping fashion, occasionally touching the ground with its hands.

Its head was round and hard and hairless, and it had pale bulging eyes that glittered hungrily as they inspected the Silver Cavern, as if the creature might be saying to itself: oho and aha: *here* is a pretty little place and *there* is a nice comfortable Throne. Its cold eyes were set below a jutting brow, giving it a brutish look, and its face was concave at the centre, as if a huge fist might have pushed the features inwards. Beneath the bulging eyes was a snout, with two deep moist black caverns for nostrils; and beneath the snout was a flat, gash-like mouth. Its skin was not the pale, almost-white colour of the Humans, nor did it have the satiny texture of Humanish skins, which the *sidh* found attractive. It had a thick, tough hide, leathery and dull and dry.

Repulsive, thought Maelduin, from his seat by the Throne. Has it indeed come from out of the Dark Ireland? And he remembered suddenly, one of the oldest and grisliest of all the legends: the immense Tanning Pit of the Dark Lords; the eternal abyss; the smoking Pit into which the Dark Lords cast those who had displeased them, leaving them there until their outer coverings were dried and smoked and until their shapes were unrecognisable. Until they were repulsive and gristly . . . *Until they were Gristlens . . .* I believe that this is a Gristlen, thought Maelduin, intrigued and repelled.

How must it be to walk the world dragging such a pitiful body about with you? What was it originally? Despite himself, Maelduin experienced a twinge of pity for the ugly, bewitched thing. The guard *sidh* had shackled it; manacles bound its legs and, when it held out its hands, they were clamped in the iron gyves used for Humans.

The Silver Cavern was filled with the cool, ice-blue light of the assembled *sidh*, and with the flickering waterlight that rippled eternally on the Palace walls. Aillen mac Midha sat cross-legged, resting his chin lightly on his hand, his eyes changing colour, becoming narrow and glittering, studying the prisoner unblinkingly. When he spoke, a stir went through the Court, for the *sidh* were unused to the spoken word, and it was always a shock to hear it. Maelduin wondered, as he always did, how the Humans could bear such a shackled method of communication, and how they understood one another fully with these ugly, restricting sounds.

'You are unexpectedly come to us, creature,' said Aillen mac Midha in his light, silvery voice, and although he used Humanish speech, a trace of the *sidh*'s own word-picture mind-imagery lingered, so that his words took shape and lay on the air for a while before melting and dissolving into droplets of pure silver.

The creature said, 'I am come to beg your help, Your Majesty,' and its voice was as cold and as ugly as its appearance. 'But in return, I could offer you something which will be of great value.'

'Why do you seek help here?' said Aillen mac Midha. 'Tiarna is heavily guarded and few find their way to us.' He leaned forward, his eyes glittering. 'Few *choose* to find their way to us,' he said. 'For to risk capture by the *sidh* is something most creatures would wish to avoid.'

The Gristlen put its head on one side as if considering its reply. 'So you still hunt the senses of Men, Aillen mac Midha,' it said softly, and for the first time there was a calculating intelligence in its eyes. 'You still drag the Humanish down into the water-caves and tear out their sight or their hearing or their speech or sense of touch.'

'For our music,' said Aillen mac Midha with perfect courtesy. 'If our music is to survive, it must be fed with the living senses of the Humanish.' He leaned forward, the cool silvery light falling across his half-Human half-*sidh* features. 'Our music must never die,' he said. 'It is the most precious thing in all Ireland, the music of the *sidh*.' He did not say, 'Without it we are powerless', but the listening *sidh* felt the thought frame in his mind.

But the Gristlen, its head on one side, said, still in the same soft voice, 'I see, Elven King. It is your music that gives you your strength and your impregnable City,' and Maelduin felt his father become more alert. A tiny breath of disquiet brushed through the Silver Cavern, and several of the *sidh* glanced uneasily at one another.

Aillen mac Midha regarded the prisoner thoughtfully, and Maelduin caught a flicker of puzzlement from his father, as if the Elven King might have heard something in the prisoner's reply that he had not expected. But he remained motionless and graceful on the Silver Throne, his head leaning lightly on one cupped hand, and presently he said, with exquisite courtesy, 'Will you tell us how you are called?'

There was an infinitesimal hesitation. Maelduin thought the other *sidh* would not have heard it – he was not sure he had heard it himself; but then his father repeated the question, and Maelduin knew his instinct had not misled him. There had been a batswing brush of uncertainty in the creature.

And then it said, 'In the world which I now inhabit, I am called the Gristlen,' and Maelduin thought: is that why it hesitated? Because it was ashamed? But it must know we would recognise it for what it is, he thought. And then: or does it want us to think it has forgotten its true name?

51

A ripple of awareness had stirred the listening *sidh*, and Maelduin knew that they, also, were remembering the legend of the Pit. This creature had dwelled there; for some reason it had been flung into the dry, smoking depths, and it had acquired the terrible carapace of the necromancers' punishment. Whatever it had been before its exile – Man or Beast or Fish or Bird or Crustacean – it might never regain its true shape . . .

The Gristlen had moved forward, shuffling its huge webbed feet, dragging the gyves as it did so. The *sidh* recoiled, for it was painful to hear the heavy, cold iron scraping the silver floor.

'I could be of service to you, Your Majesty,' it said, and although it adopted a cringing humility, there was a sneering note in its voice when it addressed the Elven King. Maelduin, motionless except for his eyes which glittered like turquoise fire, thought at once: this creature was never humble! It is not humble now! I think we have to be very wary indeed! And looked at his father, and saw that the Elven King was regarding the Gristlen through narrowed eyes.

The Gristlen was watching them, a calculating expression on its black snouted face. 'If you will dissolve the enchantment that binds me,' it said, 'I could be of service to you.'

'Say on, Gristlen,' said the Elven King, his expression remote.

The Gristlen had sidled up to the throne; its pale eyes were glittering and it held out its manacled hands.

'Once I was beautiful,' said the Gristlen. 'Once I was shining and fair and walked abroad and was admired. In my own world, I ruled.'

'And now,' said Aillen mac Midha, still in his courteous silver voice, 'now you are warped and ugly and bound by malignant spells. Now you are an outcast.'

'Yes.'

'You offended one of the Dark Lords? That is the customary reason for banishment to the Pit.'

The Gristlen's lipless mouth twisted, but it did not answer, and after a moment Aillen mac Midha said, 'Well? What was your transgression?' and the Gristlen dropped back into its cringing, shambling stance, so that Maelduin felt the flicker of distrust again.

The Gristlen said, in a soft, suddenly wistful voice, 'Once I dined at the Twelve Tables of the Dark Lords, and once I dwelled in the dark mansions of the Black Ireland. I was fêted and respected and my necromancy was sought.'

It stopped, and Aillen mac Midha waited.

'I was vouchsafed my own realm,' said the Gristlen, and a remembering greed glittered in its pale eyes. 'My own realm,' it said again, and looked round the Silver Cavern. 'I ruled there for many centuries, and my people rendered me obeisance.'

Again the pause. After a moment, Aillen mac Midha said very softly, 'You were driven out of your realm.' It was not quite a question, but the Gristlen said at once, its voice hissing with hatred, 'You are perceptive, Your Majesty.'

'It is clear that you were once a creature of power,' said the Elven King.

'I lost my realm,' said the Gristlen, and bowed its head in acknowledgement. 'I lost it in a brief and bloody war, and after that war was over, I was judged weak and unfit to rule.' It beat its breast again, and the iron gyves grated. 'My own kind judged me unfit!' it cried. 'That is why they cast me into the Pit.' It clenched its fists in bitter fury.

'That is one of the age-old laws of your kind,' said the Elven King, gravely. 'To be unable to defend a vouchsafed realm against an intruder, to be unable to keep a land in the grip of black necromancy is regarded as a severe crime by the Dark Lords.' It studied the Gristlen again. 'And so you were cast into the Pit,' he said. 'For your failure to keep and hold what had been entrusted to you, you were cast into the Pit.'

'But I escaped,' said the Gristlen, rubbing its cold webbed hands together and peering round with crafty pleasure at its cleverness. 'It took many centuries, but at last I climbed out of the Pit and I returned to the world.' It struck its scaly hide with a webbed hand. 'And I will regain what was mine!' it said angrily.

The Elven King said, 'Are you come here to seek our help? Perhaps to bargain with us?' And although he did not say, 'Are you *daring* to bargain with us?' every creature in the Silver Cavern heard the words quite clearly.

'I can pay a fine price,' said the Gristlen.

Aillen mac Midha said, very slowly, 'What do you require of us?' and the dreadful smile stretched the Gristlen's face again.

'A Humanish,' it said. 'A girl, but a *willing* girl to lie with.

53

Only that way can I dissolve this accursed carapace, and only then can I regain the realm where once I ruled.' It stood looking at them, its features evil and cunning. 'Only then can I take my place at the tables of the Dark Lords once more,' it whispered.

'Capture me a Humanish girl,' it said. 'For you it is easy. Send your *sidh* into the world above to bring me back a plump, fair-skinned Humanish female.' It grinned. 'And then lure her into my bed with your music.'

Aillen mac Midha did not move. He said, 'That would dissolve the carapace you have acquired?'

'Yes. I should take her,' said the Gristlen, its voice slurred and thick with lust. 'I should have her in my embrace and I should enter her and I should slake my body on her.' It reached between its scaly thighs and caressed itself obscenely, and Maelduin saw its withered-looking genitals swell and ripen. 'A sweet juicy Humanish,' it said. 'It is the only way.' And, looking back at the Elven King, it said with sudden arrogant impatience, 'Well? You will do it?'

Aillen mac Midha studied the Gristlen for a moment before replying, and then he said with cool, austere politeness, 'You are unable to do this for yourself?'

'They flee from me!' cried the Gristlen, and now there was a note of real anguish in its voice. It made a brief bitter gesture, indicating its monstrous body, and the gyves dragged harshly on the silver floor again. 'The prettinesses run from me,' it whispered, and Maelduin felt an unwilling pang of pity.

'But you could do it with ease,' said the Gristlen. 'You have the music that will lure the Humanish into your arms.' It paused, and Maelduin thought: that is the second time it has referred to the music's powers.

Aillen mac Midha said, 'And if we agreed, what would you give us in return?'

'In return,' said the Gristlen, 'I will show you the way through the catacombs beneath the Cadence Tower.

'I will show you how to get inside the Porphyry Palace and take the entire House of Amaranth Sorcerers.'

It leered round at them, and Maelduin said, 'But why should we want the Amaranths?'

'For your music,' said the Gristlen at once. 'That is why you take the Humanish. To add life and power to your music.' It

54

crept nearer to where Maelduin was curled half into the crystal rock, and stood looking up at him from beneath its lowering brow. 'And think, Crown Prince, only think how rich, how colourful your music would be if it had the Sacred Flame of the Amaranths coursing through it.'

The *sidh* rarely used the sunken dungeons with their cold stone walls and the constant lapping of the ocean at their walls. When they captured a Humanish, they drained him of his senses almost at once and took his soul for their music, flinging the carcass into the ocean where it would surface in the shimmering seas of Ireland's wild beautiful western coast. They took what had to be taken quickly and cleanly.

But the dungeons were still there: they were fathoms below the Palace; tiny stone cells deep in the ocean's heart, lit to dim dankness by the rippling green light of the seas. Maelduin and the *sidh* knew the eerie tales that haunted these dungeons; they knew that the dungeons had been always filled to overflowing by the fearsome Fisher King for his nightly entertainment. They knew how the Fisher King had once presided over a terrible Court in Tiarna, and how he had held grisly firelit feasts when the wretched prisoners would be dragged into the great circular Arena of Light by the *nimfeach*, to fight the Fomoire. The Fomoire hungered perpetually for Humanish victims and they had ever been allies of the Fisher King.

But if the shades of the Fisher King and his *nimfeach* walked these dungeons, they walked unseen and they walked unheard. Inse and Maelduin took the Gristlen between them, and thrust it into the deepest and the smallest of the dungeons. It crouched in a corner, its long legs drawn up almost to its chin, hugging itself with its gristly arms. The rippling green light fell across its features, giving it a twisted, sneering look.

'You will be here until we decide,' said Maelduin, using the same half-Humanish speech that his father had used, finding it clumsy and imprecise as he always did. 'Until we decide what to do with you.'

The Gristlen was unresisting. It watched them from beneath its low, brutal brow.

Inse said, 'There is Humanish food here, and water. It will not be for very long.'

'You are merciful to your prisoners,' said the Gristlen jeeringly. 'I think these dungeons have not always harboured such well cared-for victims.' It lifted its head to look round. 'The water dungeons of Tiarna,' it said, half to itself. 'A strange place to find myself.' Something that might have been amusement showed in its eyes as Inse and Maelduin left it.

Maelduin did not immediately return to the Silver Cavern. His father would have summoned the *Seomhra*, the *sidh*'s governing creatures, and the Crown Prince's presence would be expected.

But Maelduin paused in Tiarna's immense, cool, dim library, and stretched out on the banks surrounding the crystal pools, trying to glimpse the submerged annals of the *nimfeach* that lay beneath the pale water. In the deepest of those clear silken pools, was there something that would help them?

Maelduin did not trust the Gristlen. He thought that, even if they agreed to its request, it would betray them in some way. It would allow them to dissolve its terrible enchantment, but once it stood before them in its natural state – and that could be anything, thought Maelduin – it might turn on them. There had been a moment, no more than the beat of a wing, when it had looked not repulsive and cringing and beaten, but sly and triumphant. Maelduin thought it had been when the creature had said, 'So it is your music that gives you your strength.' And its eyes had gleamed, and there had been the fleeting impression of a sharp cruel mind thinking: so *that* is Tiarna's secret. That is the source of the *sidh*'s strength. How very helpful of them to tell me.

The *Seomhra* had convened in the Arena of Light, and when Maelduin slipped in, Inse was addressing them, questioning the Gristlen's motives and asking whether they really wanted the House of Amaranth and whether they needed it. The Elven King's chief advisor, Chimeara, reminded the others that to bring a Humanish to the Gristlen and to render her submissive by using their music would take up a good deal of magical energy. He did not doubt it could be done, said Chimeara, but he questioned whether they truly wanted to expend their beautiful music on such a thing.

'We use the music for just such means ourselves,' said Maelduin softly. 'We capture the Humanish with it.' He curled smokily at his father's side. 'It was for that Lure that we took the long-ago sirens,' said Maelduin.

'So that we should have the power to beckon to the Humanish,' said Aillen mac Midha, and the partly-Humanish eyes of the Elven King met the slanting turquoise eyes of the Crown Prince.

'Exactly,' said Maelduin softly.

'The House of Amaranth,' said Inse, thoughtfully. 'It is very tempting.' He looked at Maelduin, who said, in a cool, silken voice, that gave nothing away, 'Oh yes. Immensely tempting.'

One of the older *sidh* asked whether they dared risk actually releasing the Gristlen. 'For we do not know what its true state might be,' he said, and there was a ripple of agreement.

Aillen mac Midha said, very softly, 'There is a familiarity to it, I think.'

'It knew you,' said Maelduin, suddenly. 'It said, "So you still tear out the senses of the Humanish."'

'Perhaps it is something from the long-ago. There have been many creatures we have vanquished,' said Aillen mac Midha, his eyes dark and inward-looking. 'But perhaps it is only that all cursed creatures carry with them the same evil miasma.' He gave himself a shake, and turned back to the *Seomhra* to listen, and in his customary courteous fashion asked the younger ones for their opinions. They all knew that other peoples looked for advice and guidance to the Elders of their communities, but the *sidh* believed that young new ideas and outlooks could frequently be helpful.

The younger *sidh* distrusted the Gristlen. They were for pouncing on it there and then, and sucking out its horrid soul and its senses, and never mind getting into the Porphyry Palace.

'But,' said Maelduin, 'do we want the soul and the senses of such a creature? Mightn't it taint our world?' He moved to a jutting spur of rock so that he was a little higher than the others.

'It took us hundreds of years to purge Tiarna and the Nimfeach Palace of the soulless greed of the Fisher King,' said Maelduin, and the *sidh* listened, entranced, because this was no longer the cool, faintly mischievous Crown Prince; this was the dazzling, passionate being that headed the raids on the Humanish; that hurtled arrow-straight through the dim fastness of the Wolfwood, or skimmed the surface of the sparkling western seas, swooping on victims with soaring delight.

And when Maelduin spoke of the work and the dedication of the years; the decades that had been spent purging the Palace of the Fisher King's taint, and then imbuing it with their own strong, gentle bewitchments, the *sidh* nodded, and the younger ones who had been for draining the Gristlen of its soul, proffered their apologies.

'But,' said Inse cautiously, 'what about its offer? What about the souls and the senses of the Amaranths?'

He looked at Maelduin uncertainly, and Maelduin smiled the slanting smile that was uncannily the twin of his father's, but that had something far more reckless and far more audacious in it. He said, in a cool expressionless tone, 'But we are sworn to aid the House of Amaranth. As one of Ireland's Royal Lines, we are bound to the Amaranths. That was the bond made at the very beginning. In times of extreme danger, we are chained by the strictest sorcery to answer their summons if they should send it out.'

'*Humanish* sorcery,' put in Inse.

'*Amaranth* sorcery,' said someone else.

'It's nearly the same thing. The Amaranths aren't precisely Humanish but they're nearly so.'

'But,' said Chimeara, thoughtfully, 'the Gristlen said it could lead us through the catacombs and into the heart of the Palace.' He looked round. 'The Sacred Flame of the Amaranths,' said Chimeara.

'But can we in honour take it? Maelduin, can we?'

Maelduin's eyes were unreadable but there was a glint of colour deep within them.

'It is not an offer to be lightly turned down,' he said.

58

Chapter Seven

It was the most horrific situation the Amaranths could ever recall.

Theodora and Echbel were in the hands of the Lord of Chaos and the Fomoire, they were somewhere beyond the fearsome Gateway in the terrible necromancers' Realm.

The Gateway had sealed. They had all heard it happen: they had heard the great thunderous sound of the stone rolling back, and they had stared at one another in helpless dismay.

Laigne had collapsed sobbing, and Great-aunt Fuamnach and one of the younger sorceresses had helped her from the Cavern, back to the Palace.

'Understandable,' said the Amaranths, but Andrew saw that they were barely aware of Laigne, and that they were circling the Well, most of them deep in thought, and that it had not occurred to any one of them to leave the Well Cavern or the Cadence Tower, until they had found a way to break into the Dark Ireland. He found himself suddenly liking them very much for this.

Herself of Mugain was watching Rumour, who had been standing lost in thought at the Cavern's centre. 'I believe that Rumour has a plan,' she said presently, and Rumour looked up.

'Yes, I have.'

'What's that?' Cerball, who had been deep in discussion with the Mugain and Bodb Decht, turned round. 'Has somebody got a plan? Well I'm very glad to hear that.'

Rumour smiled the catsmile and came to stand at the centre. She does it naturally and effortlessly, thought Andrew. She is so used to being at the centre of everything that she moves there without even noticing.

'Really, my dears,' said Rumour, sounding amused, 'really, it ought to be quite shriekingly obvious to you all what we must do.'

'What?'

'It isn't shriekingly obvious to *me* . . .'

Rumour eyed them all, and it was impossible not to know that, although she was as worried as the others, she was beginning to enjoy herself.

'There is only one thing left for us to do,' she said. 'We must summon the *sidh*.'

There was an abrupt silence. And then Cerball said, a bit uncertainly, 'Are you serious about that, Rumour?'

'I was never more serious in my life.'

The Mugain, who had been frowning and beetling his brows, cleared his throat portentously and said he was inclined to be in favour. 'It's a weighty undertaking, of course,' he said. 'My word, it's a complex thing to do. But it *is* the obvious thing,' he added apologetically.

'Oh yes.'

'I don't know why no one else thought of it then—'

'And the *sidh* are sworn to come to the aid of any Royal House,' said Cerball, still sounding as if he might be arguing it out with himself. 'We all know that.'

'They're *bound* to come to our aid,' said somebody else. 'And to that of every Royal House in Ireland. It's a very ancient spell indeed, that of the Summoning.'

'I suppose Rumour knows the incantation, does she?'

'Of course I know it.'

'No, but really know it? Because it won't do,' said Cerball, looking unwontedly severe, 'it won't do at all to get it the smallest bit wrong.'

'I shan't get it wrong,' said Rumour with a touch of impatience.

'Then I suppose, yes, I really suppose we ought to try it.'

The ancient Summoning of the *sidh*, the powerful bewitchment that Rumour intoned, her hands lifted with the palms uppermost to call down power, was one of the most beautiful things Andrew had ever heard. He thought it would be something he would remember long after he had gone from these strange people, and he thought it would be something he would want to roll up and keep as a precious and immensely valuable experience.

The incantation was filled with gentle, rhythmic music, and with shifting, blurring patterns of light and colour, and with a soaring, pouring chiaroscuro of bewitchments and enchantry and beguilements. Rumour's soft husky voice rose and fell, reaching for the cadences with apparent effortlessness, shaping the queer, multi-syllabic words with what seemed to the dazzled Andrew to be supreme ease.

Cool light began to fill up the shadowy Cavern, and Andrew saw that the Amaranths had stepped back and were watching Rumour with mingled respect and admiration. They do not entirely like her because they do not fully understand her, he thought. But they acknowledge her strength. They respect her power and her learning. He realised with surprise that Rumour was probably very learned indeed. Would she not have been a possible successor for the dying Nechtan? he thought, and knew, in the same moment, that it would never have done. She was a gambler, a reckless adventuress. She had made that absurd extravagant gesture to the Lord of Chaos – 'Take me instead' – and although it had been courageous and generous, it had also been impetuous.

Rumour was standing alone, the cool light twisting about her, turning her hair to a streaming cascade of turquoise and silver. Her slender cloaked figure was wreathed in a pouring waterfall of blue and green iridescence. She is beautiful and exotic and utterly pagan, thought Andrew, unable to take his eyes from her. And I believe that if anyone can force open that terrible Gateway, then she can.

Rumour's voice rose and fell in the incantation, and Andrew felt, very faintly, the stirring of something from a very long way off. Something that thrummed with ancient power, and something that was so soft and cool and so achingly beautiful that it would sear your soul and brand your mind for ever . . . So that you would follow it into hell and beyond if only it would go on . . .

A huge anticipation was creeping over the Cavern now, as if every person present could hear and sense and glimpse that something tremendous was approaching . . .

The *sidh*, the ancient faery race of Ireland's ocean city answering the Summoning . . . Rushing down to the aid of the Royal House of Amaranth . . .

Andrew drew in a deep breath and waited, torn between fear and delight, his eyes scanning the Cavern, his every nerve stretched, because it would be unbearable to miss a single second. And then, without warning, in the space between one heartbeat and the next, it began to fade. At one minute it was forming, it was taking shape and substance and life, and it was going to be beautiful and powerful and marvellous.

And then it was dying. It was fading and slipping, and there was darkness and a whirling, gaping void. Andrew saw Rumour's eyes widen with surprise and fear, and he saw the Amaranths look up, startled.

It is going. Somehow she has failed. They all sense it.

Rumour whirled about, and her face was white. 'They are not answering!' she said, her voice taut with fear. 'There is an emptiness . . .'

'Try again!' cried Cerball, and several of the others called, 'Yes, again, Rumour!'

'I cannot! It is useless!' Rumour had moved from the centre of the Chamber. 'There is nothing there! Can you not hear it? Can you not feel it?' she cried angrily.

The Mugain said slowly, 'Are they refusing to answer?'

'They cannot! They dare not!'

'They *have* to answer!'

'They are *bound* to aid us, unless—'

'Unless they themselves are dying,' said Rumour, and stared at the others with horror.

The *sidh*, the cool faery creatures who had dwelled in Ireland from the very beginning, and who were constrained to aid her Royal Houses, were beyond their reach.

The Amaranths were shocked and horrified. Dawn was streaking the skies as they sat round the long banqueting table in the Porphyry Palace, stunned and appalled, eating the freshly baked bread and the honey and dishes of buttered eggs, but there was plainly no thought of resting. Andrew found himself warming to their doggedness and their unquenchable optimism, and he listened as they began to put forward suggestions, hesitantly at first, and then with more confidence. They drew strength one from another, he thought.

The Mugain, in whom Cerball's wine had wrought a remarkable upturn in spirits, said they would be sure to find spells in Nechtan's library which would force open the Gateway and get several of them into the Dark Realm. They had none of them thought of that. Somebody else remembered that there was a Spell of Keys which would unlock all doors, and somebody else suggested the White Stallion of CuChulainn which was said to be able to emerge victorious from all battles. There were Cloaks of Silence and Invisibility as well – Rumour was known to own several of those which might be helpful, and which she might be prevailed upon to loan. Great-aunt Fuamnach, who had helped to put Laigne to bed, but who had rejoined the party in time to partake of a huge breakfast, tartly said that these would be very useful indeed, always supposing that the loaning of them would not cause Rumour any deprivation.

'My entire wardrobe is at your disposal, dearest Aunt,' purred Rumour with impeccable courtesy.

Andrew had found himself seated next to Rumour. It flickered on his mind that she had deliberately arranged it, and a sudden delight surged up within him that this exotic and remarkable creature might have wished for his company. This was the closest he had yet been to Rumour, and he studied her covertly, seeing how the scarlet silk clung to her slender, supple body, and seeing that her skin had the faint ivory sheen of the other Amaranths, so that it was as if a flame had been placed behind thin, translucent alabaster. Her eyes were pure glowing violet, set aslant in her face, fringed by long dark lashes, and her long, striated, rippling hair changed from jet black to rich copper bronze, and was threaded with thin silver lace.

He had not, so far, dared to ask what would happen to Theodora and her brother, but even as the question was framing in his mind, Rumour turned her brilliant Amaranth eyes on him and said, 'Echbel will be caged and fattened, and eventually the Fomoire will flay him and wear his skin.'

'I see,' said Andrew, who had already realised this, but who was so horrified to hear it put into fact that he hardly noticed that Rumour had heard his thoughts.

'As for Theo . . .' Rumour paused, and Andrew knew at once that, although the Amaranths were concerned for Echbel, and although they would do all they could to save him, it was Theodora for whom they were really fighting.

'Theo will be held in the Castle of Infinity by Chaos,' said Rumour. 'It is many hours now since he took her, and probably they are still travelling across the Dark Realm. But they will soon be there. Every hour she is in there intensifies the danger.'

'It would have been better to rescue her before Chaos's Castle is reached?' said Andrew.

'Oh yes. There will be so many menaces,' said Rumour, frowning. 'Some we know of, but some we do not. But once she is inside the Castle of Infinity, she will be truly at Chaos's mercy.' She cupped her hands about a huge blue bowl of warm, thin mead, her eyes serious and absorbed. 'Also, it is true what Chaos said; there will be many who will try to take her from him. The Crimson Lady of Almhuin will almost certainly be one.'

'Yes?'

Rumour sent him a sideways look. 'It is whispered that the Crimson Lady bathes in the blood of young and beautiful virgins, and of course,' said Rumour, eyeing Andrew unblinkingly over the rim of the mead bowl, 'of course, virgins are always a very alluring challenge.'

'Why does she do that?'

'It is how she preserves her eternal youth and her rather grim beauty,' said Rumour. 'There are other ways to do that, you understand, but the Crimson Lady has dark and depraved hungers, and the spilling of blood serves them. She was once Chaos's paramour, although it is whispered that there has been a rift between them. But she would certainly want Theo for her slaughterhouse,' said Rumour, thoughtfully. 'And there would be others as well as the Crimson Lady.' She turned her long glowing eyes on him. 'It may be that war in the Dark Realm is about to break out.'

Andrew said carefully, 'Because of Theodora?'

'Yes, for she would be a very great prize. She has a remarkable power essence, Theo,' said Rumour. 'Chaos knew that at once, of course. Perhaps he knew it before we did so ourselves. Also, she understands something of the Lost Language of Magis, which the rest of us do not.'

Andrew said, 'I had not realised – forgive me – that there would be female necromancers,' and Rumour sent him one of her slant-eyed smiles.

'Your Order does not account females very highly, I think?' she said, and Andrew stared at her.

'There are what we call abbesses,' he said, rather coldly. 'Women of immense piety who have forsworn a husband and children.'

'How admirable,' said Rumour lightly, and Andrew had the strong impression that she did not regard it as especially admirable, but that she did not regard the gaining of a husband and children particularly admirable either. But she said, 'There are not so many female necromancers, but there are a few. They are sometimes extremely strong, and nearly always very beautiful, although I believe that some of them allow their hungers to quench their powers.'

Andrew said, with careful courtesy, 'I have had little dealing with females, madame. My creed does not permit it,' and Rumour leaned her arms on the table and allowed the silken gown to slide back, and looked into his eyes.

'Does it not?' she said, softly. 'I should like to make you change your mind, Andrew.' And smiled to herself, because although everything was truly dreadful, it was extraordinarily pleasant to discomfit this serious young man. He would be a celibate, of course, as the Druids were celibates, because it was part of this new, stark religion. I could have fun with this one, thought Rumour, with sudden mischief. There is something remarkably alluring about celibacy. There is something even more alluring about an untried lover, and I would stake my own Castle that this one is untried.

Andrew, who had eaten and drunk sparsely, sat back and studied the rest of the company.

Am I truly here, in the great Amaranth Palace, in company with creatures who profess to be able to harness magic? And am I really discussing the Realm of the necromancers with this strange exotic creature at my side? Am I eating breakfast with them and talking about enchantments and half-Human creatures, and dark evil spells, and *believing* in them? Am I believing in any of this?

And then, at a level of his mind that he hardly dared

acknowledge existed: and am I feeling the stirrings of desire for this remarkable creature who may not be entirely Human?

He had embraced celibacy willingly, seeing it as something pure and strong; something that would lead to the greater purification of the soul. But his creed also demanded self-honesty, and now, faced with the mischievous, dazzling Rumour, he thought: but did I accept that particular vow only because I did not know what I was forswearing? Is it only that I have never encountered anyone quite like her? Is it simply the strange, not-quite-Human beauty, and the flame beneath the ivory . . . ? And the rippling hair, tawny and copper, that would pour over her shoulders and cover almost her entire body like a silken cloak . . . ?

He shifted uneasily in his chair. He would quench the desire as he had quenched other desires, and he would bank down this need as he had banked down other needs. It is no different, no more difficult than resisting rich food, potent wine. I can resist this one, as I have resisted others.

At the head of the table, Cerball had risen to his feet and was regarding his family solemnly. An instant silence fell on the Amaranths, and they turned towards him, waiting.

Cerball said, 'As the direct descendant of our Ruler, I stand in his place until the Succession Ritual has been chanted.' He spoke unassumingly and rather humbly, and Andrew understood that there had probably never been any question of Cerball succeeding Nechtan, and that probably Cerball himself did not want to. But someone had to take the lead, and someone had to stand in Nechtan's place, and for the moment that someone had to be Cerball, Nechtan's grandson.

Cerball said, 'Since the *sidh* are beyond our reach, it seems that we must needs embark on a quest of immense importance and extreme danger—'

'The forcing open of a Gateway into the Dark Realm,' put in the Mugain, who would not have dreamed of usurping anybody's temporary authority, but who liked to make everything clear.

'Yes, since we are to attempt that, it would be appropriate to first invoke the Ritual of the Benison,' said Cerball. 'It would strengthen our powers.' He looked down the table, his face solemn. 'And so we will drink the wine and break the bread and call down the Benison of the Dagda,' said Cerball, and as if they had been given a command, the Amaranths rose to their feet.

Andrew rose with them from instinctive courtesy, and stood quietly in his place. But his mind had been thrown into turmoil. When Cerball said, 'We must invoke the Ritual of the Benison. We must drink the wine and break the bread', Andrew had felt a sharp jolt of shock beneath his ribcage.

The Ritual of the Benison? And – drink the wine and break the bread? What am I about to see?

Cerball lifted his hands upwards and the Amaranths brought their palms together and bowed their heads. Andrew, staring, thought: but that is the Christian attitude of prayer. That is *exactly* the Christian attitude of prayer.

In the same unassuming tones, Cerball said, 'Dagda, All-Father, we call on you to guard us from the Destroying Darkness that passes over our thresholds.' He waited, and the Amaranths murmured a soft response.

'Guard us from the passing over of the Destroying Darkness.'

Andrew was no longer aware of his surroundings, or of the presence of Rumour at his side. With Cerball's words, the tumult had begun again, and he felt it swoop and darken about his head.

The passing over of the Destroying Darkness . . . The passing over . . . *The Passover*, thought Andrew, torn between shock and creeping horror. The ancient, honourable feast, named for the exodus, the passing over of the destroying angel of the thresholds of the Israelites . . . It *cannot* be that. But the words are almost exact. Just as the prayer attitude is almost exact.

Cerball was saying, 'We render thanks, Dagda, for deliverance from the Darkness,' and again, there was the soft murmur from the Amaranths.

'Dagda, hear our plea,' said Cerball, his voice low and serious.

'Hear our plea and let our powers be strengthened.'

'Grant, we implore you, the might of your Staff of Life and Death.'

'Let our strengths be unwavering.'

'Let shine the light of your Temple about us, and let pour forth the power of your Staff.'

'Let our purpose be strong.'

Cerball paused, and then went on, 'And, if among us here present there be any creature with evil in its heart or its soul, or if we have done any thing to offend the pure Flame of the Dawn Sorcerers which is our inheritance and our vouchsafed power, let that be known now.'

Again, the response: 'Let not the evil or the wicked or the maliced-minded come to this Table.'

This Table, thought Andrew. This Table where they have broken bread and drunk wine. Where they have invoked the help of some omnipotent figure . . . *The Father-God* . . .

There was a pause as if the Amaranths were listening for the presence of evil, and Andrew felt the intense concentration of Rumour at his side.

And then came the response.

'For this is the Table of the Dagda where we have eaten the Bread of Life and drunk from the Wine of Purity and we do so in remembrance of the powerful Son of the Gods who once walked in the world of Men.'

Cerball lifted his own wine chalice and said, 'We drink in remembrance of the Samildanach, who is the Man of Each and Every Art who will come again into Ireland and free her from the Dark Powers.'

He lifted his chalice to his lips, and the Amaranths copied him.

Andrew hesitated, and then reached for his own wine chalice. But as he sipped the strong, rich wine, his mind was in a ferment. He thought: *how old is this ceremony?* And then, terribly: *But how old are the ceremonies of my people?* How old is the ceremony of the Blessing, the Eucharist? When did the Last Supper really take place? *And who truly presided over it?*

With the sudden seething turmoil, the ancient wise words of the early mission-monks, Augustine and Justus and Paulinus, slid unprompted into his mind:

'For if we put the new wine into the old casks, after a time, the new wine will smell of the cask . . .'

They adapted the pagan beliefs and the pagan rituals, thought Andrew, frantically. We *knew* that they did. So that the people, the peasants and the pagans and the simple, unschooled minds could be converted more easily.

Yes, but what about that last prayer – *The Samildanach who will come again into Ireland and free her from the Dark Powers . . .*

He thought he ought to have expected it. He ought to have known that fragments of Christianity would have reached pagan Ireland long since. That those fragments would have been absorbed into Celtic heathenism. They are believers without even being aware of it, he thought.

And then a tiny, treacherous voice said inside his head: but supposing it is the other way round? Supposing the New Learning, the marvellous, pure, clear Teachings, and the Gospels, are simply a new version of Celtic paganism? Paganism retold . . . Supposing it is we who are being given the new wine in an old cask?

Cerball had set down the wine chalice and had lifted both his hands. He said, 'The Benison of the Father-God, the Dagda, is all about us.'

'And with our quest.'

There was a further moment of silence, and then the Amaranths lifted their heads again, and there was a feeling of: now we can begin! Now we are armoured!

They went in silent procession down to the ancient Sorcery Chambers.

Cerball and the Mugain had invited Andrew to accompany them down to the Sorcery Chambers. 'You would be most welcome,' said Cerball, who had rather taken to Andrew.

'I shall be unable to further your work,' said Andrew, hesitating, but the Mugain, who had formed a very favourable opinion of Andrew's intelligence, said they needed all the wise heads they could get.

'You'll perhaps have found our rituals interesting?' he said, and Andrew said in an expressionless voice, 'Extremely interesting.'

The Purple Hour of twilight was stealing through the Palace as they descended to the Sorcery Chambers: 'An hour which is itself laden with magic,' Cerball had said seriously. 'It may help to strengthen our endeavours.'

Andrew had inclined his head, half believing, half not, but deep within his mind he was uneasily aware that Theodora had been inside the Dark Realm for more than a day already; she might already be in the bowels of the Castle of Infinity. The internal battle that Rumour had spoken of: the fight between the necromancers to gain possession of the Amaranth Princess, might already be raging. It was a fearsome thought. Andrew had not been able to forget the way that Theodora had run to him and how she had trusted him, and how he had held her in the Cadence Tower. To one unused to children, or to dependency from any other living soul, Theodora's instant and complete trust had been a remarkable experience.

He could not forget, either, that when the Lord of Chaos had held out his hands, Theodora had gone instantly into them.

'Come unto me, little children, for mine is the kingdom . . .'

It was something else he dared not explore too deeply.

Walking quietly behind the procession, Andrew felt himself falling deeper into the sensuous, twilit, pagan world of these people, and for a moment, panic touched his mind. But I cannot stop now! he thought in silent anguish. I cannot pull back now. And this is perhaps the path I must take. Was it? Yes, for if the Black Monk still lived, what more natural than that he would be within the Dark Realm itself? If everything I ever heard about him is true, thought Andrew, then he would surely have been drawn into the dark allure of Chaos and his world.

He was immensely interested in the great, silver-doored Chambers below the Porphyry Palace, and listened carefully when the Mugain explained that he must remain distanced from the Looms themselves.

'The heat,' said the Mugain seriously, 'and the power. Dear me, once the Looms begin to spin, the power is so immense that you could be blasted from the Palace!' He eyed Andrew anxiously.

'I understand,' said Andrew. 'I shall remain by the door.' The Mugain went off to tell Cerball that you had to say one thing for this new religion: at least it taught its people obedience.

The great Sorcery Chamber of the Amaranths was one of the most remarkable sights Andrew had ever seen. He stood just inside the great Silver Door with the deeply etched emblems, his eyes adjusting to the light, his senses reeling.

It was darker than he had expected, rather as if the curtain of night that had fallen outside had somehow slid here as well. Purple and silver shadows lay everywhere, and there was a huge sense of tranquillity, as if the decades and the centuries of study and concentrated thought might have permeated the stones and the bricks. There was the flickering of firelight from somewhere, and as Andrew's eyes adjusted, he saw that the Sorcery Chambers were long, rather narrow rooms, several chambers opening out of one another, linked by low stone archways, with flaring wall-sconces of pure soft silver. The Looms stood down the sides: huge rearing columns of silver and black, with silken glinting skeins of light weaving in and out of their structures. Formidable, thought Andrew, staring up at them. And also a little frightening.

He remained quietly watching, seeing the sorcerers move in and out of the Looms; seeing that the firelight came from the far end of the Chamber, from a huge brick structure that looked like a kiln that had been built into the wall. Within it was a leaping fire, burning with red and gold flames, giving out a sharp, pungent scent. Andrew thought: is it applewood? Or fruitwood of some kind? And then was not sure that it was the scent of burning wood at all. Was it the scent of burning magic? But I don't believe in magic! he cried silently.

As the sorcerers moved to the Looms, the thin, silken heat increased, and Andrew saw that the sorcerers had changed; subtly and quietly and definitely they had changed.

How? What had happened to make them different?

They were all wearing the plain dark cloaks they had worn to enter the Cadence Tower, but these did not make them look insignificant or drab. To Andrew's eyes, the Amaranths seemed to glow from some inner flame, and their eyes were lit from behind, as if flames had leapt up inside them. He understood that, in donning the cloaks, they had donned the mantles of their calling, and as he leaned forward, he saw that deep within the eyes of each one were tiny twin flames, glittering minuscule tongues of fire, twisting and spiralling.

The Power Essence, the Sacred Flame of the Dawn Sorcerers, about which the Amaranths had spoken during supper? Or something stronger? (The fire of the Holy Spirit entering the Apostles . . . ? No!)

And then Rumour touched the Looms nearest to him, and Andrew forgot about everything else.

71

Chapter Eight

The light from the rippling green water moved softly across Maelduin's slender, shining form as he darted along the water tunnels of Tiarna, to the sunken dungeons beneath the Palace.

He felt the dappled, gently moving light pour about him, and although he was very used to it, it had never lost its power to enchant him.

Beautiful. My city. I am at home here, he thought. *This is my place and this is where I belong.* He would spend hours upon hours, unmissed by the others, unlooked-for by them, roaming these closed-in tunnels, with the cool green ocean-light, occasionally hearing the dark, cold echoes of the *nimfeach*, who had created these Caves and this City at the dawn of time, and who had left a bequest of evil which the *sidh*, over the centuries, had filtered and polished, until there was no evil, only glowing light and endless music, and shining, soft beauty.

Maelduin could hear the echoes and he could feel them, and he had never feared them.

Until now.

Since the capture of the Gristlen he had felt a stirring of unease; a feeling that something was smearing a sticky, viscous trail through Tiarna. He had not been able to forget how the Gristlen's eyes had darted slyly back and forth, as if it was assessing the *sidh*, and he had not been able to forget, either, the sudden cunning alertness when Aillen mac Midha had made that reference to the *sidh*'s strength being in the music.

Now, approaching the Gristlen's dungeon, he felt a ruffle of fear and a prickling warning. *Something is wrong...*

He slowed his pace, melting into the rockface of the tunnel, and waited.

Yes, I am right... There is something here that threatens and menaces...

72

He moved on, scanning every crevice and every sliver of stone and rock, his every sense alive and alert. Beneath him was the thick bone-dust of centuries; the soft powdery particles of Humanish victims. Maelduin looked down and icy fingers closed about him.

In the thick, pale bone-dust were footprints. The marks of some creature's feet or paws or hoofs. Footprints.

Then something has walked these tunnels . . .

The *sidh* did not walk; they did not need to. They flew or they simply darted through the air, arrows of blue-green light. Sometimes they swam. But they did not leave footprints.

The footprints might be from the journey down here to bring the Gristlen into the deep, dank dungeons. Maelduin stayed where he was, considering this. Were they? He half closed his eyes, and recalled how he and Inse had brought the Gristlen down here. They had carried it between them to the dungeons, disliking handling it, but doing so firmly and steadily. Its jointed webbed feet had not touched the ground. Then these prints could not belong to the Gristlen, because no creature imprisoned down here had ever escaped. These were the Fisher King's own dungeons and he had made them impregnable.

Could it be the Gristlen? Had it somehow found or forced a way out of the sunken dungeons? Maelduin stayed where he was, considering, feeling, as he always felt, the ancient agonies of the long-ago Fisher King's prisoners, experiencing the dreadful, helpless despair that had soaked into the cold stones. A terrible emotion, despair. A giving up of all hope, a turning away from light and life.

He was framing the thought that it was even bleaker than usual down here, when he became aware that the light was changing; it was dimming, becoming colder, danker. There was a greasy look to it.

Something has happened . . . Something is happening . . . I was right . . .

He frowned and shook his head, because he knew, quite suddenly, that something had happened and something was continuing to happen. There had been one moment when everything was normal and ordinary and safe, and when Tiarna and the Palace of Nimfeach was secure. And then there had been another moment when evil – something ancient and hungry – had swooped in and swooped down, and Tiarna had become very unsafe indeed.

Something has come into Tiarna that is cold and menacing and more threatening than anything we have ever known . . .

And then he thought: *no! No – not something coming in . . .*

SOMETHING GOING OUT . . .

Something had gone from Tiarna, something magical and strong and precious.

Maelduin poured forward, a shower of turquoise smoke, and saw that his earlier suspicions had been right. The door of the Gristlen's dungeon stood open.

It had done what no other creature had ever done.

It had escaped from the Fisher King's dungeons.

The silver light that had once suffused the entire realm of Tiarna and that had its centre in the great Silver Cavern of the Elven King, was cold and dull. As Maelduin entered the Cavern, he saw that the *sidh* had already gathered, huddling together, fear in their eyes. He felt, as if it was a physical blow, their anguish and their terror gust outwards.

Something is happening to our city . . . What has come amongst us . . . ? And, from several of the more perceptive ones: *what has been taken from us?*

Maelduin thought: yes, they feel it. Of course they do.

He moved forward, seeing them fall back, hearing the ripple of trust from them. *The Prince . . . He will know what to do . . .*

But I don't know, thought Maelduin in sudden anguish. I don't know what to do, and I don't know what has happened.

But he moved with sureness, until he was standing at the centre of the Silver Cavern, facing the great Throne of his father.

And then he did know, and sick dread closed about him.

The Elven King was lying at the exact centre of the dais, still clad in the half-Human garb he had adopted to speak with the Gristlen.

His hands were crossed on his breast, the slender, beautiful fingers twined. But the opaque eyes were closed, and there was a cold, marble pallor to his skin.

Maelduin moved forward, his eyes on his father's still form, and felt the others become silent and motionless. No ripple of thought-imagery reached him, and he knew that the *sidh* were too frightened and too stunned to surround him with their presence.

I believe my father is dead, he thought. *The Elven King, the near-immortal Aillen mac Midha is dead.*

I have no idea what to do . . . I have no knowledge of what is called death. I think that none of us has any knowledge of it . . .

But the King was not quite dead. As Maelduin approached, he saw that the folded wings still moved, as if a creature beneath was breathing, lightly and sweetly; and when he touched his father's cheek, a tiny spiral of warmth reached him.

Not dead! He is not dead!

Not yet, my son . . . It came as faintly and as intransigently as the rippling water-light on Tiarna's walls and, as it did so, the *sidh* stirred uneasily.

Not dead yet, my people . . .

There was the tiniest of movements from the still shuttered features, and Maelduin stood waiting, willing his father to wake and be with them; tensing every nerve-ending.

For a terrible moment there was a silence so immense and a stillness so complete and an emptiness so vast that Maelduin thought his father had died as they watched.

And then it came again, as gently and as dimly as a breath of wind in the world above them.

The creature has taken our soul and our core . . .

Maelduin felt the *sidh* ripple into that fear again, but he stayed where he was, the cold horror engulfing him.

Our soul and our core.

Our music . . .

The Gristlen has stolen our music, thought Maelduin, and with the thought came bewilderment, for how had the creature known what to do, and how had it known where the *sidh*'s precious enchantments were stored? How had it penetrated to the deepest of the crystal pools so unerringly to snatch up the cool, beautiful music?

Somehow it did it, thought Maelduin. Somehow it found its way through the labyrinth of tunnels and caves into the world above.

There was no time to wonder how or why or when.

Their music had gone, and they were therefore surely doomed.

Chapter Nine

Rumour thought that matters were beginning to go a little better. Everyone was working quietly and intently at the Looms, and Cerball had gone round distributing Chronicles from Nechtan's library where they were wanted, trying to keep careful notes of everything everyone was doing. As the Mugain had said, they did not want to find that four of them had all been working independently on the same enchantment.

Rumour had decided to attempt the summoning of the White Stallion of CuChulainn, the great, mystical, winged horse that could pour itself and its riders through the night sky, and slice through evil as cleanly as a razor through silk. It was an extremely difficult, complex invocation, and Rumour thought it was many centuries since anyone had attempted it. The incantations were rather long, but they were very beautiful, and if they worked, it would be immensely worthwhile.

She had already woven the threads of light and the pouring fire of dawn, and as soon as they had melded and cooled slightly, she would begin the first of the twenty-seven incantations. Nine times three, one of the strongest of all numbers. Once all three of the stanzas were chanted and the incantation complete, there would be the ancient Beckoning to the Fire Stables, where the White Stallion dwelled.

Good! thought Rumour, standing back from the Loom, letting the light threads and the fire meld, seeing how they were running smoothly together. Yes, the spell could be left to cool.

She was not exactly fatigued, because the weaving of spells generated its own marvellous energy. Normally when Rumour was spinning something new or altering something already created, she was crackling with enthusiasm and brimful of such energy that she could work for days without sleeping or resting.

But there was something – perhaps not fatigue precisely, but a dragging coldness, a dank, insidious chill. Heartcold. Bonecold. As if I shall never be warm again.

If she had not known better, she would almost have thought it to be the insidious cold of necromancy. Which was patently absurd. Cerball had pronounced the incantation of the Repudiation very fervently indeed over the wine, because they dared not have anything in the Sorcery Chambers that smelt of necromancy if they were to reach Theodora. And the response of, 'Let not the evil or the wicked or the maliced-minded come to this Table' had been particularly strong, Rumour had marked it at the time. It was an immensely old and fearsomely powerful conjuration and Rumour thought that it would have shrivelled the smallest thread of anything tinged with darkness.

But for all that there was something extremely dark very near to them.

Rumour looked round the Sorcery Chamber, opening her mind to its fullest extent. Something dark and foul and leathery. Something that crept and lurked and peered slyly as it came. Cold horror touched Rumour's skin. Whatever it was, it was not quite with them, but it was very near. Perhaps it was stealing through the deserted halls of the Porphyry Palace. Perhaps it was standing just outside the door, listening and rubbing its hands together and grinning.

There was a scrabbling sound from the other side of the Silver Door, and Rumour turned towards it at once, cold horror prickling her skin.

The Silver Door was opening slowly, inch by stealthy inch. Something was standing behind it, pushing it furtively ajar, as if whoever or whatever stood there was hoping to creep in and conceal itself somewhere. As Rumour stared, black reaching fingers appeared curled around the edge, webbed and tough and leathery.

Impatient anger surged up in Rumour, for how dared something creeping and sly come prowling down into the Sorcery Chambers like this, and how dare it peer in at them and try to steal into their midst? She hurled a spear of light at the door, and saw it splinter into dozens of tiny, sizzling cascades.

There was a howl of anger and frustration, and the door swung back of its own accord.

Framed there, its evil face dark with malignant glee, was Theodora's pitiful, repulsive monster.

The Gristlen.

Cerball had felt the creeping coldness at approximately the same time as Rumour and, like Rumour, had looked round to see where it might be coming from. He had been overseeing matters generally, rather than weaving anything on his own account, and he had been worriedly watching the Black HeartStealers, who seemed to be working on something rather nasty. They did not want any necromancy creeping in. They did not really want the Black HeartStealers there either, and Cerball had been trying to discover how that branch of the family had got in. Somebody had said that they had been brought along by the Arca Dubhs who were apt to make undesirable alliances, and Cerball had been wondering, should he have a word with the Mugain about it?

At one minute it had seemed that there was nothing evil and nothing malignant in the Chamber, and everyone was working absorbedly and seriously. And then the next minute it was there, slam! a cold dark wash of necromantic power that hit you like a smack in the face and took away your breath with its suddenness.

As Rumour hurled the furious bolt of fiery light, the sorcerers turned as one, and an abrupt silence fell on the Looms' Chamber.

The Gristlen moved forward, and a myriad of colours from the half-created enchantments fell across its snouted face. Dark, thought Rumour, shivering and drawing the Sorcery Mantle more closely about her. This is an ancient dark thing. It is soaked in old, old evil.

Cupped in the Gristlen's huge, horny hands was something small and light and delicate: something that shone with gentle, prismatic incandescence.

Cerball started to speak but Rumour cut sharply across him. 'What is that you have there, filth?'

The Gristlen leered and held out its hands. Blue-green brilliance, cool and darting, trickled over its fingers and ran down its wizened skin, and Andrew, watching quietly, thought there was something obscene about such fragile loveliness spilling its turquoise and sapphire radiance over the ugly, warped body of this creature.

Rumour said again, 'What is it?' and her voice was sharpened with anger and impatience.

'The *sidh*'s enchanted music,' said the Gristlen. 'I took it from Tiarna. I stole their essence and their life-force and now they are all dying.' Throwing back its head, it bellowed its terrible triumph.

The music was a shifting, blurring kaleidoscope of rainbow colours and pouring crystal light and beckoning promise.

And it has an allure, thought Andrew. The music beckons and it sings and it is the most beautiful thing I have ever encountered. A man would be hard-pressed to resist a temptation of that strength.

It spun its soft, beckoning lures about the Chamber, so that the sorcerers stood momentarily transfixed, caught in its seductive strands . . .

Listen to me, creatures of the Amaranthine House, and you will never wish to listen to anything in the world ever again . . . Follow me, sorcerers, and never once look back, and you will not care if you are led into Hell and beyond . . .

There was the faint rippling of sound again, still distant, still barely recognisable, but light and silvery and mocking. Andrew thought: oh yes, I would follow that, I would not care whither it led me, so long as it would go on . . . Did *he* encounter this, the Black Monk? And did it lead him into dark and terrible byways and evil paths? I think I would not blame him so very much if that is what happened, thought Andrew, his senses spinning, his mind awash with the delight and the soft, sensuous pull of the music.

Rumour strode to the centre of the chamber and stood before the Gristlen. The music's radiance touched her face and her hair, so that for a moment she was bathed in the light.

The Gristlen's face twisted in a satisfied snarl, and it flung out its hands, the *sidh*'s music still clutched in its long-jointed fingers, thrusting it at Rumour.

'Prettiness,' it said, its voice so cracked and ugly with its desire that Andrew shuddered. 'The prettiness must answer the music,' said the Gristlen, edging closer to Rumour. 'I stole the music for you,' it said, and now there was such a terrible travesty of a lover's persuasion in its tone that Andrew felt his stomach twist with pity for the dreadful, warped thing. 'I took it for you so that you would look on me with favour,' said the Gristlen, its eyes beseeching.

Rumour had thrown her hands up to shield her eyes from the music's glow, and the Gristlen edged closer. 'Such a prettiness,' it crooned in its terrible voice. 'So easy to do what it tells.' It half crouched in front of her, straddling its thighs, and to Andrew's horror, the shrunken, leathery genitals between its legs began to ripen and swell. 'Love me!' it said, and reached out for her.

Rumour raised her left hand and flung sizzling, white-hot light spears into the Gristlen's face. 'Evil filth!' she cried. 'How dare you touch me! How dare you approach me!'

The Gristlen was yelping with fear and pain. It had fallen back the instant the furious light touched it, screaming and tearing at its scorched face. The music slipped from its hands and Rumour tore the Sorcery Mantle from her shoulders and flung it over the beautiful, eerie enchantment. The elusive light vanished instantly, and the music faded with a tiny, gasping breath as if something precious and vulnerable had been smothered. An aching desolation crept into the Chamber.

Rumour was facing the Gristlen, with bitter anger blazing in her eyes. It cowered against the wall, pawing at the scorch-marks where Rumour's furious fire had seared it; the stench of its burned hide filled the Sorcery Chamber. But its pale, bulging eyes glittered, and its snout-like face was twisted in a mixture of fear and angry spite. When it spoke, the power in its tone made Andrew flinch.

'One day you will pay for that, BitchHuman,' said the Gristlen, and it was quite suddenly no longer a cringing, pitiful thing, but evil and powerful and thrumming with menace. It reared up to its full height, no longer a crouching, hunchbacked distortion, but giantish and menacing. It towered over them, its elongated shadow falling across the Sorcery Chamber, and several of the younger Amaranths flinched. 'One day you will answer the music's lure, Amaranth sorceress,' screamed the Gristlen. 'And in a way that will surprise you very much.' It looked round the firelit Sorcery Chamber with cold hatred. 'One day you will all pay,' it said.

'Empty threats,' said the Mugain briskly. 'What are you doing here, creature? Why have you returned?'

'You do not make me welcome?' sneered the Gristlen. 'No, I see you do not. I am an outcast and an exile. I am welcome nowhere. Even with that—' it flung a pointing finger to the *sidh*'s music – 'even when I bring you that, you shrink from me and twitch aside the hems of your cloaks.' It lurched to the centre of the Chamber with its ungainly, lumpish gait and stood there, glaring malevolently at them, its breath harsh and rasping. But after a moment it seemed to shrink and to hunch itself into its former huddled stance, and when it spoke, it was again the cringing, whining voice, as if its earlier flare of anger had slipped out in error. It is trying to regain its earlier humble stance, thought Rumour, staring. It is trying to make us believe that it poses no threat and it is saying, Look at me, I am ugly and pitiful and I could not harm you.

But it could! thought Rumour. It is a foul, loathsome creature, soaked in terrible evil and immense ancient power. And it is far cleverer than it appears.

'I am a cursed thing,' said the Gristlen, holding out its hands in entreaty, and Rumour knew she had been right. 'I am repulsive,' it said. 'Unless I can slough off the marks of the Dark Lords' curse, I must drag this loathsome body across the world for ever.' It looked round at them. 'That is why I took the music,' it said.

'You are as mad as you are evil,' said Rumour coldly. 'I should never accept your repulsive embrace. Cerball, why have we not flung this filth into the dungeons by now? Or are we to stand discussing its future until it escapes us again?'

'Yes, it must be imprisoned, of course.' Cerball did not know what he had been thinking of. He gestured to several of the apprentices, who would probably like to try out their newly acquired knowledge, and was pleased to see that they stepped forward at once; weaving a thin, snaking chain that caught and held the Gristlen, and hauling it off to the Palace dungeons. The Mugain murmured in an aside that wasn't it altogether grand to see the youngsters so efficient and obedient?

Cerball watched them go, and turned back to find out what they were going to be doing with the *sidh*'s music. 'Because a stolen enchantment is of no use to us,' he said. And then stopped.

The Mugain said, 'Are we so sure of that?'

'Could the *sidh*'s music get us into the Dark Ireland?' asked Bodb Decht.

'Under the right circumstances,' said the Mugain, and from the fire wall, Rumour turned back to listen.

Great-aunt Fuamnach said, 'It might get *somebody* into the Dark Ireland,' and a sudden silence fell. Andrew, listening, felt the stir go through them and knew they were remembering something.

And then Rumour said, very softly, 'The *sidh*'s music and the Samildanach . . .' and several people frowned, but no one spoke.

'It's a very old belief,' said Cerball, at length. 'I don't think we could rely on it.' He looked across at Andrew and said, 'Good sir, you are learned and a traveller. What do you think?'

Andrew said carefully, 'I have not heard the legend. I only know of the . . . the being you refer to from your earlier Ritual.' And thought: but now I am about to hear more, and I am not at all sure that I want to.

'It's probably not that well known a legend, of course,' said Cerball, rather apologetically, as if it might be the Amaranths' fault that Andrew had not heard of it. 'It's so old that I don't know if anyone believes it any more.'

Rumour said softly, 'I believe in it.'

'So do I,' said several other voices.

'The Samildanach,' said Rumour, moving forward, her eyes on Andrew, her voice caressing the strange Gael syllables. 'The Man of Each and Every Art, who will come into Ireland quietly and humbly, but before whom all doors will open.'

Andrew said carefully, 'My own religion teaches a very similar belief. The One who will come into the world of Men and save them from eternal damnation—'

'But,' said Cerball, 'the Samildanach is a Human. In all the stories, he's a Human.'

'Yes,' said Rumour. 'He is a Human. Precisely.'

There was a sudden intense silence, and every head turned to look at Andrew.

Chapter Ten

The Man of Each and Every Art, who will come quietly and humbly to the world of Men, and defeat the Dark Lords . . .

I could wish I had not been told that, thought Andrew. Or, if I had been told it, I could wish I had not seen beneath it and beyond it.

The Saviour who will be born to the House of David, and who will live humbly and obscurely, but whose death will free Mankind . . .

Is the story of our Saviour simply a newer version of the Samildanach . . . ? An echo, a rewritten legend . . . Did that gentle Nazarene carpenter never really exist, and was the world turned upside down, and were men sent to their death in agony only for a palimpsest – new writing on an old manuscript . . . ?

He did not quite believe it. He thought he dared not believe it. And yet so far was he from trying to argue against it, that he was listening to their beliefs and believing in their sorcery. Little by little, he was stepping deeper into the strange, twilit world of Ireland's paganism. And discovering, along the way, that that paganism was not so far removed from the very beliefs the monks had travelled to Ireland to preach.

The Amaranths would ask him to go through the Gateway into the Dark Realm, of course. The *sidh*'s music in the hands of a Human. Powerful and unstoppable. And overshadowing it all, that eerily familiar legend. The Samildanach . . . Could I do it? Would it be arrogant of me to think I could don, even briefly, the mantle of the Samildanach? Would it help anyone? But the stolen music should certainly be returned, he thought.

But it was only when Cerball said, 'We have no means of knowing what the Gateway is like and we have no means of knowing the creatures that guard it,' that the real decision was made for Andrew.

He said, 'Guardians?' and Cerball said that there were several.

'Although they do say,' put in the Mugain, 'that the most dangerous is the Black Monk of Torach.'

A stinging awareness lashed Andrew's mind, and with it a surging exultation. Found! he thought. I have found him! And: so I was right! He did succumb to the lure of the Dark Realm, and he did travel down those evil byways!

'The Black Monk is probably in some kind of servitude to the Dark Lords,' said the Mugain, who had just remembered that the Monk might well be one of Andrew's own strange kind, and who would not for worlds have dealt an insult to this quiet, rather austere young man. 'But the story is that he prowls the boundaries of the Dark Realm, between their world and ours. What some people call the hinterlands.'

'I understand.'

'If he's still there he'll need to be sidestepped,' said Cerball, frowning.

'He would, perhaps, try to prevent anyone from entering?' said Andrew, carefully.

'Yes. And if he is held in bondage to the Dark Lords, he is probably constrained to take victims for them. But,' went on Cerball, 'we don't really know.'

'The music should protect you from him,' said Bodb Decht, a bit doubtfully.

'Oh yes. Although of course,' said Cerball, 'we don't know what the Gateway will be like.'

'That's assuming he can find it in the first place.'

'Well, I meant that.'

'A rolling-back of an immense boulder, I always thought,' said Rumour, half to herself, and Andrew glanced at her.

'There may not even be a Gateway at all,' said the Mugain. 'Andrew may simply pass from one world to the next.'

'But,' said Andrew, with gentle irony, 'the road into the Dark Realm, whatever it looks like, will be broad and straight and easy to travel.'

'Why?' The Amaranths looked at him in puzzlement, and Andrew smiled.

'It is a belief of my people,' he said, 'that the road to the dark underworld – any dark underworld – is an easy one. It is only the road to the righteous and the sinless life that is narrow and hard to find.'

'That is very profound,' said Bodb Decht after a moment. 'And rather an interesting idea.'

'We believe it to be true.' Andrew smiled at them again, and said, 'And you think the music would enable a traveller to pass between the two worlds easily? Even with the Monk of Torach lying in wait?' Saying the Monk's name suddenly gave immense credence to his existence in the Dark Realm.

'That's always been the legend,' said the Mugain. 'The *sidh*'s music and the Samildanach. They rather go together. So even though our spells failed, you should have the right tools for the job.'

'How do you know the spells failed?' demanded Great-aunt Fuamnach belligerently.

'We didn't force open a Gateway.'

'No, but we've found a way through.' She glared round. 'It seems to me that we're succeeding very nicely.'

'Yes, but not quite as we expected.'

'That is often the way,' said Andrew quietly.

He thought it remarkable that the two quests should suddenly have come together in this way. To find the Monk he must enter the Dark Realm, and by entering the Dark Realm, he would reach Theodora. Prayer was often answered in odd ways. He thanked God again that he could go after Theodora without dismissing his own task.

He stood with the Amaranths in a hand-linked circle, and listened to Cerball and the Mugain and Bodb Decht – as the Elders – pronounce a brief Benison of Light over Andrew's journey, and then a half-sung, half-chanted incantation which sounded very beautiful, but which was in a tongue that Andrew could not understand.

'Gael,' said Rumour, at his side. 'But extremely early Gael. Perhaps as early as Cruithin, or even what is called Q-Celtic or Qretani.'

'It is very beautiful,' said Andrew, gravely.

'Oh yes.'

When they finished, he thanked them courteously and said,

'Would you allow me to pronounce one of the prayers of my own religion now?' and saw the instant assent in their eyes.

'Please do,' said Cerball, and the Amaranths nodded eagerly, because it would be immensely interesting to hear something of this new Teaching.

Andrew bowed his head, and joined his hands, and spoke the lyrical, stirring words of the *Exurgat Deus*, the psalm that Augustinus was said to have pronounced over the mission monks at the beginning of their journey into the wild, barbarous northern isles.

'"*Let God arise and let his enemies be scattered . . . Like as the smoke vanisheth, so shalt thou drive them away, and like as wax melteth at the fire, so let the ungodly perish . . .*"'

A great listening stillness fell over the Amaranths, and Andrew felt the beauty and the strength and the exultation of his beliefs consuming him. How could I have doubted?

When he said, '"*The Chariots of God are twenty thousand, even thousands of angels, and the Lord is among them,*"' he felt the Amaranths stir in purest delight, and when he said, '"*That thy foot may be dipped in the blood of thine enemies and that the tongue of thy dogs may be red through the same,*"' he looked up to see their eyes kindling, and he saw them bring their hands together, the palms flat, as they had done for their own Ritual.

Andrew lifted his head and looked at them, and pronounced the final words ringingly.

'"*Thy God hath sent forth strength . . . Give thanks O Israel from the ground of thy heart.*"'

And to himself, murmured, 'Let me not fail, O Lord.'

Andrew stood very quietly inside the Well Cave, and felt the strangeness of the Tower close about him. He could think: this is the magical Cadence Tower, this is the place that was built by an overreaching sorcerer and that destroyed an ancient magical language. I suppose I am believing it, thought Andrew, but several layers down he knew he was believing it, for he was remembering all of the old stories about greedy peoples who had tried to reach other worlds and built towers, and challenged gods, and been overthrown.

He advanced to the Well, and stood looking down into the impenetrable darkness, straining his eyes, trying to catch a glimpse of light. He thought there was no light at all, and he felt a cold fear at the thought of descending by the iron ladder into such blackness.

He was slightly afraid, but not unduly so. He thought he was strung up to a pitch of immense excitement. I am fulfilling the mission vouchsafed to me, he thought. I am nearing the Black Monk of Torach. I know it. He remembered how in England, men would say that, in the act of hunting, nearing the end of the chase, the hunter sometimes entered into the mind of the hunted. I shall find him, thought Andrew, delightedly and, murmuring a soft prayer to avoid the sin of Pride, he put the *sidh*'s music in its small golden casket safely into a pocket of his robe.

He had grasped the first rung of the iron ladder, preparatory to descending into the Well, when an amused voice from the door halted him.

'If I am to accompany you,' said Rumour, 'you could at least help me over the parapet.'

She was wearing a silk cloak of a swirling flame colour, and her hair was unbound and threaded with thin silver strands, studded with tiny scarlet beads. In her left hand was a narrow hazel wand wreathed with curling symbols. Her eyes glowed with the tiny dark flames he had seen earlier on, and she was regarding him with her head on one side.

Andrew said, 'I am to go alone, madame. The one you call the Samildanach had surely not a companion with him during his life here?' And heard a tiny voice within him warning against Pride again.

Rumour laughed. 'I would not be so sure of that, Andrew,' she said, and regarded him with amused eyes. 'To begin with, at least, the Samildanach was an ordinary Human. Was not your own Leader?'

Andrew said, without thinking, 'He had the one referred to as "the disciple whom He loved".'

'There you are.'

'It is generally assumed to have been a man,' said Andrew slowly. 'Although there is no actual proof of it.'

Rumour laughed. 'Then we have good authority for me to accompany you,' she said. 'Because the Samildanach, from any tale I have ever heard, was certainly able to enjoy the company of females.' She perched on the parapet and peered into the Well's black depths. 'Dark and nasty,' she said. 'Isn't it just as well that I brought an Enchantment of Light for us to see our way.'

The Enchantment of Light burned steadily as they descended into the Well.

Andrew went first, sitting on the low, narrow parapet, and then swinging his legs over into the black abyss.

He began the descent cautiously, closing his mind to what he was doing, trying to shut out the increasing feeling of suffocation, the impression that the dank, stale air of the Well was closing over his head so that he would soon be unable to breathe.

The ladder was fixed firmly to the inside of the Well. Iron rivets had been driven into the black brickwork of the Well shaft, and there were brackets holding the ladder in position. The rivets were rusting, but Andrew thought they would hold.

Above him, Rumour stepped down lightly and easily, little silk-slippered feet barely seeming to touch the ladder, casting the warm, soft light as she moved. There was a whisper of perfume on the air, warring with the dank mustiness of the Well. Andrew found himself sending up a prayer of thanks for this unlooked-for companion. I did not wish it, he thought; I should have undertaken this alone. And then, with the self-honesty which was inbred in him: but without her, this journey would have been perilous and lonely.

The lower they went, the colder it became, and the more noxious the air. There was a sour, tainted taste to the air, as if it was the foul breath of a monster. We are crawling into the maw of a leviathan, thought Andrew, into the gaping jaws of a giant . . .

Several times, he stopped and found himself struggling for breath. Once Rumour missed her footing on the narrow rungs, and half fell, clinging to the iron staves, her feet searching frantically for the rungs. Andrew scrambled back up to her instantly, and caught her about the waist with one hand, guiding her back; and Rumour, regaining balance, managed one of her mischievous smiles at him.

'A chivalrous knight,' she said, slightly out of breath. 'And you have restored me to the path. Or were you intending that we should fall from the path together, Andrew?'

'I do not intend that either of us should fall, madame,' said Andrew, and although his voice was perfectly composed, his heart was racing and his senses had reeled at the sudden, unavoidable press of her body, and the feel and the scent of her skin.

Rumour said, 'It is sometimes extremely pleasant to fall,' and sent him her sudden, mischievous grin.

'So I have heard. If you would direct the light a little lower, I think it would make the descent easier.'

'As you will,' said Rumour, meekly.

As they neared what must surely be the Well's bottom, they were able to see tiny blind creatures crawling from the crevices in the ancient black brick of the Well shaft, tiny wriggling worm creatures, pale and fumbling. But, thought Andrew, surely that means there must be a sliver of light from somewhere? No creature can exist in complete darkness.

With the framing of the thought, he became aware of light: thin at first, and then stronger. He touched Rumour's arm and she nodded, as if she, also, had been noticing it.

'I think it must be seeping in from below,' said Andrew.

'Yes, for there is nowhere else it could come from.'

'Douse your own light,' said Andrew, but Rumour had already done so.

They stood very still, scanning the Well shaft with their eyes, trying to gauge the extent of the light, trying to see where it came from. Andrew thought, and then was sure, that the Well shaft was widening, and that the brick walls were no longer black and pitted.

But the light was not the pale, cool, elvish light of the *sidh*'s City, which they had both been hoping for; it was not the beautiful, faintly eerie turquoise-silver of Tiarna. It was thin, trickling crimson, like blood seeping from a wound.

'But whatever it is, we must go on,' said Andrew. 'We must reach the Well's floor.'

'Yes, of course.' Rumour's response was instant, as if there could be no other course for them to take. But Andrew thought he heard, for the first time, a note of hesitation in her voice, and this was the most alarming thing yet, because he had believed

Rumour to be intrepid and adventurous and impervious to danger.

'Of course I am not impervious to danger, Andrew,' said Rumour's voice softly. 'To be so would be to be insensitive in the extreme.'

'Of course. And to believe you so is to credit you with no imagination.' In the uncertain light, Andrew looked at her. 'I think you have a great deal of imagination, Rumour.'

'I am honoured,' said Rumour and, despite the danger, the note of amusement was in her voice. 'Shall we go on?'

There was only a short length left of the iron ladder, 'And I can see the Well floor,' said Andrew, peering downwards. 'But the iron rungs finish about six feet short of it. I think we have to jump from the last rung.'

'If I fall,' said Rumour, 'I shall expect you to catch me, Andrew.' And sent him, over her shoulder, the wicked grin again.

Andrew grasped the last few rungs firmly, and sought for footholds in the wall directly below. It was possible to hold the last rung, and half fall, half slide the rest of the way.

Rumour followed, descending to the Well's floor in a slither of perfumed silk, half falling into his arms, so that there was again the warmth of her body, and the sudden, strong intimacy as they stood together in the near-dark.

For a moment she was pressed against him, and Andrew felt his body harden in swift, shameful response. He beat the sweet arousal down at once, and stepped back, and turned to look about them.

Directly ahead of them were black-mouthed caves, with baleful, flickering firelight deep within. Faintly, on the air, came the sound of rhythmic singing.

> 'O give us skins of Humanish thin
> To sew and weave and clothe ourselves in.
> Give us hides and leathern skins
> Shales to warm our caverns with.'

The dungeons of the Fomoire.

The dull light oozed into the rock passage, and they could see

90

shapes moving within the caves; darting, dancing shapes that were wearing the semblance of Human appearances, but that were not Human in the least.

Behind them and above them was the Well shaft, with the iron ladder still within their reach. Beneath their feet was the hard packed earth of the floor. At their backs was a solid mass of black, pitted rock, and although there were crevices and indentations in the rock, when they tried to explore them they could see that they were simply shallow caves, niches in the wall.

There was nowhere else to go but in the direction of the singing.

Andrew was the first to move. He looked at his companion, and from somewhere dredged up a smile, and said, 'Well, *madame*? Are you prepared for the first of the dangers you wanted to experience?'

Rumour said, 'Perfectly prepared.' But her eyes went to the red glow from the caves, and Andrew saw uncertainty there.

'Is it possible to go past the caves without being seen, do you think?' he said, and Rumour frowned, considering.

'If we make no sound at all, and if we cast no shadow to alert them, we might do it,' she said.

'Mingle with the shadows,' said Andrew, and thought: well, at least I do not sound afraid. 'We must keep close together, and we must walk as if we walk on spun glass, and we must make no sudden movement that might catch their attention.'

'All right.' Rumour wrapped her silk cloak closely about her. She grinned again. 'A Cloak of Invisibility would have been so useful, Andrew, but perhaps we shall manage without it. Onwards, then?'

'Onwards,' said Andrew and, hand in hand, they began to walk softly towards the Fomoire's lair.

Chapter Eleven

Maelduin thought he was the only one left. Tiarna was already dying, as he moved through the great empty rooms, the gentle iridescence was dissolving and thin, brilliant threads of colour, like trickling spring water, were running down the rock walls. He reached out to touch the nearest rockface, and felt the cold dankness and the pale, thin sensation which meant an almost total absence of colour and light and music. He was unused to pain, but now he felt something very near to it, and panic gripped him. Many of the *sidh* were already gaunt and drab, swathes of pale colour, their narrow turquoise eyes filmed. Unable to move. *Dying*.

To begin with, he thought he might find help in the ancient magical libraries of the *nimfeach*, the silken crystal pools at the heart of the Palace. He darted along the silver tunnels, his mind in turmoil, but when he dived into the deepest pool, his body slender and shimmering, barely creating a ripple on the surface, he saw at once that there would be no help here. The cool sea-magic of the long-ago *nimfeach* – the evil, soulless water creatures who had lived in Tiarna before the *sidh* wrested it from them – was still there; but it was beyond his reach.

Maelduin's people had spent years enveloping the cold, evil sea-magic in their own gentle, pure bewitchments; they had dissolved the *nimfeach*'s necromantic magic and imbued it with their own soft, cool sorcery, and the spells that lay beneath the crystal pools were now the strongest and purest magic in all Ireland.

But to reach it now, to dissolve the ancient protective carapaces, the music itself was needed. It was the key, the talisman. It must slide into the soft water, liquid and pure, until it had coloured the rockface and tinted the pools with sparkling colours, brilliant as peacocks' tails, effervescent and elusive as herons' wings. Only then could the dawn-of-time spells woven by the Fisher King and his minions be reached.

Maelduin swirled angrily in the clear silken water, a glinting arrow of blue and green fury and frustration, churning the pool's surface to foam, emerging briefly to pour into the next pool.

In each one, it was the same. There were rows upon rows of spells and enchantments; each one exquisitely crafted and polished, each one written in the ancient mystical Cadence. Maelduin knew the Cadence as well as he knew the shining City of Tiarna. He could have pronounced any one of the enchantments effortlessly and it was certain that somewhere within those enchantments would be a spell that would revive the dying Elven King and restore Tiarna's magic and show them where the music had been taken.

But without the music, the spells could not be reached, and without the music, Tiarna and the *sidh* would die.

Maelduin emerged from the last pool, and shook himself angrily, droplets of pale, shining water falling from him.

What now?

Light still poured into the Silver Cavern, where once Aillen mac Midha had held Court, and where once the *sidh* had sung their cool music, and sent out the lures of the *nimfeach* to shipwrecked sailors whose rafts washed up at the mouths of the sea tunnels.

But it was a cold, uncertain light now, colder than ever Maelduin had seen it, fainter than he had ever imagined it could be. The Silver Cavern was no longer the shining heart of the Palace.

Maelduin stood before the immense Silver Throne, where his father sat unseeing and unhearing. Dead already? Please, no! he cried silently and, as if his thoughts had taken shape, he felt his father's response.

Not dead, my son, but fading and failing . . . And then, with a plea that went straight to Maelduin's core.

Help me.

There was a flash of time, the span of a Humanish heartbeat, when Maelduin felt panic close about him again, and when he thought: but I cannot! I do not know what to do! And then, summoning his fortitude: *Very well! What must I do to save Tiarna?*

For whatever is necessary, I will do it.

He waited, and presently, as fragile as icicles tapping against the cave walls, came the response.

You must submit to the ancient ritual, my son . . .

Yes?

That is the only way to save us.

You must seek out the creature called the Gristlen and recapture the stolen enchantment . . .

You must don Humanish garb and leave Tiarna.

And you must walk abroad in the world of Men.

Become a Humanish.

I cannot do it! thought Maelduin, appalled. There must be some other way! But hard on the heels of the thought came another: you must. There is no other way. And you are the Crown Prince, it is your right and your duty and your inheritance.

It was the only way. If he was to search the world of Men for the Gristlen, he must do so unchallenged, undetected. He must do so as a Man.

He found the idea repulsive; he could not imagine how it would be to carry about the cumbersome bones; he could make only the most fleeting guess at how it would feel to be inside their skins, to move in the clumsy, slow way they had to move, and to have, as the only method of understanding, the imprecise thing they called 'speech'. Once the Humanish had possessed the ancient magical *Samhailt*: the art of hearing and understanding one another's thoughts, but Maelduin thought this was something bestowed only on a very few, and he thought that it had frayed and ravelled until it barely existed.

Become a Humanish . . .

But I have no choice. He moved back to the great Silver Throne where the Elven King was dying.

Nearly all the *sidh* were gathered in the Silver Cavern for the ritual, but Maelduin could see that it had cost them dearly. The younger ones had dragged themselves there, crawling painfully through the tunnels, but the older ones had had to be carried.

Their eyes were dulled, their once-brilliant bodies were harsh and lustreless, and they looked at Maelduin with such desperate hope that the pity of it closed about him suffocatingly.

No one knew if Aillen mac Midha still possessed sufficient strength to summon up the ritual that would clothe Maelduin in Humanish garb; most of the *sidh* knew it, but they would all have flinched at invoking it. It was one of the oldest and one of the most powerful of all the ancient rituals. And it could rebound; in the hands of one who lacked the understanding or the power, it could play evil and malicious tricks.

Maelduin knew all of this, but as he stood before the Silver Throne, his head bowed in complete obedience, his eyes deliberately hooded, he allowed none of his fear to show. The brilliance that shone from him was subdued, and several of the *sidh* nearest him thought that he, too, was dying.

But then Maelduin moved suddenly, and the blue-green light gleamed in his long narrow eyes.

Delight touched the waiting *sidh* and with it, hope. *He is the Crown Prince, the heir to the Silver Throne, and he will not let us down.*

I cannot let them down, thought Maelduin, standing up very straight. This will be the hardest thing I have ever had to do, but I cannot let them down. But he sent his father a covert glance. How strong was the Elven King?

Aillen mac Midha had been propped up with silken, ice-blue cushions; he was still clothed in the half-Humanish form he had summoned for his converse with the Gristlen, and this struck fresh fear into the *sidh*, for the Elven King would never willingly endure the heavy thick skin and the leaden bones of a Human if he could throw it off. Had he sufficient power left?

Aillen mac Midha seemed to make an immense effort, sitting straight-backed on the silver altar, the silken cushions framing his slight, slender form. The long turquoise eyes opened, and for a brief span of time there was the inhuman, faintly mischievous, faintly contemptuous glint that the Humans feared so greatly. Like this, he was strange and alien, neither quite *sidh*, nor fully Human.

He beckoned Maelduin closer with one translucent hand, the nails curved and silver tinted.

'You are ready, my son?' It was the merest breath of a

thought, but every creature present heard it clearly.

Maelduin, using the thought-forms that all the *sidh* used, said, 'Ready, sire,' and the response was so firm and so strong that a ripple of hope went through the listening *sidh*.

Aillen mac Midha regarded Maelduin for a long moment. Without warning and apparently without summoning strength of any kind, he pronounced a string of unfamiliar words, silver-tipped and elusive, lying on the dim Cavern like quicksilver.

There was the faintest breath of something cold and alien drifting into the Cavern; something slow and ancient and creeping; something that had crawled up out of the oceans when the world was new-born and barren, and something that had once gone on all fours and that had once been finned and gilled, but that had learned to think and reason and speak.

Something that had been forged in the fires of Eternity and something that had been bestowed on the world when the world itself was still cooling.

The ancient skincloak of the Humanish.

With the feeling, there was a stir of sound in the cavern, and several of the *sidh* looked round.

At first there was nothing, the silence was heavy and stifling all about them, and they thought they had been mistaken.

And then it came again, no more than a breath of sound, no stronger than the lightest wind touching the leaves on a drowsy summer's afternoon.

Faint, far off chanting.

The exhausted *sidh* struggled to hear more fully and, presently, little by little, it came nearer, slowly, inexorably, strongly, until they could hear the words quite plainly.

> 'O give us skins for dancing in
> And give us veils of Humanish pale.
> Fleeces of fur and silken sin
> Ivory bones for living in.'

There was a whisper of delight in the Cavern, and Maelduin, standing motionless before the Silver Throne, felt his senses ripple, for he knew that they were hearing one of the oldest enchantments of all; the Humanish spell stolen away by the terrible Fomoire, the skincloak of the Mannish, taken and twisted and warped, and rewoven in the Dark Realm to the Fomoire's own, evil pattern.

'Give us fur and Humanish hair;
Silken skins and Mannish vair.
Skins for dancing, dark and fair;
Fleece and shale and bones of pale.'

This was not the deformed, ugly spell that the Fomoire had woven in the Dark Fields of necromancy, that they used to call down the writhing, squirming skins of murderers and child-eaters.

This was the gentle, strong magic of the newly born world; the true spell, bequeathed to the beings who struggled to survive at the very beginning. This was the unspoilt cloak of Man.

It was flooding their senses, sending them blind, dizzy, reeling. The voices multiplied, thousands upon thousands of times, echoing all about the cavern, singing the strong, rhythmic chant, never once pausing.

'And give us shale of Humanish pale,
Skins and bones for dancing in.
Veils of silk and cloaks of sin.
Hair to stream and limbs to spin.'

The spell was whirling round them, measured and unfaltering.

Maelduin stayed where he was, feeling, with every filament of his being, the strong, ancient cloak of Humanish come nearer.

He did not move, and those nearest to him knew sudden and complete panic: *it is not going to work!* Several of them glanced uneasily at the barely conscious King, and a terrible thought shaped in their minds:

The High King no longer possesses the power!

And then Maelduin turned to look at them, and a strange, unfamiliar glint showed in his eyes, and every one of them saw, quite clearly, the Humanish transformation begin.

For Maelduin there was a moment of complete and utter awareness, when he felt and knew, with every one of his many senses, that he was *sidh*, pure and entire. The essence of the cool blue-green creatures who had wrested Tiarna from the long-ago *nimfeach* flooded his whole being, so that he wanted to soar high above the Silver Cavern, and swoop and dart and fly. He wanted to fall on the Humanish and tear out their senses and their souls for the *sidh*'s beckoning music. He wanted to reach out and scoop up the beautiful music, and reach down and down into its heart, where the allure and the seduction of the music lived, and then pour it through his hands, as easily as he could pour water.

He did none of these things. He stayed where he was, not moving, understanding that this sudden, swift awareness of his body must be the beginning of the transformation.

And then it began.

It was slow at first; a stealing over him of warmth, a dragging sensation, the feeling of weights being hung on him, so that it would be cumbersome and heavy to move, and slow and lumbering.

There was a moment of pure panic: *I cannot bear it!* he thought, and knew that it had to be borne.

He could feel his body being compressed, cruelly and strongly, and there was a deep, wrenching pain, so that he groaned aloud.

He was on the ground now, curled tightly into a ball, but the pain closed in and closed down, and the Silver Cavern swam and wavered before his sight.

A deep solid core was forming throughout his being, and he knew it for the bones of the Humanish: hard and ugly.

Ivory bones for living in . . .

The cloak of Humanish was closing about him more tightly; there was a suffocating, smothering sensation: the shaling of skin.

Humanish pale . . . skins for dancing in . . .

For a single, absurd instant he thought: but I could never dance like this! I could never leap and dart and swoop and fly through the air! And then he remembered that the Humanish way of dancing was very different to the *sidh*'s way, and the magnitude of the appalling thing he was about to do closed about him again.

The blue-green light that had shone from him so brilliantly was dimming. He thought: it is quenching, fading . . . I believe I am almost a Human. And with the thought, came the knowledge that the iridescence was dissolving into nothing, and that the heavy, dragging, Humanish cloak was closing about him.

There was a final wrench of agony that ripped through his body and left him gasping and blinded, and with it the terrible feeling that he was anchored to the ground.

There was a sluggish warmth in his veins, and he thought: *Human blood!* and remembered about the warm, slow blood of the Humanish.

But the warmth was not as repulsive as he had expected; it was slow and gentle, and there was unexpected comfort in it. I shall do it, thought Maelduin. I shall endure it, and I believe it will not be so very bad after all.

For a brief space, he thought that he had lost all of the finely honed senses of the *sidh*, that he would no longer feel and experience in the way that the *sidh* felt and experienced, and the panic clutched him again. I shall lose it all! he thought, and with the thought, became aware for the first time of the steady pulsating inside him.

The beating of a Human heart...

There was a soft stirring, deep within his head, and a gentle strength between his thighs, and he paused, exploring these new sensations. A brief grin touched his lips: *oh yes, the Humans enjoy one another's bodies!* he thought, and with the thought was aware of a quickening heat and the faint beginnings of an insistent hardness between his thighs. The grin deepened momentarily, and he thought: perhaps after all this is not going to be all bad!

He stood up, feeling the heaviness and the clumsiness of the Human skin, but feeling, as well, an unexpected strength, and a violent curiosity as to what lay ahead.

For I am about to enter the world of Men, and I am about to follow their ways and their customs, and speak with them...

This was intriguing and arousing, but more arousing by far was the knowledge of the reason behind it all; his quest to find the Gristlen and recapture the music of the *sidh* and save Tiarna.

He caught the flash of reflection from the silver walls, and turned, briefly aware of hitherto unknown vanity. What do I look like?

And although he had expected to be repulsed and sickened by

the strange creature he had become, he found he was neither of these things.

Slender and rather pale; yes, that is what I would expect, he thought, studying the image before him. There was a tumble of pale hair, silver-gilt with flashes of golden in it, sleek and shining like a cap . . .

Fleece of fur and veil of silk . . .

He moved, and the reflection moved with him, slender and supple and graceful.

Not at all bad, thought Maelduin, and grinned suddenly, seeing his image grin back at him. Yes, not at all bad.

The eyes were not quite Human, of course. He paused, considering, his head on one side. No, the eyes were not Human in the least. No Human ever had those long, narrow eyes, or that glinting cool colour.

But taking it all in all, he thought, I believe I shall pass unchallenged.

And then he was aware that the *sidh* were making way for him to go out of the Silver Cavern, and through the sea tunnels.

The time had come for him to enter the world of Men and seek out the Gristlen.

Chapter Twelve

The Amaranths had been divided as to what they should do with the Gristlen now that they had finally imprisoned it.

The Mugain, who could not be doing with creatures from the Dark Realm in any guise, was all for forgetting about the horrid thing altogether and letting it rot where it lay, but not everybody went along with this view.

'Ceremonial execution,' said Bodb Decht firmly. 'That's what the Academy of Sorcerers recommends in these cases.'

'But can you actually kill something from the Dark Realm?'

'We could find out soon enough.'

Great-aunt Fuamnach thought they ought to talk to it, and find out as much as they could about the Dark Realm. So very little was known, she said, and the Gristlen might be able to give them some useful information. They might find out a good deal about the Dark Realm, and it might help them to rescue Echbel from the Fomoire. They could not be expecting Rumour and the monk to deal with everything. A younger cousin asked, rather hesitantly, whether Echbel mightn't use sorcery to escape on his own account, but nobody took this seriously, because everyone knew that Echbel had only the sketchiest knowledge of sorcery.

'And,' said Great-aunt Fuamnach, occupying the chair nearest to the fire and winding a few puckered skeins of one or two old enchantments, 'it might give Laigne some comfort, poor dear.'

The Amaranths nodded, a bit sheepishly, because nobody knew quite the best way to cope with Laigne.

Laigne lay in her silk-hung bed, and heard the murmurings with sadness. They would none of them admit that Echbel, the dear boy, was in fact far stronger and far more knowledgeable than any of them, she thought. They were jealous of him, of course, so handsome and so clever as he was. Laigne had secretly been hoping (and still hoped) that the Succession Ritual would name Echbel. He would make a fitting Head of the Amaranths. He would rule kindly and firmly and wisely. Laigne would see that he did.

Curiously, the thing that had given her hope had been the strange, haunting music that she had heard from the Sorcery Chambers. It had drifted up as lightly and as softly as swansdown or snowflakes; it had been as insubstantial as frost-rimmed cobwebs, but Laigne, lying in her bedchamber, had heard it clearly. She had heard its message: *follow me and all will be well . . . Come with me over hill and over dale, and there you will find your heart's delight . . .*

Follow me to the source of all joy . . .

She would follow the music to its source. She would wait until it was dark and everyone was sleeping, and then she would go quietly and calmly and no one would know.

There was probably a degree of danger in this of course; Laigne was not so foolish that she did not remember all the soft, seductive beckonings and the gentle, sly lures sent out by creatures of necromantic powers. But this was surely different. This was something soft and pure and good. It promised her her heart's desire . . . And Laigne's heart's desire was to reach Echbel. She would not disregard the possibility of danger of course, but she would not let it deter her.

The others thought she was a poor weak creature when it came to sorcery. Great-aunt Fuamnach had been known to look slightingly on her and refer, quite openly, to Laigne's dash of Human blood from three or four generations back. Laigne paid this no attention: it was extremely vulgar to mention such a thing, and in any case a drop of Human blood could be a remarkable help in sorcery.

She waited until night had fallen and the Palace was silent, and then she got up from the bed and donned a thin, silk robe. It would have been better to have dressed properly, but nobody would see her.

The music had long since faded, but Laigne could still hear it deep within her head; she could hear its haunting promise.

Come to me, Human, come into the heart of the music and I will give you the thing you desire most . . . I will show you the way to reach your dear one, and it will be a way that you never dreamed existed . . .

Echbel! thought Laigne, and slipped through the quiet Palace.

No one came out to challenge her, and Laigne walked softly through the moonlit galleries and halls, and on down the narrow stone stairway that led to the Sorcery Chambers. Wasn't it here the music had come from, and wasn't it here she must go first?

She stood for a moment in the Sorcery Chambers, the warm scents of raw magic closing about her, the quiet thrumming of the quiescent Looms purring in her ears.

Here? No, there was nothing here save the slithering gold and scarlet skeins of enchantments, the trickle of something light and silvery spilling from one of the Looms and then dissolving into tiny shards of light as it reached the ground.

Not here. Where? Laigne stood very still and whispered the light, pure words of a Trance Ritual which would open her mind to its fullest extent and allow her to follow the music to its heart. Trance Rituals were perfectly simple, but the others always had to make such a fuss. All you needed was a tranquil mind, which Laigne possessed anyway. Echbel would have made a study of Trance Rituals if he had not been torn from her. He would probably have been a Master.

She began to move through the Sorcery Chamber, her eyes wide open now and slightly filmed. Trance Rituals were really the easiest thing in sorcery. You had to have a layer of Command and a layer of Compulsion close together. And a layer of Repose and another of Silence. And then you cloaked everything in the purest of blues you could conjure up.

Come further down . . .

Yes, it was there! She had heard it, the faintest of stirrings, the lightest of touches on her mind. Not the music, but something that understood the music's pull. Something that had possessed the music, and something that might help her to reach Echbel. Something that *knew*.

It was still calling to her.

Come further down and closer in . . .

The dungeons! thought Laigne. Whatever it is, is in the

dungeons! She passed through the door that led beneath the Sorcery Chamber, and down into the ancient, dark foundations of the Porphyry Palace.

The narrow stone stair curved round sharply, and there was a rope fixed to its sides so that you could hold on while you descended. The steps were damp and slippery and not very clean because the servants never came down here. Laigne would speak sharply to them about that, and would have no patience with their silly tales about occasional demons wandering down from the Looms Chamber above. The Amaranths had never had any truck with demons, or only minor ones anyway.

The passage leading to the dungeons was cold and lit to eerie life by the flickering wall-sconces. Laigne shivered, pulling the thin robe more closely about her. Through the flimsy silk slippers she could feel the damp stones of the floor, and the slippery lichen that had crept up through the cracks.

There were only four cells down here: each of them was set back into the thick stone foundations of the Palace, and each one had iron bars which stretched from the roof into the floor. There was a small gate cut out at the centre, and the keys hung on a nail outside, near to the foot of the stone steps. Laigne, treading softly on the cold stone flags, paused and listened. Was she still within hearing of the compulsive silvery voice that promised so much?

Over here, my dear . . . Over here . . . And then, with sudden discordance, *But you must come willingly . . . You must come because you wish to come . . .*

But she did wish it. She wanted to find the creature who had had the music and who was calling to her. There was a darkness about it, but it was an alluring darkness.

When the voice again said, *You must come willingly*, Laigne said aloud, 'I do come willingly. I come because I wish to.' And reached up for the keys.

As she unlocked the cells, Laigne had the sudden impression that something cold and unclean and dank uncoiled itself, and surged towards her. Something ancient and implacable, and something that had known other worlds and ruled other creatures . . .

For a moment she could not breathe; the cold mustiness seemed to close about her throat, and there was a moment of undiluted panic. She stood very still, concentrating on Repose and Tranquillity and on the pure blue of Calm, and the smothering darkness cleared, and she could see and think properly again. She could see everything inside the stone cell at the far end.

Of your own wish . . .

'Of my own wish,' whispered Laigne.

There was very little light in the cell. There was a tiny window, high up, with thick black bars across it, and there was a spillage of light from the wall-sconces outside the dungeon. Some wisps of straw had been thrown down, and there was a metal dish containing food, with a pannikin of water close by.

The Gristlen was sitting in the far corner, its jointed legs drawn up before it, its pale eyes watching her. A shiver of cold repulsion disturbed the tranquil surface of Laigne's mind, because this was not the pure and lovely spell she had been following; this was not the silver and turquoise tracery of cobweb allure. This was something dark and ugly and soaked in blackest evil. But what lay beneath the darkness?

The Gristlen was grotesque and hideous and there was a slyness in its eyes. But Laigne was here for Echbel. She had followed the music's promise, and she would not flinch now.

But when the Gristlen spoke, it was courteous, and even humble. It said, 'You have come in search of something, Amaranth Lady?' and appeared to wait, quite submissively, for her response.

It was disconcerting to realise that this creature knew the purpose of her visit, and that it might even have been behind the music's sensuous pull. Laigne set down the candle on the floor, and stood looking down at the dark, scaly-hide being. Yes, it was steeped in evil; in old and corrupt evil. Laigne, for all that she was believed to be a little light in the theory of sorcery, knew the difference between what was called Simple Evil and what was called Corrupt Evil. Simple Evil was a young and generally straightforward evil, frequently born from something as basic as greed or lust. Corrupt Evil was different. It was ancient and convoluted; if you imagined it as a solid wedge that you were slicing through, like bread or dough, you would find many different layers: hatred and bitterness and greed and malice and perversion and depravity. Many others. If you went on slicing, right down to the core, you would find that the core was black and warped and twisted.

But nobody had ever said to Laigne that Corrupt Evil could be so compelling, and nobody had ever suggested that, once faced with it, you would want to find out more.

The Gristlen reeked of Corrupt Evil. It possessed ancient and forbidden knowledge, and it had certainly walked in dark worlds. This gave it an unexpected allure. It gave it an authority. Laigne, partly horrified, but partly fascinated, caught herself wondering what its true self was. How had it looked before the Dark Lords had flung it into the Pit? How had it looked in the days when it had spun its terrible evil and wielded its forbidden powers? Had it still been ugly and repulsive? Or had it been one of those darkly beautiful Lords whom you knew to be corrupt and wicked, but whose very corruptness gave them a mantle of seduction?

The Gristlen was watching her, and there was an amused look in its eyes, a *knowing* look. Laigne had the sudden feeling that it possessed something – some inner strength, some secret ability – that it knew would fascinate her and that might even excite her.

This was not to be permitted. Laigne had come here in good faith; she had followed something that had beckoned and promised; that had spun a light cobweb of rainbow music and that had held out the promise of rescuing Echbel. She reminded herself that she was a sorceress of the House of Amaranth; she had studied and become proficient in the Academy of Sorcerers' teachings, and they might say what they liked about that dash of Human blood on her great-grandmother's side . . .

The Gristlen's pale, bulging eyes were raking her body, and Laigne was suddenly conscious of the thin robe. Could it possibly see through to her body? Did such a repulsive, warped thing still possess ordinary physical lusts?

'Certainly I do,' said the Gristlen softly, insinuatingly. 'Oh, certainly I do, Madame Sorceress.' It moved then, suddenly and swiftly, rearing up from its half-sitting, half-crouching position, and loping across the cell to where she was standing by the iron gate. 'And I could give you such pleasure as you have never dreamed of,' it said. It was easily a foot taller than she was, but it was stooping over, so that Laigne found herself staring helplessly into the pale eyes.

'When I look at you, my dear,' said the Gristlen, its voice no longer harsh and ugly but caressing, 'when I look at you, I see your slender white body, and the gleaming thighs, and I see what lies between those thighs, and I should like to *feel* what lies between those thighs.' It stretched out a hand unexpectedly, and Laigne felt the thick leathery skin brush her neck.

'White skin,' it said softly. 'With a drop of Humanish blood.' It half closed its eyes, and Laigne thought: I am arousing it. This is a creature who has walked in the dark realms of forbidden practices and known all manner of depravities and *I* am arousing it. The knowledge gave her a sudden feeling of power.

The Gristlen was backing her against the wall of the cell, and its strong jointed fingers came up to her throat, caressing, stroking. Power rippled beneath its dark skin, and Laigne shivered in helpless fascination.

'Afraid, my white bird?' whispered the Gristlen. 'You need not be. And you came here quite willingly,' it said. 'You came here to me willingly.'

Laigne, transfixed, staring into the cold, glittering eyes, whispered, 'Yes. I came here willingly.'

'You came because you wanted to.'

'I came because I wanted to,' repeated Laigne obediently, and at once the Gristlen's face stretched into a smile. Its hand slid inside the bodice of her gown, the fingers with the thick horn nails touching her breasts, rubbing the nipples, the webbing between its fingers brushing intimately against her skin. She felt arousal swelling between its thighs. It was repulsive, of course it was repulsive, but . . . But it was once powerful and once it walked in the forbidden paths, thought Laigne.

When the Gristlen leaned closer and whispered, 'Love me,' Laigne felt the darkness within it uncoiling and reaching out serpent-fingers to her mind . . . A wave of desire, dizzying in its intensity, sliced through her, and she thought that if the dungeon wall had not been behind her, she would certainly have fallen.

The Gristlen tore aside the thin robe she was wearing, and reached beneath, the scaly skin scraping her flesh. It was

107

beginning to pant as if it had been running, and it was thrusting itself against her. There was the feeling of a hard, huge phallus, huger than anything Laigne had ever imagined, pushing against her. The shameful desire spiralled inside her again, and she threw her head back and pulled the creature's body to her.

At once the Gristlen bellowed in triumph and forced itself between her thighs, pushing her legs apart. There was the painful rasp of needle-like points tearing her skin, and Laigne gasped and looked down.

The Gristlen's monstrous rearing phallus was studded with tiny cruel spikes, so that once embedded in flesh it would tear and lacerate . . . It was barbed, it was fletched like an arrow, and in another minute it would thrust inside her . . .

Laigne screamed and struggled for the first time, and the Gristlen made a convulsive movement, forcing into her. Pain tore through her womb, and there was a sudden shameful flood of wetness between her legs as her bladder succumbed to panic and agony.

The Gristlen chuckled and thrust deeper. 'Fear, my pigeon, or ecstasy?' it hissed, and Laigne screamed again, and felt it grunting and heaving, moving inside her in terrible savage thrusts, pushing in and then withdrawing a little, so that the barbs, the wicked spiny growths, tore her skin. Her flesh was being ripped and there was a white agony, there was grinding, screaming pain . . . She could feel thick blood oozing from her, and she sobbed and struggled because it was tearing her apart; she could feel it happening. It was mutilating her beyond endurance, and she would die in the foul embrace of this evil, corrupt creature . . .

'What are you!' screamed Laigne, almost beyond reason now. 'In the gods' names, what are you?'

'You – will – see . . .' gasped the Gristlen, thrusting against her. 'You will see because you will feel the curse dissolving,' it cried, and clutched at her skin so that she cried out with the pain of her torn flesh. 'Feel it!' shrieked the Gristlen. 'Feel the curse sloughing! Rejoice with me!'

It gave a final, guttural shout, and moved convulsively. There was a wave of agony so intense that Laigne thought she would die, and there was an icy wetness as its seed spurted into her, tainted and loathsome.

She cried out, but it was a broken, mewing cry now, and no one outside the dungeons could have heard.

The Gristlen withdrew completely, and a cry of agony broke from Laigne as the barbs of its phallus tore into her again. There was the terrible feel of its seed, cold and poisonous, flooding her womb. She sagged and half fell to the floor, doubling over, hugging the pain.

The Gristlen stood over her, looking down with a malevolent smile, and she saw through a sick mist that its dark carapace was indeed sloughing. It was digging its horned nails into its skin, raking furiously at the dark, repulsive hide, peeling it back in great gobbets, like a child tearing off a scabbed wound.

Laigne, almost beyond reason now, thought: in another minute it will stand before me in its true state! And I do not want to see it! screamed her mind. I do not want to know!

Beneath the fibrous lumps of torn skin, pale thick fluid was oozing to the surface, and in places there was the glimmer of greyish scales, faintly luminous in the dark cell.

And then the creature was emerging, it was climbing out of the discarded shell, and it was standing over her, a monstrous rearing shape, palely and evilly beautiful. A shining, membraneous tail protruded like a giant fin from the base of the creature's spine, and through the new skin, Laigne could see the tiny brittle bones of a creature accustomed to dwelling beneath the seas. There was a central hollow spine with a myriad of tiny, bony rays fanning out from it, extending into the arms and lower limbs.

A sea-creature. Something piscine. Something that had walked the world many centuries ago . . . A terrible fear began to form.

The Gristlen's shrivelled black skin lay on the floor, and in its place was a sleek being with a round, hairless skull and Human features. There were bulbous eyes and a flat, wide mouth, and a thick neck with rudimentary gills.

Gills and hollow bones, thought Laigne. A lashing, jagged-edged fin. And there are scales, faintly phosphorescent, between his thighs . . .

Tumbled memories of mermen who left their sea-worlds to walk on land and spin their evil seductions over Humans churned through her mind, and with them came a searing knowledge.

Not a merman. Not something from the cool under-ocean realm of the *sidh* even.

109

This was the Fisher King. The ancient, legendary Fisher King, whose reign had been a reign of bloody terror, and whose name was even now whispered with fear.

The legend said that he had been driven from the world, that he had been vanquished by the *sidh* and that he could never again return to the world of Men. Ireland had been a safer place because of it.

And now he had returned. The Fisher King, Coelacanth himself, had come back.

The Amaranths were shocked and horrified. To think that Laigne had gone alone to the Gristlen's cell, and there been so brutally savaged, was scarcely to be borne.

The Mugain said it was all very well to say tut and pshaw and that Laigne had acted in a foolhardy manner; there the thing was, and whatever her reasons had been, now they must make the poor soul as comfortable as they could.

One of the younger Amaranths, who had made something of a study of cures and elixirs and healing spells, had spun a cool, soothing balm, made up of gentle grey cobweb substances and thin silky twines. 'It will calm her mind,' said the sorcerer, whose name was Cecht, and who had until now been rather over-awed at finding herself in such august company.

'Did she say anything about – about the Gristlen?'

'Only that it attacked her,' said Cecht, and everyone looked solemn, because you did not have to have achieved the level of scholar-sorcerer to guess what form the attack would have taken.

'Where is the creature now?' demanded Great-aunt Fuamnach, who had been sitting by the fire, unravelling the puckered enchantments for re-use. 'What happened to it?'

'It escaped,' said Cerball crossly. 'Of course.'

'And is probably roaming freely about the Palace, ready to pounce out on to another of us,' said Great-aunt Fuamnach, beckoning to Bodb Decht to sit in front of her and help with rewinding the skeins of enchantment. 'Well, Cerball, I never criticise; but how we are to sleep safely in our beds with such a creature prowling the corridors, I hope you will tell us!' She fixed Cerball with a stern look, and Cerball, who had already spent a nasty morning worrying over this one, and had assigned

110

the Mugain to organise a proper Banishing Ritual, said crossly that it was all in hand.

The Banishing Ritual was duly performed, with the Mugain leading them all. Somebody produced an especially strong Enchantment of Light to shine in every dark corner, and most people said firmly that the evil had gone.

'Self-delusion,' said Great-aunt Fuamnach. 'It's still here. Mark my words, it's still here.'

Whether it was still here or not, nobody really knew any longer. It might have scuttled into some dark hiding place somewhere, or it might have whisked itself out of the Palace altogether. And, as Bodb Decht said, there were so many itinerant enchantments wandering about the Palace at the moment, it was difficult to tell what was good and benign and what was just a little bit *grey*, and what was downright evil and black.

'And now there's poor Nechtan's funeral rites to think of,' said Herself of Mugain, and added that wasn't it exactly like Nechtan – may the gods preserve his soul – to up and die just as they were in the midst of a turmoil. Nechtan, said Herself irritably, had always been a shocking old attention-seeker, and clearly he had not altered in death.

The funeral rites would take nine days and nine nights. Nobody had the heart for it, but it was not something that could be scamped and it was certainly not something that could be ignored. Although nobody quite said it was inconvenient, most people thought it. But there it was; Nechtan must be made properly ready for the great journey to the Land Under the Ocean, so that his spirit could scale the walls of the Gates of Paradise, and unlock the Three Gates of Wisdom, of Poetry and of Knowledge.

The female sorcerers had already prepared Nechtan's body for its last journey, and the upper floors of the Porphyry Palace were redolent with the scents of natron and the burning of hazelwood. He had been dressed in the ceremonial white robe with the amethyst colours of the Amaranth House, and then his body would be placed on a silver bier draped with purple and white.

For nine days and nine nights, the Amaranths would read from the great annals of Ireland, nine of them at a time for a stretch of nine hours, after which a further nine would take over. It was exhausting and it drained their power, but it was important to

111

surround Nechtan with poetry and wisdom and knowledge, so that the Three Gates would open for him with ease.

The first three days would be given to the chanting of poetry, the most beautiful and the most evocative poetry of Ireland. There would be the verses from the famous *Voyage of Bran*:

> Unknown is wailing and treachery
> In the familiar cultivated land,
> There is nothing rough or harsh,
> But sweet music striking on the ear.
> Without grief, without sorrow, without death,
> Without sickness, without debility . . .

They would also use some of the beautiful poignant works of Amairgen the Blind, who had lived in Ireland centuries earlier and bequeathed a wealth of poetry and wisdom to generations after him:

> And it is at the Purple Hour
> When the day is handed into the keeping of the night
> When spells are cast and enchantments walk abroad,
> When the unseen creatures of the Old Ireland prowl,
> When the silver bars of the body are dissolved
> And the cag'd soul at last takes flight,
> And joy abounds for ever . . .

The next three days would encompass wisdom and knowledge, so that there would be readings from the *Chronicles of Calatin the First* and the *Annals of Sorcery*. Probably there would also be sections from the lives of some of Tara's wisest rulers; those of Grainne the Gentle and Erin the Just would also surely be chosen.

The last three days would be entirely given to music. The ancient magical runic songs of the Druids, which symbolised wisdom as well as music, would be sung, and the beautiful sad ballads of the long-ago High Kings and Queens, all of them beautiful and filled with adventure and bravery and magic.

It was unbearably difficult for them to give it their fullest concentration. Nobody could forget that the Dark Realm's most powerful necromancer had entered Ireland with ease and snatched up Theodora. Nobody could forget Echbel in the grisly clutches of the Fomoire.

'But,' said the Mugain very fiercely, 'we must pay this last homage to Nechtan, and we must do so fully and properly, for it is unthinkable that we should do other than ensure his entry through the Three Gates.'

It was unthinkable to all of them, and they would do it.

Laigne heard the slow, solemn procession set out for Nechtan's last rites.

She was trying very hard to forget what had happened to her. She was trying not to remember how he had felt and how he had looked: Coelacanth, the Fisher King... There was that remarkable image of him standing over her, virile and strong, the stance of a masculine animal who has taken and given pleasure...

Given pleasure...

There had been a surprised knife-thrust of sheer physical ecstasy that had shaken her body to its core. There had been the feeling that her womb had opened of its own volition to accept the creature's cold seed...

Coelacanth's seed. Coelacanth's son...

One hand strayed to her body low down, curving over her flat stomach, and the beginnings of a mad, secret smile lifted her lips.

Chapter Thirteen

As Andrew and Rumour drew nearer to the black-mouthed caves, they became aware of the steady rhythmic chanting again.

The caves were still some way ahead of them. Beyond them, the rock tunnel snaked into shadow, and Rumour said, very softly, 'Once we start to move, we should keep moving. Then, if they look out, they may think we are simply part of the shadows.'

Andrew nodded. The firelit shadows leapt and pranced, and by moving smoothly and ceaselessly, they might blend with them. But if they moved and stopped and moved again, the Fomoire would see a break in the shadows' pattern and would be at once alerted.

The Fomoire were dancing round the fires at the mouth of the largest of the caves, singing their horrid Hunting Song. Their skin-clad silhouettes flickered grotesquely on the cave walls and on the rock wall, and they were grisly and so inHuman, that Andrew knew a moment of near panic. He thought: I do not believe we can get past the caves without them knowing. They will *scent* us, he thought, torn between anger at his own helplessness, and fear at what lay ahead.

And then the old resolve surged back, and he thought: I will not despair! I will not believe that there is not some way in which we can reach the Dark Ireland! He glanced to Rumour, and saw that she was standing very still, her eyes narrowed so that the long lashes shadowed her cheeks, her expression absorbed. He felt at once that Rumour was summoning strength, just as he was summoning it. And although our sources are different; although we both mine a different quarry to find that strength, in the end, the result will be the same.

114

The Samildanach, who will come to Ireland humbly and quietly, but before whom all gates will fall . . .

Which of them had come first? Which was the grafted-on belief? The treacherous thought: *does it matter?* slid into Andrew's mind.

They linked hands, and began to move cautiously down the tunnel, keeping close to the right-hand side, treading in the lee of the rock, so that if the Fomoire should look out, the intruders would not be seen, and the Fomoire would see only the shadows cast by their fires.

There looked to be five or six caves, and as they moved cautiously nearer, they saw that the firelight came from the large central cave, and that the others were in deep shadow.

They were edging along with their backs against the rock wall, their eyes never once leaving the leaping figures.

As they drew nearer, they could see that at the entrance to each cave were piles of white, gleaming objects with shreds of skin adhering to them, flung down in a tumble. Andrew felt a shudder go through Rumour, and knew the objects for Human bones. Skins hung at the entrances to the caves, whole pale Human skins, spread out and nailed to the rock by the hands and feet. The skulls had been left intact, with blank staring eyes and lolling tongues, and it was dreadfully easy to imagine that at any minute the poor sightless heads might lift, and the thin frail arms would beckon, and the pinioned ankles would writhe and struggle.

A warm dry scent belched out from the caves. Andrew identified it as a cooking scent, rich and savoury, overlaid with a faint greasiness. He thought: I believe they are cooking the flesh of their victims! That is Human meat I am smelling. His mind was at once imprinted with a nightmare image of the Fomoire scraping the flesh from their victims' skins, and casting it into a pot to bubble.

The Fomoire were grouped in the centre cave. Inching stealthily forward, Rumour close behind him, Andrew felt again the immense gratitude for her presence, mingled with disgust at his selfishness. This was to have been my task, he thought; I should have approached it alone. I am taking her into a terrible danger. But as the thought took shape he felt Rumour's response.

You do not take me, I come of my own accord!

They could see into the caves now, and they could see that they stretched back and back. Deep and dark and winding away into the ancient labyrinths of legend, thought Rumour, and remembered the tales of this strange between-world where half-Human beasts were said to prowl in the shadows. The firelight cast leaping shadows as the Fomoire danced and, as they moved closer, Andrew and Rumour saw that deep within the side caves were iron bars, sunk into the ground and stretching up to the cave roof.

Iron bars, thick and harsh and so close together that once behind them it would be impossible to escape.

The Fomoire's dungeons.

The Hunting Song was all round them now, a grisly rhythmic chanting, and the red glow was falling across them, turning Rumour's hair to pouring molten gold. Andrew held up one hand and saw that it, too, had been turned to fire, so that the skin seemed transparent and he could see the bones and muscle and the flesh beneath.

They were nearly level with the first of the caves, and Andrew felt Rumour take a deep breath.

Ready?

Ready!

They flattened themselves against the rock wall and began to inch forward, level with the cave's mouth, part of the flickering firelight, melting into the shadows . . . This is the last stretch, but this will be the worst. Don't pause, don't stop, keep edging forwards . . . Andrew was repeating the words in his mind as if they were a prayer or a talisman. At any minute the Fomoire might look up, at any minute they might whip round and come pouring out of the cave.

But I think we are going to do it! thought Andrew exultantly. Only another few feet, only a dozen more steps . . . This was only a part of their journey: the descent into the Segais Well had been the first part and this was the next. If we can only reach the blackness beyond the tunnels, then we shall have left this stage behind us and have embarked on the next. And each stage will take us nearer to the Gateway itself. Am I nearing the Black Monk? thought Andrew.

His eyes flickered towards the tunnels. The deeper hinterlands, thought Andrew. The next stage. What lies within those tunnels, I wonder? Is it the borderland, the between-world where he prowls?

Don't think about it yet. Concentrate on getting past the Fomoire's caves; concentrate on blending with the shadows and the crimson firelight ... Almost there. Please God, let us be safe ...

He was bracing himself for the last, dangerous steps, when there was a check in the dancing, and the singing stopped as abruptly as if a door had been closed on it. A terrible cry went up.

'Humans!'

'Humans close by!'

'I smell Humans!'

'Out and after them!'

'Get them all and into the cages!'

The Fomoire came swarming out of the great, red-lit cave and fell upon them, knocking them to the ground, dragging them into the cave, and flinging them down before the fire.

They circled the two prisoners, grinning gleefully, rubbing their clawlike hands together and occasionally aiming a kick at them with their dead Human feet.

Rumour half struggled to her feet and lifted one hand to sketch a spell on the air, but the Fomoire were there at once, knocking her hand aside, and the spell, whatever it had been, was still-born. Black fury rose in Andrew, and he bounded upwards, hitting out at the creatures, feeling a surge of exultation when his blows sent one of them reeling backwards, seeing two more flinch and cower. It flickered on his mind that he had in some way surprised them by the blow, as if they were unused to being physically touched, and he struck out again, feeling his clenched fist punch into the nearest, feeling it go beneath the half-concealing skin cloak and sink a little way into the creature's body. There was a brief twist of nausea; it was exactly like jabbing into an overripe fruit, and feeling the crust split, and the rotten juices spurt out. For the space of a heartbeat, the Fomoire hesitated, and Andrew drew in a deep breath to hit out again, an unexpected part of his mind exulting in the angry violence.

And then the Fomoire had recovered; they were on him again, binding him with thin, cruel ropes, tying his hands behind his back, dragging him into the cave's depths. Iron cages lined the rock wall, serried rows of them, four or five all on top of one another. Small gates were inset into each one. Andrew and Rumour were lifted, and flung into a cage half-way up. The door was closed, and the key turned in the lock.

The sound of the key in the lock was the worst moment yet. They both pushed at the gate at once, finding it strong and firm.

'As we knew it would be,' said Andrew, striving for calmness, pleased to hear that his voice sounded reasonably untroubled.

'It is as well to try,' said Rumour. 'Because, of course, we cannot stay here.' She looked about her, her eyebrows lifted in disgust, but Andrew saw that, in the uncertain light, her eyes were dark and thoughtful.

The cages were cunningly wrought so that they were not quite tall enough for a captive to stand up, and not quite wide enough to lie down in. The two prisoners found themselves half sitting, half lying, and they both knew that to be unable to stand or stretch would soon become almost intolerable. There was rockdust on the floor, and hunks of bread and pannikins of water in one corner.

Rumour said, 'Do they call that food?'

'I am afraid they might.'

'It looks quite disgusting,' she said, and now it was the exotic sorceress who disdained all but the best, and who dined at the highest tables in Ireland, and would wear only the most costly silk and velvet and lace. Andrew heard this, and despite himself, smiled briefly.

He said, hesitantly, 'Is there perhaps a spell of any kind we could use to escape?' and thought: I do not believe I am saying this! I do not believe that I am asking, *hoping* that she can summon up an enchantment to free us! Prayer is the strongest force of all! That is what I must turn to! And, even while he was thinking, he knew that sorcery existed, and he knew as well that if magic could free them, he would welcome it.

Rumour said thoughtfully, 'The Fomoire are the Spirits of Darkness, the essence of what we call Corrupt Evil, and Corrupt Evil is extremely difficult to fight. Perhaps it is impossible to fight. I think it will be very difficult to summon up anything that will beat back these creatures,' she said. 'You saw how easily the Fomoire knocked my hand aside when I raised it to begin a protection spell? There was more to it than just a blow.'

Andrew said, carefully, 'There is the *sidh*'s music,' and Rumour said, 'I had not forgotten it. But we are unsure of whether it can be used against an enemy, other than by the *sidh* themselves.'

'Cerball and the Mugain said it would get us into the Dark Ireland. It must have great power.'

'It will cut a path through the Gateway, certainly. Its light should do that, for the *sidh* are creatures of light. But I do not know if it can protect us from the Fomoire,' said Rumour. 'And there is the danger that if we use it and it fails, we have placed ourselves more surely in their hands.'

'We have shown our strengths,' said Andrew, understanding this.

'Yes. I believe that if we are to outwit the Fomoire, we must forget sorcery,' said Rumour suddenly. 'We must defeat them by ordinary Human trickery.' The sudden grin slanted. 'That is by your Human trickery, and my partly-Human trickery,' said Rumour.

Andrew sat very still, and thought: of course she is not wholly Human. Of course I knew. Even so, it was a strange and not wholly comfortable feeling to be here in the cage, with the Fomoire banking up the fires, knowing that his strange, exotic companion had the blood of something unHuman in her veins.

He had heard the amusement return to her voice, and he welcomed it. He was beginning to understand that she would show that surface flippancy in any situation she found herself in, but that in fact beneath it all she was not flippant in the least.

He sat deep in thought for a moment, and then said, 'When I hit those creatures out there—'

'They flinched at once.'

'Yes.' He knew gratitude once again for her instant comprehension.

As if to strengthen this, Rumour said, 'And I think you were horrified to discover violence in your heart, Andrew.'

'Yes.' He did not say that it made him frightened about what else might lie undiscovered, but he thought she would know it.

119

Rumour leaned over and took his hand. 'But violence is in all Men,' she said. 'Perhaps for some it is never called into being, but it is the only difference. Some are never tested.'

'My Teaching eschews violence.' Andrew frowned.

Rumour, who had already felt how much he was struggling to come to terms with this deep-seated anger against the Fomoire, said at once, 'But that is a very arbitrary statement. There must surely be times when violence or anger could be justified.'

'Our Leader showed anger more than once,' said Andrew, and looked up. 'Against greed or hypocrisy. Yes, especially against hypocrisy. There is a recorded case of how he hounded the cheating money-lenders out of the Temple, and how he overturned their tables, and set about them.'

Rumour, watching his face, said, 'That is a Leader to follow.'

'Yes.' Andrew smiled at her, and then said, thoughtfully, 'Those creatures – they seemed almost afraid of being touched.'

'And yet they touch us to drag us into the cages,' said Rumour, considering this.

'But through the skin cloaks.' Andrew sat up. 'They only touch us through the skins, Rumour. Is there something – some weakness in them that we could use? Could it be so easy? What exactly are the Fomoire?'

Rumour said slowly, 'I have only glimpsed them through the skin cloaks, but they are tiny and dark and wizened. We all saw that.' She looked at him. 'I believe them to possess goblin blood,' said Rumour, and grinned as Andrew stared. 'Do you not accept such things, Andrew? You should, for there were once goblins and demons and imps in Ireland, and they walked abroad openly and easily and fought with the first Irish peoples.'

'Tell me.' Because surely the more they knew about their grisly captors, the more chance there was of outwitting them.

'The goblins dwelled in the forests and the caves,' said Rumour. 'They were creatures of the earth, dark and ancient, and they lived near to the ground. They were always vicious and greedy and black-hearted; there was one very old family of goblins who were known as the Black HeartStealers, in fact.' She paused. 'The legend is that, hundreds of years ago, they inter-married with a distant branch of the Amaranths. I think you may have met the descendants of that marriage in the Porphyry Palace.'

'Yes, I recall. Tall and rather brutish-looking.' Andrew remembered that he had felt a coldness and a greed from them.

'Cerball and Laigne were careless to allow them into the Palace,' said Rumour. 'Although perhaps they did not learn of their presence until it was too late. Every branch of the Amaranths had assembled for the Succession Ritual, you see.'

Andrew said, 'I think there is a vein of evil blood in all families somewhere.'

'There is very little known about the goblin strain,' said Rumour, keeping her voice low, occasionally glancing to where the Fomoire were seated about their fire. 'But it is known that they were imbued with what is called Corrupt Evil – which is extremely difficult to defeat – and that they were scouts for the necromancers; messengers who prowled the woods and the caves and the mountains, searching for prey for their overlords.

'When the first true Humans, the Cruithin, came to Ireland, the goblins were driven back, but they were not driven out. They hid themselves in the undersides of the earth; in the deep caves and the labyrinths and the underground tunnels.

'The Cruithin were good and gentle, and filled with the strong woodland magic that pure-bred Humans can sometimes command,' said Rumour. 'They served Ireland faithfully and well, but they, in their turn, were driven out many centuries later. The Cruithin have almost vanished from Ireland now, although you may find traces of their descendants in remote hill farms, or mountain villages. I believe that there is a community of their descendants on the western coast, within the Moher Cliffs. They are small, dark-haired, rather attractive people, and they have a slightly elfin look to them.

'But the goblins – occasionally chronicled as *ginid*, although that is a feminine term – did not vanish,' said Rumour, absorbed in her story now. 'The legend is that they traded with the necromancers, and were finally given the lands that lay between the Dark Realm and the True Ireland.'

'Hinterlands,' said Andrew thoughtfully, and Rumour said, 'Yes.'

She looked at him. 'I think we are in those hinterlands now, Andrew,' she said. 'And I believe that the Fomoire are half-goblins; perhaps the blood-descendants of the original *ginid* and some strange alliance made since.'

'You are very knowledgeable,' said Andrew, and Rumour grinned.

'I hold a very high degree in the subsidiary magical art of story-telling,' she said. 'If we escape, Andrew, one night I will spin for you the Tapestry Enchantment which I created many years ago. Woven into it are the legends and the myths and the folklore of Ireland. It took me many years to finish it – although it will never really be finished, of course, because there will always be more to add. But it is marvellous and magical and enthralling.' She did not say this as if she was boasting, or as if she was expecting him to compliment her. She merely said it as though stating a fact. 'Occasionally I have unrolled it at ceremonious gatherings, although it is rather fragile and has to be treated with care. But it is a very beautiful enchantment,' she said, seriously, and then, grinning at him, 'And, of course, it is one I can turn to good advantage if I have to. Telling a story, properly and fully, so that your listeners are held completely spellbound can be extremely useful. I have talked my way out of many a difficult situation,' she said, and then, grinning, added, 'And there have been occasions when I have talked my way into one as well.'

Andrew smiled, but said, very seriously, 'Can we use our knowledge of the Fomoire to defeat them?'

'Goblins were always believed to harbour a strong and bitter hatred for Humans,' said Rumour, frowning. 'No one ever knew why, for they possessed a dark, strong magic of their own, and they were many times victorious in battles with Humans.'

'But the Cruithin drove them back.'

'Yes, the Cruithin drove them back.' Rumour frowned.

'That must mean the Cruithin found something – a weakness—'

'Yes,' said Rumour. 'But I cannot think what it would be.' She frowned and began to say something, when Andrew turned sharply at a sound from the mouth of the cave.

Footsteps, light and darting and leaping.

The Fomoire were coming for them.

Chapter Fourteen

The Fomoire approached the cages with a sly, sideways walk, as if they were pretending to creep up on their victims, even though they must know they could be seen. Several of them had joined hands and tiptoed forward with exaggerated movements, and several more were holding a finger to their lips in hushing gestures like malignant children.

The leading one unlocked the cage, and at once the rest fell on Andrew and Rumour, pulling them out.

Andrew said, 'You are speedy in your dealings with us,' but all the while he was noticing how the Fomoire handled them through the skin cloaks, using the dead Human hands rather like ungainly gloves.

'And since you are speedy, we shall not keep you waiting,' said Rumour, and the Fomoire shrieked and jabbed at them with hard bony fingers that they thrust through their skin cloaks.

'We shall not be *dealing* with you yet awhile,' they cried.

'We shall wish to savour that pleasure,' said another.

'And you have to be fattened first,' said a third.

'Until your skins are soft and juicy,' said the first.

'Until you are plump and fair.'

'*Then* we shall peel you of your cloaks, Humanish.'

'Show them!' cried the Fomoire, prodding one another. 'Show the Humanish what is ahead of them!'

'Let them witness the feast!'

They pulled the two prisoners forward, and forced them into the largest of the caves. The fire was at the exact centre here and, as they were dragged into its light, they saw that the Fomoire were carrying in driftwood and logs which they cast into the flames.

'The gleanings from the shores of Tiarna,' said one who sat on

123

the far side of the fire, and who carried an air of authority.

Rumour said, 'So you prowl the outskirts of the *sidh*'s city?'

'We prowl the world, Madame Sorceress,' said the Fomoire. 'We are ever hungry for Humans, and so we prowl the world.' It gestured to several of the others. 'Throw on the bones,' it said. And then, with a cunning glance to Rumour, 'There is nothing so fine as the fat of Humans to make a fire burn brightly.'

As the flames leapt, the rest of the Fomoire ranged themselves in a circle about it, some of them sitting cross-legged, the heads of their skin cloaks thrown back like hoods, so that Andrew and Rumour could see their tiny, bald, wizened skulls and their grinning, toothless, leathery features, and the flat, pointed ears. Rumour looked at them, and knew she had not mistaken: there was goblin blood here. I see it and I feel it and I smell it, she thought.

The Fomoire who was seated across the fire from them lifted an arm and gestured to the five who were holding Andrew and Rumour.

'Bind them fast,' it said. 'And then bring out the other one. Bring out his cage and let us have a little fun with him.'

'Bring out the prisoner!'

'Bring out the Humanish prisoner!'

Andrew and Rumour were bound with the thin ropes again, and held tightly before the fire while several of the Fomoire went out, with their strange circling, half-dancing walk. While they were gone, the rest began the dance again at the back of the cave, almost as if they might be trying out new steps, moving this way and that, reaching down some of the skins from the cave walls, spreading them on the floor, and then dragging them behind them as they moved, as if they were ceremonial trains.

And then the others returned, and Andrew and Rumour saw that between them they were pulling a great square cage which was composed of iron bars on all sides, and which had a roof and a floor of bars. There was a small gate in one side with a massive padlock.

Inside the cage was Echbel.

He was naked and his air was matted and unkempt. He was screaming and clawing at the iron bars, begging the Fomoire to let him out, promising them all manner of things, offering them the Amaranths' secrets, offering them the Cadence itself.

'Useless,' snapped the one whom Andrew thought was the leader. 'We know your people's secrets already.'

'We inherited them from our ancestors,' said another, and Rumour knew that these were indeed the strange mutant descendants of goblins.

They grinned and crouched before the cage, prodding at Echbel with long spiked sticks. Echbel scuttled into a corner of the cage and huddled there, shielding his face with his hands, and the Fomoire sent their shrieking laughter into the glowing cave.

'String him up!' they cried. 'Hang him over the fire and let us see if he jumps!'

'For if he jumps, then we shall take his skin!'

'If he jumps, then it will be a skin for dancing in!'

'Make him jump! Make the prisoner leap and dance!'

They linked hands and began to circle the fire, singing, and as they did so, four of them dragged the cage to a great iron winch, with clamps, and fastened the cage into the clamps. The smallest of them adjusted the screws, and two more began to hoist the cage aloft, winching it higher and higher, up and up, winding it outwards then, so that at length it hung directly over the fire.

The Fomoire threw handfuls of a fine white powder into the fire's heart, and the flames leapt up, sizzling, throwing out a sickly-sweet stench of decay, licking at the underside of the cage, turning the lower bars to glowing heat. Echbel screamed and clawed at the bars, climbing to the cage roof.

'Human bone-dust!' cried the Fomoire, gleefully leaping higher in delight. 'See him jump! More! More bone-dust for the flames!'

'Burn the bones!'

They began to sing again, with a greedy, gleeful sound that made Andrew and Rumour, watching helplessly from the side, feel sick.

> 'Give us fire to burn up higher,
> Flames to roast and bones to flare.
> Burn and roast and scorch and sear,
> Singe the skins and tan the fur.'

'Tan him!' cried the Fomoire. 'Tan him and burn him! A good skin, a worthy skin! A skin for murdering in!'

Andrew said in a whisper, 'This is terrible. Surely there is something we can do?'

'Nothing,' said Rumour in a low, furious voice.

'The *sidh*'s music—'

'Save it for yourself,' said Rumour. 'Soon it will be our turn.'

The Fomoire were reaching up to Echbel now, each of them brandishing sharpened sticks and long-handled forks. In some cases they had thrust the ends into the heart of the fire, so that they glowed white-hot. They poked at Echbel, and laughed as he ran from one side to another of the cage, doubling up with mirth and holding their sides as he tried frenziedly to escape. The fire burned higher, and Echbel scrabbled frantically at the cage, trying to climb to the barred roof. His skin was already flushed and shiny from the heat, and his eyes were bloodshot.

'Enough!' cried the leader at length. 'Preserve the skin!'

'Preserve the Humanish cloak!'

'Winch him lower!'

'Yes, let us see the juices run!'

'Let us *feel* the juices run!'

'Lower! Lower!'

Three of them darted to the trivet, and began to wind the black handle, so that the cage inched its way out of the flames' reach, and then down further until it hung on a level with the fire.

Echbel was screaming continuously now; terrible, trapped-hare screams. He was clinging to the sides of the cage, as close to its roof as he could get, his hands curled about the bars, his feet twined through them lower down. He was so close to the flames now that, when sparks flew up, they touched his hair, making it flare drily and brightly. The sickening smell of burning hair mingled with that of the bone-dust stench, and Echbel fell from the sides of the cage, writhing on its floor as he clutched at his hair and tried to beat the flames out with his bare hands.

'Careful of the fur, lads!' cried the Fomoire, instantly concerned.

'Don't singe the fur!'

'For there's nothing so fine as a fur-trimmed cloak!'

'A fur-trimmed cloak of Humanish vair,
A sable lining with a veil of hair.
Singe the beard and tan the hide
But leave the fur safe behind'.

Andrew and Rumour were both struggling against the harsh
ropes that bound their hands behind their backs, and Rumour
was again murmuring a spell of light. But each time the spell
began to form, each time the narrow splinters of light began to
glisten against the cave's black walls, one of the Fomoire
knocked it away, so that it fell into hundreds of tiny, glinting
beads, useless and impotent, trickling away into the crevices in
the corners.

Echbel's skin was turning bright red and the soles of his feet
were cracking. The Fomoire leapt in delight.

'The juices! The juices are running! Don't miss them!'

'Give us the juice of Humanish blood
Give us the seed of skinflesh and hide.
Balm to smother our own hides in
Give us the sap of Humanish skin.'

Echbel's skin was splitting in several places now from the
intense heat. Andrew, unable to look away, saw that a colourless
fluid was seeping from the splits, that it was actually running
down his body and dripping on to the waiting Fomoire. For a
moment, he was surprised that there was no actual blood, and
then he realised, with a twist of nausea, that the Fomoire were so
cruelly expert, so practised, that they could judge the exact
moment when their victim's skin would exude what they called
the juice; the sluggish colourless fluid of a surface burn. They
had not left Echbel long enough over the flames to draw blood,
but they had left him long enough to make his skin scorch
slightly all over so that the fat beneath the skin oozed and ran
down.

The Fomoire were fighting one another for places directly
beneath the cage, squabbling and shrieking, tumbling over one
another in their eagerness. Several of them fell into the fire, and
shot out again squealing, bringing with them a pungent smell of
burnt hair and nail and skin; but most of them managed to stand

127

beneath the cage, their cruel goblin-faces upturned, their shrivelled claw-hands reaching upwards, cupped to catch the terrible fluids that dripped from the cage floor. They smeared their repulsive bodies with it, shrieking their delight, and Andrew and Rumour, sickened and appalled, exchanged looks, both of them frantically searching for a way to rescue Echbel.

The Fomoire were winching the cage down now, shouting to one another not to let the skin split any further.

'We have the juices, don't spoil the skin!' they cried.

The cage was on the ground, and Echbel was struggling to break out, tearing his hands and nails in the process. Thin blood smothered the stout iron lock on the door, and the Fomoire wailed.

'Make him ready!' cried the leader. 'Spread him out and make him ready!'

'Take the cloak! The cloak of Humanish thin!'

'The cloak of thin pale shale!'

'Lay him out.'

A deep and sudden silence fell on the cave as Echbel was dragged from the iron cage and forced to the ground. The Fomoire abandoned their leaping, dancing mood, and suddenly took on an air of immense concentration. Several of them drove four iron stakes into the cave floor; strong thick stakes with short ropes attached, set in a roughish square. As they lowered Echbel between these stakes, Andrew and Rumour saw that he was to be tied in a cruciform shape, his arms and legs spread wide.

And then they will flay him, thought Andrew.

The Fomoire were quiet and watchful now, and the two prisoners were aware again of the deep and sudden concentration. They circled Echbel again, but now it was a silent, watchful movement; it was the circling of predators before they pounced. Their tiny evil eyes were assessing and calculating, as if they were gauging how many knives would be needed, how many needles and razors . . .

Several of them had fetched long knives from the rear of the cave, and they held them out, so that the blades caught the fireglow and glinted redly, evilly.

'Now!' cried the leader, and the Fomoire moved.

Each one had its appointed place; each moved to it, and stood with a knife or a razor poised. When the signal was given, they moved as one, making a long, absolutely straight slit from Echbel's throat to his groin, slicing through the layers of skin and yellow fat beneath. Blood bubbled to the surface, and two of them mopped it, enabling the others to see what they were doing.

Echbel was still screaming, but it was a sobbing, hopeless sound now. Rumour thought he scarcely knew they were in the cave with him, and was glad of it, for it would surely have been torture for Echbel to hope for rescue.

It was quicker than they had thought it would be, but it was not really very quick at all.

The Fomoire inserted wafer-thin flat-bladed knives into the single cut, and began to slide them beneath the skin. Rumour, with memories of a hundred Royal banquets, found herself recalling how the High King's chefs would serve delicate pastry concoctions, and how they would ease a fragile slice from a serving dish with a silver server and lay it on the plate before the guests. Horrid! I believe I shall never want to eat again! thought Rumour. If only these goblin-creatures would ignore us long enough for me to pronounce a spell of some kind. What about a spear of lightning? But the instant she began the incantation, the guards brought their hands down and yet again the embryo enchantment died still-born.

Rumour gave vent to a brief angry curse, and then, quite suddenly, an idea slid into her mind.

A spell to disable the Fomoire was clearly impossible, but what about a spell to free them both of the ropes? What about a tiny hidden spell? thought Rumour, abruptly alert. A delicate razor-sharp spell, a miniature enchantment to slice through their bonds? Could she pronounce one without the Fomoire hearing and sensing it?

She kept her eyes lowered, in case any of the creatures should look across and see her thoughts. I do not *think* they possess the *Samhailt*, thought Rumour. I do not think they do, but I cannot risk anything. She searched her mind quickly, flipping through the layers of memory, much as she would have flipped through the *Chronicles* and the *Indexes of Sorcery*.

A mixture? A little of the Spell of Human Hands? No, for to use that, a pure-bred Human must chant it, and although Andrew was becoming close to her thoughts, he was not close enough for her to give him a whole incantation.

But there were other spells. There was the Lightning Spell she had attempted earlier; that could be used in a minuscule version, perhaps with something else. There was a fairly simple Enchantment of Slicing Fire that might do.

And then she had it. Simple and clear and strong.

The Silver Cord of the Druids.

It was many centuries since it had been chanted; legend said it had last been used by a Human whom the Druids had tried to sacrifice on a Beltane Fire in the days when Human sacrifice was still permitted. It was Ireland's ancient tongue, long since lost to Men – another Lost Language! thought Rumour – but the words of the Chant had been chronicled and recorded, and Rumour had seen the parchment bearing the words in Nechtan's library.

They had nothing to lose. She would try it, and if their bonds unravelled, then they would have a fighting chance.

For the Fomoire do not like being touched . . . Rumour glanced at Andrew, and saw the flicker of a response. She drew in a great breath of relief, for although Andrew could certainly not help her in the Silver Cord Chant, he was undoubtedly alert and aware, and he would fall on the Fomoire the instant they were released.

He is not a man of violence, thought Rumour; he abhors violence, but he will do it. How remarkable. She sent him a sideways look, and saw the strong clear line of his jaw. Yes, he would certainly fight if he had to. This was quite remarkably comforting.

The skin was being eased slowly away from Echbel's flesh now. They could see the raw meaty flesh beneath, here and there the red stringiness of muscle, and the brief whiteness of bone. The Fomoire were completely absorbed in their work; if I am to do anything at all, thought Rumour, then I must do it now, while their attention is on Echbel. She half closed her eyes, and reached deep into her mind, seeing before her the ancient, vellum-bound *Chronicles* of Nechtan's library, turning the leaves in her mind. It had been gold-tipped, the parchment, and twined with the licking, silver fire that signified it to be an ancient Druidic tongue.

The Fomoire crouched low over their victim, moving the skin inch by careful inch, giving little irritated clicking noises if they cut too deeply and caused blood to well up.

Andrew thought that Echbel was almost dead. His skin had been peeled as far as his limbs; all that they could see of his trunk was a glistening, sac-like lump, a membraneous bag of red-raw flesh and muscle, with the occasional dark streak of liver and kidney. God's bounty, thought Andrew, sickened. God's bounty, packed tight but ready to spill out on to the floor if a knife or a needle-point cuts too deeply.

The needles were used by two Fomoire who were crouched at Echbel's feet. They slid the needles beneath the skin, apparently loosening it from the flesh before the flat, thin blades were used.

The skin was the colour of tallow now; grey-yellow. Echbel's eyes were now only showing the whites; they had rolled back in his skull, and his mouth had fallen open, the tongue lolling out. Dead, or as near dead as made no difference. God take his soul, thought Andrew, and found a fleeting comfort in forming the familiar words. He half turned to Rumour, and felt a bolt of such triumph from her that, for a moment, he was very nearly blinded. But he thought: she has harnessed a spell of some kind! She has reached and caught something to free us! With the thought, he became aware that the bonds about his wrists were loosening, they were sliding over his hands, falling to the ground.

The Fomoire were standing up, holding the pale empty skin aloft, reaching out from their cloaks with their little clawlike hands, beginning a triumphant dance.

Andrew, Rumour at his side, leapt forward and fell upon them.

It was difficult, but not as difficult as they had thought. The Fomoire were taken by surprise; they were off their guard, and Andrew's first furious blows fell hard and woundingly on the unprotected goblin-bodies within the Human skincloaks. The Fomoire fell backwards, the two that Andrew knocked down slipping in the grease-spattered floor. Andrew's mind registered with horror that it was Human grease; the grisly drippings from the cage. Don't think about it! He turned to where four more were circling him and, as he did so, he saw Rumour lashing out, her long, glittering nails raking down the bodies of those Fomoire trying to hold her. As they flinched, he saw delight flare up in her eyes; the tiny flame that had intrigued him at their first meeting kindled suddenly. He thought: she has managed to overcome the darkness! and with the thought, saw lightning spit from her outflung hand, and pierce the cave.

Andrew, catching her exultant triumph, turned and reached for the dancing Fomoire, who were leaping out his reach now, grinning and egging him forward.

He bounded forward again, spurred on by the knowledge of Rumour's triumph, dragging open the skin cloaks, reaching for the scrawny necks, squeezing, throttling . . .

Rumour was at his side, shouting to him to run, and Andrew flung the two Fomoire from him, feeling surging delight at the sudden crunch as they hit the cave floor.

And then they were hand in hand, running from the cave, out into the dark tunnels, safe in the embracing shadows.

Behind them, the Fomoire were dancing in fury, shaking their fists, silhouetted against the cave fires.

'But they are not following us!' gasped Andrew, pulling Rumour with him. 'They are not following! Dear God, can it be this easy to escape them?'

Rumour said, between breaths for air, 'We defeated them! Andrew, we defeated them!' And without thinking very much about it, flung herself into his arms, sobbing and crying with delight.

Andrew's arms tightened instinctively about her, and at once there was a strong, shameful response. His body had already been aroused by the violence in the caves, and now it throbbed at her touch, and the blood raced through his veins. He felt himself become charged and stiff with desire, and he let out a low groan, and pulled her to him. The softness of her breasts crushed against him and, as he felt them, his mind spun out control.

For I have never felt a woman before, I have never known what it is to have a woman's soft body pressing against mine . . .

He brought his mouth down on hers, savagely, helplessly,

and Rumour reached up, twining her fingers in his hair, feeling his arousal through her thin gown, wanting to reach down and caress him, knowing that they must certainly move further out of the tunnels, but still standing locked in his arms.

And then Andrew put her from him, gently but firmly, and she saw that he was trembling.

'Forgive me,' he said, and his voice was suddenly remote and cold.

Rumour said, 'I see nothing to forgive.'

'Yes, you do not know . . .' He took a deep breath, and dredged up a smile. 'We are not yet out of danger, I think.'

'So it seems,' said Rumour steadily.

'Our escape was so easy!' said Andrew, frowning.

'A trap?'

'Truly, I have no idea. But we should keep in mind that it could have been a trap.'

'For what reason? Why would they let us go?' said Rumour and, in the same breath, 'But yes, of course, they might simply be driving us deeper into the Dark Realm. They might be feeding us to something lying in wait further alone.' She stared at Andrew, her eyes huge.

Something lying in wait . . . The Black Monk? thought Andrew, and felt a chill lift the hairs on the back of his neck. But he said, 'Whatever is behind it, we have to go on.'

They began to move forward, and as they rounded a curve in the rock, Rumour's grip on Andrew's hand tightened.

'What is it . . . ?'

'Look,' said Rumour, sudden delight in her voice. And then Andrew saw it as well.

Directly ahead of them, where the tunnel wound away to the left, was the cool, ice-fire, blue and green light of the *sidh*.

The ancient underwater Kingdom of Aillen mac Midha.

Tiarna.

Chapter Fifteen

The tunnels wound down and down, and the cool, blue-green light rippled gently against the rock walls.

'We are beneath the seas now,' said Rumour, softly. 'We are entering the strange, under-ocean realm of Aillen mac Midha. The kingdom of the *sidh*. And I think,' said Rumour, frowning, 'that we should not stay there for any longer than we need.'

'But – there is air?' Andrew had been visualising some kind of secret kingdom deep beneath the sea-bed, but Rumour's words gave him pause.

But she said at once, 'Yes, it is a – you could say a physical world. Secret and deeply buried. But it is no legend, no chimerical land.' She glanced at him and smiled. 'Tiarna exists,' she said. 'It is real. "*Far beneath the ocean bed and deep beneath the world's seas . . .*" One of our poets wrote that of it, and it is true. You have to go a long way down and you have to pass through strange hinterlands to reach it. But I suspect,' said Rumour, thoughtfully, 'that you pass through some kind of Gateway.'

'But we shall surely know when that happens?'

'Not necessarily,' said Rumour.

It had been precisely what Cerball and the Mugain had thought. To pass quietly through the Gateway and be barely aware of it.

Rumour said, 'You are silent, Andrew? Is it too unobtrusive for you? Should you have preferred great, glittering doorways sketched against the dark skies, and beacons of fiery light guarding the way?'

Andrew smiled, but he said, 'It seems odd, you must allow, to enter other worlds so easily.'

'We have not entered it yet,' said Rumour.

The blue-green radiance was growing stronger, and they were both becoming aware of a feeling of immense desolation somewhere close by.

'As if,' said Rumour, softly, 'something just out of sight and just beyond hearing is crying helplessly and for ever.' She glanced at Andrew. 'The *sidh*, dying, mourning for their lost music?'

'Yes. An immense desolation,' said Andrew, gently. 'And intense pain.'

As they walked on, water-light rippled and played on the rock walls, and they made out carvings on the hard rock walls, cave pictures of strange sea-beasts with horned heads and lashing, finlike tails and slanting eyes that peered sideways and saw secrets and chuckled to do so . . .

'The *nimfeach*,' said Rumour, as Andrew pointed to them. 'The ancient sea-people who once dwelled in the City of Tiarna and were ruled by the Fisher King.'

'What happened to them?'

'The *sidh*, under Aillen mac Midha, drove them out,' said Rumour. 'They vowed to return one day, of course, as all dispossessed peoples vow to return. But it is so long ago that no one now knows very much about them: where they came from or what their allegiances were.'

'Or even if they existed?' said Andrew, softly.

'Oh, they existed, Andrew. The Fisher King and his minions existed. But it is so long ago that they are simply another of Ireland's lost tribes. Ireland's origins, like that of most worlds, are lost in the mists of Time, for Time now is so old that we cannot know what was in its genesis. There are lost peoples and ancient secrets and legends in all worlds, I think,' said Rumour. 'But perhaps Ireland has a little more than most. Or so the Irish would have you believe.' She paused before the nearest of the wall carvings. 'I believe that to have been the *nimfeach* overlord,' said Rumour softly. 'The Fisher King. Called in some legends "Coelacanth".'

The Fisher King of the lost tribe of *nimfeach*. He was depicted as being much taller than Humans – 'What is called giantish,' said Rumour – but he was slender and finely boned and covered with thin, translucent skin, so that you knew that if he stood before a strong light, you would be able to see the small, frail bones. Here and there were scales on his body, scattered between his legs, and across his upper limbs. Almost like armour, thought Andrew, or like the beginnings of a carapace forming.

Rumour said, 'He was neither quite Human nor quite Fish, but a blend of the two.' She studied the carving for a moment before turning back to walk at Andrew's side.

Ahead of them they could glimpse Tiarna itself now; faint, uncertain images of shining spires and turrets and silver-tipped gates beyond the tunnels. Rumour said, very softly, 'We are leaving our own world at last, Andrew; we are very close to the boundaries.' Andrew nodded and understood her meaning and remembered about passing from one world to the next.

He said cautiously, 'Will it be difficult to get into Tiarna? Will there be—' And stopped, because he was still trying to come to terms with the idea of sentries and prowling enchantments and invisible guards. 'Will there be anything to prevent us from entering the City?' he said at length. 'Cerball and the Mugain spoke of a legend: the Black Monk . . .'

'Yes, I have heard the name,' said Rumour. 'The Black Monk who guards one of the Gateways into the Dark Realm. It is quite a new legend,' she said, thoughtfully. 'And not so very widely known. But from time to time the Dark Lords entrap those they believe can serve them. They are usually poor husked-dry things in the end, those victims, for the Dark Lords are greedy masters. They will gratify the victims' lusts, but there is usually a long period of servitude in return – sometimes several centuries of guarding a boundary or a fortress. It is possible that the Monk was one of those more lately caught.'

'And legends have to begin somewhere,' said Andrew, half to himself.

'He interests you, that one, I think?' said Rumour.

Andrew hesitated, and then thought: why not tell her a little of the truth? 'There is a belief that he was once one of my own Order,' he said.

'And – you would like to reclaim him for your strange religion?' Rumour was interested. 'Yes, of course you would like to do so, for the idea of returning a strayed sheep to the fold is always alluring and . . . What have I said?'

'Only the mention of straying sheep. But yes, I should like to find him and bring him back if I could. My people believe that his evil ways may do harm to the new Teaching.'

'That is understandable,' said Rumour. 'But I do not think we will encounter him here. If he is in thrall to one of the necromancers – Chaos himself, perhaps, or the Crimson Lady of Almhuin – then he will be much deeper in the Dark Realm than this.' She sent him one of her sideways glances. 'We have scarcely begun to penetrate the Dark Realm yet,' said Rumour. 'Even this part, even Tiarna, is only one of the borderlands.'

'Yes, I understand.'

Rumour said, 'The world of Aillen mac Midha has always been accounted the most fortified world ever known. That is why I do not think the Black Monk would be here. The *sidh* guard Tiarna themselves. They have never needed Humans.'

'But now they are injured,' said Andrew, thoughtfully. 'Perhaps dead. That should mean that at least we can enter unchallenged.'

But as they drew nearer, and as the cool turquoise light became stronger, they were both aware of a sense of unease and a creeping darkness. Rumour sketched a Banishing Ritual on the air, and with it some brief words in a tongue that Andrew thought was Gael. He glanced at her, and then joined his hands, and murmured his own plea.

'"O God, the author of peace and lover of concord, defend us Thy humble servants in this assault on our enemies, that we, trusting in Thee, may not fear the power of any adversaries, through the might of Jesus Christ our Lord".'

The words flooded his mind with calm strength. He remained still, his head bowed, his eyes closed, and thought: still there. That inner reservoir of strength, that marvellous, bottomless well of love and succour and infinite understanding. If I forgot you, God, even though it was for a brief space, you did not forget me.

There was a sense of something familiar and comforting; as if he had looked round to see a good friend whom he had not met for a time, or as if he had returned to a dearly loved place. Peace in the Lord and peace from the Lord. Of course this is right. How could I have thought otherwise? Forgive me, God, for I had almost forgotten how it felt to experience the strength and the power. *The Everlasting Arms . . .*

He looked up then, his eyes meeting Rumour's, knowing that, if she showed derision, or even incomprehension, he would feel the first stirrings of impatience and her allure would weaken.

But Rumour had joined her own hands, not quite in the Christian attitude of prayer, but in something closely akin to it. She had listened intently to the short prayer, not trying to join with it, not quite identifying with it. But sharing in it. When she spoke, she said thoughtfully, 'Those are stirring words, Andrew. There is a remarkable comfort in them. That is a God I could trust.'

And Andrew knew that she did understand, and knew, as well, that the sinful, seductive threads still held him in thrall. He said, carefully, 'It is a strong force, prayer.' And then, in a different voice, 'There is a feeling of distortion ahead of us. Would it be the *sidh*?' And then at once, 'No, of course it is not the *sidh*, for they are helpless without their music.' And barely paused to wonder at how normally he was discussing enchantments and their powers.

'It's something more than the *sidh*,' said Rumour, frowning. 'I am not sure what it is, other than that it is dark and extremely ancient.' She glanced at him, and in the soft turquoise and silver light, her eyes were amused. The iridesscence had turned her hair to rippling blue-green, woven with silver, and her eyes were lambent. 'Are you thinking you would prefer to return, Andrew?' said Rumour softly. 'To go back to your safe, ascetic world, where the rules are set down and all you have to do is follow them?'

Andrew stood very still and looked at this exotic, beautiful being and thought: she is taunting me. She is doing so deliberately and mischievously in order to provoke the response she wants. And even though the response that Rumour wanted had long since been evoked; even though he ached to touch her, he said, quite calmly, 'I believe we should go on. Remember that behind us are the caves and the cages of the Fomoire.'

'And therefore we are between a rock and a hard place,' said Rumour, thoughtfully. 'I daresay that is something your Teacher would have known about, Andrew. What would he have advised?'

138

'Prayer,' said Andrew, after a moment. 'Resolve. Faith. Certainly the determination to rout evil.'

'What of violence?' said Rumour, musingly, pulling her cloak round her more firmly as if a cold breath of air had touched her. 'What would he think of violence? Because, Andrew, I think that whatever is ahead of us must be vanquished – and perhaps physical force will be necessary.'

'The defence of one's self is permitted,' said Andrew. 'Also, violence which will defeat evil is permitted. And,' he added, 'there is Theodora to be reached.'

'I do not forget,' said Rumour. And then, taking his hand, 'Do not worry about transgressing your creed, Andrew,' she said.

They approached the gates of the ancient under-sea City of Tiarna in silence, still hand in hand. Andrew, who had been vividly aware of the touch of Rumour's soft slender hand in his, was aware that a deeper, warmer emotion was starting to bind them. There was no seduction in the touch of Rumour's hand against his, and no sexual edge to it. It was a closeness; the touch of one sentient creature seeking comfort and assurance from another. He thought: we are both extremely apprehensive, and we are both reaching out for warmth.

When Rumour said, 'I am glad you are here, Andrew,' Andrew at once said, 'I am more than glad you followed me to the Well.'

He knew he should not permit it for very long, this warmth, this pleasure in being close to another creature in this way. Already I have gone too far, he thought. Already I am taking such strength from her and such delight in her presence. It must not be. His Order decreed that a man must walk alone and cleave only to One; nevertheless, thought Andrew, for the moment, I am thankful for her warmth and her closeness and strength and humour.

The tunnels widened and the blue-green light strengthened, and there ahead of them was the fabled underwater City of Tiarna, its light gentle and muted, filled with such unearthly beauty that Andrew and Rumour stared at it in awestruck silence.

The ancient City of Tiarna. The secret kingdom of the *sidh*; the world that the Elven King had wrested from the long-ago Fisher King and the *nimfeach* . . .

It echoed softly with the *sidh*'s cool, elvish magic, and it was wreathed with shreds and curls of their misty turquoise enchantments. Directly ahead of them were the City Gates, still twined with the *sidh*'s ice-fire spells, still misty with the soft rainbow light. But silver droplets were already appearing on the glinting Gates as the ice melted, and there were tiny hissing flames as the fire licked at the dissolving ice.

Rumour said, very softly, 'Small wonder they have guarded it so jealously and so fiercely.'

To Andrew there was a silky, seductive beckoning about Tiarna. He had expected it to be beautiful; but he had not been prepared for this living radiance, this marvellous cascading light that caressed his senses. He understood why the *sidh* had ceaselessly and jealously guarded their City, and spun their ice-fire enchantments to deter travellers and invaders. Had I been born to this, thought Andrew, I should never bear leaving it. I should never bear to see it in the hands of clumsy, stupid fools, perhaps desecrated by Humans. This is something that belongs to the cool faery creatures of the seas. A world that Humans should never penetrate and despoil, but visit only in dreams and visions and longings.

The Gates stretched high above them, twenty feet at least, and they made out, very distantly, a rippling sea-green light, a ruffle of cloudiness, shot here and there with threads of vivid brilliance.

Andrew said, very softly, 'So there is to be a Gate after all.'

'Yes.' Rumour indicated the dappled light far above them. 'I believe that we are seeing the oceans of the world from beneath,' she said. 'One of our beliefs tells how, after death, the soul is taken to the place beyond and beneath the Roof of the Ocean.' She sent him one of her sidelong glances. 'There, the soul encounters the Wall of Paradise, over which it must climb,' said Rumour very softly, and just as Andrew, earlier, had looked to see if she understood about prayer and faith, now Rumour looked to see if Andrew could understand her world's beliefs.

He said, half to himself, 'The place where all the worlds converge,' and Rumour smiled with delight, because if he could

140

understand that, if he could accept the difficult ancient beliefs and set them alongside his own rather beautiful, austere teachings, he was a very rare creature indeed.

Andrew said, 'It is a concept I am not familiar with.' But he looked at her as he spoke, as if wanting to know more, and Rumour said:

'There are many worlds, and the wise men teach that, in places, the fabric between them is very thin. I have always visualised the worlds as prisms, polished diamonds, many-sided and multi-faceted.'

She looked at him and waited again, and Andrew said, slowly, 'If that should be so, then in places the surfaces of the worlds could touch. Facets of worlds could impinge on one another.'

'So that it would be possible to pass from one world to another,' said Rumour softly, and looked at him and thought: so you are indeed able to open your mind to teachings other than those of your strange Order. And if I am not very careful, I may find myself attracted as much by your mind as by your body. And that would be the most dangerous attraction of them all . . . That would be completely and irreclaimably foolish, said Rumour to herself very firmly.

'I am not sure, you know,' said Andrew carefully, 'that I can believe in other worlds.'

'But there *are* other worlds, Andrew,' said Rumour, still staring up at the glinting silver and blue City Gates, and at the misty world beyond. 'There are other worlds, and there are other beings and there are certainly creatures who have not a drop of Human blood in their veins.' She glanced at him. 'You have already met the Fomoire,' said Rumour, a questioning note in her voice, as if she might be saying: deny that if you can.

'Yes.' Andrew frowned.

'Also,' said Rumour, 'you have met the Amaranths.' And, as he turned to look at her, 'Did you truly believe us to be entirely Human?' said Rumour softly. 'We are a small part Human, but we are not entirely so. The first sorcerers of all were imbued with the ancient magic from the dawn of the world; it is in the veins of all true Amaranths, and although inter-marriages with Humans have occasionally taken place, the thin trickle of the Amaranthine flame is in us. That is why we can harness the power and channel the ancient forces that prowl the world unseen. That is

141

why a few of us were vouchsafed the Sacred Flame at the very beginning. So that we could work and rule and harness the good and pure Dawn Sorcery.'

There was a brief silence. I dare not believe, said Andrew silently, staring at Rumour. It is a dangerous, seductive idea, and I will not believe any of it. He closed his mind to the insidious bewitchment of creatures of an ancient magical lineage imbued with some kind of flamelike force, even while his mind was touching on the stories of the Twelve Apostles, filled with the Spirit of the Lord and bidden to go out and spread the Word... 'Upon thee I will build my Church, and the gates of Hell shall not prevail against it...' Simon Peter taken from the shores of Galilee to fish for men instead; Andrew his brother, James and John; Philip the lawyer who was the scholar Apostle... And what of Mary of Magdala, Mary, whom some Churchmen believed to have been the Apostle that Christ loved best...?

'*And for those who wish to enter, the Gate is always open...*'

The words repeated themselves in Andrew's head, and as if at a command, he reached out and pushed them.

They swung open with a silken whisper, and the soft, blue-green radiance of Tiarna poured outwards and fell about them.

As they passed beneath the Gates, Andrew and Rumour were both instantly aware that they were not alone in the dying City.

There were scuttlings and slitherings; cold creeping sounds, as if unseen creatures were crawling and slinking across the ground just out of their sight.

'The *sidh*?' said Andrew in a whisper, but knew at once that it could not be the *sidh*. The sounds were made by creatures who were evil and cold and who possessed a dark, cruel intelligence.

'Not the *sidh*,' said Rumour softly, looking about her, the blue-green radiance of Tiarna falling about her like a cloak, turning her hair to rippling silver. 'But perhaps some strange, chill race that has crept into Tiarna since the *sidh*'s music went.'

'*Come inside, Human Monk and Amaranth Sorceress...*' The cold, dank whispering hissed in their ears, and they whipped round towards its direction. There was a cold, dragging sound, and a sly chuckling, and there was the impression of pale, lidless eyes peering from behind the silver and blue pillars. But whatever was watching, and whatever had whispered its cold beckoning, had whisked into hiding, and there was nothing to be seen.

As they moved forward, they heard the sounds behind them again.

'Not footsteps exactly,' said Andrew, frowning.

'Something crawling?'

Something crawling . . .

Several times, as they walked on, there was muffled laughter, as if the creatures watching them were savouring their presence, and once Rumour caught a glimpse of something pale and scaled that did not quite walk but did not quite crawl either.

Something that crept and slithered along the ground . . .

The Palace was in front of them; a glistening, blue-green castle of ice and fire, lit not from within, but from without. Its topmost spires reached upwards to the rippling, silver-veined ocean, and its turrets were shining and spiralling with the pouring water-light from above.

'It looks Human,' said Andrew, and instantly wondered if this sounded absurd. 'It looks as if it was built by Humans,' he said.

Rumour, staring at the Palace, said, 'It *is* Human, Andrew. It was built by the *nimfeach* at the beginning of Ireland's history, and legend tells how, when the world was young and Tara, the Bright Palace, was new, the Fisher King crept through the tunnels we have just traversed, and walked in the world of the Humanish. He stole the designs and the plans for Tara itself, which had been created by what we call architect-sorcerers for the first High Queen of Ireland, and he and his people, the *nimfeach*, used the designs to build their own Palace. What you are seeing is almost an exact mirror-image of Tara.' Her eyes were still on the gentle, beautiful spires and turrets and crenellations. 'Tara is said to be the most beautifully perfect thing in all Ireland,' said Rumour. 'But this is a Tara soaked in centuries and aeons of the *sidh*'s soft allurements and seductions and their cold, elvish magic. And whatever waits for us in there, it is not the *sidh*, Andrew.'

Andrew was staring at the Palace. He said, 'Whatever waits for us, we must go forward.' He looked down at her. 'All right?'

'All right,' said Rumour.

There were no pathways or tracks or roads as they knew them; there was no way of knowing how the *sidh* would travel to their shining, cool Palace. Rumour, who understood a little about the *sidh*, knew that for the most part they simply poured through the air, and that they had no need of roads or tracks.

Silver grass, waving and soft, grew all round the Palace, and here and there clung to the pale substance of the walls, rather as an ivy will creep over brickwork. In the depths of the silver fronds, Andrew caught flashes of soft, turquoise light, smudges on the ground or against the Palace walls.

'*Sidh*-creatures,' said Rumour. 'Yes, they are dying. Their light is fading. Whatever has crept into Tiarna found little resistance from them.'

As they passed under the great arch of the portcullis, Andrew paused, unsure of the way they should now go, but Rumour, whose boast that she had been intimate with the High King was not an empty one, had once known Tara's layout very well indeed. She saw that the inside of the Palace corresponded almost exactly to the inside of Tara. Ahead of them were the galleried landings that led to the Staterooms: the Star of the Poets, the Skyward Tower, the beautiful, eerie Spirit Tower. Exactly the same, thought Rumour, torn between fascination and anger against the long-ago Fisher King who had stolen the architect-sorcerers' vision of Tara.

As they passed warily through empty, echoing galleries, and down silver staircases, they saw, here and there, drifting, formless, turquoise smoke, blurs of colour so faint and so indistinct that Andrew thought it was a trick of the light.

'It is no trick,' said Rumour in a low, angry voice. 'It is the *sidh*, Andrew, and they are dying a little more with every minute.' She moved forward, her silken-clad feet skimming the floor, Andrew at her side.

They heard the sounds before they reached the Palace's centre. At first, Andrew thought it was simply an echo, a lingering voice, some fragment of the dying *sidh*'s magic. And then, as they neared the centre, the sounds grew louder, and he realised that they had nothing to do with the *sidh* and their eerily beautiful world.

This was something evil and powerful; something that was

destroying the cool beauty and the lingering fragrance of the *sidh*'s music . . .

Immense double doors with etched symbols were ahead of them, partly open. Rumour and Andrew could see leaping candlelight, at first glance very nearly ordinary, and then not ordinary at all: smeary crimson, shot with frosted icy-blue, and filled with the clotted malevolence of ancient corruption and old evil.

There was shouting and jeering; bursts of goblin-laughter, screeching voices raised in revelry. A scent of food, warm and spiced and rather greasy, wafted through the doors towards them.

The whispering voice echoed about them again: '*Come inside, Human Monk . . . Come inside, Amaranth Sorceress . . . Partake of my hospitality . . .*'

The doors swung inwards. Beyond them was an immense banqueting chamber, a huge marble and crystal hall, created to reflect Tara's glittering Sun Chamber.

But it was lit to garish life, and it was pulsating with a smeary red glow from dozens of thick, evil-smelling candles, and it was alive with shrieking, grabbing, rioting creatures.

And some of them were skincloaked, wizened, dancing creatures, and some were slender, writhing fish-beings.

The long marble tables were piled high with food, great overflowing platters of roasted meats and baked game and jointed carcasses. There were dishes of glistening fruits, crystalline and shiny with syrups and sugars, and the scent of hot, greasy food, and of spilt wine.

Andrew and Rumour stood in the doorway, their senses assaulted by the sights and the sounds that filled the banqueting hall of the Elven King. Through the thick, rank heat, they began to make out the shapes of the creatures who rioted and tumbled and held such grotesque revels. Andrew's eyes were stinging from the fetid smoke, but he saw with cold horror that ranged about the tables were at least two dozen of the Fomoire, grinning goblin faces peering through slitted Human skins, tiny black paw hands reaching and snatching the food and wine. The skincloaks were shiny with spilled grease, and rivulets of fat ran from their lips. They gnawed at haunches of meat, spraying the table with fragments of half-eaten food, and then turned to the wine flagons, tilting them to their lips, spilling the liquid so that it splashed on to the tables and ran on to the silver floor. Several of them had scuttled on to the tables and were sitting cross-legged, the terrible cloaks flung back so that their wizened goblin-bodies were exposed. They reached for the hunks of warm meat joints, gnawing into them, and Andrew remembered, with an abrupt twist of nausea, the Fomoire's black-mouthed caves and the bubbling cauldrons of Human flesh.

Seated with them were nightmarish creatures, neither quite Human nor fish, but a cold, malevolent blending of the two. These were beings that could not walk upright like Men, but must go on their bellies like snakes or worms.

Slithering across the ground, thought Andrew, sickened. So it was those creatures who crept after us. He saw that they had small flat tails, jagged-edged and membraneous, that hung from their spines.

Their faces were those of the beings depicted in the tunnels: sea-nymphs, sirens, with pointed, snouted features and thick, lipless mouths. There was such greed and such cruelty in them that Andrew and Rumour both shuddered. Their bodies were pale, but not in the eerily beautiful way that Rumour knew the *sidh* to be pale; these were whitish-grey, sluglike beings: neckless and bloodless and coldly evil. Their skins were spattered with pale, faintly greasy-looking scales, and they bent over the long food-strewn table, their bodies curved, so that it was possible to see a line of thin, glistening bones that bristled outwards from their spines.

As the flickering candles burned up, distorted shadows leapt, and Andrew and Rumour both had the sudden impression that the ancient cave drawings had been woken; that the carvings had opened their scaly eyes, and stepped down from the cave walls in the darkness.

Andrew thought: the *nimfeach*! The lost people of Tiarna! And looked at the grey-scaled, iridescent creatures, and at the lashing, pronged tails and the sly, cruel faces, and felt the terrible cold evil emanating from them.

And then he looked at the creature who sat at the table's head, his pale eyes watching them, a cold, cruel smile curving his flat mouth.

The Fisher King.

The ancient, legendary Coelacanth, freed of the bondage at last, holding terrible revelry in the realm where once he had ruled.

Chapter Sixteen

Remnants of his Gristlen persona still clung to him. Shreds and fragments of the dark carapace that had shaled on to him in the terrible Pit were still adhering to parts of his sleek, pale body.

But where the Gristlen had been ugly and even pitiable, the Fisher King was not pitiable in the least. He was coldly and sinisterly beautiful, and he was imbued with such undiluted evil that icy fear formed at the pit of Rumour's stomach. For this was Coelacanth himself; this was the enigmatic ruler of the *nimfeach*.

The Fomoire were chanting a tuneless, pounding song, beating the table with their clawlike hands, their evil goblin-heads peering through the skincloaks. The *nimfeach* did not sing, but Andrew and Rumour were both aware of a high-pitched humming, a keening wailing that spun and swooped all about the chamber.

The Fisher King stood alone, a grotesque figure silhouetted against the marble walls of the banqueting hall. He was as tall as the cave drawings had shown him: he was taller as well than the crouching, hunchbacked Gristlen had been. His body was sleek and streamlined, but there was a Humanish outline, as if fish and Human had long ago lain together and this was the result. To Andrew, this Human resemblance was the most sinister thing about him. *And although his skin is not quite translucent, the bones are just visible*, thought Andrew, appalled. *I can see the bones and the pale thick flesh adhering to them.* They were not Human bones; they were thin, brittle fishbones that would break very easily; they would snap and splinter between a man's violent, angry hands . . .

There was a finlike tail protruding from his spine, as pale as the rest; jagged-edged and covered with glistening scales, and lashing like the beating of a single wing.

The Fisher King was looking straight at Andrew and Rumour

as they entered, and as he lifted his hand in a travesty of a salutation they saw, quite clearly, the light shining through the webs between his fingers.

And then he chuckled, and it was a sound so filled with cold malice, and with such evil triumph, that Andrew felt ice churn his stomach.

'Come in, my dears,' said the Fisher King, and his glittering eyes were on Rumour. 'Come in to my celebration.'

Rumour said, 'Celebration?' and moved into the banqueting hall, Andrew at her side.

The Fisher King indicated the creatures seated at the long, laden, silver table. 'My friends,' he said. 'My people. The *nimfeach* returning to Tiarna. Our good allies the Fomoire. They rejoice at my escape from the bondage of the Pit.'

'So I see,' said Rumour. 'And the shedding of the Gristlen's skin? Do they rejoice at that also?'

'Of course.'

'How did you do that?' said Rumour in a rather off-hand voice. 'The embrace of a willing female, was it?'

A leer split the Fisher King's flat features. 'So you know that, do you?' he said softly.

'Of course I know it. It is not an unusual way of dissolving a curse. In fact, I have always thought it rather common,' said Rumour disdainfully. 'I suppose it was why you wanted Theodora?' she said, and the Fisher King's eyes darkened.

'I almost had her,' he said. 'She was almost mine.'

'But Chaos took her instead,' said Rumour. 'Yes, I see. And then you had to find another.'

He smiled again. 'Laigne,' he said, softly. 'She came to me of her own accord.' He smiled again. 'She answered the music's call, as countless thousands have done,' he said, and the smile became filled with remembering lust. He reached between his thighs, fingering the repulsive phallus that hung there obscenely. 'I entered her. I invaded her flesh with mine. And she was *warm*,' said the Fisher King with thick relish. 'She was warm Humanish flesh.' His eyes glittered. 'She will never admit to it, but she *enjoyed* me,' he said. 'Deep within her, she experienced a throbbing enjoyment.' The narrow, flat eyes slid to Andrew. 'Does that arouse you, Monkish One?' said the Fisher King. 'Does it harden your loins and make the juice run?' Again the horrid, cold laugh. 'I filled her with the seed of my blood,' he said, 'Milt. Fish-sperm. I sluiced her shrivelled womb with it.' He looked back at Rumour. 'The dissolving of the enchantment happened there, in the Porphyry Palace,' he said. 'The crust that had formed in the Tanning Pit sloughed from me.'

'And then,' said Rumour, 'you returned to Tiarna.'

'And then I returned to Tiarna,' said the Fisher King. Exultation touched his voice, sending it spiralling into madness. 'And I am again in the Palace that was once mine! The *sidh* are helpless, they are dying in the place they call the Silver Cavern, which once was *my* Throne Room!' He struck his breast in triumph. '*My* Arena of Execution!' he said. 'Where my prisoners were forced to fight the Fomoire and the *nimfeach* to their deaths as I watched!' A rising note of lunacy shrilled in his voice. 'Aillen mac Midha took all that from me!' he said. 'He took my Throne Room for his own!' He paused, and then said, in a gloating voice, 'And now it is his own tomb!'

'Because you took the music,' said Andrew. 'How did you do that?'

'It was easy, Human Monk!' The cold eyes rested on Andrew with amusement. 'I crept down here and through the tunnels that once I knew so well,' said the Fisher King. 'I slunk as a supplicant into the kingdom where once I had ruled.' The madness soared in his voice again, and again he made the gesture of striking his breast. The monstrous, membraneous tail lashed with sudden, obscene excitement. 'And they threw me into the water dungeons,' he said with contempt. 'My own water dungeons that once I had filled with Humanish: the fools put me there! Into the very sea-caves that were still soaked in my own necromancy!' He made an abrupt, contemptuous gesture. 'I broke the seals almost before the guards were out of sight – the seals that I had woven myself centuries earlier. I took their music,' he said. 'And because of it, they are entombed in their own Palace. They are dying.' There was a lick of relish in his voiced and Andrew said:

'But although you took the music from the *sidh*, the Amaranths in turn took it from you.' He studied Coelacanth through narrowed eyes, trying to sense if the creature could tell that they had the music with them now.

But Coelacanth said, contemptuously, 'I allowed the Amaranths to take it because I no longer had need of it. It had served its purpose when it lured Laigne into my arms.' He regarded them both. 'And I had had my revenge,' he said. 'After centuries of exile, I had had my revenge. That is something you would know about, Monk?'

'Oh yes. An eye for an eye and a tooth for a tooth.'

'The immutable law,' said the Fisher King.

'And so the curse is dissolved,' said Andrew.

'Yes.' But the Fisher King looked down at himself, at the raw newness of his pale, bone-laced flesh, here and there oozing pale, thick fluid, as if it was seeping blood under a peeled-off scab. 'I still hurt,' he said, half to himself, and then, to Rumour, 'perhaps you will help to heal me, my dear.' His eyes narrowed and he held out a webbed hand. 'Come here,' he said, softly. 'Come here, and caress my poor, bleeding, raw flesh with your sorceress's hands.'

Rumour pronounced a word of several syllables, almost negligently, and the Fisher King flinched as if struck.

'BitchHuman!' he spat. 'Amaranth filth! I know that for the *Draiocht Tairne*! So you would sink the spikehorns into my flesh, would you! You would embed into me the barbs and the nails of the Humanish fishermen and reel me into your power! That is twice you have spurned me. You will suffer for that!' He nodded to the listening Fomoire, who leapt at once from their places and surged towards Andrew and Rumour.

Rumour lifted her hand again, but the Fisher King was before her, sending a ribbon of pale, viscous light towards her. It whipped about her wrist and dragged her forward. Andrew caught her other arm, trying to pull her back, but the Fomoire danced gleefully about him, and formed a circle, jeering and laughing. As they did so, the cold, spiny *nimfeach* moved towards him as well and surrounded him, pressing close so that he could smell the cold, dank stench of them. Their slithering, barbed tails lashed about his legs.

'There is no escape,' said the Fisher King, smiling the flat wide smile. 'Eventually, Human Monk, you will be taken by the Fomoire for their cauldrons, and you will certainly be stretched and anointed and then flayed.' He regarded them both. 'Did it not occur to you that your escape from their caves was very easy?' he said, and Andrew and Rumour exchanged a look.

At length Rumour said, 'They let us go knowing that you were here, of course.'

'Of course. The Fomoire have served me and mine for many centuries.' He flicked his hand again, so that the viscous ribbon pulled her closer. 'I think it damages your vanity to know that, Madame Sorceress,' he said, and Rumour shrugged as if it was of no account.

'Arrogant,' said the Fisher King softly. 'Oh, Madame Sorceress, you will soon be pleading for mercy. You will soon crawl to me and beg me to release you.'

'We shall see,' said Rumour equably. 'But I think you are not so strong as you believe, Coelacanth.'

There was a sudden silence, and then the Fisher King said in a slimy, purring voice, 'So you know my name.'

'I know one of your names,' said Rumour. 'Like all Corrupt Evil creatures, you have many.'

From where he stood, surrounded by the *nimfeach*, the words formed in Andrew's mind: *they are Legion; their names are many* . . .

'And you shall call me by all of the names, Madame Sorceress,' said the Fisher King with a terrible, gentle menace. And then, as if impatient, he flung out a webbed hand and stabbed the floor directly in front of him. '*Kneel!*' he shrieked, and Rumour, struggling, found herself forced downwards, as if iron weights pressed upon the back of her neck.

'Now, BitchHuman,' said the Fisher King, softly and caressingly, looking at her through slitted eyes, his face so close to hers that Rumour could see the crusting of scales, 'now, Sorceress, pleasure me.' His eyes widened, and Andrew, horrified, saw the webbed hands descend between the scaly thighs, caressing the barbed phallus, rubbing it as it swelled and became engorged. '*Pleasure me*,' said the Fisher King, and Rumour, on her knees before him, her hair falling over her face, was jerked forward.

For an instant, Rumour thought he was about to force the monstrous organ into her mouth, but, as the thought took shape, the Fisher King laughed again, and reached out to pull her to her feet.

'I am not so careless,' he said. 'Do you think I do not know the pleasure you would take in biting at my flesh?'

'A pleasure indeed, Coelacanth,' said Rumour.

'Nevertheless, you *will* pleasure me,' he said, softly. 'You will submit your body and your flesh to mine, and in ways you never dreamed existed.' The pale, glittering eyes swept over her body, and Rumour, her mind searching frantically for an escape, knew that, for the moment, she was trapped. 'I know a little of your reputation, my dear,' said the Fisher King, his eyes still on her. 'You boast many lovers.' And then, as Rumour did not speak, he said, 'And yet despite your wantonness, I think that you will be more surprised than you know at what I shall do to you.'

Rumour glared at him, saying nothing, searching her mind for some way out. And, because it was in her to face up to whatever ordeal might present itself, she stopped fighting, and shook back her hair, and smiled dazzlingly into the pale, bulging, lidless eyes. Because, after all, thought Rumour, his body is not so very different from a Human, and it is perfectly true that I have taken many lovers. Even the Wolfkings and the Beastlords, with their half-Human, half-Beast blood . . . Would this be so very different? And then panic spiralled again, and she thought: but this is the terrible Fisher King, this is Coelacanth himself. No matter. She would not allow herself to believe that it would be so very different.

Andrew was struggling to break free of the *nimfeach*, and several of them had caught and held him tightly, curling their spiked tails about his ankles, drawing blood. Rumour was facing the Fisher King defiantly; if she had to, she would probably endure his body with courage and cold contempt. But it was not rape that Andrew feared most for her; although it would hurt her, he thought, his eyes going to the immense rearing stalk of flesh between Coelacanth's scaly legs. But she would almost certainly survive being raped by this monstrous creature. What Andrew feared most was the other things he might do to her afterwards . . .

Andrew looked about him, trying to assess the number and strength of the Fisher King's Armies, seeing that there were at least a dozen Fomoire, and as many again of *nimfeach*. Too many and too strong. But there must be something we can do, thought Andrew, his mind scurrying back and forth.

What about the music? What about the *sidh*'s music, so thickly wrapped about with protective spells, so carefully placed

153

in the small golden casket. Could he reach it? Could he twist out of the spiny tails of these creatures and somehow fling it in Coelacanth's face?

But in the same minute, he remembered that, even within the dark crust of the Gristlen's skin, the Fisher King had been able to manipulate the music: he had held it out to the Amaranths in their own Sorcery Chambers, and Andrew knew quite positively that every one of them had felt its sensuous pull. I dare not risk it, thought Andrew. I may be giving him extra powers. I may be banking the fires against us.

Rumour had managed to damp down her own raging anger, because anger would be detrimental to the spinning of any enchantment. She was not trying to spin an enchantment to defeat the Fisher King because, for the moment, newly emerged from his terrible bondage in the Pit, his powers would be rampant and raging, and he was probably stronger than she was. Also, there were the *nimfeach* and the Fomoire. Rumour sent them a sideways glance. Even with Andrew at her side – and it was remarkable how his presence gave her courage! – even together, they could not hope to defeat these creatures. We should be overcome, and killed; or perhaps flayed by the Fomoire before we died, thought Rumour. And then Theodora would be beyond our reach, and Tiarna would surely die.

No. Somehow she must defeat this creature.

She stood before him, and sent him the dazzling smile again. There was a brief pause, and Rumour sensed his puzzlement, and felt a surge of exultation. I have discomfited him! He does not know what to make of me! He expected me to be subdued, to plead for mercy, and I have not done so! And then, because it was in her nature always to take the most outrageous and the most unexpected course, she leapt on to the tables with a single, catlike movement.

'Clear the tables!' cried Rumour, turning to the watching creatures, her skirts swishing about her ankles. 'Clear the tables! You! Play music!' She gestured imperiously to the little group of musicians, and at once sly, rollicking music filled the Silver Cavern.

'Better,' said Rumour and, slowly and deliberately, every movement studied, she began to dance, shaking her hair out so that it whirled about her head, silken and perfumed. The feel of it brushing her shoulders gave her courage, for she had twined into her hair a great deal of strength and a great many subtle spells. She remembered, briefly, how Great-aunt Fuamnach and the rest had called it vanity, but Rumour had laughed and said it would come in useful one day. And now perhaps it will! she thought exultantly. Now perhaps I can bemuse them and cloud their powers with lust. The Fomoire with their dark goblin-blood probably possessed Humanish lusts. What about the *nimfeach*? Could they be sexually aroused? If so, their perceptions would become clouded and she would have them at her mercy. And then, thought Rumour, *then* I can spin up something that will vanquish them!

As the music quickened, Rumour also remembered the *sidh*'s music; but, unlike Andrew, she knew instantly that it could not serve their cause. The *sidh*'s music had been Coelacanth's own spell, spun centuries ago for the sirens, the predecessors of the repulsive *nimfeach* who sat on the rocks that jutted out of the oceans and sang to the sailors and lured them to watery graves.

She moved with the music, confidence beginning to unfold, remembering how once she had danced like this at Tara, the doors locked, shedding her gown and her silk underthings to the music's pattern, her audience the High King's son, the twenty-year-old Prince and several of his Court who had stood around the table, cheering and shouting, finally carrying her off with them to the nearest bedchamber. She had made love with the Prince and his courtiers for most of the night, all of them intoxicated and laughing, tumbling together in the massive bed until dawn found them exhausted and satiated. The memory strengthened her, and she threw back her head, and began to peel off her clothes; the thin black cloak, and then the flame-coloured gown, sliding it voluptuously over her shoulders, letting it fall to the table in a whisper of softness. Beneath it she wore, as she always wore, lace-trimmed, cobweb-fine garments, wisps of Eastern silk and lawn. The *nimfeach* turned their pale eyes towards her, the gaping gills in their neck opening and closing; the Fomoire scrabbled at the table, evil lust showing on their ugly goblin-faces. Rumour laughed, and slid out of the last shreds of silk, and stood naked before them, the firelight pouring over her, her striated hair flowing over her bare shoulders, rippling copper and silver and gold.

Was Coelacanth watching? Yes! She glanced towards the silver throne and saw that he was seated motionless, his eyes narrowed with lust, the monstrous triangular fin already beginning to distend. One hand slid between his thighs, caressing his ripening phallus, and Rumour thought: unless I can harness power of some kind very quickly, I am going to have to accept that! I am going to have to let him thrust it into me. Horrid! Can I do it? The barbs will tear and hurt, and he is huger than any creature I ever saw. And he will be icy cold, as all creatures of the Dark Realm are said to be. Don't think about it! I'll avoid it if I can, I'll trap him with his own lust, and then I'll tie him up with something so strongly magical he will be helpless.

Slowly, imperceptibly, mingling it with the throbbing of the music, she began to intone the ancient gentle *Draiocht Suan*, the legendary Enchantment of Slumber, the simple, beautiful spell that had come down from the very beginning of Ireland's history, and that was so gentle and so clear-cut that a child could have chanted it and watched it form. Rumour saw it form now: thin, spun-silver filaments, tiny strong threads that would cascade about the Fisher King and his creatures, binding them into a deep, dark sleep. Yes! It is working! I have sliced through their guard, simply by arousing their horrid lusts! Triumph surged up within her.

As the silver web began to slowly descend, a howl of rage and fury burst from the Fisher King, blotting out the music, drowning the sly chuckling of the Fomoire and the strange, high-pitched, mewling cries of the *nimfeach*.

Coelacanth was on his feet, his hands outstretched, sending shards of evil, glinting sparks into the centre of the *Draiocht Suan*, causing it to splinter and fall in tiny, useless specks of light which dissolved and ran into nothing.

'Bitch!' cried the Fisher King, 'Accursed Daughter of the foul House of Amaranth! So you would cheat me, madame! You would deceive me with your seductions! You would lure me into your embrace and then spin about me another accursed spell!' He fixed his eyes on her, and the Fomoire pranced closer, their tiny claws reaching out.

'You will not defeat me,' said the Fisher King, his face lowered so that it was on a level with Rumour's. 'You will not cheat me, and you will pleasure me, and my people.' He held her, effortlessly, capturing both her hands in one of his, pulling her against him so that she could feel the horrid cold clamminess of him; feeling, as well, the triangular fin unfurl of its own accord, and stand erect behind him like a rearing cloak of hard, dry flesh.

The Fisher King threw Rumour on to the ground, and with his free hand, forced her thighs apart. And then he fell on her.

Rumour had known it would hurt, but she had not been prepared for quite such searing pain, or quite such white-hot agony. The Fisher King thrust into her at once, savagely and brutally, gripping her thighs with his webbed hands, the jointless fingers digging into her flesh. His hands were soft, but there was a hard, gristly core of soft, pliable bone at the centre.

Rumour, summoning every ounce of fortitude, lay unresisting, knowing that to fight would feed his lust.

But the touch of his cold, slabby body was so repulsive that, despite her resolve, it was difficult not to cry out, and to beat at him with her hands.

His monstrous organ was pushing deep inside her now, cold and moist, horridly intimate, and Rumour could feel the spiny barbs beginning to tear her flesh.

The Fomoire were dancing and cheering all about the hall, pulling tiny shrivelled organs from between their legs, thrusting them forward at the entwined pair with obscene glee.

The *nimfeach* were swaying, their pale, slug-like bodies writhing to and fro, emitting thick glottal sounds. Andrew, glancing at them, saw that the gills in the sides of their necks were opening and closing, as if the creatures had no conventional speech, but could only make the strange, high-pitched, keening sounds through their gills.

As the Fisher King pulled Rumour closer, several of the Fomoire leapt on their neighbours, tumbling them to the floor. Andrew, still firmly held, looked across at them and remembered the sin of Sodom. The Fomoire had cast off their grisly cloaks, and they were bending over, baring their anuses, leaping on one another's backs and clutching with tiny, clawlike hands as they thrust their mummified organs deep into each other's bodies, jerking and pumping into repulsive climax.

Several of them were seizing the *nimfeach*, knocking them flat to the ground and then straddling the creatures' thick necks and riding them obscenely, their jutting penises forced into the *nimfeach*'s lipless mouths. They shrieked with glee and then rolled off again. Andrew, horrified and sickened, looked wildly around the banqueting hall, searching for a weapon of some kind, anything . . .

Rumour's head was thrown back, and her slender white throat was pulsing as she fought for breath. The distended triangular fin of the Fisher King was swollen now, erect and rampant, fanning out behind him like a monstrous jagged wing, a frame, a tail-feather . . . It enfolded the two of them in a cloak of horny flesh.

The Fomoire were chuckling their evil delight, and the *nimfeach* were writhing between them like huge, glistening slugs. They tumbled over and over in a hideous blur of skin and scales and lashing barbed tails and claws.

Rumour was scarcely moving; she was locked tight in the embrace of her fearsome lover, and she had seen, and then felt, the terrible fin curl round them, and this was the most repulsive thing yet. The fin was cold and clammy and loathsome and, as it furled about them, the Fisher King groaned; his eyes glittered, and he drove into Rumour brutally. Rumour, the pain of the spikes tearing into her, closed her eyes, and murmured a brief enchantment of balm. Nearly there. Nearly over. Surely he will soon be done. Surely I shall soon feel the spurting of his loathsome seed, and it will be done, and we shall somehow escape.

She felt it then, the quickening, the tightening of the creature's muscles, the swelling of blood vessels, and a tiny part of her that was untouched and untarnished by the foulness, recognised that, in this, Coelacanth was little different from a Human lover. Could he be wounded at the moment of climax? For he would be vulnerable then, thought Rumour. She remained still, concentrating on calmness, keeping her mind fixed solely on remaining silent, on not letting him hear or see her agony and revulsion.

Coelacanth moved convulsively, and the barbs tore into her womb, inflicting such sudden and overwhelming agony that Rumour's vision blurred, and her mind spun. The banqueting hall, the watching *nimfeach*, the Fomoire, and Andrew – oh yes, dear Andrew was still with her! – swam and grew distant.

Finish! screamed Rumour silently, beyond thought of spell-spinning now, certainly in too much pain to be able to call down power of any kind. Spend your filth in me, and let us be done! And with the thought, the Fisher King threw back his head and gave a screeching, guttural cry, and Rumour felt razor-sharp pain surge into her, and knew it for the cold, tainted seed of Coelacanth, and thought: cold, poisonous fishblood and evil, tainted fishjuice! Icy milt, the seed of the sea-creature! I shall never feel clean again!

He pulled away from her, and Rumour fell as the spikes tore at her, feeling the repulsive cold stickiness on her thighs, knowing that she was bleeding, feeling her own blood mingle sickeningly with his cold juices, stinging and hurting, hating the pain, but hating far more the intimacy. But I did not cry out! she thought, triumphantly. I did not even give vent to a gasp of pain! And now we shall see what can be done! thought Rumour and, as she half sat, half knelt before the Fisher King, her mind was already sliding into the spell patterns that would summon power.

The Fisher King had fallen back against the Silver Throne of Aillen mac Midha, and he was watching her with his cold, pale eyes.

At length, he said, 'So still you do not submit, BitchHuman.'

A frown touched the flat, scaly features, and Rumour said, 'I shall never submit, filth.' And was glad to hear that her voice was contemptuous and defiant. 'If that is the worst you can do, Coelacanth, I do not think much of it,' said Rumour and, even as the words formed on the air, she saw Andrew's eyes darken with horror, and knew at once that the words, spoken out of bravado and out of sheer relief that she had endured the ordeal, were screamingly dangerous. It did not need Andrew's involuntary movement to tell her she had overreached.

The Fisher King was smiling, and there was such cold triumph in the smile that Rumour shivered. 'Oh, my dear, we have not yet begun,' he said. 'There is so much more I am going to do to you. So very much more, my dear.' He nodded to the waiting *nimfeach*, 'Take her to the Crystal Pools,' he said. 'Shave her hair and *anoint* her.' And then, to Rumour, who was staring

159

up at him, her eyes huge and fearful, 'Let us see how you respond to my *other* hunger,' said the Fisher King.

The *nimfeach* half dragged Rumour from the banqueting hall. She was dimly aware that Andrew was still with her: he was being guarded by several of the Fomoire and prodded by their spears to make him follow. She thought that he was fighting them, struggling against the *nimfeach* who held him, but there were too many. They twisted his arms behind his back, their lumpish muscles moving beneath the pale skin, squirming about him like monstrous worms. The Fomoire jabbed his skin with their spears. Rumour flung him an agonised look, and felt at once a bolt of comfort and strength from him.

Continue to have courage, Rumour! We shall outwit them somehow!

But they were overpowered; there were only the two of them, and physical violence was useless. Rumour, trying desperately to calm her mind, murmured yet another incantation, and saw the Fisher King deflect it with contemptuous ease. It flickered on her mind that they would take her to the great Silver Cavern – what had Coelacanth said: that it was the Elven King's tomb? – and hope rose in her, for perhaps she could in some way turn the *sidh*'s sorcery to her own ends.

But the *nimfeach* slithered and crawled along the empty, echoing galleries, dragging her into a great, dimly lit cavern with deep, clear crystal pools set into the silver floor. The cool water-light lapped against the pale walls, and there was a feeling of learning and repose and tranquillity. For a moment Rumour thought the pools were simply great shining discs of silver, but as they passed the nearest, it rippled, its reflection moving gently on the walls, and Rumour understood that this was the *sidh*'s library. *And in those pools are the stored spells of countless centuries! If I could only break free and reach them!*

But the crystal pools, where once Maelduin had dived and swum, and where he had studied the Cadence, were beyond her reach. The *nimfeach* were dragging her to the centre of the room, and the Fomoire were leaping and prancing, pointing to her with horrid glee, uncoiling lengths of thin, leathery rope. They fell on Rumour, and as they bound her hands behind her back, Rumour felt the cold smoothness of the ropes, and knew that

160

they had been fashioned from strips of Human skin.

But I think I am beyond caring about that, she thought. I think I am beyond repulsion. A part of her mind noted that her feet and legs had been left free, and she at once thought: does that mean he will do it to me again? For the first time her resolve wavered.

The Fomoire had circled her; they had produced glinting knives, razor-edged, wickedly sharp and slightly curved. Rumour struggled and, as she did so, she caught a convulsive movement from Andrew. But as he tried to break free again, the *nimfeach* dragged at his arms, twisting them behind his back, wrenching at the sockets painfully.

The Fomoire were leaping and whirling into their grisly dance, circling their prisoner, shrieking with malicious glee.

> 'Peel her smooth, shed her fur.
> Moult the Human, cast her hair,
> Let the Master swallow her.'

As Rumour shrank back, they advanced on her, still dancing, turning completely round as they whirled, and then falling back into place again. They reached for her long, rippling hair, letting it slide through their wizened hands, chuckling and nodding, brandishing the glinting knives.

> 'Leave the scalp, leave the skin,
> Let the Master swallow it in.
> Peel her smooth and peel her fair,
> Shed her hair and moult her fur.'

Rumour's head was jerked back so that her spine arched and the tip of her skull was almost touching the ground. Her hair swung loose, brushing the ground, and the Fomoire yelled with delight and closed about her. There was the cold touch of the razors then, the scrape of the thin, glinting blades against her skin. A sudden silence descended on the chamber, and Rumour and Andrew both remembered with sickening vividness how the Fomoire had worked on Echbel, how they had fallen suddenly and completely silent in this way, directing their concentration to their grisly task.

161

Rumour felt Andrew's thoughts flow out to her again.

Courage, Rumour... This will be unpleasant, but you will endure it...

Yes, thought Rumour valiantly. Yes, whatever they intend to do, I shall endure it. I endured that filth inside me. I won't let them see that I'm frightened. I'll be angry and disdainful, that'll be the thing to be.

She half closed her eyes and sent the now-absorbed Fomoire contemptuous looks, and felt, all the while, the terrible sharpness of the blades, and then the heavy, silken weight of her hair falling to the ground. There was a whisper of sound, and a cold, numb feeling, and she knew that they had taken her hair. She struggled to get her hands free, to reach up and cover her poor shorn head, because there was something so raw, so exposed about the feeling that it was scarcely to be borne. But the skin-ropes held; the Fomoire had bound them tightly, and they cut cruelly into her wrists. Real anger surged up within her then, and she thought: how *dare* these loathsome creatures treat me like this! Her mind reached for a spell, something vicious, something cruel and sharp that would tear into them and rip them apart, but anger and pain had blunted her mind, and the patterns she sought eluded her.

'And now the oils,' cried the Fomoire.

'Anoint the Human!'

'Grease her for the Master!'

They whirled and danced, chanting as they went.

'Human grease and Human fat
Slither and slime, oil and wax.'

'Bring the cauldrons!' cried several of them, and Rumour saw two of them carrying in a black cauldron, dragging its bulk across the silver floor with a scraping sound. They placed it at the centre of the room, a black menacing crucible, the rim on a level with the lolling, dead Human heads of the Fomoire's skins, the sides pitted. A rank, rancid stench gusted out from its interior.

Andrew and Rumour stared at it in horror, and Andrew fought to break free.

The Fomoire danced about the cauldron, the Human skins

flying outwards, the dead heads rolling, and then they approached the cauldron, leaning over, their tiny, clawlike hands reaching into its depths, scooping up handfuls of not-quite-colourless grease, chuckling and screeching as gobbets of it slopped on to the floor.

'Anoint her well, boys!'

'Make it slick, boys!'

'Don't tread in the fat!'

'Human fat, slither and slime!'

They leapt and cavorted back and forth between Rumour and the cauldron, standing on tiptoe to reach into its depths, ladling the repulsive, lardlike substance out in their hands, and slathering it over her skin. Thick, slightly warm fat ran into her eyes, and then into her mouth, trickling down her throat, so that she coughed and retched. It was like being smothered in mucus, in blubber, in every loathsome fluid ever imagined. She was trapped in a mucus bag, in a slimy, soupy bladder of Human grease and Human fat, boiled by the Fomoire from the flesh and the bones of their victims, melted and clarified, and then tipped into the black cauldron.

As she lay, gasping, half blinded, fighting down rising nausea, the door opened and the Fisher King walked in.

Chapter Seventeen

He stood framed in the arched doorway with the silver curlicues and the elaborate carvings, watching her, and he seemed to tower above them all, ten feet high at the very least. Rumour, her vision almost completely obscured by the warm grease, saw that the monstrous fin was distended and erect again, and that the barbed phallus reared up between the scales that covered his upper thighs.

The *nimfeach* held her firmly but, as the Fisher King moved closer, they stood back. Rumour struggled upwards, and caught a movement from Andrew, as if he might be trying to break free. But at once the Fomoire were there, surrounding them both, grinning through their slitted, Humanish cloaks, ready to pounce.

The Fisher King stood looking down at her, his eyes glittering, the scales shining greyly in the light from the pools. He nodded to the Fomoire and the *nimfeach*, as if satisfied, and stood poised on the edge of the largest crystal pool. Its surface rippled faintly, and the Fisher King dived, in a single smooth movement, into the water. There was a brief glimpse of his sleek body, streaming through the water, and then the waters churned and his head emerged, the water pouring from it in shining droplets. Torn fragments and shreds of the *sidh*'s ancient spells spattered his body, and he brushed them off impatiently, and turned to look at Rumour; and the swollen fin reared up out of the water behind him.

He turned to the waiting Fomoire and said, 'Throw her in!'

The film of grease was still blurring Rumour's vision, so that although she heard the Fisher King's imperious command, she could barely see the Fomoire move to surround her.

There was the sudden horrid feeling of the Fomoire's claws, and the clammy fin-hands of the *nimfeach* lifting her, several losing their grasp because of the slippery oil, so that she fell hitting her shoulder against the floor. And then they had a firmer hold, they were lifting her, and there was the sudden cold scent of the water as she was flung towards it.

Her body hit the crystal pool with a flat, sickening sound, and Rumour felt, through the layers of grease, the shock of the icy water stinging her skin, as if it was being pierced by hundreds of tiny, sharp needles. Her shaven scalp felt as if knives were tearing at it, and she gasped and threshed wildly, trying to free her bound wrists, trying to see better, struggling to escape.

The instant she hit the water, the Fisher King dived again, darting through the pool directly beneath her. Rumour felt him brush her legs and twine his hands about her ankles; cold, webbed, dragging her down. There was a moment when the waters were over her head, and she was seeing the wavering depths of the pool with the ancient, priceless library of magic, the beautiful, intricate enchantments created by Aillen mac Midha.

The cold water had revived her a little. Rumour kicked out, feeling her feet brush scaly thighs, feeling him pull her down deeper, guessing that his intention was not to kill her yet, only to half drown her so that she would not be able to fight. And then she was pushed upwards, and the cold wet body was pressed close to her, and it was repulsive, but he was thrusting her out into the air again . . .

The Fisher King pushed her half out of the water, so that she broke the surface, gasping and fighting for breath. His head appeared, sleek and round on the pool's surface, and Rumour was aware of his hands reaching for her under the water again.

He pulled her to him, the water slowing his movements, making them very nearly languorous. I shall bear it, thought Rumour although her courage was almost failing her now. I *will* bear it, and I will survive it! The rearing phallus pressed against her again, and she silently cried out, *Oh no, please, not again* . . .

But he made no attempt to force apart her legs, and Rumour realised that his excitement was no longer sexual.

She willed herself to be calm, feeling him holding her, feeling

165

how slowly he moved, wanting him to do whatever he intended to do, wanting him to get it over, trying to think of a way to escape.

He did not enter her. He reared partway out of the water, silver droplets streaming from his body, the scales glittering, the monstrous fin erect behind him.

And then he was above her, curving over her, his head directly over hers, his body bending over, his head was drooping forward, boneless, fluid, repulsive . . .

His mouth began to open. It opened and stretched wider than she had imagined any creature's mouth ever could stretch. Rumour writhed, churning the water to great foamy waves, but he held her firmly, his flat wide mouth stretched so wide that she could no longer see his features; he was simply a monstrous, gaping fishmaw. There were no teeth, but there were ridges of jaw-bone, gleaming whitely, crusted with some kind of growth, greyish-white and more loathsome than anything she had ever visualised.

There was a sound of chanting somewhere close by, but Rumour by now saw only the Fisher King's wide brutal mouth, and felt only the pushing barbed phallus, hard and throbbing with obscene lust.

Her stomach lifted with nausea as the tainted stench of his breath gusted into her face. There was a moment when the shape of his head was directly above her, blotting out the light, grinning and salivating, dripping thick mouth-fluids over her, and then the membraneous lips closed over her shaven head, wet, flabby, *sucking* . . . Her reason spun wildly and panic possessed her almost completely, and she thought: *he is going to eat me . . . he is going to suck me into his mouth and down through his gullet and into his stomach . . . He is pure fish now, and fish swallow their prey whole . . .*

The great grinning mouth was closing over her head; it was covering her eyes, sucking her in . . . His mouth was sliding down over her face, so that she was fighting for breath, and his stench was all about her: she was drowning in the poisonous stench of the creature's saliva . . .

There was a wet, sucking sound, and Rumour felt her waist gripped by the webbed hands, and her head pushed further down . . .

Darkness closed about her, and her vision was shot with whirling red lights... There was a suffocating, drowning feeling, and she thought: but I *cannot* drown inside the creature's gullet! and then she was being pushed down and down; his hands were reaching for her hips, he was forcing her into his mouth.

The light shut off completely, and the world was spinning and her lungs were bursting for air, and it was ending, it was ending, she was being forced down, down through the soft tissues of the creature's maw, down into the distending stomach...

As the Fisher King began to force Rumour's head into his wide, grinning mouth, Andrew drew in a deep breath and flexed his muscles to shake off the *nimfeach* and bound forward. Anger was pouring into him, for how *dared* this monstrous creature treat Rumour with such contempt?

With the anger came a sudden, cascading awareness, a cold, steely strength, and the sensation that it was not his strength, but that it was being poured into him, as easily as pouring water from one jug to another.

As if the strength came not from within, but from without...

The Spirit entering the Twelve...

The thought formed with silken ease, and Andrew seized on it, for it did not matter whence the strength came, only that it was there for the taking. He whirled about, snatching a spear from the nearest of the Fomoire, pushing the creature back, fury against Coelacanth blazing through him like a forest fire, knowing, at some deep, unacknowledged level, that it was not his fury, and it was not his strength...

The Fomoire was caught off balance at once and, as it went tumbling and shrieking to the floor, Andrew, still in the grip of the strange, alien force, plunged straight into the churning pool, feeling the water drag at his woollen robe, but barely aware of it, hardly noticing the icy sting of the pool.

The Fisher King's webbed hands were around Rumour's slender waist, and he was beginning to lift her above his head, holding her aloft, so that she would slide into his gaping maw... Behind them, the Fomoire had recovered from their first shock of surprise and were starting forward; from the edges of his vision, Andrew caught a glimpse of the *nimfeach* closing in on him.

He plunged into the foaming water, the strength that was not his strength lifting the spear, and then thrusting it at the Fisher King's face, aiming straight at the bulging, lidless eyes. He felt the tip of the spear pierce the eye-sac and meet hard bone. A cry of agony split the air, and thick eye-fluid, viscous fishblood spurted out, evil-smelling and repulsive, spattering Andrew's hands. Coelacanth fell back, the great fin hitting the water behind him.

Andrew pounced at once, dragging at Rumour with his free hand, the three of them crashing over and over, tumbling in the churning, foaming pool, its surface curdled and slimed with the Fisher King's thick, colourless blood, the Fisher King himself thrashing and screeching, flailing in his death agony.

Rumour was in his arms now, blinded, gasping, but blessedly alive. She clutched frantically at him, almost pulling them both under the water, and Andrew staggered back, and then righted them both. He lifted the spear again and brought it slicing down on the Fisher King's trunk, seeing the cold scaly skin part, feeling the repulsive juices spurt over him.

A great cry of agony rent the air, and the Fisher King writhed and threshed, the great tail-fin lashing the water and sending cascading waves over the sides. Great sheets of water drenched Andrew and Rumour, but now it was the pure cool water of the *sidh*'s pool, and it had a sharp, clean feel.

The *nimfeach* had fallen back, and Andrew, still supporting the half-drowned Rumour, managed to look back, and saw fear in their eyes; and through the threshing of the dying Fisher King, he saw the gills in their necks gaping and distorting as they fought to frame Humanish speech.

'*The Samildanach . . . The promised Humanish . . .*'

Their voices were wet and ugly, but Andrew's senses were reeling and he barely heard them. His mind was sickened at what he had done, but he was still caught in the spinning maelstrom of rage, and his entire body was throbbing with angry passion against the loathsome Coelacanth.

He dragged Rumour bodily from the pool, and climbed out after her, turning her on one side, shaking her so that the water gushed from her mouth. She was white and pinched, but she was breathing, and Andrew sent up a heartfelt prayer of thanks.

The Fomoire were moving towards him, circling the pool, but Andrew saw that they were very wary indeed. The *nimfeach* were cowering, and he heard again the ugly, unnatural gill-speech. 'The Samildanach. The mantle of the Samildanach is upon him . . . It is as it was prophesied.'

A tiny part of his mind registered that the *nimfeach* pronounced the word not as he had heard it in the Porphyry Palace, but with a different, eerily beautiful cadence of their own.

From the corner of his eyes, he caught the movement of the Fomoire as they lifted their spears and bunched together, as if to make a concerted rush. He shook Rumour again, hating himself for doing it, seeing that she was barely conscious, knowing that she should be left to healing sleep, but knowing as well that if they were to have any hope at all of escaping, she must pronounce a spell at once. Coelacanth was dead, his maimed body was now floating, face down, in the crystal pool; but Andrew knew that, although the *nimfeach* might hesitate, the Fomoire would not. He had disconcerted them, he had slain Coelacanth, and the *nimfeach* had ascribed to him the mantle of the legendary Samildanach. And that is all it was! he thought. That is all it was, and at any minute the Fomoire will be upon us.

Rumour, swimming in and out of consciousness, heard Andrew's voice shouting to her to pronounce an enchantment to beat back the advancing Fomoire.

'Something – anything! The *Draiocht Suan*!' cried Andrew, picking one of the few enchantments he had heard of. 'Rumour, you must!'

'I can't—'

'You must!' cried Andrew, desperately. 'There will be all the time afterwards to recover, but you must find that last shred of energy! I cannot do it! You *must* safeguard us!'

Rumour, clutching the remnants of sanity, heard Andrew say that they could be safe, and her mind cleared a little. Iron bands still held her lungs in a vice, and it hurt to breathe, but Andrew had said she must pronounce a spell that would safeguard them.

She summoned the last dregs of her strength, and whispered

169

the words of the ancient, powerful *Draiocht Suan*, the gentle Enchantment of Slumber, and then fell back in Andrew's arms, exhausted. She did not know if it had worked, or if the darkness of Coelacanth would stifle the spell, but there was nothing more she could do.

Holding her to him, trying to infuse the warmth of his own body into her, Andrew saw, with deep and immense thankfulness, the silver cobwebs of the *Draiocht Suan* descend about the advancing creatures, so that they fell to the ground, caught in the sticky silver cobweb of the ancient Enchantment of Slumber.

He carried her out of the chamber with the crystal pools, leaving behind the dead body of the Fisher King and his unconscious servants. He had no knowledge of the Palace, but there would surely be somewhere he could lay her down and dry her and warm her, and let her sleep.

She was dripping wet, and her skin was still streaked with the thick grease and with the spattering of Coelacanth's viscous blood. Her head was bare and shaven, but Andrew, looking down, saw the long thick lashes lying against her cheeks, and the beautiful bone structure, and felt something painful wrench his heart and his loins, because she was so beautiful, she was the most beautiful thing he had ever seen, and her pain was scarcely to be borne.

He was barely aware of her weight; he thought she felt like a trembling bird sheltering, her heart pounding against the thin cage of her ribs. The anger and the strange, invasive strength had left him, going as swiftly as it had come. I suppose, thought Andrew, that it was simply something born out of fear and out of the need to save Rumour. Yes, of course that was what it had been. Little more than a perfectly natural self-preservation. He dared not believe anything else. And Coelacanth was dead and the others locked into slumber by the *Draiocht Suan*, and for the moment they were safe. For the moment he would concentrate only on healing Rumour, on finding somewhere for them to rest.

Directly ahead was a corridor with doors opening off it, all of them etched with the silhouettes of sea-creatures and twining hazel wands and beings with rippling hair and lashing, iridescent tails. Surely there would be a room where they could rest and recover. He turned into the first, and saw with immense thankfulness that, although there was not a bed in the sense that he understood it, there was a low, wide dais with pale, silken cushions. To the left was a tiny crystal pool, with a silver fountain spouting fresh water, and behind the dais were thin, gauzy lengths of some blue-green stuff that shimmered silkily. Some kind of guests' wardrobe?

He laid Rumour on the dais, piling the cushions about her for warmth and comfort, turning to reach down lengths of the blue-green silk to wrap about her, seeing that the silk was fashioned into the shapes of loose robes, some of them fur-trimmed, several of them crusted with iridescent stones. He pulled off his own drenched robe impatiently, and pulled on the nearest of the robes before turning back to the unconscious Rumour.

The water in the tiny pool was fresh and clean; when Andrew dipped his hands into it, it slid over his hands like thin rainwater, gentle and soothing. He soaked a length of the thin silk in the pool, and turned back to sponge Rumour's lacerated body, thinking that, when she regained consciousness, at least she would be cleansed of the Fisher King's spattered slime and fishblood.

He thought: I should like to bathe her in the perfumes and the unguents I am sure she is used to. I should like to immerse her in swansdown pillows, and wrap her in down and velvet so that nothing harmful or evil could ever touch her again . . .

He was conscious of the absurdity of it, for he had only plain water, and he had only his own rough, unskilled hands, more used to the monks' harsh lye soap than to perfumes and soft lotions.

The water revived her; colour touched her cheeks, and the velvety lashes fluttered. Her eyes opened, and Andrew murmured a prayer of gratitude.

She looked up at him as he continued to wipe away every trace of Coelacanth's monstrous assault, and as he reached for a robe of peacock-blue to wrap about her, she said, very softly, 'I have no words to thank you, Andrew.' For the first time since he had known her, Andrew heard her voice falter. 'But I do thank you,' said Rumour, reaching out a hand to trace his features. 'I thank you for my life and for my sanity.' A travesty of her old mocking

171

smile showed. 'My poor man of peace,' said Rumour softly. 'Had you to wrestle with your conscience and your god to kill him, Andrew?'

'No,' said Andrew, staring down at her. 'There was no fight. The creature had to die.'

Because if he had not died, you would not be here, my love . . .

'There was no fight,' he said, again. 'And what I began, you finished. I could not have held off the Fomoire if you had not pronounced the *Draiocht Suan*.' He looked at her, seeing all over again that, even without the rippling hair framing her face, she was beautiful; there was no part of her that was not beautiful. Eyes, skin, teeth, shoulders, breasts . . . The peacock-blue robe turned her eyes to pure turquoise, the colour of the *Gaillimh* coast on a brilliant summer day, the colour of dragonflies' wings. The robe was loosely tied, and beneath it her skin gleamed ivory white . . .

Rumour half sat up, propping herself up on one elbow, looking about her; Andrew, knowing that, despite his resolve, his body was betraying him, sat back. At length, Rumour said, very softly, 'If you would enfold me in your arms, as I think you have been wishing to, I should be so grateful.'

Andrew said, 'That creature has – hurt you . . .'

'The hurt is deeper. Please,' said Rumour and, unexpectedly, there was a thread of amusement. 'I have never before had to plead for an embrace,' she said, and Andrew saw that, although the familiar mockery lit her eyes, behind them was hurt; pain and terror, and the dreadful memory of what Coelacanth had done to her. He could have coped with the mockery; he had schooled himself to cope with it ever since they had descended to Tiarna, and he could have withstood the lingering fear. But the knowledge of her pain unmanned him. He could not bear to think of her hurting. He thought: after all, I am only Human, and after all, she is asking for no more than warmth and closeness. He held out his arms, and Rumour went into them.

There was more sweetness, more warmth and more pure joy in holding her than he had ever imagined possible.

Her skin smelt of the clean water, and of her own special fragrance, and Andrew held her, not daring to do more, feeling that she was still shivering, knowing that he was shivering also, although whether from cold or from some other cause, he was unsure.

He thought: there is no sin. She has been used cruelly, and there must only be this closeness, this warmth. But all the while, he was aware of his traitorous body, throbbing with wanting, aching with desire, hard and sinful and sweet.

At length she fell asleep, and Andrew moved away cautiously, because it would be sensible to make sure that the *Draiocht Suan* still held their enemies, and it would be practical to find if there was food and wine in the Palace, lotions for Rumour's torn skin.

But each time he moved, she cried out, like a child frightened of the dark, and clutched him, and at length Andrew crept beneath the silken covers and the cushions, and held her.

There was no dawn in Tiarna; Andrew, lying with Rumour quiescent at his side, thought that, where there was no sky, no sun, there could not be day or night, as he knew it.

But gradually he became aware of a faint softening of the rippling water-light, and a silvering of the shadows. There was the feeling of renewal, of the darkness receding, of an awakening.

And imbued with the new Teaching of the Nazarene as he was, he found himself remembering the ancient beliefs, pagan but suddenly comprehensible. The sun-worshippers, the many peoples who had lifted their voices in paeans of praise and thanksgiving for the dawn and the light. The legendary Mansions of the Gods in the East, and the ritual sun-dances of primitive tribes.

I understand it, thought Andrew, watching the light grow grey and then silver, feeling the creeping shadows retreat. There was something strong, reviving, about the beginning of a new day.

Andrew silently offered up prayers of thanks, and a simple brief supplication for strength to continue. He looked down at Rumour, sleeping peacefully, and thought: there must be no more nights like this one, the two of us alone, our bodies tangled together for warmth and comfort . . .

Moving cautiously, he washed in the cool, pure pool, and found it refreshing and faintly scented. His Order decreed that a man must wash and cleanse his body regularly. 'For,' had said

Brother Stephen, 'the body is God's creation, and must perforce not be abused.' But Andrew had guessed that the Brothers' rule of regular washing in cold water and the scouring of the rough drying cloths was intended to quench sensuous thoughts and desires.

Now, rinsing his entire body in the pool, he felt not just cleansed but purged, refreshed, silken clean all over.

Donning the blue-green robe, so different to the serviceable but rather coarse wool robes the Brothers wore, he remembered Brother Stephen's edict against any material other than homespun for robes. And, in truth, there was a soft, insidious sensuality about the very act of sliding his arms into the whispering silk; there was a caress in the cool, slippery robe, there was even pleasure in the colours of the silk – azure blue, shot here and there with a thin silver thread. Andrew stood very still, feeling the glossy robe stroke his skin, brush his thighs, and with a twist of irony, he made brief acknowledgement to the wise Brother who had known that men could be vulnerable, and that the sexual appetites could be aroused by things other than a woman's body.

Andrew and Rumour found food in one of the adjoining rooms: fruit and honey, exotic and unfamiliar, but wholly delicious. There was wine in exquisite silver casks, fragrant and sweet, tinged with the scent of fruit and with the colours of the oceans, blue-green and heady.

'I do not know if Coelacanth's creatures would have fed on this,' said Rumour, wrapped in the vivid turquoise robe, eating and drinking with industrious pleasure. The long Amaranth eyes glanced up and filled with amusement. 'I am ravenously hungry,' she said. 'I daresay it is indelicate of me, but there it is.' She reached for the wine.

Andrew said, 'The *sidh* would eat this?'

'In fact, I have no idea,' said Rumour, reaching for the platter of strange-looking fruits with crisp, spicy outer crusts and strong, sweet hearts. 'It is said that they feed on the senses of their victims,' she said, and bit into the fruit, and although the look she threw him was not quite the old mischievous one, it was a creditable attempt at it. Andrew smiled back.

But he said, after they had eaten and drunk, 'Perhaps you

174

should stay here while I explore?' and looked at her, and knew this for only a token attempt at chivalry.

Rumour said, 'Rest and recline on the silken couch?'

'I did not really think you would. Also,' said Andrew, draining his own wine chalice, 'to explore Tiarna together will be more interesting.'

'So it will.' Rumour set down the wine chalice and stood up, and then, suddenly serious, her eyes sliding away, 'my strength is gone,' she said and, lifting one slender hand, indicated the shaven ivory scalp. 'Therefore I must find a carapace, a covering until it is restored. And also,' said Rumour, looking up and grinning, her eyes filled with the light of self-mockery, 'I could not possibly be seen abroad looking like this.' But she reached for his hand as she spoke, and Andrew heard the fear and the note of self-doubt.

He took her hand, and said, 'Like this you are even more beautiful.' Reaching out, he touched her face with his other hand, tracing its outline, lingering over the satiny feel of her skin. 'Truly, you are the most beautiful creature I have ever seen.'

There was a sudden silence. Andrew thought: her closeness is almost unbearable. I dare not remember how she lay in my arms.

And then Rumour withdrew her hand, gently and naturally, and said, 'Well, I shall feel better properly covered. And therefore, I must plunder the *sidh*'s cache.'

'Will there be something?'

'Oh yes. For there have been times when the *sidh* have donned the garb of Humans, and walked abroad in our world. They do not like to do so, and they only do it in extreme danger. Perhaps at a time such as this, when they have lost their music and their very existence is threatened.' Her eyes narrowed. 'Yes, that is entirely possible,' said Rumour, thoughtfully. 'If they had time and sufficient strength left to them, they may have sent out one – perhaps more – of their number to try to find the lost enchantment.'

'They could do that?'

'Yes, certainly. Although the danger to them would be almost overwhelming,' said Rumour. 'They would find it difficult to survive in the world of Men, because of the extreme differences in the ways of living. But if one of them was sufficiently courageous and sufficiently resourceful, he might do it. He might almost pass as Human. But he would not dare live like that for very long.'

'He would acquire Humanish appetites and thoughts?' said Andrew, tentatively.

'Yes. How extremely perceptive of you. But as well as that,' said Rumour, 'he would begin to acquire an accretion of Humanish essence. To begin with, the donning of Humanish garb would be only like the wearing of an unfamiliar gown or a cloak. But if he lived like that for too long, the gown, the garb, the Humanish covering would begin to blend with the *sidh* beneath it.'

'He would be changing from *sidh* to Human?'

'Yes,' said Rumour. 'Exactly that.'

'Then that is why they keep Human garments,' said Andrew, remembering how he had found the silken robes.

Rumour grinned. 'These robes do very well,' she said, 'but I believe that, if I can find them, I shall array myself in the regalia of the Elven King. Shall we explore?'

It was an eerie experience to walk through the empty, echoing Palace, knowing that the *nimfeach* and the Fomoire slept the deep, enchanted slumber of the *Draiocht Suan* close by. Rumour entered the chamber of the crystal pools unhesitatingly, Andrew at her side, and pronounced the spell again: 'To strengthen it,' she said. They stood silently, and watched the fragile filaments form on the air, and descend in a cobweb cloud over the slumbering creatures.

Andrew said, 'Coelacanth?' and Rumour sent a quick look to the pool, where the Fisher King still lay on the water's surface.

'When the *sidh* return, they will know how to deal with that one,' she aid, and her face was shuttered, so that Andrew knew that, although she was already recovering from the Fisher King's terrible assault, deep within her mind must still be areas of raw agony.

But she surprised him again. As they stood together outside the *sidh*'s ancient, beautiful library, with the slumbering enemies still held by the *Draiocht Suan*, the barely perceptible dawnlight of Tiarna silvering the Palace, she said, 'Andrew, I cannot think of any other man who would have drawn my attention to Coelacanth, as you did just now. Almost every other man would have tried to pretend that he was no longer there, and would think that I must not be reminded of what had happened. That I must be shielded.'

'Should I try to shield you? Should I pretend it did not happen? I can't do it,' said Andrew. 'And you would see through it. I cannot . . . *unmake* the horror of what happened to you. Perhaps I can help you to heal; I can offer you comfort and friendship and love, but I cannot unmake Coelacanth's brutality.' He watched her, seeing the play of the silver light on her face, seeing it find tiny silver lights in the dark pools of her eyes. 'I think you would not wish for any pretence,' said Andrew softly. 'I think you would not want well-meaning deceptions. If I had stood in front of Coelacanth's body, so that you could not see it, you would still have known it was there.'

Rumour said, 'I cannot bear pretence or falseness.'

'No.' He took her hands. 'You are stronger than anyone I have ever known.'

'You are stronger still.' Her hands lay in his, unresisting. 'I think I could have killed Coelacanth,' she said. 'If sorcery failed me, then I think I could have killed him as you did. I should have hated it very much, but I think I could have done it. But I do not know if I could have sufficiently overcome such deep-rooted beliefs as you did.'

'The Man of Peace?'

'Yes.' She withdrew her hands with the same gentle, natural gesture. 'It is not in your nature to offer violence to another living creature. It is not in your creed.' The grin slid out. 'I do not altogether understand your creed,' said Rumour, child of a people who enjoyed warmth and comfort and love and wine and music. 'But I understand that violence, killing, is abhorrent to you. And still you killed Coelacanth without hesitating.'

'I was lent the strength to do it,' said Andrew, so softly that Rumour barely caught the words.

But she said, 'The Samildanach . . .' and Andrew looked at her.

'So you heard the *nimfeach*.' He had wondered about this.

'I heard them, but I do not understand it any more than you do. But it is an old, old belief, and an old, old legend, that of the Samildanach. Perhaps the *nimfeach* had their own version of it.'

Andrew said, 'To us it is a very new and a very wonderful belief. The One who walked the world and redeemed Men of their sins. And who will one day return—'

He stopped, frowning, and Rumour said, 'I think you are beginning to question that prophecy, Andrew.'

'No.' His eye met hers. 'But perhaps to question its origins,' he said.

'Would your priests have . . .' Rumour paused, searching for an expression that would not sound too brutal, 'would they perhaps have manipulated the legends and the beliefs they found already in existence?' she said.

The new wine in the old casks . . . ? No, thought Andrew. Please, no. If I lose the trust in that belief, the Nazarene carpenter who saved Mankind and who will one day return; if I lose that, I shall have lost everything. He said, carefully, 'For what reason would they do such a thing?' And waited to see her reactions.

'To make their own new teachings more acceptable. To make them a little familiar. Oh, Andrew, you know it as well as I do. And I could understand it if it were so,' said Rumour. 'I could understand it very easily.' She glanced at him. 'It is not difficult to adjust truth and it is not hard to make people believe what they would like to believe,' said Rumour, and her eyes met his coolly, with no trace of expression in them. 'When a quest or a task, or when something of immense importance is at stake, it is surely a thing frequently done,' she said. 'Are you sure that they were not looking for a way to impose their own authority on the gullible?'

'If they were,' said Andrew, slowly, 'they did so purely to show the people the Truth. There would be no selfishness behind it.'

'People are rarely selfless,' said Rumour, and touched his face lightly. 'Most people are driven by some kind of self-interest. Remember that, Andrew.'

And then, as if suddenly impatient with herself, she shook her head, and with an abrupt change of mood, turned, indicating the galleried landings ahead of them. 'I think that along here is the Elven King's legendary Silver Cavern,' she said. 'If the Palace is a replica of Tara, then we are close to what is called the Throne Room at Tara.'

As they entered the Silver Cavern, light lay across the floor in great pearly swathes, and there was a thick, soft silence, as if swansdown lay everywhere, or as if a great fold of stifling velvet was enclosing the chamber. The walls were fashioned from some kind of pale, shimmering rock, exquisitely beautiful, veined with glinting crystal and delicate ivory, studded and crusted with great opalescent stones. Here and there were soaring, ice-blue formations, crystalline stalagmites, and within them were the outlines of slender shapes with slanting, mischievous eyes and sinuous, beautiful bodies. Andrew stood looking, thinking he had never seen anything so strange and so eerily beautiful, unable to tell whether the shapes were natural formations, or whether they had been hewn.

'The *sidh*,' said Rumour softly, looking up at them. 'That is how they appear to anyone who is foolish enough to look directly upon them. Or at least,' she said, 'that is how they are believed to look, because no one ever looks on them and lives to tell of it.'

Andrew had been aware, ever since they entered the Cavern, of blue-green smudges, darting threads of turquoise light, moving on the outer rim of his vision.

'They are not dead,' said Rumour softly, when Andrew indicated this. 'But do not try to look too fully upon them, Andrew.'

They moved forward, across the shining silver floor, and there, in front of them, was the Silver Throne of the Elven King . . .

Rumour stood very still, and her hand came out to Andrew. In a whisper, she said, 'So he is here. Exactly as Coelacanth said.'

Directly ahead of them, seated in the great carven Throne of the *sidh*, still wearing the eerie, half-Humanish form he had donned for Coelacanth's repulsive Gristlen, the Elven King was unseeing, unhearing. His skin was ivory pale, translucent, dull, and the long turquoise eyes were filmed over. His hands, thin and slender, lay supine on the arms of the Silver Throne, the fingers delicate and curving inwards, indicating the predatory vein in his chill faery blood.

Aillen mac Midha, the strange, icily beautiful High King of the *sidh*, the most magical, most inHuman creature in all Ireland, bonded by ancient sorcery to the Royal Houses of

Ireland, constrained to give his people's aid to them in times of extreme danger, but now silent and helpless, poised in a half-world . . .

'*Is* he dead?' said Andrew, at length, staring at the Throne.

'No, he will not be dead, for the *sidh* do not die as we know it,' said Rumour, also staring. 'I think he could be revived.'

'The music?' Andrew started to reach for the golden casket with the shifting, beautiful enchantment, because surely this was the time to return to the *sidh* the stolen magic of their race; surely this was the time to restore their life and their world to them?

He started to open the delicately crafted lid, and at once Rumour put out a hand to stop him. 'No!' And as Andrew looked up, startled, she said:

'It is only that I believe we should keep the enchantment ourselves for a little longer.'

'But that is why we brought it.'

'No. We brought it to force open a Gateway into the Dark Realm. Into the necromancers' kingdoms.' Her eyes glittered and Andrew, staring, thought: the idea of that excites her. Because she wants to enter the Dark Realm? Because, despite all she has said, there is something there that calls to her? Chaos?

But Rumour said, 'If we are to truly help the *sidh*, we shall do so by destroying Chaos and his evil.'

'And in order to reach Chaos and the Dark Ireland, we need the *sidh*'s music. Yes, of course.' But Andrew looked back at the slender, unearthly creature on the throne, and he remembered that he knew very little indeed about the exotic Amaranth sorceress. A prickle of unease brushed his skin, and he thought: I must remember that there are many forms of temptation. I must remember that, even while she is tempting me, something may be tempting her.

Rumour had moved to the Silver Throne, and then behind it, where the soaring rock was a shifting, blurring cascade of cool blue ice-fire, threaded with glistening pearl and ivory. There was a moment when Andrew caught a whisper of entreaty – '*Help us!*' – and there was a glimpse of slender, shining forms, wingless dragonfly bodies swooping and darting and then falling to the ground. And then the visions faded, and the heartbreaking whisperings died away, and there was only the sad silence, and the still figure on the ancient Elven Throne; blind, deaf, locked into helpless silence.

Rumour stood for a moment at the Cavern's centre, her hands lifted, her head thrown back. The silver and blue light poured about her shoulders, and Andrew received a fleeting impression, not of the exotic, wilful, Amaranth sorceress, but of something that was imbued with the cold eerie light; something in whose veins might run the chill, faery blood of the under-sea creatures . . .

And she is withholding the music that would surely pour the life back into them . . .

And then Rumour moved, and the light changed, and the vivid image vanished. She slipped behind a jutting rock that was crusted with pale, translucent gems, and Andrew, watching, saw that she moved with assurance. *Because she has been here before? Because she has consorted with these creatures?*

He stayed where he was, looking about him, seeing that in places rock ledges gave way to alcoves, niches, seeing the blur of colour deep within the niches. And then Rumour reappeared, and Andrew caught his breath, for here, once more, was the beautiful exotic Amaranthine, the daughter of Ireland's Royal Sorcerers, the creature composed of fire and magic, of twisting spells and cascading enchantments. He stared at her, momentarily unable to speak, and saw, as he had seen in the Porphyry Palace, the candle shining strongly through the pure alabaster of her skin, the rippling vein of mystical Amaranth blood that gave her the strength and the power to spin bewitchments.

Rumour was clad in a shining turquoise garment that slid over her body in a silken cascade, and clung to the slender outline. Here and there were scatterings of blue-green gems that moved and glistened and caught the light, making it seem alive. Woven into the gown's substance were threads of living silver; rearing, licking tongues of pale light, exotic and dazzling.

On her head, she wore a close-fitting jewelled helmet, made up of the same turquoise and silver stones, glittering with icy fire, banded with pure silver. Beneath it, her eyes gleamed, slanting, tiptilted, filled with power and light.

Andrew knew he could not fight his desire for her for very much longer.

* * *

Andrew and Rumour supped together that night, in the room with the dais and the pouring crystal fountain, eating the sweet, crisp fruits, drinking the fragrant, brilliant wine.

Rumour had curled on to the cushions, graceful as a cat, the silken gown rippling sensuously over her limbs. As the light dimmed and softened into the strange night of Tiarna, shadows touched her face, making great, mysterious pools of her eyes, silvering her skin to purest alabaster, to cool, seamless marble . . .

Andrew ate little, as was his custom, although he found the fruit palatable and sustaining. He drank the wine, thinking it would calm him, knowing all the while that, so far from calming him, it was firing his ardour, it was feeding the sweet, strong throbbing of his body, sending his desire soaring as high and as hard as the cascading rock walls of the Elven King's Throne Room.

He felt his heart begin to beat more slowly, and a great dark heaviness seemed to hover over him as he reached yet again for the chalice of wine at his place. When he moved, she moved with him, as if she had been sharing his thoughts, as if she had walked alongside his thoughts for every step of the way. She had travelled the path with him, her desires matching his, and when he set down the wine chalice and put out his hand to her, her hand was there, waiting.

The touch of her skin, soft, cool against his, fired his body to unbearable longing; he looked at her, and his mind tumbled with delight and fear; and passion, hot and hurting, raged through him.

He thought: I am sliding towards surrender; I am reaching the point where I shall not be able to stop . . .

Let me have this one night with her . . . Let me know, just once, the sweetness and the delight . . . Let me have that, thought Andrew, and I will forever suffer penance for it, I will go fasting all my days, I will embrace celibacy for ever more. But let me know it, just once, let me *possess* her, just once . . .

He traced the line of her face, moving over her neck, feeling the scent of her warmth reach out to engulf him. Of their own volition, his hands slid beneath the silk gown, cupping her breasts: exquisite, beautiful, sufficient to make a man cry with longing . . . Just this once, said his mind, and I will go barefoot,

182

dressed in sackcloth; I will take the scourge upon my back willingly . . .

From somewhere came the strength to pull away from her, to move back and stand looking down at her. A tiny frown twisted Rumour's face, and Andrew saw anger behind her eyes. He went abruptly from the room, feeling her eyes upon him, knowing that, if he looked back, if he saw her amidst the silken jewel-colours, he would be lost.

He went blindly through the great Palace, scarcely noticing where he went, his mind seething with a dozen different emotions, his body on fire with raging, hurting desire.

At last he found himself in the desolate Silver Cavern, the great rock-lined chamber with the eerie, silent figure of the Elven King and the strange, drifting, blue-green colours. He was trembling violently, but at length he sank to his knees, and bowed his head, reaching blindly, frenziedly for the calm, still centre that he had always been able to touch: the huge tranquil pool that he thought of as God's love and that had always been his strength and his inspiration.

Am I so weak, so easily lured? he thought, horrified and wracked with self-disgust. He remembered how he had always felt slightly superior, slightly contemptuous of the poor frail men who had allowed themselves to be tempted by women. He had seen those women – the Jezebels and the Delilahs – as no better than the harlots in the Temples, as flaunting, unclean creatures; painted-faced, vulgar-minded, raucous-voiced. He had seen the men who consorted with them as dissolute, debauched libertines, bestial and crude. Wasn't there something in one of the Epistles – to the Ephesians, was it? – that warned against such consorting? Such behaviour was not the stuff that made saints; '. . . therefore fornication and all covetousness should be avoided . . . Walk as children of light . . . For unless ye be as children ye can not enter heaven . . .'

And it is not the stuff that saints are made of.

But now, struggling with the violent desires that Rumour had aroused in him, Andrew found himself remembering again those women he had always found contemptible and beneath notice. He remembered that they had been of high birth and considerable scholarship: Delilah had been sought out by the Philistine lords to entice Samson and learn the secret of his strength. Jezebel had been a King's daughter, a lady of power who had forced the Phoenician religion in Israel and persecuted the Israelite prophets. And Salome was a Queen's daughter. They might have been evil and calculating, but they must also have been clever and beautiful and courageous in their own way. As Rumour was beautiful and courageous and clever.

Rumour was worlds and years away from the harlots and the painted whores. And has, as those creatures had, her own motives?

For what do I truly know of her? They were thoughts to instantly quench, just as his response to her allure was to be instantly quenched. For to succumb to that, to fall into the temptation of the flesh is not the stuff that saints are made of! cried Andrew in silent anguish, and at once there was the answer:

Are you being so arrogant, so insufferably proud as to think you are in the mould of a saint?

The sin of Pride. There it was, clear as a curse. And he had not even seen it. He had been striving for something that was beyond his reach and out of his grasp.

For I am no saint.

He was never aware, afterwards, of returning to the cavern with the crystal fountains, of moving to the silken couch, of lying once again next to her, the press of her body curving into his, naturally, softly, making them almost one creature.

Her arms closed about him, gratefully, warmly, and he was no longer fighting the sweet, sensual singing of his blood: he was almost drowning in the soaring joy.

She peeled the robe from him and he felt her hands against his skin; soft, caressing, at once soothing and exciting. She moved closer, her breasts against him, and desire, so long banked down, flared out of all control.

He no longer thought of such sweetness as mortal sin. He no longer thought: for this I may burn for ever, but: this is the woman I love, and I shall do so for always.

He wanted to know every part of her, every separate bone, every shred of skin, eyes, flesh, lips . . . The eternal fire would be no punishment for this, for even its searing heat could never match the fire that was scalding his body now . . . And I believe I shall not care if Hell opens and its flames consume me for ever, he thought.

There was the feeling that he was fusing with the one creature who understood him, the one living creature with whom he could share everything and for whom he would do anything in the world.

He paused only once, as her hands reached for his manhood, and a low groan was forced from him, for he had never before known a woman's touch there, and it was exquisite, it was beyond any emotion he had ever imagined. He looked down at Rumour and saw that her eyes were half closed with longing, and that her skin was glowing with desire. But even with his control snapped and with the restraints of years gone, he paused, remembering how Coelacanth had savaged her, hesitant.

She understood his hesitation at once, for she said, 'Andrew, I am aching with desire for you.'

'But there could be pain...' He stopped, conscious of ignorance, and Rumour pulled him closer and kissed him, not gently, not even lovingly, but savagely, as if she had been driven to the brink of endurance. Her lips were warm and soft, and she tasted of wine and love, and the last vestige of Andrew's control dissolved. He moved to her, trembling, feeling the sweet, sinless warmth.

His last conscious thought was that he no longer knew whether he was forsaking his god, or whether his god was forsaking him, but that he had ceased to care.

Chapter Eighteen

To leave Tiarna was the hardest thing Maelduin had ever had to do. To walk like this through the dark, whispering tunnels, in the strange, bone-filled garb and the pale skincloak of the Humanish, and somehow enter their alien world, filled him with dismay.

But there had been no other way. The Elven King had been helpless, beyond their reach, and the *sidh* were ailing and fading. Maelduin and Inse and two of the others had carried Aillen mac Midha to the great Silver Throne in the ice-blue cavern of the *Seomhra*. Maelduin had seen Inse begin to shiver and miss his way, as if he could no longer see properly, and he had known that the darkness was quenching Inse, as it was quenching them all.

And I have only escaped it because my father pronounced over me the ancient Humanish Enchantment, and I carry the flesh and the skin and the warm Human blood now.

There were still unexplored territories about his new self; feelings, emotions, pain, pleasure, fear. He could feel them all, one level below conscious thought, and it was a strange, rather alarming knowledge that, before his quest to find the *sidh*'s music was over, he might have known some of these feelings. *And passion?* said a tiny silver voice. *Will you know the passion of the Humanish? Will you take their women in the way of their strange love-making?* His thoughts formed no answer, but a smile curved his lips.

Before he left Tiarna, he went to the crystal pools of the *sidh*'s library, in search of the *nimfeach*'s priceless marvellous maps, so that he might find his way through the tunnels and into the world of Men. There was a bad moment there as he realised he could no longer dive into the pools, arrow-straight, his slender, glinting body making scarcely a ripple on the surface. He could

186

no longer swim at his leisure below the water, searching in the ancient, carefully preserved spells for this enchantment or that.

But he had managed it; he had discarded the thin silk robe he had donned after the Enchantment, and he had plunged into the pool naked, feeling, with a shock, the extreme coldness of the water, remembering in the same instant that Humanish blood was warmer than the chill faery blood of the *sidh*.

There was unaccustomed pain from having to hold his breath for so long, and having to come back to the surface many times to fill his lungs with air and to rest, and he found that Humanish sight became blurred under water.

It was a tedious, long-drawn-out exercise, for there were many pools to search, but at length he found the maps, locked deep into a silver cage with the curiously wrought doors that showed it to be of *nimfeach* crafting.

He had pushed from his mind the strong feeling that dark forces were closing in on Tiarna; it was absurd to think that the minute he left, Tiarna's enemies would pour in, and it was illogical to imagine that they had been there all along, waiting, watching, wanting just such an opportunity as this to wreak their vengeance. He went at once, leaving the Palace, his movements swift and graceful, not entirely quite Humanish, although he did not realise this; despite the strong Enchantment, he had still traces of the *sidh*'s cool, sensuous bewitchment.

His feet, lightly shod in thin hide of roe deer, made prints in the bone-dust that had thickened on the tunnel floors over the centuries, and the soft cambric shirt and pale leather jerkin and breeches felt heavy. But this was Humanish garb, this was how they dressed and how they travelled. He must become accustomed. He had taken a last look at his reflection, in the rippling silver walls of the fountain room, and he had thought: yes, I believe I am not ill pleased! And then he had put the thought from him, for it did not matter so much how he looked, only that the Humanish would not question him too closely. Only by being accepted into their world could he find out about the Gristlen and the *sidh*'s music.

Several layers below conscious thought, he was aware that it was the shining citadels of the Humanish that drew him, rather than their forests and their villages and the hill-farms. The palaces and the castles and the great legend-haunted fortresses of the High Kings . . .

The Grail Castle, sometimes called *Scathach*, the Shadow Place, only accessible by means of a long dark road and a dark dangerous journey from which not all travellers returned . . .

The *Dun na nGed* on the banks of the Boyne River, built by Domnall, who had so feared the ancient Curse of Tara that he would not live there. Maelduin knew of the Curse, he knew that the High Kings held it at bay only by the strongest and most intricate magic, but the Curse still lived, for no curse that had been properly pronounced could ever be destroyed.

And what of Tara itself, the seat of every High King and Queen of Ireland? The legendary glowing Bright Palace, the Shining Citadel, raised from the rock by the Amaranth sorcerers for the first High Queen of all, the beautiful, mischievous Dierdriu. Tara, so close in design to his beloved Palace of Nimfeach, that Maelduin had always thought he would surely feel at home there. He would like to see Tara.

And the Porphyry Palace of the House of Amaranth. A mischievous grin touched his lips. The Porphyry Palace, the home of the Royal Sorcerers, the Amaranths, the magical line who had served every High King and Queen, and who could trace their lineage to the long-ago Dawn Sorcerers, when Tara was no more than bare rock and the magic yet to be spun; to the days when Ireland was still inhabited by the small, elfin Cruithin race, and when Coelacanth still ruled in Tiarna . . .

It might be very interesting indeed to visit the Porphyry Palace, and to see the Cadence Tower, the great dark *Tur Baibeil* created from a clever blend of sorcery and architecture, whose building had resulted in the loss of the Cadence, the *sidh*'s magical gift to the Amaranths . . . The *sidh* did not fully understand what had happened, for the Amaranths could be secretive, but they knew that the Cadence, given to the Amaranths so long ago, could no longer be reached by the sorcerers.

If Maelduin could somehow recover the Cadence, it might assist him in his search for the *sidh*'s music. The Amaranths had lost it, but Maelduin thought it would still form at the bidding of one with sufficient understanding of it. And he understood the

Ancient Language of Magic as well as he understood Tiarna's shining halls.

The grin became very slightly malicious.

Why should he not enter the ancient, spell-ridden Tower, and reanimate the Cadence and reclaim it for his people?

Why not indeed?

It felt strange and unexpected to find himself approaching a world where night and day were sharply delineated, and where dusk fell in great purple and violet swathes over the land, spattering the skies with stars. Maelduin, used to the gentle fading of the Tiarnan days into a soft half-night, walked cautiously forwards to where the tunnels widened, remembering as he walked the countless times he had poured along these tunnels with the other *sidh*, sometimes bringing a Humanish whose senses would be stolen and poured into the music, occasionally bringing a raw length of magic from the sorcerers.

And sometimes we paid for the magic, and sometimes we did not, he thought, and there was a bitter knowledge in that memory, for had not the *sidh* been repaid in their own coin now? Their most precious possession of all had been taken; the Gristlen had vanished, and with it the music of Tiarna.

He came fully out of the tunnels, into the strange soft twilight that the Humanish called the Purple Hour, and which was laden with its own strong, gentle magic, and saw, directly ahead of him, the pale, lilac-tinged turrets and the soaring crenellations and the mist-wreathed spires of the beautiful ancient seat of the Royal Sorcerers of Ireland.

The Porphyry Palace of the Amaranth sorcerers.

Cerball was always ready to extend a welcome to unexpected guests, even when they came at such an awkward time as this. And as well as it being awkward, it cost money. Another place at the table meant another mouth to be fed, and Cerball was already finding the entertaining of the entire Amaranth clan more expensive than he had bargained for. But it could not be avoided; Nechtan had established a tradition of lavish hospitality, and it had to be maintained, unless you wanted to be branded as a miser. Cerball was many things, but miserly was not one of them.

189

So he made Maelduin welcome, thinking that, although it was all adding to the bills, this rather unusual-looking young man would be an interesting addition to the company. And Cerball would be glad to have any kind of diversion to take his mind from Theodora and Echbel, and from the really very awkward matter of Laigne.

But there was not, of course, anything so very extraordinary about the fact that Laigne was expecting a child. There ought not to be any need for concern.

But Cerball was very concerned indeed. He went about the Palace wearing a bothered look, because wasn't there something extremely worrying about it; and, if he was honest, wasn't it just the smallest bit sinister? He did not quite like to come out and tell people that he had not shared his lady's bed for rather a long time; Laigne did not care much for that kind of thing, and Cerball, while he could enjoy the company of the saucy young cousins and the giddy young nieces who came to the Porphyry Palace, was not overly fond of it himself lately.

Laigne had presented the information about the child to him a few days before Maelduin's arrival, using the most fadeaway of all her fadeaway voices, lying on her bed in a darkened room, a soothing draught of camomile tea at her hand and a length of cobweb-fine *Draiocht Suan* on her pillow, left by the conscientious Cecht.

Too tiresome, she had said, her face turned to the wall. Too tiresome and really almost embarrassing. She did not, of course, say, 'At my age,' but Cerball knew that everyone else was going to say it for her. In his hearing or out of it.

They had all had to be told. There had not been any way out of it; the Mugain had already said hadn't they all better be staying on a while, so that they could pool their strengths and continue to bombard the Dark Realm with spells to reach Theodora and Echbel. His lady had supported this – 'Saving servants' wages and food bills at Mugain,' said Great-aunt Fuamnach – and Cerball had not been able to think of a polite way of asking them to please all go home. It was very heartening to think that his family were rallying round him, of course; Cerball admitted to being very heartened indeed. The trouble was that there were so many of them. At the last count, there had been forty-five people sitting down to a light midday repast (which had still taken two hours to consume and consisted of five courses), and there would have been more than that if several cousins on the distaff side had not become so involved in a new idea to reach Theo and Echbel that they had forgotten the time and missed the meal altogether. Cerball began to wake up at the unreasonable hour of the First Dawn Song, with a steady parade of mounting bills for food, wine, table-linen, firewood, and laundry marching past his eyes. He felt it tactless, as well, of a young cousin of Rumour's to start a discussion on an increase in Partholon's Pence, which apparently involved an exact head-count of people in your house several times a year. The more people you were found to be housing, the higher your Pence. Cerball listened to this glumly. He had previously been feeling quite warmly disposed to the cousin, whose name was Murmur, and who had large, soulful eyes, but clearly his feelings had been misplaced.

Still, since he must needs continue to extend hospitality towards the entire House of Amaranth for an unspecified time, they had to know about Laigne. It was not something you could hide, or not for very long. Cerball had made the announcement directly after they had all finished eating supper, and had felt sheepish and extremely silly. (He had also had to remember not to look at Murmur while he made his speech, because it could have been distinctly embarrassing in view of certain recent exchanges between them.)

There had been a moment of startled silence, and everyone had glanced at one another uneasily. And then the Mugain had risen to the occasion, and said wasn't this the grandest news, and wouldn't they all drink to the newest scion of their House (which necessitated ordering up three more flagons of best tawnyfire wine to refill everyone's chalice, because you could not be drinking the health of anything in inferior stuff)? Herself said that, in the light of this, they must certainly stay, because hadn't somebody to be supervising the scullery staff? And everyone drank to the health of the unborn Amaranthine, and several people drank to it more than once, which meant yet another round of tawnyfire, and it was all extremely depressing.

Cerball was glad that nobody had made any bawdy remarks (which would have been embarrassing) and that nobody had congratulated him (which would have been inaccurate). He was very glad indeed that it did not seem to have occurred to any of them that the announcement had come sinisterly soon after poorest Laigne's quite dreadful experience at the Gristlen's hands.

It had occurred to every single soul at the table, of course. People had got together as soon as possible, congregating in worried clusters, posting the youngest apprentice sorcerers to keep watch in case Cerball should come along and hear them talking about him. It was probably a good thing that Cerball had not thought for himself that the unborn child might be the Gristlen's.

The Mugains had called a proper, sensible meeting of the older Amaranths in the Tapestry Room, because this was the sort of thing you should do in such an ominous situation. They had drunk some more of the tawnyfire wine, just to help them along, but they had held a responsible and solemn discussion despite this.

The Arca Dubhs had declined to attend the Mugains' meeting, because wasn't Himself of Mugain always taking the running of the entire clan on his shoulders and him with no more right to do so than the stable cat. The Arca Dubhs had long since thought that their own branch had the better claim to the Porphyry Throne, and in fact had expended a great deal of time and energy grooming Iarbonel Soothsayer for the Ritual at the Well. It had been extremely annoying when their plans had been spoiled. They commandeered the winter dining-hall, which meant they could quite openly order up a bit of a noonday banquet just to help them think, and told one another that if Laigne, poor soul, was to give birth to the Gristlen's son, it would be a very good reason to depose Cerball's branch of the family. You could not be having that sort of creature born into Ireland's Royal Sorcery House. They became quite animated, and drew up plans for taking over the Porphyry Palace and manning the battlements, and sending Cerball and Laigne into exile.

Bodb Decht and several cousins held a learned and scholarly meeting in Nechtan's manuscript room, where they became sidetracked from their original purpose by the discovery on one of the dustier shelves of a hitherto unknown spell of Nechtan's composing, about infiltrating the barracks of the Dark Lords' armies, Almhuin itself.

Several ladies, under the aegis of Great-aunt Fuamnach, got together in Laigne's still-room under pretext of brewing some soothing potions, but in reality picked over the more sanguine details of what might occur at the birth. Poor Laigne had never been strong to begin with, of course (that very undesirable strain of Human blood!), and she was certainly not as young as she had once been. They brewed up one or two infusions of camomile tea and some mugwort broth, and enjoyed themselves hugely.

And while the Mugains had done a good deal of table-thumping (which had made the wine flagons jump and dance), and the Arca Dubhs had spilt mushroom soup on the best table-linen and eaten the last of the pressed duck; while Great-aunt Fuamnach's coterie had clashed with Bodb Decht's scholars over who should have the use of the *Book of Medicinal Herbs and Potions Gathered at the Dark Midnight*, in the end they had all come to pretty much the same conclusion.

'We cannot be sure that the – ah – child has anything to do with the Gristlen,' said the Mugain rather portentously, when they all gathered in the banqueting hall, with sentries posted at both ends again. 'It is highly probable that it will be a true Amaranth, a son or daughter of Cerball and Laigne. Cerball thinks so, anyway,' he said firmly.

It was unfortunate that Murmur should choose that precise moment to giggle; the Mugains both glared and thought, couldn't you trust any close relation of Rumour to be frivolous and silly at a serious meeting? Murmur drew breath to say that it was extremely unlikely that Laigne's unborn child had anything to do with Cerball, since she had what was virtually incontrovertible proof that Cerball (even under the most encouraging of circumstances), could not raise his flag much above half-mast. This was the kind of thing that her Cousin Rumour would have said, but Murmur, who had not yet Rumour's panache (but was working on it), looked round at the company, and doubted her ability to carry the thing off. She apologised and relapsed into subdued silence.

'I believe,' said the Mugain, removing his frown from Murmur and tucking his chins into his neck solemnly, 'I believe that it behoves us to keep our suspicions to ourselves, and not put extra anxiety onto Cerball at this difficult time.'

Several people nodded, because hadn't they all been saying this, and the Arca Dubhs sneaked conspiratorial looks at one another, and remembered the very good suggestion of Iarbonel Soothsayer to involve the Black HeartStealers in the plot to overthrow Cerball.

'We'll continue to work on the spinning of spells to reach Theodora and Echbel,' went on the Mugain, who was rather enjoying himself by this time. 'We'll continue to do that, but meantime, what we'll do is, we'll be weaving a few extra bits as a protection against anything *nasty* that might be born.'

Great-aunt Fuamnach wanted to know what kinds of bits of protection Himself had in mind, and the Mugain, who had not visualised anything more definite than a length of Rainbow Light, or maybe conjuring up the Mirror of the Sorceress Reflection, said firmly that they would work something out.

They all gathered for supper that evening, a bit strained and a bit wary, and it was into this strained and wary company that Maelduin, watchful as a cat in the dark, came. He stood for a moment in the doorway to the banqueting hall, amused and curious about this Humanish practice of eating and drinking round a table, the food scents and the fragrance of the wine touching his senses. Hunger and thirst. A need for the companionship of their own kind. Yes, these were things the Humanish found important.

He moved forward at Cerball's bidding, and was made known to the Mugain and his Lady, and to several of the younger sorcerers. When asked his name, he replied, 'I am called Maelduin,' and heard his voice fall on the air with a faint silvery tone. He looked at them to see if they had detected any strangeness, but although Great-aunt Fuamnach looked at him sharply, and the Mugain paused in the act of replenishing wine chalices, no one appeared to find anything unusual. Cerball, who seemed to be some kind of Elder, said he was very welcome; there was always a place at their table for a traveller, and a bed for the night to follow.

This was entirely keeping with what Maelduin knew of Humanish, and particularly of the Amaranths. They enjoyed the company of people not from their own territories; they liked to hear about other ways of life. Presently they would ask him, with perfect courtesy, where he had come from and what his journey's end was. There were a number of replies to this; some truthful, some not. He would wait to see if the Amaranths were likely to be of any use to his quest, and also, whether he thought they could be trusted.

He sat at the table, watching to see how they ate, interested in the instruments they used for eating, copying them with the oddly fashioned silver implements laid out for his use.

The food was unfamiliar but very good. Maelduin, fastidious by nature, perceptive and receptive, precise and delicate in his movements, found it surprisingly easy to segment pieces of meat with the silver utensils, to scoop up portions of sauce, and then to sip at the wine placed next to his hand. The food was brought by servants; Maelduin, unused to such a concept, found this intriguing. Was this all they did? How did the Amaranths secure their subservience? Were they in some way a slightly lower form of Humanish? The *sidh* had known that the Humanish world had grades, levels, so that some were richer and better housed than others. But how was it decided? Was it just luck?

He looked round the great banqueting chamber, interested to see how the Amaranths arranged their possessions and embellished their rooms. There were wall-hangings – a bit stifling, but interesting – and standing against the walls were massive wooden frames, on which were placed tureens of soup and platters of meat and fish and bread. The rich reds and vivid blues of the walls were oppressive to one used to the cool ice-fires of Tiarna; the floor was covered here and there with very beautiful silk, the colours glowing and vivid. And they had a rather attractive way of making light: positioning small burning twists of wood or perhaps wax in silver holders on the walls. The tiny flames burned up, casting a soft radiance over the assembled company. Maelduin found this beautiful and intriguing.

He listened to them carefully, hearing how they addressed remarks to one another, and then interposed comments of their own. A kind of tossing to and fro of speech, as if it were a game. If he half closed his eyes, he could see, very faintly, the glistening threads of their discourse, twining and spinning, touching first one of them and then another, occasionally rolling up into a huge silver globe, being thrown to someone else, and

195

then unravelling again. He found it rather endearing that they should share their thoughts and their feelings in this way. Was it something he could do?

When Cerball, turning to this unexpected, rather unusual-looking guest at his table, said, 'And may we know whence you come, Maelduin?' Maelduin said, choosing his words with care:

'I must carry out a quest for my family who have suffered grave illness.' And thought: I believe that is ordinary and acceptable.

It was ordinary and entirely acceptable to everyone. The Amaranths were used to people engaged on quests and pilgrimages and crusades. It was not considered to be in the best of good taste to ask for details of the quest or the pilgrimage, unless of course the traveller proffered the details voluntarily. Then it was usually very interesting, and everyone listened and asked questions and sometimes offered advice. Rumour, in fact, had woven a whole series of enchantments simply from listening to travellers' tales; she had called them the Tapestry Enchantments, and when they were invoked, each one was in the form of a huge, glittering tapestry which Rumour could unroll and spread at people's feet like a vivid carpet.

But the young man called Maelduin, with his brilliant turquoise eyes and hair like a cap of molten silver, did not say very much about his quest. He was quiet and appeared interested in his hosts, and although he was not like anyone they had ever seen before, most of them were used to the heterogeny of people who came to the Porphyry Palace, or to the smaller castles of the rest of them. Hospitality to all comers was an Amaranth tradition.

Great-aunt Fuamnach murmured to Bodb Decht that the boy had not the look of a pure-bred Human, and Bodb Decht, who was still engrossed in the newly discovered spell to infiltrate Almhuin, looked round and said, 'I daresay he isn't entirely Human. A great many people in Ireland aren't.'

Cerball, slightly puzzled by Maelduin, saw that he was listening to the various conversations that were going on round the table, his head tilted, almost as if he might be hearing their voices at a different level. Cerball thought: I hope we are not being infiltrated by something from the Dark Realm, and knew a stab of panic. Surely there were no more horrors for them to meet? Surely they had their share at present?

Maelduin was beginning to enjoy himself. He found the Amaranths attractive and interesting, and he found their way of life intriguing. He had seen at once that each of them possessed the ancient vein of Amaranth blood, the strange, mystical, flame-like power of Ireland's true sorcerers, and he had seen that some possessed it in greater quantity than others. The Arca Dubhs caused him some disquiet, for he had seen at once the black stirring that was fermenting within them. He studied them, thinking there was something there that threatened the others, and that it would be a pity if these charming creatures were thrown into disruption or civil war. But it was nothing to do with him; he was here purely to find out if he could reach the Cadence, and then to embark on his search for the Gristlen and the *sidh*'s lost music.

He was not aware that he was being inspected with strong interest, or that several of the ladies, particularly Murmur, were eyeing him with anticipatory delight. One or two felt the brilliant narrow eyes rest on her for a moment, and felt in that moment a bolt of such shattering light that it was necessary to look away instantly. A sorcerer? But he was not anyone that any of them had ever heard of. Like Cerball, they began to wonder about this exotic, beautiful young man who was most certainly not entirely Human.

Maelduin retired to the bedchamber allotted him, and regarded his surroundings with a faint air of amused curiosity. So this was how they slept when they rested; this was how they lay down, covering themselves with lengths of silk and velvet and fur. He stroked the bed-coverings, finding them soft and sensuous to his touch, and then turned to examine the ewers of hot scented water put out for him (servants again!), and the thick, thirsty towels, and the silver combs and brushes. In the oval mirror, he could see his reflection more clearly than he had done in Tiarna's silver walls; his eyes were smoky in the candlelight, and his hair was so pale as to be nearly colourless. He studied his reflection, and thought that, in a world where a goodly number of creatures were not entirely Humanish, he passed as well as any. If there was a difference, it was in his eyes and his long-fingered, slender, sensitive hands.

He plunged them into the warm water, and then splashed his face, liking the freshness it gave him, intrigued by the idea of lying down in the great deep bed, seeing the nightfall of the Humanish, and then the thin, beautiful dawnlight.

He undressed only partially, for he was still not entirely accustomed to this habit of discarding certain clothes at certain times, and donning others for different occasions. The bed, as he had thought, was soft and comfortable and warm. Did they lie beneath the coverings or on top of them? He tried both, and found it was warmer and more comforting to lie beneath. Humanish luxury. Someone had lit a fire in the hearth, which he had believed he would dislike, but which was actually rather pleasant. He could lie and watch the flames wash the walls with vivid colour.

He was not exactly falling asleep, for he would have said that sleep was not a thing he understood. But he was very close to it, for it had been a long and arduous journey, and he was still finding the fleshly cloak and the ivory bones awkward and unfamiliar.

He was totally unprepared for the tap on his door, and the sound of the door being pushed open. There was a drift of feminine fragrance, and the sensuous sound of silk brushing the floor.

Murmur had dressed – rather say undressed, she thought with a grin – very carefully for this really rather daring adventure. At times, you had to take what you wanted, and at times you had to risk a rebuff. Rumour had taught Murmur this, although it was difficult to imagine anyone ever rebuffing Rumour, who was the most dazzling creature Murmur had ever seen.

The exotic young traveller called Maelduin was fascinating. Murmur had sat quite quietly during supper, not really listening to the conversation, certainly trying to avoid Cousin Cerball's eye. Cousin Cerball, nasty old man, had subjected her to a bout of rather embarrassing fumbling in the library, and Murmur, who believed you should find out all you could about these things, had actually felt a bit cheapened by Cerball's puffing exertions. She had allowed him to stroke her breasts and her thighs, and had even slid her hands obligingly into his breeches. It had been really quite insulting to discover that his manhood was barely aroused, and that even Murmur's attentions could not arouse it any more. In the end, the whole thing was reduced to a middle-aged sorcerer, a bit stout, standing with his breeches round his ankles, sweatily trying to get himself into the necessary physical condition. It had all been very embarrassing, and Murmur thought it served her right for being so vulgarly curious.

Maelduin was different. He was so different that Murmur had barely been able to take her eyes off him. He had looked across at her just once, his eyes seeming to see straight into her mind, and Murmur had experienced a bolt of longing so intense that she had thought she might faint. But he had looked away then, and continued his rather quiet discourse with the others.

But you have to take what you want, my dear, and risk the occasional rebuff... Murmur could hear Rumour saying the words.

And so, following her cousin's excellent example, Murmur had perfumed her small, feline body, and rubbed aphrodisiacal ointments everywhere, and had brushed her hair until it shone. She slid into a thin wrap of cream-coloured silk with silver embroidery, and tied it loosely, so that it would fall open at the least touch, and thrust her feet into dainty slippers, in which she could tiptoe along the corridor to Maelduin's room.

As she slipped into the room, the silk robe parted a little, showing slender hips and gleaming thighs and pink-tipped breasts. The musky perfumes were heavy on the warm room.

Maelduin regarded his unexpected guest from the bed, and something totally outside of his experience leapt within him. He thought: *seduction*. And by this remarkably lovely Humanish female. He lay back and watched her approach, his eyes raking her body with such cool allure, his lips curving in such a beckoning smile, that Murmur fell a little deeper into his strange, fey bewitchment.

The small core of Maelduin's mind that was still purely *sidh* knew that he was about to be initiated into the Humanish custom of love-making, and he found it amusing that he should be embracing the ways of the Humanish so fully. But alongside the amusement was a deep sensual stirring, a hard warm arousal between his thighs. So this was how it felt. This was how the

Humanish felt when they took their women and laid their plans for love-making and feasting and libation to their gods of love and eroticism.

Murmur dropped the silken wrap to the floor, and stood for a moment looking down at him. Maelduin said, very softly, 'I believe you are well come, madame,' and smiled the beckoning smile again; the smile that said, *Come closer, my dear, and come nearer . . . Let me see you and let me touch you and know you and let me feel you . . .*

He reached out a hand and traced her body, feeling with delight the soft smoothness of skin, and the gentle curve of bone and muscle; feeling, as well, the heat of alien Humanish blood . . . Lovely! thought Maelduin, pleasure and passion flooding his entire body now. Hair and eyes and skin and teeth . . .

Murmur found herself swept into the most remarkable maelstrom of emotions she had ever known. There was a moment when there was nothing but pounding anticipation, the knowledge that he had not rebuffed her; that, so far from rebuffing her, he had welcomed her with his cool, alien beauty and his secret, exciting smile.

And then there was another moment, when something else entered her mind, slyly and insidiously, but so strongly that she felt it happen, as clear as a curse, as definitely as a door opening . . . Fear trickled through her mind and into her body . . .

He was regarding her with amused delight, as if they were about to share something marvellous and secret and entirely wonderful, and she was naked now, standing before him, the warmth of the room and the rising heat of her body making the musky fragrances stir. The fear receded, and in its place was only the purest, most undiluted delight, and with it exultation. Rumour was right! There are times when you have to reach out and take the things you want!

And then he reached for her, and Murmur arched her back with pleasure, half closing her eyes, waiting for the ecstasy, more ready for his touch than she had ever been for any other lover. His touch, when it came, was gentle and strong; his hands were exciting and silky and it was going to be the most exhilarating thing she had ever known . . . But as Maelduin

200

caressed her body, his hands pouring over her skin like thin water, she felt again the flicker of fear.

His hands were soft and silky, but Murmur opened her eyes startled, because there was the sudden feeling of a creature in the bed who did not possess ordinary Human blood, and who was cool and shining and alien. A half-forgotten memory stirred in her mind, that of strange half-Human beings who lured victims into their arms and so to their deaths, using cold, sly bewitchments, and she thought: But he did not seek me out! He did not beckon to me! I came here of my own accord! A tiny treacherous voice said: oh, but did you? Can you be sure? Can you be sure that the beckoning was not so subtle, so *practised* that you did not even feel it?

I am sure! cried Murmur silently, but the fear swam a little nearer, and the throbbing desire lessened.

He was pulling her down beside him, his skin against hers, his eyes brilliant with passion, and surely it was all right, surely there was nothing to be afraid of . . .

But they were together in the deep soft bed, and his body felt light and supple, and in some curious way weightless, so that you could visualise him as a soaring creature of light and speed, not needing, not wanting Human limbs and Human strength and muscle and bone . . . able to pour effortlessly through the skies and the seas and the worlds . . .

He was covering her with his body now, and yes! he was very nearly weightless, there was no sense of heavy masculinity, there was only slender, glinting strength, the flare of brilliant aquamarine eyes with, deep behind them, iridescent colours . . .

But his hands were like ivory and his skin was like silk, and her senses were spinning into such strange and dangerous rapture that she no longer knew whether to cry with fear or with passion . . .

She felt him part her thighs easily and smoothly, and of course it was all right, of course this was no cold sinister being from some eerily beautiful race . . . Passion rose again, so that she pulled him closer, unable to bear it any longer, wanting to feel the hard masculine strength, wanting to explore this faintly menacing feeling, wanting to know more of this remarkable intoxication.

Maelduin's mind was soaring into wild delight, and his body

was spinning with ecstasy. Exhilaration engulfed him, and deep within it, the small *sidh* vein of amusement was saying, wasn't it easy, wasn't it the easiest thing in all the worlds, smooth and seamless, a silken melding of their bodies, a marvellous, magical uniting.

Ecstasy rocketed upwards, and with it the urgency of need, a pulsating throbbing that he would not be able to bear much longer . . .

He slid easily and smoothly into her body, feeling at once the extraordinary Humanish heat, flinching briefly, and then, swept along by the soaring delight, unable to control his wild desire.

Murmur's mind was in chaos; she was tumbling helplessly from passion to fear and then back to passion. She felt the icy coldness as Maelduin penetrated her, and gasped because he was cold, he was colder than any living soul, and it was as if he had thrust a glinting frozen spear into her body . . .

She cried out, feeling icy fluid like frosted milk already beginning to fill her, and Maelduin, hearing her pain but beyond control, made a convulsive movement and felt, in a terrible searing ice-blue sheet of agony, the cold seed flow from him and flood the warm, Humanish blood.

Chapter Nineteen

Cerball and the Mugain, Bodb Decht and Iarbonel Soothsayer sat behind the great purple and silver desk which had been Nechtan's, and looked at the slender, brilliant-eyed young man before them.

Cerball had said, and the Mugain had agreed, that there should be just this small private inquiry. Murmur's death in Maelduin's bed had stunned the entire Palace, although Great-aunt Fuamnach remarked that she had always said that Murmur would come to a bad end. She did not say it with very much force, however, because she had rather liked Murmur – naughty, frivolous child, who might have no more moral sense than her Cousin Rumour, but who could usually be relied on to lend a sympathetic ear to a friend in trouble, or come up with a light-hearted remark if you were a bit low.

They had all liked Murmur. Charm, said the Mugain dolefully, that was the thing. There was nothing quite like it, and Murmur, poor, dear child, had possessed it in great measure; well, didn't all Rumour's side of the family possess it? There would be a fine old sending off, the Mugain made no doubt of that. Cerball would see to it, of course, and wouldn't they all contribute a bit towards the funerary rituals? To which Cerball, driven nearly to distraction by the thought of another funerary ritual, thought: I hope you *will*!

They had decided that they would talk sensibly and quietly to Maelduin to find out what had happened. The Mugain had said that to be sure they did not want to be knowing the *exact* details; Murmur's relationships were her own affair, and no doubt so were Maelduin's. Cerball thought, but did not say, that you might almost call it an abuse of hospitality when a guest was welcomed into your home, given one of the nicest bedchambers (a south-facing view, it was, and caught the early sun), and then up and seduced your fifth cousin to death, plunging you into yet more unwelcome expense.

They decided that there should be just a representative from each of the main branches of the family to talk to Maelduin and decide what ought to be done. Nothing official. There might be a very good explanation for Murmur's death. As to the representatives, well, there would be Cerball himself and the Mugain on behalf of all the other Mugains; they would include Bodb Decht, who would speak for what were usually called the Scholars. They had hesitated a bit about inviting Iarbonel Soothsayer, because it was a moot point as to what standing the Arca Dubhs had in the family.

'They haven't any,' said Great-aunt Fuamnach, who thought she should have been included and was a bit waspish as a result. 'They haven't any standing at all. There's nothing but rubbish on that side of the family. I'm surprised Cerball considers it.'

But Cerball had had to consider it, because there was the very worrying fact that the Arca Dubhs had recently been seen consorting somewhat furtively with the Black HeartStealers: not once, but several times. Cerball had asked, as politely as possible, if the Black HeartStealers would very kindly return to their homes, but he had received an evasive reply, and the outcome had been that they were all still in the Palace. This was worrying, because they all knew that the Black HeartStealers practised a type of sorcery which was beyond the Codes of the Academy of Sorcerers, and there had been some rather sinister marriages. Great-aunt Fuamnach said that Iarbonel Soothsayer's grandmother had actually borne twins to a necromancer, and that the family trafficked with the Dark Realm, but this might have been an exaggeration. The Mugain and Bodb Decht were trying to keep watch on the Black HeartStealers' activities in case of anything really nasty, such as out-and-out necromancy in the Looms Chamber, or a mutiny within the Palace walls, but the trouble was that you could not be watching people every minute of the day.

In the end, they included Iarbonel on the grounds that not to do so might seriously upset the Arca Dubhs and provoke real rebellion, which was the last thing that was needed just now.

Maelduin, called to stand before the great Desk of Sorcery

that Nechtan had coaxed out of the hands of one of the High Kings, ought to have been subservient. His stance, facing them all, should certainly have been that of a supplicant, but he was neither supplicating nor subservient. His eyes glowed, and his head was tilted arrogantly, as if it was the Amaranths who were called to account, and Maelduin who was interrogating them. Cerball, unsure as to how they should deal with all this anyway, found himself thinking that surely the boy ought to be showing some remorse.

Maelduin said at once, 'I feel more remorse than you can know, Cerball,' and Cerball thought crossly that the careless use of his name was all of a piece with the rest of this strange creature.

'Should I then call you "my lord"?' said Maelduin, picking this up at once, but speaking in a voice that said, quite plainly, he had no intention of using such a form of address.

The Mugain, scenting antagonism, said, 'I think it is immaterial what anyone calls anyone. That is not what we are here to discuss.' And frowned at Maelduin with the expression that generally caused lesser members of his house to blench.

Maelduin did not blench. He said, 'I offer you my extreme regrets for the death of your . . .' and hesitated, searching for the right term. 'Of your sister,' he said. Was that the right word? 'I had not intended harm.'

'Yes, but look here, young man, she didn't just die of no accord!' said Cerball. 'You must have done something!' He caught the flicker of a prurient grin from Iarbonel Soothsayer, and thought that matters had come to something when you could not make an ill-worded remark without your own kith and kin smirking offensively.

'Murmur came to my bedchamber unasked,' said Maelduin, and the Mugain looked very shocked, because such a statement was outside the code of politeness about seductions. The Mugain would not have dreamed of telling people that a young, attractive lady had visited his bedchamber unasked, even if it had happened, which unfortunately it had not. He shook his head and wondered where such behaviour would end, while Iarbonel Soothsayer made a note on the vellum-bound book he had brought, in which he was listing all the things they would use when they threw Cerball and the others into exile.

Bodb Decht said firmly, 'Could we at least know how Murmur died?' and regarded Maelduin.

Maelduin returned the look unblinkingly, and at length said, 'I do not know myself.' And then, as Cerball drew breath, he said, 'But I believe it is because she lay with one who is not Humanish.' And then, as they stared at him, he said, 'If I had known it would happen, I should not have permitted it. That would not have been in accordance with my creed.'

There was silence. None of the four Amaranths knew quite what to say to this. At length, Cerball, choosing his words with care, said, 'You're telling us you are not Human?'

'Of course I am not Human,' said Maelduin. 'Neither are you.'

Cerball thought this was nothing to do with the matter, and the Mugain began to tell how the Amaranths had started out as pure-Human, and how it had only been with the advent of the Dawn Sorcerers that they had been given the Sacred Flame of Sorcery, but Cerball and Bodb Decht squashed this hurriedly, because once you got the Mugain off on the exact balance of Human blood against sorcerous he was apt to get carried away.

In any case, said Cerball, weren't there any number of people who had their blood mingled with other species, and how would Tara itself survive if it had to be inhabited by Humans?

'It will be one day,' said Iarbonel, putting on the rather distant look he kept for prophecies. 'At some far-away time, the Humans will take Tara. And then the Curse of Tara will—'

The Mugain said be bothered and be blowed to the Curse of Tara, because didn't they all of them know that it would one day overtake them, it could not be kept at bay for ever, but so long as it happened after he, the Mugain, had departed to the Place Beneath the Ocean Roof, he did not much care.

'To return to this matter of Human blood,' began Bodb Decht, and looked inquiringly at Maelduin, who said in his cool, silver voice:

'I have no Humanish blood in me at all.' And regarded them, his narrow eyes piercingly brilliant.

Bodb Decht, staring, said, quite suddenly, 'You're a *sidh*.'

'Yes.'

'How—'

'I am the Crown Prince,' said Maelduin, and now the

arrogance was unmistakable. 'I am the son of Aillen mac Midha, and the heir to Tiarna and the underwater Palace of the Nimfeach.' He looked at them with the slant-eyed look that quite clearly said: and since in my world I bow my head to no creature, I do not intend to do so here. Cerball experienced a sudden compulsion to kneel before this eerily beautiful, imperious creature.

Bodb Decht, staring at Maelduin in complete fascination, said, 'It's your eyes. I once saw a cave drawing of one of your people, and there were long turquoise eyes depicted by some kind of gemstone – I don't remember what exactly. But there was the same look: like the western oceans with the sun glinting on them.' He studied Maelduin. 'And your voice is different. Cooler.'

Maelduin said, 'So that is how you knew.' He regarded Bodb Decht. 'Then our sorcery is not quite as perfect as we had believed,' he said. 'I had hoped to be unchallenged.'

'Why are you here?' said Cerball.

'Because our world was invaded by a being who had been chained in the Pit of the Dark Lords—'

'The Gristlen?'

'Yes. So you know of it also.'

'It has been here,' said Bodb Decht.

'And will again,' said Iarbonel Soothsayer, shaking his head.

'It came to our world,' said Maelduin, and now the brilliant eyes were misty with pain. 'And it stole the one thing that we cherished and valued; the thing that was our life-blood.'

'The music,' said Bodb Decht, very softly.

'Yes.' Maelduin regarded them again. 'And so I have submitted to the Ancient Enchantment so that I may walk in your world and recover the music. I have donned the Cloak of Humanish Skin.'

The Mugain said slowly, 'Your people frequently hunt ours for sport and slaughter. Even if we believe you, we cannot trust you.'

Maelduin lifted one shoulder, as if to say: trust me or not and believe me or not, just as you choose, and the Amaranths looked uneasily at one another, each of them thinking: ought we to tell him? Ought we to tell him how the Gristlen brought it here, and how Rumour and the monk Andrew took it with them to help them to reach the Dark Realm and Theodora?

Maelduin said, in his soft, beautiful voice, 'So that is what happened. I see.'

'You hear our thoughts?' This was the Mugain.

'Yes. If your thoughts are near to the surface, I hear them clearly. Although it is forbidden most strictly to pry beneath that surface.'

Cerball said, cautiously, 'You possess the Samhailt?'

'A form of it,' said Maelduin, tranquilly. 'Although for your people I think the Samhailt is almost lost. You have misused it and sometimes you have abused it, and it has become frayed and worn, almost to extinction. You rely on your Humanish speech. Perhaps that is why you lost the Cadence.' He frowned, and said, quite suddenly, 'So the music was here but is here no longer. I have missed it. I was so near, but it has eluded me.' There was suddenly such pain in his voice that no one dared to speak.

Maelduin appeared to withdraw, as if considering the matter, and then, without warning, the ice-blue fire blazed back into his eyes. 'Your people took the music to penetrate the Black Ireland,' he said, accusingly, and his stare was so piercing that the Amaranths shifted uncomfortably in their seats.

Cerball said, 'They intend to return it to Tiarna,' and was annoyed to find a note of self-deprecation creeping into his voice. 'After they have managed to find Theodora,' he said.

'Theodora?'

'Well, she's—'

'She is your heir,' said Maelduin, suddenly, looking at Cerball as if he thought him a fool. 'And – she is in the hands of the Lord of Chaos?'

'Well, yes. You see—'

'But that is extremely serious,' said Maelduin. 'Why did you not summon my people? Why did you not invoke the ancient law that binds us to help you?' And stopped speaking suddenly, because the answer was perfectly clear. 'You did call to us,' he said, staring at them. 'You called and we could not hear you.'

'Well, yes,' said Cerball awkwardly. 'That's what we did. The music—'

'The music had by then been taken,' said Maelduin, half to himself. 'Yes, I see it now.' He looked back up at them, his eyes blazing. 'This is a situation of immense gravity,' he said. 'But you will know that. The Princess is in Chaos's hands. How long has she been his prisoner?'

Cerball found himself apologising again, and explaining that they had not thought of Theodora in that way.

'But she is your House's Ruler,' said Maelduin, impatiently, and Bodb Decht said thoughtfully, 'You know, Chaos himself said something of the same kind. That Theodora was the heir.' He looked at Maelduin with renewed respect.

The Mugain who was still goggling at Maelduin said, 'But she's a child of six—'

'Yes?' said Maelduin, politely.

'There was the Ritual,' said Cerball, frowning. And then, to Maelduin, 'That is the Ritual of the Segais Well.'

'I know of it.'

'But it wasn't finished,' said Cerball, still trying to remember exactly what had happened. 'We didn't complete it because of the Fomoire and the Lord of Chaos . . .' He broke off again, staring at Maelduin. 'Even if the Ritual would have pointed to Theodora—'

'She is your House's Ruler and without it you're dangerously vulnerable,' said Maelduin.

'But a child—'

Cerball said, 'She is only six—'

'That does not matter. Without your Ruler, your House is weakened. Also,' said Maelduin, 'it is possible that they intend to hold the Princess to some kind of ransom.'

'We had not thought of that,' said Bodb Decht, and Cerball did not like to say that *he* had thought of it, but that he had been hoping it would not happen, because he was not sure if there was enough money to pay a ransom.

Maelduin said, 'The music of the *sidh* will be of immense protection to your emissaries, and since the Princess must be reached, I cannot deprive them of it.' He stopped, frowning, and at length he said, 'No, it would be impossible. It would break the ancient law that requires my people to help the Royal Houses of Ireland. I cannot do it. Even if I could reach them, I would not take the one thing that might aid their quest.' There was anger in his voice, and frustration, but when he looked back at them, something shone in his eyes. 'But there is the Cadence,' he said, softly, and felt their start of surprise with amusement. Had they not expected him to refer to the Cadence?

The Mugain said defensively, 'What about the Cadence?' and Maelduin grinned inwardly. But he said, politely, 'It is here. My father made your House a gift of it.'

Maelduin was bitterly disappointed at finding the music beyond his reach, but he had seen what he thought might be another way to save his people. He was beginning to enjoy the Amaranths' discomfiture; clearly they were rather ashamed of having lost the Cadence, and equally clearly they had been intending on keeping its loss a huge secret. He leaned back in his chair and crossed his arms and waited to see what they would do.

'Well,' began Cerball. 'The thing is—'

'Unfortunately,' put in the Mugain, 'we no longer—'

'That you lost it is known to us,' said Maelduin, impatient and suddenly losing interest in the game. 'You lost it, but you lost only the understanding of it. It is still here.'

'Is it?' Cerball looked to Bodb Decht for guidance, and Bodb Decht said slowly:

'It must be. Yes, of course, it must be.' He turned back to Maelduin. 'Within the Cadence Tower, would it be? Yes, for Nechtan wove it into the walls and into the substance and the fabric of the place. It was then that it became lost to us.'

Maelduin, listening and watching, thought: so it is nearer even than I hoped! Good! But he said in his cool, silvery voice, 'Would you permit me to revive it?'

'Well, it—'

'If it is truly there, it can be revived. And it is the matrix spell, the core. Inside Tiarna we use a version of it in our spells, but it is – I think you would say – a pale copy. The genesis enchantment would be quite immensely powerful...' He leaned forward, suddenly and endearingly youthful. 'If you would permit me to try, you would find that I would be no trouble to you. I am accustomed to long hours of study. And if you would prefer that I do not eat at your table and sleep beneath your roof, I can fend for myself.' A sudden mischievous grin. 'I am accustomed to fending for myself,' he said. 'But if I could revive the Cadence, the true, original heartspell, perhaps I could use it to save my people.'

The Mugain, who had the feeling that things were slipping

from their control, said, 'Well I don't think there could be any objection to that, of course. And I daresay that one more mouth at table, and one more bedchamber to be prepared makes little difference.'

He looked to Cerball for confirmation of this, and Cerball at once said, 'Oh, no difference in the world.' And supposed he might as well be made bankrupt this year as next.

'But,' said the Mugain firmly, 'we have not resolved the matter of Murmur,' and Iarbonel said nor they had, and oughtn't there to be some kind of reparation made.

'The High King Erin,' he said cunningly, 'once made a law in this country that the punishment given for an offence must fit that offence very exactly.'

'Well, what do you suggest in this case?' demanded the Mugain, who was beginning to think they should never have included Iarbonel, silly old fool. 'We can hardly arrange for the boy to be shafted to death – dear me, I beg your pardon . . .'

Maelduin, suppressing the amusement he was feeling at the way the Humanish squabbled, said smoothly, 'When I have refound the Cadence and restored it, and when I have set in action the means to save my people, you should pronounce sentence on me for Murmur's death in accordance with your laws.'

'How can we trust you not to run away while we aren't looking?'

'You have my word on it,' said Maelduin, raising his brows at Cerball in surprise, and, as Cerball was to say afterwards, there was such frosty hauteur in the look, that you found yourself believing the boy – and even trusting him.

'It may be,' said Maelduin, 'that in your House's present turmoil, there will be a service I can render. Perhaps a danger will threaten which I can help you to avert at some cost to myself. That I would consider a just penance. To risk my life to help your House, and to avenge the death of the Lady who died in my arms.' He looked across at Iarbonel Soothsayer, and said, with silken courtesy, 'Your High King Erin would have considered that just.'

'Would he? How do you know he would?' demanded Iarbonel suspiciously.

'My father once had the great pleasure of meeting him and

211

speaking with him,' said Maelduin with immaculate politeness; and the Mugain whispered gleefully to Cerball that *that* should show Iarbonel Soothsayer where he stood in the pecking order, silly old fool!

Iarbonel Soothsayer, who was not going to be squashed by this cold-eyed upstart, said sepulchrally that he could foresee a danger.

'You always can,' said the Mugain.

'A journey,' said Iarbonel, portentously. 'An exile.'

Maelduin looked at Cerball very intently. 'This is so?' he said. 'One of your people wishes to embrace exile?' Cerball thought he said this as if he found it entirely natural, and as if a self-imposed exile was not in the least unusual.

He said, 'It was something that occurred to me; I had not discussed it with the others . . .' He stopped and frowned, and then said, firmly, 'The creature called the Gristlen assaulted one of the Ladies, and it is possible that a child will be born as a result.' And thought that this explained it as neatly as anything could. He did not see the look the others exchanged, which said quite clearly: so he *did* know!

'And – you would wish to exile the child?' said Maelduin. 'If it should bear the mark of the Gristlen, you would wish it to be imprisoned? Cast into some dungeon where it could not trouble you?'

Cerball said, 'That is putting it rather starkly . . .'

'What else would you do with it? If it is in truth the spawn of a Gristlen, you could not kill it, for it would possess necromantic blood. It would be difficult to kill it.' He looked at them, waiting, his head tilted to one side. Cerball looked at the others and saw that they were watching him closely. He thought: they knew it may be a son of the Gristlen that Laigne carries! Of course they knew! But he clutched at the remnants of his dignity, and said firmly, 'Yes, that is what I . . . what we would wish.'

Maelduin said, 'I understand.' And looked at them and thought that, if the Gristlen had indeed left its pawmarks on an Amaranthine lady, the results could be horrifying in the extreme. Had they any concept of what such a child might be? He thought: I have injured them by the death of the one called Murmur, and I should make reparation. He did not fully understand death, but he knew that it was something that the Humanish regarded with extreme awe. If a Humanish caused a death, reparation had to be made. Supposing he offered to cage the Gristlen's creature when it was born? It would fit with their laws, it would gain more of their trust. And the further they trusted him, the more he could use them.

Aloud, he said, 'If you consider it fitting: firstly, I will work to find the Lost Language of Cadence, not only to save my people, but to re-present it to yours.' Were they accepting this? He listened with the level of his mind that was above speech and beyond words. Yes. They had been ashamed of losing the Cadence, and they were ready to be grateful to him for restoring it. Good! He had judged them accurately.

'It will take some time, I think,' said Maelduin, softly. 'I have not your measuring of time, but I think you would say . . . many weeks.' His eyes held Cerball's unblinkingly like a cat's. 'If your lady is in truth to bear the fruit of the Gristlen's seed, then that fruit could be more horrendous and more monstrous than anything your Humanish minds can encompass. You will know that the creatures who become Gristlens were once necromancers in their own right?'

'Yes.'

'They are outcasts,' said Maelduin, very seriously. 'Evil, warped beings who had offended the Dark Lords. They are called, and rightly, the damned of the Dark Realm. Many of them carry the taint of old and evil lineages: there is goblin blood in many of them, and giantish blood also. Some of them are descended from the terrible Northern Houses of necromancers.' He studied them. 'If the House of Amaranth is about to witness the birth of the seed of such a one, you're in very great danger. The creature will assuredly have to be caged and bound.' He paused. 'I will do that for you,' he said. 'I will take the child to the strongest of all Ireland's many strongholds, and to the blackest and most remote of all the many fortresses.'

There was a silence, and then Bodb Decht said in a horrified voice, 'The Grail Castle?'

'The Grail Castle,' said Maelduin, grimly. 'It is sited in the loneliest part of all Ireland, and it is surrounded by thick stone keeps and guarded by iron yetts and jagged-toothed portcullises. There is nowhere else in Ireland where the walls are so thick, the dungeons so deep, and the bars so strong.'

'How do you now so much about it?' asked Iarbonel Soothsayer suspiciously. 'It is said that no living creature ever returns from journeying to the Grail Castle.'

'My father has journeyed there and returned,' said Maelduin.

'But,' said the Mugain, quite as horrified as Bodb Decht, 'my dear young man, to attempt that journey is almost certain death. Iarbonel is right; no living creature has ever returned from the Grail Castle.'

'I am aware of it. But I pledge to you that I will do it. If a monster-child, a spawn of the Gristlen, is born, I will carry it along the dark road that is said to end in the Grail Castle, and I will cause it to be caged and imprisoned in the deepest of all the deep dungeons so that it can never escape.'

He looked at them all, his eyes blazing. 'Even if I forfeit my life in the process,' he said.

Chapter Twenty

Laigne had become accustomed to being left by herself for long stretches at a time. It was all of a piece with their treatment of her; she no longer expected anything better. It was heartless of them to say she must join in the life of the Palace, emerge from her bedchamber. They did not understand. They did not know that she was becoming engrossed in the creature growing inside her: the Fisher King's son.

The memory of him was still with her. Not the poor, piteous Gristlen thing the curse had made of him, but the strong, powerful Sea Prince with his pale, compelling eyes and his extraordinary dominance. The remarkable sleek being who had called to her and whose embrace she had suffered to dissolve the ancient curse. She no longer saw it as a suffering, but an honour and a privilege. And he had chosen her to bear his son, he had chosen her out of them all to receive his seed and give birth to his spawn. It was something to hug to herself, something to enjoy in deep, dark secrecy. It was something to gloat over. The Chosen One . . .

Cerball visited her and he was dutiful and kindly and well-meaning, but he was dull and plodding as he had always been dull and plodding. He tried to talk about the pain and the ugliness of the Gristlen's attack, never once guessing that the pain had been fleeting, and the ugliness had given way to the shining creature of the ancient legend. He did not know, and Laigne was not going to tell him.

The others had talked uneasily of finding a spell to free her; if she harboured the Gristlen's fearsome seed, they said, it ought to be dispersed. It ought to be killed before it could live, even though the killing of an unborn creature was a risky business, they added worriedly. Even when you used sorcery it was risky.

215

'Especially when you use sorcery,' said Great-aunt Fuamnach tartly.

Laigne thought vaguely that it said a good deal about their opinion of Cerball that they had all jumped to the same conclusion. And of course they would be fearful of the Gristlen's spawn. But she would not tell them that she would never let this child go; she would birth it even if they subjected her to torture of the most extreme kind. It was *his* child – Coelacanth's – and he would return for her and for it; she knew it quite surely and quite definitely.

She did not let any of them suspect the true identity of the Gristlen because it was nothing to do with any of them. She remained in her bedchamber, lying on her bed most of the time, dreaming of the child, watching the days slide past, waiting for the Fisher King's return.

Her body thickened and became swollen and gross, and she began to suffer odd, slithering pains, as if the child within were moving in an unnatural fashion. She clasped her hands to her body when that happened, trying to hear it, feeling the child circling in exactly the way a forest beast circled when it was making a nest or a lair ... Coelacanth's spawn circling within her womb, moving and sniffing to find its way out into the world ...

After a time, it became possible to shut the others out completely; to lie quietly on the bed, but to withdraw the real part – the small central core that was her real self – into a dark, safe cave.

She thought that the cave had been there for a little while, almost as if somebody (something?) had prepared it. It was faintly disturbing to think of a 'something' preparing a dark cave for her; but then people could not get at you if you lived deep in a cave. They could call in things to you, and sometimes you heard and sometimes you did not; they could leave food at the mouth of the cave, which you did not need to eat if you did not want to. The cave was safe and dark; she could stay in it for as long as she liked. Perhaps she would never come out. She retreated into it, liking the dry darkness closing about her. She need never bother with the absurd people of the Palace again.

The strange creature whom they had told her was attempting

216

to revive the Cadence came sometimes. He did not say very much; he stood at the opening to her cave and watched her. Laigne wanted to ignore him, but he was more difficult to ignore than the others. She could not work out why this should be, and it puzzled her. But she always looked up at him, by this time so deep in the grip of the dark insanity that was creeping over her, that she saw Maelduin framed in the cave's mouth with the light behind him, a clear, silhouetted figure.

He upset her. He seemed to know things and to see things that the others could not: the memories of Echbel, for instance, over which she brooded sometimes and which she had so painstakingly buried in the floor of her cave so that no one else should share them. That night in the Gristlen's cell. The circling child inside her. Once, she even thought he had known about that wild, dizzying pleasure from the Fisher King's body; that deep, scalding wash of delight.

It was all plainly absurd but, just to be sure, Laigne scuttled further back into the safeness of the dark, and began to bury the treacherous pleasure, scrabbling at the hard-packed earth with her hands until a cache had been scooped out; laying the memory in the earth until she should want to dig it up again. It should be a twice-buried thing, and it should be buried so deeply that no one would ever know it had existed.

Maelduin found the sight of Laigne unexpectedly distressing. She was so plainly in the grip of a dark madness, and he had the feeling that she was retreating into some sinister shadowland. And then he thought: retreating? *Or being pulled?*

Darkness worried him. Even the suggestion of it was almost like a physical pain, lancing through that part of him that was still pure *sidh*. He felt it surrounding Laigne, swallowing her, blotting out her mind. At times he could almost see it, stealing slowly and inexorably over her.

By offering himself as gaoler for the Gristlen's spawn, by striking that strange bargain for Murmur's death, Maelduin knew he had taken Laigne's plight on his shoulders. He had almost felt it descend on him physically; a heavy, stifling weight, dark and turgid, shot here and there with dull crimson. He thought he might have been absurdly foolish: what the

Humanish called 'chivalrous', and he knew as well that to journey to the Grail Castle would hamper his real quest, and delay the time when he could return to Tiarna with the means to revive the *sidh*.

But as a Prince of an ancient House, he could have done nothing else. Murmur's death had been his fault and reparation must be made.

It had been an odd experience to feel the life suddenly drain from Murmur. It had been a rather dreadful reminder that the Humanish lived only for a short time. Maelduin had felt no sense of loss for Murmur, but he had felt something. Coldness. Sadness at the briefness of Humanish lifespan. How could you accomplish anything, how could you leave any kind of imprint on your world if you had only a few short decades? And he had shortened it further for the pretty, feckless creature. That he knew to be unforgiveable by the Humanish belief – and perhaps by my own beliefs also, he thought.

A life for a life. The High King Erin had lived by that creed, and Maelduin, living in the Ireland that had once been Erin's, would live by it also.

Even if, said a sly, silvery voice within his mind, even if it means journeying to the terrible Grail Castle and incarcerating the monster-child in its dungeons?

Even if it means that.

He had commenced the task of reviving the Cadence at once, going alone to the Cadence Tower, the fearsome, legend-ridden *Tur Baibeil*, at the time the Humanish called the Purple Hour. The Amaranths had wanted to accompany him; the Mugain and Bodb Decht had wanted him to allow the reciting of the Chaunt of Banishment, and perhaps the Cadenzas of Light. Didn't he know that the Tower was where the Fomoire had found a bridge from the Dark Realm?

Maelduin was not swayed. He knew the legends and he knew the tales. He did not quite say that he would be able to deal with the Fomoire, but he indicated it. To himself, he thought that a single creature slipping through the shadows would be far less likely to attract attention than half the Amaranth clan chanting spells and brandishing torches. It was strange how they spurned solitude, the creatures of this Humanish world. Were they afraid to be alone for any length of time? He remembered again

218

the shortness of their lives, and thought perhaps they clustered together for assurance.

But to Maelduin, born to the near-immortality of the *sidh*, long periods of silence and solitude were very natural indeed. He was well used to lonely towers and dark citadels soaked in sorcery.

But the Cadence Tower gave him pause. He stood in the great cobbled courtyard, with the creeping shadows reaching out purple and black fingers, and stared up at the immense black citadel, and thought: yes, they are right to be afraid of it, and to approach it with the protection of Light and Banishment Rituals. It is steeped in evil and it is soaked in malevolent necromancy. Profane Evil is here, thought Maelduin, his eyes narrowed in concentration. Profane Evil and also Eclectic Evil. Had it leaked through from the Black Ireland? Yes, perhaps.

The darkness was a deep ache in his mind, so that he wanted to put up his hands to shield his eyes from the suffocating, pain-filled blackness. But he stayed where he was, remembering Tiarna, remembering that by reaching the Cadence he might save his people, and presently thread by fragile thread, cobweb by cobweb, he felt the silver and gold filaments of the Cadence, the Lost Language of Magic filter through the darkness. Excitement gripped him, and he thought: yes, I was right! It is here! The ancient sorcerous tongue, the runic language of mysticism and enchantment and magic. The talismanic chronicles of sorcery.

They have lost it for their people, but it is still here! It is still here and I can reach it! he thought. I could recapture it and take it back to Tiarna!

And little by little, their powers – the ancient, flamelike vein of sorcery that they are so proud of – would erode, and the House of Amaranth would die . . .

I could steal the Cadence from them and they would never know.

The smile that was so uncannily not Human curved his lips, and he slipped through the shadows and into the Cadence Tower.

At first, he thought that after all he would not be able to do it. The Cadence – the beautiful, intricate enchantment, woven by the long-ago *nimfeach*, taken by Aillen mac Midha for his

219

people, and polished by them before it was given to the Amaranths – was so deeply buried that it was almost impossible to reach.

Maelduin had gone warily to the central, star-shaped chamber, knowing that this would be the heart and the core and the powerhouse, slipping through the courtyard with the creeping shadows, and through the jagged-toothed gate with the massive iron rings. The Dark Evil had been all about him; he had felt the anger of the sentry spells, left there by the Lord of Chaos and his henchmen; he saw them almost materialise: slithering black creatures, low in intelligence but high in cunning.

But he ignored them. He walked calmly through the dim halls and the ebony satin of the Sable Stair, and stretched his mind to its furthest point, reaching for light, feeling for the silver strands, the elusive mesh of the Cadence. The shadows retreated as the light within his mind touched them, and swift exultation rose in Maelduin's mind. He thought: so it is still there! The cool, elvish light of my people is still within me! I am still my father's son, and while I can still feel the ice-blues and the frost-greens, I am safe. While I feel that, I can still look upon the Humanish as creatures to hunt, creatures to hound for their souls. I can see them for the absurd beings they are!

And then, hard on the heels of that thought came another: but how involved am I becoming with them? Already he had found himself experiencing sadness at Murmur's death, wishing to make reparation.

I dare not! thought Maelduin, his eyes flashing turquoise fire. I must look on these creatures as my prey! I must remember how it feels to chase them and swoop on them and drain their souls! There must be no involvements, no sympathies.

He dared not permit Humanish feelings to seep into his mind, for the more the Humanish garb shaled on to him, the harder it would be to return to his natural state. And I could not bear never to see Tiarna again!

The Cadence Tower was silent and secretive. Maelduin seated himself cross-legged at the centre of the star-shaped room, his eyes glittering turquoise slits, his head tilted, as if he was listening for something.

He narrowed his mind to a single, silver point, a speartip, a

220

glinting pinhead of light in the darkness. If I am right, he thought, if I have the strength and the knowledge and the – yes, the perception! – and if the Cadence is truly here, then I shall see it. He would see it irradiating from the silver speck of light; beautiful, powerful, exquisitely wrought, intricate and complex. He did not yet know if he would be able to capture it.

He did not reach it on that first attempt, nor yet the second, nor the third. Despair threatened to cloud his mind, but he pushed it back fiercely, for despair – that terrible desolation of the spirit – could not be permitted.

He spent most of his days in the Tower, seated silent and still in the star-shaped chamber. Despite his resolve, there were times when he found himself beating back hopelessness, and there were times when he almost despaired of reaching the lost Cadence, for he knew it for an elusive, chimerical spell, faithful and loyal once caged, but mischievous and prankish and as transient as the will o' the wisps that danced across the night marshes, beckoning mockingly to foolish travellers.

He took his place at Cerball's table each night, grateful for the food and the wine that was always there for him, listening to the discourse of the Amaranths, beginning to find this Humanish custom of gathering together over the evening meal to share and discuss the events of the day rather attractive. They had celebrated the funerary rites for Murmur, and Cerball and the Mugain had courteously invited him to take part.

Maelduin had looked at them both thoughtfully, and had said, gravely, 'I do not think your people would welcome it.' And had stolen out of the Palace before dawnlight, leaving them to their strange nine-day ritual, seating himself on the hillside that rose behind the Porphyry Palace, hearing the rather beautiful chants and the singing; seeing the torchlit procession that set out at the Purple Hour with Murmur's embalmed body in a silver casket. He sent up his own plea for Murmur, calling up strands of light, and weaving them into a thin shining veil to wrap about her soul, chanting a Halcyon that would enfold and protect her with its strength and its tranquillity.

He found the Amaranths interesting and companionable. They made him welcome, and they shared their work with him. They were still trying to reach the child, the Amaranth princess who had been taken by the Lord of Chaos, and they discussed their attempts openly, which Maelduin listened to with absorption.

When Bodb Decht talked of the spell for infiltrating the Rodent Armies, or Cecht and Great-aunt Fuamnach told how they were trying to conjure up the Looking-glass of the Sorceress Reflection, Maelduin thought: but those are enchantments of light, and you are surrounded by such darkness! You will never succeed! And then: do they not feel the darkness? he thought. Do they not sense the stifling, heavy shadows that lie over the Palace?

He wondered if the Amaranths were aware of the growing menace from the Black HeartStealers, and whether he ought to warn them. But he was still unsure about the ways of the Humanish: wars and feuds and battles were a part of their world, and he was aware that Humanish emotions were already seeping into his mind. Unsafe! he thought. I must not! And already he looked forward to the nightly gatherings with more keenness than was safe; to hearing about the progress of their day's work, to learning whether this spell or that was taking shape; whether they had decided to attempt the difficult summoning of the White Stallion of CuChulainn, or if the Looking-glass of Reflection had materialised.

Several times he found himself wanting to tell them of his own endeavours; of how the Cadence stayed elusively out of his reach, but how he was determined to capture it. It would have been heartening to have talked about it, but he would not do so. Humanish weaknesses! This is my battle and that of my people. I dare not be drawn any deeper into this world.

But when Bodb Decht said to him that they believed their powers to be hampered by a darkness, Maelduin said, carefully, 'It is a belief within my people that the greatest threat is sometimes from within the ranks of one's own race.' And let his eyes move to where the Black HeartStealers were gathered at the far end of the table.

Bodb Decht frowned, and Maelduin, seeing it, was satisfied. For although I do not care what happens to these creatures, they have been hospitable; they have not driven me out and they have accepted my help. He thought it was not in any creed that he should not try to warn them of the uncoiling evil in their midst.

He had found that the best time to pursue the Cadence was

the Purple Hour; the magical drowsy time between day and night called dusk, when shadows thickened and there were drifting scents on the air, and the feeling that creatures from other worlds hovered. At these times, he knew the Cadence to be very close, a thread of light on the rim of his vision that would expand and open into the great silver chronicles of the Cadence if he could pin it down.

As the shadows thickened about the dark lonely Tower every night, Maelduin sat on, bending every ounce of his will to calling the Lost Magical Language to him, heedless of fatigue or thirst or hunger, barely aware now of the restricting Humanish cloak of skin and flesh and hair and bones. Every night, the scents of the Purple Hour closed about him, and every night he pursued the flickering lights; until at last he felt the Cadence within his reach. Slowly, stealthily, so gently that Maelduin could not be sure his senses were not tricking him, a glimmer of light began to form on the rim of his vision, a disc of pure, solid silver.

He stayed where he was, not moving, barely breathing. Was this to be the night? Was he about to capture the vagrant Cadence, the Language of Magic created all those centuries ago?

Slowly, with infinite patience, he wrapped his mind about the slivers of light, spinning a cage of enchantment so strong and so bright that after a time he began to see it before him: the bars slender and strong, the vagrant spell inside.

And then finally and at last, strand by exquisite strand, the Cadence began to form. At first there was only the faint glimpse of symbols on the darkness: strange curlicued shapes, scrolls and whorls and half-formed emblems and fragments of inscriptions and incantations, and torn shreds of runic signs.

Maelduin thought: it is closer! It is so close that I believe that I could reach out and hold it in my hands!

He knew that he must not. The beautiful fey spell was not a thing of the body; it was ephemeral, a thing of the mind and the spirit. The silver cage he was spinning was as ephemeral as the Cadence itself, but it was the only symbol that could be used. Capture, imprisonment, silver bars and golden cages . . .

You could not reach out and hold the Cadence in your hands, you could not spread it out before you. You could only conjure it by the force of your understanding, and if you were very lucky,

223

you could harness it and yoke it, so that you could pronounce its beautiful complex patterns in speech, and so open up the door to the entire storehouse of sorcery, and reach every enchantment ever spun.

A key. A door. A gateway into the glittering, shifting, chimerical world of magic.

The light was stronger now, and the patterns were lying, harlequin and beautiful, across the floor, silver and violet and pink and turquoise and gold. The great Chronicles of the Amaranthine sorcerers were unfurling before him, like a series of great, silver-leaved books, the pages studded with live enchantments and breathing spells. On and on they went, reaching back and back into the mists of time, stretching back into the dawn before the world began, when Men walked on all fours like beasts and could understand one another without words . . . On and on, back into the darkness that existed before the dawn, when ancient magic stalked the world, and Men were unborn . . . Magic and Enchantment and Bewitchment and Allure and Beckoning and Beguilement . . .

Maelduin could see the shapes clearly now, he could see the awesome silhouettes and the outlines and the shifting, blurring shapes. The symbols danced and darted all about him, but now he could look on them with understanding. He could decipher the symbols, and pronounce the strange, multi-syllabic incantations, and see them form at his bidding. He thought: I can conjure it all up; I can summon the whole history of magic if I wish.

The entire Tower was suffused with light; it was a soaring, flaming mass of brilliance that was soaking into the blackened and pitted walls, driving back the shadows, lying like a great silver and rose tapestry across the floor at his feet.

And within that tapestry are the dreams of the world and the hopes of Mankind and the skills of the sorcerers, and within it lies the intricate weaving of every spell ever spun and every incantation ever pronounced, and every enchantment ever woven on a Silver Loom . . . And they are all there for the taking . . .

I have done it! thought Maelduin, his mind rocketing into purest delight, exultation filling his entire body. I have reached out and captured the Lost Language of Magic.

* * *

224

Maelduin walked slowly back to the Porphyry Palace, aching and bruised with exhaustion, but still filled with such deep delight that his tired body ceased to matter. So this was what it felt like to experience deep contentment and immense satisfaction; the all-embracing joy of something fought for and finally achieved.

Above him, dawn was silvering the sky, and he thought: yes, but which dawn? How long was I in the Tower? He was strongly aware of hunger now and of thirst. It would be good to enter the banqueting hall and eat and drink and be in the company of the others again.

I have begun the journey, he thought. I have battled with an immense strength and imposed my will on it. And somewhere within those silken, silver paths I must find a spell to save my people.

And what of the Amaranths? whispered a mischievous voice in his mind. Are you going to simply hand back the Cadence to them?

My father's gift, thought Maelduin, frowning. Yes, it was my father's gift, and they should have treated it as the precious thing it was. They should have guarded it. If I took it from them now it would only be what they deserve.

He approached the Palace, and slipped in through a side door. He would go to the room allotted to him, and lie for a time on the bed, letting his mind wander in the half-conscious state that was so refreshing. Perhaps he could ask for food and wine to be brought, or go down to the great, stone-flagged sculleries and fend for himself.

But as he closed the door behind him and turned to mount the stairway that led to the upper floors, he felt, as abruptly as if it was a blow, the angry, struggling darkness inside the Palace.

He stood motionless, his eyes looking upwards, their brilliance filmed with exhaustion, and after a moment, he knew the angry evil for what it was.

A monstrous creature clawing its way into the world. The dark, evil fruit of a terrible rape, tearing at the womb in its hungering desire to be in the world of Men.

The birthing of the Gristlen's spawn.

The Amaranths had tied Laigne down to the bed. Herself of

225

Mugain had done it, with Cecht and Great-aunt Fuamnach. Cerball had wanted to help, but he had been so upset by the sight of Laigne writhing and screaming, and by the thick dark blood oozing out between her thighs, that he had had to be sent out of the room. Great-aunt Fuamnach had said it was better anyway; you did not want to be doing with Men in a birth-chamber, it was not their place. Cerball was please to go away and leave the ladies of the family to get on with the matter.

Laigne's lips were bitten to shreds and her nails were torn where she had scrabbled weakly at the straps and the lengths of sheet they had used to tie her down. She had flung herself to the floor at one point, clawing at the ground, fighting them off. She had screamed imprecations in an ancient tongue, which nobody had quite followed, but which Great-aunt Fuamnach, frowning, thought was a kind of libation to the Fisher King.

'He will return for me!' shrieked Laigne, rearing up, her hair sweat-soaked and rank, the flesh of her face pinched so that her nose jutted out like a snipe's beak. 'Coelacanth will come for me!' she gasped, her voice hoarse with pain and exhaustion, sobbing and struggling.

It was then that they had tied her down, fearful of such insanity, frightened that she would injure herself. It had been a truly appalling thing to do, and the gentle Cecht had had to go away to be sick afterwards, but in the face of such demented torture, there had been nothing else for it.

They had pronounced all of the usual spells, of course; there were any number of soothing balm-enchantments, and a good many had been created precisely for birthing.

But the spells had all failed; Cecht's potions and infusions had failed. The monster-child was tearing its way out of Laigne's body, fighting and clawing, and Laigne seemed to be falling deeper and deeper into the terrible, tormented madness. They could see the child heaving within her; a great, lumpish creature, struggling and churning, rippling her distended body from within. Great-aunt Fuamnach, who liked to think she had no trace of squeamishness, found herself likening it to a stunted, warped beast trapped inside a pale sack, punching and squirming to find its way out . . .

Maelduin had gone quietly and unobtrusively to the room allotted to him. He was drained and exhausted with the final effort of recapturing the Cadence, but he was unable to rest. His body ached with fatigue and his mind was dizzy with exhaustion, but he could feel Laigne's agony and her terror lacerating his mind and smothering his senses. He had not known that the Humanish must suffer such terrible torments, nor that his mind would be so open to it. Every time Laigne screamed, Maelduin felt white-hot agony sear his mind. Am I becoming more Humanish? he thought in a sudden agony of his own. Am I feeling their pain and their torment, and am I acquiring another layer of Humanish emotion? The tiny *sida*-core of him could distance itself from the agony tearing through the Palace; the creature that Maelduin was becoming could not.

He felt a cold horror at what lay ahead, but would not renege on the bargain he had made.

He would take the creature while it was still blind and helpless, and he would embark on the treacherous journey to the legendary fortress whose name had crept into every sinister tale and every dark myth in Ireland's history.

The Grail Castle.

Chapter Twenty-one

Even though he was dead, Coelacanth still walked through Rumour's dreams: evil, monstrous, rearing up to torment her.

She knew he was dead; she had seen his body cold and lifeless in the crystal pool. She had watched him die and she had heard his death throes. But she could not rid herself of the feeling that something of him lived . . . That somewhere was still the seed, the core, the cold evil that had dwelled in the black void of his soul . . .

The *nimfeach* and the Fomoire lay in the sticky web of the *Draoicht Suan*, sealed into the room with the crystal pools, and Rumour knew they could not reach her. But the nightmares remained, so that she would wake crying, clutching at Andrew.

And every time the nightmares attack me, he is there, she thought. Every time I am afraid, he is with me, calm and gentle and strong. I can lose the nightmares in his arms.

He intrigued her as much now as he had at the beginning. She found herself continually remembering the ancient legend of the Samildanach, the strange, myth-wreathed figure, the Man of Each and Every Art, who would release Ireland from the dark bonds of the necromancers. The one who would return to slay the evil that threatened Ireland . . .

Legend told how the Samildanach possessed all the gifts and all the graces; how he was poet and scholar and lover and musician and artisan.

And I believe he is all of those, thought Rumour, studying Andrew in the days that followed, as they explored the threatened City of Tiarna, and talked and ate and made love, and regained their strength. I have seen the scholar, for he is certainly learned. As for the lover – oh yes, she had seen the lover: fiercely passionate, and gentle and strong. And within the

228

lover was surely the poet. He had said, 'I would quote to you every beautiful verse ever penned and every love-poem ever spun had I the learning, but I have not; you will have to take me for what I am, my love.'

Take me for what I am, my love . . . But that had been poetry, thought Rumour; there had been poetry in his voice and there had been music in his touch. Yes, he was lover and poet and scholar and musician . . . What of the artisan, the worker and the craftsman? He had told her a little of the strange, enclosed community where he had lived. He had told her of how each man must work with his hands: tilling the land when it was his turn, scrubbing floors, helping with the preparation of food, occasionally brewing wine for their feasts and festivals. And there had been the maintaining of the fabric of the austere, stone-walled building where they all lived; there had been carpentry and stonework and thatching at times . . .

'I turned my hand to most things,' he said, dismissively, as if it was of small account.

And so, thought Rumour – half fascinated, half fearful – the artisan is there as well.

What had started as an amusing challenge in the safety of the Porphyry Palace; a determination to lure the austere, attractive young monk into her bed, was now something very different indeed. She understood that Andrew had broken some kind of deep and solemn promise, and that it troubled him very deeply. She tried to understand this. But I was born into a world where love and music and wine and laughter hold the greatest sway, she thought wryly. I cannot enter into his mood when he talks of fasting and prayer and scourging. I can listen but I cannot share that. He was violently passionate, as if he had been thirsting for this for most of his life, and must now take it before it slipped from his grasp, and it was this, above everything else, that wound its way into Rumour's heart and fastened on to her emotions with treacherous sweetness.

When Andrew talked to her of the unfamiliar religion; the queer, harsh beliefs of his Leader who had died for all men, she felt the passion in him, only now it was in his mind. Can I compete with that? thought Rumour, curled at Andrew's feet, wearing one of Aillen mac Midha's extravagant robes, listening and trying to understand.

229

To begin with, she had tried to hide her poor shaved head from Andrew, believing it to be ugly and feeling it to be repulsive. But he had hardly seemed to notice. When he had taken her in his arms, and when he had lain with her that first night, there had been such fierce longing and such blind, helpless need, that Coelacanth's maiming and Coelacanth's brutality had ceased to matter. There had been a soaring satisfaction, and he had taken her again and again, she forcing him on, neither of them able to hold back the relentless passion that swept through them.

When Rumour said, very softly, 'I think this has been a long time in the making, my love,' Andrew said, 'All of my life, I think,' and took her face between his hands and stared into it, as if he was trying to learn her, as if he believed that one day soon they would be parted for ever.

And when that happens, my dear forbidden love, I must have your beloved face for ever imprinted on my mind, so that I can store it in the groves of memory, and call it up from my heart, and look on it, and say: ah yes, of course, that was the time when I knew true happiness . . .

It had been soon after that that Rumour had raided the Elven King's storeroom of gowns and robes and headdresses, selecting the most beautiful, folding them inside a large cloak which could be carried easily and lightly when they left Tiarna.

'Vanity, of course,' she said to Andrew, partly serious, partly inviting him to laugh at her. 'I am known as wanton and extravagant, and I should like to continue to be so known. The slant-eyed grin slid out. 'If we are to take on the Dark Lords and reach Theodora,' said Rumour, demurely, 'I would like to do so properly dressed for it. I shall go into the necromancers' Realm dressed as they will expect me to be dressed, or I shall not go at all. A fanfare of trumpets to announce my entrance would help,' she said thoughtfully, amusement and self-mockery dancing in her eyes. 'The sorceress Reflection never made an entrance to her Court without one. But perhaps it would be impractical.' She grinned. 'And in the meantime, it will be rather fun to try out Aillen mac Midha's things.' Rumour did not see why she should not extract what fun she could from the situation. The

230

stories told of how, when Aillen mac Midha walked in the world of Men, he always did so garbed in shining robes and iridescent cloaks, occasionally with jewel-studded headdresses: silver and gold helmets, tiaras with great cabochon rubies and pearls, exotic pearl and ivory creations. Rumour, plundering his store, discovered shimmering satins; silken gowns woven in the magical Caves of Seiricia, where no Human had ever penetrated; robes and cloaks veined with silver, helmets with lapis-lazuli and firegems and chalcedony and turquoise. Beautiful. Yes, she would dazzle the Dark Lords with these. A tiny, treacherous voice, deep within her, whispered that she might also dazzle Chaos: Chaos with his evil, cruel smile and his dark sinister eyes . . . The cruel Lord of the Black Ireland, with his beautiful, seductive voice that almost certainly owed its allure to the ancient Enchantment of the necromancer Medoc, but that had beckoned to her and evoked that swift, shameful response . . . Dangerous! thought Rumour. And then: but when did danger ever deter me?

Andrew was watching her. He said, 'You will dazzle me, also,' and Rumour forgot about darkly dangerous seductions, and remembered that it was sweet and warm and safe to be loved. Of course she would not succumb to Chaos's dark romance. She tried on all the gowns, and the headdresses, using the crystal walls of the Silver Throne room for mirrors, half serious, half amused at herself, because surely there was scant room for this kind of vanity in their quest.

They left Tiarna after several days, taking what little food they could, taking the maps that Andrew had found, which would lead them towards the hinterlands of the Dark Realm.

As they walked, they could hear the faint lapping of water somewhere, as if there might be hidden shores and unseen coasts, against which the oceans constantly washed. At times the tunnels widened into great, echoing caverns, where the waterfalls had created pale icicle pillars and immense, sweeping walls of glistening, frosted water. Above their heads were arched roofs, veined with the silver and ivory and pearl of Tiarna's kingdom, almost unbearably lovely and exquisitely shaped.

'Shall we actually see the borderlands?' asked Andrew as they walked warily through these great, echoing caverns. 'Or shall

231

we simply pass from Tiarna into the Dark Realm without knowing it?'

'I have no idea. I am not sure if we shall see the borderlands, or how they will look to us if we do see them.' She frowned. 'There are only a very few ways in which one may pass from the True Ireland into the Dark One.'

'Yes?'

Rumour said, 'The best known is by using one of the existing Gateways. That is how the Fomoire came into the Cadence Tower, and how we passed into Tiarna. The Cadence Tower and the Well of Segais are both . . .' Again the frown. 'I think you would say, flaws in the weave,' said Rumour. 'Breaks in the pattern. There are a few here and there in Ireland. There is a very ancient one in the Cruachan Cavern of the Soul Eaters, although that is many days' journey from here. And there is another deep in the heart of the Wolfwood, but that is difficult to find. An even older legend tells of a third Gateway somewhere in the Cliffs of Moher on Ireland's western coast, although most people give that scant credence.

'But just as a door is a break in a wall, a break that allows people to pass through the wall, so those breaks, those flaws in the fabric between the two worlds, will allow people to pass through the worlds.' She glanced at him. 'For those people brave enough or foolhardy enough to go into the Dark Realm, those are the Gateways that are nearly always used. But very few people have attempted it, because it is fraught with appalling dangers.'

'I understand. But here we are using a – you called it an interface,' said Andrew, questioningly.

'Yes. Tiarna is neither quite of the True Ireland, nor the Dark Realm, but is between the two. A buffer world. Nechtan and the Amaranth Scholars taught how it was diamond-shaped, multi-faceted, and how several of its facets impinged on the other worlds.'

She paused and Andrew said, 'Your voice changes when you speak of Nechtan.'

'Does it?' Rumour looked up and smiled. 'He was good to me, that incorrigible old man. When I was an apprentice sorcerer, he taught me many things that are not normally taught to sorceresses.' Mischief shone in her eyes. 'We are generally believed inferior to the men,' she said. 'And generally we *are* inferior. I do not like to say it, but it is true. We have not the power.' She paused.

'But Nechtan believed that some females could be stronger than the men,' she said. 'He saw no reason to – to make differences. When I asked to study for higher levels than are normally permitted to sorceresses, he fought for me. That is why I hold much higher degrees than most of the others.' The mischief showed again. 'That is why many of them dislike me,' she said.

'And,' said Andrew, gently, 'that is why you are here now. Because Nechtan would have believed you could succeed.'

'It was something I could do in repayment,' said Rumour seriously. 'In gratitude for the way he fought on my behalf; the way he forced the Academy of Sorcerers to permit me to study for the advanced levels of enchantry. For the time and the patience he expended on me – hours and hours, Andrew.' She paused and then said, 'In the way I believe he was tutoring Theodora.'

'Yes. I understand that.'

'She must be saved,' said Rumour. 'Or everything I have ever believed in – everything Nechtan believed in – will have been for nothing.' And then, directing her mind to what was ahead of them, said, 'The maps you found will be invaluable to us. I think we are nearing the borderlands of the Dark Realm now.'

'Yes.' Andrew had traced their journey carefully. 'I think we shall be faced with mountains which form a natural barricade to the eastern boundaries,' he said now.

'Yes, they would be the *Sliabh Ciardhubh*, which means the Black Mountains. Fearsome. Within them is the Crimson Lady's grim fortress at Almhuin, and within the mountains prowl her creatures.' She looked up. 'If the Black Monk is still within the necromancers' realm, it is very likely he will be there, Andrew.'

'In thrall to the Crimson Lady?'

Rumour paused, and then said, carefully, 'The Crimson Lady is known to have a voracious appetite for the unspoilt bodies of young men. If the Black Monk strayed into her realm, and if he was comely—'

'Of that I have no idea,' said Andrew.

'Well, she may somehow have captured him and forced him to work for her. But if that is so, it will be a harsh fight to release him,' said Rumour, frowning. 'She is said to be immensely powerful.'

'We have overcome immense darknesses already,' said Andrew.

'And we may have to overcome others.' Rumour half unconsciously touched her head with the concealing silver helmet. 'Coelacanth and the *nimfeach* may have taken some of my strength,' she said, and her voice was suddenly uncertain. Andrew thought: she is afraid.

Rumour said, 'There is an ancient belief that much of the strength of sorcery exists in the hair.'

Her brilliant eyes rested on him, and Andrew said, slowly, 'My own people once held a similar belief. That to shear a man of his hair was to take his strength.' He looked at her. 'But you do not believe it?' he said. 'Not truly?'

'Of course not,' said Rumour at once, but her expression was thoughtful.

Andrew said, 'Since Coelacanth attacked you, you have attempted no sorcery of any kind.'

'So you have noticed.'

'Oh yes,' said Andrew, softly, 'I have noticed, Lady.' He reached out to trace the lines of her face. 'But the strength is not gone. I think it will be there for you when you need it.'

'I hope so.'

The journey through the tunnels was much shorter than either of them had envisaged. Because the beautiful tragic city of the *sidh* was even closer to the Dark Realm than they had realised? Perhaps. Andrew, following the charts carefully, finding it surprisingly easy to choose a left-hand fork or a right, or to take the road directly ahead, thought that it was simply that Rumour's description of the interface between the worlds had been a true one: they had travelled through the surface of Tiarna that abutted on to the fearsome Dark Realm of the necromancers, and now they were reaching the interface itself. Light was seeping into the tunnels, and it was no longer the soft water-light, the rippling gentle sea-light that had cast eerie green shadows and turned Rumour's eyes to emerald.

It was a thick, smeary light; sluggish and heavy and brooding.

And then the rippling water-light receded, and the tunnel widened, and they came out into the hinterlands of the Dark Realm.

Rumour caught her breath and reached for Andrew's hand, and they stood silently together, the caves behind them, knowing that finally and at last they were in sight of their goal.

The Black Domain of the necromancers . . . The Dark Realm of the Evil Lords of Ancient Magic. The terrible mirror-image, the underside of everything that was good and true and strong, and where all was warped and twisted and soaked with the black sorcery of ages and the vicious corruption of countless centuries.

The Other Ireland.

It was directly ahead of them; perhaps it was a walk of three miles across a flat expanse of pale, barren land that darkened as it neared the borderlands of the necromancers' empire.

The Black Realm, the Domain of the Lord of Chaos and the Crimson Lady; the necromancers' world . . . From where Andrew and Rumour stood, it spanned the entire horizon, spreading out in front of them like a dark, glowing tapestry, a grim crimson and black vista of mountains and turrets and wide flat plains and dark oily lakes, wreathed in shadows, shrouded in darkness.

The skies were black and lowering, veined here and there with pulsating magenta light. To their left, in what Andrew assumed was the west, they could see the silhouettes of the terrible fortresses of the necromancers; turrets and citadels and ancient strongholds, all of them soaked in old, old evil. They would have harboured immense wickedness, those turrets and strongholds; their windowless dungeons would have witnessed centuries of torture at the hands of the Dark Lords' servants. Chaos's henchmen would be there somewhere now: Anarchy, Murder and Misrule. And others . . . Rumour remembered, and wished she had not, the sinister tales of the Flesh-eating Trolls of the Red Caves . . . the Manhunts of the Rodent Armies who pursued Humans for sport across the NightFields . . . And I suppose those are the NightFields we can see to the east, thought Rumour. Flat, endless plains, blackened and charred and streaked with crimson, scattered here and there with mounds – what looked like burial heaps or barrows. Above them hovered screeching, crowlike shapes, swooping and diving and fighting. Carrion creatures and Harpies, voracious and pitiless.

The sky was low and menacing; Andrew thought it was so low that it was almost as if a massive black lid had been clapped over the landscape, shutting off the air. If they stood on tiptoe and stretched their hands up, they would be able to touch it, that stifling black lid. There was a stale dryness to the air, as if this was a place where fresh breezes never blew, or clean white clouds never scudded, or where rain never fell.

Away to their right, limned clearly against the lowering skies, were the crouching outlines of a vast jagged mountain range.

Rumour, looking towards them, said in a low voice, 'Sliabh Ciardhubh. The Black Mountains. The Jagged Tors of Necromancy. Soaked in evil and imbued with every dark power ever known. They are the western bastions of the Dark Realm.' She paused. 'And in their heart is Almhuin itself. We cannot see it from here, but it is there.' She fell silent, her eyes on the terrible menacing mountains, and Andrew thought: yes, she is right. I can *feel* that it is there. The Crimson Lady, the Beast of Almhuin . . .

He remembered that Rumour had said that Almhuin's Lady had a voracious appetite for comely young men. Had the Black Monk been comely? Am I drawing nearer to him now than at any other time? he thought. He studied the jagged mountains thoughtfully, and said, 'It looks to be a dangerous path to take.'

'Oh yes.' Rumour was watching the mountains intently.

'But,' said Andrew, gently, 'even if we must pass by Almhuin itself, I cannot see that there is any other path for us to take.'

'No.' Rumour had feared that they would have to pass through Almhuin all along, and now, faced with the terrible landscape, she saw her fears were founded. They dare not go straight into the City itself, and although the NightFields would be easy to cross on foot, they were sentinelled by the screeching carrion birds. The creatures would dart and swoop on them and tear them apart before they had gone more than a dozen steps.

Andrew said, as if he was thinking aloud, 'If we go quietly and stealthily through the Mountains, perhaps we can be unnoticed.' He took her hand and they walked warily towards the foothills of the Mountains, the terrain becoming clearer as they neared it. Beneath their feet, the silvery sand of Tiarna's borderlands thinned and melted, and Tiarna itself became no more than a blur behind them. The ground was harsh and rough and there was a dry heat to it now, as if an immense fire might lately have blazed across the land.

The western horizon had a damaged look to it as they drew closer. The dark skyline of the citadels and the fortresses was ravaged, split, here and there crumbling. There were gaps, great jagged holes where towers had collapsed, or turrets torn away. To the extreme west, on what Andrew thought must surely be the furthermost City boundary, was a great elaborate edifice with onion spires and domes and battlements. But it was gutted and torn open; the domes were pitted and ruined, as if a giant hand had come down and crushed it.

Rumour, puzzled, thought: it is as if the castles and the citadels have been attacked. As if they have been *ravaged*. What could have done that? What power has attacked the castles, and was so great that the necromancers could not defeat it?

They had kept the NightFields to their left as they walked, skirting them carefully, wary of the screeching birds. And although they were making for the scree of the Black Mountains, they were sufficiently close to the NightFields to see across their desolate face. And they are not simply black, they are burned, thought Andrew. They are smoking ruins. I think they are not even cooled yet.

The NightFields glowed redly and evilly, the crimson light glowing upwards into the darkling skies. Andrew and Rumour, shading their eyes from its glare, saw that it came from great stagnant lakes of blood, from huge, glistening pools of gore that lay across the NightFields and oozed slowly across the plateaux. The small, untidy mounds that Rumour had thought might be barrows, were tumbled piles of rags and skulls and pieces of bone. As they stood looking, a dry, sour wind ruffled the tattered mounds and puffed the sickly-sweet stench of decay into their faces.

'Corpses,' whispered Rumour. 'And the carrion crows are eating them.' As she spoke, three of the birds swooped, screeching, and tore at the tumbled heaps, and then ascended into the air again, tearing and clawing at gobbets of bleeding flesh, two of them with protruding stained bones, the other with a single eye hanging from a reddened shred of skin. Their dark harsh features were matted with blood; their talons dripped with gore.

Rats and weasels scuttled within the heaped bodies, their little eyes red and baleful, their thin, boneless tails twitching and slithering. The mounds heaved and undulated with their scurrying, lending them a semblance of grisly life.

Rumour nodded to the hovering birds. 'Carrion vultures,' she said. 'And Harpies. The bodies of birds, but the faces of voracious women. They also will eat the flesh of the dead bodies.'

'I have read of Harpies,' said Andrew. 'But I had hoped never to see them.'

They stood still, watching, and as they did so the Harpies shrieked in eldritch glee and swooped again on to the gore-soaked fields, scrabbling and tearing at the piles of rotting corpses, several of them scooping up the scurrying rats and flinging them bodily across the NightFields, and then rising into the air again with the gobbets of decomposing flesh. Andrew saw two of them fly at the same piece of bone and tear the flesh that adhered to it, flapping their blood-soaked black wings as they did so.

Rumour was standing very still, watching the Harpies. 'I believe,' she said, after a moment, 'that Chaos's prediction has come true. Do you remember, Andrew? Do you remember what he said in the Well Cavern? That the Lady of Almhuin would fight him for Theodora? That there might even be war and schism within the Black Ireland? I think it has already happened. I think it is still happening. The Crimson Lady is leading her people against Chaos. She is waging war on him in an endeavour to get Theo from him.'

'The necromancers fighting one another for the Amaranth Princess,' said Andrew, slowly, and Rumour at once said:

'Yes! We are seeing the carnage of a War of Necromancy, for only one thing would have been powerful enough to destroy the Castles of Necromancy—'

'More necromancy,' finished Andrew.

'Yes. They are fighting one another. They are at war.' She turned to face him, her eyes huge with apprehension.

'If they are still fighting for Theodora, she must be safe.'

'Yes. But this is Civil War, Andrew! We will be walking into a land where necromancers are fighting one another! Where they will be using the darkest, most evil sorcery they can summon.'

Rumour's eyes went back to the ravaged skyline.

'This will be the most dangerous part of the whole journey,' she said.

Chapter Twenty-two

The Black Mountains of Almhuin were dark and forbidding; Andrew thought they gave the impression of leaning over, so that you felt that at any minute they might topple forward and crush you. But as they began to ascend the scree, neither of the two travellers sensed anything stirring in their depths.

And then there was a moment when the Mountains ceased to be quiescent, and became something very different indeed, something menacing and watchful, as if some concealed beast had woken and looked up, and seen them approaching, and had rubbed its hands together and licked its lips . . .

The sentries of the necromancers, alerted by two Human intruders? Or the Crimson Lady, Almhuin's Beast Woman, who immersed her body in the blood of young virgins and whose servants were ever on the watch for fresh victims . . . ?

There was the feeling of something dark and immensely powerful passing overhead, and so strong was the sense that they flinched, and Andrew saw Rumour throw up her hands to shield her eyes. He flung his arms about her, both of them diving for cover beneath a jutting overhang of rock.

There was the sound of dark wings beating on the air, and the skies flared to angry life. Rumour shivered, and a scorching flare of scarlet tore over their heads, splitting the darkness wide open. The skies were lit to brilliant, hurting colour: great sheets of molten fire, livid and pulsating, shivered above the jagged Mountains, and huge, vicious starbursts exploded everywhere.

At once an answering volley of flames erupted from the west, and great, arrow-shaped tongues of fire poured over their heads, straight to the centre of the fiery heat, a white-hot wake sizzling its path across the burning sky.

There was the sound of rocks falling, and boulders and stones and rocks came tumbling and spilling down on to the mountain path. Andrew and Rumour pressed deeper into the shelter of the jutting rock, trying to avoid being hit. Andrew heard Rumour cry out, and knew she must have been hit. He moved instinctively to shield her, but the avalanche had already slithered to a halt, and the sounds were dying away.

At length Andrew stood up, and peered cautiously about them. The fiery lightning was dying, and the thick, stifling darkness of the skies was creeping back. And although rocks and stones lay everywhere, the narrow mountain path was not blocked as he had feared. He turned back to Rumour, and saw that she was bent over, her face white, her eyes dark with pain. Fear flooded him. He said, 'You are hurt . . .'

'Only a rock; but it crushed my foot.' She was half lying, half sitting against the mountain wall, and Andrew saw that her left foot was bruised and torn where the rock must have fallen on to it. Blood soaked her shoe, and her foot was already swollen. Andrew winced inside, knowing that to suffer a blow on the soft fragile instep is excruciatingly painful.

'I think it is only bruising,' said Rumour. 'I think the bones are not broken. I can go on a little way. And there is a healing spell I could call up, unless this place is smothering my powers.' She looked up at the skies uneasily.

'Were those things directed at us?' said Andrew.

'I think they were part of some kind of battle,' said Rumour and, as she spoke, they heard, very faintly, the sound of hoofs thudding across a hidden terrain. 'Cloven,' said Rumour, very softly. 'Cloven-hoofed stallions.'

'A battle?'

'Yes, almost certainly.' Rumour looked about her angrily. 'We are so vulnerable here,' she said. 'I am slowing you down, Andrew.'

'Then I'll carry you,' said Andrew at once.

'No.' Rumour gestured to the narrow path with one hand. 'It is far too narrow and dangerous. We shall have to walk very cautiously as it is. If you were carrying me, you would very easily miss your footing and we should both be at the foot of a ravine, or dashed to death against the crags.' She straightened up, and tried putting her foot to the ground. Andrew saw a fresh jag of pain go through her, and looked about him. Could they rest here? But it is the open mountainside, he thought. We would be at the mercy of any creatures that prowl here. As he framed the thought, he saw the screeching Harpies rise into the air.

Rumour said, 'We have to keep moving, Andrew. The Harpies were alerted by the fire and the lights of the battle. They have seen us, and they will have sensed that I am wounded. They will be watching to see if we are weak enough for them to attack us.'

'Yes.' Andrew understood this. 'If we could go a little further up,' he said, scanning the mountain; 'if we could reach the shelter of a cave or a crevice, perhaps it would be sufficient.'

As they moved back on to the path and began the ascent again, Andrew had the feeling that the mountain was becoming more evil, as if its shadows had been disturbed, and as if lurking evils had woken and looked up and seen them. The fiery skies had dimmed, but they could still hear, to the west, the pounding of the cloven hoofs.

'And there is a scent of blood,' said Rumour, softly. 'Can you smell it, Andrew? A taint on the air.'

'Yes. Then a battle is being fought somewhere.' He took her arm. 'We should go on,' he said, and thought: we should go on, because something ancient and evil is uncoiling here. The clinging mists are hiding peering eyes and reaching bony fingers . . .

As they struggled up the narrow, winding path, Rumour supported by Andrew's arm, the path twisted around to the left, and Andrew saw something that the sheer mountain face had hidden from them until now. He paused, letting Rumour take the weight from her injured foot, and pointed.

'What is—'

'Lights,' said Andrew. 'A little cluster of lights, about a third of the way up the mountainside.'

'Houses? A mountain village of some kind?' And then, in a different, sharper voice, 'Almhuin?' said Rumour.

'I suppose it must be.' But Andrew thought that the lights had a rather warm, friendly look to them. He found himself remembering his own world, where travellers, pilgrims, wayfarers of all kinds were welcomed and given food and shelter. Perhaps the lights indicated a mountain village of some kind, where there might be ordinary people, Humans, who would allow them to rest, so that Rumour could pronounce the healing spell over her damaged foot.

The mountain was becoming darker. Several of the Harpies had flown in the direction of the blood-tainted battle, but a number were still hovering, a little distance away, their cold, greedy eyes glinting in the red light from the skies.

'If we stop for longer than a few minutes, they will be upon us,' said Rumour. 'They know I am wounded and unable to fight.'

'Yes.' It tore at Andrew's heart to force her on, but there was no choice. They must reach somewhere where they could rest.

The mountain was alive with strange, prowling movements; stealthy, furtive, creeping rustlings that seemed to come from out of the swirling mists above them. Andrew thought it was exactly as if a lair had been disturbed, and as if the beast that had its nest there had woken and was prowling and sniffing and scenting Humans... Was the Crimson Lady, the Beast of Almhuin, already watching their approach, and was she already eyeing them with her greedy lips smiling, and curving her voracious predator's talons as she savoured their capture...?

Andrew tightened his hold on the limping Rumour, wrapping the black, fur-lined cloak she had donned for the journey more tightly about her, glad to think that at least she was protected from the cold, sour wind that blew into their faces. He still wore the plain robe of his Order, and although it was not as warm as Rumour's cloak, still it was good, strong wool. He touched the crucifix that hung at his waist, almost without realising it.

The lights were not as far up the mountainside as it had seemed; they were quite close. It would not take long to reach them.

Rumour was plainly in a good deal of pain, but she had not complained. Andrew glanced about him, seeing that it was much darker, feeling the cold wind increase. If Rumour had not been injured, they would have been through the mountain by now and Almhuin would be behind them.

As they rounded a curve in the narrow mountain path, several pairs of red eyes peered at them from deep within a crevice in the mountainside. Andrew drew a deep breath, and lifted Rumour in his arms, ignoring her protests. He carried her past the crevice, and there was a brief spiral of delight that he had done so without showing any fear. But Rumour was clearly unable to go much further, and so we *have* to risk stopping in this place! thought Andrew. He pushed from his mind the knowledge that this was Almhuin, and that they were now deep inside the war-torn Dark Realm, and they were in the terrible mountain realm of the Crimson Lady.

Rumour was angry at the misfortune that had injured her foot, and she was trying to think of a way of avoiding Almhuin. She had tried several times already to call up the power, the flickering Amaranth flame that would summon the healing enchantment, but every time she attempted it, the pain smothered her strength. But there had been a brief shoot of delight at finding the power still with her. She thought: so Coelacanth did not kill it!

The beckoning lights of Almhuin were warm, but they were sinister. Rumour thought there would be some kind of mountain village, a little self-sufficient community that would have grown up around the Castle, because although some of the Lady's people would live inside her Citadel, there would be others that would not: cooks and scullions and smiths and masons and their families. She found herself remembering, all over again, the tales of how the Lady sent her creatures out into the hill farms and the mountain passes in search of prey, for the Crimson Lady's bathhouses must always be kept stocked. This was a daunting thought, but, like Andrew, she could see no other path for them to take. At least I am still able to touch the power, she thought, with a spiral of confidence.

The skies were still black and heavy overhead, but as they climbed higher, Andrew still carrying Rumour but beginning to lag, jagged lightning began to vein the skies again.

'As if the skies are tearing,' said Rumour fascinated. 'As if they are bleeding. But this time there is no sound.'

'Should we be wary of it?'

'I think we should not look directly at it,' said Rumour, and Andrew remembered how she had shielded her eyes earlier. 'Any sort of light here is sure to be spurious.' She glanced at him. 'This is the Dark Realm, remember. The Black Ireland. Any form of light must be evil. Normal, harmless light could not live.'

'Yes, of course.'

'They do not have night as we know it,' said Rumour. 'But there will always be a time when it is darker.'

As the track wound upwards, the mountain face on each side of them, the jagged scarlet tears widened, and sluggish red light oozed out. The path became lit to eerie life, and a malevolent crimson glow bathed the black crags and the granite mountain faces.

Through the strange livid tears, they glimpsed crimson-eyed stallions, gleaming black steeds, pouring across the skies, their riders thin, ravaged-looking beings with wild, streaming hair and clutching hands. They crouched low over their mounts, and Rumour and Andrew caught, very faintly, the screeching of their eldritch laughter.

'The Lord of Chaos summoning his armies,' said Rumour, softly. 'I believe they are the WarMongers, riding the NightMares.' She looked at Andrew, her eyes fearful. 'Chaos is indeed a Master,' she said. 'For if he can call up the WarMongers, then he is unrivalled in this world.'

They went on, keeping their eyes downwards, determinedly not looking up at the red-soaked skies with their eerie dark armies, climbing the path doggedly.

Behind them they could see the spreading carpet of the Dark Realm; when Andrew stopped to rest, keeping careful watch on the Harpies, Rumour drew his attention to a large fortress on what they thought was the northern boundary, set apart. There were several towers and a massive central portion made of gleaming black stone.

'Chaos's Castle of Infinity?' said Andrew, leaning back against the rockface, and looking to where she indicated.

'I think it could be. It is the largest and it is set apart from the others. That is what I would expect of him.'

'It is where the NightMares were riding,' said Andrew.

'Yes.'

The NightMares had vanished now, swallowed up in the dense, swirling skies, and Andrew looked carefully at the great black fortress, trying to fix its position in his mind, thinking that Theodora could be somewhere within those grim, sheer walls, deep in the ancient black vaults. They must reach it as soon as they could.

'I believe I could walk a little,' said Rumour, trying her weight on her injured foot. 'Yes. And it is not so very far. If I lean on your arm . . . Yes, that is not so uncomfortable.'

'I would rather carry you.'

'I would rather try to walk.'

They eyed one another, and Andrew made an abrupt gesture of submission, and thought: after all, we are almost in the village.

'Also,' said Rumour softly, 'it may serve to deceive those creatures behind us.'

The mountain path wound upwards, and thick red light still lay across their path. And then it curved sharply to the right, and Rumour stopped, and clutched Andrew's arm, and pointed.

Directly ahead of them, set half into the mountain, was a cluster of tiny houses with deep, low roofs and tiny, square windows. Lights shone from the windows, and there was a small cobbled square with two or three tiny streets leading off it.

And, rearing up against the mountain, seeming to be built half into it, was a great dark fortress with twin turrets and a central portcullis and narrow, slitlike windows.

The Castle of the Crimson Lady. The Mountain Fortress of the Beithioch.

Almhuin.

It reared over them, seeming to overhang the little mountain village with its cobbled square and friendly huddle of buildings.

Almhuin, the sinister Mountain Fortress. The grim rearing stronghold that guarded their way into the Dark Realm itself. The lair of the Crimson Lady, the Beast of Almhuin who scoured the Mountains of the Dark Ireland for prey to drain of their blood, so that she might bathe her white limbs and slake her terrible thirst . . . The necromancess who had once been Chaos's paramour, but who now seemed to be his enemy.

I could wish I knew none of her legend, thought Rumour, leaning against Andrew, and feeling the pain tear through her crushed instep again. How did they live, these poor people out here in the shadow of Almhuin? How did they live, knowing that the Lady nightly held her gruesome revelries? Did they live in constant and abject terror? Or was it the other way entirely?

Perhaps they entered into the Lady's grisly appetites, and perhaps they served her, not because they were forced to, but because they enjoyed it.

'Someone has been quaffed tonight...' Rumour could not remember when she had first heard the grisly expression, and she did not know by whom it had been coined. Had there once been a fearsome necromancer about whom it had been said? The Erl-King, was it?

They moved forward, Andrew carrying Rumour again, keeping to the shadows, seeing the yellow squares of light lying across the cobbled streets of the tiny mountain village.

Andrew paused, and looked about him, scanning the mountainside. 'The road leads out of Almhuin as well as into it,' he said. 'Do you see? Almhuin is clustered about the mountain path itself. If we can once get this place behind us, we would be able to walk straight through the Mountains to the centre of the Dark Realm.'

'And so to Chaos's Castle of Infinity,' said Rumour, nodding.

'But first there is Almhuin to be traversed. I think we must approach someone here – perhaps enter the inn over there – and rest,' said Andrew. 'Perhaps we have to stay here for the night, or what passes for night here. And then we must go on.'

'It is possible that the Lady and her servants are so involved in the battles that they are not thinking of victims for the bathhouses,' said Rumour, looking at Andrew hopefully, and Andrew said, blandly, 'It is a useful thing, a war,' and Rumour grinned, and was glad that he had a dry sense of humour, this strange monk.

'I had not until I knew you,' said Andrew softly. 'I had thought life a serious and a solemn thing.' Rumour looked at him sharply, because although she had been able to hear a little of his thoughts, this was the first time he had heard hers.

But he simply grinned at her, his teeth very white in the darkness, and Rumour studied him, and saw how his hair had grown a little since their first meeting, and how it tumbled over his brow, dark and untidy. He had not shaved since they left the Porphyry Palace, and a dark, silky beard framed his face now, emphasising the lean, strong bones, making him look altogether tougher, harder, more worldly. She thought: I wonder whether any of your Order would know you in this moment, Brother

247

Andrew? I wonder if I know you, even. I can barely see the gentle, serious young monk who ate and drank so sparingly and who eschewed the pleasures of the flesh . . . All I can see is a rather reckless young man who has already vanquished one fearsome enemy, and who looks as if he might almost enjoy vanquishing another . . . and who makes love with gentle, fierce passion, and has begun to find humour in danger. And who is even now regarding the terrible Fortress of Almhuin with a speculative light in his eyes. I believe he would almost welcome an encounter with the Lady of this place, thought Rumour, torn between exasperation and admiration.

The mountain village was larger than they had thought. There was a central square, with an iron pump and a well: 'Spring water from beneath the mountain,' said Rumour. There were two or three narrow streets leading away from the square, and little huddles of houses. Looking out on to the cobbled square were buildings which plainly carried on trades of various kinds: they picked out a blacksmith's with a forge and benches, and a bakeshop and tiny wineshop, which Andrew had pointed out earlier.

'So they are permitted a little relaxation, these people of Almhuin,' murmured Rumour, her eyes on the inn.

'So it seems. That, Lady, is where we must seek sanctuary.'

'Yes.' Rumour was finding the little village reassuringly ordinary. There was something normal and everyday about a place that had a forge and a village pump, and that had a rather friendly-looking inn with a brightly painted sign over its door. The bakeshop had jutting bow windows, with a display of wares: crusty loaves and gingerbread men and dark, rich fruit cakes. Next to it was what looked to be a sempstress's, with bales of silk and velvet and swathes of lace arranged colourfully.

They looked across at the square of yellow light that shone from the inn's windows and, as they did so, someone walked across the window, and a hand – an ordinary white Human hand – unlatched the window and pushed it open to the night. To Andrew and Rumour there was suddenly something heart-warmingly reassuring about the normality of a person who could reach out and open the window of an over-heated room to let in the cool night air.

With the opening of the window, the scents of food drifted

248

out to them: roasting meats and newly baked bread and simmering soup, and they heard a shout of laughter followed by derisory cheering, as if somebody within the room might have told a good joke, or perhaps as if a game of some kind had been in progress, and somebody had scored an unexpected point. There was a brief burst of music, and several voices raised in a snatch of song.

At length Andrew said, 'It *sounds* very ordinary and normal.'

'Yes.' Rumour frowned. 'But we have to think of a story to tell them. They will surely ask us. What could we say?'

'Are there not quests of any kind here?' Andrew was thinking of the pilgrimages made by his Order; of the arduous but rewarding journeys several of the monks had made to the Eastern Lands to learn more of their Founder. Would there not be pilgrimages here? Dark pilgrimages, but still involving journeys?

'I don't know,' said Rumour, when Andrew asked this. 'But a pilgrimage, by its very nature, is an arduous and long undertaking. The Crimson Lady and her people would not comprehend the concept of hardship in return for reward.' She frowned, thinking.

'Could we simply say we are in pursuit of the Gristlen who has stolen an enchantment from our people?' said Andrew, thinking that the closer they could keep to the truth, the less chance there would be of being caught. He was rather horrified to discover that he was having less regard for truth itself than for a credible tale. But he said, 'I believe we could tell them that and be believed.'

Rumour said, slowly, 'I think you are right. And Gristlens are outcasts in any world. They are sometimes spoken of as the damned of the Black Ireland.'

'They would surely know that here. If we told how we had been cheated by one, and said we were seeking to be revenged on it; and that you had been injured by a rockfall . . .' He stopped and looked at her. 'Your injured foot would be more than sufficient reason for our seeking shelter,' he said.

Rumour grinned suddenly, and Andrew saw again the reckless, extravagant creature who had dazzled him in the Porphyry Palace.

But she only said, 'Trust a monk to find a truthful solution,

Andrew. I should certainly have spun an elaborate web of deceit.'

'And been caught out the sooner,' said Andrew.

'Yes, but I should have had fun spinning it,' said Rumour. And then, sobering, 'But you are right, Andrew. We should keep our story simple and near to the truth if we can.' She looked across at the tiny inn. 'There are lights in the windows,' said Rumour. 'And there is food and wine, and there are people. All I need is an hour or so to quench the pain, and then I could pronounce the healing spell. And it is a quiet, gentle spell; I think no one would even hear it.' She studied the tiny, low-roofed building, and the familiar glint of humour showed. 'Of course, I have never before been in such a humble place,' said Rumour. 'And after the splendours of Tara and the Porphyry Palace it is very modest . . .'

She grinned at him, and Andrew said, thoughtfully, 'I have never been in a wineshop of any kind,' and sent her a sudden, sweet smile that said: but I should rather like to experience it. 'Shall we go in, Lady?' he said.

Chapter Twenty-three

The people of Almhuin were not altogether unaccustomed to seeing strangers in their mountain village, but it was a rare occurrence. Travellers shunned Almhuin – the Almhuinians knew why, of course. The Lady's ways and her appetites were well known, and even better known were her revelries.

Better not to admit to too much, they said, glancing at one another from the corners of their eyes and grinning. Better to simply do the work you were assigned; shoeing horses, baking bread for the Castle, laundering, maintaining the Castle's fabric. It was nothing to do with outsiders what else they might do for the Lady, and what other needs they might help her to satisfy.

And it was all of it work which put food on your table and clothes on your back. Since the War, times had been prosperous. The Lady had martialled her Armies. Just as Chaos – they would no longer give him the courtesy of calling him *Lord* of Chaos – just as Chaos had called up the WarMongers and the NightMare Stallions, so the Lady had summoned the Rodent Armies: the ancient, half-vermin creatures who dwelled in the Caves of Cruachan, but who would serve any master who would pay them enough. They had been Chaos's servants for a very long time, said the Almhuinians proudly; although the Lady had not lured them all to fight for her, she had lured a very great many of them. Those of the Rodents who still swore allegiance to Chaos and his henchmen could soon be dealt with.

Almhuin had done pretty well out of the Rodent Armies. There had been the feeding of them and the housing – a whole section of the Castle had been turned into barracks for them before the immense Battle of the NightFields had been fought. There had been the fashioning of armour for it, which had been very profitable indeed. Halberds and spears and breastplates

251

and javelins. Silver and black helmets with the Lady's emblem etched deeply into them had been the design, which the Almhuinians had thought very tasteful. There were places within the Army for the Almhuinians as well, for the younger ones who had a taste for blood and fighting, as who in Almhuin had not? You did not grow up in the Lady's service without learning about the dark pleasures of pain and torture . . . And although this was a War of Necromancy, and although black powerful sorcery was being used, the Lady and her opponents had not been able to do without plain, ordinary broadsword battles. Most of the younger men had ridden out, either on the march to Chaos's Castle of Infinity, or in the Battle of the NightFields itself. Very nasty, that had been, with the Fomoire riding for Chaos, galloping hard across the battlefield on the NightMare Stallions, and summoning up the creatures of people's nightmares as they went. The outcome had been indecisive, neither side managing to claim total victory, but it had been a fine battle. It had set the tone for the entire war. Fierce and bloody and merciless.

Chaos's Armies had used the ancient magical NightCloak of Ireland's first High Queen to call up the NightMares, of course: it was one of the Dark Lord's most jealously guarded possessions, and it had taken many years of intrigue and scheming to acquire it. That was how he had been able to call up the NightMare Stallions: fearsome and strong creatures that trailed with them the terrible aura of the NightMare Domain they inhabited. They had ridden into the fray, dozens of them drawing the NightMares across the battlefield, and hundreds of people from both sides had been slain and left to die in their own gore and that of their comrades.

And now the Lady wanted the Amaranth Princess whom Chaos had brought out of the Other Ireland. She wanted the pure Dawn Flame of Sorcery that the child possessed, and she would stop at nothing to get it. She was using every spell and every strength she possessed, but she had not been able to compete with the NightCloak, and Chaos still held the Princess deep within the Castle of Infinity.

And so there would be no more revelries at Almhuin with Chaos the honoured guest, and the Lady presiding over the banqueting tables. There would be no more nights with the villagers cudgelling their wits to think up new ways of entertaining Chaos and his train.

But the Lady was generous to those who served her faithfully. She was gracious and benevolent to those of her people who scoured the Mountains for lone travellers, and who sometimes even slipped through the Gateways into the Other Ireland to bring back plump young maidens for her. As for the war, hadn't she already bestowed honours on those of her people who had ridden out in the great siege on the Castle of Infinity and been wounded in the battle? Hadn't she sent down money and the deeds to land for the families of those who had been slain fighting for her against the Lord of Chaos and his henchmen? She was a fearsome and powerful necromancer, their Lady, and terrible tales were whispered about her in the Other Ireland. But she looked after her own, and when you had wives, children, perhaps elderly parents to look to, it was a grand thing to have your own bit of land and a house on it.

The war had made extra work, of course. The Lady must still have her victims; she must still have her plump, fair young virgins to tease and torture (yes, and do other things to!), and finally to suspend from the great black hooks in the bathhouses. They dug one another in the ribs and said, slyly, hadn't there been nights when the Lady had thought she had true untouched virgins gushing their fluids over her limbs, but hadn't she been very much mistaken! It was a hard old life if you couldn't relieve your own needs on the Lady's victims at times. A man on Castle night duty got ragingly frustrated watching the Lady work off her passions on the poor pretty fools that they captured for her; best just take one or two of them for yourself before the Lady's attentions rendered the poor creatures so mutilated that they were scarcely recognisable as Humans at all. Not that the Almhuinians differentiated particularly between Humans and other creatures. If Humans couldn't be found, (and occasionally there was a shortage), the Lady had been known to make do with young deer or the silken-skinned panthers that sometimes roamed the mountains.

And when you had a frustration on you the size of a gatepost, where was the difference between Human and beast? You could strap down a panther or a deer and ply your stalk between its rear quarters as easily as a Human. You could still steal along to one of the Lady's cells and bring out the manacles and the muzzles. Panthers fought and bit, but deer were gentler, apt to freeze into immobility in fear. Humans screamed and struggled and implored to be set free, which could be a good game, because you could pretend to bargain, and see their gratitude. It was a game that could be played indefinitely before you finally did whatever you wanted to. Every creature was different. It all made for interest.

It had made for great interest when the Summoning had come from the Other Ireland. To begin with, opinions had been divided as to the wisdom of answering it, especially with their own War here to be fought. But Black Aed, whose wife was said to be an illegitimate descendant of Medoc himself, and who therefore ought to be able to judge such things, had said it sounded perfectly genuine. A matter of a rebellion, so Aed's wife believed; a mutiny within the Porphyry Palace itself, and the rebels wanting a little *dark* assistance.

'Necromancy?' said one or two people suspiciously, because there was no use pretending that any of them had a shred of power between them. Fighting and serving and spying, that was what the Almhuinians did, and very thoroughly too! But they had not a smidgen of necromancy anywhere in them, and it would not have done to say they had. These things had to be made clear at the outset.

But it had appeared that it was the Black HeartStealers who were wanting assistance, and as Black Aed had said, didn't they all know perfectly well that the Black HeartStealers had their own necromancy? They simply wanted a show of force, he said. A smallish but strongish Army to lead against the Amaranths. The leader of the Black Hearts, who as they all knew was the Fer Caille, was prepared to pay extremely well, said Aed, rubbing his thumb and forefinger together suggestively, and people said, oh well, if it was only *fighting* that was wanted, they could very likely get through a Gateway and help out a bit. So long as it was understood that they were properly paid.

Black Aed cracked his knuckle-joints happily, and told everyone they would all do very nicely out of this, what with the Black HeartStealers being such a very prosperous branch of the Royal Sorcery House. They were an actual branch of the

Amaranths, a *bastard* branch, added Black Aed's wife, sniggering; and everyone chuckled slyly, because didn't they all know exactly what she meant: a necromancer had somewhere or other inter-married with the Black HeartStealers, and infiltrated a vein of dark sorcery into the line. And very nice too.

As Diarmuit, the innkeeper, had pointed out, wasn't it high time that they sneaked a few of their own kind in to rule the Amaranths? And wouldn't it be the Amaranths' own fault if they were soundly and roundly beaten and driven from the Porphyry Palace? Old-fashioned in their ways, said Diarmuit wisely; old-fashioned and narrow-minded. It would be a fine thing to have their own Black HeartStealers serving the High King, he said with one of his sly, gravelly chuckles, and everyone had chuckled with him and agreed.

And so there was plenty to discuss on the night that the Lady sent over the Blinding Lightning, and told them all to stay safely indoors. There was the progress of their own War to chart, and whether or not Chaos could be beaten, and if not, whether the Almhuinians might not be better to change sides altogether because you had to watch your own interests.

They had taken shelter in the inn, because you might as well have a bit of company and a bite of supper while necromantic forces were rampaging across the skies outside; they were engaged in drawing up a bit of a list of the younger ones who could be spared to send through a Gateway in answer to the Black Hearts' summons, and debating the merits of using the Moher Gateway, which was guarded by the Flesh-eating Trolls, as against the tunnels of Tiarna, which were guarded by the *sidh*, when the two travellers came into the inn.

This was intriguing, because most travellers who had to pass through Almhuin scuttled through the streets without stopping. But these two – a dark-haired, bearded young man and a lady – seemed not to care or perhaps not to know about the Lady's legend. They came quite openly into the inn, the lady limping from an injury to her foot, coming up to the tables where the wine flagons and the bite of food that was always available were all set out.

They asked for wine; 'And if you could provide us with a bite of supper, we should be grateful,' said the young man.

'We will pay you well,' said his companion, and people looked up at the sound of her voice, because it was a soft, rather attractive voice.

They were served with wine – very good wine they would find it – and bowls of steaming soup with newly baked bread and wedges of creamy-yellow cheese, and slices of roast beef. There was a dab of freshly made horseradish to go with the beef.

'A feast,' said the young man to his companion, carrying the food to a table by the fire. 'We thank you, good sir.'

He was dressed a bit oddly, and several of the villagers found that they were made uncomfortable by the carved symbol he wore at his waist, to the extent that they could not look directly at it; but the two strangers sat quietly enough, drinking their wine and supping their food. The pinched, cold look faded from the lady's face after a while, and she looked about her with interest.

Glances were exchanged, because would she be a good one to take up to the Castle? She would be no maiden, of course – a man with half an eye could see that – but still, she might provide their Lady with an hour or so's pleasure. As for the man – yes, he would do for the Lady's bed. He would die during the night, of course, but so did all the Lady's guests die. They glanced at one another, and one of them produced the thin ivory sticks, one much shorter than the other, that were used for deciding who should undertake various tasks. Whoever drew the short stick would engage the travellers in conversation and allay their suspicions. It was an old tried method, and no one had ever questioned it. They could not let the travellers see the drawing of the sticks, but weren't they very used to hiding this ploy under cover of dice-throwing?

Rumour and Andrew had found the inn reassuringly ordinary. It was a somewhat larger room than it had appeared from outside; it was long and low-ceilinged, and there were perhaps eight or ten round wooden tables, with stools standing around them. Andrew thought there were far more people here than they had expected: at each table were seated three or four men, and at most of the tables, wine was being drunk, and games involving dice and carved wooden figures were in progress. There was a thick, faintly sour smell of spilt wine, and a warm, slightly greasy feel in the air.

But still, thought Andrew, looking round, still it is a welcome refuge. Rumour can rest and with God's will she can heal her foot.

He helped Rumour to sit by the fire, and sat next to her, looking with interest at the Almhuinians who were drinking and engaged in their gambling games and their dice-throwing. Rumour's face was already less pinched and the lines of pain were smoothing out, and Andrew was immensely relieved, because he had thought that perhaps the darkness here would smother her attempts to pronounce the spell, as the darkness churned by the Fomoire in the Cadence Tower had smothered the Amaranths'.

But Rumour, schooled by the wily Nechtan in a great many levels of sorcery, knew that one of the first and most basic principles of magic of any kind was to be able to recognise the scents and the feel of necromancy, and to assess its potential menace. She recognised, in the rather stifling heat of the inn, and in the thickness of the air, that strong, ancient evil dwelled here, but she recognised as well that none of these people were able to harness any power on their own account. Good! thought Rumour. Then I should be able to heal my foot without their powers quenching the healing spell.

The pain was already easing. Andrew had drawn up an unused stool for her to rest it on, and had quietly and unobtrusively bound it with a linen napkin he had requested from the innkeeper. The pain trickled away, and at length Rumour murmured the gentle words of the healing spell, the *Draiocht Cneasaim*. She felt it form in her mind, and for a brief instant it hovered on the air, light and transient, but unmistakably there. Rumour held her breath, waiting to see if the Almhuinians should see it, but they were all engrossed in their dice-throwing and their talk, and no one looked round. So far so good, thought Rumour, and felt the caress of the spell on her bruised foot already lifting the pain and restoring the torn flesh.

The food was very good. Rumour, eating hungrily, studied the inhabitants of the inn, and saw the faint traces of an ancient and malevolent ancestry in them; the narrow, slitlike eyes, the sharp features, the curving hands. And for all their powerful muscles, they had narrow, sloping shoulders, and an unmistakable, rather repulsive, boneless look. As if it might be more natural to them to slither and dart and scuttle across the ground ... Rodent blood! thought Rumour with an inward shudder. It is only a thin vein, but is there. They have the blood of rats and weasels and jackals and stoats. It is from very far back, but it is there. She remembered how some of the Rodent Armies had inter-married with Humans over the centuries, and how, although the Dark Lords had carefully preserved the dark, evil strain of the first Rodent Creatures for fighting and guarding, mutant strains had evolved. I think we are seeing one of those mutant strains now, thought Rumour. I think we shall have to be very careful.

But they had been made welcome by the innkeeper, whose name was Diarmuit, and who appeared to find nothing unusual about them; and whose tone was exactly that of a genial host, wanting to put unexpected guests at ease.

It was generally agreed in the inn that Diarmuit had done a very neat job of work on the two travellers.

Diarmuit said, modestly, that it came of practice, and of working sensibly together. They'd worked together tonight, he said, nodding his head portentously. It had been easy enough to just slip the draught into the flagon of wine, and then to take it across to the travellers' table, as nice as could be. And he had resisted the temptation to pour the wine into chalices, said Diarmuit, because that might have aroused their suspicions.

No suspicions had been aroused. Andrew and Rumour, tired from their journey, had already been lulled by the warmth of the fire and the good food. Andrew had poured two chalicefuls of the wine, and they had drunk it gratefully. And then they had slipped into drugged unconsciousness as swiftly and as easily as the Almhuinians could have wished.

And with them drugged and helpless, it was the easiest thing you'd ever know for Black Aed to just tap them on the head, so that they slid to the floor without giving the smallest trouble. And even that had to be judged, because too hard a tap and you'd killed your victim, and the Lady would have flown into a towering rage if that had happened! Alive they had to be, with blood running warmly and richly in them.

But all had been well; the travellers were only stunned. The Lady would be pleased with them tonight. Diarmuit and Black

Aed and a couple of the others tied Andrew and Rumour hand and foot.

The Lady would be very pleased indeed, and doubtless she would reward her people in her customary generous fashion. The deep dungeons of Almhuin would be open tonight, and those of them who were on Castle duty tomorrow night would be kept busy.

Someone would be quaffed . . .

It was all in a night's work.

Chapter Twenty-four

The Black HeartStealers, under the aegis of their leader, the Fer Caille, met with Iarbonel Soothsayer and the Arca Dubhs in a small, rather dark panelled chamber in the cold east wing of the Palace.

The Fer Caille had summoned them in secret, and as soon as they were all in the chamber, sealed the doors against any of the other Amaranths who might be prowling.

'They won't come here,' said Iarbonel. 'They're too taken up with Laigne and the birth.'

'Fortunate,' murmured another, and several of the Black Hearts laughed rather gloatingly, because wasn't this going to be the smoothest rebellion in the entire history of the Amaranth House. Before long the Black HeartStealers would ascend the Purple Throne; they would head the Royal Sorcery House and take precedence over every other sorcerer in Ireland.

'Even so, it is as well to be sure that we shall not be overheard.' The Fer Caille moved slowly round the room, studying each of the plotters in turn, his huge, dense shadow falling over them. Several of the Arca Dubhs, who had wavered a bit about joining in, remembered with unease the stories of the Fer Caille's ancestry. He was a towering creature, broad-shouldered and with a brutish cast of countenance. He had the small, mean eyes of all who possessed Giantish blood, and the coarse, brutal mouth of the ogre-people. He did not often smile, but when he did, he showed tiny, stumplike teeth. The Arca Dubhs shivered and thought that you might say what you liked: it was as well to be very wary indeed of those with Giantish blood in them.

But if Cerball and the rest were to be driven out and new ways brought in, somebody had to lead. The Arca Dubhs murmured this to one another, because while none of them had wanted actually to instigate the rebellion, they were all agreeable to following somebody else. It had been explained to them that Cerball and the Mugains and even Bodb Decht were becoming too old and set in their ways. Why, you could not so much as whisper a spell that had even a sliver of darkness in it without incurring their anger these days. And, said the Black HeartStealers persuasively, didn't any sorcerer of scholarship know that you had occasionally to make use of the blacker side of enchantry, and shouldn't any sorcerer with any decent power be able to control it?

What was wanted was younger blood heading the House, they said firmly. Younger blood and newer, more exciting ideas. The Arca Dubhs had been rather flattered to be thought of as being sorcerers of scholarship and power. They were not as a rule greatly given to excitement, which was apt to be exhausting, but they told one another that you had to see the force of the argument. And wasn't it an enormous compliment to be invited to take part in this really very important plot? They would make history, they said, pleased.

Two of the Black HeartStealers had murmured a Sealing Incantation over the doors, and as the words fell on the air, there was a sudden spiralling of dark, greasy smoke. The sorcerers averted their eyes, recognising the whiff of necromancy, and Iarbonel Soothsayer started to say that surely the utilising of necromancy for a minor door-sealing was a waste of energy, but the Fer Caille looked across at him, his eyes cold and hard, and Iarbonel found the words dying at birth.

The Fer Caille explained how he had called them together to tell them that the Dark Summoning put out earlier had been effective.

'It has worked very well,' he said. 'We reached the mountain community of Almhuin, deep in the *Sliabh Ciardhubh*.' He looked at them, and waited.

'The Crimson Lady's people?' asked an Arca Dubh, a bit uncertainly.

'Yes.' The Fer Caille turned his huge stare inquiringly on the Arca Dubh who had spoken, and waited, as if inviting a challenge. No one spoke, and after a moment he said, 'The Almhuinians themselves – at least a section of them – have answered our Summoning.'

'They will help our cause?'

'Oh yes. And,' said the Fer Caille, a sudden, rather evil relish in his voice, 'they will help us to squash these die-hards. And they are the most savage, most vicious fighters in the entire Dark Realm.'

A sudden silence fell, and at last, one of the Arca Dubhs said, 'It's a mutant branch, of course,' as if this made it more acceptable. He looked round him a bit doubtfully, because none of the Arca Dubhs had expected the involvement of Almhuin. Most of them had visualised a quite peaceful, almost cosy little fight, more of an argument really, at the end of which Cerball and the Mugains would go into comfortable retirement and the Arca Dubhs themselves would be given lucrative posts in the Palace. They'd seen themselves being invited along to Tara to advise the High King now and again. It would all have been perfectly amicable.

'They might be mutants, but they have the strongest traits of all sides,' said a Black HeartStealer instantly, and the Arca Dubhs began to look even more worried.

'Oh yes.'

The Fer Caille said, 'The Almhuinian Armies are already armed and accoutred, ready for our final call. They are waiting within the shadow of the Gateway inside the Cadence Tower.'

'So close?' murmured the Arca Dubh who had been doubtful about the Almhuinians.

'Yes. They would normally have selected one of the other Gateways to enter – perhaps the Moher Gateway, although that would have meant passing dangerously close to the Pit of the Dark Lords, which is in the keeping of the Flesh-eating Trolls. The Gateway in the Cadence Tower was the easiest and the nearest.'

'And next?' asked Iarbonel.

'And next,' said the Fer Caille with a throaty chuckle, 'next, we shall let them in. And then, by the bones and the blood of my ancestors, we shall sweep aside these ineffectual creatures who hold this Palace, and take the Amaranth Throne for ourselves.' He looked round at them, and the Arca Dubh who had said that the Almhuins were mutants, asked what about the Succession Ritual? You could not ignore something so ancient and so powerful as that.

'We do not ignore it,' said the Fer Caille in his huge voice. 'But rituals can be adjusted.' He grinned slyly. 'Rituals can be forced to obey the one who invokes them,' he said, and the Arca Dubhs all began to feel very worried indeed.

The Fer Caille turned back to the waiting BlackHeart Stealers. 'So,' he said, his voice thick with relish, 'so, my friends, do you permit me to call up our Armies? The Crimson Armies of Almhuinian? The Rodent descendants who will ride as our combatants? Who will fall on these paltry half-magicians and drive them out?'

A cry of assent went up, and the Arca Dubhs added their voices a bit raggedly. They had been rather shocked to hear the Fer Caille dismiss Cerball as a 'magician', which was, of course, the greatest insult you could deal anybody. But it was too late to back out now.

The Fer Caille moved to the centre of the small chamber, and raised his hands above his head. The shadows surrounding him reared up, and as he began to intone the dread lines of the Dark Summoning, the ancient and malevolent Beckoning, the shadows shrouded him so that he became a great solid column of blackness.

The Black HeartStealers and the Arca Dubhs made a circle about him, linking hands, joining their voices with his in the last and most powerful stanza of the Summoning. The light became tinged with crimson, and thick, fetid evil began to form like a vapour in the chamber.

Iarbonel Soothsayer, at the centre of it all, nodded to himself, and thought they'd made a wise move in throwing in their lot with the Fer Caille and his people. They would open the Cadence Gateway to let in the Almhuinians.

The Black HeartStealers would have ascended the Purple Throne of Porphyry Palace before the night was out.

Laigne was weakening. The Amaranth ladies around her bed saw it and heard it and felt it. She was flailing helplessly at the bonds that still held her down, but they were poor, weak struggles, and her screams of agony had faded into pitiful, mewling cries, as if the poor soul had barely the breath left in her lungs. Cecht, unable to bear the sight of Laigne's thin hands plucking feverishly at the leather thongs, bent to untie her,

'For,' she said, 'she can no longer hurt herself; she has not the strength left. And it is only *merciful*,' said Cecht, angry tears starting to her eyes.

The Gristlen's child was moving frenziedly beneath the distended body, struggling in its birth throes.

'It is huge,' murmured Great-aunt Fuamnach. 'It will surely kill her.'

Herself of Mugain said, rather tartly, that the creature was like to split Laigne in twain, but she said it quietly because there was no sense in distressing their poor cousin any further.

'Although I believe she is beyond hearing now,' said Cecht, bending to mop the pouring rivulets of sweat from Laigne's face, seeing, as she did so, that the skin was taking on a waxen look. Laigne was no longer moving; only the beast inside her was moving, making the great swollen mound ripple and heave with sinister life.

'Try the balm again,' suggested Great-aunt Fuamnach, and Cecht turned to the little side-table, where they had arranged the jars and boxes and flagons.

Herself of Mugain said, urgently, 'No, wait. Something is happening.'

A ridge was appearing in Laigne's swollen body now, as if the creature inside was pushing at the womb in which it was enclosed. There was a sharp look to the ridge, as if the pressure from within was being exerted by something pointed . . . A long fingernail. A claw . . . As they watched, appalled, a thin line of dark, sluggish blood appeared where the skin was splitting open.

'It is tearing its way out,' said Cecht. 'This is dreadful. It is ripping her open from inside. Cannot we . . . ?' And stopped as the tear gaped open, like a hideous dark wound.

The skin of Laigne's swollen body began to split, not neatly and cleanly, but jaggedly, the skin parting only with difficulty. There was a sickening glutinous sound, and dark blood welled up and trickled down over her white body, staining the bed. Laigne moaned and moved restlessly, but seemed barely aware of what was happening any longer.

Within the opening, they could make out a thick membraneous sac, smeared and clotted with blood and birth fluid, heaving and pulsating with horrid life. The point of a claw was protruding from the birth sac, a horrid, hard, grey claw, slicing and tearing at the thick membrane that enclosed it. There was a rather terrible efficiency about it, as if the creature knew that it must cut its way out.

The sac burst open, spattering thick yellowish fluid over the bed, and the Gristlen's monster-child started to clamber out of the torn, blood-slimed womb.

Its eyes were matted and closed, the lids crusted with blood and pus. It could not have known, in any sentient way, what it did, but it was struggling out of the dark, soundless womb into the world. It was struggling and fighting; its upper half was already freed, and it was pushing back the lips of the gaping wound in Laigne's body, heedless of the fearsome mutilations it was inflicting.

And then it was out; it had heaved itself out, and there was a terrible sticky sucking as the birth sac collapsed into a wrinkled pouch. Laigne gave a little sigh, and then was still.

'Dead,' said Great-aunt Fuamnach, softly. 'Poor soul.'

The creature crouched on the bed, shaking its head to rid itself of the slimed blood and the thick, discharged fluids, so that they dripped to the floor in curdled ropes of gore. Its hands came up in a flailing motion, rubbing at its eyes, trying to wipe away the clotting mucus and blood. Strings and gobbets of semi-liquid blood hung from its claws and its face, slopping down on to its body. Its hair was matted and wet, plastered to its head with dark blood.

It turned its head from side to side, and its flailing hands seemed to be searching for something, and this blind seeking movement was at once piteous and terrible. It was as if something alien and monstrous had been flung into a cold hostile world and was trying, in its sightless, newly born state, to seek assurance.

But beneath that, the Amaranths could see that there was calculating intelligence in its movements; it knew what it had to do to make itself ready for the world. Once its eyes were open, it would be sighted, it would not be blind and helpless in the manner of most newly-born things, it would not make those pitiful, searching gestures to where the dead Laigne lay . . .

It would be alive and sentient and rampant; there would be cold intelligence in the eyes, and there would be the undiluted

265

evil and the raging greed of its sire in its cold, black soul . . .

The Gristlen's seed, the foul spawn of the dark, evil creature who had dwelled in the noisome Tanning Pits, was in the room with them.

The three Amaranth ladies instinctively murmured a brief Ritual of Protection, and Great-aunt Fuamnach sketched the outline of the great Amaranthine Star before them.

Even like this, smeared and still partly blind from the thick dark blood and the pus-like matter, the Gristlen's monster-child was the most evil thing any of them had ever encountered.

There was a deep overhanging brow, shadowing the eyes and almost obscuring them. The eyes struggled to open, and for a moment there was bewilderment and incomprehension in them. The creature turned again to Laigne's body, reaching out with its hands, and the horrified watchers saw understanding dawn in its face.

She is dead and I am alone to fight these creatures before I have the power . . .

And then it seemed to gather huge strength into itself, and now its eyes shone with cold malevolence. It turned back to the room, and such bitter fury poured from it that for a moment it shone on the dark room, a baleful, crimson stream. Cecht, directly in line, felt it scorch her eyes, and flung up a hand to shield herself, falling back against the wall.

'Cecht? Child, are you all right?'

Cecht said, 'Yes. Yes, only dazzled.' And put out a hand to pull herself up.

'Anger,' muttered Great-aunt Fuamnach, helping Cecht to her feet with one hand, and grasping her hazel wand more tightly with the other. 'A nasty thing to fight, anger. But we'll see what we can do.' She lifted the hazel wand, and set a shaft of pure light sizzling through the air.

The creature lifted one claw-tipped hand, almost without looking, and deflected the light easily and carelessly, splintering it in mid-flight, so that tiny shards of glittering white fell to the ground.

'Strong,' said Great-aunt Fuamnach, shaking her head. 'By all the gods, it's strong. Cecht, child, are you sure you are all right?'

'Yes.' Cecht was bruised and a bit dizzy by the shaft of fury that had seemed to spit from the creature's eyes. The scorching light had stayed on her vision, playing tricks with it, as if she had been staring into the bright noon sun. Blinded by the Gristlen's spawn? Oh no! Aloud, she said, 'But I think we must send for the others . . .'

'Of course we must,' said Great-aunt Fuamnach. 'Mugain, what are you thinking of?' and Herself of Mugain muttered something and scurried from the room at once, banging the door behind her.

'Coward,' said Great-aunt Fuamnach, turning back to the bed. 'Still, I daresay we can't blame her! Please the gods she'll bring the Tiarnan. Now, child, is there anything we can do to render this monster harmless for a time?'

But they both knew there would be little either of them could do by themselves. The creature was watching them; it was crouching on the bed, naked and still wet. From time to time it made a scuttling, circling movement on the bed, like an animal burrowing out a nest, and its hands plucked at the blood-drenched bed-gown of the dead woman who had given it birth, as if trying to wake her.

They could make out the creature's features more clearly now. There was a flat, slash-like mouth, wide and lipless, rather horridly reminiscent of a sea creature. But its body was not hairless; there was a thatch of dark hair, coarse and ragged, and beneath it, they could see small ears, flat to the creature's skull.

Cecht, who had never before encountered Corrupt Evil, was trying not to be afraid, but the Gristlen's son was the most repulsive thing she had ever seen. It was the blending of ordinary Humanish blood and ordinary Humanish features with something that was not Humanish at all, that made Cecht's skin creep with horror. She thought: it has ordinary ears, and although its nose is flat and wide-nostrilled, that is not so very inHuman. And it has eyes and lips and hair, it has arms and legs and bones and muscles . . .

But there was no neck; the creature's jowls widened and sloped outwards until they joined the shoulders, and Great-aunt Fuamnach, who was sharp-sighted, said in a low voice, 'Fins. Gills. Do you see? In its neck at the sides.'

'Yes. Horrid.'

Great-aunt Fuamnach was becoming extremely angry at the way in which this bloodied morsel of repulsive life was able to send out its waves of fury and the billowing Corrupt Evil of the ancient Dark Realm. She pronounced again the Protective Ritual, this time snatching up her hazel wand, using it to trace the Amaranth Star on the floor around the bed. The creature was plainly gaining strength now; it darted at the constricting circle, and punched a hole through it with one taloned hand, and a low, throaty chuckle, glutinous and mocking, filled the room.

'It is able to deflect everything we do,' said Cecht, her eyes wide with horror.

'We shall do better when the others arrive. That fool Mugain has had time to gather up the entire Palace by this time.'

'Don't take your eyes from it,' said Cecht in a low, urgent voice, because it would be the most unbearable thing ever if the creature slid from the bed, and darted into hiding somewhere while they were not watching. It would be rather like having lost track of a particularly huge, particularly loathsome spider in your bedroom, or a slithering, writhing snake . . . Only it would be a million times worse.

'I don't intend to take my eyes from it,' retorted Great-aunt Fuamnach.

They could see that its body was nearly shapeless and faintly scaled. But, thought Cecht, it is difficult to tell if it is scale or Humanish skin. Perhaps it was a blending of the two. Yes. Humanish and fish-creature. Disgusting. Between its thighs was a thicker sprinkling of scales, and large, perfectly formed genitals; the penis, barbed like a fletched arrow, hung down pendulously.

And then it moved slightly in the bed, a horrid, sudden, slithering movement, its muscles bunching and rippling, and they saw that at the base of its spine was a triangular shape, a tightly furled membraneous structure, pale and cold-looking. A fin.

The two Amaranthine ladies looked at one another in horror, and then Cecht said, very softly, 'Coelacanth.' And then, 'Coelacanth's spawn,' she said.

Great-aunt Fuamnach was watching the creature closely. When she spoke, there was a note of fear in her voice that no one had ever heard there before. But she said, 'I believe so.'

'The Fisher King's seed. Then the Gristlen must have been Coelacanth himself,' whispered Cecht. 'Coelacanth thrown into the Pit of the Dark Lords and left for centuries until he became a Gristlen.'

'Yes. He must have somehow incurred the wrath of the other Dark Lords,' said Great-aunt Fuamnach, staring.

'This is his heir. This is the Fisher Prince,' said Cecht, horrified, and at once the creature turned its terrible head to regard her, as if it had heard and understood. Its eyes were cold and filled with an implacable, soulless evil.

Cecht shuddered and stepped back, but Great-aunt Fuamnach stood her ground.

'Is the Star holding it?' whispered Cecht.

'We will hope so.' Great-aunt Fuamnach regarded the Fisher Prince grimly. 'But we dare not lose any time in caging it. I hope that fool Mugain has the sense to bring the Tiarnan,' she said again. 'He's the only one who can deal with this.'

Cecht said, carefully, 'Can we do anything for Laigne?'

'She is dead,' said Great-aunt Fuamnach. And then, because she was a merciful soul at heart, murmured, 'Poor thing,' but because she was also Great-aunt Fuamnach, spared a thought for Cerball's pocket, which was going to be sorely stretched by yet another death.

They could hear people coming along the corridor now, and it was suddenly immensely comforting to hear voices and footsteps and doors slamming.

The door was flung open, and Cerball, with the Mugain and Bodb Decht at his side, stood on the threshhold. Behind them was Maelduin, slender and silent.

There was a moment when the newcomers stood horrified, frozen into uncertainty, each of them recognising, as Cecht and Great-aunt Fuamnach had done, that this was the spawn of the terrible Fisher King, the son of Coelacanth himself.

And then Maelduin moved forward, and the others fell back silently. Night had crept into the bedchamber without anyone realising, and as Maelduin moved across the room, he moved through dark, creeping shadows that lay thickly across the floor, and stole out towards him as he moved. But he paid them no heed; he simply moved silently forward, across the shadow-splashed floor, and as he approached the bed, the Amaranths saw that everywhere he trod was a faint sprinkling of cool, silver light. His eyes, brilliant blue-green pools of colour, shone as he eyed the thing on the bed, and a whisper of fear ruffled the surface of the silent room.

The creature was watching Maelduin's approach; it was eyeing him from the corners of his eyes: sly, furtive, gleeful, as if it knew it could not be attacked physically.

Come and get me, Tiarnan Prince . . .

Light poured outwards from Maelduin's slender form now, and he stood motionless and alone, eyeing the terrible thing that squatted in the drying blood and the pools of foul-smelling fluids.

The others did not know it, but his courage almost broke, for he saw, as they had seen, that this was indeed the Fisher King's creature, the child of Coelacanth, forced upon the poor Amaranth lady who lay dead. The *sidh* had driven Coelacanth out of Tiarna, but only the Elven King himself and Maelduin, the Crown Prince, knew how close-run the battle had been, and how nearly Coelacanth had overpowered the *sidh*'s Armies.

And Coelacanth had vowed to one day return . . .

He summoned up every ounce of resolve, and reached far down into his mind, plumbing memory's depths, down and down, until he felt his mind close about the living silver veins and the cords and the glittering pure strands that would harness and yoke the Cadence.

For a moment, the fear threatened to quench his strength; he thought: I cannot do it! I have forfeited the elven garb and donned the cloak of the Humanish. I no longer have the power!

But he beat the fear down and began the searching, the reaching out, the reaching *down* that would enable him to control the Cadence.

The Cadence was like the crystal pools of Tiarna, where the cool sea-magic of the *nimfeach* was stored. He would see it like that and he would force it to submit to him. A great library, an endless storehouse of spells and enchantments, each one catalogued and referenced and indexed . . . All I have to do is grasp the Cadence and bend and force it to my will. He half closed his eyes, his mind a single, vivid stream of concentration.

It was within his grasp. Maelduin felt his mind strongly in

control; he felt it spinning and darting through the immense magical library of the Cadence; the library that did not consist of vellum chronicles and shelves of manuscripts or cupboards filled with documents, but that was filled with every enchantment and every spell ever written or created or spun . . .

And then it was before him, opening up to his inner vision, the silver scrolls, the great tapestry of magic, the lore and the wisdom and the knowledge culled by every sorcerer who ever lived . . . Maelduin felt himself submerged in it, he felt it closing over his head, so that the beauty and the strength and the ancient wisdom was soaking into his skin, drenching his eyes, obscuring his sight . . .

And then it was there. The incantation that would not destroy the creature, but that would certainly cage it. The ancient pure Sea Ritual. The great far-reaching enchantment spun by the beings who had inhabited the seas and the oceans of the world; who had built Tiarna before the *sidh*, before even the *nimfeach*.

For the nimfeach *were themselves usurpers and despoilers, just as the* sidh, *in their turn, were the same* . . .

He saw that it had no formal name, that it had been known only as the Sea Ritual. But it was the long-ago incantation; it was the enchantment that Aillen mac Midha had used to drive out the *nimfeach* centuries ago. It had vanquished Coelacanth and it would vanquish Coelacanth's son . . .

Maelduin stayed where he was, completely still, his face colourless, his hair silver gilt, only his eyes showing colour, two narrow slits of brilliance. To the watchers it seemed that a gentle radiance began to enfold him, and for a moment there was the faint outline of slender, iridescent bodies, silver and blue and green, shimmering with the cool sea-magic of the fabled City of Tiarna . . .

Maelduin was no longer aware of the dark bedchamber. He was immersed in the great marvellous Language of Enchantment. It was all about him, so that he could see the words, the symbols, the silhouettes of the incantation forming; the Cadence was unrolling its wisdom at his feet like a great silken carpet: ice-blue, silver-green, the outlines tipped with silver, strengthened with gold and ivory. Great soaring curlicues of turquoise and pearl were woven into it, all of it within his understanding now, all of it waiting for him to call it into being,

271

so that the dark, monstrous being, the Fisher Prince, could be imprisoned . . .

Yes! thought Maelduin, his mind soaring. Yes! This is the one that will cage the creature, and this is the one that will imprison it! With the knowledge, he glimpsed the first faint forming of the immense silver cage, the Sea Ritual created when the world was still cooling . . .

The creature on the bed reared up, its face hideously distorted with blind rage. Its muscles bunched and rippled as it braced itself to spring, but for the first time it hesitated, and the watching Amaranths saw the faint glimmer of the Star sketched by Great-aunt Fuamnach earlier, and knew that, frail as the protection was, it was quenching the creature's powers a little.

Maelduin held out his arms, the palms turned upwards, and pronounced the beautiful, fearsome words of the Sea Ritual.

There was a howl of black bitter rage from the creature, and the repulsive membraneous fin unfurled and distended. Its eyes spat the baleful light again, but Maelduin was encased in the soft radiance of his people, and in the pouring silver silhouettes of the Sea Ritual, and the red glare faltered and died.

The shimmering shapes moved – forming, solidifying, glistening on the air – until they were a silver cage, the bars strong and brilliant, the cage itself doorless, invincible . . .

There was the deep echoing reverberation of a great door being closed somewhere above their heads, and another howl of fury came from the creature. The Amaranths blinked and put up their hands to shield their senses from the sight and the sound, for the silver bars, strong and transient though they were, shone so brightly that it made your eyes ache to look at them for too long.

But the creature was caged. The Gristlen's spawn, Coelacanth's evil seed, the monstrous Fisher Prince who had killed Laigne in its entry into the world, was penned inside the silver cage of the ancient Sea Ritual.

And from here, it must be taken to the deepest darkest dungeon in the bowels of Ireland's ancient haunted fortress.

The Grail Castle.

Chapter Twenty-five

Bodb Decht had found a tinder box and gone across to the lamps; now squares of glad yellow light flooded the room.

Maelduin was white and drained; there was no colour in him anywhere now, for even his eyes were the colour of the ocean with grey dull skies above it.

He said, in a rather faraway voice. 'The creature will be safe for a time. But it must be taken – to the place we agreed – at once.'

'You will do that?' said Cerball.

'I will do that,' said Maelduin, and looked at Cerball in surprise, as if he might be saying: but that was the promise. That was what we agreed.

'We shall make horses ready for you,' said Cerball. 'And provisions for the journey.'

'Thank you.' Maelduin had not moved, but as he stood framed in the window, the dying light of the day behind him, the candleglow touching his hair, he was suddenly and sharply remote from them. Cerball found himself remembering that this was the Crown Prince of Tiarna, the heir to the *sidh* kingdom, and that he came from the same world and perhaps even the same ancient roots as Coelacanth.

And he will have with him Coelacanth's spawn . . .

I suppose we are right, thought Cerball, staring at Maelduin. I suppose it is all right to let these two creatures come together.

But he could see no other way; and when Maelduin reached for the silver cage, he was conscious of a flood of thankfulness.

The cage was lighter than Maelduin had expected; he lifted it cautiously at first, and then with assurance. He crossed the room, and then paused and, setting down the cage carefully, he moved back to the bed where Laigne lay, and murmured a string of words in a cool, unfamiliar tongue.

273

Cerball said, 'What is . . .' and Maelduin looked across the bed at him.

'The words of an ancient *sidh* Halcyon,' he said. 'They will bring peace and balm to your lady on her journey to the Place Beneath the Ocean Roof.'

And without waiting, he slipped out into the vast corridors of the Palace, the silver cage tightly in his grip.

It was then that the Mugain said, 'Listen.'

'What?'

'I hear something . . .'

'It's only the others in the Looms Chamber,' said Bodb Decht, uncertainly. 'We're directly above the Looms Chambers here, aren't we.' And then, suddenly unsure, 'Or is it only that?'

'Perhaps travellers have arrived,' said Great-aunt Fuamnach.

Cecht and Bodb Decht had gone to the windows; Cecht was thinking that of course they would see only the normal reassuring arrival of travellers; pilgrims of some kind, perhaps.

But there were no travellers below. They could see the moon-washed courtyard clearly. There were no cries of 'Welcome, good sirs!' or shouted instructions to stable their horses, to bring out lights, to please to come along inside for a bite of supper and a firkin of wine. There was none of the jostle and bustle, the rather friendly sounds that always filled the large cobbled courtyard when travellers arrived at the Palace.

There were solid dark shapes lining the courtyard, standing sentinel around its edges. At first they all thought that they were shadows, nothing more. Cerball drew breath to make some reassuring remark, although he did not know what it would have been.

And then, quite suddenly, the shadows were no longer ordinary or harmless; they were creatures, beings; silent, motionless figures standing in the shadows, waiting . . .

There was the glint of spears and the glitter of javelins, and of black armour . . .

And eyes, dozens of pairs of sly red eyes . . .

'Red eyes,' said Bodb Decht. 'Whatever they are, they are not Humanish.'

'The Rodent Armies?' whispered Cecht, her eyes huge with fear.

'I don't know.' The Mugain was trying to see down into the

274

courtyard. 'Bless my boots, I don't like the look of this.'

'How did they get in?' demanded Great-aunt Fuamnach.

'That is easy,' said the Mugain rather grimly. 'Someone has let them in.'

He looked at the others, and Cerball, staring, said, 'A rebellion.'

'Yes. Someone inside this Palace has mounted a mutiny. Someone inside this Palace has sent out a Beckoning to the Dark Ireland. And the Dark Ireland has answered. The forces of the necromancers are waiting outside.'

Cerball had ordered them down into the central hall at once. 'All of us!' he gasped. 'Find everyone! Don't miss a single one!'

'Everyone into the central hall!' cried the Mugain. 'That's the place to put up a fight!'

Great-aunt Fuamnach stumped along gamely in his wake, because if there was going to be a battle, she was not going to miss it. Cecht took her arm, which was kind of the child but not necessary; her legs had not yet failed her.

The Mugain was importantly directing everyone to spread the word as fully as ever possible. No corner of the Palace was to be missed. He had sent everyone scurrying hither and yon, he said, coming up to Cerball, puffing a bit with the exertion of it all. But he thought no one had been missed.

The great central hall was immense; it was a hundred and fifty feet long and eighty feet wide, and it took up almost a whole quarter of the entire ground floor. When the Palace had been built for the long-ago Amaranths who had served the first High Kings and Queens, its architects who designed it, and its builders who raised it, had visualised the central hall as the great heart of the Palace: the nub and the cornerstone. The pity was that the vast gatherings and the great and splendid pageants of those days were no longer practical. Sorcerers these days liked to have their own castles, their own dwellings, no matter how modest. And there was not the money to entertain on such a lavish scale any longer.

The hall was paved with marble and white alabaster; there were doors leading from it, several of them only going down into sculleries and pantries and wine cellars, but four great iron-studded doors with pointed arches leading directly into each of the Palace's four wings. As the Amaranths came tumbling and running in from all parts of the Palace, Cerball, who was trying to make an overall plan, thought that here they would have four routes of escape. And was at once angry with himself, because they were not going to need an escape route, they were going to beat back these marauders. He spared a thought for Laigne, poor dead soul, for whom they had not yet been able to render any of the proper funerary rites, and for whom he, Cerball, had not even been able to grieve properly. To his credit, he did not even remember that this would be the third set of ceremonies in a row, and that funerary rites were expensive.

'But there are so few of us!' cried Bodb Decht, standing in the hall and looking round, dismayed. 'We cannot possibly fight with only this number!'

'Does anyone know what we're fighting?' demanded Great-aunt Fuamnach.

'The Mugain thinks they're Almhuinians,' said Bodb Decht, and Great-aunt Fuamnach compressed her lips disapprovingly, because it was no more than you would expect to be attacked by Almhuinian gutter-sweepings.

The Amaranths bunched together on the south side of the hall, just beneath the Star Ceiling, directly in line with the great arched entrance that led out to the portcullis and the main Palace gates. Cerball had said, and everyone had agreed, that the Almhuinians, when they came, would surely come this way.

'We must form a line so that they cannot break through,' he said. 'A straight, solid line, right across the hall. That way we should be able to force them back the way they came.'

'Yes. And we must arm ourselves,' said the Mugain firmly, because hadn't one of the Elders to take proper charge of all this, and he was not letting Cerball appropriate all the authority. 'See now, there're some swords and cutlasses – somebody brought them from the armoury – oh it was you, Bodb Decht, well, it was very quick thinking. Hand them round, and sharp about it.'

'We'll range ourselves here with the west wing at our back,' said Cerball, who had not been thinking about being authoritative, and was still trying to map out a plan that would meet all contingencies. 'That way, if we have to retreat, we can do so into the west wing, and we can seal it.'

'And then what?' demanded Great-aunt Fuamnach.

'Well, and then we . . . Cerball stopped and looked worried.

'I say we fight tooth and nail before we even think of a retreat,' put in a younger brother of Cecht's, who had never seen a battle, and who was truth to tell rather relishing being involved in this one. 'We ought to be thinking about fighting and winning,' he added, somewhat belligerently.

'But we aren't fighters!' cried Cerball in cross frustration. 'We aren't trained in fighting!' He glanced back at the door to the west wing, as if to reassure himself that it was still there.

'We can fight them with sorcery!' said Great-aunt Fuamnach, who had planted herself firmly at the forefront of them all, and was already drawing out circles and diagrams on the floor in front of them with her hazel wand. 'What's wrong with using sorcery as weapons! It's been done before, and it can be done again!'

'Yes, what about the Sorcery Wars with the Tyrians?' cried Cecht's brother, who had been named after Calatin, the famous hero of the Amaranth Sorcery Wars, and had consequently read his ancestor's remarkable *Memoirs*. 'Didn't we win then!'

'Did we?'

'Of course we won!' cried Calatin. 'And very thoroughly as well. What we did once, we can do again!'

'That's the spirit!' said Great-aunt Fuamnach. 'My word, I never thought to see you so lily-livered, Cerball! That boy's right, I always said that branch of the family had guts. Almhuinians! We'll see how far *Almhuinians* can get,' she said fiercely. 'By the gods, those miserable creatures shan't prevail against the House of Amaranth! Now then, Cerball! Where's your fighting spirit!'

A rather ragged cheer went up at this, and everyone began to hurriedly assemble spells and enchantments. There were a great many that could be used against an enemy when you came to think about it. And as Calatin said, these were *beatable* enemies; they were not the grim, darkness-soaked Fomoire. They might have come out of the Dark Ireland, but so far as anyone knew, they had no actual necromancy of their own. There would be no sorcery to deal with.

'If we lay a good strong wall of sorcery,' said the Mugain gleefully, 'they'll never be able to penetrate it. That'll be the

277

thing to do. Now form a line right across the hall, with the west wing to our back – just in case – yes, that's right. Facing the south entrance, the *south* entrance, I said. That's better. Quickly now, or they'll be upon us!

'And now for the spells,' he said. 'Have we decided what we're using, does anyone know?'

'Swamplands at the edges, I thought,' said Cerball, and several people looked at him approvingly, because wasn't this a very good idea indeed. They could fairly easily create a belt of Swamplands, strong thirsty Quicksands, across the entire breadth of the hall, so that when the Almhuinians attacked, the leading ones would certainly be trapped by it, and sucked down.

'Very good,' said the Mugain, who was not going to allow the control of this very important event slip from his grasp. 'And then, Cerball, if you and I are *here* to control the Swamplands, and Bodb Decht and Calatin are stationed *there*—'

'With a stock of Lightning Bolts?' asked Calatin hopefully, because you might as well have a bit of noise and excitement if you were fighting a battle.

'Yes, that's a good idea, you can direct them straight into the centre. What else?'

Several of the younger sorcerers who, like Calatin, enjoyed a bit of colour and fizz, suggested that the Twisting Fire Columns were always an effective deterrent, and were at once detailed to the centre. The air began to sizzle and hum, and the Fire Columns began to form, directly behind the belt of Swamplands which Cerball and the Mugain were creating across the length of the hall.

'And Great-aunt Fuamnach and the rest of the ladies could spin the Web of Mab,' said Bodb Decht, eyeing the defences critically. 'Just behind the Fire Columns, so that it will trap any of them who manage to get through.'

'Yes, we ought to take some prisoners if we can.'

'We'll take them all right,' said Great-aunt Fuamnach, who did not know what things were coming to when the ancient magical stronghold of Ireland's Royal Sorcerers could be invaded in such an impudent fashion. She marshalled her ladies at once, telling them to fan out directly behind the Twisting Fire, and not to get singed. 'You'll all know the incantation for Mab's Web,' she said, glaring at two fifteen-year-old nieces of

Rumour, twins, who were looking alarmed. 'Remember to work together, so that the Web joins up properly. We don't want any gaps in it,' said Great-aunt Fuamnach, stumping down the line. 'Strong and thick, that's what we want. My word, we'll tie the wretches up and fling them into the dungeons!'

'Anything else?' asked Cerball. 'What about a NightMare Spell?'

'Isn't that a bit – well, strong?' said Herself of Mugain, who found the NightMare Spell – which summoned the creatures of your adversary's nightmares (and sometimes your own) – very nasty. 'We are only fighting Humans. Well, nearly Humans.'

The Mugain remembered that the Academy was rather severe these days about people using NightMare Spells against Humans, and Cerball, who had forgotten this for the moment, said, 'Yes, all right. We'll keep that in reserve.'

'And for the NightMare Spell to be truly effective, you'd really need the NightCloak,' put in Bodb Decht, rather wistfully. 'You can't really do much in the way of nightmares without the NightCloak.'

'Yes, and that's *long* since lost to us.'

They could hear the scufflings and the scurryings more loudly now, and as they turned from their various tasks, several people caught, quite plainly, the sound of the portcullis being raised.

'Raised?' said Cerball, looking across at Bodb Decht. 'How have they done that?'

'Does it matter? They'll be with us at any minute. Stand firm!'

It was then that the Mugain, who, satisfied with the defences they had created, turned to make a quick count of everyone present. It would not do to find later that someone had been left forgotten in a pantry somewhere, or maybe the lone north tower, which people were apt to retreat to in order to harness a bit of star power which could be useful in spinning the odd spell. He strode up and down, seeing that everyone was working well; the Fire Columns were burning strongly, and ready to be sent gusting out at the Almhuinians, and the Web of Mab had formed very nicely indeed. And although he did not know, not to the last person, how many people ought to be there, he knew pretty quickly that there were some people who were not there at all.

279

He said, in a stricken voice, 'Cerball. The Black HeartStealers are missing,' and several of the Amaranths looked round.

'So they are,' said a voice, worriedly.

'And,' said another voice, 'the Arca Dubhs.'

Nobody was especially concerned about the Arca Dubhs' absence, but everyone was very concerned indeed about the Black HeartStealers'.

A sudden silence fell. People began to remember how the Fer Caille and his family had several times been seen brewing up very *dark* spells, and how a number of the Black Hearts had been spotted more than once going furtively off to the abandoned east wing of the Palace, and the absence of these two leading branches of the family began to assume sinister proportions.

It was Bodb Decht who said, 'So it is a mutiny. We were right.'

'Surely not,' said Cerball, because sometimes if you said a thing strongly enough it became fact. 'I won't believe it,' he added for good measure.

'I will,' said Great-aunt Fuamnach grimly. 'I always said no good would come of inviting the Fer Caille and his family, and now we see.' She glared at Cerball. 'We'll be under the rule of the Black HeartStealers before dawn if we aren't careful, mark my words.'

'Listen,' said Cecht, lifting a hand.

'What is it?'

'They're coming.'

They could all hear it now; since the portcullis had risen protestingly and screamingly, they could hear stronger, more definite movements within the Palace confines.

'Marching,' said Herself of Mugain, white-faced.

It was the soft, inexorable marching of feet that were nearly but not quite Human; the swishing of arms and hands that were not Rodent, but that possessed a thin trickle of cold, sly, Rodent blood. The feeling of a terrible darkness closing in . . .

There was a moment when absolute stillness held them in its grip; when the defensive enchantments spun and shimmered and spat; when the intricate Web of Mab, carefully spun by the ladies, glistened and caught the moonlight that silvered the floor, and glinted red from the Fire Columns and the Lightning Bolts.

And then there was another moment when the stillness was shattered, and they heard the marching – suddenly and shockingly close now – and felt the evil darkness approaching the hall.

And then they were there. The sly evil Almhuinians were with them, crowding through the arched entrance, leaping and darting, pointed swords held aloft, daggers and knives and wicked fletched arrows, shiny with poison, ready to fire.

They led the attack. They came storming across the great hall, their black armour gleaming, their eyes sly inside their visors.

Directly behind them were the Black HeartStealers, led by the Fer Caille, his huge shape towering over the rest. He brandished an immense sword, but the Amaranths saw at once that the air all round him was thick with necromancy, and veined with crimson and horrid pulsating strings of viscousness, and knew that the sword was unnecessary. The Fer Caille had called down a great dark cloud of malevolence; those at the front of the Amaranth line could already see the vapour of Simple Evil forming.

Cerball said, very softly to Bodb Decht, 'He has already gone over to the Other Ireland.'

'Yes. This is terrible.' Bodb Decht was staring at the Fer Caille, the Simple Evil as clear to him as it had been to Cerball.

'Can we beat them?'

'I don't know.'

But further along, the younger Amaranths were already piling into the battle, and if they had seen the clouds of Simple Evil already about their opponents' heads, they paid scant heed.

Calatin directed half a dozen of the Lightning Bolts straight at the centre of the Almhuinians. There was a sizzling sound as the Fire streaked forward, leaving scorch marks on the marble floor as it went, and a cheer went up. Calatin's little band flung four more Bolts after it, and several of the others were sending out knife-tipped spears of pure white light, which they had brewed as back-ups to the Lightning.

The leading Almhuinians fell, burned and injured, a dreadful acrid stench of hot steel billowing out. They rolled over, clawing at the hasps of their breastplates, shrieking and writhing. Howls of pain were filling the great hall, but the Almhuinians were already recovering, and the uninjured were re-forming and holding their spears and javelins ready.

'They are coming at us again!' cried Calatin. 'Again! Hurry!'

The Almhuinians ran in a solid block straight at the waiting Amaranths, and as they did so, the heaving, turgid Swamplands slopped into life. The six Almhuinians leading the charge fell at once, sinking knee-deep and then waist-deep into the oozing mires. They threw up their hands, their swords clattering harmlessly to the ground, and the Amaranths heard the Swamps begin the horrid, inexorable, sucking, lapping sounds.

The Almhuinians struggled and screamed for help, but the Swamplands were too strong. They heaved with grisly life, and the sucking took on a sudden, dreadful intelligence. The nearest Almhuinian was screaming, terrible trapped-hare screams, as the slopping, semi-liquid mud bubbled over his voice. He threw his head back, and with the one hand that was still free, tried desperately to reach his companions.

'Help m-e-e-e—'

For answer, the Swamplands lapped over his face, in slabby waves, and there was a choking, mucus-filled scream. The other Almhuinians hesitated, watching their colleague's struggle, hearing his screams, seeing that the other five were already floundering, shoulder-deep in the glutinous mud.

And then the Fer Caille effortlessly and very nearly contemptuously reached up into the thick cloud of vapour over his head and pulled down a twisting mucus-like string, which he spun and whirled about his head.

The white substance solidified almost immediately, and the Fer Caille, chuckling throatily and evilly, cast it across the surface of the Swamps, and flung out a hand, pointing.

'See, my friends! We can with ease form a bridge across the puny defences of these charlatans! Across the bridge and slay the weak-kneed creatures who would rule Ireland!'

'Kill them all!' cried the Almhuinians, rushing forward, the Black HeartStealers and the Arca Dubhs in their wake. 'Kill the paltry magicians!'

'How dare they!' cried Cerball, his face scarlet with rage. 'How dare they call us *magicians*!'

But there was no time to think; the Almhuinians and the traitorous Black HeartStealers poured forward across the white, pulsating bridge, formed from the Fer Caille's necromancy. As they did so, the Fer Caille himself, together with Iarbonel, hurled more of the thick smothering whiteness straight on to the Fire Columns. There was a furious hissing sound, and spirals of evil-smelling grey smoke rose.

'As for the Web of Mab you have striven to create,' cried the Fer Caille, 'that is easily dealt with!' As he spoke, three of the Black HeartStealers to his right flung sizzling knives and red-glinting spears at the web, slicing it to shreds instantly.

'The Porphyry Palace is within our reach!' cried Iarbonel. 'Fall on them! Slay them if you must!'

The Almhuinians were already across the defences, and falling on Calatin and his group of friends, recognising that these were the strongest physically, stabbing them with their knives and spears. The air became tainted with the stench of spilled blood, and through the thick acrid smoke that had doused the Fire Columns, Cerball and the Mugain could both see that several of the Amaranths had already fallen. Cerball looked round wildly; Great-aunt Fuamnach was standing her ground, the famous hazel wand brandishing in the air. Light spat forth, and one of the Almhuinians fell, wounded in the shoulder. The hall was a seething cauldron of fire and whirling smoke and darting, hissing knives and swords. Clouds of thick, mucus-like vapour poured down from the ceiling, opening to rain down stringy clots of blood straight on to the Amaranths. Several of the Almhuinians were still struggling in the belt of Swampland, and several more lay shrivelled and dead, burned by the Fire Columns earlier.

Cerball thought: we can beat them if we can call up other spells! But to do that we must be able to concentrate.

Raising his voice above the shouting and the screams and the hissing spitting daggers, he cried, 'Get back! All of you! Into the west wing!' And turning, pulled wide the great studded door.

At once a howl of triumph went up from the Black HeartStealers and the Arca Dubhs. The Almhuinians surged forward towards the retreating sorcerers, screeching their glee.

'Cowards! Defeatists! Craven creatures!' They bounded across the great blood-spattered, smoke-filled hall, unsheathing their swords, aiming longbows and crossbows, beginning to swing fearsome broadswords and cutlasses.

Cerball, pushing his people frantically to safety through the door, glanced back at them. Calatin and a couple of his friends were covering their retreat, inching backwards to the studded door, facing the on-coming Almhuinians, their own swords striking out. Calatin snatched a spear of light from the air, and hurled it into the midst of the dark Armies, where it splintered and sent dazzling shards of light flying. The Almhuinians hesitated, and Calatin and his friends flung several more. The Fer Caille deflected them this time, and Cerball knew that, although Calatin had bought them a few precious minutes to escape, there was no more time now. They must barricade themselves in the west wing; they must combine their strengths and call up something so awesome and so overpowering that it would sweep these adversaries away once and for all.

He began to push the last few people through, shouting to them to be quick, for they dared not let these creatures follow them. He saw Great-aunt Fuamnach and the twins station themselves in the doorway just inside, hidden from the Almhuinians' sight, and saw the great purple and silver Seals of the Amaranthine House of Sorcery begin to form. He half pushed the last of his people through, and saw the Seals fly to the door at once, tiny tongues of flame shooting from them as they covered the lock and the frame and the hinges . . . He watched for a moment, and was satisfied. No crack, no sliver of egress or ingress showed. Not even the tiniest thread of enchantment could slip through from outside, and the Seals were invincible. The only person who could break the Amaranth Seal once it was properly in place was the person who had created it.

As they mounted the stairs, they heard from over their heads the immensely comforting sound of gates closing and bolts being driven home.

The Seals of the ancient Amaranthine House of Sorcery locking into place.

Cerball waited just long enough to draw the ordinary iron and steel bolts across the door, and to turn the key in the lock. He turned to regard the Amaranths, who were standing uncertainly at the foot of the stone stairway. At the head of the stairs was the ancient west wing unused these two centuries past, but as safe a refuge as any they would find anywhere.

In the dim light the sorcerers were pale, and several of them were wounded. Cerball quickly counted them. Twenty-seven, including himself. Then eight? ten? were lying dead outside. He spared a brief thought for them. But there were twenty-seven here. Twenty-seven. The mystical three times nine. Not as bad as it might have been. The number would help to strengthen any enchantments they might weave.

Bodb Decht was unharmed, as was Cecht and Great-aunt Fuamnach. Calatin had a knife-slash across one cheekbone, and the twins were wounded, but only slightly. The Mugains, dusty and dishevelled, were here. Several others. It could have been much worse.

But they were barricaded inside the west wing, and their numbers were severely depleted.

And outside the door were the Almhuinian Armies of the Beastwoman of the Dark Realm, and the traitor Fer Caille and his people.

Chapter Twenty-six

Maelduin stood in the shadowy courtyard and saw and felt the creeping darkness of the Almhuinian Armies.

Advancing on the Amaranths. Exactly as I guessed, he thought.

There was a moment when his resolve wavered; he looked about him and thought: perhaps I should stay here. Perhaps there is something I could do to help. And with the thought came a derisive, silvery voice, somewhere deep inside him.

Help the Humanish . . . ?

I suppose not, thought Maelduin. And it is not part of my mission to do so. But he found himself remembering how the Amaranths had been friendly and welcoming; how they had invited him in and given him a place at their table and been unfailingly hospitable. Even after Murmur's death, the vow he had made to free them from the Gristlen's creature had been courteously discussed, as if there might be another way, and then, when it was apparent that there was not, as courteously accepted. But there had been reluctance in their acceptance. They were concerned for me and I ought to help them.

He was uneasily aware that he was becoming bound to this Humanish world, and to this vast Amaranthine Palace – *and I dare not!* he thought. I dare not acquire any more Humanish emotions and Humanish thoughts. Already there are too many.

And the thicker the carapace, the harder it will be to return . . .

The harder to return. Yes. That was a better way to think. Of course he would return, of course he would re-enter Tiarna and restore his people. Already there was the Cadence, harnessed lightly to his mind. Even if the music was beyond his reach, somewhere in the vast storehouse of magical knowledge, there would be a spell, an enchantment, a bewitchment that would free the *sidh* and allow them to live again.

He slipped unseen through a tiny side door, ivy-covered and set deep into the thick walls of the Palace. Cerball had talked of a horse, provisions for the journey, but Cerball and all of them would be caught up with the dark adversaries that had slunk in. Maelduin thought he could find the stables for himself from here. He glanced down at the creature in the cage, and saw that it was somnolent, curled into a dark mass in one corner. Maelduin hesitated. Could he simply kill it now? Could he plunge a knife into its black heart?

With the framing of the thought, the thing uncoiled at once, and a clawed hand came snaking through the bars, raking at Maelduin's hand. Blood poured out, spattering the cage, and the creature grinned and leaned close to the bars. Blood touched its jowls, and it licked, savouring, grinning. Maelduin, his arm stinging with white-hot pain, stared down at the caged being.

His senses were swimming, and he put out a hand to the wall for support. So this was Humanish pain, this was wounding, bleeding, *hurting*. He mopped the blood as best he could, using the cambric shirt he had donned in Tiarna, seeing it become wet and stained.

'I would put an arrow through your heart if I could,' said Maelduin, very softly, and the sly flat eyes regarded him, red amusement within them.

You know me for a near-immortal, sidh *Prince . . .*

Maelduin said, 'We shall see,' and moved towards the stables. For the moment the creature was imprisoned; the cool, elvish spell of the Sea Ritual held it. For the moment, he was safe.

But it is growing stronger with every hour . . . It is feeding on the darkness from the Almhuinian armies, and it is gaining sustenance from the battle that must be imminent . . .

And if there should be bloodshed, it will feed from that, also . . .

The stables were directly ahead of him, and although he had never entered them, he knew that within them were the great strong beasts the Humanish used for travelling.

He entered cautiously, unused to such a place, and felt the scents of horse and leather and straw close about him, with unexpectedly comforting warmth. He placed the silver cage carefully on the ground, and stood eyeing the creatures in the stalls. Could he take one? Could he control one?

287

I have to try, he thought. For on foot I should be vulnerable and prey to anything that cared to attack me. I should be at the mercy of every prowling danger. I have to try to use one of these beasts as the Humanish use them.

He moved forward.

In the end it was easier than he thought. He had no knowledge of the methods of saddling and bridling, although at home in Tiarna he had sometimes harnessed and ridden the *Uisce*, the silken-skinned, floss-maned sea-horses that occasionally romped and danced on Tiarna's shores. He had used the thin silken cords that were spun in the caves of Seiricia by strange, little-known beings who lived in a twilight world, but whose silk and spiderweb gauze and wafer-thin lace was sought by eager pilgrims.

The *sidh* had traded for the Seirician's exquisite and costly spinnings; using them to embellish the Silver Cavern of Aillen mac Midha, or for the garments and robes that must needs be donned along with the Humanish spell.

And now, Maelduin, used only to the pale flosslike threads and the smooth silken skeins, must somehow handle thick leather straps for his mount, and cumbersome steel trappings.

He thought he managed it well. To begin with the horses shied from him, their eyes rolling back so that the whites showed. Maelduin murmured the Halcyon he had used earlier, and then thought: but perhaps it is the blood they scent. He glanced down at his torn arm, and saw that it was drying over, but that blood still soaked his shirt.

He rinsed his arm carefully, using a bucket of water left in the adjoining room. There were Humanish clothes here as well; shirts and breeches and leather jerkins. Maelduin took one of the shirts and donned it and slid into a pair of soft warm boots. There was a thick woollen cloak which could be slung about his shoulders.

In a room adjoining the stables (tack-room, did they call it?), he found harnesses and saddles. The horses were quiet now, regarding him with interest, and he managed to lead the nearest one out, and fasten a saddle and bridle to it. The buckles and the straps gave him a little trouble – although it is only a question of plain sense, he thought – but in the end, he did it.

288

There were saddlebags with panniers, clearly intended for transporting food and provisions. Very good, he had no provisions that he could take, but he had his prisoner. He led out a second horse, and found it easier, this time, to fasten on the pannier. Then he fastened the cage firmly to the pannier, and pulled a square of blanket over it. If he must ride the dark sinister road to the Grail Castle, then he must. But I should infinitely prefer to do so without the Fisher Prince's baleful stare on me, he thought.

It was generally believed in Ireland that the road to Grail Castle, the fearsome, myth-shrouded stronghold of legend, was almost impossible to find.

Tales were told about it the length and breadth of the land, for wasn't there something altogether fine about a dark fortress that everyone had heard of, but that no one had ever seen? It was a well-known fact that no one who ever attempted to journey along the dark, eerie road to the Grail Castle ever returned. People went boldly off on quests and adventures, but none of them came back to tell the tale.

If you were really clever (or especially imaginative), you could weave a few extra strands of your own on to the existing tales. It was not telling an untruth to do that, it was only making the tale a little bit better. And although nobody ever came out and said so, making a tale – any tale – a little bit better was meat and drink to the Irish.

But the legends that clung to the Grail Castle needed little embellishment. There were the solemn and severe tales of the many prisoners who had been cast into its grim fastness, and who had sat out the dreary years of exile in its vasty dark halls. Maelduin, who knew the stories as well as he knew the silver and green tunnels of Tiarna, knew that he was riding towards a place of great and ancient magic. The Grail Castle had been old when Ireland was young; it had been raised when Tara was still only barren rock, and it kept its secrets. Some people believed that it was Tara's dark underside, just as the Black Realm was Ireland's dark underside.

Maelduin's father had visited it once, many centuries earlier; he had said little about it, other than that it had been a place of shadows and strange, lingering echoes, but the story of what happened to him there had never been told. Maelduin caught himself thinking that this was surely odd in itself, for the *sidh* loved to foregather in the Silver Cavern on feasts and at festivals, and tell stories, sometimes scooping up sparkling handfuls of music from the crystal pools and setting it to the tales there and then. There were many stories of many journeys in the land of the Humanish, but there was not a one of the Elven King's sojourn in the Grail Castle.

I do not even know if I can find it, thought Maelduin. The ancient belief was that you must ride directly into the setting sun, but other sources said you rode away from it. Many tales said it could only be found in the depths of the night, when the ancient lost enchantments of Ireland stirred, and when prowling evils walked abroad.

Maelduin, riding warily along, keeping the Porphyry Palace behind him, delved far down into memory, and the words of his father were strongly in his mind.

'The Grail Castle is the Humanish place of suffering. It is used for exiles and outcasts and failed spells . . . There are many strange things to be found there, and many strange Guardians on its road to challenge and trap the unwary . . .

'And the road that leads Men to it is the darkest and the most desolate place in all Ireland . . .'

The darkest and the most desolate place in all Ireland . . .

A rather grim smile touched Maelduin's lips, for he knew precisely where his father meant. The Ireland of the Humanish was a remarkable place; a place of fields and villages, and remote settlements where traces of almost extinct races still lived: a place where there were ancient forests, with blue and purple shadows stealing through the trees at twilight, and soft prowling enchantments . . . And soaring mountains, veined with tiny trickling streams, and studded here and there with the fortresses of Ireland's warrior lords and chieftains . . . And marvellous awe-inspiring coastlines, where the ocean lashed against the rocks, and where there was nothing to be seen for miles other than glinting, rippling sea, and shining, endless sky . . .

The coastline where the ocean lashed against the rocks . . .

Ireland's dazzlingly beautiful western rim, where once the Twelve Tribes of *Gaillimh* had ruled, and where Maelduin had frequently darted and swooped joyously, skimming the surface of the water, sparkling and iridescent in the sun's reflection on the sea.

And where there were lonely forbidding crags and cliffs that were said to be the haunt of strange, evil creatures and where, according to an ancient belief, there had once been a Gateway into the Dark Realm.

The loneliest place in all Ireland.

The Cliffs of Moher.

The day was dying, and the sun was sinking into the ocean on Ireland's desolate, beautiful western coast, as Maelduin neared his journey's end.

He had stopped to rest several times, unsure of how far or for how long the horses could travel. They had passed through several clusters of houses, through sparsely populated villages and along narrow forest paths, where the ancient trees fringed the road. Lovely! thought Maelduin, drinking in the sights and the scents and the sounds of this Humanish world. He thought that the vivid greens of the forest and the fields, and the deep rich blues of the small streams and lakes were no longer so garish. Ireland is mellower out here, he thought; far more beautiful than ever I realised. And then, in sudden fear, he thought: *or is it that my vision is becoming more Humanish?*

He pushed the thought from him at once, and rode on, noting the road, guiding the horses due west all the time.

When the noonday sun was high above, he stopped at a farmhouse, and asked if he might beg a crust of bread and perhaps a drink. The farmer's wife brought him a meat-filled pasty, together with a pitcher of creamy, still-warm milk, and a dish of pears, sweet and wine-scented.

'You are generous,' said Maelduin, and at once heard the thought that formed in her mind: *and could be even more generous to one such as yourself . . .*

He considered her briefly, but he knew he dared not turn aside from his quest. And he had not forgotten the ill-fated Murmur, he had not forgotten the sudden cold desolation, the feeling of a life draining away. I should not like to experience that feeling again, he thought. I should not like to cause another death. And I must do nothing that would draw attention to me.

He ate the pasty and drank the milk, and bade the lady farewell, and did not notice that his first emotion had been to avoid sadness and death; and that it was only afterwards that he had thought of the danger to himself.

The sun was setting into the sea as he finally approached the great sea-washed, sun-drenched edge of Ireland's west coast. As he turned his mount's head towards the blazing light, he saw for the first time the great, towering shapes of the Moher Cliffs, silhouetted sharply and blackly against the horizon. The narrow roadway sloped sharply upwards, so that he must approach them from below. Fiery light from the dying sun poured in between the great rocks, laying fingers of brilliance across the road. The horses' manes were turned to molten gold in the blaze, and Maelduin felt as if he was riding into the centre of an immense fire. He thought that he was surely going in the right direction – *ride directly into the setting sun* – and he felt confidence well up inside him.

I am riding into the setting sun, I am following the oldest, most enduring story ever told about the Grail Castle. I am surely on the right road. I shall cage this monster, and then I shall return to my people.

Ahead of him, the skies were washed in the fiery sunset, so that it was as if the entire western edge of Ireland was burning. He reined in his horse, and sat motionless for a moment, seeing the great swathes of flame and pink and crimson pouring across the skies, turning the ocean to a river of dazzling brilliance. Beautiful and awe-inspiring. And how often had he flown recklessly through that fire-drenched ocean, chasing the shrieking seagulls, leading the other *sidh*, all of them gleefully hunting the Humanish.

And now the Humanish are my friends, and I am seeing the dying sun from the ground, and I am chained and manacled in Humanish skin and bones and flesh.

He touched the horse's flanks lightly to move it onwards again, for the sun was slipping down into the ocean, and night would soon be creeping over the great stark Cliffs.

The road continued to climb, and as the two horses climbed with it, Maelduin heard the ocean roaring and tasted the sharp clean scent of the pounding waves. At the summit of the incline, straight ahead of him, were the great Moher Cliffs, standing sentinel to Ireland's western edge. He could not see beyond them, but at any minute, he thought, I will reach the crest of the hill, and I will stand on the summit of the Cliffs, and I shall look out over the endless ocean.

And somewhere there will be the Grail Castle.

He looked back yet again to be sure that the other horse was still with him. Yes. It followed faithfully and steadily, the silver cage securely strapped to its pannier. Maelduin turned back to the road, thinking that he had come this far without incident, thinking that after all it had not been so very hard a task.

The great crags seemed to be leaning forward towards him now, and he saw that, at their exact centre, standing directly in his path, were two vast columns, great black pillars, either natural or Man-made, he did not know which, starkly outlined against the glow of the setting sun.

The disused Gateway to the Dark Realm.

The pillars tapered towards their summit, and at the tip of each of them was an eyelet, a round fissure, through which the dying light streamed, giving the pillars an eerie appearance of sight. I could easily believe that those are single eyes, and that they are watching me, thought Maelduin. I could very easily imagine that they are giants, cyclopic ogres, twin colossi standing guard to the dark inner world of that Other Ireland . . .

He gave himself a shake, and looked back at the columns of stone. Nothing but hard, dark rock, immense stone pillars with some kind of freak formation at the tip. But he felt, as if it were a physical coldness, the shadows of the pillars fall across his path; and he felt as well the trickling, seeping, *draining* feeling of evil quite close by. An icy wind stirred the air, and blew dank, sour breath in his face, as if an ancient tomb had been unsealed. In the cage behind him, he heard the Fisher Prince uncoil, and he heard the scrape of its claws against the silver bars of its cage. So it also sensed and smelt the ancient evil, did it? Maelduin shivered and drew the woollen cloak more tightly about him. I am on the edges of the necromancers' Realm, I am approaching a Gateway to the Black Domain, and the sun is sinking, and night is falling all about me . . .

And only in the darkest depths of the night can the Grail Castle on its lonely, desolate road, be found . . .

He rode on, occasionally glancing back to where the second

293

horse followed faithfully, and as he rode, he felt the night begin to wake.

The depths of the night, when the ancient lost enchantments of Ireland stir, and when prowling evils walk abroad . . .

He could feel the old enchantments all about him as he guided his horse on to the narrow path that led to the Cliffs, but they were no longer the soft woodland enchantments that lived in Ireland's heart and that stirred the depths of the ancient forests or walked abroad in the magical Purple Hour of twilight.

These were the dark, warped creatures of necromancy; the twisted, grotesque beings that patrolled the boundaries and that were sometimes glimpsed in the deepest thickets of the night. I can feel them and I can scent them, thought Maelduin, his every nerve stretched to its furthest point. There was a thickening in the air, the fleeting vision of something – several somethings? – darting ahead; not quite on all fours, but not quite walking upright either. There was the beating of wings overhead several times, the soft, insidious sounds of slithering boneless creatures, or claw-footed beasts with slavering jaws and hungry muzzles . . .

The Dark Ireland waking and walking close by . . . Yes, I believe that I am very close to one of the Gateways now.

He was not afraid. He was curious and fascinated; in his mind he touched the glistening, silver-tipped Cadence and felt himself protected. He feared no creature; for, he thought, I believe that nothing in this Humanish world could kill me.

As he drew nearer, the great black columns were framed against the sky, and he saw that, just in front of them, a thin reddish vapour rose into the air, tainting it, as if blood were oozing from a wound, or as if someone – several someones – were sitting round a fire. His mind at once conjured up an image of a group of people talking quietly, perhaps cooking a meal over the fire, the shadows gathering beyond the leaping warmth, but the circle of light safe and bright and friendly. Perhaps they would invite him to share their fire and their supper. And then he thought: *but what kind of people would make camp out here in the lee of the Moher Cliffs, on the very threshold of the Dark Ireland . . . ?*

As he neared the light, he saw that it lay over the road and the foot of the great black stone pillars, and that it seemed almost to be a dull phosphorescence, a faintly luminous glow that was escaping from the crags and the boulders and the sudden jagged quarries out here. Not a fire after all. Or is it? thought Maelduin. It had the feeling of fire; there was a dry, rather evil-smelling heat to it.

He reined in his horse and remained motionless, trying to identify the light, feeling the harsh dry heat quite strongly now, thinking that perhaps the phosphorescence might be coming from the earth's core; a cavern or a chasm of some kind.

Behind him on the second horse, the monster-creature was peering through the silver cage, his clawed hands curled about the bars, his flat, evil eyes fixed unblinkingly on the glow. Maelduin felt something inside him spark a warning, for if the monster-creature was attracted by the lights, then they must have a sinister meaning.

A quarry. Some kind of natural crater. An abyss. Or a chasm. Or a pit.

As they rounded a curve in the road, Maelduin saw directly ahead of him, yawning redly and evilly in the light of the dying sun, the great smooth-sided abyss, with thick, fetid smoke rising slowly from its depths.

The Tanning Pit of the Dark Lords.

He recognised it at once, for the tales told about it were many and vivid. The great Chasm, the Pit, where servants of the Dark Lords who displeased or injured them were summarily flung to bake slowly in the hard, dry heat. The terrible gaping abyss where the unfortunate wretches who incurred the necroman-cers' wrath and transgressed their laws were chained and manacled to the hard rock. Where they were left to dry and wither, to tan and harden until their outer coverings became thick and horny and scaly; covered with the crusted carapace that branded them for what they were.

Gristlens . . . Many of them once perhaps necromancers of some power and some standing in the Black Ireland. Disgraced, outlawed Dark Lords. And this is their place of punishment.

Maelduin dismounted and tethered both horses to a jutting piece of rock. The silver cage he covered with the blanket, so that the creature should not see what lay ahead. He felt the waves of hatred emanate outwards from it as he did so, and he felt, as well, angry red fire spit from its eyes; and although he paid this no heed, he thought: it senses what is ahead and it wants to see.

He moved forward warily, feeling even at this distance the harsh heat belching out, brushing his skin and making his eyes dry and gritty.

And the prisoners condemned to be chained to the Pit's bottom must dwell there for decades, perhaps centuries even. Maelduin thought: what did they do to deserve such a sentence? In the evil world where they dwelled, what was their offence that they must be cast into this place, and left to flay and shrivel and acquire the repulsive appearance of Gristlens?

He walked forward, padding soft-footed, silent as a shadow, a slender, colourless figure blending with the moonlight; only his eyes a vivid, glowing colour. The light from the Pit fell about him, clothing him in golden fire and, as he drew closer, he saw that around the Pit's edges were flambeaux, huge flaring torches that were thrust into the ground at regular intervals. The flames leapt and danced, sending out eerie, flickering shadows, so that for a moment he could believe that strange, distorted beings cavorted and pranced in silent and unholy glee around the Pit's rim.

But as he drew closer, he saw that it was only the leaping flames; that nothing moved in the shadows beyond the flambeaux. He stood still, his mind working furiously, studying the torches. They glistened with nearly colourless grease of some kind; there was a sickening meaty scent to them which made his stomach lift with revulsion. He thought: Humanish flesh! I can *smell* that it is Humanish flesh! And knew the torches to be fuelled by the remains of Humanish bodies, torn into pieces, impaled on stakes and lit so that the wretches in the Pit might see their grisly surroundings.

The smoke stung his eyes, and for a moment his sight blurred and wavered. He blinked hard, unused to such a feeling, and brushed a hand across his eyes. At once tears ran down his face, stinging slightly; unfamiliar, but unexpectedly cleansing. He moved forward, making out details more clearly now.

The edges of the Pit were blackened and scorched; here and there they were charred, and cracked from the endless dry heat from below. Maelduin moved as delicately and as fastidiously as a cat, testing every inch of the ground before putting his weight down, aware that at any minute the ground might crumble and fall away, sending him plummeting helplessly into the abyss.

The stench was stronger here. He looked up at the glowing torches, and saw that he had been right. Humanish torsos; stumps of Humanish limbs. Dreadful, bloodied fragments of bodies, some more complete than others, impaled on the stakes. Several had the heads still attached, so that the necks lolled and the dead, sightless eyes rolled. Maelduin, remembering the physical content of the Humanish, thought: the eyes will be *cooking. Poaching.* And tried not to think that it was entirely possible that the victims had not been completely dead when they were impaled. How would it feel to be caught and forced down on to sharp stakes, to feel your skin split and your bowels tear, and to know that you were to be burned alive; that you were nothing but faggots for the fire; that your flesh was about to be lit to provide eerie light for the prisoners of the Pit?

Without warning, a tiny voice on the edge of his mind said: Lit? And who lit them? And then – not who, *what*?

Fear uncoiled deep at the base of his stomach: a cold, curdling fear that sent out icy tendrils despite the belching heat. The spikes were quite tall, they were at least six feet high. Six feet high . . . To reach up and impale the grisly kindling on to them would only be possible for something that was seven or eight feet tall.

What, in the normal Humanish world, was eight feet tall?

There was movement on the edge of his vision, a rather horrid lumbering movement, as if something – several somethings – might be creeping towards him. There was the pale blur of something, neither quite skin nor fur, and the glimpse of a twisted, stunted body. Maelduin narrowed his eyes, but the shape eluded him. He thought: Giants! Or perhaps half-Giants! Yes, the size was about right. Eight or nine feet tall. But Giants did not move in quite such creeping, stealthy fashion. They were huge and brutish, but they were not very clever. They were certainly not stealthy or creeping. What, then?

Maelduin glanced uneasily behind him. The horses were tethered to the rock, the one still bearing its firmly tied burden. He thought: I could be on their backs and away into the darkness. Safe.

297

But ahead of him was the Grail Castle, and he was bound by his word as Crown Prince of Tiarna to take the Fisher Prince to it and imprison him there.

Even, said the scoffing, silvery voice within him, even if it means crossing the Tanning Pit of the Dark Lords? Even if it means braving whatever creatures lurk out there in the shadows?

Even then.

Deep in his mind, he touched the silver-tipped Cadence, and felt it respond, as if he had twitched lightly on a thin, shining thread. Every enchantment ever spun or written or imagined...

He walked to the edge of the vast, sinister abyss, the greasy, meaty scent of the burning flesh almost overpowering him, but moving until he was midway between two of the torches, looking into the shadows beyond the firelight, searching the darkness for whatever moved there.

The shadows stirred, and six lumbering creatures, with blood-smeared maws, huge, leather-pad hands, and with great, heavy faces with thick jowls, moved out of the shadows.

Flesh-eating Trolls.

Chapter Twenty-seven

The Trolls surrounded Maelduin at once, standing in a circle looking down at him. There were six of them, and they all had the large, lopsided, slightly lumpish faces of their kind, rather as if their faces had been poured into a mould, but had slipped, or as if a giant hand had been wiped over the surface of their features, smearing the wet clay before it had properly hardened.

Their skins were thick-looking and pallid, but their jowls were bulbous and darker than the rest of their faces, as if the blood of the victims they ate had collected there, and coagulated in a heavy, dark pool. Their skin was rather coarse, and in places it thickened into matted, bristly fur. Their hands were enormous paws, covered with greasy-looking fur, the palms hard and leathery, the claws crusted with dirt.

All the better to tear my flesh with . . .

Maelduin reached for the Cadence in his mind again, and felt it near him, cool and silvery and obedient. Yes. All right. I can defeat these creatures if I am watchful and if I do not allow them to read my thoughts. I can defeat them if I do not permit fear to enter my mind or my heart. Fear would cloud his concentration, and send the Cadence out of his reach. And fear was a Humanish emotion.

The Trolls were grinning down at him, showing tiny, stumplike teeth. Their feet were bare, the soles horny and leathery, with thick, rather dirty claw-tipped toes, and they were dressed alike in leather breeches with square aprons with deep pockets, from which protruded the handles of hammers and chisels and knives. Labourers, thought Maelduin. Manual workers. They are the labourers of the Dark Lords. The artisans. Probably not very intelligent, and certainly brutish and coarse-natured.

'Here's a tasty morsel,' said one, eyeing Maelduin and

smacking its thick, blubbery lips with relish.

'Wouldn't make three bites,' said the second, contemptuously. 'Throw it on to a spike, I says. Let it burn over the Pit.'

'Fillet it for its rib-bones,' said a third. 'I likes a nice juicy rib-bone to gnaw.'

'Suck its marrow and then fling it into the Pit to let the Gristlens play with it.'

'That's a waste of good ManFlesh.'

They had rough, coarse voices, as if their lungs were filled with gravel, and as if they might have rather revolting coughing fits when they first awoke from slumber. Maelduin, who found them brutish and repulsive, but who knew himself outpowered physically, eyed them calmly, and said in a cool, silvery voice, 'Good sirs, may I not express a preference for the method of my own death?' and the Trolls looked at him in surprise as if he had interrupted a serious and important discussion, and ought to have known better.

'We don't let Humans choose their death,' said the one who had spoken first.

'We lets them *roast* slowly,' said the second, moving to stand over Maelduin, so that Maelduin could smell the onion-tainted breath and the stale body juices.

'Or we *minces* 'em.' The third licked his greasy lips and reached out to pinch Maelduin's arm with his great paw. 'This one'd mince well,' he said. 'I likes minced Human.'

'Rib-bones,' put in the fourth. 'Fillet it, I says, and suck its rib-bones, and then let the Gristlen have it.'

'And what about the fire?' The first pointed with a hairy, muscular arm to the stakes at the edges of the Pit. 'We're bound to keep the fire going all through the night.'

'And through the day.'

A sudden silence fell, and Maelduin, watching through half-closed eyes, saw that the mention of day had disconcerted them. He searched his mind. Was there an escape here? Were Trolls somehow threatened by daylight?

But then the first, who appeared to be some kind of leader, said, 'At any rate, we'll bring it to the cave, chaps. And then we'll see whether it's worth filleting. It's a long job, filleting a Human, and it's not one as you'd want to undertake lightly.'

'We'll light the fire and we'll take a look,' said another,

nodding; and he reached out to the nearest of the stakes that lit the Tanning Pit, plucking a burning gobbet of flesh. 'Bring it up then, chaps. It'll squirm and be off into the night if we don't watch it. They're cunning, Humans. I knows all about Humans.' The Troll leered rather horribly at Maelduin, and tapped the side of its lumpish nose in a knowledgeable gesture.

'Bring a bit of meat from the stakes while we're about it,' said the leader. 'Just a bit, mind.' He turned to watch as two of them reached up to the partly charred bodies. 'Be sure there's enough left to burn through tomorrow's daylight.'

'Leg bones here,' said one, producing one of the sharp knives.

'And good meaty flesh over here,' said the other. 'We'll have us a bit of supper out of this.'

'Leave enough for tomorrow's light,' said the leader again, and the Trolls glared at him.

'We *knows* there's got to be enough to burn,' said the nearest. 'We knows as there's got to be enough to burn all night *and* all day,' it added, and Maelduin, listening with every fibre of his being, thought: then they are unable to replenish the torches during daylight.

The Trolls lumbered back carrying their grisly feast carefully, distributing gobbets of partly cooked meat, the hot fat running down over their hands and darkening the thick, matted fur.

'Plenty for all,' said one, grinning. 'And maybe more to come when this one's cooked.' He eyed Maelduin greedily.

For the moment Maelduin could see no escape. The Cadence was within his grasp, but to study it, to search it, to find a spell that would help him, he would have to concentrate. He could not do so here, like this. For the moment he must let the Trolls take him, and hope to outwit them by some ordinary Humanish means. But as they half dragged, half carried him around the edges of the fearsome Pit, their horrid, greasy-fur, stale-food stench in his nostrils, he felt fear uncoil again, and knew himself in the grip of the one Humanish emotion he had thought he could avoid. *Fear: one of the destructive ones . . .*

The Trolls were carrying him to their cave. As they moved, they held aloft the burning torch of flesh they had taken from the stake. The light fell eerily across the ground, red and flickering, casting huge, lumbering Troll-shadows.

301

The cave was set part-way into one of the rearing black columns. Maelduin looked up and saw that the red glow of the setting sun was no longer filtering through the single eyelet near the top of the column. Night, black and thick with malevolence, closed about the desolate Moher Cliffs, and the ocean lashed against the rocks far below.

The Trolls threw their prisoner on to the ground at the back of the cave. Maelduin lay motionless, letting the Trolls believe him to be subdued. But he studied the cave through half-closed eyes, seeing that it had a hard earth floor scattered with bones – some brittle and sapless, as if they might have been sucked dry – and coarse hanks of hair. There was a tiny pile of glinting gold coins, spilling out of a drawstring canvas bag in one corner, and in another he glimpsed a cache of silver chalices and goblets. So they were venal, these great, misshapen beings, were they? Could he in some way bargain with them for his freedom?

The Trolls had set light to a bundle of kindling lying ready in the cave's mouth. They cast the grisly torch from the Pit's edge into the centre, and at once flames, scarlet and yellow, burned up, crackling and spitting. A greasy stench rose on the air, and Maelduin thought: Humanish fat! They will have no compunction about roasting me, or impaling me to add light to the Tanning Pit. What did they say earlier? Something about keeping it properly lit. Are they in some kind of bondage to the Dark Realm to do so, I wonder? And surely I did not imagine their fear of daylight. He glanced up at the sky, and saw that the moon had risen, and that dark clouds scudded across the sky behind it. The night had only just begun. He turned his attention back to the Trolls, who had seated themselves round the fire at the cave's mouth, avidly devouring the hunks of half-charred Human flesh brought from the Pit, tearing gobbets of flesh with their claws and gnawing at the bones.

'Over-cooked,' said the leader, grease dribbling down over his chin. 'You don't want to over-cook ManFlesh. It gives you wind.'

'I likes it over-cooked,' said another, sucking the end of a protruding thigh bone from his portion.

'Dries the juices,' said a third. 'Where's the swipes? Nothing like a mug of swipes to wash down over-cooked ManFlesh.'

'I can't abide it over-cooked,' said the leader, reaching out a great paw and lifting a massive wineskin. He drank deeply, wiping his lips on the back of his hand, and then belched loudly, his mouth open, so that the warm, half-digested stench of cooked meat gusted nauseatingly into Maelduin's face.

The Trolls finished their supper, and flung the gnawed bones and pieces of gristle into the fire's depths. The leader stirred the fire, and the others leaned forward, wiping their paws on the front of their leather aprons, and then resting their great heavy chins moodily on their hands.

'Now,' said the leader with the air of one preparing to make a decision, 'what'll us do with it?'

Maelduin was half in and half out of the flickering firelight. The Trolls were suddenly not quite so stupid-looking: their meaty faces held a sly intelligence, and there was a glinting cunning in the little eyes.

'I says mince it,' repeated the Troll who liked minced Human. 'It'll go much farther. There'll be a taste for everyone.'

'If we adds a bit of the roast meat from the torches at the Pit, it'd go even further,' agreed another. 'There was plenty left. If we takes a morsel from each of them it wouldn't harm the light.'

'But the light's a bit dim,' said the one next to him. 'And we're here to keep it burning.'

'We ought to use this one for light,' said the leader uneasily, looking across at the torches around the Pit. 'They're burning very low, those Humans. Flimsy things they were. That light'll never last through tomorrow's daylight.' He picked his teeth with one claw, glowering.

'Let's take this one to the Pit and see what light it'd give,' suggested another. 'Then if we decides to eat it, we can say as we *considered* using it as light. We can say as we *thought* about it, but it didn't *burn*.' He grinned knowingly at the others. 'That'd sound *loyal*,' he said. 'It'd be in keeping with the bargain. '

This was thought a good idea. The Trolls nodded to one another, pleased, and two of them lumbered over to where Maelduin lay.

'Off to the fire with it,' they said. 'See if it'll light the Pit and the Gristlens, and if it won't, why, then we'll have it for ourselves.' They stood looking down at Maelduin, their paws resting on their hips, grinning.

303

'I says we ought to have it for ourselves anyway. It was us as caught it, wasn't it?'

'It was that. But the light's got to burn without ever going out. That's *his* orders – Chaos's.'

Maelduin had become very still. As the Trolls bent over, he felt the nauseating, grease-tainted stench of them close about him, and saw the blood-heavy faces loom closer. Two of them lifted him and carried him out of the cave, towards the torchlit Pit, and Maelduin, his stomach churning from the stench of them, fought to remain calm. Their bristly paws scratched his skin and tore his flesh, and pain – *Humanish* pain – lacerated him.

But when they set him on the ground and stood before him grinning, he said, very coolly, 'I see from the possessions in your cave that you are fond of silver and gold.'

The Trolls looked at one another, and then the leader said, suspiciously, 'What if we are?'

Maelduin said, softly, 'I could pay you well for my freedom.'

'O-ho,' said the Trolls, digging one another in the ribs. 'O-ho, here's one as likes to bargain.'

'We knows about bargains,' said the leader, cunningly. 'We made a good bargain with the Lord of Chaos, we did.' He hooked his meaty thumbs in the bib of his apron and rocked knowingly on his huge feet.

Maelduin seated himself cross-legged on the ground, the livid torchlights of the great Pit behind him, and felt the Cadence swirl silver-gilt on the outskirts of his mind. His mind was working furiously and he was horridly aware that physically he was no match for these creatures. They would overpower him before he could summon the Cadence. Could he keep them talking? How many hours until dawn?

He was barely aware of the Humanish cloak and the cumbersome Humanish bones; for the moment he was all *sidh*, cold-blooded and merciless and filled with the unearthly allure of his people.

Cool, strong power flooded his mind, and if it was not quite the incisive, sea-sorcerous essence of Tiarna, it was sufficiently akin to it to be of use.

And I must make it of use! he thought angrily.

He fixed the Troll leader with his eyes, and said in a soft, caressing voice, 'Tell me about the bargain you made with the Lord of Chaos.'

The Trolls seemed not averse to telling their story. The leader said, warningly they were not to be fooled; Maelduin was to understand that. There was to be no sneaking away under cover of some kind of story-spinning.

'But we likes to tell a story,' he added. 'We're good at telling stories.'

'We're *known* for it,' added another.

'This ain't a trap, is it?' demanded a third suddenly, and Maelduin said at once, 'I do not try to trap you. But if you will tell me a little of yourselves, in turn I will tell you of my own world.' He fixed them with his narrow eyes. 'You do not know what I am?' he said softly. 'No, I see you do not. But you must believe that, if you tell the Lord of Chaos how you have caught the Crown Prince of the *sidh*, he will be extremely pleased with you. Your standing would be vastly increased with him.'

'A *sidh*, are you?' said the Trolls, and rubbed their paws together, pleased. 'And the Crown Prince. We'd like to hear about that.'

'We'd like our standing increased.'

'I will tell you with pleasure,' said Maelduin. 'But in return you must first tell me of *your* world and of how you come to be here. It is the age-old law,' he said, lowering his voice to a soft, persuasive allure. 'A story for a story. And I should not wish to offend against that law.'

The Trolls said at once that they knew all about that. 'We don't offend against age-old laws,' said the leader, looking very wise.

'And we'd like to hear about a *sidh*,' put in another, greedily.

'*He'd* like to know as well – Chaos.'

'We'd like to *burn* a *sidh*,' added one, smiling horridly to show its teeth, wet and shiny with greed.

'But you ain't to try to escape,' repeated the leader, thrusting his huge lumpen face close to Maelduin's. 'There's to be no sneaking away into the darkness.'

'We'd catch you if you did,' said a second. '*And* we'd make you pay for it.'

'There's *games* can be played with Humans.'

305

'I understand,' said Maelduin, his heart pounding, but still using the silvery, persuasive voice that his father had sometimes used when dealing with Humanish travellers; hearing with sudden joy that deep within it was a faint, sweet echo of the *sidh*'s music itself. *So, after all, something of it lingers. And although it was not the music, there was a thread, a vein of its essence. Not good, but better than nothing.*

He sat perfectly still on the ground, cross-legged and straight-backed, his hands resting lightly on the insides of his thighs. The glow from the Pit fell about him like a crimson-tinged mantle, turning his hair to molten gold. His eyes were thin, glittering slits of colour. The Trolls watched him uneasily, but when he said again, 'Tell me of your Guardianship of the Pit,' they glanced at one another and then nodded and seated themselves on the ground in a half circle around him. As the leader began to speak, over their heads, the moon rose to its zenith.

Dawn was many hours away.

It was important to keep holding on to the tenuous reins of the perilously frail bewitchment that held the Trolls. Maelduin knew that, if his concentration slipped, even for a second, the Trolls would look up and look round and the thin spell would shatter.

But for the moment I have them! he thought exultantly. *For the moment they are thinking only of talking to me.* He sent a covert glance to the skies. *How much time had passed?* He thought it must be several hours, although his perceptions of the Humanish methods of measuring time were still uncertain.

As a *sidh* he would have held the Trolls until dawn with ease. He would have scooped up his people's music and thrown out twining, blue-green threads to entrap the creatures. He could have surrounded the Trolls with any number of different sorcerous chains, and escaped into the night with supreme ease.

But as a Humanish he must rely almost solely on his wits. His body, the pale-cloaked, ivory-boned, Humanish body, was already feeling the strain. His legs were beginning to ache from sitting absolutely still, and his mind was tiring too. To his left, the Fisher Prince moved uneasily inside the Silver Cage, but Maelduin dared spare it no attention. He heard it make one of its circling movements, and there was a light, scraping sound as it explored the confines of its prison again, before curling back into a corner of the cage.

The Trolls were telling the story of their Guardianship of the Pit, pouring it out, interrupting one another like ill-mannered children, telling the tale clumsily and inarticulately. Maelduin, his mind concentrating on keeping the light fragile threads spun from the music's echoes, caught a jumble of facts.

It seemed that there had been some kind of encounter with Chaos himself, followed by meetings with Chaos's henchmen.

'Because you don't do these things in the flick of a bat's wing,' said the leader, solemnly. 'Us knew that.'

'Of course not.'

'The Guardianship of the Pit,' said the leader, staring at Maelduin from his small, mean eyes, 'that's what we was given. And an honour it was to be chosen,' he said, his eyes fixed on the slight figure silhouetted against the Pit's fiery light.

Maelduin did not move but, as the Troll spoke, his eyes flicked to the sky. No thread of light broke the blackness, and a tiny wind ruffled the surface of the ground, stirring the dry, fetid scents of the Pit. I am not sure if I can do this, he thought in sudden panic.

The Troll was explaining how they had talked with Chaos, trying in a clumsy, childlike way to make it sound as if Chaos had sought them out and beseeched them to help him. But the one who liked minced Human was contradicting him loudly.

'We was captured,' it said, leaning forward and pushing aside the leader. 'Captured and given a choice: the Lord of Chaos's nasty Castle or the guarding of the Pit.' Its little eyes glowed redly. 'And we all know what's done to them as gets imprisoned in the Castle of Infinity!' it added slyly. '*Worked* on. *Bred* on to unnatural creatures.' It slid a hand between its huge, greasy thighs and rubbed itself suggestively with a finger and thumb, grinning. 'Your juices taken from you and *fed* to Goblins and Giants,' it said.

'Fed while they're still warm,' added another.

'*Mixed* with snakes and rats and worms,' said a third, shuddering.

Maelduin was dizzy with the effort of forcing the Trolls to talk, but at these words his mind sharpened. 'That is what

Chaos does?' he said. 'Inter-breeding between species?'

'He don't call it that,' said the Troll. 'He gives it a long name – necromantic race-breeding, or some such. Us don't bother with it.' He leaned forward and jabbed a horny finger at Maelduin. 'But when we was caught by Chaos's servants – yes we was, Lumpkin, no point in making it sound otherways – when we was caught, we was given a choice. Have your juices taken from you or guard the Pit. And I ain't letting no necromancers take *my* juices,' said the Troll aggrievedly.

'Unnatural,' said Lumpkin.

'Painful, I heard.'

'I heard they do it with hollow needles until you're sucked dry.'

'I heard that as well.'

'So,' said Maelduin, keeping his voice deliberately low and caressing, 'so you chose the Guardianship of the Pit. That was a very good bargain indeed, I think.'

The Trolls looked wise. 'Trolls don't make bad bargains,' said Lumpkin. 'People thinks Trolls're stupid, but we knows what we knows.' It made the familiar gesture of tapping the side of its nose. 'The guarding of the Pit and the patrolling of the Moher Gate,' it said. 'That's what we was given. There was no Guardian, see, on account of the Black Monk having offending Chaos.' He shook his head. 'Reckless, that. Nobody offends Chaos and lives to walk free.'

'The Black Monk had the guarding of the Pit and the Moher Gateway,' explained one of the others, eager to add his mite to the story.

'For years it was—'

'He thought he could challenge Chaos and win.' The Troll shook its head sadly.

'And so we agreed as we'd do it,' went on Lumpkin. 'And it's an important task.'

'Chaos couldn't do without us,' put in another.

'Even if he didn't get our juices,' said the one who had told about Chaos's necromantic race-breeding.

The Trolls leered. 'We keeps our juices to ourselves,' they said, nodding their misshapen heads.

Maelduin stole another glance at the sky. Was there the faintest lightening, over to the east? He was beginning to doubt his ability to keep the Trolls' attention for much longer; his mind was becoming blurred and his muscles were locking into painful, cramping agony.

But I must! Only a very little longer! They must be kept here until the sun rises!

Help came from an unexpected quarter. Just as he thought he must give in to the waves of sick exhaustion, he felt a ripple of strength, and something cold and bloodless and ancient lay across his mind, bolstering it up, pouring cool sea-sorcery into it. He thought: the Fisher Prince! and glanced at the Silver Cage.

Yes, the Prince was at the front of the cage, hands curled about the bars, the cold, colourless eyes fixed unblinkingly on Maelduin. Maelduin at once understood that the Prince wanted him to escape these creatures: it was possessed of tremendous power, but it was still too young to fend for itself. It needs me! he thought, and derived a surprised strength from the thought.

He fixed the Trolls with his slanting eyes and said, 'What of the Gristlens? Have you the guarding of them, also?' and for the first time saw the cobweb-strands of his frail enchantment shiver on the darkness. Still holding! And now I may learn something of Coelacanth, who escaped from the Pit!

'It's part of our task, guarding the Gristlens,' said the Trolls, proudly.

'They . . . do not escape?'

'Oh no,' said the Trolls, shaking their heads solemnly so that the blood-filled jowls quivered. 'We never lets them escape.'

But Maelduin saw them steal uneasy glances at one another. He said carefully, 'And if ever one did escape, there would be nowhere for it to run to? You would catch it at once?'

'After it and fling it back,' they agreed, nodding firmly.

'Unless—'

'Yes?'

'Unless it might escape by *daylight*,' said Lumpkin. 'We can't be responsible for what happens by *daylight*.'

'*He* knows that – Chaos.'

'It was all part of the bargain.'

'We can't be out in daylight, see. Anyone knows Trolls can't be out in daylight.'

Maelduin felt the sudden unease stir their slow, coarse minds, and knew they had remembered the menace of daylight again. At any minute they would look up at the sky. He spoke swiftly, not giving them time to think. 'Tell me of the Court of the Dark Lords?' he said. 'The pronouncing of the punishment for the banished ones.'

'Well it's . . .' the Troll leader stopped and frowned. A look of fear crept over his face, and now Maelduin dared to glance up, and saw that across the eastern skies a thin finger of pale grey light was appearing; ephemeral and transient, and so faint that for a moment Maelduin thought he had imagined it.

The Troll said, in a voice thick and gravelly with fear, 'Getting on for dawn, chaps.' He pointed to the sky. 'Time to be back into the cave.'

Maelduin summoned his last shreds of strength. Leaning forward, he said, 'You must tell me of the punished necromancers who are flung to the Pit,' and saw terror and indecision in their faces. The leader began to lumber to his feet, and in the slowly breaking dawn, Maelduin could see immense spiders' webs, like the skeletons of bats or octopuses crawling across the Trolls' faces. The nearest shuddered and put up a bristly paw, as if to brush off a huge, smothering hand, and the others moved to him.

'Dawn,' said Lumpkin, and turned the mean little eyes on Maelduin. 'And us out in it if we aren't careful! And that's responsible!' He pointed to Maelduin. 'Get it now, chaps!'

'Impale it afore it has chance to run!'

'Afore the light gets to us! Make haste!'

Maelduin no longer thought about whether he could summon power. He no longer thought about being tired and cramped and almost drained. He felt the Fisher Prince pouring cold, piscine strength into his mind, and for a glorious, soaring moment, the Humanish mantle wavered and dimmed, and the *sidh* was in the ascendant, arrogant and imperious.

And I am the Crown Prince of Tiarna, and I will devour you as I have devoured countless others! There was a moment when he almost thought he could have soared above them, as once he had soared above the Humanish, swooping about their heads and then closing in on them and tearing out their coarse, sluggish souls.

Above their heads, the first rose and gold streaks of dawn

310

flooded the eastern sky, veining it with the pure, pale colours of the new day. As the light fell across the rearing black pillars, the Trolls bellowed and fell back, throwing up their great paws to shield their eyes, and Maelduin thought exultantly: I have done it! Dawnlight!

He sprang to his feet, the cool sea-essence filling him up, reaching joyously for the shining pages of the Cadence, hurling pure shards of scalding light across the ground.

The Trolls were bellowing in agony, rolling over and over, clutching and tearing at their faces. As Maelduin stood watching, torn between exultation and horror, he saw that, as the light fell upon them, it burned them, so that their thick skin bubbled and boiled, forming hundreds upon hundreds of tiny, sizzling blisters. A dreadful stench of singed bristle and hide began to taint the plain.

The Trolls' tallowy skin was melting and, as they clutched their faces, Maelduin saw that the thick flesh was running between their fingers like candle grease. They screamed and writhed, rolling over and over on the ground. Lumpkin was trying to crawl back into the cave, blinded by his own melting, runny skin, groping his way along the ground, dripping thick, oily flesh as he went. Maelduin shuddered and stepped back, and Lumpkin, sightless and deaf, dragged himself nearer to the cave by some still-alert instinct. Maelduin thought: he is smelling his way back to his lair! and was sickened and appalled.

The Trolls were almost dead. Two of them made a final huge effort, struggling to their feet and lumbering across the ground, their faces dissolving and melting and trickling over their bodies to lie in great, evil-smelling pools on the ground. They flailed wildly at the air, bellowing their torment, cursing and screeching for help.

And then the nearest of them, as if by the same instinct that had driven Lumpkin, turned suddenly and staggered straight at Maelduin, his head lowered as if to charge. Maelduin moved, but the Troll made a sudden sideways lunge, and toppled forward.

Maelduin was knocked from his feet at once. He felt himself rolling across the ground, away from the dying Trolls, spinning and sliding, unable to stop himself.

And then the ground was suddenly uneven and dryly hot, and

he knew himself to be on the very brink of the Pit. There was a moment when he clawed at the ground, for he could not fall, he must not fall . . .

The ground, dry and baked, crumbled and fell away, and Maelduin tumbled helplessly into the Tanning Pit of the necromancers.

Chapter Twenty-eight

The Almhuinians were feeling extremely pleased with themselves. It said a good deal for the people of Almhuin when a proper fighting force, a strong, *dark* force could be sent out to give aid and lend strength to people as important as the Black HeartStealers.

They had been pleased to hear that the Royal Amaranth House was to be overthrown. They all remembered that the Black HeartStealers had been the guests of the Lady a few months ago, and that there'd been a certain closeness between the Lady and the Fer Caille at the time. It had not lasted very long, because the Fer Caille, although a worthy enough bed-partner, it was thought, had not fully shared the Lady's appetites for fresh warm blood, or not as fully as she would have liked.

But they were all hoping that he would succeed, and that the Amaranths would be killed and vanquished. It would be a grand thing altogether if the Royal Sorcery House could be in the hands of strong necromancers.

And it did your heart good to see your sons and nephews and grandsons – and the sons and nephews and grandsons of all your friends – so eager to fight against the Amaranths, and so aroused by the thought of killing and pain. Chaos's people had said, rather contemptuously, that the blood was running thin; the Rodent strain was disappearing and the Almhuinians were becoming Humanish, but this was a complete untruth. The Almhuinians could kill and maim as viciously as ever, and they could certainly steal into an enemy's Palace at dead of night, and slit his throat while he slept. Becoming Humanish indeed! said the Almhuinians crossly, and spread a few sly stories about Chaos's own people by way of revenge.

313

The young ones would see a good bit of the Other Ireland during the mutiny, and a nasty pallid place they would find it. But it would broaden their outlook, and it would all help to spread the force of the Dark Lords. It was true that the Almhuinians did not want to spread Chaos's force at the moment, on account of him being on the other side, but you had to take a broader view at such times.

Sending off the young men had been an important event. You could not let your sons and grandsons present themselves to important people like the Black HeartStealers without due preparation. They would go fully armoured and properly prepared, and the village would turn out to send them off.

They had a bit of a procession by way of farewell, only very quietly because of the War, but a procession all the same. They had been sure to march past the Castle, because the Lady had been very interested in their venture. She had sent down a message commending her people for answering the Black HeartStealers' Summons so promptly. The Almhuinians must do all they could in the way of spying and creeping into the Porphyry Palace by night, she had said. They might consider infiltrating the Palace while the Amaranths slept, and creeping into their bedchambers and slitting their throats. She would expect them to return victorious, and bathed in the warm blood of the accursed Amaranths, she said, a lick of relish in her voice. She had even sent down two spells which they could take with them, and which would help them to vanquish any sentry enchantments the Amaranths might have posted.

With all this going on, it had been several nights before they got properly around to dealing with the two prisoners taken in Diarmuit's tavern. Presently they would be taken up to the Castle in the tilt cart, but they were safe enough for the moment. They were tightly tied up, although Black Aed and Diarmuit had been careful not to draw blood because the Lady couldn't abear not to be the first one to draw blood from a prisoner. But they were bound securely; their food was drugged to stop them escaping, and they would not harm for keeping for a day or so. In fact it added to the enjoyment to keep them for a while; it gave everyone a good feeling, a feeling of power and sexual arousal, to think of the two of them lying down there in the dark cellar, knowing the death that awaited them.

Diarmuit visited them and took them a bite of food and pannikins of water: the Lady would not have liked her victims to become dried out, and the Almhuinians would not have liked the Lady's wrath if such a thing had been allowed to happen. Diarmuit would remind them what was ahead for them each time he took their food and water down, and Black Aed's wife would have judged the drugging to a nicety. Enough to drain their strength and prevent them from fighting or escaping, not enough to cloud their senses and make them unaware of what was ahead.

Diarmuit and Black Aed believed one of the prisoners, the female, to be an Amaranth sorceress of quite a high degree, which was extremely gratifying. They'd all enjoy seeing her humiliated. Black Aed's wife was preparing the food very carefully indeed this time, because they were not going to risk any nasty Amaranthine spells being furtively spun. The very thought of pale, pure, Amaranth magic in Almhuin was enough to make most people feel ill. Properly drugged the creature must be, and her companion as well. They'd mistrusted the both of them the minute they'd entered the inn, and although they'd all spotted Rumour for what she was, most people had also been made very uneasy indeed by the strange symbol Andrew wore at his waist. Aed had said, and everyone had agreed, that the horrid thing should be removed and summarily burned at the first opportunity, but the really remarkable thing had been that, when they went tiptoeing into the shed later that night, the prisoners lying drugged and helpless, not a one of them had been able to bring himself to touch the symbol. Clearly it was a focus for power of some immense strength. The Almhuinians wanted nothing to do with it. They tiptoed out again, and told one another that, if the Lady wanted to destroy the nasty thing, she would have to do so herself.

The two would be taken in the traditional procession to the Castle, of course, but it would have to be a rather quiet procession. If they were to go marching up and down the mountainside carrying flaring torches, they would all be an easy target for the Harpies, and they would certainly be sitting ducks for the screeching vultures whom everyone knew, quite positively, to be in Chaos's pay. The Almhuinians naturally had a few spies inside Chaos's Castle, but spying was a two-way

315

affair. Chaos would have his own people watching Almhuin, and whatever else you might say about his people, you had to admit that they were efficient.

And so, although they all talked wistfully of the grand days before the War when, not only would there be torches, but the singing of several Dark Chaunts to accompany a prisoner's last journey, everyone would be sensible. The two prisoners would be taken quietly and unobtrusively to the Castle, under cover of a moonless night, using the small tilt cart. To be sure, it was a sad old day not to be having the usual ceremonies, but doubtless the prisoners would not know any difference. If you were going to your death, it would not matter to you whether you went to it quietly and inconspicuously, or whether you went with the full panoply of Almhuinian ceremony and the full complement of Chaunts echoing in your ears.

All the same, it was rather a pity . . .

Andrew had prayed for strength in the dark, low-ceilinged cellar, kneeling on the dusty, bare floorboards, reaching for the strength and the love and the deep inner consciousness of power that had never yet failed him. But he knew how perilous their situation was, and he knew that the only help would be from within themselves. There could be no flaming swords splitting the skies, or fiery-lined clouds descending to the earth to disgorge warriors with heavenly strengths.

Rumour, curled like a cat in the far corner, slept an uneasy, drugged slumber. They had both eaten hungrily of the food that the Almhuinians had brought, and although Andrew had felt only dizzy and drowsy, Rumour had been violently sick within a couple of hours, choking and retching miserably.

'Poisoned,' she said, gasping and blinded by the tears that streamed down her face.

'No.' It tore Andrew apart to see her like this, but he was so firmly chained that he could not get near to her. He said, 'It is not their intention to kill us.'

'You think not?' Rumour sat back, exhausted and drained, and regarded him from eyes made huge by the dark smudges beneath them, her face white and pinched but the wry irony still discernible in her voice.

'They will not dare to kill us, Rumour.'

316

Rumour stared at him, and then said, 'Of course. They have to keep us for the Crimson Lady.'

'I am afraid so.'

'Well,' said Rumour, leaning back against the cellar wall tiredly, 'whatever they intend for us, I do *not* care for this place.' She looked about her and managed to dredge up a grimace of disparagement.

The cellar was a small, dry place, boarded with planks of wood that had an ancient dry smell to them, and lined with great sour-smelling wineskins and barrels of ale. There was a trapdoor in the ceiling; a square hatch, just large enough for a man to climb through. When Diarmuit brought their supper, he had pulled the hatch back and let down a narrow, iron ladder. Andrew had watched carefully how this was done, thinking there might be some way to overpower the innkeeper, but Diarmuit did not come near enough. He simply placed the food at the foot of the ladder, and then pushed it across until it was within their reach, using a hooked pole.

The cellar seemed to be used as a storeroom of some kind. Near to the ceiling, beyond their reach, were shelves on which were stored huge wheels of cheese wrapped in muslin and waxed paper. Close by the cheeses were huge smoked hams and flitches of bacon.

Andrew regarded the smoked hams and the bacon and cheese, and then glanced involuntarily into the dusty corners of the cellar, thinking that surely there would be vermin in such a place, and thinking as well that to encounter rats in their present helpless state would have been unbearable.

But I do not think there are any rats down here, he thought, and at once Rumour said, 'Of course there are not, Andrew. The rats are upstairs, waiting to pounce on us.'

Andrew said, softly, 'Your sense of humour is still with you then, madame.'

'The last thing I shall lose,' said Rumour, but her voice was blurred and her eyes were sunken and dull. She looked exhausted, and Andrew caught himself thinking that their captors might have administered stronger doses of the drug to Rumour with the idea of preventing her from calling up sorcerous forces to defeat them.

Rumour said, 'I am not defeated, Andrew. It is only that the darkness in this place is so stifling . . . I have tried to call up the power . . ' For the first time there was a break in her voice. 'I have tried, so hard,' she said, and there was such humility in her voice, such contrition, as if she was asking for his forgiveness, or as if she had failed, that Andrew felt as if a giant hand had squeezed the breath from him.

He said, very gently: 'Rumour, we will get out of here. I promise it with everything I ever held dear. On the body and soul of my own God, I promise it.' He looked at her across the ill-lit cellar, trying to pour strength into her and trying to pour hope in as well. He knew the danger of despair; the monks had called it *accidie*, and had believed it to be the most grievous and the most dangerous of all sins. Once you gave way to despair, real black, lonely despair, you had given up hope of anything and everything. You had stopped trusting God. They *must* continue to hope and they must continue to believe that they would escape from Almhuin.

'Do you feel your God may have forsaken you, Andrew?' said Rumour softly, and at once he turned.

'No!' His eyes met hers, but in his mind a cold serpent of memory uncoiled, and he remembered the agonised bitterness of the dying Christ, who had cried aloud to a God whom he thought had forsaken him. But I will not think like that! said Andrew in silent anger. I will not accuse God of forsaking me! I will believe and I will trust!

'But perhaps he seems . . .' Rumour paused, searching for words that would not be offensive. 'He seems very far away,' she said, the hint of a question in her voice.

'He is not a god like your gods,' said Andrew.

'He will not fight the battle for us?'

'He will not. You understand.' Of course you do, said his expression. Aloud, he said, 'He would not send warriors into the world to lead us against enemies, or armies to fight for us. He would expect the strength to come from us.'

'I do understand,' said Rumour. 'Not completely. But a little.' She looked at him, and thought: but for all that, your God *has* sent help, Andrew. He has imbued you with something that I am very sure you did not possess when you came to the Porphyry Palace. You are no longer the gentle, ascetic monk, the pale, unassuming young man who supped so quietly with the Amaranths, and who listened so politely as we chanted our rituals. I think he has gone for ever, thought Rumour. And in his place is a fiery-eyed adversary, a thin, dark-haired young man with a lean hard body and a burning anger.

She studied him, caught momentarily in fascination, and thought that even the black woollen robe no longer gave him the cool aloofness he had once possessed. He is awake and alive and he is *feeling*, thought Rumour, still curled into the dusty cellar corner. I suppose I did that. I suppose I tore aside the armour he had so carefully built up and made him live and hurt and care. But what was beneath the armour is infinitely stronger and infinitely more human. I wonder if his God finds him better like this? I wonder if I am indeed seeing the Samildanach reborn, she thought with a thrill that was half fear and half delight.

The sickness from the drugged food had been disgusting and humiliating. Sickness was something you hid, something you dealt with alone. You certainly did not inflict it on a lover. But it could not be helped, and since it could not be helped, she would try to turn it into something to smile at. It was important to remain brave and flippant, to find lightness in any situation, because these were the things that armoured you against the world. Rumour was aware of reaching for bravery and flippancy, rather in the way she might have reached for a gown appropriate to an occasion. The simile amused her, and with the amusement came a thin vein of courage that was no longer a pretence, but almost the real thing. She managed to dash cold water on to her face from the tin cup left for them, and to rinse her mouth. The water was cold and pure and untainted by any drug, and Rumour began to feel better. And if I had hair that I could brush out, I should feel ready to face anything! she thought. But she sat up determinedly, and said, 'You have to admit, Andrew, that I could not be accused of showing a false picture of myself to you. You have seen me in every conceivable humiliation now.' And thought that, if this was not quite her old mocking carelessness, it was not a bad attempt.

Andrew said, very gently, 'None of it matters, of course.'

'No.' She looked at him, waiting, and after a moment, Andrew said:

'Love is not a matter of silken gowns and perfumed bodies,' and Rumour smiled the old smile, the catsmile that said: now I have made you admit it! And felt considerably better, because after all she was not so beaten by the Almhuinians; she could still present the glittering image; she could still look across at Andrew and feel the swift, secret delight at loving and being loved. They would get through this and they would find a way to escape.

After the first makeshift meal, she had left the food untouched, but Andrew, who had already wrestled with this one, said, 'I believe the food is only lightly drugged. And you should eat a very little if you could.'

'To retain strength for escape?' Rumour was glad to hear that her voice sounded as much mocking as questioning.

'Yes,' said Andrew, seriously.

'Very well.' She regarded the food disdainfully. 'It is quite disgusting, of course. I am not accustomed to plain bread and cheese. But I will get through the ordeal.' She leaned forward, her eyes glowing. 'When I was very small, Andrew – perhaps Theodora's age – Nechtan once taught me that the best way to get through an ordeal was to visualise something that existed beyond the ordeal. On the other side of it. Something pleasant and familiar that you knew without doubt would happen after the ordeal was over.'

'Yes?' He smiled slightly, thinking that for all her dazzling extravagances, she was possessed of an unexpected ingenuousness at times.

Rumour said, 'It was the best advice ever, but then Nechtan was the wisest, wiliest man I ever knew.' She smiled in the dim cellar. 'The thing you look forward to, the thing that you know lies beyond the ordeal can be something quite small. Perhaps as small as a favourite meal for supper. But the trick is to look beyond. To look forward to that favourite dish. Or perhaps to the playing of a new song.' She looked at him, waiting for his reaction, thinking, as she had thought in Tiarna: and if he does not understand, or if he ridicules, the feeling I have for him will surely weaken. But let him understand, thought Rumour, and was surprised at the vehemence of her plea.

Andrew said, 'My Order – that is, my religion – requires many hours of fasting and prayer. At the beginning, during the years of what are called novitiate, there is the scourging of one's own flesh.'

He paused, and Rumour said cautiously, 'To subdue the appetites of the flesh?'

'Yes.' Andrew frowned. 'I found it immensely difficult,' he said after a moment. 'The scourge is a light whip with several knotted ends, and the novices had to apply it to their own bodies once every week for as long as it took to chant the Miserere – that is a prayer we find of particular strength. To me, such self-inflicted pain was a needless humiliation and a – a degradation.' He sent her the sudden, sweet smile. 'Also it was unnecessary,' he said. 'For then the lures of the flesh did not trouble me.

'But I did it. I was obedient. But in order to get through it, I would set my mind on what always followed the scourging and the chanting of the Miserere.'

'Which was?'

Andrew's thin face lightened into the sudden smile again. 'The one good midday meal of the week,' he said. 'Roast beef.'

Rumour laughed, because of course he had understood. She said, 'Well, for now I am looking beyond this place, and I am looking beyond our visit to the Crimson Lady's fortress.' She leaned forward again, hugging her knees, the iron manacles dragging against the floor. 'I am looking forward to being inside my own castle,' she said. 'To ordering up a banquet – roast swan and baked goose. Almond pudding and crystallised fruits piled high on silver dishes. And wine: the richest, sweetest, the most *expensive* wine there is. I shall believe it will happen, that banquet, and that is how I shall endure what is ahead of us.'

'A banquet on the other side,' said Andrew softly.

'Yes.' She leaned back against the cellar wall. 'Will you be there with me, Andrew?' she said, quietly. 'Will you share that banquet?'

Andrew drew breath to answer, to say that they would share it – they would eat the rich food together and drink the strong, sweet wine – when a sound from above made them both look up sharply.

Footsteps came across the room over their heads, and the trap door was lifted and the iron ladder let down. Diarmuit, followed by Black Aed and some half a dozen of the others, climbed down into the cellar and stood grinning at them.

Rumour, staring, thought: of course they are Rodents. I

never really doubted it, but down here, with barely any light, it is very obvious indeed. Rats and weasels and stoats. They are enjoying our captivity and what they believe is our humiliation. They are gloating. Horrid creatures! thought Rumour, and a tiny spurt of anger spiralled inside her, stinging her into renewed life. How dare they treat us like this! she thought, and waited, and there again was the anger, and the rushing strength with it. That is interesting, she thought. Anger is a – a *reviving* emotion. I shall remember that, she thought, and being Rumour, tucked the knowledge away until it might be of some use.

Diarmuit and the others clambered down the narrow ladder, and stood in the small cellar, eyeing their prisoners avidly. In the dimness their eyes glinted redly and their teeth were sharper, their features narrower, more vicious. Rumour was aware of the thick feral stench emanating from them.

As they pulled her roughly to her feet, one of them pressed her against him, so that she could feel the hard stalk of arousal between his thin thighs, and she shuddered in revulsion, because there was something so coarse, so unclean about feeling the swollen desire of a creature you found completely repulsive. The Almhuinian grinned at her, his teeth gleaming wetly, and thrust a hand into the bodice of her gown, fingering her breasts. Rumour turned her head away and struggled and the Almhuinian laughed gloatingly.

'Modest, Madame Sorceress? Perhaps you will prefer the embraces of the Lady? For she is not particular whether she explores the flesh of men or women.'

The sick feeling and the slight dizziness left by the drugged food were not a deterrent to a show of courage. Rumour took a deep breath, and reached again for the core of anger, and found that it enabled her to stand firm and send the Almhuinian a haughty stare.

'I am selective in my choice of lovers,' she said, and Andrew heard with something approaching delight that it was once more the arrogant, I-am-beyond-the-law tone that had intrigued him from the beginning. Rumour continued icily, 'I do not permit *Rodent Creatures* to touch me. Remove your hands, or I shall shrivel your phallus where it hangs.'

The Almhuinians laughed and nudged one another. 'We'd

like to see you try,' said Diarmuit, and Andrew looked up, hearing the derisive, challenging note, knowing at once that Rumour would certainly make some attempt to meet the challenge.

'The Lady has Almhuin wrapped safely in the Girdle of Gold,' said one of them. 'Nothing ever got past the Girdle of Gold.'

'Did it not?' said Rumour, and her eyes glinted.

Black Aed, who was watching and listening, hooked his hands in his belt and looked at the others. 'She's a haughty BitchHuman, this one,' he said. 'Shall we take her to the Castle now, or shall we – *enjoy* her ourselves first?'

'Enjoy her first!' cried the others, and at once formed a circle about her.

'And Searbhan to have first taste!' cried Diarmuit, and the Almhuinian who had grasped Rumour and fingered her breasts, chuckled lasciviously and moved forward.

'And we'll untie her,' he said, and nodded to Diarmuit to do so. 'Less *restricting*,' said Searbhan, his voice thick with lust.

Rumour had backed away from the evil, greedy creatures, but Diarmuit untied the ropes that had bound her ankles, and unlocked the iron gyves that had tethered her arms to the wall, and then pulled her forward. The Almhuinians stood in a circle about her, grinning and nudging one another suggestively.

'One at a time, remember,' said Black Aed, already beginning to unbuckle his iron-studded belt. 'And no tearing of her white skin, or we'll have the Lady's anger to contend with.'

'Onwards then, Searbhan,' cried another. 'Or shall we warm her for you?'

'I can do my own warming, friend,' said the ugly, black-visaged Searbhan, unbuttoning his breeches and easing them downwards over his thin, hairy thighs. He eyed Rumour, who let her eyes wander over his body and then laughed contemptuously.

'Weakling,' she said. 'I had thought you were *proper* men here in Almhuin. You will have to produce better flesh than that to satisfy me, milksops. I have been accustomed to quality in my lovers.' She directed her gaze between Searbhan's legs. 'Also to *quantity*,' said Rumour in a silken purr. She turned her back disdainfully, and Andrew, watching his every chance to help, wanted to hug her for her cool contemptuousness of these horrid, sly creatures.

Searbhan said, angrily, 'You'll regret those words, Madame Sorceress,' and reached out to pull her to him. Rumour felt the hard, bony fingers dig into her skin, and the anger welled up again, swirling through her entire body.

She thought: how *dare* this weasel-faced Rodent speak to me thus! How dare these evil, ugly things humiliate us both and taunt us with their absurd puny necromancy! And although she knew, in the corners of her mind, that they were inside the fearsome Dark Realm and that they were in the dread Almhuin itself, still her mind sought and closed about a strong and vicious spell, just a little *dark*, read and learned in secrecy when she was studying at the Academy, tucked away in her mind, because you never knew ... You never knew when a lover, a partner, a Human, might become importunate ...

And if any spell would work in this dark, evil place, it would be a spell tinged with a little necromantic malice ...

She seized on the incantation with delight – I *knew* I should need it one day! – and whirled about to face the weasel-featured Searbhan. With her eyes flashing angrily, she pronounced in a furious voice, a string of syllables in an ancient, ugly tongue.

A huge, whirling blackness reared up from nowhere, and the cellar was suddenly filled with the evillest, most gloating chuckling Andrew had ever heard. He shivered, and pulled his woollen robe more closely about him.

'*I am the Collector*,' said the chuckling, clotted voice. '*I wear the phalluses of my victims about my waist ... I* collect *lumps of flesh*,' it said. '*I take them.*'

There was the fleeting impression of an impossibly tall, skeletal-thin man, dark and cavernous-featured, with hands that reached and clutched. It darted across the cellar, its hands outstretched, the nails glinting, and closed about Searbhan's groin.

He staggered back, flailing desperately at the air, trying to fight off the shadowy figure, screaming in pain and fear. As he fell against the far wall, his legs were suddenly forced wide apart, and blood and urine and thick, nearly colourless fluid spurted out, soaking his breeches and running down his legs to puddle on the floor. Shreds of pinkish skin and flesh tore in bloodied tatters and the greedy, chuckling laugh filled the cellar again.

'*A new piece for my collection*,' whispered the voice. '*I have nothing from the Rodent descendants of Almhuin. I thank you, Madame Amaranth.*' The huge dark shape bent over, in the act of stringing a lump of pale, bloodied flesh on to a massive belt.

The Collector seemed to turn his huge head towards Rumour. '*Madame Amaranth, I am indebted*,' he said in a soft, satisfied voice.

'The indebtedness is entirely mine,' responded Rumour with amused courtesy, and the Collector gave his fearsome laugh again.

'*There are few of your kind who know how to summon me*,' he said. '*But I am always there for those who pronounce the incantation. Remember it, madame.*'

'I will remember it,' said Rumour, and the Collector made another of his courtly bows, and vanished.

Rumour turned to face the Almhuinians. 'Well?' she said softly and challengingly. 'Would any other creature care to make the attempt to rape me?'

'What did you do?' said Diarmuit, as two of the others went to help the sobbing, moaning Searbhan.

'Summoned the Collector,' said Rumour coldly. 'As you saw.'

'That is necromancy,' said Black Aed.

'Yes?' *What about it?* said her tone. 'I did warn you,' said Rumour. 'And it was a fitting punishment.' The malicious grin lit her face. 'Well, gentlemen?' said Rumour. 'Are there any more who would like to challenge me? The Collector will certainly return if I call. He will not be so very far off yet.'

And then Black Aed moved forward, Diarmuit and several more at his side, twisting Rumour's arms painfully behind her back. Rumour felt the pain instantly cloud her strength, and knew herself unable to summon any kind of power. She bit her lip to stop herself from crying aloud with the pain, and concentrated on maintaining a cool disdain.

'Into the tilt cart with them both,' said Black Aed. 'And then take them to the Castle.

'We'll let the Lady have her way with these two.'

Chapter Twenty-nine

The skies were heavy and dark and streaked with menace as the tilt cart jolted its way up the mountain path towards the Castle.

The Almhuinians seemed uneasy and Andrew, listening and watching for any chance that might present itself, realised that they were afraid of being seen.

When Black Aed said, 'Watch for the Harpies now,' and Diarmuit replied, 'Nasty spying things,' Andrew knew he had been right; these creatures were engaged in War; they were fearful of spies.

They could hear, very faintly, the sounds of a battle somewhere beneath them. Andrew caught the thudding of hoofbeats, and several times the darkness was split by livid flashes of light. Once Black Aed halted and pointed to the east, where a line of what Andrew guessed to be more of the WarMongers were galloping hard through the night towards the Castle of Infinity. The manes of their gleaming stallions streamed out wildly in the night wind, and their ravaged silhouettes were black and menacing against the sky.

The path was steep and narrow and there was the feeling that you could travel this way for many cold, dark nights without meeting a single soul. As they went deeper into the mountains, the two prisoners felt a sour wind gust in their faces. The sounds of the faraway battle faded, and as it did so Andrew felt Rumour shiver, and understood that, compared with the wild desolation of the mountains, there had been something very nearly cosy about the noise and the clash of a battle being fought.

And then the Almhuinians pulled the tilt cart across the last rough patch of ground, and there was a sudden break in the great rearing mountain walls ahead of them. Directly ahead of them, set half into the mountain itself, was the Crimson Lady's

Citadel, the Mountain Fortress of the BeastWoman of Almhuin.

The immense shadow of the evil Fortress fell across the cart, and Rumour shivered again and pulled her cloak about her, staring up at the rearing Citadel, her eyes huge.

The great Stronghold of the Crimson Lady had been hewn from massive black stones, rough and pitted and harsh, with here and there pale, blind growths crusting the surface.

As they drew nearer, Rumour, still feeling sick from the drugged food, felt a creeping coldness steal over her. The evil that emanated from the Castle was Complex Evil at its strongest; it was noisome and filled with pulsating malevolence. Rumour could smell it and feel it and taste it; it struck at her senses with the wincing pain of raw flesh being scraped by a knife.

There was something dark and ageless and hungering about the jagged-toothed turrets and the black crouching bulk. Rumour thought: this is a place of pain, a Citadel of agony . . . A torture house, seen through a darkling glass, silhouetted against crimson-streaked skies.

It was immense. Between the huge, rearing turrets with the narrow slitted windows was a long, low, central portion, which Andrew thought might have once been a keep, but which Rumour identified as being probably the ceremonious halls and banqueting chambers.

The Almhuinians had paused and, on the still air, the two captives heard the sound of the drawbridge being lowered, followed by the unmistakable winching up of the portcullis gates, with a slow, and rather dreadful inexorability.

The Crimson Lady's gates opening to let us in . . .

The drawbridge stretched before them, bridging the deep chasm that surrounded the castle, and the portcullis was raised to its highest point. Black Aed looked down at his prisoners, and said in a voice of satisfaction, 'Almhuin. The Fortress of the Lady.'

'It is not quite what I expected,' said Andrew in a thoughtful tone, and Rumour at once said:

'It is certainly not what *I* am accustomed to.' And regarded Black Aed haughtily.

Black Aed grinned, and in the darkness his teeth showed white and feral, but Diarmuit who had been watching the sky nervously, pointed suddenly upwards. 'Harpies,' he said. 'See? Over to the west.'

'Yes.' Black Aed followed Diarmuit's pointing finger. 'And the sound of more WarMongers,' he said, and Andrew and Rumour both thought he looked very slightly fearful. But he turned back, and said, 'Chaos and his people were ever watchful. We'd best get these two inside.' He stood for a moment longer, scanning the dark mountainside, and Rumour, half lying against the cart's sides, caught the flicker of a movement deep within the creeping shadows. WarMongers? No! thought Rumour, her senses alerted. Something much stealthier.

She looked up sharply, trying to see, trying to feel, aware of a new menace. Chaos's people? Spies? The Almhuinians appeared to have heard nothing other than the thudding hoofbeats, and Rumour guessed that they did not possess sufficient perception. They could see and hear things that were intended to be seen and heard, but they were unaware of sly, creeping darknesses. But I feel them, and I see them. And then: could we turn this to our advantage? she thought. Does Andrew feel them? And sent him a quick glance from beneath her lashes, and knew that for all Andrew's truly remarkable perception and for all his sensitivity, he had not heard anything. Then it is up to me, thought Rumour, and hard on the heels of that thought came another: am I beginning to depend on him? Or is it that his strength is simply increasing?

The Almhuinians were pulling the cart on to the drawbridge which was extended across the deep, dark moat. Directly ahead, the gateway at the centre of the Castle-keep yawned, the iron grille of the portcullis raised to its highest point.

And we must pass under that portcullis . . . We must enter the Castle of the Crimson Lady, the pain-filled Citadel of the Beithioch. It reeks of old dark necromancy, and it is soaked in the agony of its victims, thought Rumour. And we are being taken into its bowels.

The cart bumped and jolted forward, its wheels reverberating hollowly on the wooden planks of the drawbridge. Rumour looked back, but there was only the dark mountain, and the stretch of drawbridge they had already covered. There was no sound, save the trundling of the cart's wheels, and the firm, light tread of their captors. Nothing stirred in the darkness.

But as they were pulled towards the waiting portcullis, into the shadow of the immense Fortress, she caught the sound she had heard earlier. Soft light, furtive footsteps creeping towards the Castle behind them ... Something – perhaps several somethings – stealing along behind them.

Chaos's spies following them into the grisly lair of the BeastWoman of the Mountains ... ?

The iron grille of the portcullis was ahead of them, huge and black and menacing; as the cart passed into the clotted darkness beneath the drawbridge, Rumour felt the suffocating, smothering darkness of Almhuin descend over her head, so that for a moment she could hardly breathe.

Behind them the drawbridge was lifted, clanking upwards on its immense iron chains and crashing home, and the portcullis was lowered.

And so we are shut in ... We are shut in with one of the most evil necromancers ever known, thought Rumour, sick with horror and fear. We are shut inside the Castle of Almhuin.

But if I am right, she thought, trying to see about her, if I am right we are not entirely alone. There is another enemy here with us. I feel that there is.

Something followed us, and something stole stealthily along the drawbridge after us, and slipped under the portcullis. And now that something is inside the Castle with us ...

They were shut inside the Citadel of the Crimson Lady of Almhuin. And it seemed likely that, shut in with them, were the dark, evil servants of the Lord of Chaos.

The portcullis did not open into a courtyard or a quadrangle as they had expected, but into the central portion of the Castle itself. They were in a stone chamber, with narrow windows set high up, criss-crossed with thin strips of lead. Slivers of crimson-tinged twilight lay across the uneven stone floor, and dust motes danced in and out of it, showing up the decaying interior of the Castle.

Great swathes of dark red velvet drapes covered sections of the walls, but the velvet was worn and rubbed, and in places it hung in threads. There was a dry, musty smell, and the smothering feeling of stale air and dirt, and as the tilt cart was pushed forward, there was the pattering of mice scuttling away beneath the hangings.

The Almhuinians moved purposefully about the stone hall, lighting branched candle-holders and setting them in front of several oval mirrors with damp-spotted silver surfaces and tarnished rims. But each candle was reflected in the mirrors a dozen times over, so that the hall was illuminated to a great flickering cavern filled with tiny, glowing flames. The shadows receded and Rumour thought with a start of surprise: this is a place of decay and dust, but once it must have been very beautiful.

Immense silken tapestries hung between the mouldering velvet, all of them dimmed with extreme age, damp stains obscuring most of the depicted stories. But in some of them it was possible to make out crouching Beast-Humans bending over the mutilated remains of prey, their jowls blood-smeared, fangs jutting down from curled-back lips.

Beneath the tapestries were long oak tables and settles, black with age, the cushions on the settles crumbling, the silver plate and the gold chalices and platters on the tables tarnished and dull. The wall-hangings stirred with the entrance of so many people, and a dry, fetid breath of air gusted outwards.

Black Aed and three of the others pulled the two prisoners out of the cart, tipping them on to the uneven stone floor and untying their ankles.

'No tricks,' said Black Aed. 'No attempts to escape.'

'They won't escape,' said Diarmuit. 'We've left their wrists bound. And even if they do try, they'll be caught and brought back.'

Rumour and Andrew, both conscious of slow agony in their ankles as the blood began to flow again, stood up and looked round, trying to take in as much as they could. Rumour thought: yes, it once was extremely lovely here. But something came in and tainted it. She could smell the smothering stench of decay and age, but stronger by far was the sour taint of Complex Evil, of a strength and a quality Rumour had never encountered. She thought: was it the Crimson Lady's evil that tainted this place? Or is it simply that it has seen centuries of agony?

At the far end of the hall was a small raised area, set with a high-backed chair draped in black velvet. Rumour saw that

330

woven into the velvet was the ancient and terrible symbol of the Northern sorcerers: the race of malevolent necromancers whose beginnings were so old that no one knew now whence they had sprung.

Behind the dais was an immense, almost intact tapestry depicting a long table set for some kind of meal. At the centre, seated in a high-backed chair, was a slender, dark-haired man with a cruel, beautiful mouth and high flaring cheekbones. Twelve guests sat with him, ranged along the table, most of them apparently engaged in eating and drinking, but all of them clearly subservient to the cruelly beautiful man. At the table's centre was a platter of what Andrew recognised as unleavened bread, and he saw that the dark man was holding up a golden chalice brimming with blood. Over his head was twisted a symbol of crimson and gold and ebony, and black rays, irradiating outwards, had been woven into the fabric about his head.

Rumour said, very softly, 'The Last Feast of the *Casca Dubh*. Medoc holding the Revel of the Twelve Necromancers on the night before he entered the True Ireland and was slain.'

At her side, Andrew said, '*Dubh* is darkness or blackness, I think. But what is *Casca*?'

'The Passing Over,' said Rumour, her eyes on the beautiful, cruel creature who presided over the sinister revelry. 'That is the Dark Passing Over, Andrew. The terrible underside of the Banishment Ritual you heard in the Porphyry Palace.'

'Yes. Beautiful. Then this is the Passing Over, not of the Darkness but of the Light,' said Andrew, softly, and behind them, Diarmuit said, 'The plea that the Light will not cross the threshold of the necromancers.'

'A good plea,' put in Black Aed, chuckling hoarsely.

'The reverse side of our Ritual,' said Rumour, and Andrew, staring at the darkly beautiful revelry said, almost to himself, 'The Dark Passover. The evil mirror image of the Paschal Supper. The old wine that has been in the cask for so many centuries that it can never be completely drained.'

'Medoc is lifting the chalice of blood so that his Twelve Lords may drink it in memory of him,' said Rumour. 'The legend is that he knew at that feast he would be vanquished on the morrow.'

331

'And that he wanted to leave his House a Ritual that would ensure that his work and his word would live on,' said Aed.

'We still celebrate that Ritual today,' said Diarmuit, and a soft voice from behind them said,

'"Take ye and drink, for this is my blood".'

Rumour and Andrew wheeled sharply round.

The Crimson Lady stood watching them from the doorway.

She was smaller than either of them had been visualising, and far more beautiful than they had expected. Andrew, staring, thought they had been expecting a towering, menacing being, and he found himself taken aback by this slender, graceful creature. She wore a dark cloak with a hood, but the hood was thrown back, and as the light from the flickering torches fell across her face, he saw that she was pale-skinned, and that her face was a perfect oval.

'Of course I am beautiful, Human,' said the Lady, moving to stand before him. 'It is the blood and the juice and the *sap* of Humans that makes me so.' She smiled, and it was a smile of such perfection that Andrew blinked.

Her skin was as smooth as ivory. Andrew thought it was like pale, pure alabaster, or soft, polished silk. But it is made so by bathing in Human blood and Human juices, he thought, sickened. Beneath that truly remarkable beauty is a loathsome, evil thing. As the Lady moved to stand before him and reached out to touch his face, he felt his skin shrivel with the coldness of her hand. The sleeve of her robe had fallen back, revealing a velvety white arm, with a wrist so fragile and so delicate that Andrew almost believed he could reach out and snap it in two between his hands.

She had black silken hair coiled into a jewelled snood, so that her features stood out sharply, a pure, clear cameo. There was a high, pale forehead – and there is learning there, thought Andrew, staring. There is scholarship. This is no untutored peasant.

'You are perceptive,' said the Crimson Lady to Rumour. 'You have recognised not only the emblem on my Throne, but also the famous depiction of Medoc's Last Feast.'

'Who would not recognise it?' said Rumour at once. 'The

legend is well known. And your evil House is also well known, madame.' She looked straight at the Crimson Lady. 'The Northern necromancers, who swore a vow to destroy Ireland and possess Tara. But none of you have ever been able to make good that vow,' said Rumour.

'You think that, do you?'

'You are still here,' said Rumour. 'And Tara and the Porphyry Palace of the Amaranths are still in the hands of their rightful owners.'

'But not for very much longer,' said the Lady. She studied Rumour. 'But you recognise my House correctly,' she said. 'I *am* a daughter of that old and powerful House.'

'I believe you to be the last of your line, madame,' said Rumour, and Andrew realised that she was according the creature the courtesy of one sorceress addressing another.

The Crimson Lady said, 'I am the descendant of the Erl-King of ancient days, and as such the head of my House. I am the descendant of Medoc, the dark, evil, beautiful Medoc who so nearly gained Tara, but who was vanquished by a Human.' She looked at Andrew suddenly. 'For that I have a deep and abiding hatred for Humans,' she said. 'I have vowed to rid my Realm of all Humans.' There was a lick of pleasure in her voice now, and Andrew and Rumour both felt icy fingers of fear touch them.

She looked back at Andrew, her eyes holding his, and Andrew felt as if he had been plunged, neck-deep, into an icy lake of dark, evil water. 'I am versed in many arts, Human,' said the Crimson Lady, softly. 'We shall shortly explore some of them, together.' Her eyes held his and Andrew, unable to look away, felt himself drowning, smothered . . . With an immense effort, he dragged his eyes away.

But I am right, he thought. The power is there. The eyes have it. They were huge swirling pools of blackness, twin lakes of evil, of pitch, of charred jet. A man might drown in those eyes and know himself suffocated by foul, ancient darkness.

O, but I shall smother you with other things first, Human creature . . .

Andrew looked up, startled, and saw that the Crimson Lady was smiling, a terrible smile, hungry and brutal and filled with greedy anticipation.

For someone will be quaffed tonight . . .

Her lips were wide and sensuous, dark red and livid against the whiteness of her skin. Andrew thought inconsequentially: I wonder, does she paint them, or are they naturally that colour? The smile was that of a predator, scenting and sighting its prey, hungering for blood. Tiny, even white teeth, razor sharp, gleamed in the dimness. How would it feel to be bitten by them...? Incredibly Andrew felt a stirring of hard, crude desire. He beat it down at once, horrified and repelled, and drawing his eyes away with an immense effort, he said quite coolly, 'We are interested in your Castle, madame.' And heard, with relief, that his voice was calm and unruffled.

'There are more interesting parts of the Castle than this,' said the Lady. She studied Andrew with the detached air of one who studies a strange beast or an insect recently caught and caged. 'All of them are now imbued with Complex Evil at its strongest,' she said, and then, to Rumour, 'I think you have already felt that.'

'Yes. But then,' said Rumour, her tone as bland as buttermilk, 'but then, madame, I hold an extremely high degree in the Theory of Sorcery. I could not possibly miss or mistake the level of Complex Evil that encloses this Castle. I could not mistake the density of Profane Evil at the outer edges.'

The Crimson Lady said, very sharply, 'That is either the statement of a fool or a very clever sorceress,' and for answer, Rumour said:

'The level of Complex Evil is Demonolatrous and the density is Vulpicide. It is well beyond the Magenta Boundary of Slaughterous, close to the Cannibalistic Vortex at the centre.

'As for the Profane Evil, that is Tyrannical, which I should expect of you. But there is an outer crust of Abyss-Mal.' She paused, and Andrew heard that she gave the last word a rather strange emphasis. Abyss-Mal: an evil from the Abyss...

Rumour said, as if bored with the entire subject now, 'And there is a layer of Eclectic Evil to the degree of Virulence, which, as you know, is not quite so high as Vulpicide, but still very high indeed.' She regarded their captor. 'Shall I continue?'

The Crimson Lady said, 'In my Realm, we would call that boasting, Madame Amaranth.'

'Oh, in mine also.' Rumour smiled contemptuously. 'But then in my world, I am already known to be boastful and extravagant and immodest. I see no reason to change simply because I am visiting your world, madame.'

The Lady turned back to Andrew. 'For a monk, you keep strange company,' she said.

'So I understand,' said Andrew in a tranquil, that-is-my-business tone.

The Lady shrugged. 'Your absurd word-games will not save either of you, of course,' she said. 'And presently, I shall enjoy showing you my Castle. The slaughterhouses and the sheds. The dungeons deep beneath the Castle-keep . . .' The hungry smile touched her red lips again. 'After all,' said the Lady, 'you *are* within my world, and you *are* in my power. There is no escape, you know.' She studied them. 'Once a prisoner is shut away in those deep dungeons, he would be for ever lost to the world.' She leaned closer. 'Shall I shut you both away? In a windowless, lightless cell? There are many such here. There are many halls in my Fortress . . .'

And many mansions in my Father's House . . .

Andrew thought: I must maintain a calm exterior. I must preserve a feeling of disdain. Rumour is treating the creature with such contempt, and I must match that. Above all, I must not let either of them guess that her voice – beautiful, sensual – rakes at deeply buried senses, and at longings so secret, I had not known, until now, that I possessed them . . .

How would it feel to lie with this beautiful, evil creature, and feel her teeth and taste the blood . . .

The Lady had moved away a little, the silken skirts of her cloak brushing the floor in a whisper of sound. 'You will see it all, Human Monk and Amaranth Sorceress,' she said, and the dark eyes flickered back to Rumour. 'I believe you know some of the legends, madame,' said the Crimson Lady politely.

'Yes. I know also that it is told how, within this Castle, are rooms, dungeons, each one containing a worse torment than the last,' said Rumour. She regarded the other. 'I have always felt that rather *obvious*, but I daresay that having practised necromancy for so *long*, you are running out of new ideas.' Poor burnt-out soul, said her tone.

The Crimson Lady drew back and hissed faintly. 'You shall pay dearly for that, BitchAmaranth,' she said, her voice sibilant and filled with hatred.

'Dear me, how tedious,' said Rumour at once, and the Lady turned back to Andrew.

The smile curved her lips again, and she said, 'When I have done with the Amaranth Bitch, I shall introduce you to the pleasures of extreme pain.'

The taste of blood, Human...

'You will be a worthy partner for a night for my bed,' she said softly. 'And when once you have tasted blood, when once you have felt it cascading over your naked limbs, you will know it for the sweetest, most potent wine you have ever taken.' She studied him again, and Andrew stared back. The Lady said, 'The line between pain and pleasure is a very fine one. Perhaps you have already found that? Perhaps you have already experienced arousal when flagellating yourself in your lonely, monkish cell.'

Scourging the flesh with the Miserere chanting all about your ears...

'I am afraid you are going to be disappointed in my response, madame,' said Andrew, with immaculate courtesy tinged with apology, and something dark and serpentine flickered in the Lady's eyes.

She said, very softly, 'I do not think so.' She was standing directly in front of him, and Andrew felt the cold, sour evil billowing out from the creature, as if the door to an ice-house had been opened. She leaned nearer, so that Andrew smelt the fetid stench of her breath, and knew it must come from the constant imbibing of warm blood.

'You will never destroy me,' hissed the Crimson Lady, 'although before we are done, you may wish to.' For a moment, her great black eyes seemed to distend, so that Andrew had the sensation of falling down a deep, dark well.

The Lady stood back, regarding them both, and then, turning to the waiting Almhuinians, said, 'They will do very well for a night's pleasure. Take them to the slaughterhouses.

'Make ready the silver troughs.'

The Almhuinians took their two prisoners through echoing galleries and narrow stone passages. Black Aed led the way, holding the torch aloft in the darkness, and Diarmuit and the other Almhuinians walked close behind, their knives unsheathed. Andrew knew that any attempt to escape would be useless. Their captors were armed and watchful, the tunnels narrow and dim. He glanced at Rumour, seeing that her eyes were in shadow and unreadable, but that her expression was calm, even rather disdainful. He saw her twitch the skirts of her cloak aside from a thick patch of dust at their feet, and grimace in disgust.

'Keep moving,' said Diarmuit harshly, and Rumour stopped and turned round to regard him, and said, in a faintly surprised voice:

'You cannot expect me to *walk through* this filth? In *slippers?*'

'You'll endure far worse presently,' said Diarmuit, and Rumour sighed, and said in a low, confiding tone to Andrew, 'Do you know, I had always heard that the Crimson Lady was *much* more particular than this. Really, it goes to show that gossip is not to be trusted, because who would have thought that Almhuin would be so disgustingly *dirty*.' She sent Andrew one of her sudden grins, and said, with a shrug, 'But then of course, she is one of the Northern necromancers and they were never overly fastidious.'

'Were they not?' said Andrew, as if he found this interesting.

'Oh my dear, disgracefully unclean.' Rumour glanced back at Diarmuit, and leaning closer to Andrew, said in a conspiratorial whisper, 'They do say that after the Erl-King died – at the hands of a Human, naturally . . .'

'Naturally.'

'. . . his entire Citadel had to be burned down, because no one would live in it.'

Andrew would have given all of his sparse possessions to have got Rumour away; he would gladly have rendered homage to any god who would take her back to the Porphyry Palace, even if he himself had to be left behind to face the Lady of Almhuin. But he was boundlessly grateful for her air of flippancy and her reckless, challenging bravery in front of these creatures.

For, he thought, I cannot be sure if I would have shown such courage without her. I cannot be sure if I could have faced the Crimson Lady so contemptuously and with such disdain.

The Crimson Lady, who would rake and stir up a man's deeply hidden desires until he was bursting his skin with longing, and who

*would draw him across the thin line, the first threadline that separates
pain from pleasure . . .*

*Pain . . . The scourging that had sometimes aroused a crude,
throbbing lust . . . So strong, so hard that sometimes the only relief
was to commit the sin of Onan . . . The spilling of the seed, scalding
and sinful, shameful but exquisite . . . How had she known about
that?*

The stone passage widened, and there was the feeling of
something ahead, waiting, watching . . . Something that had
hungering black eyes and greedy, clutching hands, and that
might already be seated on a black throne, with an immense
silver chalice held in place, waiting to catch the gleanings from
the bodies of the two new prisoners . . .

For someone will be quaffed tonight . . .

*Yes, but before that, that someone will have been drawn down a
dark and terrible path . . . How would it feel to lie alongside that
alabaster skin, to feel its coldness drawing the throbbing heat from
your own, to feel the icy flesh surround your desperate passion . . .*

Andrew tugged angrily at the ropes around his wrists, and felt
a stinging pain. With the sharp, scraping pain, the insidious pull
on his mind ceased, and he knew his thoughts his own again. He
thought: she is trying to bewitch me! The creature is sending out
some kind of dark seduction, some kind of evil beckoning. She
is spinning black necromancy about my mind! And he glanced
at Rumour, and remembered how, in the Cavern of the Segais
Well, Rumour had, just for a moment, stared at the Lord of
Chaos, her eyes wide and dark. Yes, Rumour would understand
about the evil, beautiful allure.

Rumour was not thinking about the Crimson Lady's possible
powers over Andrew. She had seen, for a fleeting moment that
the creature was attracted to him, of course, and she had known
that the Lady would almost certainly send out the Dark
Beckoning to him, more or less as a routine. The Amaranth
Charter forbade the Dark Beckoning of course but everyone had
used it at one time or another. Rumour herself had woven her
own version of it, but she had spun into it as many
Enchantments of Light as possible, and her Lures had always
been soaring, joyous things, filled with light and love and
washed with music and wine and firelight.

She thought that Andrew was strong enough to resist the

Crimson Lady's dark, evil Lure. He might succumb briefly, but he would almost certainly recognise the Beckoning for what it was, and he would throw it off. And after all, thought Rumour, her mind going fleetingly back to that moment when she had responded so strongly and so shamefully to Chaos; after all, who am I to criticise, or even mind if he does respond to it? She glanced at him in the ill-lit passage, and knew an overwhelming gratitude that he was with her, and that his strength and his belief that they would escape flowed out ceaselessly. She thought: without Andrew, I could certainly not have faced the Crimson Lady as – as *insolently* as I did earlier.

Directly ahead of them was a massive double door, studded with iron nails, and with huge iron ring-handles. Black Aed reached to open them; they swung to with a soft, well-oiled whisper of sound.

'Frequently used,' he said, grinning the rat-grin at Andrew and standing back, holding the torch aloft for them to see. 'Frequently used and carefully looked after. The Lady would not wish this place to be neglected.'

'Indeed? Then how very sad she does not apply the same rules to the rest of her Castle,' said Rumour, standing on one foot and then the other to inspect the soles of her slippers, and frowning.

'Onwards,' said Diarmuit angrily, pushing them forward. And there, ahead of them, was the place which every person in Ireland, the true, real Ireland, feared and spoke of in whispers. There, waiting for them, was the nightmare sanctum, the grisly temple of blood raised by the last daughter of the Northern necromancers . . .

The Lady of Almhuin's slaughterhouse.

Chapter Thirty

It was larger than they had expected, and it was shadowy and dim, so that to begin with they could only make out crouching shapes, formless, sinister outlines. And then Black Aed moved forward, holding up the torch to the rusted wall-brackets, and flames leapt up, vivid orange and scarlet, illuminating the slaughterhouse to grisly life. A warm, faintly meaty scent hung on the air.

As the light steadied, they saw that at the far end of the chamber were four stone tables, oblong in shape – *Human* in shape, thought Andrew. The tables were waist-high, and set on thick, dark plinths engraved with symbols and runic hiero-glyphs. Around the edges were culverts, deep narrow channels with drainholes at each corner, and at each of the tables' corners lay iron gyves and manacles with long, snakelike chains hanging down.

At the sides of the chamber were deep stone troughs, each one placed directly beneath one of the evil-smelling wall-sconces. Andrew thought they were a little like the huge drinking troughs used for horses, but Rumour, whose eyes were still adjusting to the flickering torchlight, thought they bore a sinister resemblance to stone coffins. Each one was partly sunk into the floor, with stone steps, worn away at the centre, leading down.

The sunken blood-baths.

The symbols used on the tables were carved around the edges of the baths, and Rumour recognised them as belonging to the House of Medoc and the Erl-King. In her own terrible world, this creature is royalty of a very high order indeed, thought Rumour, with a cold trickle of fear.

The windows of the slaughterhouse were barred, but, as Andrew had seen earlier, they looked directly on to the bleak northern face of the Black Mountains. So that no matter what agonies were inflicted on you, no matter what mutilations you suffered, no one would see and no one would hear...

The roof was low and intersected by massive rafters, blackened with age and centuries of candlesmoke. Protruding from the central beam was a row of huge black iron hooks, glinting in the flickering torchlight. Butcher-hooks, thought Andrew, shuddering inwardly. At the room's centre was a small, square platform some three feet from the ground. Steps led up to it, and a silver barrel, rather like a huge elaborate water-butt, with several small pipes protruding from its base, stood on the platform beneath the hooks. A gigantic earthenware jug stood close by.

Andrew, who had for a time been responsible for the fabric and the upkeep of his monastery, saw that the pipes ran from the silver butt along the floor to the stone troughs, and understood that their purpose was to discharge whatever fluids collected in the silver butt directly into the sunken troughs.

Set against the inner wall, facing the barred windows, was a squat iron brazier, cauldron-shaped but fashioned from thick iron, and resting on elaborately carved iron legs. Black Aed moved to it, holding a flaring torch to heat the bricks inside, and Rumour, remembering the whispered tales of the Lady's methods of torture, felt a sick dread clutch her.

They could both feel the rising heat from the Almhuinians now, and with it, a feral scent, dry and warm, as if thick, unclean fur were standing before a furnace. Rumour felt a stir of sexual heat from their captors, and knew that the Rodent side of them was strongly and grotesquely aroused by what was ahead.

A door at the far end of the chamber was flung open, and the Crimson Lady, clad only in a thin scarlet silk wrap, stood before them.

The Crimson Lady moved forwards with a slow, snakelike grace, the wrap falling open to reveal pale, marbled flesh. Her hair was still drawn back from her white brow, but the snood was gone, and her hair cascaded over her shoulders in sinuous black coils. Her eyes were on the two prisoners and, as she approached them, her fingers curved in a predatory fashion, the great burning-pitch eyes unblinking. 'So you are in my Temple at last, Humans,' she said, softly.

'We had little choice, madame,' said Andrew.

'We would certainly not have *chosen* to be here,' said Rumour.

The deep hungry eyes flickered. 'You are insolent,' said the Lady. And then, turning to Andrew, 'But you, Human, have a certain courtesy. I find it to my liking.' Her eyes raked him. 'I believe I shall enjoy you,' said the Lady, her voice clotted and thick. 'I shall find immense pleasure in your body and, at the end, when you are exhausted and begging for mercy, I shall enjoy seeing your agonies cross the line to the greatest sensuality you have ever known.' She glanced briefly at Rumour. 'Did you think this posturing Amaranth creature, this charlatan had given you pleasure?' she said, her voice filled with amused disdain. 'Did you think she had brought you to the peaks of fulfilment?' She reached out a cold, long-fingered white hand and traced the lines of Andrew's face. 'Yes, you are lean and firmly muscled,' she said, half to herself. 'And I shall take you to the peaks of agony and the exquisite heights of the purest pain in the world. And when you have scaled those peaks with me, then I shall permit you to die so that my beauty will survive. And your death will be a whisper of sheerest delight to your exhausted body.'

Andrew said, quite calmly, 'An interesting fate, madame.'

'How tedious to have to continually *feed* beauty,' said Rumour, bored.

There was the flicker of acknowledgement in the black eyes, as if the Lady might be relishing this interchange, and certainly as if she might be finding both Andrew and Rumour of more than usual interest. But she stepped back, turning her gaze on to Black Aed and Diarmuit and the waiting Almhuinians.

'I see you are already excited by the thought of the blood and the pain ahead,' said the Crimson Lady, in her soft, harsh voice. 'I see that your bodies are already hardening and ripening with anticipation.' She moved to stand before them. 'Perhaps I shall permit you to play a more active part this time. Perhaps I shall even take one or two of you to my bed later,' she said, and at once a low groaning murmur stirred the Almhuinians, and they glanced at one another from the corners of their eyes.

The Lady laughed, flinging back her head, so that the dark hair caressed the white flesh of her shoulders. 'First,' she said, 'we must show these two prisoners what is ahead, for anticipation was ever a part of pleasure.' She moved amongst them, studying each of them intently, coming to stop before Black Aed. A sudden hush fell on the Almhuinians, and Andrew and Rumour both felt their senses alerted, for something was about to happen, something unexpected, thought Rumour, and felt Andrew's awareness. Was this the moment for them to stage an escape? A diversion?

The Lady was staring at Black Aed, and there was such black fury in her eyes that he flinched.

'You have failed me,' said the Crimson Lady, and her voice was suddenly cold and hard, and filled with such authority that the Almhuinians flinched. Black Aed stayed where he was, transfixed by the staring, pit-like black eyes.

'You permitted that Amaranth creature to harness sorcery while she was in your keeping,' said the Lady. 'You permitted her to summon the Collector.'

'It was not—'

'Be silent, rat,' said the Lady, and although she did not say it very loudly, or even very aggressively, Black Aed was at once still. But Rumour could see that his eyes were shifting uneasily, as if he were searching the chamber for a means of escape.

'You are kept by me to ensure a supply of prisoners,' said the Lady, and now she was standing very close to him. 'You are kept very well by me to do that, Black Aed,' she said. 'And yet you sat drinking and carousing while that Amaranth creature laid her plans. And one of your number was killed by her sorcery,' said the Lady, and from the waiting Almhuinians, there was a murmur of 'Searbhan'.

'Yes, Searbhan. His manhood torn from him to adorn the Collector's hoard. And now dead of his wounds. Simply for trying to spear the Amaranth.'

She looked at Black Aed again, who said, 'It was – we had not expected—'

'I *keep* you to expect,' said the Lady. 'I *pay* you to expect. And the summoning of the Collector was a very *obvious* ploy.' She glanced contemptuously at Rumour, who grinned and said:

'But it worked.'

The Lady's eyes flickered with anger, but she turned back to Black Aed.

He had stood his ground. He eyed the Crimson Lady and said, 'Searbhan ought not to have approached the Amaranth. It is not permitted that we should tamper with your prisoners.' He said it in a cringing, unctuous way, as if he was reminding the Lady how slavishly they obeyed her laws, but his face was the colour of tallow and a faint sheen of sweat stood out on his brow.

'Absurd mutant-creature,' said the Lady in a tone of cold fury. 'Did you truly imagine I did not know your little ways?' She glanced back at the others. 'Did you all believe me to be ignorant of your rutting and your crude, brutish lusts?' She walked slowly round them, looking deeply into each narrow, rattish face as she did so. 'Of course you sample my prey before it reaches me,' she said. 'All of you do so.' She regarded them, her face white with fury, her eyes blazing such power that Andrew and Rumour felt the icy chill brush them. 'Did you truly think I did not know of it?' she said, and Diarmuit, whom Andrew had already seen to be the bravest of these people said, 'Ma'am, the virgins are never—'

'I know the virgins are never touched,' said the Lady at once, turning back to face Diarmuit. 'I *feel* them to be sure that they have not been touched before I embark on their torture.' A rather terrible smile touched the sensuous lips briefly. 'That is one of my pleasures,' she said. 'For once I have felt that the maiden's veil is still between their thighs, I have *other* uses for them.' She glanced across at Rumour. 'Virgins' blood was ever potent for many spells,' said the Crimson Lady, and Andrew heard with horror, that she spoke in a suddenly crisp, businesslike voice, rather as one craftsman to another; rather as if she was saying: and of course, *you* will understand about that.

Rumour said, in an uninterested voice, 'I have heard that it is so. I have never needed to have recourse to such crude methods.'

The Lady only smiled, as if she were amused by Rumour's disdain. She turned back to Black Aed, who stood silently before her.

'You tremble,' said the Lady, eyeing him. 'And you *will* tremble. You are going to *suffer*, Black Aed, and I am going to enjoy seeing you suffer.' She gestured impatiently to the other Almhuinians.

'The stone table first,' said the Crimson Lady. 'For the mood is on me to *play* a little before the final grand feast.' She glanced back at Rumour and Andrew. 'In your world, you would perhaps say – an appetiser, I think?'

'No, we would not say anything of the kind,' said Rumour, and the Lady smiled again and turned back to the Almhuinians. Andrew saw that they were waiting to obey their Lady, that no matter the atrocities they were called on to assist in, they would obey her instantly and unquestioningly. He thought: but surely between them they could overpower her? Surely they will make some attempt at rescuing one of their own people? And saw that they would not, and that whatever the Crimson Lady told them to do would be done.

'Strap him down well,' said the Lady, lifting one slender white hand to indicate the nearest of the stone tables. 'Strap him down well.' She paused, deliberately.

'And then heat the pokers.'

Black Aed fought every inch of the way. The Almhuinians leapt on him, instantly obedient as Andrew had foreseen, dragging him to the nearest of the stone tables. He kicked and clawed at them, his eyes bolting from his head, showing red in the flickering torchlight, his face hardly human now, but that of a cornered rat, baring its teeth.

At one point, he half broke from his captors and flung himself across the room, scrabbling at the closed door, only to be caught and dragged by his feet across the floor, his head scraping harshly against the rough surface, clawing and grasping at the stone flags as he was dragged, trying to gain purchase, his fingernails tearing backwards, so that his fingers were bloodied, nailless stumps. He was lifted to the stone table by four of the Almhuinians – four people who had once been his friends and his companions, or even his kin, thought Andrew.

'Face downwards,' said the Crimson Lady, standing at the table's head, her face lit to evil life, her arms crossed on her breast. 'Face downwards, and spread his legs.'

Black Aed was thrust on to the stone table top, and the gyves were snapped tightly and cruelly about his wrists and ankles. He writhed and threw himself against their restraints, shrieking in terror, cursing and threatening.

But he is caught, thought Rumour, unable to look away. The gyves are holding fast, and he is caught.

A rat caught in the trap . . .

At the centre of the room, Diarmuit had placed a slender, wicked-looking iron rod into the centre of the brazier, and the scent of hot iron filled the room.

The Lady slipped the thin robe from her shoulders, and let it fall to the ground in a whisper of silk. She stood before them, naked and slender and beautiful, and for a moment, the great evil eyes were turned to Andrew, and the strong beckoning stirred in their depths.

Andrew felt the flicker of arousal again, and stared at her angrily, understanding that she was throwing out her seductive lures, but for the moment, helpless against them.

Did I not tell you, Human, that I should take you to the peaks of the darkest and most sensual pleasures of all . . . ?

With an immense effort, Andrew dragged his eyes away from the great black eyes, and the Lady said, in an amused voice, 'Afraid, Monk? Let us see how you fare when it is your turn to face the hooks and the razors. When it is your turn to be strung from the iron hooks so that I may feel your warm, pulsating blood caressing my skin.' She stopped, breathing fast as if she had been running, and shook her head slightly like an animal coming out of water.

'The rod, ma'am,' said Diarmuit softly, and she turned back, taking the rod from him, using a thick velvet pad to hold it. She lifted it up, so that they could all see the thin, smooth steel shivering with heat, white-hot from the brazier, and the smile touched her lips again; avid, sexual, greedy . . . Andrew felt again that treacherous stirring. What would it feel like to inflict pain, to bestow screaming agony on another living creature . . . ? You would know yourself to be possessed of such power . . . He stared at the Lady, and felt his mind spiral downwards into crimson swirling desires and deep, dark passions, and then, without the least warning, Rumour's thoughts pierced the smothering evil: *Close your mind to her, Andrew, for she is casting the Beckoning Darkness about you . . .* Andrew felt something cool and clean touch his mind, rather like a shower of rain on an

346

autumn morning, he felt the insidious lure release its hold, and with the feeling, came a deep gratitude to Rumour, who understood and sympathised, and who had managed to break through the darkness and brush the surface of his mind in that cool, gentle way.

Black Aed was spreadeagled on the table, and his captors had peeled his shirt and breeches from his body. Andrew and Rumour saw that, although his body was covered with pale, more or less ordinary Human skin, along his spine was a band, a stripe, a striae of thick, bristly fur, dark brown and coarse. As Aed struggled again, Andrew saw that Aed's spine extended approximately six inches outwards from his body, jutting over his buttocks, making a rudimentary tail.

The Lady approached softly and sinuously, the heated rod held firmly in her right hand. Black Aed flung a terrified glance over his shoulder, and his body sagged suddenly.

The Lady nodded to the two Almhuinians who stood at Aed's head, and they leaned forward, silently, forcing his thighs wide, so that the embryo tail jutted rather horridly upwards. The Lady pushed it aside impatiently, and Andrew and Rumour saw that it was not bone, as they had thought, but a gristly, fibrous growth. Rumour found herself trying to decide whether this made Black Aed more Humanish and therefore more pitiable, or more Rodent-like, and thus evil and repulsive. She shook her head angrily, because there was no time to be feeling sorry for these evil beings. They had to think of themselves; of getting away and finding Chaos's Castle of Infinity, and reaching Theodora. She glanced to the doors, but three Almhuinians were standing guard, and one of them caught Rumour's eye and grinned knowingly, shaking his head.

There will be no escape from this place, Amaranthine . . .

Black Aed was sobbing, his head and his face pressed into the rough surface of the table. His nose and chin were grazed and bleeding from having been dragged across the floor, and the tips of his fingers were in bloodied rags from where he had fought to avoid being dragged to the stone table. He still flailed helplessly against the gyves that were about his wrists, but his legs were held firm and immovable by his captors.

The Crimson Lady stood savouring her prey, and then nodded to the Almhuinians holding the prisoner's legs. At once they jerked his thighs apart, and two of them moved to pull open his buttocks.

In a single clean movement, the Crimson Lady thrust the white-hot iron rod down between Black Aed's thighs, and as it rested there, lying against his skin, there was the terrible sound of skin scorching and flesh searing. Black Aed was screaming – dreadful, trapped-hare screams – and Andrew saw the Lady throw back her head and shiver with anticipation. A frown of concentrating ecstasy touch her brow now, and, still holding the fibrous, gristly tail out of the way, she grasped the rod more firmly, and slid the tip inside Black Aed's gaping anus.

A truly dreadful shriek rent the air, and there was a faint hissing sound, as if water had gushed on to the hot iron. Runnels of urine trickled between Aed's thighs, hissing and bubbling. Tiny droplets of moisture ran down his legs, leaving a thin trail of scarlet, blistering flesh, and the Lady laughed contemptuously.

'The creature cannot even hold its water in the face of a little pain!' she shouted, and her eyes were blazing madly now, flecks of bloodied spittle on her lips. 'See how its filth and its excretions are boiling within its miserable carcass! An inch of the heated iron – no more! – and it is writhing in agony! Puny being! Weakling! I am better without such cowards to serve me!'

Black Aed was sobbing, his face was contorted in such agony, that Andrew made an involuntary movement and then was still.

'And now,' said the Crimson Lady, stepping back, and surveying her victim, 'and now, to the hook with him.' She gestured imperiously to Diarmuit, and the Almhuinians sprang forward, unfastening the gyves and the manacles, dragging the moaning, shivering Aed from the stone table.

'To the hook!' screamed the Crimson Lady, stretching out a pointing finger, and the Almhuinians began dragging the barely conscious Aed across the floor. Andrew, his mind reeling with horror, saw for the first time that thin, iron-runged ladders were embedded into the walls, and that the Almhuinians were swarming up them, hauling Aed with them. They moved easily and agilely, and although they all wore leather shoes or boots, there was the impression that their toes curled like thin claws around the ladder's rungs.

They dragged Aed up carelessly, scraping his already mutilated body against the iron rungs, and at once the Lady screamed in anguish, 'Do not let him bleed! Preserve the blood!'

The Almhuinians reached the top, and crawled along the thick, wide rafters. There was the soft creaking of ancient, well-seasoned wood, and Andrew saw that the rafters were easily four feet in width, and that the Almhuinians were able to drag Aed along with them. They neared the centre and knelt there, lowering Aed over the edge.

'Carefully!' screamed the Crimson Lady, suddenly. 'Do not spill any more of his blood!'

The Almhuinians had lowered Aed and they were holding him by his arms now. His chin was resting on the hook, its point against the bony ridge of his jaw. Aed's eyes were bolting from his head with terror, and he was still struggling, but the Almhuinians held him firmly and he was helpless.

The Lady was watching avidly, her fists clenched and her eyes blazing with inHuman excitement. Thin fingers of colour painted her white face, and Andrew felt the treacherous ripple of admiration stir the surface of his awareness again. He thought: she is caught in the grip of her evil hunger, but like this I believe she is the most beautiful thing I have ever seen!

'Position the cask!' said the Crimson Lady, her voice suddenly urgent, as if she could scarcely contain her hunger. 'Do it!'

She bounded forward, moving like a great cat, and as the Almhuinians dragged the immense silver butt directly beneath the moaning, writhing Aed, she held out her hands and they lifted her into it. Diarmuit reached for the huge earthenware jug and stood watching Aed.

'And now,' said the Crimson Lady, her voice languorous and sensual, 'impale him. But do it *slowly*. Let him feel the caress of the cold iron in his cowardly mouth. Let him feel it biting into his bones and his teeth.'

There was a moment when no one moved, and a sudden waiting silence descended on the slaughterhouse. Rumour thought: is this the moment to reach for a spell? Something filled with light? Something made up of slicing knives and white-hot spears? Would the Collector come again, and if so, would he be a match for her?

349

The Lady had thrown back her head, and her eyes were fixed on the dangling figure of Aed directly above her. The lower part of her body was hidden by the silver cask, but her nipples stood out hard and erect, and her eyes were avid.

'Impale him!' she screamed frenziedly, and ran her flattened hands over her body with such absorbed sensuality that Rumour shuddered.

'Drive the hook into the creature's cowardly flesh!' cried the Crimson Lady. 'Make him dance on air! Do it! *Do it!*'

Aed was fighting again, struggling to break free, but the Almhuinians held him. He began to jerk convulsively with terror, his legs kicking and writhing.

'The dance of the hanged-man!' screamed the Lady triumphantly. 'See him dance! See the fool dance on air! Impale him! *Now!*'

The Almhuinians lifted Aed several inches, the muscles in their stringy arms bulging. And then, with dreadful precision, they brought his jaw down on the hook. There was a wet, splintering crunch and Aed jerked convulsively, an animal grunt of agony bursting from him. Blood and spittle gushed from his mouth, and the point of the hook burst through his nose bone, jutting out of the centre of his face so that, from below, it appeared that his nose had been replaced by the great black hook.

His body sagged, and he moaned with thick, grunting sounds. Rumour, sickened, realised that his mouth was shattered and that he was screaming through his nose. Blood, flecked with splinters of bone and teeth, trickled down over his chin.

The Lady stared up at him with the hungry intensity of a lover. 'And now let us have the traitor's blood!' she cried. 'Let us have every drop and every trickle and every ounce and every tear-drop of moisture in his puny body! Now! Now, when he is poised between pleasure and pain! Slit his veins! Shed his juices! Quickly! Do it! Or must I slaughter more of you! *Do it!*' And then, with unmistakable lust clotting her voice, 'Let me feel the blood,' she said, and her voice lingered on the word.

But the Almhuinians were already reaching down, the razors held out. Their eyes glinted redly in the dim light and, for a moment, it was not Humans who crouched along the ceiling beams, but huge rats, red-eyed and feral. At the Lady's side, Diarmuit stood with the great earthenware jug.

'Open his veins!' screeched the Lady. 'Open his veins! Or must I twist your manhoods from their roots and force them into your cowardly throats! Let me feel the blood, Rodent-mutants!' And then, in a different voice, 'But do it *slowly* to begin with. Let it fall slowly, like a caress. *Now!*'

The Almhuinians reached forward, and held Aed's arms up, the razors glinting redly.

'*The blood!*' screeched the Crimson Lady, and as the razors sliced into Aed's flesh, blood and juices and terrible fluids began to gush.

The Lady threw back her head, the veins standing out in her neck like cords, and the blood began to splash on to her. It came in a thin, steady flow, spattering over her white skin, running into her hair and over her face. Her tongue came out, licking at the terrible fluids, and her eyes were half closed in evil ecstasy. With the palms of her hands, she caressed her naked body, stroking the skin, sliding her hands between her thighs. Black Aed moaned and struggled, and there was the sound of tearing flesh and muscle as the hook, embedded in his jaw and his face, shifted a little. He grunted agonisedly through the shattered bones of his nose again.

Diarmuit, his expression absorbed, held out the jug, and as more of the gore ran down, there was the sound of it dripping into the jug's cavernous depths. He held it aloft, and poured it with a slow steady trickle over the writhing, blood-drenched figure of the Lady.

'He is draining,' she cried. 'Let me have *all* his juices! He is a paltry specimen of manhood, but I will have it all nevertheless! Be ready to slit him again!'

She reached her slender white arms upwards, and the Almhuinians wielded the glinting razors again. Blood ran into the Lady's cupped waiting hands and slopped over, and she cried out in obscene ecstasy.

'The remainder!' cried the Lady. 'Drain the traitor of everything!' As she spoke, the Almhuinians plied the razors for the last time, slicing with grisly expertise at the pulsing veins in Aed's neck. Blood sprayed outwards, a thick, gore-filled fountain, and the Lady moaned in dreadful pleasure, catching the flow and smearing it into her limbs. Her white body was clotted with gore, and her hair was matted and slick with the fresh, warm blood – and she is dangerously and soul-scaldingly beautiful, thought Andrew. Even as he framed the thought, the Lady turned and regarded him through eyes that were slitted with dreadful ecstasy. Her lips curved in a hungry smile.

And you will be the next one, Human . . .

Black Aed's body had sagged; it was turning slowly and swinging, exactly as a carcass of a slaughtered animal will hang in a meat-safe. Great livid bruises had appeared on his skin, and the last drains of blood trickled out now, clotted droplets splashing on to the Lady's shoulders.

He is raining blood on her, thought Andrew, still caught in the evil fascination, unable to tear his eyes away. This is her god, her worship, this is the thing she believes keeps her beautiful and young. And perhaps it does.

The Lady was gesturing to the Almhuinians who held Andrew.

'And now, Human,' she said, her voice purring with anticipation, 'and now, you see a little of my pleasures.' She glanced to Diarmuit and the others. 'This one interests me,' said the Crimson Lady. 'His body draws me.' She raked Andrew with her eyes. 'Lean and strong,' she said, softly. 'Muscular. Strong arms and powerful thighs.' She leapt from the blood-butt, as agile as a panther, and moved to stand in front of him. Blood dripped from her, smearing the stone floor, and Rumour saw that blood had collected under her fingernails and toenails, and that her scalp was crusted with drying gore.

The Crimson Lady was standing close to Andrew, and her bloodied hands were caressing his body, her eyes holding his, her whole bearing one of terrible and evil beauty. Rumour thought: of *course* he is caught in thrall. Of *course* he is feeling his body respond. He cannot do otherwise. That is the terrible allure possessed by the necromancers of the House of Medoc, she thought, and knew that, although she had reached him earlier, Andrew was helpless in the Lady's allure now.

'Strong and lean and hard,' whispered the Lady, her blood-smeared body pressed against Andrew's. 'Pure Humanish blood. Untainted Humanish sap and Humanish juice.' She opened her eyes and deliberately ran her hands over him, caressing his thighs. 'Oh, monk, I am going to enjoy you,' she said. 'I am going to enjoy your agony, and then I am going to enjoy seeing it cross over to the most exquisite agony of all.' She stepped back and nodded to the Almhuinians. 'Strap him down,' she said.

Chapter Thirty-one

Rumour's mind was working furiously.

She knew that she was hovering perilously on the brink of throwing herself on the Crimson Lady's mercy, begging her to spare them, certainly begging her to spare Andrew.

Could I? she thought, watching him being carried to the centre of the room and strapped to the stone couch. There was the cold, cruel snapping of the gyves as the metal slid home. Could I ask the creature's mercy, promise her some kind of evil pleasure? thought Rumour. Offer my own flesh for her to satisfy her horrid lusts? Her skin crawled at the thought, but she would have done it save for one sure thing: the Crimson Lady would accept her offer, would use her in a dozen warped, twisted ways, and at the end would still slaughter Andrew. She will not give him up, thought Rumour.

Diarmuit and the others had strapped Andrew to the table they had used for Black Aed, and two of them had moved to Rumour, not chaining her in any way, but twisting her arms behind her back so that she could not move. But she could see that Andrew had been forced to lie amidst the half-dried gore and blood, and the expelled urine from Aed's body. A deep anger kindled and she thought: I *will* outwit this one! Somehow I will do it!

The Lady waited until Andrew was manacled, but there was an impatient glitter in her eyes, and Diarmuit's people, glancing at her uneasily from the corners of their eyes, worked quickly. The instant they finished, she leapt forward, as quickly and as suddenly as an uncoiled spring, and leaned over the table, her eyes raking Andrew's body, her fingers curving in a predatory gesture. Her hair was matted from Aed's blood and her eyes were wild. There was barely any trace of the icily beautiful creature who had confronted them on their arrival, this was the creature beneath the thin veneer of culture, and it was a creature red in tooth and claw.

The Lady took a razor from one of the Almhuinians, and her movements were slower now, deliberate and studied. She held the razor aloft in her left hand, her eyes glittering, the other hand stroking her white, blood-spattered body in a monstrous, self-indulgent caress.

Andrew's dark woollen robe had been torn from him, and Rumour could see that the gyves were cutting cruelly into his wrists and ankles. Tiny bubbles of blood welled to the surface, and at once the Lady bent over, licking them, savouring the taste, her tangled, crusted hair brushing Andrew's bare skin. Rumour saw him flinch, and remembered with sharp poignancy how the silken swing of a lover's hair against bare skin was one of the most intimate and joyous sensations of love-making. She felt a cold sickness at seeing this parody of something soft and precious and loving being inflicted on Andrew.

The Crimson Lady padded silently round the table again, her eyes never leaving Andrew's body. She is savouring him, thought Rumour, struggling uselessly against her captors, feeling their hard, bony fingers digging into her flesh. She cast a quick look back at the door through which they had entered, listening for the soft footfalls of Chaos's people. Did I imagine it after all? If they would only come, thought Rumour in anguish; if they would only come pouring down on their Lord's enemies, I believe we should be able to escape. But although she thought there was a faint stirring of something beyond the double iron-framed doors, the shadows remained quiescent, and there was nothing in the chamber with them, save the soft padding of the Lady's bare feet, and the harsh struggles of Andrew, manacled and chained on the stone.

At last the Crimson Lady moved to stand over him, her eyes glittering with lust and hunger, her hands still reddened from the blood of Black Aed, her lips slicked and red with Andrew's own blood. She reached for the great earthenware jug, still spattered with Black Aed's blood, and positioned it beneath the table, directly under one of the drainholes, lining it up with such absorption and such minute attention to its exact placement that Rumour had to choke back a scream of frustration and anger. As if sensing this, the Lady turned and sent Rumour a thin, hungry smile, with something dreadfully intimate in it, as if she believed that Rumour might understand and enter into this fearsome bloodlust. Rumour looked away, as if bored, and the Lady smiled, and said, very softly, '*Someone will be quaffed tonight*. Oh yes, Amaranth sorceress, I know what they say of me.'

'I suppose,' rejoined Rumour, sounding as if the matter was of scant interest, 'that it is better to be known for something – even the quaffing of Humanish blood – rather than not to be known at all.' She studied the Lady. 'But for your warped tastes,' said Rumour, 'you would probably live in obscurity. Unheard of. Rather sad,' said Rumour and, looking across at Andrew, said in the coolest of all her cool voices, 'We should try to be kind to her, Andrew, for this is really the poor soul's only claim to fame.'

The Lady stared at Rumour, and Rumour felt the icy darkness uncoiling deep in the creature's mind. At length the Lady said, 'You will pay very dearly for that remark, Amaranthine,' and Rumour said at once, 'But I seldom pay my debts, madame. You should know that I seldom pay for anything.' And smiled blandly.

The Crimson Lady looked at Rumour for a moment longer, and Rumour felt a stir of triumph, for she thought she had succeeded in disconcerting the Lady very slightly. If I could somehow throw her off balance, she thought, I believe I could quench the smothering darkness and reach power of some kind. If only Chaos's spies would come swarming in.

The Lady was reaching out to caress Andrew's skin, stroking the inner part of his thigh. Rumour felt fury sweep her mind, because there must surely be some way to defeat this evil creature, there must be something she could do. To summon a dark power would be better than nothing, and here of all places, a dark power would be easy to summon.

A dark power . . .

Of course.

Rumour did not hesitate. She flung back her head, and in a ringing voice, pronounced the ancient, distorted incantation that she had used in Diarmuit's tavern cellar.

As if in answer, the slopping liquid chuckling reverberated around the room, and Rumour knew she had reached him again.

The Collector.

He materialised almost at once, the huge black shadow falling half across the chamber, the remembered stench of old blood and ancient evil gusting in their faces. The Almhuinians fell back fearfully, and Rumour twisted from their grasp, laughing in delighted triumph.

'See your victim, Master Collector!' she cried, pointing to the Crimson Lady. 'Take whatever you will of her!' And as the Lady turned, a snarl twisting her beautiful, cruel features, 'The biter is about to be bitten, madame!' cried Rumour.

The Lady fixed her black eyes on the hovering shadowy outline. 'You are not unknown to me, sir,' she said, and the Collector gave vent to his terrible laugh again. The torches flared, and although the light did not quite reveal his whole body, it seemed to alight on portions of it in turn, never quite revealing the whole, but almost appearing to say: see, *here* is one grisly aspect, and *here* another; showing the great slung belt with the grisly gobbets of flesh and the pieces of his victims' bodies: phalluses and hanging, sagging breasts . . . The necklace of eyes and teeth . . . The bracelets of bloodied hair and the glimpse of his cloak hem, plaited with the glistening, still wet ropes of pale intestines, bowels . . .

Rumour shuddered, but the Crimson Lady was moving towards the huge, loping silhouette, her eyes blazing with strong emotion.

'The Collector,' she said, in a purring, sensual whisper. '*Bailitheoir* . . .'

The Collector's huge head came round, and for an instant the torches flickered, showing a gaping, yawning face, a face stretched into an impossible elongated shape, tallow-pale and the edges indistinct, but with great black chasms where the eyes should have been. In his soft, dark voice, the Collector said, 'You know my name,' and there was a different, sharper quality to it now, as if he might be suddenly interested.

The Crimson Lady had come to kneel before him, her hands upraised with the palms uppermost. 'Who of my House does not?' she said. 'The Collector, whose name in the ancient Gael is Bailitheoir. The one who takes the gleanings of the Humanish bodies. The one who permits corners and fragments of his dark self to be glimpsed, but never the whole.' With the words, the great shadowy cloak stirred, and Rumour caught the edges of torn-apart lips, dozens upon dozens of them, and wide-open, silently screaming mouths behind.

The Lady smiled, as if she, also, had seen this and understood it to be a response from the shadowy entity. She said, 'No living creature has ever beheld you in your entirety, Bailitheoir. And you value your privacy. But you are well come, sir,' she said.

Rumour strode forward, her cloak brushing the stone floor angrily. 'This creature is my servant!' she cried. 'Called up by my sorcery and my strength! He will answer to me!'

'But,' said the Crimson Lady, her eyes still on Bailitheoir, 'but if he should find himself in accord with one who springs from the same root . . .' She paused, and her eyes swivelled to Rumour, mockery in her expression. 'If he should find himself faced with one who may be kin to him, one who could strike a very profitable bargain with him,' she said, 'then his allegiance might very well turn.' The dark eyes rested on Rumour and the amusement was there again. 'You did not think of that when you summoned him?' said the Lady. 'I see you did not. Well, I had heard you were a gambler, madame, and now I know it to be so.'

'The Summoning was clear!' cried Rumour angrily. 'He is answerable to me!' She whirled around to the dim outline of Bailitheoir. 'Tear this creature's head from her shoulders and wear it for a trophy!' she cried. 'I *command* you to do it! By every ancient law of sorcery and by every *Chronicle of Enchantry* you are *bound* to obey me!' She stopped, breathing hard, and from behind caught a movement, as Andrew struggled helplessly against the iron gyves of the table. If Andrew could somehow be freed, together they might flee from this dreadful place . . .

The Crimson Lady was reaching out to stroke the Collector's swirling, indistinct cloak. 'I could give you so much, Bailitheoir,' she said, her voice heavy with sexual promise. 'We could share in the pain and the blood. Join me at my banquets, and take what I do not need. Rule at my side.'

The Collector appeared to be sunk in thought. He dipped his great head to Rumour, and said, 'You summoned me, madame,' and the courtliness that Rumour remembered was in his voice.

'I summoned you, and by the ancient law of sorcery you must obey me,' said Rumour again. 'Tear that creature into collops!'

Unexpectedly the Lady laughed. 'A terrible choice!' she cried. 'You are caught between the law and the promise of far more than that puny Amaranth can give!' She moved to the shadowy outline again, and lifted one slender arm almost negligently. 'Serve *me*,' she said, softly. The Collector turned his great head, and Rumour saw, as clearly as any manifesting curse, the Dark Beckoning, the seductive lure of necromancy spin outwards and curl about the Collector's head.

'Ride with me against the Lord of Chaos,' said the Crimson Lady in a soft voice. 'Join with me in battle against him, and together we will vanquish him and rule unchallenged.' She paused, and the tip of her tongue came out to lick her full red lips. The Collector remained silent and motionless, but Rumour felt him listening.

'And then it would be all ours, Bailitheoir,' said the Lady, and now the rising note of sexual hunger was in her voice. 'The NightFields with their bloody harvests and the sprawling piles of rotting carcasses. The gore-soaked Crimson Lakes, and the Black Pits of Ireland's ancient, fire-drenched Hell: *Ifreann* itself.'

The Collector said in a quiet, breathy whisper, 'But you have a servant, madame. All the Dark Realm knows of your servant,' and the Crimson Lady made a quick, dismissive gesture.

'There was a fool who served me,' she said. 'A Human who fell for a time into my vassalage. He was weak and gullible.'

'And?' Rumour, watching carefully, saw that the Collector was listening with absorption. Across the room, Andrew turned his head.

'He betrayed me as Humans always betray in the end. I discovered that he was prepared to sell his services to any in the Dark Realm who would gratify his needs. He was serving Chaos at the same time as he was pretending to serve me. And no man in this Realm can serve two masters,' she said, her brow drawn down.

'Or two mistresses,' said Bailitheoir softly. 'So you cast him out, madame,' he said, and the Crimson Lady smiled, remembering.

'I cast him out,' she said. 'Into the howling night of the Dark Realm, where Humans are constantly at the mercy of the Harpies and the Crones and the roaming WarMongers. I have had many pleasurable nights imagining what his fate was.' She looked up at the towering shadow standing over her. 'That was when I issued the ancient challenge of War to Chaos, who had tried to steal one of my people.'

Rumour drew in a quick breath of understanding, because after all it was not Theodora who had caused this War of Necromancy, but simply the revenge of Almhuin's Lady. Her eyes met Andrew's, and she saw that he also had understood.

'What became of the Human?' said the Collector, and Rumour saw Andrew's eyes fixed with intensity on the Crimson Lady.

But she said, 'I have no idea. If he survived out there, he may have fallen into the thrall of some lesser necromancer. He may even have managed to reach the Castle of Infinity. But he is of no account. Once I discovered his disloyalty, I had no further use for him.' She fixed her great black eyes on the Collector. 'So you see,' she said in a soft, purring voice, 'you see, Bailitheoir, apart from the rat-mutants, I am alone. And to those who give me their loyalty, I am generous. Since the Wars there are many rich gleanings for such as you.'

Bailitheoir said, thoughtfully, 'The corpses of battle.'

'Yes. Chaos's people.'

'You are able to overpower him in battle?'

'Certainly,' said the Crimson Lady. 'Our Armies have met and fought several times now. The famous Battle of the NightFields was my greatest victory. But the War is not yet entirely won.'

'No?'

'Chaos still lives,' she said, coldly. 'And so there must be many more battles. A quarter of all the prisoners we take could be yours.'

The Collector's teeth gleamed with sudden predatory hunger. 'Not enough, madame. Half.'

The Crimson Lady hesitated, and then said, 'As you will. Half. You drive a hard bargain, Master Collector. But to have you with me will be worth it.'

The Collector bowed his head again. 'It is my pleasure, madame,' he said. And then, turning to where Andrew lay, 'Shall we attend to the first of our shared victims?' he said, and the Crimson Lady laughed, throwing back her head.

* * *

The Almhuinians had again sprung to Rumour's side, holding her captive. She struggled and raked her mind for a means of escape, but they held her firmly, their hands digging into her like tiny claws.

The Crimson Lady stood behind the stone table, the blurred figure of Bailitheoir with her. She looked directly at Rumour, malevolent triumph gleaming in her eyes, and Rumour glared. When the Lady spoke, her voice was a silken purr. 'You gambled on summoning and controlling a dark power, Madame Amaranth,' she said. 'And in the manner of all gamblers, you must occasionally lose.' She looked down at the helpless Andrew and smiled. 'You have lost, madame. He is mine.'

Rumour looked up furiously at the towering figure beside her, and it seemed to her that the two of them conferred, Bailitheoir's massive blurred head bending over, his outline so blurred that at times it seemed that the Lady slid inside the dark shadow of his body. The two of them looking down at Andrew, touching, stroking... Rumour saw the Lady's hand slide insinuatingly between Andrew's thighs, and bit her lip in rage.

Then the Collector spoke, and it was the courteous, cultured tones that Rumour remembered. 'I shall remove his legs,' he said. 'That will be of immense interest to me, for with a little *dark* sorcery, I may then walk with the tread of the Humanish. I may prowl the world of Men at will, in search of further prey.'

The Crimson Lady silently held up the razor, but there was a curdling of the shadows as Bailitheoir declined it.

'Of knives and razors and Humanish weapons I have no need,' he said, and turned to the table.

Rumour saw Andrew's shiver, and she saw the shadows surrounding Bailitheoir thicken, and the sudden silver glint of dozens of tiny, vicious teeth.

The Lady flung herself beneath the table, writhing in an ecstasy of anticipation; and as the Collector raised his head, Rumour glimpsed the stretched wide mouth now, the rows of teeth smothered in blood. And then he descended on Andrew's helpless body, a great smothering cloud of evil, and for a brief instant, Rumour saw the outline of his face again, and saw how the black glistening hair swung outwards, framing his head in a black aureole.

The Collector buried his face in Andrew's flesh, and Rumour thought: he is *biting* through Andrew's leg . . . He is *eating* it!

She knew the exact moment when the eerie core of teeth tore into Andrew. She was concentrating so furiously that she thought she almost felt the pain in her own flesh: a tearing, a wrenching, agony of unbelievable intensity . . .

Andrew's skin had taken on a waxen quality, and Rumour knew that he must be held in a vice of mind-shattering agony. Blood poured from his leg, and when Bailitheoir raised his head, the barely glimpsed jowls blood-smeared, she saw deep within the gaping wound the white glint of bone. A groan broke from Andrew and he writhed against the gyves, his head threshing from side to side. The Collector moved again, this time shaking his head from side to side as a dog shakes a rat to subdue it. Rumour fought down the rising nausea, because she would not be sick, she would not be so weak . . . And very soon it will be me on that couch! she thought, her eyes huge with fear.

'Humanish blood,' cried the Lady. 'Humanish blood, pure and clear and undiluted.' She smeared the dripping blood into her skin a further time, her eyes half closed with dreadful delight.

The Collector was chuckling evilly, but now it was a thick, clotted chuckling, and Rumour knew his mouth was filled with the fresh warm blood. Despite her resolve, her stomach lurched, and she thought: he is severing his leg. He is doing it slowly . . . I cannot bear it! thought Rumour. If I am to save him – if I am to save either of us, I must move! She braced herself, ready to throw off the Almhuinians, drawing in a deep breath and reaching desperately for the shining, Amaranthine power, even the thinnest vein of it . . . There must be a chink in these creatures' dark carapaces! If only I could find it, I believe I could save us both! Her mind touched on and rejected a dozen enchantments. To defeat the Crimson Lady and her servants, she must use a spell that would turn the darkness upside down and inside out.

From deep within the Castle came the sound of light, soft feet, dancing and whirling, approaching the blood-smeared chamber. And over the sound, the unmistakable chanting of a grisly Hunting Song.

> *'O give us skins for murdering in*
> *Cloaks of pale and Humanish shale.'*

The Fomoire were in the Castle with them.

The great double doors to the slaughterhouse burst open, and the baleful red light that Rumour remembered so vividly streamed in. Silhouetted against it were the grinning, capering figures of the Fomoire, their cloaks of Humanish skin flying wildly about them, their tiny goblin faces grinning wickedly and lasciviously through the slits.

> *'O give us skins of Humanish thin*
> *Husks to hide our evil in.*
> *Murderers' cloaks and child-eaters' hair.*
> *Robes of hide and fur and vair.'*

They streamed forward, malevolently triumphant, and the Almhuinians fell back, clearly terrified, plainly unable or unprepared to fight the evil goblin creatures from Chaos's dark Armies. The Fomoire came swarming forward, filling the blood-tainted slaughterhouse with their own terrible darkness, dancing and shrieking with malicious glee, chanting their grisly Hunting Song.

> *'Fleeces of crimson, blood-soaked skin;*
> *Pelts with trims of silken sin.*
> *Give us fur and Humanish hair,*
> *Rodent cloaks and rattish fur.'*

They surrounded the Crimson Lady and the Almhuinians, leaping and jeering, their wizened claws reaching out, grabbing the razors and the thin iron rods and the knives from the cowering Almhuinians.

'Spies!' screeched the Lady, falling back against the stone table and staring up at them with distended eyes. 'Spies and snooping, prying vermin! Chaos's evil, sneaking spies!'

'Rats and jackals and bloodied fur,' shrieked the Fomoire. 'Paws and claws and whiskers and hair.

Hides of Rodent and weasels' skin,
Husks to hide our true selves in'.

The Collector jerked back from his grisly work and, whirling
about, melted into the swirling shadows in a vortex of blood-
tainted darkness. At once, the Lady gave a howl of fury, and
turned this way and that, her huge eyes blazing with fury.

'Coward! Back to my side and help me fight! Bailitheoir! I
command you!'

'Bailitheoir is not to be commanded, madame!' cried
Rumour. 'The biter is bitten indeed!'

From the whirlpool of crimson-streaked darkness, there was
a breath of a whisper, a soft polite murmur. 'I do not fight for my
prey, madame . . . Farewell . . .' And then he was gone in truth,
leaving only drops of dark blood splashing to the floor where he
had been.

The Fomoire fell on the Crimson Lady, dragging her by her
hair to the stone tables, shouting their glee, their empty-eyed
heads lolling and jerking, the skins of several of them falling
back, exposing their horrid wizened pates and their evil,
shrunken, goblin faces. On the stone table, Andrew was barely
conscious, blood pouring from the dreadful gaping wound in his
leg, his skin waxen and grey. There are probably no more than a
few minutes left if I am to save him! thought Rumour
frantically.

The Lady was still trying to fight the Fomoire back. She was
screeching and hurling imprecations at them, and Rumour
thought that, if ever there was a moment to rescue Andrew and
get out of Almhuin Castle, then this was the moment.

The Almhuinians were penned in the circle by the leaping,
cavorting Fomoire, and the others were closing in on the Lady,
their glinting, inward-slanting eyes avid.

'Weaklings!' cried the Lady, on her feet now, facing them
with her eyes wild, her naked body caked with the blood of her
victims. 'Goblins, creatures of ancient filth and earth! Does your
Master think to insult me by sending such puny creatures
against me! Get from my Castle!' She hit out at them again, but
the Fomoire leapt and darted, grinning and jeering.

'No power!' they cried. 'The Crimson Lady of Almhuin
cannot even call up a spell to protect herself!' And then, with

one of their abrupt changes of direction, 'Get the Rodent one
down, chaps!' they shrieked. 'There's a creature up there with a
good skin!'

'A skin of Rodent fur!'

'We'll sew the veins!'

'We'll sew the nose!'

'And then we'll hang it to cure!'

'Rodent fur, chaps!'

> 'Rats and jackals and bloodied fur,
> Hides of Rat and weasels' fur
> Paws and claws and whiskers and hair.
> Coats of hide and murderers' vair.'

They swarmed up the ladders and across the beams to where
Black Aed's body still hung, swinging slightly in the movements
from below, the head drooping, the huge black hook still
protruding through his shattered nose.

The Lady was cowering in a corner, and Rumour stood for a
moment, summoning courage, reaching for strength, knowing
that even as she stood there, Andrew was bleeding to death, and
knowing with a terrible clarity that there was barely any time
left.

And then the Fomoire lowered Aed's drained body, and
began their strange Chaunt, the Chaunt that had marked the
entry of Chaos into the Cadence Tower; and with the words,
Rumour felt light exploding within her mind, and knew, in that
instant, what to do.

The Fomoire were singing the fearsome Chaunt mockingly.

> 'Carpet the world in Human misery,
> Strew thick the harvest of the creatures of night.
> Lay down the gleanings of the soul eaters.
> Kill the veil of the world of light.'

Rumour knew the Chaunt as well as she knew any other
incantation, for it ran like a sticky black snails' trail of evil
through every *Book of Magic Lore*, and every *Sorcery Chronicle*
ever written. The Entry of the Dark Lords ... Unutterably
ancient and immeasurably potent.

The words fell on the air as if they were tangible things, a creeping dark slime entering the castle.

But for every darkness, there is light, thought Rumour. For every dark spell, there is a counter-spell. The age-old law.

And they are pronouncing the Chaunt of the Entry of the Dark Lords, and there is a counter-spell, and I know that counter-spell. It was the original Chaunt, the true and dazzlingly beautiful incantation written and spun for the first Amaranth sorcerers by the *sidh*, bestowed on them by Aillen mac Midha. And I know it! thought Rumour, exultantly. I can pronounce the Chaunt as it was written and as it was planned before the Fomoire stole it away and warped it to their own evil ends. It was the chink in the dark armour of Almhuin that she had tried so desperately to discover. And I have discovered it! she thought. A great surge of confidence filled her, and the Amaranth light, the ancient pure flame of her ancestors, streamed into her mind.

She moved to the centre of the chamber, and lifted her arms above her head, palms upwards in the age-old gesture that reached for the power, that harnessed it and turned it into pure living magic.

'O give us skins for dancing in
And give us veils of Humanish pale.
Fleeces of fur and silken skin
Ivory bones for living in.'

And this time the power was there. As if a door had opened and permitted the ingress of a sliver of light from another room, the marvellous mystical power began to flood her mind.

It was a slow trickle at first; it came to her in rivulets and thin runnels, glittering and silken-smooth. But as she reached for it and seized it to weave into the Chaunt, it intensified, until it was a pouring torrent, a huge, almost overwhelming fountain of cascading light.

But I must be quick! thought Rumour. I must be quick, for I do not think there is very much time left if I am to save Andrew! The door is open, but I must be sure that it is pushed wide.

But the Fomoire were already falling back, screeching in

366

furious pain, their clawed hands scrabbling frantically at the air in front of them, as if blinding white light was swooping at them. They tumbled backwards, falling over one another, shrieking and wailing.

'The light, the Chaunt of Light!'

'The creature knows it!'

'It will kill the Darkness!'

'Slay the Amaranthine!'

'Slay her and *skin* her!'

'Take her fleece for the Lord of Chaos and his henchmen!'

'You dare not touch me!' cried Rumour, confidence filling her whole body, because she had forced open the door, she had let in the light and the strength and the power. She felt it streaming about her like a shimmering mantle, and when she flung out her hand, light sizzled and spat from the ends of her fingers.

'You dare not even approach me, evil, snooping creatures!' cried Rumour, and even at such a moment, she felt a tiny inner spurt of amusement at the sheer extravagance of the gesture. 'Back to your lord!' cried Rumour in ringing tones, and thought: well, if you can't be dramatic at times like this, I don't know when you can be!

'Back and report your failure, Goblin spies!' cried Rumour, and although it would be too much to have said she was enjoying herself, she was aware of a sudden relish and an uplifting of her spirits.

'Back to your wretched Master, and tell him that you were vanquished by an Amaranth!' shouted Rumour, thinking she might as well bring out all the rhetoric while she was about it.

The Fomoire squeaked and shouted in shrill and angry fear, but they were already tumbling across the floor, scuttling and scrabbling, climbing over one another in their haste to be out of the reach of the sorceress who had been able to defeat their Chaunt.

The Almhuinians were huddled against the far wall, trembling and cowering, and Diarmuit was fumbling with the door handles. As the Fomoire reached them, the door fell open, and Almhuinians and Fomoire tumbled through it in a seething, frightened mass of skin and fur and claws and flying skin-cloaks.

Silence fell over the slaughterhouse, and Rumour saw with infinite thankfulness that Andrew had revived a little, and had

367

even managed to half raise himself, and reach down to press the wadded folds of his woollen robe to the terrible wound. Blood still flowed, but it had slowed to a sluggish trickle now.

Rumour looked at the Crimson Lady. 'So, madame,' she said, softly, 'it seems that we are evenly matched at last.'

The Lady was on her feet, thrusting bloodied fingers through her tangled hair, combing it roughly into place. When she addressed Rumour, a semblance of the former cold authority had fallen about her.

'We would never be evenly matched, Amaranth,' said the Lady in a cold, contemptuous tone. 'My powers are greater and darker and more ancient than anything you could ever hope to summon.'

Rumour said, rather as if it was a matter of minor importance, 'Oh, I don't think so, you know. Although it is a pity you did not make use of your ancestry, madame. I find it sad that the last of such an ancient line could not even turn back the Fomoire. I find it heart-warming that you can not deflect *this!*' cried Rumour, and flung a spear of light straight at the Lady, aiming it so precisely that it fell within a foot of where the Lady stood, following it with another, and then another, lining them exactly and deliberately, until the Lady was fenced in by dozens of spears of white, hurting light. She flinched and cowered, covering her eyes with her hands, her face contorted with pain.

'A small revenge,' said Rumour. 'But it will serve for the moment. It will prevent you from being a nuisance to me while I see what has to be done here.'

'How dare you refer to me so slightingly!' cried the Lady, but she eyed the glinting light warily, and Rumour saw that she avoided looking at it directly.

'Well, madame?' she said. 'Do you still say we are not evenly matched?' And without waiting for an answer, went to where Andrew still lay, his face grey and his eyes closed, blood still seeping out from under the makeshift dressing.

At first Rumour thought that, despite his valiant effort to staunch the blood earlier, he was dead, and such cold desolation closed about her that the blood-smeared slaughterhouse and the caged creature blurred before her eyes. And then she remembered that dead men do not bleed, and saw that a tiny pulse was beating at the base of his throat.

Horridly conscious of ignorance, she pushed the gaping edges of the wound together, and bound it about with the makeshift wadding he had already managed to fashion from his robe. She thought it might be possible to effect a stronger healing, with sorcery, but it was one of the few magical arts of which she had little knowledge. And I cannot do anything here with that creature glaring! thought Rumour. Practical ordinary help first, and then she would think about magical aid.

Although she could not move him yet, she could surely make him more comfortable. She dragged off her own cloak and threw it over him, for although the bleeding was lessening he was icy cold and his flesh had taken on a grey pallor. As she did so, his eyes fluttered open, and although they were pain-filled and blurred, they were aware.

He said, in a thread of a voice, 'Rumour . . .'

'I am here and the Lady is caged,' said Rumour at once. 'And you are safe, Andrew, and I shall heal your wound.'

She thought he whispered a thank-you, and then his eyes closed again and Rumour thought: well, I suppose he will gain strength from unconsciousness. At least while he sleeps, he will be free from pain. She glanced back to the Crimson Lady, but the creature was still held inside the light spears. Safe so far, thought Rumour, looking about her. But I believe I shall have to leave him here to get linen and water to bind his leg. Can I leave him? I think I have no choice. I cannot move him as he is. But she pronounced a further enchantment before she did so, this time surrounding Andrew with light for protection, drawing gratefully on the power that was still obedient to her summons.

And then she went from the terrible slaughterhouse with its stench of spilled blood and its taint of ancient evil, out into the dank coldness of the Castle.

If there had been a sunrise it would have been so much better. Rumour prowled through the great silent Castle cautiously, hating the darkness and the thick shrouding shadows, fearful of every creature that she disturbed and that went scuttling or slithering out of the wavering light of her flaring torch.

She thought that the knowledge that there would never be a dawn here made the desolate night a truly dreadful thing to endure. If I could know that there would be a sunrise in this terrible place, thought Rumour, prowling warily through the dark Castle, I believe I could explore with a better heart. It was a futile hope, of course. This was the Black Ireland where there was only endless night and perpetual dark.

She searched the Castle cautiously and swiftly, disliking the great empty rooms and the crimson-swathed chambers that reeked of dirt and decay; finding it necessary to summon every shred of courage to push open doors and venture into deserted and dusty wings that had plainly been disused for many years. The stench of ancient malevolence pervaded the whole Castle, so that Rumour felt sick. She thought, half amused, half fearful, that she might be hard put to it to call up any light, any powers out here, but she put the thought from her at once, because there was no time to be having doubts, there was only time to get Andrew out from the slaughterhouse, and imprison the Crimson Lady properly, and go on to find Theodora.

At last she found a small, relatively dry room near to the portcullis entrance, which was warmer and cleaner than the rest, and which she thought was not as heavily tainted with evil. There was a small stone hearth where a fire could be laid, and a pallet bed near by. Perhaps a porter's room? It was surprisingly easy to imagine this Castle humming with life, peopled by servants, nightly revels held in the great banqueting hall. The dungeons would be filled, and the banquets would be grisly, bloody feasts, for this was a necromancer's citadel. But Rumour could see beauty in the carved plaster mouldings, and in the oak panelling in some of the rooms, and the crystal windows that must once have looked out over flower gardens and fountains and terraces.

The small porter's room would do very well. It was close to the slaughterhouse, on the ground floor, and there was bedding in a cupboard at the side of the stone hearth. Rumour set light to the fire before she went back for Andrew, thinking that at least here they could be warm and dry and safe for a time.

She bound Andrew's mutilated leg as well as she could, packing it with wads of tightly folded linen from the hearth cupboard knowing that this was crude and inexpert, but knowing of nothing else that could be done. And then she turned back to the Crimson Lady.

She had reinforced the light cage at regular intervals, not

daring to leave the creature for more than an hour at a time.

'For,' said Rumour, regarding her captive, 'although I think your powers are weak, and although I think you have built your reputation purely on your ability to coerce those poor weaklings of Almhuinians, still I do not trust you.'

The Crimson Lady snarled and lunged out at Rumour, but the spears of light held firm, and she flinched, nursing her hand as if she might have burnt it.

Rumour said, in a voice suddenly cold and stern, 'For the moment, you are held, madame. For the moment you are under *my* enchantment, and you cannot escape. But we will devise something a little stronger presently, I think. We will ensure that you are imprisoned properly.' And went back to Andrew.

'I cannot carry you, Andrew, but I can act as a crutch,' said Rumour, nearly in tears of frustration at her physical weakness.

'I should not have let you carry me anyway,' he said, but his voice was blurred with pain, and sweat poured down his face as he held on to Rumour and slid agonisingly down from the table.

The Lady jeered and laughed from behind the light spears, hurling curses at them as they went.

'Useless,' said Rumour to Andrew in a conversational tone designed to reach the creature. 'Do you know, Andrew, she has no real powers at all?'

'Has she not?' said Andrew, valiantly joining in the game, suppressing the cries of pain that welled up inside him, certainly suppressing the almost overwhelming need to simply curl into a tight ball of agony and let his mind slip into pain-free oblivion again.

'Nothing but a charlatan,' said Rumour, in one of her confiding whispers, and sent Andrew a sudden grin.

Andrew was dizzy, half blinded with pain and shivering with cold, but he managed to say, 'Then there is little to worry about.'

'Nothing in the world to worry about,' said Rumour. 'We are nearly at the door now, and there is a fire laid and a bed of rugs made up for you.'

'Yes?' Andrew's consciousness was slipping away again, but they must get away from this dreadful place, they must find a refuge for a few hours where they could consider what to do next. Rumour was showing such extraordinary courage and

371

strength that the least Andrew could do was try to match it. He was grateful for her courage, and he was immeasurably thankful for the wry humour she was managing to dredge up. He found himself reaching for and holding on to her matter-of-fact tone. She had said there was warmth and a bed: he would reach it somehow.

Between them they managed to cross the stone hall; but they had to stop many times, and by the time they reached the little room, Andrew's skin had again taken on the frightening grey pallor, and Rumour was trembling and aching in every bone. Andrew staggered and put out a hand to the wall to right himself, and then fell forward, unconscious again. Rumour, sobbing with exhaustion now, bent down and curved her hands under his arms, pulling him across to the makeshift bed. The fire had burned up and the flames were casting leaping shadows on the dingy stone walls. But it is rather cosy, thought Rumour determinedly; it is small and warm and I believe we can be safe here.

She pulled the unconscious Andrew on to the pallet, and arranged the fur rugs over him, and then, straightening up, took a burning twist of wood from the fire, and reached up to light the wall-torches on each side of the chimney breast. I suppose that is Humanish flesh in the sconces, thought Rumour. But the poor creatures were long since beyond their pain, and they needed light and warmth if they were to survive. This was no time to start being squeamish. But whoever you were, forgive me, she murmured silently.

Andrew was lying under the pile of cloaks and fur rugs, and Rumour stood looking down at him, seeing that the dreadful pallor had receded a little, hearing that he was breathing evenly and gently. She would go back to the slaughterhouse several times to reinforce the spears of light that held the Crimson Lady captive. She thought they would hold the creature for a few hours – and when we have both rested, we can discuss what to do with her, she thought, her mind already considering several spells of imprisonment. Yes, there would surely be something. But I must have a respite, she thought; if I am to break through the darkness again, I must rest, even for an hour or two. I reached the light earlier, but I think it has drained my strength. She paused, remembering how it had felt to force open that door and feel the light begin to trickle through and despite the dangers, a smile touched her lips.

But Andrew was maimed and mutilated, and even with Rumour's help he would be unable to travel for several weeks. She was angrily aware that she knew only the most basic of healing spells. She would try them anyway but she knew that Andrew would be physically unable to cope with the dangers ahead. And Rumour knew that the greatest of all those dangers would certainly be Chaos's Castle of Infinity.

She crawled, shivering and exhausted, under the fur rugs beside him, inexpressibly thankful for a brief respite before she need return to the slaughterhouse. But as she slipped over the edges into sleep, she knew that she might very well be forced to continue the journey to Chaos's castle alone.

And leave Andrew here in Almhuin.

Chapter Thirty-two

Deep within the old west wing of the Porphyry Palace, the Amaranths were holding a Council of War.

They had Sealed the doors, and then they had gone in hasty procession through the great deserted wing, pronouncing the Sealing Enchantment around all of the windows as well. As Great-aunt Fuamnach said, traitors within your midst were nasty things to have, but when those traitors had thrown in their lot with the Almhuinians, you had to be prepared for anything.

'And don't you think,' said Bodb Decht, 'that we ought to post look-outs? Just in case?'

Cerball thought this very sensible, and detailed Cecht and the twins to keep watch. You could not be too careful.

The younger Amaranths would have quite liked to explore this disused part of the Palace, because nobody in living memory (which was quite a long time for people such as the Mugains) had ever been here. But, as the Mugain himself said, they really had not the time to be going off on expeditions. They had to discuss this matter of the Almhuinians and the Black HeartStealers trying to take over the Palace, and they had to think what they were going to do about it.

Cecht had found a small pantry, with a few casks of wine which was excellent news, and somebody else had discovered sacks of flour and wheat and some jars of honey and dried fruit which they might be glad of, but the Mugain said they could not be giving their minds over to eating and drinking just now. Not but what they mightn't be very glad of the stuff presently, of course, and come to think of it, there was no reason not to fetch in the wine.

Herself said she might dredge up a bit of a Scullery Spell to fire the ovens, always supposing that there *were* ovens. They'd be glad of a bite to eat, said Herself, at which several people, to whom it had not occurred that the sojourn in the west wing would need to be other than a couple of hours, or an afternoon at most, looked startled.

The Mugain unbunged the wine-casks on the grounds that you needed a bit of sustenance when there was a battle to be fought, and directed everyone to assemble in the long, rather dusty gallery at the centre of the wing.

It was very dusty indeed. Great-aunt Fuamnach tutted with disapproval, and fetched over a length of curtain to sweep the dirt, because you could not summon proper sorcery in such a disarray.

But there was a long oak table, with chairs drawn up to it, and there was room for them all to sit down; even the twins, who were fetched up from their posts as look-outs, and who had not until now been considered far enough into their apprenticeships to be included in family conferences. As Cerball said, this was no time to be excluding the younger ones; even the rawest of them might have an idea to contribute. And if they couldn't trust their own Seals to keep out the Fer Caille for a half-hour, then they were none of them fit to hold any rank in the Academy at all! said Cerball, looking quite fierce. The twins, round-eyed at being in such important company, sat very quietly in case anyone remembered that they had only reached the degree of Artisan, and made them leave.

Cerball took the chair at the head of the table – 'But the Mugain has taken the one at the foot,' said Calatin, grinning.

Cerball was not thinking about authority or about being at the head of the table. He was wrestling with himself over what they should do. He thought that the only way in which they could overpower the Fer Caille and the Black HeartStealers was to summon something ancient and powerful, and something that they could be very sure would defeat the Fer Caille.

But something that might be beyond their power to control once they had summoned it . . .

Bodb Decht was talking about the NightMare Spell, and saying wasn't it the only way to drive back the Armies? He looked round the table, his thin scholarly face unusually bright-eyed, and Cerball saw the others react with mingled doubt and excitement.

Cecht said, 'But do we know the NightMare Spell?'

'Yes, nobody's pronounced it for – well, a very long time,' said Herself, who did not hold with NightMares, nasty unpredictable things: and further along the table, Great-aunt Fuamnach nodded in agreement. You did not want NightMares rampaging about all over the place and getting out of control.

'And surely,' put in the Mugain, 'we'd need the NightCloak to invoke the Spell fully. Wouldn't we?' He looked at the others for confirmation of this.

'I always heard that only a pure bred Human could wear the NightCloak anyway,' said Herself.

'Well it doesn't matter because we haven't got the NightCloak.'

'It was lost to the High Kings – oh, centuries ago.'

'Like a lot of other things,' said Great-aunt Fuamnach sourly.

Cerball cleared his throat nervously, and everyone turned to look at him.

'Yes?' said the Mugain. 'Have you got an idea?'

'Out with it if you have,' said Great-aunt Fuamnach. 'Battles have been lost before now by folks dithering.'

Cerball said, 'The NightCloak is certainly in the hands of the Black Ireland, but it is possible that we – that we might be able to invoke one of the other great enchantments. Something that might turn back the Fer Caille once and for all.' He relapsed into silence, chewing worriedly at his lower lip, and everyone stared at him.

'What did you have in mind?' said the Mugain.

'Well,' said Cerball, beginning to wish he had not spoken, but going on doggedly. 'Well, for instance the – the opening of the Temple of the Dagda.'

There was a rather startled silence. Cerball thought: well, I've said it. I can't unsay it. I suppose they all think I'm a bit unhinged. Laigne's death and Echbel's capture by the Fomoire, and Theodora being taken by the Lord of Chaos. It's enough to unhinge anyone. But he eyed them and said, 'If we could open up the Temple, we should bring the gods down into Ireland.'

'Which would certainly drive back those miserable wretches below,' said Great-aunt Fuamnach.

'Yes, but to open the Temple of the Dagda,' said Bodb Decht, 'would require the Key.'

'Yes.'

'But it's lost,' said Bodb Decht, staring at Cerball.

'Would opening the Temple really bring the Dagda storming out?' demanded Calatin, hopefully.

'Well that's what they say,' said the Mugain, sounding doubtful.

'Out from the Temple of Eternal Fire? And the – what do they call them? – the Men of Art as well? The lesser gods?'

'Danaan the Mother-god . . .' began someone.

'Brigit the Poetess . . .' put in somebody else.

'Neit the God of Battle and Manannan mac Lir the Pilot . . .'

'Ruad Rofessa, the Lord of Great Knowledge . . .'

'Ruad's another name for the Dagda: he isn't a separate god.'

'Are you sure? I thought—'

'Look here,' said the Mugain, who felt that matters were getting out of hand. 'Look here, this is all speculation. We haven't got the Key any more than we've got the NightCloak. We can't possibly force open the Temple.'

'We could try,' said Calatin hopefully.

'No, no, it's impossible. We'd be shrivelled in an instant – well, we'd very likely be shrivelled anyway, even if we had the Key, which we haven't.'

'The Key was stolen by the Dark Lords,' said Herself of Mugain, in a surprised, doesn't-everybody-know-that voice.

'During Grainne's rule, wasn't it?'

'I heard it was Erin's.'

'No, that isn't right, it was much earlier, because—'

Cerball cleared his throat again and they all looked up.

Cerball said, 'The Key isn't lost.' And, as they turned to stare at him, 'We've got it,' he said.

'Where?'

'It's here with us. In the west wing.'

It had been one of the secrets that Nechtan had preserved jealously and had only disclosed to Cerball on his deathbed.

'And I'm only telling you now because there ought to be two of you knowing about it,' he had said, glaring at Cerball from under his bushy brows.

'Two of us?'

'That minx Rumour coaxed the story out of me,' Nechtan had said irritably.

'Yes, she'd coax anything out of anybody,' Cerball had said, half to himself, and Nechtan had at once reared up and said that Rumour was worth a dozen of any of them.

'She'll surprise all of you one day,' Nechtan had added, and Cerball forbore to tell Nechtan that Rumour had surprised them already; she had surprised them all very much. The thought that Rumour might have gone into the Dark Ireland as much for Nechtan's sake as for Theodora's crossed his mind.

But now, seated at the long dusty oak table in the deserted west wing, Cerball looked round at the assembled Amaranths and thought: well, we have lost nearly everything that matters. Nechtan is dead, and Laigne. Echbel and Theodora are somewhere inside the Dark Realm. And, so far as we can know, the young monk and Rumour are in there with them. I wonder if Rumour *did* do it for Nechtan, he thought again.

But there was no time to spare for speculation; if the Fer Caille and his people took the Palace, the Amaranths would be truly exiled. We shall have lost everything, thought Cerball. I'm not the selected head – I don't want to be. But somebody's got to make these decisions and, since it has to be me, I'll probably be the one to get blamed if the Black HeartStealers take the Palace. I'll go down in history as the Amaranth sorcerer who lost his people everything, thought Cerball glumly. Well there's nothing else for it; it'll have to be the Key. Oh dear. We'll have to try to open the Dagda's Temple. He found himself remembering all of the things ever told or written about the great Father-god who was believed to be the Lord of life and death. Fearsome and all-powerful. Able to deal out death with one end of his staff and restore life with the other. Oh *dear*, thought Cerball, again.

Nechtan had been dying when he had passed on the secret to Cerball, but he had not been incoherent or astray in his wits.

'I schemed and plotted for many years to regain the Key for the Wolfkings,' he had said to Cerball in the flickering candlelight of the deathchamber. 'And when I finally got it out of the Dark Realm, I hid it away.' He had glared at Cerball. 'And now I'll have to pass the secret on to you for safe-keeping,' he had said, rather grudgingly.

'I schemed and plotted,' Nechtan had said again, and a dry, papery chuckle had broken from him. Cerball had thought: yes, *and* enjoyed doing it! and Nechtan had at once said, 'Of course I enjoyed it. Meat and drink and the breath of life, dear boy, and don't be forgetting it!'

Cerball had known vaguely the history of the legendary Key to the Dagda's Temple, of course. It was one of the most strongly magical possessions in Ireland, ranking alongside the NightCloak itself.

The legend told how the Keys had been given by the sorcerers to the first High Queen of all, in the days when Tara, the Bright Palace, the Shining Citadel of Ireland's Royal House, had been raised from the rock.

'Our ancestors,' said Nechtan, grinning unexpectedly. 'The first Royal sorcerers. They presented the Key of the Dagda's Temple to the Royal House. There was a very famous set of injunctions given with it, although of course the exact words have long since been lost.'

Cerball said, 'Something about building the House of Ireland on a rock, was it?'

Nechtan shot him a piercing look from beneath his bushy brows. 'So you did pay attention to some things, after all, did you? Yes. The High Queen was commanded to build Tara as the seat of Ireland's rulers, and to preserve it as the rock for the True Ireland, so that the Gates of the Dark Realm should never prevail against it.

'But of course,' continued Nechtan, 'the Wolfkings lost Key. Well, they're good rulers on the whole, the Wolfkings, but now and then you get a rogue, a strug. I mention no names,' said Nechtan so virtuously that Cerball thought you might easily be pardoned for forgetting that the rascally old sinner had been responsible for spreading some of the juiciest scandals about the Wolfkings for nearly an entire century.

'I mention no names, but the High King Erin had a *cousin*,' said Nechtan darkly.

'What did—'

'Never mind the details,' said Nechtan, so hurriedly that Cerball suspected him of having forgotten most of them. 'We'll just say the Key was lost,' he said. 'It got into the hands of the necromancers and the Dark Lords – well, it would, of course. Aren't they for ever on the prowl for the best and the strongest of our treasures? Shocking state of affairs.' He coughed and turned a bit white, and Cerball remembered that, rascally old sinner though Nechtan might be, he *was* on his deathbed; so he poured a chaliceful of wine, which Nechtan supped gratefully.

'I got the Key back,' said Nechtan, grinning reminiscently. 'I got it back, but I—' He shot a suspicious look at Cerball, as if wondering how far to trust him. 'I kept it,' he finished baldly.

'You kept it?'

'I did.'

'The most ancient heirloom of Tara? You didn't return it to the High King?'

'I don't know why I have to be interrogated as if I was no more than a pup apprentice sorcerer,' said Nechtan, crossly. 'Nobody ever knew I got it back – it was a commission from the High King Erin. He called me to Tara, and asked me to regain it, and so I did. Eventually.' He chuckled the dry chuckle again. 'My word, it took some scheming and some intrigue, and a great many years of spell-spinning. And by the time I finally got it out of the Dark Realm, Erin had long since gone to the Place Beneath the Ocean Roof. So I thought: why hand it back? Nobody at Tara knew I had been working to regain it. And by that time there were sons and grandsons of that *cousin* skulking around the High Throne,' said Nechtan virtuously. 'People you wouldn't trust from here to that window. And I didn't want the Key getting back into the hands of the necromancers.' He eyed Cerball beadily. 'I knew if it was kept here, in the Porphyry Palace, it'd be safe. On hand if it were ever wanted . . .'

'It's here in the west wing,' said Cerball again, facing the astounded Amaranths rather defiantly. 'We've had it for – well, I don't know how long we've had it, but it's here, and I think we ought to use it now.' He looked round the table. 'I think we ought to try to open up the Temple, and call the Dagda.'

Bodb Decht said, carefully, 'Of course, we don't want to know why it's here or how it got here, Cerball—'

'I wouldn't mind knowing,' said Great-aunt Fuamnach.

'The question is whether we should use it, and whether we dare use it,' finished Bodb Decht.

'Why can't we use it?' demanded Calatin, who found the whole idea of the legendary Temple of Dagda so utterly enthralling that he had forgotten to drink the wine placed before him by Cecht.

380

'I didn't mean we oughtn't to use it, I meant we ought to be very careful.'

'Why?'

'Well, because they're tricky things, gods,' said Bodb Decht, a bit uneasily. 'You never quite know how they'll react.'

'Yes, but look here,' said the Mugain, 'if the Keys were given to Tara in the beginning, with the command to – what was it again?'

'Build the House of Ireland on the rock of Tara, so that it would prevail against the Gates of the Dark Realm,' said Cerball. 'At least, that's as near as I can remember.'

'It's near enough,' said the Mugain, frowning. 'If that was the command, then surely it meant that the Dagda was on the side of the True Ireland.'

'He's always been regarded as a *good* god,' said Bodb Decht, slowly and thoughtfully.

'The Father-god,' said Great-aunt Fuamnach, nodding.

Cecht said the Druids had held the Dagda in very high regard.

'So they did,' said Cerball.

'They called him the *Draidecht*,' said one of the twins, speaking rather nervously for the first time, but sure of her facts, because hadn't they just been studying this part of Amaranth history for their Artisan level degree?

'If the Dark Lords got their hands on the Key—' said Great-aunt Fuamnach.

'They stole it,' said Cerball, who felt himself to be on rather thin ice over the entire thing. 'They wouldn't have bought it.'

'If the Dark Lords got their hands on it,' continued Great-aunt Fuamnach, who could not be doing with folk who interrupted when you were about to say something important, 'that means they thought they could make use of it.' She rapped the floor with her hazel stick. 'Why didn't they do so? Why didn't they open the Temple?'

There was a thoughtful silence. 'You know,' said Cerball, 'that's quite right. They must have believed they could force open the Temple, or they'd never have taken the Key in the first place. But it wasn't any use. It couldn't have been. They were never able to open the Temple. We'd have heard about it.'

'My word, I should hope we would,' said Great-aunt Fuamnach.

'And the fact that they didn't use it rather suggests that they *couldn't*,' said Bodb Decht.

'They'd certainly have tried to use it, the black-hearted scoundrels,' cried the Mugain, who was becoming very fired up at the idea of the Dark Lords, impudent creatures, getting their nasty hands on Ireland's ancient magical treasurers.

'Yes, of course they would,' said Bodb Decht. 'But they didn't succeed. They didn't open up the Temple. The Dagda wouldn't respond to their spells—'

'Because he isn't on their side,' finished Calatin, beaming.

'I think we could be sure of that,' said Bodb Decht.

'Of course the Dagda isn't on the side of the Dark Lords,' said Great-aunt Fuamnach, impatiently. 'I never heard of such a thing!' She glared at Bodb Decht, who said quite mildly that he was only pursuing a logical line of reasoning.

'Logic my bottom,' said Great-aunt Fuamnach, and Herself of Mugain frowned and wished Great-aunt Fuamnach would not be so coarse.

'Well, I say we find the Key and invoke the spell at once!' cried Calatin, on his feet, his chair pushed impatiently backwards. 'Find it and open up the Temple, and let loose the wrath of the Dagda and the – the lesser gods on those traitors downstairs! Neit the God of Battle, and the rest!' He looked round, and several people called out in agreement. The younger ones stood up excitedly, but looked to Cerball and the Mugain for permission, because there was a strong ritual of respect in the family, and it would have been extremely impolite to have gone dashing off through the west wing in search of the Key before the Elders of the party had given the scheme their blessing.

Bodb Decht said, 'We do know where it is, do we, Cerball?' and Cerball, who had been pulling worriedly at his lower lip, said, 'Well, there's the problem. I haven't the smallest idea.'

But in the end it was easy. They simply searched each of the rooms in turn. The twins were once more detailed to keep a watch on what was happening below, and to make a round of all windows and doors to be sure that the Seals were holding.

'The search will be easy, because there's hardly any furniture in here,' said Calatin, who had been told to cover the rooms at the top of the wing, and was being very important about it.

'I expect Cerball moved all the best stuff into the main part of the Palace,' put in somebody else.

'And there aren't all that many rooms to search.'

They made a careful list, and divided into three groups.

Cerball, leading the Mugains and Cecht round the central portion of the wing, stopped once or twice to listen to the sounds below.

'Are they breaking the Seals?' asked Cecht.

'I don't think so.'

'Amaranthine Seals are unbreakable,' said the Mugain firmly.

'We can't be sure of that, not with the Fer Caille there.'

'The twins will tell us if they start to dissolve.'

'Even so, I don't think we ought to waste any time,' said Cerball, rather nervously, because he was becoming aware of an unease, a feeling that eyes were peering out from the shadowy corners of the empty rooms. He remembered that there were a great many enchantments which could send rather repulsive, but amorphous creatures into an enemy's camp as spies. There was a particularly loathsome one called the *Draoicht Spiaire* which meant, quite literally, the Enchantment of Spying, and which the Lord of Chaos was supposed to own and keep chained and muzzled in his dungeons, and only let out at night. Supposing the Black HeartStealers and the Arca Dubhs had summoned something similar to Chaos's *Spiaire*? He moved more quickly, opening doors, scanning cupboards and chests.

In the end he found the Key himself, which rather pleased him. It was lying quite neatly and quite quietly in an ancient oak chest that had stood beneath a window of the corridor overlooking the south courtyard, and had lain in the streaming sunlight of centuries, and soaked up the warmth and the scents of several generations of Amaranths. Lovely, thought Cerball, reaching out to touch the blackened surface of the chest, liking the smoothness that centuries of usage had given it, and the elaborate carving with the Amaranthine symbols of the Tree of Fertility and the Hazel Wands.

The chest was quite small, perhaps the size of a jewel coffer, and Cerball carried it back to the long gallery, and set it on the table and opened the lid.

'Be careful,' said Herself of Mugain, who was not at all happy about getting involved with gods and ancient mystical Temples.

'Oh, do hush. Has somebody fetched those twins? They oughtn't to miss this. It's an historic moment,' said Cerball firmly.

The twins came pattering up the stairs, bright-eyed and out of breath, to report that the Seals were all secure, with the exception, they said rather worriedly, of the Seal at the door leading out into the banqueting hall.

'It's a bit fuzzy at the edges.'

'Calatin, go and reinforce it.'

'Can I just see the Key first?'

'Well, all right, but don't lose any time.' Cerball glanced uneasily in the direction of the stair that led to the main Palace.

And then Cerball and the Mugain between them lifted out the ancient legendary Key to the Temple of the Gods, and a great stillness fell upon the long, dusty gallery. Cecht, who was seated next to Cerball, thought that even the little stirring winds outside ceased, as if they, too, were listening and watching.

The Key to the Temple of the Dagda, the all-powerful Father-god of all the gods. The Lord of Great Knowledge, the *Draidecht* of the druids of Ireland. The father of Brigit the Poetess and Dian Cecht the Sage for whom their own Cecht had been named . . . And of the two sons, Neit the God of Battle, and Manannan mac Lir the Pilot . . .

Dare we use it? thought Cerball. Dare we call them?

The Key lay before them, shining with its own inner radiance. It was much larger than they had imagined, although most of them had not known what to imagine. But it was easily the length of a man's arm, and half as wide. There was a thick shaft etched with ancient symbols: 'The Symbol of Eternal Life, and the Symbol of the Tree of Knowledge and of Good and Evil,' whispered Bodb Decht. At the narrow end of the shaft were the symbols for light and strength, and at the other end, the handpiece was shaped like the winged fruit of sycamore and ash, inlaid with turquoise and firestones.

The Key to the Temple of the Dagda. The ancient, most magical gift ever bestowed on Tara's Royal House, given by the sorcerers to the Wolfkings and their descendants, with the exhorted promise that they would build Ireland, the True Ireland, on the rock of Tara, and guard her against the Dark Realm for all time . . .

Bestowed on the first High Queen of Ireland, handed down to her descendants, and rescued from the Dark Realm by Nechtan.

'Well,' said Cerball, reluctant to break the silence, but knowing that somebody had to do so, 'well, now that we've found it, we have to decide whether we dare use it.'

'Do we know the spell to use it?' asked the Mugain.

'I know *a* spell that might work,' said Bodb Decht, rather doubtfully. 'But I don't know if it would be the right one.'

The Amaranths looked at one another dismayed, and Cerball started to say that they would simply have to try every spell that seemed to them appropriate until they hit on the right one, when there was the sound of breaking glass and drawing back of bolts, and the scampering of feet below.

The Fer Caille and his armies had broken through the Seals, and were swarming through the ancient west wing towards them.

Chapter Thirty-three

There was no time to think and no time to plan. The Fer Caille and his followers were inside the west wing, and with them came the fetid stench of old evil magic and the clotted aura of necromancy.

'Re-Seal the doors!' shouted Herself of Mugain frantically.

'It's too late!' cried Bodb Decht, who was already at the door, Calatin behind. 'They're already here!'

The gallery door was pushed contemptuously in, crashing back against the wall. The Fer Caille, huge and grinning and surrounded by his followers, stood on the threshold. Behind him were the Black HeartStealers, and the Arca Dubhs stood with Iarbonel Soothsayer and the uninjured Almhuinians, who were armoured and accoutred, their narrow, mean eyes glinting through their dark visors.

From the corner of his eye, Cerball saw Calatin inching forward, but even as he did so, one of the Almhuinians flung a spear effortlessly, and Calatin was knocked back, falling helplessly to the ground, his left arm hanging at an awkward angle. Anger welled up in Cerball, and with it came a surge of power. He felt, for the first time, the immense, locked-in power of the great golden Key.

He closed his eyes and concentrated on the force, the strength, the ancient and undying Amaranth stream bequeathed on his ancestors, which flowed like a great silver river in the veins of every member of his House. I think I can do it, thought Cerball with sudden astonishment. And then, with terrified entreaty: let me do it! Let me force open the doors of the Great Temple of the Dagda, because if I can only do this one thing, then perhaps after all I am not so unworthy of the name of my House . . .

He felt the power stream into his hands, scalding and fierce. *Help us* . . . thought Cerball, concentrating his mind on the single, shining thought. *Help us to drive back the Dark Ireland . . .*

The great Key seemed to shiver and hum with life, and there was a searing heat from it, so that Cerball dropped it at once, and saw it slide a little way across the floor, and then stop at the centre, its shining, silken shaft pointing towards the east, glowing with fiery light.

The Fer Caille and his people drew back instantly, and the Almhuinians began to shriek in fear and to scrabble for the door to the stairs.

There was the distant sound of humming, of some immense force whirring and spinning over their heads. The Almhuinians, who had not reached the door, fell back on the floor, cowering there with their hands flung up over their darkly visored faces for protection.

Light was pouring into the dusty gallery; soft, glowing light, flame-tinted and pure, and the Amaranths moved back, the Key's irradiating light directly before them. Through it they could see the Fer Caille and his followers cowering by the door.

'Beyond the light,' thought Cerball, seeing how the glow illuminated their faces, showing up the fear, but showing, as well, the twisted evil and the sly eyes.

The Fer Caille was standing in the doorway, a massive, brutish figure, his wide greedy mouth closed in a hard line, his small mean eyes flickering with a mixture of fury and terror.

There was a moment, searingly beautiful and very nearly blinding, when the pure flame-light lit the entire gallery, so that every object in it was silhouetted in sharp black relief. The Amaranths, clustered together at the centre, saw deep within the fiery light the massive outline of a glittering Temple; a shining, Golden Palace, so immense and so beautiful, but so mystical and so transient that they fell back in awe.

There was the sound of bolts being thrown back, and for a moment Cerball thought that more of the Seals were dissolving. And then he realised that it was nothing to do with the Seals; at the centre of the great Temple, massive, elaborate double doors were opening slowly, and rays of light were pouring outwards.

The Opening of the Temple of the Gods . . .

A great stillness fell over the gallery, and with it a feeling that they stood on the brink of some unguessed-at world, or as if they might have been ripped out of the Porphyry Palace altogether,

387

and were on the edge of undreamed-of forces. But also as if they might also be within reach of silent blessed wells of tranquillity, and of deep and ancient wisdoms that far transcended the sentient world. Cecht and the twins, standing with the wounded Calatin, the four of them holding hands for courage, felt suddenly helplessly young and shamefully unlearned.

There is so much you will never know on your side of the barriers, mortal creatures . . .

There was a brief, never-to-be-forgotten moment when they all saw, quite plainly, the wise, implacable features of a being who dwelled deep within the ancient mystical Temple; a being somehow composed of the fire and the light, but somehow Humanish as well. There was an agelessness about him, and there was the aura of every eternal legend and every undying myth . .

As the light increased, they saw, quite clearly, wise slanting eyes that saw into Men's souls and read their innermost thoughts, and that understood Men's frailties and pettinesses as well as their kindnesses and their generosities. There was the feeling of immeasurable understanding and compassion, but there was the feeling as well of avenging anger and cold and dispassionate judging.

And then fire burned up more brilliantly, enveloping the wise, solemn eyes, and the doors began to move to a close again, and as the Amaranths flinched in the blinding heat and the fierce light, the Dagda's face wavered and blurred, and finally dissolved.

In the last flicker of the dying flames, darkly silhouetted against the light, there appeared the figures of two slender young men, the taller clad in glinting golden armour, with a breastplate bearing licking tongues of fire. His hair was not ordinary hair that moved and became dishevelled or tousled, but a solid gold cap of carven curls sculptured to his head and clustering over his brow. His companion wore a silken robe of grey-green, and his skin had a pearly, luminous sheen, rather as if moisture clung to it. He had eyes the colour of the ocean on a dull day, and shining grey-green hair that rippled like thin water.

The Dagda had not come in response to their summons.

But he had sent two of his sons.

388

Neit the God of Battle, and Manannan mac Lir the Pilot.

The Fer Caille and his followers fell back at once, tumbling over one another in their haste to get down the stairs and out of the west wing and to some kind of safety.

The Amaranths could hear them running for cover, the Almhuinians shrieking and squealing – 'Like the mutant-rats they are!' thought Cerball, still bewildered and torn between triumph and fear. The Black HeartStealers were pounding down the stairs and along the corridors with their great, heavy tread, and they could hear the Arca Dubhs hurrying along in their wake.

Neit stood watching them go, his back to the dazed Amaranths, the golden armour gleaming, and a spear held in his right hand. Manannan mac Lir had turned to survey the Amaranths, and grinned suddenly and rather humanly at Cecht.

The God of Battle and the Pilot . .

Cerball thought: I suppose it is up to me to say something. And tried to remember what was the correct way to greet a couple of gods, and glared at the Mugain, who might have been thought to know these things, but who was being no help at all, and was in fact staring at the two creatures with his mouth open.

Neit turned back into the gallery and strode to Cerball, holding out both his hands.

'You are the Amaranth leader,' he said, throwing back his head, so that the golden sculptured curls caught the light. His voice was strong and rich. It was the sort of voice you would instantly trust, and the sort of voice that made you feel, quite suddenly, that things could be put right after all.

Manannan mac Lir had followed his brother, but he seemed to be more interested in studying the female Amaranths rather than thinking about reassuring anybody about anything. In fact, so far from making them all feel safer, there was a glint in Manannan mac Lir's cool, clear eyes that made Cerball a bit uneasy. He remembered that the younger gods had sometimes rather carnal appetites, and hoped there was not going to be one of those awkward situations where their guests invoked some kind of godlike privilege which might place everybody in an embarrassing situation.

Great-aunt Fuamnach said in a loud whisper, 'Cerball – the

389

Welcoming Speech of Erin,' and Cerball, who had by this time realised that the Welcoming Speech of Erin was the correct protocol, but who could not remember how it started, turned round to glare.

Neit appeared not to notice any of this. He was looking down at him – Cerball thought he must be quite seven feet tall, although he was not in the least bit Giantish – and smiling. It was probably coincidence that he had positioned himself directly under the central torchlights, so that the glow fell across his sculpted hair and made it shine like newly minted coins.

Manannan mac Lir had moved to where Cecht and the twins were watching, huge-eyed, and was inspecting them with deep interest.

Neit said in a rich, strong voice, 'Well, Amaranths? You called to us to rout the Dark Armies. And we have come in answer to your call. We are here.'

'And Neit's presence makes *everything* all right,' said Manannan mac Lir, and his voice was low and faintly mocking. He sounded as if he might be rather enjoying himself. He sounded, in fact, as if he enjoyed most things. He said, 'Neit has only to arrive, and *all* will be put right. He will tell you so himself, I daresay.'

'We – welcome you both,' said Cerball at length, having abandoned any attempt to remember the Welcoming Speech of Erin. The Mugain, standing next to him, said, 'Indeed we do, and are grateful to you for answering our call,' because Cerball was not going to have all the glory when it came to welcoming a pair of gods. If the Mugain had been able to recall the Welcoming Speech he would certainly have delivered it, and in proper oratorial style, too! As it was, he added his welcome to Cerball's, and sent a covert glance to Manannan mac Lir. They might have to have a word with Cecht, who was blushing and lowering her eyes. And those twins – saucy baggages! – were giggling in a way which suggested they had more in common with their Aunt Rumour than had been hitherto suspected. The Mugain remembered that that branch of the family had never been noted for its high moral tone.

Neit said, 'May we be seated?' and without waiting for an answer, strode to the long oak table, his head flung back as if he were breasting a great ocean. Manannan mac Lir followed, looking amused. They sat down, Neit using smooth, fluid movements, and arranging his bronzed limbs gracefully, Manannan mac Lir simply curling carelessly into the nearest chair.

Neit said, 'This is perhaps a little overbearing of us, to sit before we are invited, but—'

'But gods have no manners,' said Manannan mac Lir.

'We have simply walked into your Palace – although not uninvited, of course – and taken over,' said Neit. 'Ah, we know better than to do that, I should hope.'

'Even though we have been quite appallingly brought up, we have a modicum of good manners,' said Manannan mac Lir.

'Manannan was appallingly brought up because he was the youngest of us all, and the youngest of any family is always spoiled,' said Neit in an indulgent voice. 'Do not concern yourselves; I shall not allow him to offend you.'

'I'm not spoiled,' said Manannan at once.

'Nonsense, Dian Cecht spoiled you from the time you entered the world. Not that it mattered to *me*,' said Neit, laughing slightly as if such an idea was absurd.

'Dian Cecht might have spoiled me just the *smallest* bit, but Brigit certainly spoiled *you*,' said Manannan at once.

'Can I help it if I am the sort of god that people like to write poetry to? My sister Brigit is the Goddess of Poetry,' he added in an aside to Cerball, who said, 'Um, so I understand.'

Neit repositioned himself, and it suddenly struck Cerball that he was in fact arranging his pose so that they should be presented with his profile. He glanced at the young man and thought: well, I daresay he *is* alarmingly handsome.

'I am the beauty of the gods,' said Neit, at once very grave. 'It is a great responsibility. I take it very seriously.'

'He does not like to offend his thousands of worshippers,' said Manannan, in a voice so devoid of expression that every person present knew that Manannan was baiting his brother. 'It would never do for them to hear that he had been splashed by the mud of a carriage for instance. Or become bedraggled by rain . .'

'There is not a soul who has ever seen me mud-splashed or bedraggled,' said Neit, smiling in a rather superior fashion. 'I cannot bear dirt in any form.'

'Even when we ducked you in the fishpond? I remember—'

'Manannan will have his little joke,' said Neit very crossly indeed. 'And we waste time.' He turned back to the Amaranths, who were listening round-eyed to this interchange, and he smiled so dazzlingly that even Great-aunt Fuamnach, who liked to tell people that she had never been one to be misled by a fair face and well-formed body, blinked.

Cerball, who felt that the situation was slipping out of his control, asked if they might discuss the matter of their attackers.

'Ah!' said Neit, richly, sitting up and eyeing them all with a flashing look, 'A war council, is it? I was about to suggest such a thing myself.'

'My brother is *very* good at war councils,' murmured Manannan.

'I am even better at *fighting* wars,' said Neit instantly. 'Now, what is your battle?' he said in a businesslike voice, and the Amaranths had the impression that he might be shuffling papers together and thumbing through a sheaf of possible strategies.

Manannan said, 'Oh *really*, Neit, anyone with half an eye can see that there are traitors in this rather fetching Palace.' He leaned back in his chair and looked round him with approval. 'Very nice,' he said, and then, to the twins, 'I expect you'll show me over the rest of it, will you? I like Palaces.'

The Mugain, who felt that some kind of explanation was called for, said that they were in fact fighting their own kith and kin, and it was to the shame and the disgrace of them all.

'Oh, every family has the odd rogue gene,' said Manannan mac Lir, and grinned mischievously round the table. 'I could tell you—'

The Mugain felt it was time to intervene. He did not altogether trust Manannan mac Lir (in fact now that he came to think about it, he recalled hearing a few rather colourful stories about him) and so he said firmly that oughtn't they all to be concentrating on the situation. 'Aren't those black-hearted traitors away downstairs plotting up fresh evil?' he demanded.

'Are they?' said Manannan. 'Dear me, I suppose they are. Shall I find out what they have in mind for you?'

'I don't think it . . How?' demanded Cerball.

'Easy,' said Manannan, standing up and grinning. There was a brief spurt of light, and the impression of a great swirling wave of grey-green ocean and Manannan vanished.

Neit said, pettishly, 'He only does that for effect.'

'Really?'

'Our father used to punish him when he was small to try to stop him from showing off all the time.'

'Yes?' Nobody dared to ask what form the Dagda's punishment might have taken, although everybody would have liked to know.

'It did absolutely no good at all,' said Neit. 'And of course my sisters thoroughly spoiled him.' He glanced towards the door, and said, 'And d'you see he's back with us already,' and as the words were said, Manannan mac Lir reappeared inside the door and walked thoughtfully back to his seat at the table.

'Well?' said Cerball, leaning forward anxiously.

'Well,' said Manannan mac Lir, 'your adversaries are below.'

'Dear me, anyone could have told that!' said Neit scornfully.

'Anyone with any *sense* would not be sitting up here studying maps and drawing up strategies,' retorted Manannan. 'It'll be the Battle against the King of the Marshes again if you aren't careful.'

There was a rather nasty silence. Then Neit said, very haughtily indeed, 'I suppose I may be allowed one single small failure in a lifetime.' And then, to the Amaranths, 'I was betrayed by a lady,' he said. 'It is something that can happen to *anyone*, and I assure you that it is the only time I have ever—'

The Mugain and Great-aunt Fuamnach both said in a single voice, '*What is happening below?*' and Manannan eyed them both thoughtfully.

'I am afraid they are invoking a very great force to send against us.'

The Amaranths looked at him and waited.

Neit tossed his head back and said, 'Oh, we can deal with very great forces, you know. I shall fling them to the jackals.'

Manannan said in an expressionless voice, 'The Fer Caille has in his possession one of the most fearsome weapons ever to come into Ireland. And I am afraid he plans to use it against you.'

Cerball started to say, 'What is it?' but knew, in the same moment, what Manannan mac Lir was about to say.

Manannan said, 'They have the NightCloak of the first High Queen of Ireland. And they are going to summon the NightMares and the WarMongers.'

Chapter Thirty-four

Maelduin lay at the bottom of the Tanning Pit of the necromancers, the grisly light from the Human torches above casting its eerie red glow, his senses blurred and his mind tumbling.

His perceptions were still hazy, but his mind was clearing. He lay where he had fallen, every bone bruised, every muscle wracked, stinging with the pain of a dozen lacerations. He thought he might be bleeding, but he was not sure, and then he remembered that in any case he did not know what it felt like to bleed.

I escaped the Trolls, he thought. I outwitted them and they are dead.

But I am on the floor of the gaping abyss, the terrible Pit of the necromancers. And in every tale ever told, in every legend ever recounted, no creature has ever escaped from the Pit.

He felt black despair threaten, and then a tiny, silvery voice deep within him said: the Gristlen escaped.

A small shoot of hope unfolded, and he thought: yes, of course. The Fisher King was here, Coelacanth was cast into the Pit by the Dark Lords, and he escaped; he dragged his foul body down to Tiarna and stole the music of the *sidh*.

If Coelacanth could escape, so can I.

He sat up cautiously, looking about him, seeing that he had fallen on the edges of the Pit's floor, half against one of the steep, baked-rock walls. He could feel the heat, dreadful dry waves of it glowing somewhere beneath him, so that when he stood up, a bit shakily, finding it necessary to put out a hand to the rock wall for support, he felt the burning heat penetrating the soles of his boots. The cold silvery *sidh*-blood that still ran deep in his veins flinched in pain, and Maelduin thought: I don't think I can bear this. And remembered that it had to be borne.

The grisly torches, thrust into the ground above him, burned strongly, lighting the Pit to vivid, terrible life. Maelduin stayed where he was, his senses clearing, aware that he was not badly hurt, simply bruised and jolted and scraped.

The Pit was larger than he had expected. He had no knowledge of the Humanish's methods of judging size or distance or a room's dimensions, but he thought that the Pit was much larger than the great banqueting hall in the Porphyry Palace, and it was certainly larger even than Tiarna's massive Silver Cavern.

At the far side, almost directly opposite him, was an expanse of boiling heat, a bubbling, oily, crimson-streaked lake that surged and eddied angrily. Its shores were crusted with black embers, glowing coals vomited by the molten fires.

Maelduin stared at it, and into his mind slid the ancient *sidh* Chaunt.

> The vast unbottom'd pit
> The flaming furnace and the parched pavements;
> The beds of fire and the flames of revenge.
> The brimstone sea of boiling fire where blows the
>   dragons' breath and the ogres' delight;
> Where the Dark Lords' wrath burns for ever.
> Where the Gristlens have their nest
> And spawn their kind.

The *sidh* had sung the Chaunt mischievously to the Humanish they had hunted, for although it was not one of their Hunting Songs, they had sometimes used it to taunt the fleeing Humanish victims. And now I am in the unbottom'd Pit itself, though Maelduin. Now I am in the Gristlens' nest, and I can see no way of escaping.

The Gristlens' nest . . . The dark and foul abyss where all must eventually acquire the repulsive hides and the warped features and the deformed, fibrous muscles . . .

Maelduin looked down at the slender limbs and the ivory-pale skin with the faint sheen to it. Humanish cloak . . .

> Fleeces of fur and silken skin
> Ivory bones for living in . . .

I fought against it, he thought; I fought against it but in the end I endured it. Now I think I do not want to be shrivelled and darkened by the Pit's fearsome heat, and I do not want to be warped and deformed.

There was an acrid stench of old evil and ancient, heavy sorcery, and, overlaying it all, were the terrible, warm-meat scents of the burning gobbets of Humanish flesh at the Pit's edges.

The light from the torches burned strongly, the dull red glow sending leaping, prowling silhouettes across the baked rock-face, so that he could see everything plainly.

Red-tinted waves formed on the lake's surface, washing angrily against the ash-crusted shores, dashing their glinting moisture on to the blackened banks. Maelduin thought: so that is the brimstone sea, that is the boiling lake of legend, and here, all around me, are the parched pavements and the beds of fire . . .

Blown on by dragon's breath . . .

The floor of the Pit was not entirely flat. It undulated and sloped sharply, and there were mounds and rocks and protruding crags. The grisly light cast weird shadows so that, for a moment, Maelduin saw not boulders and crags, but crouching beasts, the silent guards of the necromancers, glowing red eyes within the crags, lips parted in grinning greed . . .

And then the light waned slightly, and after all they were only rocks, formations of the crags.

At the foot of the crags were gashes in the floor, gaping chasms, as if someone had been digging down into the rock. Maelduin studied this, trying to understand their purpose.

Someone had been digging . . . Why? *Who?*

He could see the Pit's occupants quite plainly now. In the flickering red light he could see them with cruel clarity: dreadful creatures; warped, distorted beings that toiled endlessly to and fro, their misshapen heads bowed in patient acceptance of their terrible existence, their great, unnaturally developed muscles lifting and carrying and hammering as they laboured ceaselessly at the tasks assigned to them by the Dark Lords they had offended.

The damn'd ones who incurred the wrath of the necromancers . . .

The Black Abyss, where accursed slaves drudge for infinity . . .

The Dark Lords had dungeons deep within their evil fortresses; dank cells and underground stone chambers where they imprisoned their victims and satisfied their dark lusts.

But the dungeons were for the Humanish. The Pit was for the creatures of the Dark Realm itself.

Maelduin thought: and so I am here with the Black Domain's traitors and with its outcasts. Murderers and child-eaters and creatures so foul that they have even been dishonoured by their own kind. And almost certainly some of them will have been necromancers who transgressed the laws of the Black Ireland.

He could see that there were at least twenty of the creatures here with him. They were all in different stages of transformation, but they were all acquiring the unmistakable carapace of Gristlens. Their skins were becoming blackened and dried, leathery from the harsh, endless heat. Several of them still had ordinary, pale, Humanish flesh, but others were already completely covered by the dark fibrous skin that Maelduin remembered. It had crept over them, inch by dreadful inch, until it had covered them entirely. They were chained and manacled; they dragged their chains as they worked, huge, clanking iron and steel gyves protruding from cruel bracelets clamped about their feet and wrists. They could walk and they could wield the hammers and the axes and chisels, but they could take only short, shambling steps, and when they swung the great axes over their heads, the manacles about their wrists kept their hands closely and painfully together.

Their faces had all acquired the repulsive ugliness of their kind. The skin had shrivelled and dried around their lips, contracting so that the lips were pulled back in a snarl, giving them long-toothed, sneering grins. Their eyes bulged and Maelduin thought: the heat is drawing their eyes from the sockets, and heating the jellylike mass until it is nearly boiling. Sick repulsion closed about him; his own eyes already felt sore and gritty from endless dry warmth. He blinked and felt for the second time Humanish tears, salty and stinging.

Each one toiled at what Maelduin thought must be a set task;

most of them wielded instruments which were unfamiliar to Maelduin, but which he recognised as being for Humanish quarrying and pit-labour. There were great heavy-headed, T-shaped weapons, which the prisoners swung above their heads, and then buried deep in the Pit's floor, chipping away doggedly at the rockface.

Several of the Gristlens wheeled tiny, box-shaped carts which ran on minuscule wheels, and which were piled with the rough, unhewn rocks. They trudged to and fro, tipping the boulders into careful piles at the other end of the Pit, returning to refill their carts. It seemed to Maelduin rather pointless; and then he realised with a sick pity that there was indeed no aim and no purpose in what they did: this was part of the Dark Lords' fiendish plan, that the creatures should toil endlessly and meaninglessly.

The creatures paid Maelduin no heed, and he thought that they would be accustomed to seeing new victims flung down here from time to time. Probably they would simply wait for him to find his place with them: presumably soon I shall be expected to toil and labour and drudge alongside them. This was a truly terrible thought, but alongside it ran a far worse one: before long, I may be grateful for the companionship even of these creatures, and I may be thankful to have a task to work at, no matter how pointless.

He was forming in his mind words of greeting to them, knowing that he must make an approach, trying to decide the best way to do it, when a voice, quite close to him, said, 'I would not bid you well come, sir, but I would acknowledge your presence here. You are come to a harsh and unforgiving world.'

Maelduin turned sharply, and saw, seated on a rock near to him, a tall, thin Humanish, clad in a dark robe of some kind, with a hood which was pulled up, shadowing his face. Maelduin received the impression of thin, ravaged features and dark, ragged hair, and of eyes of a burning intensity. He tilted his head, trying to see more, listening for the essence of this unexpected being. He thought: he is certainly Humanish, but there is something clinging to him that is not in the least Humanish. Something that he was not born with, but that he has acquired and that he is trying to slough off; a skin not of

398

scale, but of darkness, is it? He half closed his eyes, and felt, with those extra senses, the shell and the crust of evil which this unexpected figure wore. It is cracked in places, and in places he has managed to shed it, thought Maelduin. But it is still there. This is a strange one. This is something I have never before encountered.

But he seated himself cross-legged on the ground and regarded the robed man with his brilliant turquoise eyes, and said, very courteously, 'I am grateful for your words, sir.' He studied the other covertly, seeing that there was little outward sign that the dry, acrid heat was affecting him so far, seeing that he had still the pale, soft, Humanish skin, and that the eyes had not yet been made bulbous, but were deeply set and intensely black. Then he has not been here for so very long, thought Maelduin.

The robed figure seemed to sense Maelduin's thoughts; he said, 'You are right; I have been here for a short time as time is measured here. The heat has not yet begun its devilish work on me.' He held out his hand, and Maelduin saw that, although it was dry-looking and slightly puckered with the heat, it had not taken on the hard, gristly fibrousness of the others.

He said, 'It is – generous of you to speak to me.' And waited, his every sense stretched to learn as much as he could.

The robed Humanish said, 'I am glad to have a fellow being to speak with, for I have nothing to say to these other creatures, nor they to me.' And then, as Maelduin made to speak, he said at once, 'I see, of course, that you are not a Human, but I think you are close to being a Human. And I have been without Human companionship for a very long time.'

'Yes?' Maelduin's interest was caught, but he was wary. He said, 'These Gristlen-creatures are not Human at all, I think?'

'Many of them are what are called mongrels; partly Human, but also partly necromancer or beast.' The man's eyes flickered over the Gristlens. 'In the world I once lived in, it would be said that they have the worst of their mixed ancestry, and nothing of the best of it. I think that several possess Giantish blood or snake blood. It is possible, here and there, to tell the ancestry. You see that they are not completely alike.' He pointed to one wrapped in a leaden cloak who had a brutish, snout-like face, the nubs of horns protruding from its skull and a dry membraneous tail. 'That one I would guess to be a descendant of the Harpies,' he said. 'Perhaps an alliance between a Harpy and an Almhuinian Rodent-mutant.' He indicated one of the hod-carriers. 'And that one has the flat fish-eyes and the rudimentary gills of one of the *nimfeach*, although there is a trace of Humanish blood.'

'The ancestry is clearer in some than in others,' said Maelduin, as if there was nothing other than this on his mind.

'The Pit eventually douses all individuality,' said the man. 'When the transformation is complete, it is difficult to tell one from another. Do you see there?' Again he pointed, and Maelduin saw that, seated a little apart from the rest, were four or five creatures who were so devoid of Humanish or any other trait that it was impossible to tell what they might once have been. They were completely encased in the terrible scaly hides formed by the Pit's constant heat. Only their eyes showed in their distorted, snout-like faces, pale and so bulbous that Maelduin saw that the eye-stalks behind had become visible. They had the huge-jointed knuckles and hulking shoulders he remembered, and they sat by themselves, their legs drawn up, the knees on a level with their shoulders. They had not the patient acceptance of the creatures who toiled at the meaningless quarrying work, but there was a sly furtiveness about them, as if they might be engaged in some mean intrigue. Maelduin felt a shudder of repulsion laced with apprehension at the sight of them.

At his side, the robed man said softly, 'You do right to feel fear, friend. They are the rulers down here.' His eyes rested on them. 'There is little order here,' he said. 'But what there is is ordered by those.'

'Elders,' said Maelduin, half to himself.

'Yes.' The man shot him an approving look. 'In every community there will be those who serve and those who rule.'

Maelduin said, 'You are very knowledgeable about this place.' He looked at the other one, and the man said, as if in response, ' I am what you could call a pure Human. And there is little else to do here, unless I wish to carry the meaningless loads of rock or pointlessly quarry the endless stones. Or enter into the sly plots of those creatures who set themselves apart.' He glanced at Maelduin, and Maelduin said, half to himself:

'So it *is* a part of their punishment to have no proper work.'

The man studied Maelduin thoughtfully. 'It is perceptive of you to have understood.' He paused, and then said, 'Have you also seen that some wear steel muzzles over the lower part of their faces? And that others must carry on their shoulders cloaks fashioned from iron sheets?'

'I have seen it,' said Maelduin. 'The muzzles are to prevent speech, perhaps?'

'Yes, those are the ones who betrayed the Dark Lords by speech. The cloaks are for those who allowed Human prisoners to escape from the dungeons of the Black Citadels.'

'To remind them of restriction,' said Maelduin softly. 'Yes, I see.'

The man sent Maelduin another of his sidelong glances. 'There are other impositions which are not instantly apparent,' he said. 'Some of them have had hands struck off or noses cut out. Several have been deprived of their sexual organs for daring to vent their lusts on Chaos's harem women.'

'Yes?' Maelduin stayed where he was, sensing the man's need to talk, but watching the slowly moving Gristlens, seeing more vividly than ever now the chains and leaden cloaks; seeing as well that several of them wore spiked iron helmets clamped about their heads, and that dark, old blood was caked about the rims.

'Those are the most damned of all,' said the other, following Maelduin's line of vision. 'For they are the ones who offended against the Dark Lords in thought.'

'The Samhailt?' said Maelduin, startled.

'Its dark side. In the True Ireland it is known as the *Stroicim Inchinn*.' He looked to Maelduin to make sure that Maelduin understood, and Maelduin said, softly, 'Yes, I know of it.'

'The Dark Lords ruled that their servants might not summon it, but many risked this Pit to do so. In the eyes of the necromancers, the acquiring of the *Stroicim Inchinn* by those unworthy of it – that is, unworthy in their eyes, you understand – is one of the gravest offences of them all. The prisoners are forced to wear the spiked helmets about their skulls so that their thinking shall be restricted.' He fell silent, and Maelduin waited. Presently, the man said, 'And now you are wondering about my own transgression.'

'If you wish to talk about it, then I should listen; it is not a part of my beliefs that I should pry,' said Maelduin, and the man smiled rather wryly.

'A good creed,' he said. And then, 'Perhaps I can tell you.' He frowned, and Maelduin did not move. Presently the man said, 'I am here because I once served the Dark Lord of Chaos as a Guardian of one of the Gates between the Black Realm and the True Ireland.' He paused, and Maelduin said, 'You have dwelled in the True Ireland? The Ireland of Tara and of ordinary Men and Women?' And waited, because no true servant of the Dark Lords would ever genuinely acknowledge the True Ireland.

'I was once a part of it,' said the man, and there was a deep, aching sadness in his voice. 'I was part of the True Ireland, although I was never inside Tara, and I only once saw the High King.' He stopped, and Maelduin relaxed very slightly, for he had heard the wistfulness in the man's voice, and he knew that one who was still in thrall to the Dark Lords would not have spoken thus.

'I lived there,' said the man, 'and I served a far better Lord there than any who ever ruled in the Black Domain.' He lifted his head and the deep hood fell back a little. Maelduin saw his thin face was ravaged and marked with some inner suffering.

He said, 'Tell me how you are called. For if we are to be –' he glanced about them – 'if we are to be companions here, we should know one another's names.' This was something the Humanish did, this exchanging of names. It was one of their small rituals and important to them. And I do not know that I disagree with it, thought Maelduin. There is comfort, the sense of touching another's mind, and of greeting in the giving and receiving of a name.

The robed man said, 'In the world I come from, and within the community where I lived, I was known as Brother Quintus.'

'Yes?'

The dark eyes looked at Maelduin, and something so pain-filled showed there that Maelduin felt a wrenching in his own vitals.

'But inside the Dark Domain,' said the man, 'I was called the Black Monk of Torach.'

* * *

The Black Monk of Torach. The dark and menacing figure who had served the Lord of Chaos and the Crimson Lady of Almhuin. Who had prowled the hinterlands between the True Ireland and the Dark Realm, trawling for victims for the evil ones whom he served.

Even in their underwater caves and in the secret heart of Tiarna, the *sidh* had heard of the Black Monk. It was told how, if you approached one of the Gateways – perhaps the magical hidden one in the heart of the Wolfwood, or the most ancient of them all deep within the Cruachan Caves – you would feel the dense black shadow of the hooded and cowled figure fall about you, and then, before you could slip through and find yourself in the Dark Realm, the thick blackness would fall about you, smothering you, choking you, so that you could feel the stifling evil driving the breath from your body. You would die before you could get through the Gateway and reach the necromancers' lairs, and it would be a slow and painful death.

Here is here with me, thought Maelduin, staring. This is the Black Monk himself. But why is he here? What has his offence been?

Quintus seemed to hear this. He said, 'I came to the Dark Realm because of lust and greed. It is as simple as that. I served evil masters and I performed many terrible tasks for them. All to satisfy my own needs.' He studied Maelduin, his head on one side, and Maelduin said, carefully, 'I think that lust and greed are not unusual traits.'

'They were forbidden by my creed,' said Quintus. 'The One I served permitted neither lust nor greed.'

'That is surely a harsh Master.'

A light kindled in Quintus's eyes. 'It is a new creed,' he said. 'But it is the Truth which I, with my brethren, had sworn to bring from England so that all would see the Light.'

He regarded Maelduin from out of his deeply set eyes, and Maelduin said, 'Light and Truth are always good things to follow.'

'Oh yes. And in the beginning – in the days when I first came to Ireland, it was the message I preached. Love and hope and redemption.' The sunken eyes shone with unexpected ardency, and then Quintus's eyes flickered to Maelduin, as if looking to see how this would be taken.

Maelduin thought: he would have me believe he has repented of his sojourn in the Dark Realm, and returned to those beliefs. I think perhaps he may even have done so. But I am not entirely sure. And I certainly do not trust him. Aloud he said, 'What happened?'

Quintus said, 'I preached fervently and determinedly in every town I came to, and in every settlement and every cluster of cottages I found. Perhaps I was a little too insistent, a little too forceful. Perhaps I was even arrogant. "This is what you *must* believe." Yes, I said that to the wild, pagan Irish.'

He glanced at Maelduin again, and Maelduin said, softly, 'They will always listen to a good story, the Irish. They will always tell one, as well. But their beliefs are very deep-rooted. Your task would not have been an easy one.'

'You are very courteous,' said Quintus, eyeing Maelduin. 'Perhaps it was a little like that.' He paused. 'At length my preaching came to the ears of the Dark Lords.'

'And they sent out . . . something to stop you? Something to prevent you spreading the new religion? Yes, of course they would,' said Maelduin, thoughtfully. 'They would have been very quick to destroy anything that was tinged with light and hope.' He looked at Quintus. 'What did they do?'

'They sent the highest of their dark evil Order,' said Quintus, bitterly. 'They sent the Lord of Chaos himself.'

There was a brief silence. Then Maelduin said, 'They must have accounted you a very serious threat. They must have been afraid that your beliefs would spread and take root. And so Chaos confronted you?'

Quintus leaned back against the harsh rockface, his eyes suddenly distant. He said, 'Yes. He brought me to the Moher Cliffs.'

'Yes.'

'The wildest, most desolate place in all Ireland,' said Quintus. 'A wilderness, but a beautiful wilderness. Chaos faced me here. At first he tried to mock my faith, saying that if the One I worshipped was so strong, then I should cast myself from the cliffs and into the raging seas below and see if He would protect me.' Again the pause. 'When I declined to put my God to such a ridiculous test, Chaos changed his attack. He turned about, and

404

stood with his back to the raging oceans and the sea-lashed cliffs. It was twilight,' said Quintus, his eyes far away. 'The blue-tinted dusk was stealing over everything, but the sun had not quite set. It was a remarkable sight . . .

'He indicated the land before us,' said Quintus after a moment. 'He gestured to the rolling fields and the mountains and the dark, misty forests. I remember how the blue and green twilight lay everywhere, so that it was as if all Ireland were at our feet, and it was as if all Ireland were shrouded in ancient magic and pagan myth. He said – and I believe I can repeat the words exactly – he said, "Look on the beauty of Ireland, Monk. Look on the power and the glory. All of that is yours if you will leave your God and swear your allegiance to me."' Quintus stopped abruptly, and Maelduin had the feeling that the monk was not only repeating words said to him by Chaos, but words that had been said to someone else a very long time ago.

But that time the offer was turned down . . .

As if in response, Quintus said, 'I had not the strength of mind to turn it down. So beautiful. All Ireland . . . I had lived in the austere, celibate world of an English monastery. You cannot know what it meant . . .'

Maelduin said, 'I understand a little. And so you fell under the thrall of the Lord of Chaos, as many others before you have done, and doubtless many after will do.'

'Yes,' said Quintus. 'And he was so dark and yet so beautiful . . . Surely one of the most powerful necromancers ever known. Yes, I accepted. He appointed me as his Gatekeeper; he vouchsafed to me the Enchantment he had taken from the ancient Isle of Torach so that I could use it in his service. A dark, coiled thing it was. But so powerful. He taught me how to use it, and I used it cruelly. For many years I lived in great sin.'

'Yes?' 'Sin' was not a very familiar word to Maelduin, but he understood Quintus's meaning.

'I served Chaos faithfully in the beginning,' said Quintus, the burnt-out eyes staring straight ahead, so that despite the dry heat of the Pit, Maelduin shivered at the fierce pain in them. 'I kept faith with him. Every Human creature who tried to penetrate the Dark Realm, I caught and offered up to him for his terrible work.'

'Necromantic race-breeding,' said Maelduin, half to himself, remembering the Trolls' story.

'Yes. Yes, that was his quest,' said Quintus. 'But there came a time when I turned my back on Chaos.'

'The rewards he had promised you turned out to be empty?'

'Yes. I cannot even plead that I sickened of what I did. Chaos had promised such gratification; every sense to be satisfied. I had practised the celibacy required by my Order for so long . . . But there was no satisfaction and no gratification,' said Quintus. 'The bodies of the women he flung to me gave me no pleasure. He had cheated me.'

'It is the way of all necromancers,' said Maelduin, softly.

'I began to barter with the other necromancers,' said Quintus. 'If Chaos would not give me what he had promised, I vowed I would serve those who would. And because I had lived in the Dark Realm for many years by then, I was deemed a valuable servant. There was no dearth of necromancers prepared to take me into their dark citadels. But because I had lived alongside the blood-lusts of Chaos and his people, those blood-lusts were burning within me and I craved true gratification.' He sent Maelduin another of his sideways looks. 'The sweet, sensuous pleasures of warm, fresh blood,' he said, very softly. 'The taking of life, the feeling when the life-force gushes out . . .'

He stopped, and Maelduin said, 'And so you decided that, of them all, you would serve the BeastWoman of Almhuin.'

'Yes.

'The Enchantment found on the Isle of Torach was a subtle one,' said Quintus. 'It smothered and stifled, but it left the victim's blood warm and pulsing,' he said, and Maelduin heard the sudden lick of prurience in the Monk's voice. Quintus said, 'Warm and fresh. *Living* blood. And the Lady of Almhuin Castle was ever greedy for fresh, warm blood. And I was greedy for it, also. And so for a time, I served both Chaos and the Crimson Lady.'

Maelduin said, 'And it was that that caused the schism between them?'

'Yes.' Quintus looked back at Maelduin. 'I gambled and I lost,' he said. 'The Crimson Lady flung me out. She turned me into the terrible Dark Realm, to live or die as the fates decreed. And Chaos also flung me out.'

'Into the Pit,' said Maelduin.

'Yes. He would not, any more than the Lady of Almhuin, permit a traitor, a double-dealer, to go free. He summoned his dark brethren, and I was brought before the Dark Council of the Twelve.'

'And sentenced to banishment to the Pit.' Maelduin sought for the right words, the *Humanish* words. 'For treachery against Chaos,' he said. 'For disloyalty to him.'

Quintus, his eyes dark and pain-filled, said, 'Yes.' He turned his intense stare on Maelduin. 'According to his lights, Chaos was fair,' he said. 'He is . . .' A small smile touched his lips. 'He is a gentleman,' said Quintus. 'He abides by the rules of his kind. I was a traitor, and it was a traitor's punishment he would have pronounced.

'Perhaps he would have banished me here anyway, but perhaps he would only have flung me into some miserable dungeon.' Light glowed in the Monk's eyes. 'But at the end, I humiliated them,' he said. 'I stood before the Dark Council at the heart of the Castle of Infinity, and I remembered the teachings of my own Leader. I remembered the gentle goodness and the final sufferings of the One whose creed I had once followed.' A flicker of anguish passed over his face. 'I was reclaimed by the One True Religion,' he said. 'And, facing them all, I renounced the Dark Ireland and all its beliefs; there before the most powerful necromancers ever known.' A brief smile touched his thin face. 'I did so loudly and ringingly,' he said, 'as I should have done when Chaos first tempted me on the Moher Cliffs. I repudiated the Dark Ireland once and for all, and proclaimed my undying allegiance to the Nazarene. I tore Chaos's wickedness to shreds before his people, and flung his darkness, and that of his henchmen and his evil brethren, in his face.' He looked at Maelduin, and wry amusement touched his lips. 'You understand, perhaps, why I was cast into the Pit.'

'You humiliated him,' said Maelduin, studying the Monk. 'That took extreme courage, I think.'

The man said, 'You have not heard of my Master?'

'The . . . Nazarene? No.' Maelduin would have liked to hear of this new austere religion which was being brought into Ireland, and which had apparently given Quintus such extraordinary courage. He knew, in a vague way, that it preached asceticism and fasting and long hours of silence, but little more. It occurred to him, rather bitterly, that at least there would be time to spare for him to talk with Quintus and learn about his beliefs.

And while I sit here and learn of the world's religions and the new teachings, Tiarna will surely die . . . Anguish pierced him again, but he beat it down, and turned back with courtesy to listen to the ending of Quintus's strange story.

Quintus said, 'He had extreme courage and immense fortitude, my Master. He believed what he believed, and did not allow anything to sway him. Perhaps we shall talk more of him. But I have told you my story.' He looked at Maelduin more fully and, as he did so, Maelduin felt the man shed a little more of the dark crusted shell that he carried. When Quintus said, 'Will you tell me, in turn, how you come to be cast into this place?' Maelduin, still unsure how far to trust Quintus, said, lightly, 'Oh, I simply fell into it.' And, despite his fear, and despite his deep inner horror at being trapped in the fearsome Pit, he grinned at the Monk. 'A mistake,' he said. 'I encountered a band of Trolls who would have minced me for their supper. I outwitted them, but in the fight I rolled over the Pit's edge.' He stood up and looked about him and, as he did so, he heard a slithering movement above him.

A shower of stones came hurtling down from the Pit's edges, and the Gristlens stopped in their work and turned to look.

Against the red-lit sky, sharply limned by the evil light of the Human torches, a monstrous outline was staring down into the Pit. The torches flickered wildly, and the sickly warm-meat odours gusted downwards.

In the glowing firelight, Maelduin saw the deformed outline of a squat, evil being with a flat, noseless face and slyly intelligent eyes set askew in its head. At his side, Quintus made as if to speak, and then was silent, and Maelduin felt the sudden fear course through the man's body. Behind them, a low growling sound of angry fear came from the watching Gristlens, and Maelduin sensed the sudden concerted movement of the six who sat apart.

The dark, misshapen silhouette at the Pit's rim moved then, flinging a webbed-footed leg over the edges and beginning to clamber down the steep sides.

The Fisher Prince, the monster-spawn of Coelacanth, had escaped from the silver cage and was descending into the Tanning Pit.

Chapter Thirty-five

The creature was descending easily, seeming to find footholes and crevices to cling to the steep rockface. The red torchlight cast its thick, clotted light over the creature as it moved, showing it for the dreadful warped monster that Maelduin had seen in the Amaranths' Palace. As it moved, he had the eerie impression of something boneless wriggling its way down the Pit's walls, and he remembered the legends of Coelacanth's ancestry, and that Coelacanth was believed to be part-fish, part-snake, part-worm. This was unmistakably Coelacanth's spawn: loathsome, unutterably evil. And yet, try as he might, he could not think of it as other than the son of the Fisher King, and therefore a Prince of a Royal House . . .

As the light burned up, Maelduin and Quintus saw that the creature was using a thin silver rope, which it had clearly fastened to something – perhaps a jutting rock – beyond the Pit's edges.

Maelduin stared at it and felt a tremor of fear again. He thought: it is using a rope. It is only a few days old, but it has had the intelligence and the cunning to do that. A *silver* rope. Then it must have somehow made use of the silver bars and the silver lights I caged it with. I bound it with one of the Cadence's enchantments of captivity, thought Maelduin, but it has broken out, and it has snapped the bars and fashioned a rope from them.

It has escaped with ease and it is coming to fetch me.

The Prince was nearing the floor of the Pit, and Maelduin saw that evil amusement was glinting in its flat, ugly eyes. He thought: it scents my fear! It *smells* it! It finds it amusing that I am prey to Humanish emotions. Deep within his mind he sought for the silver threads that would summon the Cadence, and the fear deepened as he felt the thin, elusive strands slide from his mind's grasp.

410

So that, also, is beyond my reach. Panic tore at him, great, scarlet, clawlike rents, and for a moment, his cool *sidh* mind spun out of control. And then Quintus's mind brushed him lightly, unlooked-for and unexpected, but filled with such resolute courage that his own mind steadied.

The Gristlens were watching the Prince's descent with silent concentration. Maelduin could smell the dry, sour stench gusting forward as they moved from their work, and stood at the Pit's centre.

The Prince – I *cannot* think of it otherwise! thought Maelduin – was still climbing steadily downwards, its webbed hands curling about the rope with apparent ease, its gristly feet searching out footholds in the rockface. The membraneous fin that protruded from its spine was darkly limned in the glowing torchlight.

At Maelduin's side, Quintus said softly, 'Dear God, what is it? Maelduin, what is it?'

'A son of the Gristlen,' said Maelduin. 'Of a creature that once dwelled in the Pit, but found its way into the True Ireland.'

Coelacanth's Prince, evil and malignant beyond belief . . .

'A mutant,' said Maelduin, 'born of a rape inflicted on a . . .' He stopped and amended his next words. 'Inflicted on a lady of one of Ireland's noble Houses,' he said.

Quintus said, 'Its kin recognise it.'

'Yes.' Maelduin looked back once more to where the Gristlens were standing in a silent mass, their pale, bulbous eyes watching the Prince unblinkingly. 'They will certainly try to use the rope,' he said. 'They will try to escape.'

'Oh yes.' Quintus looked back at the watching Gristlens, and Maelduin received the impression of a sudden strength uncoiling in the Monk, as if he might be tensing his muscles to fight. But he only said, 'Is the creature coming to join its kindred?'

'No,' said Maelduin, in an expressionless voice. 'No. It is coming for me.' He looked at Quintus. 'It needs me,' he said. 'It cannot fend for itself in the world yet, and it needs a protector. I caged it, but has broken out, and it is coming to find me.'

As the words were said, the Fisher Prince reached the floor of the Pit and turned to look at Maelduin again. Maelduin knew he had been right.

411

I can still get it to the Grail Castle, he thought with a surge of hope. It is going to bargain with me: if I will agree to take it to the Grail Castle, it will get me out of the Pit. It knows that inside the Grail Castle it will be safe from the world until it is sufficiently strong to venture out. And once it is there, I shall be free of it. I shall have paid my debt, and shall be free to pursue the music or explore the Cadence for a way to save Tiarna.

He moved to the foot of the steep Pit walls, and grasped the waiting rope that would take him out the Pit. As he did so, there was movement behind him. He half turned, and saw that the Gristlens were moving forward, their eyes fixed on the rope, the manacles dragging and scraping across the hard rock floor.

Quintus had moved to shield Maelduin, but his voice was low and urgent. 'They are going to attack you! If they get past that creature they have a means to escape! The rope is a way out! You have to go quickly!'

Maelduin had already swung himself upwards using the rope, feeling it cool and easy to grasp. He began the ascent, and as he did so, he caught a movement from behind. He turned back and saw that the Gristlens were creeping towards him, their leering faces sly, their great, swollen-jointed hands lifted as if to strike, the thick iron manacles held out threateningly. Several of them glanced uneasily at the Prince, who was standing silent and still by the rope end, but they came on relentlessly.

Quintus was facing them, standing below Maelduin, his back pressed against the rock walls. Maelduin thought: I cannot leave him behind! I cannot leave him to be torn apart by these creatures!

He leaned down, and cried, 'Quintus! After me! Take the rope and begin climbing! Quickly!' and at once, Quintus reached for the rope, and swung upwards at Maelduin's heels. Maelduin had the brief, vivid awareness that Quintus had had no thought for his own escape, that his mind had been wholly on facing the Gristlens, fighting them off if necessary to allow Maelduin to climb out.

They were several feet above the Pit's floor now, and Maelduin could feel his wrists – Humanish bones and muscles and skin! – aching almost intolerably with the strain, when the Gristlens moved again. Maelduin and Quintus both stopped, and the Gristlens surged forward towards the motionless figure of the Fisher Prince, their faces leering, their horrid, bulbous eyes avid and their long-toothed snarls more pronounced. The six Elders stood back, not joining in, not moving, but Maelduin and Quintus, from their precarious position, shared a thought: it was they who incited the others! They are the strongest!

The Gristlens moved to the Prince, their great hands reaching for him, their lips curling back, their misshapen teeth gleaming wetly. A low growling of greed and bloodlust broke from them, and then they moved as one towards the Prince, holding out the gyves and the manacles threateningly. There was a moment, the span of a heartbeat, a breathspace, when the black heaving mass of dark leathery bodies and reaching hands and clawing fingers engulfed the Prince as the creatures of the Dark Lords' Tanning Pit fought to reach the silver rope. Maelduin, still clinging to the rope several feet above the ground, thought: it will be slain by its own kind! They will tear it to pieces and then they will swarm up the rope and out into the world! He stayed where he was, his feet finding a crevice for support, his eyes never leaving the fighting, clawing throng below him.

And then the small, slithering shape of the Fisher Prince detached itself, stepping back from the angry Gristlens with apparent ease; its cold eyes regarded its attackers, and the pale, membraneous fin lashed angrily at its legs. The Gristlens turned, and seemed to draw in breath, as if gathering themselves for a final concerted rush at this evil creature who was barring their way to freedom.

The Prince stood waiting, watching its attackers move towards it, silent and menacing; and a twisted smile lifted its lips.

But the Gristlens crept forward, their eyes wary, but inching closer, fanning out as they came, to surround the one who was trying to prevent them from reaching the rope that would lead to freedom.

Maelduin could see that the nearest of them wore one of the cruel mesh muzzles, and that it had a thin sly face above the muzzle, and the huge flat ears and high pointed skull of one possessing the black and evil blood of Goblins. Its fingers were not webbed like most of the others, but long and fleshless, with huge burrlike knuckles and joints and long, pointed nails. Goblin blood for certain.

As the Goblin-Gristlen reached the Prince and swung the manacles it wore above its head, the Prince stepped easily and neatly aside and, reaching out, tore the muzzle from the Gristlen's face contemptuously. A howl of dreadful agony rent the night, and bright red blood, speckled with fragments of white bone, covered the Gristlen's jowls. Maelduin, unable to look away, saw that the muzzle must have been somehow fused into the creature's jaw, so that it had been a part of its flesh and its bone. In ripping it away, the lower part of the Gristlen's face had been ripped away also.

The Gristlen fell back, its bony Goblin-fingers covering its mutilated face, screeching with agony, blood and teeth covering its hands. Its moans had a dreadful guttural tone, but as it stumbled away, the Prince turned to the one who stood behind it and smiled. Maelduin saw that the second Gristlen wore a spiked iron helmet, and that the nubs of hard black horns protruded through the iron. It had a cruel, evil intelligence and a furtive look to it. As it moved forward, Maelduin saw that it had pointed features and that its lips were curling back in a snarl, revealing the tiny, needle-sharp teeth of a Rodent. A thin boneless tail slithered behind it, but the tip had become jagged and shrunken and mummified with the Pit's relentless heat.

The Gristlen was advancing on the Prince warily, its eyes bulging. It lifted both hands above its head, so that the chains that bound them clanked and grated, and Maelduin saw that instead of hands, it had huge, leather-palmed paws, covered on the backs with black matted hide. Its neck and shoulder muscles rippled as it tensed to strike the Prince, but even as it did so, the Prince reached out again, chuckling contemptuously, and with one webbed hand, and a single horizontal stroke, sliced the helmet from the creature's head.

The Gristlen fell back instantly, clutching at its forehead and its eyes, braying in agony; in the thick, smeary light, Maelduin saw that the top of its skull had been sliced completely away, exactly as if it had been an egg, so that its brainpan was exposed. The Gristlen fell sprawlingly on to the ground, howling. Its long jointed legs scrabbled helplessly at the ground, and its tail twitched and curled. Thick grey brain matter, streaked with oozing, glutinous fluid, spilled and bubbled out of its skull and ran down into its eyes. It howled again and rolled on to its back, drawing up its knees, writhing in purest agony, bringing up its paws as it tried to wipe its eyes free.

Maelduin, sickened and horrified, felt his stomach lifting with nausea, and a tiny part of his mind recognised that his feelings were almost wholly Humanish; he ought not to be feeling sickened, and he certainly ought not to be feeling pity.

The Fisher Prince moved forward, and stood regarding the Gristlens, as if inviting more of them to pit themselves against him. The six Elders glanced furtively at one another and remained motionless, but a smaller Gristlen crept towards the waiting Prince. It wore a thick, dull breastplate of black iron about its upper body, and had short, sticklike arms and legs, so that it had the appearance of a monstrous beetle.

The armoured Gristlen stood its ground, and malevolence glinted in its pale eyes. The Prince turned from its scrutiny of Maelduin, and eyed the Gristlen thoughtfully. It did not move, but the other Gristlens backed away from it.

The armoured Gristlen was moving forward with a scuttling, creeping gait which increased its likeness to a huge, upright insect. The Prince stayed where he was, and the Gristlen began to grin, showing tiny, stumplike teeth in double rows.

All the better to rip you apart . . .

The Prince moved then, bounding forward, cleaving the air with his monstrous body, landing on the Gristlen's chest, clamping tightly about the upper part of the repulsive torso. The Gristlen fell back, pushing vainly at the thing that had fastened on to it, trying to dislodge it. It fell back, and the Prince fell with it, limpetlike, levering at the breastplate with sharp questing fingers.

There was a wet, sucking noise, and the sound of rib-bones snapping. The iron breastplate came away with the Gristlen's ribcage; the ribs gleaming wetly, spattered with blood, with slopping kidneys and liver and bile-filled sacs still adhering to it. Blood spurted upwards in a thick, dark fountain, and the other Gristlens fell back, cowering and moaning, flinging their clawed and webbed and leathery hands up to protect themselves.

The Fisher Prince stood directly in the fountain's fall, the dark, evil blood showering over it, the fragments of skin and bone and glistening wet entrails adhering to its face and arms and skin.

And then he stepped back from the dying, partly eviscerated creature at his feet, and turned his eyes upwards, sending the cold, evil, compelling light directly on to Maelduin.

Without a sound, Maelduin turned back to continue his climb up to the edges of the Tanning Pit.

The Human torches had long since ceased to burn, but there was sufficient light to see. Maelduin pulled himself over the edges of the Pit, and lay for a moment, summoning his strength. He breathed in the cold air thankfully, seeing that, although it had been perpetually dark in the depths of the Pit, here it was the strange, faintly eerie time that the Humanish called the Purple Hour.

So a day, perhaps two or three days, passed while I was imprisoned down there, and now it is twilight.

Twilight, when creatures not entirely of this world walk . . .

The two horses were still tethered where he had left them, and Maelduin glanced at Quintus, and nodded in their direction.

'You can ride, Quintus?' he said.

'I have ridden,' said the Monk. 'I should be grateful for your company a little longer.' He looked at Maelduin questioningly, as if he might be saying: *I will not ask if I may come with you in your strange quest, but if you invite me, I should accept.*

Maelduin studied Quintus, remembering that strange dark shell that he had sensed earlier. *Still there? Yes, I think so. But he helped me in the Pit, and I think he would be a strong ally. I could take him with me as far as the Grail Castle at least.* He narrowed his eyes thoughtfully, and remembered the Humanish notion of 'gaoler', the guarding of prisoners. *Could he leave Quintus as the Prince's guard? Dare he?* But he was already dreadfully aware of time trickling out, and he had no idea of how long the *sidh* could survive without the music.

He made a swift decision. *Nothing must get in the way of restoring Tiarna. Nothing was as important.* And so he would make use of Quintus if he could. He looked back at the Prince, who was standing submissively by the silver cage and then turned again to Quintus. 'I have given my word that I will take that creature to the Grail Castle,' he said. Quintus's eyes flickered, and Maelduin felt the sudden stirring of the darkness that clung about the Monk, as if something that had been quiescent was raising its evil head and sniffing the air. A warning note sounded in his mind. *Quintus and Coelacanth's son together? And the Prince has bowed to captivity at my hands again. I think I must be very wary indeed of these two,* thought Maelduin.

But Quintus only said, thoughtfully, 'The Grail Castle is a fearsome place, and difficult to find, I believe.'

Maelduin said very softly, '"*Ride directly into the setting sun, and in the depths of the night, when the ancient lost enchantments of Ireland stir, on the darkest and most desolate road in the land . . .*"' He stopped, and regarded the Monk through eyes that suddenly slanted mischievously.

Quintus said, half to himself, '"*The darkest and most desolate road in the land . . .*"'

'. . . and there you will find the Grail Castle,' finished Maelduin. 'So you know the legends.'

'All Ireland knows the legends,' said Quintus evenly. And then, in a different voice, 'Do you know the road? That is – do you know where it is?'

For answer, Maelduin turned and pointed beyond the rearing Moher Cliffs.

'There is the road,' he said, and looked back at the Monk, his eyes shining brilliantly in the twilight. 'It winds through the Moher Cliffs, a little inland, and it is dark and desolate and its galleries and its halls will be filled with the pounding of the seas against the cliffs below. It will be shrouded in the thick sea-mists that creep across the cliffs, and it may be difficult to see it. But that is the road I must take.' He regarded the Monk with his cool *sidh* authority. 'You may take it with me if you wish,' he said. 'Although if you do, you must be prepared for danger and also for difficulties.' *If you have the courage, then you may come,* said his tone. *But it is all one to me.*

Quintus said, very calmly, 'You mistrust me.'

'A little.' Maelduin turned back to gaze into the darkening night, beyond the mist-shrouded cliffs. 'Do you wonder?'

'No. No, for the darkness of the Black Realm is still within me,' said Quintus, and then, as Maelduin looked up sharply, 'We both feel it,' he said. 'I am not sure exactly what you are, although I know you are not wholly Human. But you are aware of the darkness, the taint that is within me and that has still to be plucked out by its roots.' His face was in shadow, the eyes sombre. 'And yet I have repented, Maelduin,' he said. 'I sinned grievously, but I repented, and there in the Pit I was serving my penance.'

'"Penance"?'

'The means by which one makes reparation for sins. For crimes.' Quintus looked at Maelduin. 'That is why I did not instantly take the escape to freedom that the silver rope offered,' he said. 'For I must serve whatever penance is imposed on me.' His eyes filled with the darkness again. 'I was sentenced to the Pit—'

'By Chaos.'

'The instrument of the sentencing does not matter. It was my punishment, my atoning. We forge our own chains. And if I did not serve the full sentence, then there will be further sufferings ahead,' he said. 'The payment can never be avoided. It can sometimes be delayed, but it can never be avoided.' And then, his expression suddenly shrewd, he said, 'You should find it easy to understand, Maelduin, for I think you chose to cast this evil being into a dungeon in reparation for a sin you once committed. This is your own penance.'

'Payment,' said Maelduin, half to himself, but understanding Quintus. 'Murmur's death. And the honour of my people which required it.'

'That is not so very different. To call a penance payment for a sin is not so very different.'

'Perhaps not.' Maelduin was still unable to tell if the Monk was exactly what he purported to be – a creature who had committed great evil while in the thrall of the Lord of Chaos, but who had later repented. I must remember that this is the Black Monk of Torach, he thought. But I think it will be all right. I think I will take the risk. After a moment, he said, 'Our path lies along there.' He lifted a hand, pointing. 'Do you see?'

Quintus narrowed his eyes, following the line of Maelduin's hand. 'Yes,' he said at length, very softly. 'Yes, I see it.' And then, almost to himself, 'So I am to return to the wilderness where Chaos tempted me. I am to see the place of my sinning again. There is an irony in that, I think.' He paused, and Maelduin felt again the presence of something dark and ancient and threatening deep within the Monk. But he turned his horse about, and set it to the narrow cliff path. On their left, the cliffs fell sharply away, and far below they could hear the sea pounding against the shore. Fine spray rose, shrouding the cliffs and the crags, veiling them in thick, swirling mists. Inland from the cliffs, the Moher Crags rose steeply and starkly; a black outline against the sky. But as Maelduin narrowed his eyes, trying to penetrate the darkness, he saw that further inland were small, winking lights; the huddle of hill farms and cottages, perhaps the occasional flare of lanterns in windows. The tiny lights ought to have given him comfort; he ought to have felt warmed by this evidence of Humanish occupancy, for, he thought, it is only the Humanish that light their windows in the dark night in that fashion . . .

But for some reason, the lights made him feel colder and more desolate than he had ever felt before. What must it be like to live your life out here, to be so far distant from life and warmth and colour? To know only the dark, craggy cliffs and the pounding of the ocean − surely the most fearsomely lonely sound in the world? − and to live in the endless, swirling sea-mists?

What had Quintus called this place? Ireland's wilderness.

What kind of creatures lived out here?

The Purple Hour was all about them as they left the Tanning Pit behind. Beautiful, thought Maelduin, hearing and seeing and feeling the ancient heady magic of Ireland, the soft, sly whisperings, the scurrying, furry-footed sounds. The feeling of three-cornered faces peering out from the shadows, and the brief vivid glimpses of sly, grinning faces with pointed muzzles and pointed ears . . . Cloven hoofs and the beating of wings overhead . . . The lingering not-entirely-safe enchantments that had been poured into Ireland at the very beginning, before Men could speak and understand one another, before they could walk upright . . . The Other Ireland, waking and walking . . .

And this is the hour when the Grail Castle can be reached, thought Maelduin.

I believe I am touching the deepest of Humanish feelings now, he thought as they rode warily along, the narrow path winding sharply upwards and inland. I believe I am experiencing Humanish race-memory. A deep fear closed about him without warning. Am I, then, now able to hear the ancestral echoes and feel the atavistic fears of a people, a race, a species to whom I do not belong? I dare not allow that! thought Maelduin. I must not allow it. For if I am able to reach into the centuries-old memories and fears of the Humanish, then for sure I am becoming too deeply entwined in the ivory cloak and too strongly enmeshed in the silken skin. And that may mean that I shall not be able to rid my true self of them later.

He gave no indication of any of this; he guided the horse along the narrow cliff path, Quintus a little behind him, with the great cage with the Prince strapped firmly to the saddle panniers. The creature had gone willingly into its captivity, eyeing Maelduin from its sly flat eyes with mocking amusement, and Maelduin had known, quite surely, that the cage would not hold the Prince for longer than it wished.

The Moher Cliffs were behind them now, fading into the distance, but thick sea-spray still wreathed the cliff path, obscuring their vision, and clinging to their hair and their eyelashes. Maelduin thought there was still the occasional glimmer of lights from the hill farms farther inland, but the mist played tricks, and it was difficult to be sure. Tiny stunted trees loomed up on the roadside, their skeletal branches resembling long bony fingers that reached and clutched, droplets of moisture clinging to them. Maelduin shivered and drew the woollen cloak more tightly about him. The horses slowed, picking their way cautiously now, and the sound of their hoofs, muffled in the mists, echoed eerily against the cliff walls. Clouds scudded across the darkening skies, and Maelduin, his eyes adjusting to the uncertain light, made out tiny footprints on the ground; the spoor of creatures who pattered through the night, some of them tiny and light, but others larger and hoofed and cloven . . .

Because the Grail Castle is guarded by every darkness and every prowling, slithering, creeping servant that walks the land by night . . .

The mist closed in on them, thick, heavy, quenching all sound. Maelduin thought that it was as if there were dozens of eyes within it, listening and watching. But they do not approach us, he thought; they do not challenge us. Because they sense that we carry with us an immense evil and are flinching from it.

When Quintus said, very softly, 'There are creatures

prowling within the shadows and within the mists, but whatever they are, they feel the prisoner's darkness, and they fear it,' Maelduin nodded, but thought: is it only the Prince's darkness they feel? What of the darkness you carry, Monk?

And then they rounded a curve in the road, and there was a sudden break in the cliff face. The mists parted without warning and there – against the scudding skies, rearing against the moonwashed cliffs and partly shrouded in mist – was the Grail Castle.

As they approached, they saw that the Castle was made of some kind of rough dark stone, with a square central portion and huge circular towers with battlements and machicolations at each corner. At the centre was a gateway, an opening, deep in shadow where the grille of the portcullis, the great iron gates that rendered the Castle safe, should have been.

But somebody had raised the portcullis, and somebody had lowered the drawbridge.

As if they were expected.

But, as they drew nearer, they saw that the Grail Castle had an empty, desolate air. When they paused at the edge of the narrow drawbridge, they could both see that moss grew thickly over the lower part of the towers, and that several of the windows were broken and gaping, giving them the appearance of huge, yawning eyes that stared endlessly down at the waiting drawbridge, and that watched ceaselessly for any creatures that might approach.

Oh yes, send these two inside, let the gates swallow them, they will do very nicely, they are tasty morsels both . . . They can add a little more to the legend of the Grail Castle . . . They can weave a few more dark strands into the lore of this desolate place . . .

Against his will, Maelduin remembered again the many creatures – some Humanish, some not – who had set out in quest of this place and been lost for all time. He remembered his own father journeying here in Erin's reign, and maintaining that strange silence ever afterwards.

At his side, Quintus said softly, 'They tell odd stories of this place,' He looked up at the towering black shape, his eyes unreadable.

Maelduin said, 'You know of it?'

'Every creature who ever lived in Ireland knows of it.' A shadow fell across his face, and for a moment something red gleamed in his eyes. He said, very softly, 'There is an immense darkness within those walls.' He looked back at Maelduin, and Maelduin repressed a shiver. Quintus's eyes were huge black pits and his face was drained and bloodless.

Maelduin stared at him, and thought: there is something looking out of his eyes that is no longer the quiet, rather interesting creature I met earlier. This is his dark inner self; the being who served Chaos and the Lady of Almhuin, and who plumbed the deepest abysses of Necromancy to serve his lusts.

He still carries the taint of those dark years, thought Maelduin. It still lives.

And whatever is inside the Grail Castle is calling to it.

This is no longer Brother Quintus, a renegade Human from an English monastery.

This is the Black Monk of Torach once again.

Chapter Thirty-six

As they passed under the great square arch of the Castle portcullis, a darkness and a cold, keening desolation fell about them. Maelduin, his every sense alert, felt as if a thick, stifling cloak had been thrown over them. The terrible crushing weight of every exile who had ever been cast into this place pressed down on him.

Niall and the Nine Hostages, condemned by an evil necromancer . . . The lost Tribes of Ireland, sometimes called the Cruithin, who had vanished from Ireland one night centuries earlier, and had never been seen again . . . One legend told how they had taken refuge here when their existence was threatened, and had lived for several generations within the darkness of the Castle's echoing halls. Maelduin remembered the lonely little huddles of light they had seen through the swirling mists. Were they still here, those Lost Peoples, Ireland's long-ago Cruithin, living still in secrecy in the cliffs and the hills that surrounded the ancient Castle?

Yes, it had its secrets, this place, it had its mysteries, but it kept them to itself, and some of them were terrible and some of them were pitiful, and all of them were woven inextricably into Ireland's rich tapestry of legend and lore and myth.

And now I am about to add a dark strand to that tapestry, thought Maelduin, glancing back at the caged Prince, and at the set features of the Monk. I am about to imprison here the son of the dread Coelacanth, and I am about to force the creature who wore the guise of the Black Monk of Torach to act as his gaoler.

Could he then escape? Or would he in turn become one of the Grail Castle's sad, forgotten exiles? The lost *sidh* Prince, Tiarna's vanished heir . . . The thought was like a knife-twist in his vitals.

Moonlight silvered the great hall as he entered, and dust motes swirled in and out of the thin light. Maelduin looked about him, seeing that the hall was a vast, stone-floored place, but feeling with a shock of surprise the gentle scents of old timbers and the faint drifts of lavender and beeswax enfold him. There was the lingering scent of peat, the ghosts of comfortable roaring fires, around which people might have gathered to eat and tell stories and sing songs.

He stood very still just inside the door, and thought: this is a place where people – some of them quite ordinary – have lived and laughed and been sad, and shared companionship and work.

And left their mark as firmly as those other poor creatures, Ireland's exiles, who were flung here for Ireland to forget them. Just as Ireland might one day forget the *sidh* . . .

The moonlight filtered in through two narrow, high windows, set on each side of the door. At the far end was a low stone archway, and beyond it Maelduin could see passages leading away from the central hall. Sculleries? Stillrooms?

The floor was strewn with skin rugs of some kind, and to the left a wide, shallow-tread staircase led away from the hall and curved upwards, vanishing into the thick shadows.

On Maelduin's right was an immense, stone-backed hearth, black with age. Above it, engraved in the stone chimney-breast, were the ancient arms of the Wolfkings.

So this was once a Royal House . . . thought Maelduin, caught in fascination, feeling the ancient memories close about him. This was once one of the great strongholds of the High Kings of Tara.

And, he thought, we are inside, and nothing has challenged us so far. All that remains is to penetrate to the dungeons and lock the Prince away. His thoughts were sane and practical and ordered. But, just beneath the sanity and the logic and the calm, ran another stratum, another layer that was none of these things.

I am standing in the heart of the fearsome, haunted Castle of every dark legend and every sinister story ever told, and with me are two creatures whom I cannot trust . . .

And it is night, thought Maelduin, and shivered suddenly. It is the darkest hour of the night, midnight's arch is above us, we are held fast in the dread lonelinesses of the night's watches . . .

He blinked and shook his head, and turned to the task of fetching in the silver cage which held the Fisher Prince, he and Quintus carrying it between them, and setting it on the floor of the great central hall.

'Will it be safe here?' said Quintus, frowning.

'I have no idea.' Maelduin was already moving across the floor to the archways that led to the rest of the Castle. 'But the sooner we cast it into the dungeons, the better.'

'Through here?' said Quintus, following him.

'It is somewhere to start.'

The shadows seemed to reach out as they moved warily out of the moon-washed hall with its strange echoes and its drifting memories. Maelduin trod slowly, waiting for the faint luminosity that still glimmered softly from his skin to show them their way. As he did so, he felt memory slip, and he was again in the Silver Cavern of Tiarna, enduring the fearsome, bone-wrenching agonies that had been a part of the Ritual of the Humanish. He had glanced down at his slender limbs, and seen the faint phosphorescence and had grinned: *so there is something that even the Ritual cannot quench* . . .

Now, standing with the Monk in the dark vastness of the ancient, deserted Castle, there was no luminosity, no faint glimmer of phosphorescence. No light at all. *There was no light* . . .

Then I am closer to the line dividing Humanish from *sidh* than is safe. Panic brushed him with icy fingers. I am so close to the line that I no longer have the light! And then: *perhaps the line has already been crossed* . . .

He thrust the thought from him, and began to move purposefully along the dark passage, Quintus at his side. They had reached some kind of intersection – Maelduin thought they might be nearing the sculleries which would be lower than the hall for coolness – when a movement from the hall stopped them. Maelduin felt ice form at the pit of his stomach, and there was a moment when he wanted to run away. I could be out of here, I could be astride the horse, and out into the night! I could be inside Tiarna and trying to shed the Humanish cloak, the ivory bones . . .

And then he remembered that Tiarna was dying, that it might already be dead, and that he was bound to the world of the

Humanish for as long as it took to regain the *sidh*'s ancient music. He struggled for mastery, but within the space of time it had taken the thoughts to tumble through his mind, Quintus had turned and was already running back to the stone hall, towards the source of the sound. Maelduin thought: for all his sinister history, he does not lack courage. He followed the Monk quickly, trying not to notice the dense blackness of the shadows, trying not to remember that once he could have lifted a hand and seen the faint shimmer of elvish light.

At the centre of the hall, the cloth that Maelduin had used to cover the cage had been thrown back, and the cage itself lay in sticks of gleaming light across the floor. Broken. Discarded.

'Then the creature has escaped,' said Maelduin very softly, and turned to rake the shadows.

'I am here, sidh *Prince . . .*

Maelduin stood very still, and felt the cold horror trickling down his spine again, for although the Prince was speaking aloud, and although the speech was comprehensible, although it was ordinary Humanish speech, the words were clumsy and pronounced in a brutal, ugly manner.

Maelduin saw again the birth-chamber at the Porphyry Palace; the monster-Prince's flat lips, the gills in its neck, the jaw that was neither quite Humanish nor piscine.

It was not shaped for Humanish speech . . .

He remembered how one of the terrible legends surrounding Coelacanth told how he had had to learn Humanish speech from the necromancers before he could enter the Humanish world.

And this is Coelacanth's son . . .

'You thought to imprison me, Maelduin,' said the voice, and Maelduin heard more clearly this time how it was struggling to form the words and the syllables; how it was using a method of communication that was unnatural to it. He found himself thinking of Humanish deformities: of cleft palates and roofless mouths and of empty, gaping gullets that could not close properly on the clumsy homespun mechanics of Humanish speech.

He stayed where he was, Quintus at his side, both of them trying to penetrate the shadows. Maelduin caught a slithering movement near to the stair. Over there? Yes!

'Do not try to touch me,' said the Prince, and now the slurring

426

had faded a little. It is already learning how to make itself understood, thought Maelduin, and remembered, with horror, that Coelacanth had spent months – perhaps years – in studying Humanish speech. Coelacanth's spawn was learning it in minutes.

'Do not try to injure me,' said the Prince again, and as they stood, motionless, it moved from the shadows, and stood in the shifting, thin moonlight, its evil eyes malevolent. Maelduin saw that the membraneous fin was spread out behind it, erect; grotesque in one so young.

'Young only in Humanish time,' said the Prince, and Maelduin heard with a shudder how it could not quite manage the *y* of *young*; how its flat mouth and jawless face did not close properly over the *m* in *time*.

The creature moved forward across the stone floor with its slithering gait, and as Quintus stepped towards it, it rounded on him, the gills in its neck opening and closing.

'Do not approach me, Monk,' it said, hissing faintly. 'Do not approach me, or I shall call down the chains that bound you to the Dark Lords.' It studied Quintus, and the evil amusement bubbled from its tone. '*Shall* I call them down, Monk?' it said. 'It would amuse me to do so, I think.'

Maelduin thought: it has still not quite mastered it. It still cannot quite reproduce Humanish speech.

'But I am learning, *sidh*, I am learning,' said the slurred deformed voice. 'I shall learn a little each day. I shall learn as my father did, until I can walk unchallenged amongst the Humanish.' Its eyes slewed back to Quintus. 'But while I am learning,' said the Fisher Prince, 'I must be served.' It fixed Quintus with its baleful glare.

Quintus backed away, and Maelduin caught the swift movement as the monk threw up a hand to deflect the creature's icy malevolence.

'You are accustomed to serving,' said the Prince, and now its voice dripped with a horrid, phlegmy note. Maelduin, sickened, thought: it is striving for the pitch of Humanish.

'You are accustomed to serving,' said the Prince again. 'That will suit me very well.' It moved again, and Maelduin saw it lift its webbed hands upwards. Almost before it had completed the gesture, great heavy black chains, immense manacles and gyves, had formed from the clustering shadows and slithered across the floor to Quintus.

The Monk fell back, his face distorted, but the chains coiled about his ankles, and so heavy and so cruelly thick were they that he sank to his knees, unable to stand for the dragging weight. There was the hiss of metal, and tiny spirals of smoke rose from the iron where the chains had fused.

'Chained,' said the Prince, its thick, slurry voice licking the word with pleasure. 'Chained by the ancient forgings of the *nimfeach* to do my pleasure. A good spell.' It pointed to the doors through which they had entered, its webbed hands making a flapping sound. 'Out to the stables, Monk, and make ready the trappings of your servitude.'

'My servitude . . .' Quintus's face was drained of every vestige of colour and his eyes were deep black pits.

The Fisher Prince said, 'I shall need victims to feed on. Prey. *Humanish* prey. Warm fresh blood and tender young flesh to devour. Whole, unspoiled bodies.' Its monstrous, lipless fishmouth stretched open, and the flat eyes gleamed. 'You will become adept again,' said the Prince. 'You served the Lord of Chaos and the Lady of Almhuin, and now you will serve me.' It moved closer to Quintus. 'And my appetites are large, Monk,' it said in a slimy, insinuating whisper, the sibilants hissing again.

Quintus said in a low voice, 'I will never serve you, filth.'

The Prince did not move, but the repulsive mouth opened again in a gulping, swallowing motion. The gills in its neck gaped, revealing slimy white under-flesh.

'Your Teacher,' hissed the Prince, 'the upstart Nazarene, whom you revere so highly, knew of many lessons and many punishments. And amongst the meaningless writings of his people, is recorded a punishment used many times by the old gods.' The creature paused and Maelduin heard how it was curling its loathsome tongue more agilely about the unfamiliar cadences of speech now.

With the thought, the knowledge of the real Cadence slipped into his mind, and he sought for the gentle silver radiance. But even as he did so, the remembrance of how his own inner radiance had dimmed in the dark passages flooded his mind, and he thought: I cannot! The light has dimmed!

The Prince was still studying Quintus. 'You know the

pronouncement, perhaps?' it said. 'It is one that my father used against those whom he wished to snare into serving him. It bound even the *nimfeach* themselves at one time.' And then, as Quintus stared unflinchingly back, the creature whispered in its clotted voice, the words of the old and terrible malediction.

'"*They shall be accursed, and they shall be afflicted with a terrible burning in their privily parts, so that they shall be forced to douse them in the cooling bodies of women . . . but there will be no relief for them . . . And sores and buboes shall fester them so that all shall shrink from them . . . Cancers and blisters shall festoon their bodies . . . And they shall crawl the earth like the lowest, laidliest worms . . .*"'

Before the Prince had finished speaking, the black chains coiled like thick black snakes, dragging Quintus down to the cold stone of the floor, so that he was lying on his front. Maelduin, horrified, saw sudden pain twist his face, and something very like despair flood his dark eyes.

'A *burning*, Monk,' said the Prince, its face distorted with evil glee. 'Does it hurt? Does it burn and itch? Do you ache for the embrace of women? But what of the rest of the curse? What of the final, subtle, exquisite agony?'

In the thin light that still silvered the floor, Quintus's pale skin began to bubble and split as if a great heat was bursting it open. Thick fluid oozed out, and then ceased, and instantly the split skin began to dry and to crust over with ugly scabs, leprous and so utterly repulsive that Maelduin, who had thought himself armoured against most things, felt his stomach churn with nausea He watched, helplessly, as Quintus tried to stand.

They shall crawl the earth like laidly worms . . .

Laidly worms, thought Maelduin, staring at the squirming, struggling thing that was Quintus. The Prince has made of him a repulsive worm, and he will be forced to crawl like this, he will be forced to endure those evil, suppurating sores, and the terrible burning desires until the creature chooses to release him.

'That is to ensure you do not cheat me,' hissed the Prince. 'To ensure that, even if you try to despoil the creatures you snare for me, they will recoil from you. And now go out and find the trappings of your servitude, Monk. Go out and make your bed where you may, and find, if you will, creatures who will not shudder from you, even in the darkest night. Satiate your hungers where you can.' The short squat figure seemed to tower above them suddenly. 'But bring me Humanish victims!' screeched the Prince, its slurry voice out of control now, spittle flying from the flat, piscine jaw. 'Bring me the beasts of the ocean so that I may satiate my lusts! Bring me creatures that I may devour slowly. Creatures whose juices I can suck and in whose blood I can wallow.' The gulping mouth opened and closed again, but the webbed hand moved impatiently, indicating the oaken doors. 'Begone from my sight, foul thing, and be about my work!' it cried and, as it did so, Quintus gathered the great black chains up, and half crawled, half scuttled across the moon-washed stone flags, and into the dark night outside.

There was a long silence. Maelduin's eyes were fixed on the Prince and his mind was churning.

The Prince was grinning, the fish-eyes resting on Maelduin with piercing malignancy. Maelduin knew at once that it possessed the *Stroicim Inchinn*, the forbidden dark underside of the Samhailt, which enabled the possessor to claw into the mind of an enemy, to tear out deeply buried thoughts and emotions, and to plant alien thoughts and emotions in their stead. The Prince had not needed to acquire it slowly and painfully as most of the Dark Lords did; he had been born knowing it, he would have inherited the knowledge from his terrible sire.

He lowered his eyes at once, but it was too late; he could already feel the cold pincers of the *Stroicim Inchinn* probing deep into his mind, searching out his weaknesses . . .

Your will is mine, sidh *Prince . . . Your will must bend to mine, son of the Elven King . . .*

Maelduin struggled against the dark, overwhelming tide of the creature's mind. It was like plunging breast-deep into an icy cold river, it was like falling fathoms down into a dark, bottomless well, it was every dark, desolate thing ever felt or sensed or feared . . .

Old, evil darkness, creeping from its hole . . .

I am drowning in the creature's darkness, thought Maelduin, fighting desperately, clawing upwards for a shred of light, a sliver of moonglow, a thin, tenuous thread of the Cadence.

430

. . . ancient, terrible blackness stealing over its prey . . .

Through the dark mist that was obscuring his vision, Maelduin was aware that the great fishmaw was gaping again, stretching impossibly wide, gusting the sickening stench of rotting fish and decaying flesh into his nostrils. It loomed nearer and nearer, and he thought: he is eating my mind! He is leaving my body, but he is eating my mind . . .

He was aware of his mind, his being, the tiny core that was ineluctably himself, being drawn nearer and nearer into that thick, lipless mouth, and he clutched desperately at the Cadence.

I am the Crown Prince . . . You will never send me into the darkness . . .

But the light was far from him now; it was beyond his reach, behind the spiked darkness of the Fisher Prince's evil powers.

There was a final wrenching, a moment of such complete agony at the core of his being, that he heard himself cry out.

The darkness closed about him and awareness drained away.

Chapter Thirty-seven

The Amaranths thought it was just as well that they had found wine and provisions in the west wing, because their sojourn there was beginning to seem as if it might be much longer than any of them had anticipated.

They had marshalled their forces in readiness for the attack by the Fer Caille and the Black HeartStealers seriously and efficiently. They had held a hasty discussion, with everyone seated round the long table in the west wing, because it was as well to be prepared for every eventuality, and it was as well to have some kind of battle plan. They had all looked expectantly at Neit and Manannan mac Lir, because wasn't this the whole point of having them there. As Cerball said, they could probably have worked out a plan on their own account, but they did not want to be impolite to their important guests.

Herself of Mugain said that, if their important guests could find a way to defeat the NightCloak, it would be the first time in Ireland's history, and they were all wasting their time, but nobody paid this much attention. As Great-aunt Fuamnach pointed out, they could not just sit up here in the west wing – nasty dusty place – with their hands folded, with black evil rampaging about below. She glared at Herself as she said this, and demanded of Cerball what was to be done. Cerball, who was beginning to feel beleaguered on all sides, said it behoved them all to put up a show of bravery, and the Mugain tucked in his chins and looked wise and said to his way of thinking, they'd be needing to put up a bit of a fight for themselves, what did Bodb Decht and Cerball think?

'Well, our two guests do not appear to be contributing a very great deal,' said Bodb Decht cautiously.

'They aren't contributing at all,' said Great-aunt Fuamnach.

'It's a difficult situation,' put in Cerball.

'Very.'

None of them quite liked to say that the two gods were being of no help at all, and that the invoking of the ancient and precious Ritual of the Key had been pretty much of a useless exercise.

The Mugain had remembered a spell to call up the Four Winds. 'See now, couldn't we try that? That would cause some havoc.'

'If only we had the Cadence,' groaned Cerball.

'Well, we haven't. We'll make do with our own knowledge. Let's think now, do we need the Incantation of the Storm, or is it the Tempest Runes?'

Calatin and the younger cousins were planning on a concerted rush. 'Off down the stairs and lay about them with our swords,' said Calatin, brandishing his own sword by way of illustration, but doing it a bit awkwardly because of his injured arm.

'There will be time for that when we have turned back the NightMares,' said Neit, smiling at Calatin rather indulgently. 'When you are a little better versed in these things, you will understand about wars. First things first, young sir,' he added, and Calatin, who had been all ready to accord Neit a wholly uncritical admiration, turned bright red and stared at the floor.

And then Cecht, who had been standing near to the door, held up a hand and said, 'Listen.'

'What is it?'

'I can't hear anything. What's going on . . .'

'Oh do hush, Cecht thinks something's starting to happen.'

'Well, tell those noisy cousins of Calatin to stop chanting battle cries.'

Great-aunt Fuamnach thumped the floor with her stick to stop the younger cousins from chanting things like, 'Death to the invaders' and 'Drown them in boiling oil' and 'Ireland for the Amaranths'. Calatin had even remembered an old battle song of some long-ago warrior called CuChulainn, and was rehearsing it with the twins. You could go very valiantly into a battle with a good rousing war song.

But they all fell silent, and Bodb Decht, going quickly to where Cecht stood still listening intently, said, in a low voice, 'There's something creeping up the stairs.'

* * *

433

Something creeping up the stairs. Something slithery and slimy, and something that flopped wetly and squirmed and then sniffed at the door into the gallery. But something that had rattling claws as well, and was scratching at the closed and Sealed door leading into the gallery. The Amaranths held their breath, and waited.

Calatin said, very softly, 'If it's an ordinary mortal force we can kill it,' and at his side, the Mugain said, 'And if it's a nasty spell of some kind, we can blast it with lightning bolts.'

'Cerball and the Mugain are calling up the Four Winds.'

'If they can remember the Incantation.'

The creeping, slithering thing was fumbling at the door-latch now, and there was a nauseating stench of old blood and rotting meat and vegetation that has turned slimy and brackish.

Neit was standing at the centre of the room, his eyes on the door, a tiny frown creasing his brow. Cerball, who had left the Mugain to finish the Incantation to the Four Winds, thought: I suppose he *does* know about battles and wars, does he? and at once, Manannan mac Lir, who was standing next to him, said very softly:

'Do not be too sure of it, my friend.' And then, as Cerball looked up sharply, 'He *does* rely rather heavily on his reputation, you know,' said Manannan blandly.

Cerball said, 'But he was sent to us – you were both sent to us when we used the Key . . .'

'Oh, *that*.' Manannan's eyes went to Neit. 'The truth is that our father is usually so glad to get rid of any of us for a time that he sends us down here willy-nilly whenever anyone calls for help. And then goes off on his own ploys,' he added. 'And you wouldn't *believe* some of the things he—'

'But the Key . . .' said Cerball, so aghast that he broke in on Manannan's words, which he would not normally have done, on account of Manannan being a God and one of the Dagda's sons to boot. 'We had the legendary Key to the Dagda's Temple—'

'And very nice too,' said Manannan approvingly, as if they were discussing a possible supper dish. He glanced at Cerball mischievously. 'There are a number of such things, of course,' he said. 'Keys to unlock doors, and Mirrors and Forest Pools to be stared into. All of them are supposed to summon my family, although I don't know that any one of them works above another when you come down to it. And then of course there're Golden Horns to be blown – my sisters were always *very* rude about those, because for all Neit's golden strength and muscular build, and for all he would have you believe *otherwise*, he is *very* poorly endowed.'

'Ah. Indeed?'

'Oh yes. *I'm* the one our father sends if there's any *wooing* to be done,' said Manannan, puffing out his chest a bit, and Cerball, who felt the situation sliding from his grasp all over again, looked worriedly to where the Mugain was determinedly chanting the Tempest Runes.

It was Calatin who said, in an urgent cry, 'It's opening the door! The thing outside, it's opening the door!' He looked round. 'To arms, everyone!'

'Death to the Black HeartStealers!' cried the cousins, and Calatin brandished his sword again, his face set and his eyes shining with excitement.

'Destruction to Ireland's enemies!'

'Confusion to the Dark Realm!' shouted the twins.

'The Four Winds' Spell!' cried Cerball. 'Mugain, what—'

But there was no time to remember the Spell to the Four Winds, and there was no use in relying on it, even if the Mugain had been anywhere near finishing it.

The door to the disused gallery was pushed open very slowly. It inched its way open, with the tortuous creaking of seldom-used hinges. A wavering, blurry light slid into the gallery, and a huge amorphous shadow fell across the floor. Cecht and the twins, standing together, grasped one another's hands, and Great-aunt Fuamnach took a firmer grasp on her stick.

Slowly, with a crawling, groping movement, a great jagged-nailed hand slid around the edges of the door, the fingers curling about the edge of the wood, the movement horridly copied by the black shadow. In the deep darkness beyond the door, there was the rasp of clawed feet, and then, above that, the sound of hoarse breathing.

Something in the hall . . . Something fearsome and monstrous standing in the dark shadows watching them and awaiting its chance to burst through the door and get them . . .

The shadow of the thing lay blackly across the gallery floor, crepitating slightly, stumplike protruberances sprouting from its upper half, as if it were trying to grow rudimentary arms.

Cerball, standing with the Mugain and Bodb Decht, Calatin and the younger ones with them, stared at the black void with horrified expressions and pounding hearts. *What had the Fer Caille sent to them? What was standing there in the shadows, listening and watching . . . ?*

No one moved. Everyone stared helplessly at the blackened, horny nails of the monstrous hand that had crept round it, and at the bloated-looking skin of the thick, fleshy fingers.

At last Cerball, who could not bear it any longer, said, 'If there is anything there, come out and fight!' And was pleased to hear that his voice sounded really rather fierce.

'Come out and fight the Royal Amaranth Sorcerers,' he added, and was just thinking that this sounded even better, when Bodb Decht said, 'I don't think there's anything there at all.'

'But it's—'

'Don't you understand? It's beginning,' said Bodb Decht. 'It's part of the NightMares.'

Cerball started to say, 'Oh, but . . .' and stopped.

Great-aunt Fuamnach said, 'Well *something*'s climbed those stairs, whether it's a NightMare or a plain ordinary demon.'

'Yes, but whatever's there isn't anything *temporal*,' said Bodb Decht. And then, in a worried voice, 'Or is it?'

A dreadful throaty chuckle came from beyond the door and Cerball, firmly grasping what little courage he had left, took a step closer to the door and said, 'Who are you?'

There was a brief silence, and then they heard the hoarse chuckling and the harsh, difficult breathing again. And then, '*I am Tromlui, a Servant of the NightCloak*,' said a throaty, whispering voice that made Cecht and the twins jump back.

'*When a sorcerer with sufficient power invokes the Cloak's forces, then I am woken . . .*' The gloating chuckle broke from it again.

Bodb Decht said, half to himself, '*Tromlui*, meaning "a nightmare creature" . . .' and they heard Tromlui's quickened, excited breathing again.

'*Yes, Amaranth, that is what I am.*

'*I am every NightMare you have ever encountered . . . Every dark slithering beast and every horned creature you have ever feared . . . Every slimed, loathsome reptile, and every squirming giant worm . . .*

436

'*I carry the seeds of each and every race within me. I am Giant and Hobgoblin and serpent and snake . . . I am the faceless Ogre who chased you across the blood-red landscape, and I am the huge clanking machinery with the Humanish face that will waddle across the bedchamber to gobble you up . . .*

'*Fear I am, and terror also, and every distortion and every warped being that has ever haunted your dreams, so that you woke drenched in sweat, reaching thankfully for the night candle so that its light would chase away the shadows and its warmth would dry the cold fear on your bodies . . .*'

There was a pause, and again came the wheezing, wet-lung breathing, and the clotted laughter.

'*But supposing you awoke and I was still there?*' whispered Tromlui, and the blurred shadow palpitated again with evil amusement.

'*Supposing you fought your way out of your terror-ridden slumbers, and found that I was still with you? Crouching in the shadows, slithering beneath the bed-covers . . . The dark cloak you have hung in your cupboard that will suddenly rear up to smother you . . . The gown you have laid on the chair-back that will gather up its folds and glide noiselessly to strangle you . . .*'

'A lot of rot,' said Great-aunt Fuamnach loudly, and thumped the floor with her stick.

'Of course it is. See now—'

'*Are you sure I am not with you now?*' said Tromlui, its snuffling, bubbling breathing seeming to creep nearer. '*Are you sure that I do not already lurk unseen in the corners of the room, peering at you, ready to pounce? Perhaps I have an axe already dripping with blood, or perhaps I have a razor to slash your pretty Humanish flesh to tatters . . . I like Humanish flesh,*' said the wheezing, phlegmy voice, and Cecht and the twins shuddered.

'Pay it no attention,' directed Cerball. 'Nasty whispery thing.'

'Why doesn't it come out into the open and fight honestly?' demanded the Mugain.

'*I shall come,*' whispered the creature. '*I shall certainly come, my dears . . .*' it went on. '*And when I do, I shall fold the pretty little Amaranth ladies in my embrace.*' The greed clotted its voice. '*Ripe for my embraces,*' it said. '*Perhaps I shall creep into their beds when it is dark and the Humanish world sleeps, and perhaps I shall press my noseless face to theirs, and push my skinless body close to their warm, soft flesh...'*

Cecht and the twins gasped, and clutched one another's hands, and Calatin took a firmer grip on his sword.

The Mugain said, very loudly, to the room in general, 'I don't think we believe in any of this, do we? The NightCloak was always on the side of the *True* Ireland. I don't give much credence to it serving the necromancers.'

'That's quite right,' said Cerball, gamely backing the Mugain, but still casting worried glances to the half-open door. 'I've never even heard of Tromlui,' he said firmly.

'One of the northern lot, I shouldn't wonder,' put in Great-aunt Fuamnach, as if this dealt with Tromlui and there was nothing more to worry about. 'I daresay we could banish it in a gnat's eyeblink. Bodb Decht?'

Bodb Decht said, 'The NightCloak was created by the first Amaranths for Ireland's first Queen, and as such has always been used by those practising only pure sorcery.'

Great-aunt Fuamnach had started to say that this disposed of Tromlui, when the creature laughed derisively. The Amaranths heard at once that the throaty, snuffling note had vanished, and that now it was the hungry and over-powering laugh of the nearly-extinct Giantish race.

'I did tell you, Amaranths, that I possessed the blood of all the races,' it said, and now its words were impossibly loud, magnified a dozen times. *'Perhaps I shall summon my Giantish blood, and my Ogre-ish appetites,'* it blared. *'Perhaps I shall scent the blood of Humans and crush them in my great fists and pound their bones for my bread...'*

Cecht, who was standing with her arms about the twins, thought it was the kind of laugh that said: o-ho and ha-ha, here is *Manflesh* and here are *Humans* for the supper table. It was the kind of sinister laugh that made you think of things like seven-league boots, that could stride across the land and catch you no matter how fast you ran, or of coarse, Ogreish faces that leered and smacked their lips in anticipation of eating you, and of huge Giantish fists that came down and crushed your bones in their hands...

And then the dreadful hoarse whispering died away, and the thick grotesque shadow became very still. Cecht thought: it has not gone, it is still there, watching and listening, but its attention has been diverted. And could not decide whether to be glad about this, or afraid of what might have caught Tromlui's attention sufficiently strongly.

The Mugain, who happened to be nearest to the windows, caught a flicker of movement from down in the courtyard, and turned at once.

'What is it?' said Cerball, half turning to see. 'What have you seen?'

The Mugain said, in a whisper, 'There's something down there in the courtyard.'

'What sort of something?'

'I don't know.'

Calatin walked determinedly across to the window, deliberately turning his back on the partly open door, and clambered on to the window-seat to look down, because although he was actually extremely frightened of the unseen creature's whispering (*huge, clanking gobbling machinery*, it had said, and Calatin had felt rather sick), he was not going to let anyone know he was frightened.

In fact, several people had followed him to the windows, which was remarkably comforting, and were beside him staring down into the shadowy courtyard directly below.

'I can hear hoofbeats,' said Great-aunt Fuamnach, who liked to let everyone know that her hearing was as sharp as ever it had been.

'*Muffled* hoofbeats,' said the Mugain.

'As if the hoofs are covered with a thick cloth.'

'Or as if they are cloven,' said Bodb Decht, his face suddenly white.

Cloven hoofs . . . Dark shadowy beasts pouring through the night towards the Porphyry Palace, pounding the ground with cloven hoofs.

Cerball said, 'What's that?'

'Where?'

'Over there.' He pointed to the far corners of the courtyard, where a low stone arch led out to the surrounding countryside. 'There's something moving out there,' he said. 'It's—'

'It's horses,' said Bodb Decht in a whisper. 'Dozens of them. Black rearing stallions with red eyes and cloven hoofs.'

'They're each pulling a chariot,' said Calatin, staring in horrified fascination.

Bodb Decht said, 'And in each of the chariots is something dark and shapeless . . .' He turned sharply as the thick chuckle of Tromlui sounded from behind the door again.

'*So unlearned you are, Amaranths . . . You are seeing the Beasts of the NightCloak bringing with them my brethren . . .*'

Bodb Decht said in a voice from which the breath had been driven, 'The NightMare Stallions. And they are bringing the creatures of the NightMares with them.'

They were pouring into the courtyard, their slanting red eyes glinting in the shadows, their skins gleaming like polished ebony. They were sinisterly beautiful and darkly menacing, and they dragged with them the foul miasma of the terrible Black Ireland.

The NightMare Stallions, answering the summoning of the legendary NightCloak of the High Queens of Ireland . . .

Each one drew a black chariot with huge, viciously spiked wheels, and the Dark Star of Necromancy glinted on their prows. The wheels of each chariot were clogged and fouled with gobbets of blood and with trailing, slimed skeins of flesh and mangled bones.

The Mugain said softly, 'The NightMares are said to gallop across the fields of battle carrying death and mutilation with them. Whoever can enlist them as allies is believed fortunate.' He stared down at the massing stallions. 'They can call up not only the Lord of Chaos's henchmen, but the lesser creatures of war,' he said, and at his side, Bodb Decht said, 'Chaos's henchmen: Murder, Anarchy and Misrule.'

'Yes. But also there are Mutilation and Agony and Spite and . . . I forget them all,' said the Mugain.

'Torment, Thirst, Starvation,' said Cerball, frowning in an effort of memory.

'And Loss and Despair, isn't it?'

'Yes. And there're several more as well. The NightMares draw them to the battlefields. They'll be down there now,' said Cerball, his eyes still on the courtyard.

Neit pushed back a lock of hair with one hand and said, 'Oh, I have met *those* ones many times.'

'And defeated them, brother dear?' inquired Manannan mac Lir sweetly.

'They're nasty creatures.' Great-aunt Fuamnach could not be doing with such things. 'WarMongers we used to call them in my younger days. Now then, Cerball, those things are rampaging through the courtyard.' She eyed Cerball and the Mugain sternly. 'They'll be inside the Palace at any minute. What are we doing about them?'

The Stallions were beneath the windows of the west wing now, smoke pouring from their flared nostrils, the fetid stench rising like poisonous fumes from a swamp. They tossed their heads, so that the silver and black harnesses rang out coldly on the night air, and their cloven hoofs stamped the ground impatiently.

The Amaranths could not see the occupants of the chariots fully, but as they stood looking down, they caught glimpses of terrible and fearsome beings.

Giants and Ogres with brutish, greedy faces and coarse red lips . . . Squat stubby lumps of metal and iron that would waddle after their victims, their steeltrap mouths snapping hungrily, their grinding, threshing machinery whirring and gobbling. *All the better to mince you with* . . .

In the far chariots, they could see horrendous mutilations, creatures with their skulls split and with eyes dangling on the ends of bright red strings. Creatures with their skins bubbling and festering with plague and disease and filth. Others with their skulls sliced off at the top, so that their exposed brains pulsated and heaved . . .

'The NightMares,' said Bodb Decht, leaning over as far as he could. 'They have not quite solidified, but they are there in their embryo forms.' He glanced back and saw the twins shudder. 'Nasty,' he said gently. 'But we shall find a way to beat them.'

The chariots were forming themselves into a circle, and they could see that several of them held creeping snakes with serpents' heads, and cauldrons of turbulent oil that would boil and ferment over the sides, scalding any who went near. Close by were huge spiders with the heads of Men, and scaly-skinned, batlike reptiles with great gristly jointed legs and arms.

At the far side of the circle of dark chariots, they could see thin grey beings, skin-covered skeletons with hungry, reaching fingers and empty eyes.

'The WarMongers,' said Great-aunt Fuamnach grimly.

'Mutilation and Torment and Hunger and Thirst,' said Cerball.

'Yes. Present on every battlefield.' Bodb Decht was looking very solemn. 'Not only has the Fer Caille summoned the NightMares, he has also summoned the creatures of war.' He stepped back from the window and regarded the Amaranths sternly. 'I don't think we can fight against this,' he said. 'The Fer Caille and his followers are sending the strongest forces of the Dark Realm against us. He is determined to take the Amaranth Palace at all costs.'

There was a moment of terrible silence. Then Cerball said, 'You are not – surely you are not suggesting surrender?'

'I hope he is not!' said Great-aunt Fuamnach at once. 'Surrender! Well, you'll do so over my dead body, Cerball!' She stumped across the room and sat down at thee table, glaring.

Cerball said, 'Of course we do not surrender. Only . . .' He sent a desperate look to Neit and Manannan mac Lir, who had taken no part in the rush to the window, but had stayed within the room.

'Yes, but you know, I don't think we can fight those things,' said the Mugain, and paid no heed to his lady who tutted crossly, and wished that Himself would not show such defeatism. 'We should be overpowered in minutes,' said the Mugain. 'I am only being practical,' he added, and Herself sniffed and remembered that her dear mother had frequently said that the Mugains possessed a lily-livered streak.

Cerball turned angrily to Neit and Manannan mac Lir. 'Do something!' he cried, flinging out his hands. 'We called on you for help! Help us!'

'They are at the main entrance,' said Calatin suddenly. 'Listen – can't you hear them? Cerball, Mugain – we can't simply stand here and wait for them to come pouring in . . . He grasped his sword and strode to the door, and at once the terrible black mass that was Tromlui's shadow lurched menacingly. There was the sound of grinding machinery, a rhythmic, clanking, grating sound, and Calatin turned rather pale, and fell back as if he had been struck.

Cerball was looking at the two gods. 'Help us,' he said.

'Yes, but we cannot fight the creatures of the NightCloak!' said Neit, and then, rallying, said, 'Even *I* cannot do so. Those things are the brethren of Tromlui! They possess black sorcery of the strongest kind!'

Great-aunt Fuamnach started to say that Gods of War who were afeared of Tromlui, whoever he might be, were neither use nor ornament to folk, but Cerball, who was back at the window, said, 'They are searching for a way in! All of you! Look!'

The terrible black stallions, the fearsome NightMares of the Dark Realm, were rearing up, pawing the air with their wicked split hoofs, whinnying derisively. They turned about, their silken black manes rippling behind them, the dark chariots with their grisly burdens sending sparks shooting from their huge wheels. The horrified Amaranths saw the dripping, ravaged creatures begin to emerge from the depths of the black chariots, and swarm across the stones of the courtyard.

'The Four Winds' Spell!' cried Calatin. 'Mugain . . .'

'It will be useless,' said Manannan mac Lir, his eyes on the terrible creatures below. 'Already Tromlui has broken the Seals. You are at the creatures' mercy.'

The NightMares were shrieking in triumph now, the disease-ridden faces of the WarMongers avid and greedy. The maimed and mutilated creatures who were spilling from the chariots were leaping on to the backs of the Human-visaged spiders, bridling the creeping snakes and serpents, clinging to their backs and forcing them to carry their grisly burdens into the Palace. The creatures that Great-aunt Fuamnach had identified as WarMongers were running and scuttling across the ground, several of them swarming straight up the sheer Palace walls, climbing easily and swiftly. From the half-open door, Tromlui chuckled, and there was the sound of clawed, leathery hands being rubbed together.

'*All the better to eat you, my dears . . .*'

The Amaranths stared at each other, knowing that it could be only minutes before they would be facing the NightMares and the fearsome WarMongers. Tromlui's great black shadow swelled and crepitated with malicious anticipation, and the twins, standing with Cecht and Calatin, clung together, white-faced.

'Tromlui is taking shape,' whispered Cecht. 'The NightMare Stallions are giving him strength and life.'

'*All the better to* embrace *you, my dear*,' came the throaty whisper, and there was the sudden sound of claws scratching on the timbers of the floor outside the gallery.

'There must be something we can do!' cried Cerball, staring about him in anguish. 'There must be something!'

Neit said, 'There might be a way . . .' And glanced at his brother, who said impatiently, 'Oh get on with it, Neit, and let us be rid of these disgusting creatures!'

'What can you do!' cried Cerball. 'If there is something you can do, then do it at once!'

'Yes, he *always* drags out the anticipation. I remember the King of the Marshes—'

'I am thinking of a plan,' said Neit, disdainfully.

'Can we not simply deny the creatures' existences?' said Cecht, suddenly. 'If we simply refuse to believe in them . . . They are only NightMares,' said Cecht angrily. 'Not real at all.'

'Yes, surely they can exist only if we believe in their existence,' said the Mugain.

'The WarMongers are real,' said Manannan mac Lir. 'Mutilation and Spite and Agony . . .'

Bodb Decht said, slowly, 'If we could put ourselves beyond their reach . . .'

'How?' said Neit, and even in the heat of the moment, the Amaranths shared the thought that Neit was really rather stupid.

'By sending themselves into a deep slumber of course,' said Manannan mac Lir impatiently. 'Dear me, I should have thought that even *you* would have thought of that, Neit!' He turned to Cerball and the Mugain. 'I believe you have the answer,' he said, and his eyes were suddenly bright.

Cecht said, very softly, 'The gods help those who help themselves,' and Manannan shot her an approving look.

'Precisely, my dear,' he said. And then, turning back to Cerball and Bodb Decht, 'It's the only way you'll defeat them,' he said, and now his voice was authoritative. 'Don't wait for that fool.' He indicated Neit contemptuously. 'If you do, it'll be the Battle against the King of the Marshes all over again.'

Bodb Decht said, 'The *Draoicht Suan*—'

'Yes,' Manannan looked at them. 'The Enchantment of Deepest Slumber. Swift and simple. And an enchantment so light-filled, that the Fer Caille and his armies will never dissolve it.'

'In any case, the *Draoicht Suan* can only be dissolved by those who spin it,' put in Cerball.

'Yes,' said Manannan. 'Do it,' he said. 'It's the only way! You can each direct the spell to one another. And once inside the *Suan*, once *properly* inside it, you'll be beyond the reach of the NightMares and Tromlui.'

Cecht said, 'But the *Draoicht Suan* is so strong that we shall all succumb to it as soon as it is pronounced . . .'

'Yes?'

'That means there will be no one left awake to dissolve the spell when the danger has passed.' She looked at them, her eyes huge and fearful.

'But we can't leave anyone awake,' said Cerball. 'Anyone left unenchanted by the *Suan* would be horribly vulnerable. Whoever we left would quite certainly be killed and his soul taken into the Dark Realm for Chaos.'

'I volunteer to die,' said Calatin promptly, and was told by Great-aunt Fuamnach to be quiet and not to be foolish.

'We shan't leave anyone to die,' said Cerball. 'We have to put ourselves beyond the reach of the Nightmares and the Warmongers. We have to lock ourselves inside a light-filled sleep of our own spinning. Because,' he said, looking very solemn, 'we know that the NightMares will never penetrate the *Draoicht Suan*. We shall have to pronounce it and take our chance on the rest.'

'But once we're inside the Enchantment it could be days – years even – before we awake.' . . .

'Then,' said Cerball, rather grimly, 'we shall simply have to stay asleep for years.' His eyes went over them all. 'Is everyone here? There's no time to lose now. Ready?'

The Mugain said, 'Who knows the incantation best?'

'We all know it.' Cerball looked round. 'I think we should all pronounce it. It'll be stronger that way.'

'And therefore deeper.'

'Exactly. And if we form a circle, we can each of us direct it to the person in front of us.'

'Are we ready?' said Cerball again, and raised his hand. 'Exactly in unison now.'

The Amaranths moved silently into a circle, their palms raised upwards, their faces intent.

And then Cerball brought his hand down, and the gentle, strong chant of the ancient *Draoicht Suan* flooded the disused west wing.

Chapter Thirty-eight

It was only when Andrew had finally fallen into a deep, calm slumber, and Rumour was sure that she had managed to quench the pain, that she summoned every ounce of her strength and descended to Almhuin's bath-house once more.

The Lady had not moved since Rumour had caged her; she had simply crouched in her cage, the blood-caked hair tousled and curtaining her face. But now, as Rumour entered, and as the torchlight fell across the blood-smeared stone flags, she looked up, snarling and trying to strike out at Rumour with bloodied, talon-tipped hands.

Rumour stood in the centre of the room and regarded the creature. She saw that there was already a film over the Lady's great pit-like eyes, and understood at once that the light was already quenching this creature who had for so long served darkness. The knowledge lent her extra strength, and she was able to stand before the creature calmly.

'Well, madame,' said Rumour. 'It seems that the time has come to make your imprisonment a little more secure.'

For answer, the Lady spat and sprang at the bars, her long pale fingers curling about them.

'Useless,' said Rumour crisply. 'My sorcery is too strong for you. The bars of light will hold.' She studied the creature. 'I am considered to be really rather good, you know,' said Rumour.

'You are considered to be the whore of the Amaranth House,' said the Lady in a voice of icy fury.

'Am I really? Now that pleases me enormously.' Rumour moved round the room thoughtfully. 'I do think it is gratifying to know that one's reputation has preceded one. You, on the other hand, are really hardly known at all outside your Realm, are you? It's such a pity, my dear, because I do think you could have had quite a *useful* career if you had not been so vain.'

447

'Chaos will send his Armies against you,' snarled the Lady. 'The Fomoire will already have returned to his Castle to report that Almhuin is in the hands of an Amaranth. And,' she said, with sudden vicious hatred, 'he will certainly know *which* Amaranth.'

'Oh yes,' said Rumour at once, but a swift, small smile lifted her lips. Of course Chaos would know which Amaranth. He would be furiously angry that the Fomoire had not taken the Almhuin Citadel, but he might also be intrigued. And I almost believe I can handle Chaos, thought Rumour. At the moment I believe I could take on the entire Dark Realm and win.

Because I forced open the door to the light, and that door is still ajar . . .

She turned back to the snarling creature with the tangled, matted hair and smeared white skin. 'There is nothing for it,' said Rumour in a bored tone. 'It is really quite stultifyingly tedious, but I am afraid there is only one thing I can do with you.'

The Lady glanced slyly at Rumour from the corners of her eyes, and Rumour felt the animal fear emanating from her. At length, she said, 'Well?'

Rumour smiled rather pityingly. 'I am going to brick you up in the dungeons and leave you for ever in the dark,' she said.

For ever in the dark. To be bricked up, to be shut away for ever in a tiny lightless, windowless cell, without hope of reprieve, without even the sound of another voice. A truly terrible fate, thought Rumour. I can scarcely believe I said it.

But I will do it.

The Dark Realm had little light, of course; it had no day and no dawn and no sun. But there was light of a kind here. It was told how the Dark Lords enjoyed their dissolute, flame-lit banquets, and how, when they travelled in the Black Domain, they did so by the lights of hundreds of flambeaux carried by servants. And Rumour had already seen that Almhuin was well provided with wall-sconces. Yes, the Lady served the dark powers, she exulted in darkness itself, but she would not find it an easy punishment to bear.

Bricked up and left in the dark for ever . . .

There must be no possibility of a rescue. The sentence must

last until the creature died. It must be immutable. It would have been better to have killed her outright, but Rumour knew she had not sufficient strength. She knew that she had overcome massive forces simply to cage the creature; to end her life and render up her soul would require the strongest, purest sorcery ever spun. Rumour thought if she had had with her the entire House of Amaranth, they might have managed it. The slaying of the necromancess . . . Yes, together, their several strengths combined, they would surely have been victorious.

And all the time, beneath the cool logic and the cold planning, ran a seething anger. *Why should the creature not be made to suffer for what she has done to Andrew and all those other poor wretches? Why should she be accorded a swift, painless ending . . . ?*

She left the slaughterhouse and went quickly down the narrow curving steps that led to Almhuin's dank dungeons, wrapping her cloak about her, but feeling how it still dragged in the seeping moisture of the stone floors and brushed against the crumbling walls with their thick crusting of lichen. Horrid! thought Rumour, shuddering. But she began to play the old, childish game again, that was not really childish and was not quite a game, of looking beyond.

Look beyond. When I am out of here – when Andrew and I are both out of here – I shall lie for several hours in a deep scented bath with every expensive perfume and every sensuous oil I can find.

When I am in my own Castle again, I shall hold a tremendous banquet with every exotic food and every potent wine I can think of.

There was no light down here and she held aloft the flambeau, seeing with a shudder how it showed up the creeping mould and the pale fungal growths on the walls.

Somewhere close by, water was dripping steadily, echoing bleakly and coldly in the enclosed stone tunnels. Rumour shivered and held the flambeau up, trying not to see how tiny scuttling things ran away from the rays of light, or how there were stagnant pools of moisture on the floor.

Don't notice it. Don't see it. Think about hot scented baths and thick fluffy towels, and velvet robes and silken underthings that slither over your skin with a soft, sensuous whisper . . .

The dripping of water was exactly the sort of thing that would prey on your mind and fray your nerves. Drip-drip-drip . . . It was better to ignore it. It was better to look forward to the silks and the perfumes . . . A deep soft bed with a fire burning and silver wine carafes with diamond-bright chalices set out. Two chalices, of course, thought Rumour, the corners of her lips lifting in a sudden, mischievous smile. There was no point in scented baths and perfumed silks and firelit bedchambers if you were not going to share them with a lover . . . Oh Andrew, my love, there must a way to get you of this terrible place.

She thought she was directly beneath the keep now. She had stayed in innumerable Castles throughout Ireland, sometimes as a guest, sometimes as a business arrangement when a sorceress was required; occasionally clandestinely, when the Lady of the Castle was away, and the Castle Lord engaging in a little dilettante dalliance. She had many times slipped quietly through dark galleries and halls, sometimes with a torch to see the way, sometimes not. And she knew that the general layout of such places varied very little.

Even so, there was something overwhelming about knowing that the immense weight of a great dark Castle was directly over your head. Rumour lifted the flaring torch cautiously, and saw that above her were the curved, undressed stones of the tunnel roof, but that here and there were huge joists, great iron rivets and groynes.

The smallest of the cell-like dungeons was at the far end of the long narrow passage; it was very small and very cold and very dark. Rumour stood surveying it, frowning a little, holding the flambeau up to see the solid stone floor and the thick walls. How large? She paced it carefully. Four paces its length; three paces its width. Enough for the creature to lie flat if she wanted to. I am inflicting a terrible revenge, thought Rumour, and for a moment, standing there in the dank, foul-smelling cell, with only the thin torchlight, her resolve wavered.

And then: but the creature wounded Andrew! she thought angrily. She wounded him, and she would have killed him slowly and agonisingly. She has done so to countless others. Let her suffer! thought Rumour in silent fury.

The door was narrow and very low; Rumour had had to bend almost double to get through. She thought it would be fairly easy to block it up. There had been a partly crumbled and collapsed section of wall further back. She could move the bricks and the stones; there was actually a brief and very easy Spell of Labour that would do it for her. She would force the evil creature down here, keeping her inside the cage of light, and she would fling her into this cell, and she would have the Spell of Labour ready and waiting. And then, once the tiny door was bricked up, and the creature helpless, the bars of light could be withdrawn. Rumour stood in the tunnel, considering.

Was she then going to leave the creature to die of hunger and thirst and madness in the dark? Could she do it?

But if she was not to die, then someone would have to remain in the Castle as Gaoler. Someone would have to be here to pass the creature food and water through a hatch.

Who?

Andrew said, 'She must not be left to die. Punishment if you will, but she must be allowed the opportunity to repent of the evil.' He sat hunched over the fire in the small stone room, his face haggard and white with pain, but his eyes sensible.

Rumour had found the Lady's sculleries – grim, vaulted chambers below the great dining hall – and had brought up a cask of good red wine which they had heated over the fire, together with wedges of some kind of dark rye bread, and a wheel of rich, ripe cheese and a spicy preserve to go with it. There was a dish of velvet-skinned plums.

Andrew cupped his hands gratefully about the silver wine chalice, feeling the warmth soak into his skin. His mind was still reeling from what had happened to him, and he knew that there would still be days of pain for him: he knew he had been so severely wounded by the one called Bailitheoir that he might never walk normally again. Lamed. *Mutilated*.

But I am alive, he thought, rallying. I am alive and I am whole. I am surviving, and Rumour is surviving with me. We shall beat this Dark Land and Theodora will be safe. And I believe I am drawing nearer to the Black Monk, he thought. He served the Crimson Lady for a time, she told Bailitheoir so. I am nearer to fulfilling the quest for my Order, he thought, and derived an unexpected comfort from this. As Rumour had been able to look beyond Almhuin to the scented baths and lavish banquets of her own Castle, Andrew found himself looking beyond it to the resuming of his quest; the taking back of the traitor of his Order.

Near to the fire, Rumour was getting out food. She had even brought up the Lady's silver table utensils and squares of white linen for napkins. Through the pain that still gnawed, Andrew found himself smiling as she bent over the small task, because it was so very like her to remember knives and forks and linen, and to choose the best.

Without turning round, Rumour said, 'There is no reason for us to live in an uncivilised fashion, Andrew.'

'Of course not.' Andrew accepted the plate she handed to him, and reached for a sharp knife to slice the bread for them. Rumour sat facing him, the warm glow from the wine in her own chalice casting a deep rich shadow over her face.

She said, in a level voice, 'I intend to take the Lady down to the dungeons presently, and pronounce the spell that will cause her to bricked up for ever.' She looked at him, not precisely asking for his view on this, not quite asking for his permission, but certainly waiting for his reactions.

Andrew said, 'And then? Afterwards?'

Rumour met his eyes straightly. 'She will be left for ever in the dark,' she said. 'There will be no light, no sound, no companionship for her ever again.' She looked at him very directly, and her expression said that she did not care. 'It is a fitting punishment,' she said, aloud, but even to her own ears there was a defiance in her tone which should not have been necessary. Am I convinced that what I intend is right? thought Rumour. I suppose I cannot be, or I would have done it hours ago while Andrew slept. She touched, in her mind, the spells that could be used; simple Enchantments of Labour and Construction – what were called Artisan Enchantments – that would do the work and that would not be in the least quenched by the darkness of Almhuin.

Andrew's eyes were thoughtful, and Rumour waited. At length he set down his wine and, leaning forward, took her hand. 'My dear love,' he said, 'you cannot do it.'

'Yes, I can do it.' Rumour put up her chin challengingly.

'No. The creature cannot be left to die like that.'

'She is unutterably evil.' But Rumour had known for several hours that she could not leave the Crimson Lady to die.

'Revenge belongs not to us,' said Andrew.

'More of your Leader's tenets?' The defiance was still there, but Rumour could hear that it rang false.

Andrew said gently, 'There may come a time when even this one will repent of her evil. If that should happen, then she should be allowed to—'

'Pay her debts? Make reparation? Andrew, this is the Crimson Lady!' *And already she has helped to mutilate you . . .*

If Andrew caught the thought, he gave no indication. He had picked up his wine chalice again, and was sipping it slowly, his eyes shadowed and unreadable. He said, very gently, 'It is not permissible that any creature should take the life of another.'

'You killed Coelacanth.'

'And you killed Searbhan. And each time it was in defence of my life and yours!'

'It is permissible to kill in self-defence, but not mete out just punishment? I do not understand these teachings you follow!' said Rumour in angry frustration. 'I do not understand your rules!'

'I do not understand them either,' said Andrew quietly.

'Do you ever question?'

'Constantly.' His hand tightened about her. 'I did not understand the beliefs of your people,' he said.

'And yet you paid them a surface, more than a surface courtesy,' said Rumour, staring at him.

'Of course. I *think* that my way is right,' said Andrew. 'I believe it is. But I do not *know* that it is, not with absolute certainty.' He looked at her, his eyes suddenly filled with self-doubt. 'For all my deep convictions, I cannot help occasionally wondering—'

'Whether the other ways, the old ways, the ways of the ancient Ireland might be the true ones after all?' whispered Rumour.

'Yes. It is difficult for me to explain, but they seem to share the same roots and the same bases. There are so many parallels. You have the Samildanach—'

'The Man of Each and Every Art who will come humbly and quietly, but who will fling wide the doors that will let light into the Dark Ireland.' Rumour smiled softly. 'I have always loved that belief,' she said. 'I have always found such comfort in the

453

thought that perhaps one day the Dark Realm will be for ever vanquished.'

'We have a similar belief,' said Andrew, watching her. 'But we believe that He has already entered the world.'

'Was it . . . humbly and quietly?'

'Yes.' He looked at her. 'Yes, it was very humbly and very modestly. During His life, He endured immense suffering. But He was a healer of extraordinary powers, and also he was a very remarkable . . .' He paused. 'I think you would say "orator",' he said, and Rumour nodded, for the concept of one who could exercise charisma over a listening throng was not unknown to her.

She said, thoughtfully, 'They say that when Chaos calls his people to gather together in the great open square outside his Castle, and addresses them standing in Murder's Chariot, such are his powers of oration, that the people would follow him into Hell if he asked.'

Andrew, remembering Chaos's dark, strong beauty, understood this at once. He grinned suddenly, and said, 'Quite aside from the many similarities, your people's beliefs are deeply interesting.'

'The Samildanach?'

'Yes.' Andrew reached for her hand. 'We may hold differing beliefs,' he said. 'And it is true that I have always questioned some of my religion's ways. But I know without having to question it that you must not leave the Beithioch to die. If you had slain her in a fight, or if I had, that would have been—'

'Permissible?'

'Acceptable,' said Andrew.

A small detached part of Rumour's mind noted that he had said: you must not leave her to die, and not: you must not punish her. She said, 'You cannot stop me.'

'I can.'

They stared at one another. Rumour thought, with sudden terror: is this a measure of his love for me? That the instant I conflict with his strange beliefs, he chooses those beliefs and not me? She put the thought from her, for she would not be so small-minded as to ask or expect him to choose her above something that mattered to him so deeply. But all the same, she felt a sudden deep pain.

454

At length, she said, 'If the creature is not to die, she must have a Keeper. Someone must be here to pass food and water to her. Someone who will not allow her to escape.'

'Yes.'

'But that is not possible,' said Rumour, knowing already that it was very possible, that it was pre-ordained and that the decision had already been made.

Andrew said, 'I will do it.'

He was horrified and afraid, but he knew there was no other way. For I, also, must serve my penance, he might have said. I also must pay a debt for the sweet stolen nights and the golden forbidden slaking of my desires.

I also must make my *mea culpa* to my Lord, and sit out the time of my penance.

A soft voice inside his mind said: and share your penance with the Beithioch, the BeastWoman inside the fearsome Almhuin Castle? Roam these halls and dwell at the heart of this terrible Fortress, where evil still stalks the darkness?

Yes.

And what of Rumour? said the insidious voice. What of the strange exotic creature who has already risked so much for you, and who has been unfailingly courageous, and unflaggingly high-spirited?

Already I have wounded her, he thought. By making the decision to remain here, to guard the evil creature of this Castle, I am deliberately putting her from me. A tiny spiral of agony threaded through his mind. But it could not have been otherwise! he thought. I cannot be other than I am. Against his will, the words of his Teacher and Leader, the gentle Nazarene carpenter, echoed across his mind's surface . . . *I am what I am* . . .

Aloud he said, 'There is the question of my lameness.' And was pleased that he had been able to refer to it quite normally and quite lightly. Lameness. Yes. It was an acceptable word. He touched the stout ash branch that Rumour had found to assist him in walking and that stood nearby. 'I would slow you down,' said Andrew, watching her, seeing how the firelight fell across her face, lighting the planes. Shall I ever forget her? Do I ever want to forget her? But he said, 'You must go on to Chaos's

455

Castle of Infinity, as we planned. There will surely be horses in the stables – it would be a swift enough journey if you could ride.' He paused and then went on, in a different, anguished voice. 'I think my heart will be torn from me when you do,' he said simply, and felt at once that the warmth flooded her body again, and understood that a deep, lonely coldness had been encasing her.

She said, 'But I have to go?' And at once, 'Yes, of course I have to. There is still Theodora.' She looked at him. 'I vowed I would find Theodora for Nechtan,' she said. 'I cannot go back on that. And Nechtan would have said—' she paused, and a sudden smile curved her lips – 'Nechtan would have wanted it,' said Rumour softly. 'He would have said the danger ought not to count.'

'It ought not.' Andrew was remembering the small, slight child who had turned to him with such trust but who had glared at Chaos, and who had sought in her mind for some way to defeat him. Yes, he could not let Theodora down. 'I would be an encumbrance,' he said. 'We both know it. Alone, you will do better. There will be danger, but you will be less vulnerable without me.'

He eyed her steadily and, after a moment, Rumour said softly, 'Very well. Will you come with me now to imprison the creature below?'

'Yes. All right.' Andrew reached for the ash branch. He hesitated for a moment, and Rumour turned in the doorway.

Andrew said, 'Bring the bread and wine.'

The Enchantment of Silver Bars had held strongly and well. 'Although I did not expect it to do otherwise,' said Rumour.

'You can summon the – the power again?' asked Andrew as she raised her hands in the gesture he had come to know.

'The Lady is caged,' said Rumour. 'And therefore I am able to touch a little of the power again.' She looked at him. 'The door to the light is still ajar.'

She murmured a brief incantation, and at once, silver reins materialised in her hands and slid across the room, to loop about the bars of the cage. Rumour moved slowly towards the door, drawing the silken reins with her, and the silver-barred cage moved with her, gently and easily. At once, the Lady let out a terrible animal howl and threw herself against the bars, reaching between them with her blood-stained hands, clawing at her captors. Andrew thought: she knows what we are about to do. She is struggling to get free. And then, with the framing of the thought, came another: *but she is not using necromancy to do so . . . She cannot match her power against Rumour's.* He knew a brief spurt of pride in Rumour, who could outclass this creature who had wielded such power.

Rumour paid the Lady no attention, but her face was white, and her lips were set in a rather grim line. Andrew thought: it is hurting her to do this. She hates the Crimson Lady, and she will carry out the sentence she has decided on. But is still causing her anguish.

Rumour was moving carefully out into the darkened halls, the silver skeins shimmering behind her, sprinkling their quicksilver light across the floor. Andrew followed, awkwardly and painfully, but finding that the ash stick was surprisingly strong. The rather thin healing spells that Rumour had managed to summon had dispelled much of the pain, but even so, he was trembling and soaked in sweat as they reached the narrow walled stair leading down to the dungeons. Rumour had not looked back, and Andrew could feel that her entire mind, her whole will was concentrating on drawing the cage with its snarling, lashing victim down the narrow tunnels. He stayed where he was, regaining his strength, trying to push back the pain that was sending spears of agony through his leg.

He had thought they would have to fumble their way through the dark, for Rumour's hands were both occupied with the silver cords, and Andrew's right hand leaned heavily on the stick, while his left was occupied with the flagon of wine and the bread which they had packed into a small drawstring bag. Neither of them had been able to carry any kind of light. There had been a moment when Andrew had thought: am I really doing this? Is it a madman's whim? But he knew it was not; he knew he must bring his own beliefs and his own strengths to bear against the creeping evil of Almhuin Castle.

The silken skeins and the glinting bars of the cage shed a soft radiance of their own as they moved through the shadows. Andrew thought that Rumour pronounced a spell of some kind, and that the shadows had flinched back from it, but he could not be sure.

He found himself trying to feel pity for the caged and doomed Lady of Almhuin. But I have only hatred, he thought, and wondered if this would fade with the passing of time. Would he come to feel compassion for his malevolent prisoner? I should try to do so, he thought, and then, in sudden fear: but how long shall I be here? How long is the term of the Lady's imprisonment to be?

They had reached the small, dark cell, and Rumour drew on the silver cords again, pulling them with her hands, drawing the cage through the narrow, low door carefully, until it stood at the centre of the tiny stone room. Andrew, watching from the passage, felt a terrible dark coldness descend about him. How did it feel to be caged like this, to know that in a few minutes you would be sealed away from the world, bricked up for the rest of your life, with no human companionship, no light, no sound . . . Only the twice- or thrice-daily ritual of bread and water being pushed through a tiny hatch. Shall I weaken? he wondered. In time, shall I find myself bringing better food, perhaps even wine? Shall I finally enter into discourse with the creature?

For you, also, will be friendless, surrounded by silence, perpetually alone, Human Monk . . .

He closed his mind at once, understanding that the Lady was reaching for his inmost thoughts, that she was snaking her dark evil seductions about his consciousness, as she had done in the fearsome slaughterhouses. I dare not let that happen! he thought. I must perform this dreadful task boldly and unthinkingly. But even as the thought formed, his mind was racing ahead, to the days and months and years when all there would be for him would be the wearisome journey here to send in food and water, perhaps a blanket if it was cold. Would he find himself falling prey to pity for her at those times?

And you may be glad of another living creature to talk with, Human Monk, for Almhuin is a cold and lonely place, and there will be none of your kind here . . .

I shall walk the land and try to grow things, thought Andrew with silent determination. I shall find solace in mending and renewing. He remembered the satisfaction he had felt in the monks' house when a wall had had to be rebuilt, or a roof mended. And there would be prayer . . . The observance of the rituals of his house. He thought that, although he no longer had any notion of time, he could draw up a chart, what the monks had called a calendar, with the feast-days marked. Yes. Perhaps he could write a little, telling the story once again of the great Leader whose beliefs he followed, perhaps even telling a little of the story of his brotherhood. The idea fired him; he remembered how his Order had contained several monks gifted in the making of illuminated manuscripts, lovely painted books chronicling the events of the day and the miracles of Christ.

I could do that, thought Andrew, fixing his mind on the idea in an endeavour to shut out the terrible swirling evil of the Castle. I could write the story of this battle, perhaps. There would be more than enough to occupy him. And one day this terrible task will somehow be ended, and I shall be on the other side of it. I shall have returned to the world and I shall have found and reclaimed the Black Monk.

He took no part in the brief ritual which Rumour performed, although he listened attentively to the short incantation – 'The Spell of Labour,' said Rumour. He thought it interesting, as he thought all other religious rituals interesting, and for the first time he found himself able to differentiate between some of syllables, recognising that they were rather terse and abrupt, comparing them to the gentle, light-filled chant that Rumour had used to create the silken reins.

The bricks and the undressed stones were obedient to Rumour's chanting; they had tumbled forward, and begun to lay themselves in a neat serried row, one atop another, so that a fourth wall to the tiny dank cell was forming. Soon she will know nothing but the impenetrable blackness of that cell, thought Andrew. Soon she will have no sound, no sense of closeness to the world . . . She will never see or hear anything ever again, only the faint rasp of the hatch opening as food is pushed through to her. In time she will become blind and deaf, and the only one of her senses left to her will be that of smell, and with that she will eternally smell the dank sourness of the tomb and of her own bodily excretions . . .

He thought: and in her own world she is a Lady of a Royal House! and felt fear close about him once more, for he could not and he dared not show any shred of pity for the creature.

As Rumour's voice rose and fell in the chant that was so eerily familiar, Andrew found his voice murmuring, almost of its own volition, the joyous words of the *Te Deum*.

'*We praise thee, O God... To thee all Angels cry aloud ... the Heavens and all the Powers therein... Cherubim and Seraphin cry...*'

His voice mingled with Rumour's, both seeming to touch the soft, pure notes of praise and entreaty and worship together. But beneath the ordered layers of prayer, Andrew thought: am I lending my strengths to paganism? Is paganism buttressing Christianity? Or is this the common ground? The meeting of the two worlds, Christianity blending with paganism at last ...

The Lady of Almhuin was crouching behind the silver bars of the cage, black hatred burning in her terrible eyes, and Rumour stepped back, and chanted the ancient spell that invoked the Amaranth Seals. As they began to form, great purple and silver crests with licking curlicues of flame, Andrew moved forward, unhooking the small ebonywood crucifix from about his waist. Without pausing in her own incantation, Rumour handed him the bread and wine.

And now their voices mingled more strongly and more evocatively than before: Andrew's rising and falling in the warm, comforting rhythms of Christianity, Rumour's in a lighter, more musical chant.

The common ground. The two beliefs, one so new it had barely made its mark yet; the other immeasurably ancient, its genesis lost in the dark that existed before Time dawned. Blending and mingling, running from one mind to the other, until it was impossible to know where one began and the other ended.

Two streams of wine joining to make one ...

When Andrew reached the part that he always thought of as the heart and the core and the great living centre of his religion, he felt the answering response from Rumour.

'"*This is my Body which is given for you... This is my Blood of the New Testament, which is shed for you...*"'

In the same moment, they heard the fiery sounds of the great Amaranth Seals fusing over the cell door and, from within, a terrible shriek that rent the air with agony.

Andrew stepped forward and wedged the crucifix between the tightly layered bricks and, as he did so, a small, pale face with great burning-pitch eyes appeared framed in the tiny hatch opening.

'*You will pay dearly for this, Human Monk and Amaranth Sorceress . . .*' Maniacal laughter exploded in the quiet dungeons, and Andrew fell back, feeling vicious hatred slice his mind.

Rumour caught him as he fell against the far wall, but he stood unaided, the ash stick supporting him. There was a moment when he silently regarded the prisoner, black eyes meeting grey, and then with Rumour at his side, they went from the unbroken darkness and the lonely dungeons, clinging to one another for warmth and comfort.

Rumour moved closer to the leaping fire they had kindled in the small stone room. She said, 'Andrew, you will have to be extremely careful of this one. She would kill us and eat our hearts if she could get out.'

'Yes.' *Yes, for she will reach for my mind, and there may be times when I shall be lonely or despairing, and in need of the sound of another creature's voice . . . And she would be learned in the legend and the lore of this strange, evil Realm*, said the tiny treacherous voice within his mind. *She would surely know much of its history, and all of it would make interesting hearing . . .*

He shut his mind to the slithering, treacherous thoughts, and passed Rumour the chalice of wine.

'I am aware of the dangers,' he said, sipping the hot, fragrant wine gratefully. 'I shall be on my guard.'

Rumour's eyes were shadowed and her face was drawn as she stared into the leaping flames. But she only said, 'You will be able to construct a hatch over the opening in the bricks?'

'Yes.' They had left the opening deliberately, so that food and water could be passed through. It was a small oblong aperture, perhaps eight inches square, near to the ceiling, and Andrew considered it, glad to concentrate on the practicalities of the situation. He said, 'Once my wound has healed a little more, I believe I could fit a small door with hinges.' His mind sped on, thinking that there must a stout lock, strong spring-hinges that opened outwards only; planning how he could pass food and water through with a long hooked pole, rather like the one the

461

Almhuinians had used in Diarmuit's cellar.

'Once a hatch is in place,' said Rumour, 'the cage can be withdrawn. But until then, it will hold her.' She looked at him, her face serious in the fireglow. 'Your ritual – your prayer – was very powerful. I could feel the power and the strength.'

The power and the glory and the strength . . . Andrew smiled and thought: yes, of course, that is what I shall hold on to. That is what will give me the courage to endure this task.

He said, 'I was adding the beliefs of my people to the beliefs of your people,' and smiled at her.

'I think that this is something both our gods would unite over,' said Rumour seriously.

'Yes.'

'She seemed to recognise the symbol of your Leader. The wooden carved emblem you left.'

'There may have been other travellers who passed through here,' said Andrew. 'Or she may simply have recognised it as a symbol of light.' He leaned back, grateful for the wine and the fire, trying to visualise a pattern, a shape to the formless time that lay ahead of him.

As Guardian to the Crimson Lady, the BeastWoman, Almhuin's necromancess . . .

He could not be sure that she would not work some terrible dark seduction. He could not be sure that he would be able to resist it if she did.

Rumour said, 'No emotional farewells, Andrew. I cannot bear it. Let me simply go, let me just saddle one of the Lady's horses and ride away. Let it be as if I am simply going into another room.'

'If you wish.' He handed her the small casket containing the *sidh*'s music. 'You will return it to Tiarna?'

'Of course.'

They looked at one another. 'I shall await your return, Lady,' said Andrew at length.

'In my world,' said Rumour, 'there was once an expression which has now fallen into disuse. But its meaning is still potent.' She reached out and touched his face, tracing her fingers lightly across his eyes. 'You will be in my thoughts for a part of every day, Andrew,' she said very softly.

462

'Thank you.' He looked at her. 'In my world, in my religion, we also have an expression,' he said. 'It is that you will be in my prayers every day,' said Andrew.

'That is . . . more than I could wish for,' said Rumour, and bit her lip so hard that it bled, because she would not cry, she would *not . . .*

He took her face between his hands then, and stared down at it very intently, as if he was trying to learn her, as if he wanted to imprint her face on his memory for ever.

Only that I shall never forget you, my love, you will always be with me, you will always be a part of me, even when I cannot recall your face . . .

Rumour, fighting back the tears – stupid, emotional, she would not give way – stared at him, and saw how far removed he was now from the gentle, ascetic monk. His eyes burned with a fervour and a belief in what he was about to do in Almhuin, and Rumour recognised fully, at last, that he must make his peace with his strange God and he must make the reparation he believed was necessary.

But you no longer wear the mien of an ascetic or a celibate, she thought. The passion that swept us so fiercely has left its mark. It is there in your eyes, my love, and in the curve of your lips . . .

I wonder if your brethren would recognise you, Andrew, thought Rumour. I wonder if you would recognise yourself, even. He still wore the black robe of his house, but he had grown thinner, and beneath it his body was as lean and as hard as whipcord. Only the ash stick, propped close at hand, betrayed the terrible mutilation that the Crimson Lady had inflicted on him. His dark hair tumbled about his brow; his eyes were glowing and filled with passion – whether for me or for his strange, self-imposed hermitry I cannot tell, thought Rumour. But this is no true hermit, this is no austere pietist or anchorite. This is a fiery-eyed man of the real world, an activist, a militant, a player rather than a watcher. A Man of Each and Every Art . . .

I wonder how long Almhuin will contain him, thought Rumour.

She thought that he heard none of this. She stayed where she was, holding his eyes steadily, trying to imprint his face on her mind, as he had done with hers . . . *You will always be a part of me, even when I cannot recall your features;* and in the end was beyond caring about the ridiculous tears that had spilled over, and that were pouring down her cheeks.

She went then, running out to where the laden horses waited in the courtyard, running from him before he could stop her, before her stupid, *senseless* emotions betrayed her completely, out into the dark world that waited, and on to the lowering mountains that girdled Chaos's Castle of Infinity.

Chapter Thirty-nine

Rumour approached the Castle of Infinity, riding one of the Crimson Lady's gleaming black stallions. She led a second, which bore the robes she had brought out of Tiarna and the precious cask containing the *sidh*'s music.

As she drew nearer the great, gleaming Fortress, she saw that it was not dark and sombre and forbidding as she had expected, but shining and sleek. 'And extremely well looked after,' thought Rumour, whose own Castle of the Starlit Night had always been carefully maintained, but at considerable expense.

It was so vast as to be almost a small township, set within high walls; gold-tipped gates led up to its central entrance, and glinting diamond chippings shone from its hundreds of windows.

Rumour thought: somewhere inside there is Theodora. She touched her mount's flanks and rode on towards the entrance.

She had expected to be questioned, and she had certainly expected to be barred from entering. She had evolved a rather sketchy plan, deliberately not making it too precise, because anything might lie ahead and she must be prepared to adapt to the moment.

But she had donned the most dazzling of all the dazzling outfits she had brought out of Aillen mac Midha's store of robes, and she was wearing a shining blue-green robe of pure, soft silk, with a sleeveless garment, a little like a surcoat, of midnight blue velvet over it. After deliberation she had donned only the plainest of headdresses: a thin circlet of silver studded with sapphires.

'Plain but *good*,' she had said to Andrew before that last soul-searing farewell. 'I do not wish to be taken for a second-rate sorceress, you understand. If Chaos accepts me, he will be accepting me as an enemy; but I will at least be an *equal* enemy.'

465

Riding up to the Castle gates, she derived confidence from the plain but good headdress and the slither of silk against her skin. I am tipped with silver and wrapped in the gown of the *sidh* High King, and I have a whole store of enchantments at my beck. And if you welcome me, Chaos, Lord of the Dark Realm, then you will welcome me as a very high-ranking sorceress indeed.

She approached the entrance with her head high and a look of faint boredom. They might repel her and they might imprison her, but they certainly would not ignore her.

Inside the Castle of Infinity, the great banqueting hall was laid for one of the Lord of Chaos's immense elaborate feasts. Gold plate glistened the length of the huge banqueting table, and every place was set with pure golden chalices, and ruby-studded eating implements. The deep red jewel flowers, grown and tended in the *Saraigli*, where Chaos's concubines were kept, glowed brightly at every place.

There had been some competition over the picking of the flowers. The concubines had all wanted to have the arranging of them, because wasn't it a known fact that Chaos noticed these things, and wasn't the whole point of being in the *Saraigli* to get noticed? They had all drawn sketches of how the tables could be arranged, and what colours could be used. They had thought the designs very imaginative, and had asked Meirdreach, who oversaw the *Saraigli*, please to be sure to present them to the Reachtaire who held sway in the Castle kitchens and dining halls. The Reachtaire would be glad to have such good ideas.

Several of them, who thought that food should be arranged prettily and temptingly, had thought up ideas and decorations for the food itself. There were all kinds of things that could be done, they said, very busy with the thin paints they had coaxed out of Meirdreach, anxiously consulting with the Reachtaire's servants as to whether there would be lobster or crab, which you could not do a great deal with, or whether it might be Twilight Fish and salmonidae, which could be made to look very attractive indeed.

One or two of the concubines had affected to disdain such slavish attempts to attract Chaos's attention, and had turned their attention to the selecting of gowns and jewels and to the perfuming of their pampered bodies for the banquet.

'As if they think they are already selected to attend,' said Meirdreach, grumpily. She stood at the centre of the warm-scented rooms, and glowered at them, arms akimbo. The concubines sighed for poorest Meirdreach, who was fat and grey-haired and had the tiniest strain of Giantish blood in her, poor soul. You could see it in the incipient beard and in the thick coarse hair and you could hear it in the flat, heavy tread. They tried to be sympathetic because it must be a shocking thing to have to be seen abroad looking like Meirdreach. AnCine, who had been fourteen when she came to the *Saraigli* and had therefore seen a bit more of the world than the others, whispered that Meirdreach had certain unwholesome appetites. If you wanted to get to Chaos's bed, you might first have to go to Meirdreach's, said AnCine, and the concubines had listened round-eyed, but opinions had been divided as to whether it was true or simply one of AnCine's lurid stories.

But when Meirdreach said they would not all be going to the banquet, her chins wobbled crossly, and the concubines did not know where to look for fear of giggling. 'Don't think that more than one of you will go,' said Meirdreach, regarding them all grimly. 'Have you understood that, you bed-cats?'

They all said they had, and nudged one another and whispered behind their hands that Meirdreach was stouter than ever, and that a new sprouting of black hairs had grown from her chins. They curled up on their silken couches and velvet beds, and eyed their own sleek bodies and shining hair with pleased complacency.

AnCine said loudly, wouldn't Meirdreach be plotting and intriguing away on her own account, and maybe soliciting her nasty favours from those of the *Saraigli* who were that way inclined. *Some* people, said AnCine, tossing back her long hair, would do anything at all to get a place at Chaos's table for the evening.

This was extremely bold of AnCine, and the concubines had looked uneasily at one another in case there should be a row. You had to be careful about that, because rows sometimes led to fights, and fights usually meant disarranged hair or even scratched faces.

Meirdreach said that was as maybe, but hadn't she the running of the *Saraigli*, nasty thankless task it was, nobody need

467

think it was a sinecure, and hadn't Chaos himself given her the complete controlling of it?

The concubines did not know what a sinecure was. They giggled together after Meirdreach had stumped off and said that, as for the suggestion that only one of them would be on display at the banquet, pooh! didn't they all of them know perfectly well that the Lord of Chaos was easily capable of dealing with eight or ten of them in one night!

AnCine said that Meirdreach was a *Leispiach* and the concubines shrieked at such daring, but wished AnCine would not use such a word in front of the little one.

AnCine did not care. 'She will learn what a *Leispiach* is if she is in Meirdreach's hands for very long,' she said, and picked up a hand-mirror to study her reflection. Hadn't there been the suspicion of a spot forming that morning; you could not be having a spot with a grand banquet ahead of you and Chaos's eye to be caught.

The concubines had made rather a pet of the little girl that their Lord had brought back with him from the Beyond Ireland. She was a pretty little creature with her huge dark eyes and soft white skin. It was rather like having a kitten or a baby. Something to stroke and pet and dress up. They fed her with sugared fruits and devised games for her, and tried the effect of scarlet ribbons – no, *emerald green!* – in her hair.

She had very nice manners. She listened to their stories of how they had all come to the *Saraigli* with polite interest, occasionally asking questions, not saying very much about her own world.

The concubines liked to tell the stories of how they had come to the Castle of Infinity. They all told Theodora, taking it in turns, listening quite politely to the others, but in reality only waiting for their own turn. They held little secret feasts of their own, bribing the Reachtaire's servants to smuggle in extra food and flagons of rich, syrupy wine; and they giggled a great deal, and peeped out of the tiny high windows, standing on chairs to reach, making sure that no horrid guards were lurking below and listening.

They were mostly daughters of chieftains whose lands lay on the hinterlands between the two Irelands, where allegiances were apt to become a bit blurred. Most of them had been captured or sold when they were very young indeed. Theo thought it was probably a bit uncharitable to think that they did not seem to have grown up.

Their lives consisted of perfuming their bodies and painting their faces and learning the small, rather useless skills which they remembered or had devised, and which might make Chaos notice them. They taught one another the skills because, between them, they had really rather a great deal of accomplishments, they said, tossing their hair vainly.

'Some of us have *secret* skills,' said AnCine, whom Theodora found the most interesting of all the concubines. It was AnCine who had called Meirdreach the bad name. AnCine had long red hair and soft white skin, and had once spent three nights in a row with the Lord of Chaos, which the other concubines regarded with awe, because wasn't that more than anyone else in the *Saraigli* had ever done?

Theodora tried very hard to be quiet and polite to them all, because Mamma had said that this was something you should always do. You never knew when you might be glad that you had been polite and gracious, said Mamma. Even when it was the oddest of people, you had to remember that you were a daughter of the House of Amaranth and therefore required to behave well at all times. Great-grandfather, putting it a bit differently, had said with a chuckle that you never knew when you might need to make use of somebody.

So Theo had been polite and quiet; she had listened attentively to the stories that the concubines told, and she had thanked them when they included her in their little feasts, and when they gave her hair ribbons (which she thought made her look like a dressed-up doll, but which it would have been very impolite to refuse) and fed her with the sickly sugared berries and the sweet sticky cordials they liked to sip from jewel-encrusted chalices.

She had not said anything about the Porphyry Palace, and she had especially not said anything about being an Amaranth. She was unsure how the concubines would feel about her being an Amaranth, and stolen away solely on account of it, and so she pretended that she had lived in a quite ordinary place with a quite ordinary family. This was telling lies, which was not something you ought to do, but it was a lot safer than the truth.

It was interesting to hear about the banquet, which had sent the concubines into such a flurry. At least it was something to look forward to: Theo had in fact been getting extremely bored in the *Saraigli*. A banquet might mean that all kinds of people would come to the Castle, and perhaps there would be someone who would help her to escape and get out of the Dark Realm.

She knew about banquets, although she had not been allowed to attend any, of course, on account of not being old enough. But when Great-grandfather had given banquets, Theo had slipped into the great hall at the Porphyry Palace before the guests assembled, to peep at the sparkling tables, all laid with Great-grandfather's nicest gold plate; there would usually be huge silver bowls of fruit, from which you could, if you were very careful, steal a handful of berries: perhaps the glossy blackberries that grew along the road to the Palace, or maybe the soft, sharp raspberries. Mamma had usually decorated the tables: there would be rowan at Samain to keep out the evil creatures, and there would be the marvellous nine bronze burners at Beltane, elaborately wrought and burnished by many generations of Beltane fire. You had to keep the sacred fire burning throughout the Palace for the entire festival of Beltane, of course; it was extremely important, although Theo was not sure why.

The banquet tonight was to be a very grand affair. The concubines told one another that Chaos had summoned the heads of all his Armies: one story said he had called in the Fomoire as well, but nobody knew if this was true.

He was going to launch a final and overwhelming attack on the Crimson Lady and take Almhuin Castle for his own, which would mean he would at last rule the whole of the Dark Realm.

'And then,' said AnCine, who usually told the concubines what was happening in the Palace, 'and then he will be strong enough to storm into the Beyond Ireland and rule there as well!'

They all knew that this was well within Chaos's powers. They listened to the stories while they were gilding their soft, pampered bodies for the banquet, and threading seed pearls or rubies or tiny winking diamonds into their hair and painting their faces. They had to look their very best tonight, they said importantly. They had not really time to think about battles and wars and the Beyond Ireland.

AnCine said it would be an historic evening, and so of course they had all assumed serious expressions at once, because knowing about historic evenings and wars was a grown-up thing and they all wanted to appear very grown-up.

But then Meirdreach came plodding in with the keys to the jewel caskets, and they all forgot about silly boring things like battles and historic events, because it was much more interesting to see inside the jewel-boxes, which they were not normally allowed to do, because Meirdreach and the Reachtaire said that they could not be trusted not to steal the prettiest. They had tossed their heads and affected not to care, but when the boxes were opened, they all clustered about them, asking Meirdreach in their best voices which of the jewels they might have; begging to be given that one – no, *that!* – trying the effect of pearls against a length of cream satin, or rainbow diamonds on gold damask. Even AnCine liked jewels.

As the hour of the banquet approached, they became very excited indeed, giggling and primping, running to ask Meirdreach which of them was to attend because there was *such* a lot to do: there were scented baths to be taken, and oils to be rubbed in, and gowns to be chosen. They furrowed their brows over this last, until AnCine reminded them that frowning caused wrinkles.

There was a great deal of trying-on of gowns and silk slippers, and laying-out of paints and powders and perfumes. AnCine tied her red hair up in a new shape, and twined a diadem threaded with rubies through it, but it was discovered that she had appropriated the rubies from Meirdreach's private cache, and was ordered to give them back by Meirdreach, who said that, in any case, rubies with red hair were vulgar, and she was not having any of them appearing at a banquet looking vulgar.

Light flooded the huge banqueting hall, pouring down from the crystal and diamond wall-sconces that had been fashioned for Chaos by the captured salamanders of Fael-Inis's Fire Country many years earlier. Chaos was known to be rather proud of having enslaved the salamanders – albeit briefly – and his people knew that this streak of pride was one of his very few weaknesses. You might, if you were sufficiently brave or

471

sufficiently foolhardy, almost call it a nearly *Humanish* weakness, although of course nobody even whispered this, or anything else defamatory about Chaos, on account of the *Draoicht Spiaire*. This was the ancient and fearsomely strong Spell of Spies, one of the ugliest enchantments ever woven, and which Chaos kept chained and locked behind a massively thick iron door in the depths of the Castle keep. It was unchained and let out every night to prowl the dark corridors of the Castle; it would stand outside bedchamber doors, and sometimes slither through keyholes and down chimneys, so that it could watch exactly what every single creature was doing and hear every single thing that was said. Nobody had ever seen the *Draoicht Spiaire*, because nobody ever dared to venture out at night, but everyone heard it pattering through the empty halls and sniffing at doors and chuckling greedily to itself over its accumulated knowledge.

There would not be as much revel-making as usual tonight, because the banquet was rather in the nature of a war council. But there would be some, because the Castle of Infinity was famous for its lavish entertainments. This was Misrule's province, and most people were interested to see what he would come up with, because it was being whispered that Chaos had been displeased with Misrule's last efforts. One rumour even said he had been threatened with a spell of exile in the Tanning Pit. If that happened, Anarchy might be appointed in Misrule's place, and opinions were divided as to whether this was a good thing or no, because Anarchy had an original, inventive mind, and would probably come up with some splendidly gory and gruesome entertainments; but say what you liked, he was disgracefully disorganised.

And most people enjoyed Misrule's masques and dances. He it was who had devised the now-famous Human-baiting, which everyone enjoyed, and then of course he had actually managed to capture some of the *sidh*'s *Uisce*, the floss-maned SeaHorses that inhabited Ireland's wild beautiful western coasts, for the Palace to stage ManHunts across the NightFields. This had proved even more popular than Human-baiting, and Chaos had frequently taken a party of guests out to the NightFields, all of them riding the *Uisce*, who had been beaten and cowed into submission so that they would carry Chaos's guests at a good fast pace along the hinterlands of the Realm, to where you could often find a party of lurking Humanish. The Hunting Parties nearly always brought back upwards of a dozen of the creatures for the Castle dungeons. And everyone in Chaos's Realm knew that, once you had Humanish in your cells, once you had imprisoned them and chained them and manacled them (and sometimes muzzled them), there were any number of uses they could be put to.

It was into this fermenting and anticipatory Castle that Rumour, proceeding with extreme caution, came.

The entry was, in fact, far easier and far less attended by suspicion than she had expected.

'For the banquet, I daresay?' said the doorkeeper, glancing at her rather carelessly, seeing that she was garbed richly and had about her the aura of power. And hadn't Himself all manner of strangers coming along up to the Castle tonight, on account of the fine old battle they were all going to mount against the Lady of Almhuin, the black-hearted, traitorous bitch! Necromancers and black sorcerers and all manner of important beings were expected. He'd bathed in the reflected glory of it all, because wasn't it the finest thing ever to be in the service of the most powerful of all the Dark Lords? He let Rumour in through the gates without thinking very much about it.

Rumour stood just inside the immense central portion of the Castle, seeing at once that this was the heart and the life of the Castle. Chaos's servants were everywhere; they ran and scurried and fetched and carried. Great silver tubs of wine were trundled across the hall, and scullions ran distractedly to and fro with haunches of venison and carcasses of oxen and sheep for the spits. Huge containers of flowers were carried carefully towards the far end of the hall, and heavy-featured females, whom Rumour at once recognised as being half-Giantesses, were dealing with white linen and damask for the tables, and bales of lavender-scented sheets for guest chambers.

But Rumour, for the moment unnoticed, saw that, with the exception of the half-Giantesses, who were probably laundresses and scrubwomen, Chaos's servants were a breed of the Rodent-mutants that she and Andrew had encountered in Almhuin.

473

But it was a subtly different breed from the Almhuinians, and Rumour, her attention momentarily caught, studied them, seeing signs not just of the Rodent strain, but of other, more ancient lineages.

As well as the Rodent-strain, Chaos's servants showed traces of the ancient sea-creatures, the little-known beings who had lived in Tiarna before the *sidh*, and long before the *nimfeach*, and whose origins were so far back that even the name had been lost. But Rumour thought the signs were there in the long, sea-green eyes and in the pale, faintly luminous skins and long-fingered hands.

And there was certainly a vein of Humanish blood and also Giantish, for they moved with an odd blending of Giantish strength and Humanish quickness. Rumour stayed where she was, partly in the shadow cast by the great bastions of the Castle, watching the servants going about their Lord's business, and began to see, quite clearly, that they possessed, in addition, the unmistakable characteristics of the Cruithin, the little dark elfin people, believed by most to be the first true Irish race, long since lost.

Rumour, torn between fascination and repulsion, recognised that this was a blending of many and diverse creatures, of creatures who were natural and ancient enemies.

They are mutants, she thought, but I do not believe they are natural mutants. This is deliberate and calculated, this is the result of forced mating and planned breeding, controlled by dark, evil magic.

Fear stirred again, but this time it was not simply fear of the powerful necromancer who ruled here. It was a deeper, more ancient fear, the atavistic revulsion and terror of natural laws harnessed and then deliberately warped and distorted.

So the whispers about Chaos's secret work were true, thought Rumour, staring about her.

Chaos's servants were the products of the forbidden practise of the *Draoicht Roghnacht*.

Necromantic race-breeding.

As she stood watching, a thin, rather spindly-legged creature wearing a black cloak and elaborate mask said, very softly, 'Are you here to assist with the revels, my dear?' and Rumour turned sharply. She knew at once that at her side was one of Chaos's foremost henchmen.

The Lord of Misrule.

Dark inHuman eyes glinted behind the slits in the mask, and Rumour was conscious of a cold, sly assessing, as if he might be wondering who and what she was, and whether he could make use of her. 'I bid you welcome to the Castle of Infinity,' he said, and his voice had a slightly taunting, but not unfriendly note.

'Thank you,' said Rumour carefully.

Misrule regarded her, his head on one side. 'I think we have never met,' he said, 'but I have sent out the call to all creatures who have the subsidiary necromantic degrees of Turmoil and Discord. 'I think you are one of those creatures.'

Rumour stared at him, understanding that, in the necromantic world, there were degrees and gradings and hierarchies, exactly as there were in the purer magic of sorcery.

Misrule said, in his rather mocking voice, 'You have a remarkably strong power essence, madame, and I see that it is tinged with the blue of the *Scealai*.'

The *Scealai*. The Narrator. The Story-Teller... Rumour thought: so he is able to see that, is he? He is able to see it easily and within minutes of meeting. She felt cold fear touch her skin again, for if the perceptions of these beings were as sharp and as finely honed as all this, she had been fortunate even to get through the Castle gates without being challenged.

But she said, carefully and courteously, 'You see rightly. I am versed in the art of Story-Telling.' And then, picking the words as warily as if she were treading on spun sugar, 'I have the degree of *Scealai*,' she said, and although in her world, the ancient Gael word was not utilised, she spoke with perfect truth. The Amaranths had simply called it the Art of the Story-Teller, and Rumour held a very high degree in it.

Misrule was looking at her, clearly waiting for more. Could she possibly bluff him? Dare she? But Rumour had always taken the reckless, the daring way. She eyed the Lord of Misrule with apparent tranquillity and said, 'I also have a degree in Saturnalia.'

The partly hidden eyes narrowed. 'Saturnalia? I do not know that,' said Misrule, and Rumour felt the spun sugar crack. She knew the theory and the history of sorcery as well as any living creature, but her knowledge of the mechanics of necromancy was sparse. It might betray her at any moment.

But she would not turn back now. She said, in a rather contemptuous voice, 'Indeed? Of course, it is a little obscure. A practice brought from Eastern lands. A feast of wild revelry,' said Rumour in a surprised, did-you-not-know-that tone. 'The god of the Saturnalia is sometimes known as Cronus,' she said, in the extra-kind voice of one addressing an untutored inferior, and Misrule said, glacially, 'The god Cronus is known to the Lord of this Castle.'

'Yes, I am sure he is.' Rumour smiled the most catlike of all her catlike smiles. 'In the Legends of Prophecy, is not Chaos usurped by Cronus, son of Gaia?' She moved to the centre of the hall, the silken blue-green robe of the Elven King brushing the floor with a soft, sensuous whisper. 'In the Prophecies, Cronus is the son of Gaia,' said Rumour, her voice as soft and as sensuous as her silken gown. 'Your Lord should beware of any creature approaching this Castle bearing that name.

'But perhaps Cronus has a female immanence. Perhaps he has a twin, an alter-ego, a doppelganger.' Again the smile. 'And so,' purred Rumour, 'perhaps you will tell your Lord that it is the Sorceress Saturnalia who has come to his Castle.'

Chapter Forty

Rumour was shown to a large, well-lit bedchamber with a deep soft bed with rich, silver-embroidered hangings. A bright fire glowed in the hearth, its leaping flames reflecting in the copper cans of scented hot water left for her.

The windows were set deeply into the thick ancient stone of the Castle walls, and beneath them was a wide, velvet-covered seat strewn with cushions. Through the half-curtained windows, Rumour could see the NightFields spread out to the west and, beyond them, the stark silhouettes of the Black Mountains. And somewhere in there was the lonely desolate Fortress of Almhuin, with its terrible prisoner and its solitary Guardian. She touched the memory of Andrew, because it was something good and something warm and safe and something to be trusted. While I have that, I can feel safe, and while I have that I can be immune to Chaos's dark beckoning necromancy. She turned back.

Tonight's banquet, whatever its purpose, was clearly to be a very grand affair. The guests would undoubtedly be glitteringly clad; there would be silks and velvets and taffetas; rich jewels and scented bodies and elaborate masks and ornate headdresses. I have to take part in it, thought Rumour. I have to go down into the brilliantly lit banqueting hall and mingle with the evil creatures that will undoubtedly assemble there, and I must hope I am not recognised. I think it is the only way to find out where Theodora is.

She grinned suddenly, and turned to the gowns she had brought, selecting, after thought, one of Aillen mac Midha's most beautiful robes; a soft gauzy gown of palest cream Seirician silk, the cobweb-fine stuff woven in the strange hidden water-caves of Seiricia, the seams bound with pearl and opal. There was a narrow circlet of pure soft silver. Rumour slid into the gown, lacing it so that it fell open across her breasts. Too much? Not enough? She smiled the catsmile, and allowed the laces to part another inch. Exactly right.

Her hair was still very short, but she thought it was not grotesquely so any more. It was like a boy's cap of hair, soft and dark, here and there with reddish lights. But it could be improved on. She unwrapped her small pots and the ivory boxes, and commenced to tip the short dark fronds with glinting silver. She would add a sprinkling of tiny silver stars to her bare shoulders, and perhaps she would sprinkle her breasts with them as well. Should she? She tried the effect, and was pleased. *Good.* She grinned again and reached for the soft tints of the face-paint, and the vivid colours she sometimes used to outline her eyes. Green eyelashes tonight, and a sprinkling of tiny silver specks to emphasise her cheekbones.

She set the casket containing the *sidh*'s music carefully in the garde-robe where her gowns and cloaks hung, and murmured a brief spell of protection over it. She thought there was a faint fragrant sigh from it, as if it was unhappy at being consigned to the dark, airless corner, and she thought there was a ripple of soft blue-green light. But she dared not leave it anywhere that it might be seen.

She gave her reflection a last inspection in the long oval looking-glass and, taking a deep breath, left the room to make her way to the banqueting hall of the Lord of Chaos and his dark servants.

It took more resolve than she had expected to walk through the Castle in the direction of the music and the sounds of the revelry. In a few minutes, I shall have to enter a room that will be filled with strangers, every one of them evil, any one of whom may recognise me for an intruder and an imposter.

But I'll do it, thought Rumour determinedly. I'll do it, I'll walk in with my head in the air, and somehow I'll outwit them.

She found the banqueting hall easily, and there was a thin trickle of confidence at that, as if she was being reminded that she was very used to walking through Castles and finding her way about, and that she was accustomed to taking part in glittering assemblies. She would pretend that this would not be so very different to any of those other banquets and gatherings and revelries.

But she paused outside the great double doors, summoning every ounce of courage, feeling the palms of her hands wet with nervous perspiration. This would be the most dangerous part yet.

The Lord of Chaos's guests were assembled in the huge brilliantly lit hall; the long tables were set with a sumptuous feast. Deferential servants stood ready to serve wine from immense silver tubs. Musicians were grouped on the dais at the far end, and the strange, faintly discordant music, which Rumour knew must be the dark strains created to assist the necromancers in their evil magic, spun and shivered about the hall.

Rumour knew she was in the presence of the greatest and the most evil necromancers ever gathered together under one roof. The beautiful hall was thick with the dark, swirling forces of necromancy, and suffocating waves of every one of the Seven Evils closed about her. Behind her, the door swung to with a little click, and Rumour knew a moment of panic. I am shut in with them. I am shut in with creatures who will certainly fall on me if they recognise me for an intruder. Don't think about it. Look about you as if looking for friends and acquaintances. Appear slightly disdainful.

She took another deep breath, and stood looking about her.

Misrule, with Anarchy and Murder, stood at the far end of the hall. Misrule was wearing a solid gold mask, shaped into the likeness of a fire demon, studded with rubies. His eyes, red and sly, glinted through the slits, and beneath it his thin, rather frail-looking body was clad in scarlet and black robes. Between his thighs was slung a narrow golden belt with its centre thickening into a huge jutting phallus, solid gold and monstrously lifelike, resting over his own genitals. On his feet were black boots laced with silver, with heels studded with rubies.

Murder wore his swirling crimson cloak and a black, deep-brimmed hat that shadowed his face. He did not appear to speak, only to watch and listen, but Rumour caught a glimpse of cold, merciless eyes and felt a cold shiver of fear. Anarchy was dressed as if for war, in black chainmail, with a breastplate engraved with Chaos's emblem. A white velvet cloak was slung negligently from his shoulders, and Rumour could see that it was spattered with blood and streaked with gore. But Anarchy's eyes were bright and alert; he was studying the guests in a lively fashion, as if he found them interesting and wanted to know them better.

Rumour was unexpectedly drawn to Anarchy. She found his air of bright interest attractive, and she found his extreme youth endearing. Murder was cold and sinister; he would stand silently and watchfully inside a room, watching his victim from under the deep shadow cast by the wide-brimmed slouch hat. And Misrule looked shallow and vain. But Anarchy would probably tumble headfirst into all manner of ill-judged battles and unwise rebellions. You could very easily visualise him rampaging through towns and cities and across battlefields, calling to rebels and dissidents, overturning laws and rulers and toppling governments. He would be lively and reckless and enthusiastic, and Rumour liked enthusiasts.

Among the guests were armoured and visor'd soldiers, and Rumour recognised them as being Captains of the ancient lineage of Rodent Armies, probably summoned by Chaos from the dread Caves of Cruachan, where they guarded one of the most ancient Gateways between the two Irelands. As they moved and mingled with the guests, she saw with a shiver of revulsion that many of them had slithering, boneless tails, which some of them had hung over their left forearms, rather as a soldier will accoutre himself with a dress sword if attending a very formal event. Beneath the black visors and helmets were the nightmare lumpish blending of jackals and rats and stoats and weasels with Humans, so that whiskers and feral teeth and snouts mingled grotesquely with Humanish lips and nostrils and ears.

Many of the silk- and satin-garbed Lords wore on their breasts the legendary Silver Star of Medoc, and again, Rumour received the impression of a military gathering, where all badges of honour or valour must be displayed.

The females were richly clad, but they were nearly all thin, ravaged-faced creatures; rapacious and avid, their lips painted the colour of blood, their faces alabaster-white and their eyes huge dark pits. Rumour remembered how the Crimson Lady had possessed exactly those dark, abyss-like eyes, and understood that the greeds and the lusts that male necromancers turned outwards, turned inwards for the females. The hungers had corrupted their powers, and they had become so dependent on the dark, lustful side of their craft, that they perpetually craved blood or sexual gratification. She knew a brief anger at the poor-spirited necromancesses who had allowed the power to master them instead of mastering the power.

Several of the females had live snakes coiled in their hair, for the snake is one of the highest servants of the necromantic Houses. The snakes were moribund and turgid, but Rumour saw the occasional flicker of a thin, forked tongue or the gleam of a basilisk eye, and knew it would not take very much to waken them. Some of the necromancesses had tiny black Goblin-creatures walking at their heels, many of them carrying the satin and velvet trains of their mistresses' gowns, sometimes simply holding golden, jewel-encrusted pouches which would probably hold mirrors and brushes and salves and pomades. Rumour glanced at these tiny, ugly train-bearers warily, knowing the limited but sometimes vicious powers of those who possessed Goblin-blood, but she saw at once that the creatures were stunted wizened beings, probably deliberately starved and made to sleep in cramped dark cupboards by the rapacious necromancesses, who would use them for grotesque sexual relief.

The Dark Royalty of the Black Ireland, all gathered together for the Lord of Chaos's fearsome War Banquet . . .

The musicians suddenly struck a harsh cacophony of notes, and a stir of anticipation brushed the company. Heads turned, conversation stilled, and the scarlet velvet curtains at the back of the banqueting hall rippled from the movement of an unseen creature, and the cold, unmelodious music rose to a massive crescendo.

Rumour felt the cold fear twist her stomach again, because this was it, this was the moment when he would appear – the moment when she could be caught.

The Lord of the Castle, the Suzerain of the Dark Ireland was about to appear . . .

The curtains parted with a whisper of sound, and he was

481

there. Chaos, the legendary dark sorcerer, the most powerful necromancer of them all.

Chaos, who had held the Black Domain firmly and impregnably against all assault for two centuries, who had waged war on the terrible Crimson Lady of Almhuin in the grisly, blood-soaked NightFields, and who commanded instant obedience and total allegiance, and hunted Men for sport and roasted their carcasses for torchlight . . .

And who, by the Well of Segais, had spun the Dark Lure over Rumour and evoked that swift, never-to-be-admitted response . . .

Rumour had thought that they would all be summoned to sit at the long tables, in order to partake of the dazzling array of dishes and to drink the wine and the spiced punch, but this did not seem to be the custom here.

There was no move to the tables, no announcement or request that the guests seat themselves. As Chaos stood framed by the scarlet velvet hangings, a slender, darkly garbed figure with slanting, glowing eyes, the guests sank on to their left knees in some kind of obeisance. Rumour, watching covertly, copied them. She would acknowledge no creature master, although she would be respectful to the Amaranth Head, but she dare not do anything to draw attention to herself.

As Chaos moved down from the dais, several of what Rumour thought would be Elders of some kind – cold-eyed, cruel-looking necromancers – moved to his side, and with them the Captains of the Rodent Army. As if this was a signal, the waiting servants began to move about the hall, each of them bearing platters of food which they offered to the grouped guests. There was roast venison and oxen and green goose and pressed duck; other dishes held portions of baked lakefish and salmonidae and ingot fish. Two of the servants were carving several sucking pigs and the foetus of young cows, which Rumour knew was considered a great delicacy, but which she did not care for very much. A side-table bore huge silver dishes of sugared fruits and honey cakes and confections of rose petals and tansies and elaborate concoctions made from pounded chestnuts and cream. Six of the servants stood beside the immense silver tubs, ladling wine into exquisite silver and gold chalices, which they handed to the guests.

Rumour thought it was an unusual, but rather interesting arrangement. She watched carefully to see what was done, and saw that, as the servants moved to and fro with the platters, they handed small silver bowls to each of the guests. The guests then simply helped themselves to portions of whatever they chose, eating and drinking and talking, and then moving on to other groups.

In fact, thought Rumour, momentarily intrigued, it was an extremely sensible way of giving a banquet, for it meant it was possible to move about and meet and talk with as many guests as you liked. She began to play the 'look-beyond' game again. If I get out of this alive, I shall give just such a feast. She visualised her own star-shaped banqueting hall inside her Castle of the Starlit Night, and saw how tables could be set in the points of the stars, and how guests could move about comfortably. A new fashion.

She moved slowly and quite composedly through the necromancers, smiling and nodding as she did so, as if she were entirely at home and as if she had a perfect right to be here.

But all the while her heart was racing, and from the corners of her eyes, she was watching Chaos and the small group that stood with him. Elder necromancers: not rulers exactly, but perhaps Dark Lords who had attained some kind of higher power? Yes. And the Rodent Captains – six of them, were there? – were being deferential, and Chaos was listening to them, his head tilted courteously.

War talk, thought Rumour, sipping her wine. Battle talk. I believe that this banquet is something to do with the War between Chaos and the Crimson Lady. And with the framing of the thought came another: but if that is so, then Chaos does not yet know that the Crimson Lady has been imprisoned in her own fortress! Dare I believe that? thought Rumour. Did the Fomoire after all not return here to tell their tale? But why not? And knew the answer at once: the Fomoire had been beaten – Rumour herself had beaten them – and they would not dare to face Chaos with such an admission.

This was unexpectedly heartening, because it made Chaos

seem less all-powerful than he had previously seemed. But Rumour thought she dared not believe in it too wholeheartedly.

But it was plain that the Rodent Captains were here to plan a battle. Rumour watched them under cover of taking a further portion of the food, and saw that they were all looking very serious. So whatever they are planning is something important, and probably something they have not yet attempted in this war. *Could* it be the storming of Almhuin? Cold fear gripped her, and she thought: but Andrew is still there! He is alone and he is lame in that great dark Fortress!

Anarchy and Murder stood together, Anarchy laughing and drinking wine as fast as his chalice was filled by the silent servants, eyeing the females rather leeringly and calling out ribald jokes to the males. But Murder said very little; he stood wrapped in his crimson cloak, the slouch hat pulled over his face, eating and drinking sparingly. Once the deep sunken eyes seemed to meet Rumour's, and she tensed her muscles, waiting for the shout, the pointing finger that would unmask her, but Murder's eyes slid over her and passed on. Rumour, her every muscle aching with the tension of fear, drew in a breath of relief.

Misrule was everywhere, peering at people's plates to see what was being eaten, whipping up the musicians to provide louder music, occasionally leaping on to the table to caper amidst the wine-flagons and the silver dishes and the arrangements of flowers and bowls of fruit. Everywhere he went, a crackle of laughter broke out and a buzz of alert conversation, and Rumour saw that, despite the deep and serious nature of Chaos's conversation, the necromancer's eyes frequently turned towards Misrule, as if he was watching that Misrule did not miss any opportunity to entertain the guests.

As she turned back to where Chaos stood with the four Dark Lords and the Rodent Captains, Misrule darted suddenly to the centre of the room, and flung up his hands, calling for the guests' attention.

'For, my friends,' he said, 'we have a little amusement devised for your pleasure now.' The mischievous eyes behind the slanting golden mask gleamed with malicious mirth, and Rumour moved to the far wall, where she could be partly concealed by a fall of gold brocade that swathed a window.

Misrule said, still in his light mocking voice, 'My alter ego,

Murder, is arranging for better *lights* for us, friends,' and at once an amused cheer went up, and Rumour, guessing what lay ahead, felt cold horror clutch the pit of her stomach. Misrule flung out a hand, pointing to the thick wooden spikes standing around the hall, each one nearly eight feet in height, its end set into a heavy-looking base of what Rumour thought was beaten copper, or perhaps even solid gold. As she stared, not daring to move lest she should be spotted as an interloper, the doors at the far end were flung open, and Murder, now clad in a black cloak that brushed the floor, stood there, with behind him six chained and manacled Humans, bedraggled and dirty, their bones showing through the skimpy rags that clung to them, their eyes pale and bewildered by the sudden brilliant light of the banqueting hall after their dark, windowless dungeons.

Rumour glanced round, seeking a way to create a diversion that would enable the prisoners to break free, but knowing that they would almost certainly have been kept in the Castle dungeons for so long that their wits would be dulled and their strength so feeble that all alertness would long since have deserted them, and that they would be incapable of grasping at any sudden opportunity.

And then she saw that, surrounding the prisoners, leaping and whirling, the horrid slit Humanish skins flying wildly, were the Fomoire.

The necromancers and their attendants moved back, leaving the centre of the floor clear. A hum of pleased anticipation went up.

Misrule was dancing around the edges of the room now, the golden mask glinting cruelly, the ruby heels of his shoes sending out sparks of baleful red light. Rumour, still partly concealed by the curtain, saw that he was dancing nimbly and agilely beneath each of the rearing wooden stakes, and that, as he did so, the sparks from his ruby heels collected and coagulated, until a tiny pool of crimson formed; thick, viscous fluid that coiled and swirled and sent up tiny hissing spirals of smoke. Within the smoke there appeared glowing coals, black as ebony, but emitting such fierce heat that the necromancers drew back.

Rumour heard someone say, 'Misrule has made sure of the heat tonight,' and another answer, 'Can you blame him? We all remember the time when the Humanish had to be set alight

485

from the wall-torches, and how long it took for them to burn up.'

The heat glowed in fierce pools of molten brilliance, and Murder moved forward, the prisoners shuffling after him in horrid obedience, the Fomoire prodding them, leaping and jeering, singing their terrible Hunting Song.

> 'Give us fire to burn the hair
> Flames to light the Humanish vair.
> Give us heat and glowing meat;
> Sparks and flames and smoke and fire.'

They pushed the prisoners forward, jabbing with their long, bony fingers, their wizened faces just visible through the Humanish cloaks, the mean little eyes gleaming with malevolence.

Misrule stood at the centre of the room, his hands on his hips, and Murder stalked forward and stood beneath the first of the stakes. He looked round at the watching throng, and the smallest of smiles touched his thin lips. Rumour thought that it was if he were saying: ah, you puny creatures, you laugh and cavort with Misrule, but it is *I* who can command your full attention now! It flickered on her mind that there might be jealousy between Chaos's three henchmen, and there might certainly be rivalry, and for a moment she wondered if this was something she could use.

The Fomoire had reached for one prisoner's chains, skittering excitedly across the floor on all fours, the empty-eyed skulls of their cloaks jerked backwards as they did so. They began to drag the prisoner forward and, as they did so, the crimson pool of fire created by Misrule flared up, washing the scene to eerie glowing horror. The prisoner, who had seemed bewildered and barely aware of his surroundings, looked up as the monstrous shadow of the stake fell over him, and terrible comprehension dawned in his eyes. At once he screamed and jerked away, trying to free himself. The Fomoire shrieked gleefully, and four of them bent down in front of him, seizing the slithering iron chains that trailed from his legs, hauling him forward to the waiting stake and the leaping flames.

The swirling crimson pool flared up again, and as the flames licked the base of the stake, a scent of burning wood drifted across the banqueting hall. Rumour, who had sat before innumerable blazing fires stoked high with applewood and pearwood, found it unbearable that such beautiful and evocative scents should be so horribly mixed in with such grisliness and such pitiless torture.

The prisoner was at the foot of the stake now; the leaping flames were before him, and he was screaming like a trapped hare.

Anarchy, who was standing in a semi-drunken state nearby, lifted his wine chalice and shouted, 'Misrule has neglected to sew the prisoners' mouths again!'

'Shame on him!' cried the necromancers, and low chuckles broke from them.

Misrule grinned and capered around the circle of the watchers, holding out the jutting golden phallus, thrusting it obscenely at the females.

'Let the Humanish squeal!' he cried. 'Let us hear them squeal and smell them roast!'

Murder was standing directly behind the wickedly sharp stake, the black cloak wrapped about him, the deep-brimmed hat pulled over his eyes. The flames leapt higher, illuminating his silent watchful figure, black against fiery red, and Rumour shivered, knowing that, although Misrule might be vain and malicious and Anarchy feckless and shallow, Murder was far and away the most evil of Chaos's henchmen.

Misrule was urging the Fomoire on, dancing around the watching guests, starting up little chants and rhythms wherever he went. Rumour heard the low murmur of sound begin, and swell, and mount to fill the entire, red-lit hall.

'Burn the Humanish . . . Burn them . . . Burn them . . .'

The entire banqueting hall was echoing with the rhythmic chanting now.

'Burn them . . . Burn them . . .'

Misrule leapt and capered, laughing and darting, holding out the jutting golden phallus again, and presently, above the steady chanting, Rumour heard another refrain start up.

> 'Feed the flames, appease the fire;
> Boil the skins and scorch the hair.
> Catch the juices, poach the eyes,

The Fomoire had started it, but now the necromancers were joining in, and the terrible grisly words rose to a painful, deafening pitch.

The guests were swaying with the steady, rhythmic chanting, and Rumour heard the sexual note in their voices. Several of them were pulling up their robes and caressing their swelling organs, and from where she stood, Rumour could see that most of the men possessed the unmistakable barbed penises of all who harness the true Darkness.

A low cry came from the necromancesses, and they pounced at once, their ravaged faces hungry, reaching out, clawing and tearing their gowns aside, exposing withered bodies, empty hanging breasts, fleshless thighs.

They are eaten up with their own hungers, thought Rumour, staring in sick disgust. They are burnt up with their unnatural lusts and desires.

Several of the necromancesses had forced the Dark Lords to the floor, and had leapt to straddle them, forcing the monstrous organs between their thighs, moaning and panting.

Misrule shrieked with delight, and began his capering dance again, and Anarchy flung the wine chalice on to the floor, and plunged into the centre of the heaving, writhing mêlée.

Murder and the Fomoire had lifted the screaming Humanish prisoner high, and were chaining him to the stake. When they stepped back, the flames from Misrule's molten pools leapt, engulfing the screaming prisoner, and the truly terrible scent of roasting meat filled the banqueting hall.

From his stance at the far end, the Lord of Chaos stood alone, watching his people as they moaned and writhed in obscene ecstasy. The light from the roasting Humanish burned upwards, making him a creature of dark fire, beautiful and sinister and evil beyond belief. He moved to the back of the dais, and seated himself on a black carven throne, high-backed and lined with ebony velvet. Rumour looked at him, and instantly dragged her eyes away, because even at this distance, he would see that she was not of his people.

The second prisoner was being chained to the next stake now, and his hair had already caught fire, so that the stench of its burning was tainting the hall. The first one was still screaming, but the flames were engulfing his body, and all that was visible of him now was his face, splitting open with the heat, emitting the thin, colourless fluid from just beneath the skin, which ran into the flames with grisly, crackling noises.

Rumour thought: and he will burn slowly, they will all burn slowly, their agony will be long drawn-out, for the necromancers want the light for their repulsive couplings.

As she framed the thought, the Fomoire dragged out the next two prisoners, and Murder again moved into place.

It was then, at the moment when Rumour had been least expecting it, that the Lord of Chaos turned his dark, glowing eyes upon her, and said, 'Stop. All of you. We have an enemy in our midst.'

At once the quality of the revelries altered. The Fomoire scurried backwards, and Misrule and Anarchy turned to regard their Master.

The necromancers and their partners stood up, their robes still disarrayed, some of them partly naked, some of them completely so. From a great distance, Rumour was aware that the first prisoner had sagged on the wooden stake, and that his screams had stopped, but that the second one was still writhing, although his cries were growing weaker.

She moved forward, the thin pale-as-floss gown whispering across the floor as she walked. There was a murmur from the necromancers and the Rodent Captains, and Rumour understood that the agony and the flames had cast over them all a cloak of such unbridled lechery and such rampant hunger that they were still held fast in its grip. Red lust showed in the faces of the necromancers, and also – Rumour shuddered inwardly – in the faces of the females. The Goblin-creatures who attended some of the necromancesses scampered out to her, and tugged on the hem of her gown, chuckling with evil glee as they did so.

Rumour was standing before Chaos now, a little below him, so that he looked down on her. Anger rose within her, and she thought: I may be caught and exposed, but I will not allow this evil creature to look down on me as if I am of no account at all!

With the searing anger came courage, and she walked calmly to stand on the dais beside him and regarded him straightly.

She thought that a gleam of appreciation showed in the dark, glowing eyes, but he only said, 'You are welcome, madame, even though I think you are unexpected.'

Rumour said, 'Indeed? Did you not, then, believe I should one day come in answer to your beckoning, Chaos?' and saw the dark eyes gleam again.

'You are here in answer to no beckoning of mine, Rumour,' he said. 'But since you are here . . .' He looked down to where Misrule was listening. 'Since you are here,' said Chaos, 'I believe we shall ask you to provide a little entertainment.'

Rumour stared at him and thought: he is going to burn me! He is going to order Murder and the Fomoire to chain me to one of the stakes, as they have already chained two of their prisoners. And then they will let me burn, and they will continue to satisfy their evil lusts in the light of my burning body! Shall I scream as those poor wretches screamed? She was dimly aware that the second prisoner had sagged into a charred mass, and that his screams had ceased. But before he does that, he is going to force me to spin something for these obscene creatures' amusement.

Misrule said, 'Master, she is a *Scealai*,' and Rumour heard with disgust the sycophantic note in his voice. 'I believed her to be one of the guests . . .'

Chaos did not speak, but he turned on Misrule a look of such searing contempt that Rumour saw Misrule fall back and fling up his hands to shield his eyes. A low murmur came from the listening necromancers, and several of them began to look uneasy.

Chaos turned back to Rumour. 'You are here to rescue the Amaranth Princess. We both know it.' He made a brief gesture with one hand. 'Therefore I cannot allow you to escape,' he said with a note of what Rumour could almost have believed to be regret. She understood at once that Chaos rather admired her, but that he could not afford to let her live. She must be summarily put to death, here, before all of his subjects, so that they should see his might and his merciless dealings with spies and enemies.

Chaos said, softly, 'You are right, my dear, of course you must die. But you know, I believe it would add a touch of refinement to your torture to delay it a little.' His eyes went thoughtfully to the waiting stakes. 'Not necessarily the flames of course,' said Chaos, as if considering the matter carefully. 'There are several other punishments I can order for you.' The dark eyes hardened suddenly. 'You should know that I do not care very much for intruders here, Madame Amaranth,' he said, and now there was no faintly amused respect and no rather grudging admiration. This was premier Lord of the terrible Dark Ireland; the pitiless necromancer who consorted with the darkness and could summon whatever black sorcery he wished.

'But since you have chosen to risk my anger and my punishment, then let us play the charade a little longer,' said Chaos. He gestured to the banqueting hall, still lit by the dying flames from the stakes, the breathless anticipation of the guests so strong that Rumour could feel it gusting towards her.

'It is a pity,' he said softly, 'that you did not choose to serve me in other ways, Rumour.' His eyes slid over her body and, despite her resolve, Rumour felt the treacherous stirrings again. How would it be, how would it feel to lie alongside this slender, cruel, beautiful being, to see his face twist not with cruel, cold authority, but with passion and longing . . .

Chaos smiled again, as if perfectly aware of her thoughts. 'Only think what we could have been together, my dear,' he said, and now it was the dangerous soft voice of the seducer. He looked at her, and Rumour understood him again. He was offering her her freedom . . .

If you will bow your head and embrace my dark world . . .

'No,' said Rumour, very softly. 'I shall never do that, Chaos.'

'You could share it all,' he said. 'The power and the might and the glory.'

'No,' said Rumour again, and their eyes met and locked.

Then Chaos said, dismissively, 'A pity. Misrule was deceived into believing you came here to make part of the entertainments,' he said. 'He is a gullible fool and he will pay dearly for his mistake.' As he spoke, he flung, almost negligently, a sizzling tongue of flame in Misrule's direction. Misrule screeched with anger and fear, but the flame had reached him, and curled about his waist a thin lash of white-hot fire. Misrule screamed and tore at the fire, his fingers blistering and bubbling from its furious heat, the flesh charring almost instantly. He fell back, rolling over and over in agony now, and Rumour saw with sick horror that the fire-lash that circled his waist was burning through his flesh, cutting him in half . . .

The necromancers had moved back, their faces uneasy now. Misrule was rolling on the ground, still frantically trying to claw the fire-lash from his body. His nails were black and smoking, and there was a terrible stench of burning. He writhed frantically, screaming and begging for mercy, but the fire had bitten deep into his flesh now. He arched his back, trying to throw it off, and Rumour saw that blood and bone showed and that the flesh was being neatly sawn through; that there were no jagged-edged wounds, only a clean severing, a slicing in twain.

He knew what was happening. Through the golden mask his eyes were fiery red now, and starting from his head. He threw himself back once again, his head cracking against the hard floor, his body arching once more, so that it rested on the tip of his head and his heels, his neck muscles straining and standing out.

And then, quite suddenly, he looked down at his body, and the watchers saw that the fire-lash had almost succeeded in its grisly work; there was the glint of blood-soaked rib-bones, the dark gleam of liver and the wet purple sac of entrails beginning to spill out over the floor . . .

Misrule gave one final scream and fell to the floor, blood seeping from the two halves of his body. His hands scrabbled feebly at the ground, as if still trying to reach the dais and plead for forgiveness. His feet in the dazzling, ruby-heeled boots were twitching, as if trying to show that they still had the power to dance and leap.

There was a choking, bubbling cough, and blood – thick dark blood – dribbled from the slits in the golden mask.

Silence fell on the banqueting hall.

'A fool and a creature of no judgement,' said Chaos dismissively. And then, to the Fomoire, 'Remove it.' The Fomoire leapt at once, dragging the two halves of Misrule's body across the floor, leaving smeary trails of blood as they did so.

Rumour found herself wondering, with sharp irrelevancy, whether they would use Misrule's skin, and then, as she felt Chaos's eyes on her again, turned back to him.

'And now,' said Chaos, smiling thinly, 'now, Rumour, it is

your turn to entertain us.' He moved back to seat himself on the black, velvet-lined throne.

Rumour thought: oh, why not do the thing in full? Why not summon up the most dazzling, most extravagant enchantment I can think of? And why not do it with such style and such elegance that it will have these horrid greedy necromancers and these stupid hungering necromancesses speechless with admiration?

And that may give me time to formulate a plan to escape them.

She stepped forward, allowing the front of her gown to slide open a little further as she did so. As she moved, the skirts parted to show the soft gleam of slender thighs and narrow ankles. Rumour moved down from the dais, and walked to the centre of the hall, seeing that Chaos's guests moved back at once.

She stood at the centre of the great banqueting hall, feeling how thickly it was tainted from the lusts and the greeds of the company, feeling as well that it was smeared and clotted with the bewildered death agonies of the two prisoners, and Misrule's final, terrible torment, knowing that none of it must matter to her now.

For she must spin something that would dazzle and capture; she must blind these creatures, render them helpless, deaf – lifeless, if only it were possible – so that she could escape and reach Theodora.

For I will *not* die at these creatures' hands!

As she lifted her hands to call down the power, her mind was racing. What should it be? Chaos would certainly dissolve at birth anything that would be harmful; he would take a warped delight in watching her try to summon the Enchantment of Slumber, or aggressive spells of knives or fire or lightning that would injure his guests.

Nothing so crude! thought Rumour, turning slowly to regard the waiting necromancers, seeing that anticipation glittered in their eyes, that they were all regarding her with the red lust again. They had already dismissed Chaos's terrible vengeance on Misrule; they were avid for the revelries again, and it would not take very much to make them tear off the flimsy silk gown

493

and slake their hungers on her helpless body. And although, said a tiny unquenched part of her, although I could cope with the males, I think I must really draw the line at the females and the Rodents!

The sudden wry irony made her feel instantly better. She thought: I am at the centre of Chaos's Castle; I may well be within yards of Theo and I may be within inches of a nasty death. But for now everyone is looking at me: it is my moment of power, and I must, I absolutely *must* dazzle them!

The power was there, waiting, shimmering, easily and fluidly obedient to her summons. Whatever she summoned would materialise within seconds. What should it be?

What?

And then a tiny smile curved her lips, and as she looked round at the silent watching necromancers and the Rodent Captains, and at Murder and Anarchy, she thought: well, of course there is only one enchantment I can use! Of course there is only one that will dazzle and bewitch them, and that will show them that I am easily as powerful as they are, and that may even give me the chance to escape!

The beautiful rich spell she had woven herself over so many years, that had never been completed, that never would be completed, because its story would never be told, it had no end . . .

The glittering, iridescent enchantment that she could conjure so easily, and that would unroll and unfold its immense shimmering pageantry and its brilliant, compelling magic, with pouring rivers of molten gold and silver strands and incandescent blues and greens, and blazing oriflames of scarlet and orange and tawny.

The Unfinished Spell.

The Enchanted Tapestry of the Amaranths.

It formed at her bidding almost instantly, and although Rumour was concentrating on keeping the silvered symbols of the Enchantment firmly before her inner eye, she heard the ripple of admiration that went through the hall. She thought: I was right, I was right to suspect they had not so very much power, these creatures! How easy it is to dazzle them!

The stories were spilling over now, beautiful and enthralling and magical; each one a precious piece of history, each one a page of the chronicles of Ireland; of sorcery, of necromancy, of battles and intrigues and usurpings; invasions and Wars and Golden Reigns and Evil Tyrannies . . . The Wolfkings and the Druids and the *sidh*, and the strange, half-Human beasts who had ruled from Tara, all pouring out and marching past, whirling about the heads of the Dark Lords with lambent light and flaring colour.

Rumour stood at the centre, the pageantry all about her, glittering and shining, dazzling in a hall that had been dazzling to begin with; a marvellous chiaroscuro, a shifting, blurring kaleidoscope not only of light, but also of elusive sounds and vagrant scents, and the marvellous woodland magic and the deep mountain sorcery, and the glittering intrigue of the Courts of the High Kings. The lovers and the poets and the warrior Queens of Ireland; the fighters and the traitors and the courtiers . . . The lost loves and the forbidden passions and the strange spells and the lingering curses that ran through Ireland's great and wonderful history in glittering threads of scarlet and gold, and in coursing rivers of twilit sorcery and dawn-filled magic . . .

There was unwilling respect in every face now; the necromancers were staring and Chaos was watching from the black throne, his eyes unreadable.

Rumour thought: if there is a moment when I can run from the hall and try to reach Theo, then surely this is the moment! Strength coursed through her, and she thought: this is the moment, now, when they are all dazzled, and when the brilliance is blurring their vision and their senses. She lifted a hand again, causing the pouring swathes of brilliance to spiral upwards, gathering the Enchantment up as she would have gathered up a glittering ball of thread, seeing the tumble of the marvellous tapestry whirling about in a maelstrom of rainbow beauty.

And then she stepped back, and slipped out through the doors of the hall.

Chapter Forty-one

The concubines did not know *what* to do. They had been waiting for AnCine to return from the banquet, because of course, AnCine had been chosen to attend: they had all known that she would be. But she had promised to tell them all about it, and so they were going to sit up, just as they did when one of them was sent to Chaos, so that they could hear all about it.

She had looked very nice indeed. They had all helped, running to and fro to fetch scented water and oil for her bath and trying the effect of tawny brown – no *yellow!* – for her gown and cloak. It had all been so exciting.

Most of them had actually been a bit relieved not to have been chosen to attend the banquet, because there were to be all manner of important people there, and it might have been difficult to know what to say to them. AnCine said it was easy, but the concubines did not think it was easy at all. It was all very well for AnCine, who had spent three nights in a row with Chaos, and who, moreover, had been all of fourteen when she was brought to the *Saraigli*, and could therefore be considered more worldly than most of them.

It had been quite a long time after the banquet had started (they had been able to hear the music and the revelries so they knew), that a complete stranger had stepped into the *Saraigli* and stood looking at them.

This was not something that anyone could ever remember happening before. The *Saraigli* was not a place where people simply stepped in. It was secret and safe; it was not kept locked because it did not need to be locked; everyone in Chaos's service knew that it was death – and a slow, bad death – to enter the *Saraigli* illicitly.

And so the only people who came to it were Meirdreach and

the Reachtaire and his servants. Chaos did not come, of course, he simply sent a message to Meirdreach that he would be wanting one of them for the night, and Meirdreach chose who would go, and whoever it was was escorted by two servants to the velvet-hung bedchamber.

But here was a slender, silk-clad figure standing just inside the door, looking at them with a small, friendly smile. The concubines glanced uneasily at one another, because they had no idea what to do. The intruder was very beautifully dressed, they could not help seeing that. The pale ivory gown was of the finest silk, and the tiny pearls were of a very high quality. They all knew the difference between good jewels and inferior ones, of course. They could not help wondering how ever the stranger had the courage to wear her hair in such a short, stark fashion, although most of them were already trying to visualise how the shape would look on their own hair. And they noted the sprinkling of silver stars, which was certainly something different and new, and something they might all like to copy, and also the carefully painted silver tips to the short hair. You might even use gold paint, or – this would be *very* daring – turquoise or emerald-green. They began to feel interested.

Rumour had understood instantly that these were Chaos's sequestered women; his harem, the sheltered, pampered creatures, one or two of whom he would occasionally summon to his bed, but most of whom might never even see him. She thought that this rather odd custom of imprisoning pretty brainless creatures for random, unthinking sexual gratification, had originated in one of the Eastern lands, and she looked at the twenty or so concubines, and felt anger at the Lord of this Castle who had condemned them to such useless, narrow lives.

But this was almost surely where Chaos would have put Theodora, and so she moved purposefully forward.

'Please do not be afraid,' said Rumour in a low, urgent voice. 'I do not wish any of you any harm.' She saw them glance at one another, and understood that the making of decisions, the shouldering of responsibility was wholly outside their experience.

'I shall not hurt you,' said Rumour, trying again. 'I understand that you are – are not permitted to receive guests,

497

and I promise you that no one need know I was ever here.'
She studied them. 'But I must take the child,' she said. 'The
Princess.' And saw fearful comprehension dawn in their eyes.
'If she is here,' said Rumour, glancing behind her at the
half-closed door, 'you *must* let me take her.' And saw at once
from their expressions that Theo was indeed here, and knew a
rush of gratitude so vast that for a moment the room swam
before her sight. She had been almost sure, she *had* been sure,
but there had always been the faint chance that Theo was
somewhere else entirely, shut away, used in some monstrous
fashion...

The concubines did not know what to do. They withdrew a
little, chattering anxiously. They did not want to call for
Meirdreach; you never knew what Meirdreach might do, and in
any case, she was probably spying on the banquet.

On the whole, they were rather inclined to believe that
Rumour was a friend. Also, people who could think up such
remarkable ways of dressing and wearing their hair ought not to
be dismissed without a hearing. They reached this conclusion,
and felt rather pleased with themselves, because it seemed to be
very sensible. One or two of them said that Rumour might even
be somebody extremely important, and therefore they would be
glad, later, if they had obeyed her, although several said: no,
they must be careful, she might be an enemy of Chaos after all.
But since they had no idea what they should do if Rumour was
an enemy, they found this point of view very worrying, and
decided to ignore it.

And then, without the least warning, without anyone being
aware of it, the inner doors to the sleeping chambers were
pushed rather hesitantly open, and Theodora, the dear, pretty
little creature they had all enjoyed dressing up and petting and
devising games for, stood on the threshold, her dark eyes huge
in her little pointed face, a trace of colour touching her high
cheekbones.

Theodora said, in a whisper, 'Rumour – I *knew* you would
come!' and straightaway launched herself across the room into
Rumour's arms.

Theo had known all along that someone would come to get her.
Of course they would not leave her here inside the horrid Dark

Realm, and of course they would somehow come in and rescue her. She had dreamt about it happening nearly every night, only sometimes the dreams had got muddled, and she had been glad to wake up, because they had been all about dreadful things happening in the Porphyry Palace, and about Mamma and Papa being threatened and harmed, and the rest of the Amaranths in some dreadful danger.

But here was Rumour, her beautiful and dazzling Cousin Rumour, smiling at her with the remembered amusement, as if they might be sharing some kind of delightful secret, and here was one of Rumour's marvellous, extravagant gowns. As Rumour's arms closed about her, Theo could smell the beautiful expensive scents her cousin always used, and feel the silken brush of her skin. She would not cry, because it would have been very childish, and anyway, there would not be time for anything like that. But for the first time since the Fomoire had broken through the Gateway in the Well of Segais and carried her into the Dark Ireland, Theo began to feel safe.

The concubines were in a flurry of excitement, because hadn't the decision been made for them, with the dear loving child clasped in her aunt's arms, was it? Ah, her *cousin* – well, in any event, it was all very affecting.

They bustled about importantly, eager to help, and it all began to be rather exciting. The cousin must be offered refreshments before her journey, they said, remembering their manners; three of them running for the wine-flagons, two more for the little sweet cakes they had baked by themselves only the day before.

But Theo's cousin said, no, they must not trouble themselves, because there was not really time for such things, and so the concubines next bethought themselves of warm clothes for the journey. Theodora could not possibly go out of the *Saraigli* clad only in her sleeping things, they said, shocked. They fetched the little store of things the child had used while she had been here, and they opened the cupboards where they hung their best gowns, and found her a warm, fur-lined cloak and the dearest little red boots.

Rumour, frantic to get Theo away before the necromancers burst out of the banqueting hall, but knowing they must pacify these pretty, frivolous creatures, accepted the cloaks and the slippers, and also the cambric shirts and breeches, which, said the concubines giggling behind their hands, had been left behind by the Reachtaire's men, although they did *not* know how that had happened!

Rumour said, 'You are extremely generous, and we will bid you farewell now,' and the concubines at once looked alarmed, because they had not realised that the unknown lady would actually be leaving at once, and it would be quite dreadfully dangerous to go prowling along the corridors and the empty halls by night.

'Why?' said Rumour, who was wrapping Theo in the cloak and helping her to lace up the red boots.

The concubines glanced uneasily at one another, and finally mustered up the courage to explain about the *Draoicht Spiaire*, the fearsome Enchantment of Spying that Chaos would by now have let loose to prowl the Castle. Rumour thought: so that is why he allowed me to go! That is why he did not order his minions to come in search of me after I left the banqueting hall! That is why I have been inside this place for the last half-hour without hearing Chaos's servants, or Chaos himself, coming to find me! Chaos had known that the *Spiaire* was loose, or perhaps he had ordered it to be let loose. He knew it would find Rumour as she crept through the deserted halls and galleries of the Castle. This was a rather daunting thought, but they could not let it stop them. The *Spiaire* would have to be faced.

She looked round at the pretty, empty-headed creatures of the *Saraigli*, and said, very gently, 'The *Draoicht Spiaire* is certainly a formidable thing to confront, but nevertheless it must be faced. And you have been more helpful than I had looked for. We cannot thank you sufficiently,' she said, and Theo at once said:

'You have all been so very kind, and I do wish you . . .' She paused, unsure of the correct, the polite expression. 'I do wish you all happiness,' she said, and the concubines sighed, because the dear child had such pretty manners, and they would all miss her so much, they did not know what they would do when she had gone.

Rumour had been wondering, should she offer them something by way of thanks for their kindnesses to Theo? She had no jewels on her, which was probably the one thing they would appreciate. Was there something she could spin for them, something quick and easy but dazzling that would appeal to their light, shallow minds?

Stepping back, she lifted her hands, palms upwards, to harness power. 'We have not very much time,' she said, 'but I think there is time for me to make you a small gift to show my gratitude for the way you have cared for my cousin.' She smiled at them. 'It will only be very little, because there is not time for anything more, but it would please me if you would accept it,' said Rumour, and Theo gazed up at her admiringly, because this was her marvellous cousin, this was the famous Amaranth sorceress who had dined with the High Kings, and had dozens of lovers, and who could take her place at the high table when the Amaranths gave their splendid banquets, and make all the important people smile and relax and enjoy themselves. Theo was immensely proud of Rumour who was speaking in exactly the right way to these ladies, who were a bit silly but who had been kind to her.

Rumour had reached down a brief, rather garish Spell of Seduction, scarlet and gold phallus-shapes etched clearly against a pale swathe of gauze. She thought it was exactly the sort of colourful, slightly obvious thing that the concubines might like, and she coiled it into thin silken folds, and presented it to them.

'With my heartfelt gratitude,' she said, and the concubines thanked her, twittering excitedly over the unexpected gift, telling her how they would store it away carefully, and use it very often, and how no one should ever guess they had it.

'As for the escape of Theodora,' said Rumour, 'I think if you simply say you woke up this morning and found she was gone, your story will be believed.'

The concubines had in fact been quite worried about this, but Rumour's suggestion at once found favour. They said, very seriously, that they would all go to bed the minute she left, they would close their eyes very tightly, and they would pretend that they had not heard a thing.

'You will be believed,' said Rumour, with certainty, because no one could possibly suspect these empty-headed little creatures of any kind of intrigue.

She looked down at the expectant-eyed Theodora, and smiled. 'Well, little one?' she said. 'Are you ready to brave the *Draoicht Spiaire* with me?'

But Theo would have braved anything in the whole world with Rumour at her side. She at once said, 'Oh yes!' and together they went through the doors and out into the vast Castle.

Theo had thought that the journey through the deserted Castle would be the most frightening thing you could imagine. She held Rumour's hand, although she was careful not to hold it too tightly because of not letting Rumour know how frightened she really was.

It was important to show Rumour that she was not a silly baby, no better than the concubines. Theo thought she might have begun to get a bit impatient with the concubines if she had had to stay locked into the *Saraigli* for much longer. She explained this to Rumour as they walked cautiously through the Castle, not whispering, because whisperings were full of hisses and people could sometimes hear you very clearly indeed if you whispered and hissed, but speaking in an extra-quiet voice.

Rumour listened, and Theo, momentarily diverted, remembered that this had been one of Rumour's best qualities: she listened to you, really listened, not just pretend or polite listening.

Rumour seemed to want to know all about the *Saraigli*. She asked quite a lot of questions, some of which Theo did not see the point of, but all of which she answered, because of not being a nuisance or impolite. She explained that they had come into the Dark Realm through the Moher Gateway, which had been quite frightening really on account of it being near to the Tanning Pit, but which you might, if you looked at it all sensibly, describe as a new experience, especially if you had not seen that part of Ireland before. Theo had not seen it, and she had been astonished at the dark beauty of the Moher Cliffs and at the dazzling splendour of the endless oceans that pounded and lashed Ireland's west coast.

Rumour asked if Theo had been in the *Saraigli* for all of the time she had been here, and Theo said, 'Oh yes,' only that it had been dreadfully boring, on account of never seeing anyone except the concubines, and not being allowed even to go outside for a walk.

Rumour said, her voice carefully expressionless, 'Did you not see Chaos or any of his servants at all?' and Theo explained about Meirdreach, whom they had all giggled over, and about the Reachtaire, who sometimes came into the *Saraigli* with sugared fruits or little sweet buns for them all, and who was very fat and smooth-skinned and loved a little gossip with them all.

Rumour said, in a sympathetic voice, 'Horridly boring,' and Theo was glad that Rumour understood.

They had reached Rumour's bedchamber now, and it was all safe and very nearly normal, and Theo was beginning to think that it was all turning into a very good adventure. The bedchamber was faintly scented with Rumour's perfume, which Theo had noticed all Rumour's bedchambers were. She had sometimes gone into Rumour's bedchamber at the Porphyry Palace, after Rumour had gone back to her own Starlit Night Castle, just for the pleasure of being enfolded in Rumour's beautiful, elusive fragrance and the lingering essences she always left, even when she had only been in a room for a few hours.

They managed to fold some things into a large bag shaped like a box, with tapestry patterns on the outside, and Rumour said they must be very careful indeed to take it with them, no matter what might threaten them, because there were some very precious things indeed inside. Theo touched the tapestry box-bag, and looked up at Rumour, because she had felt at once that there was something deeply magical inside it.

'There is,' said Rumour. 'That is why we must take it out with us at all costs.' She grinned at Theo. 'I have brought that with me out of the Porphyry Palace, through Tiarna, and even out of the fortress of Almhuin,' she said.

'Almhuin?' Theo had heard Almhuin mentioned in a general way.

Rumour said, 'Andrew is at Almhuin, Theo,' and saw the sudden pleasure in the child's face.

'Waiting for us?'

'I hope so,' said Rumour, and something that Theo had never seen shone in Rumour's eyes for a moment. 'Yes, I hope so.'

Theo thought the journey through the Castle began to be frightening as soon as they stepped out of Rumour's bedchamber. The shadows crept forward at once, so that you could almost imagine they were alive and waiting for you. Theodora stared at them and came up with the word, 'menacing'. The shadows were menacing, and the whole Castle was menacing; it crawled and shivered with dark things you could not see, although you knew they were there, and it throbbed and hummed and whispered with secret, peering creatures. Theodora cautiously drew Rumour's attention to this, and Rumour said at once, 'Yes, I know. I hear it all. Don't worry,' and Theo was instantly comforted, because if Rumour could hear and feel the dark slithery things and say, 'Don't worry', in that very ordinary voice, then probably there was not very much to worry about. Probably whatever the things were, Rumour could deal with them quite easily.

They moved onwards, hand in hand. Rumour was not the sort of person you would mind holding hands with at a moment like this, although Theo would not have done it with anyone else, because she would not have let anyone else know she was beginning to be very frightened indeed. But Rumour would understand all this.

There was a moment when all that they were hearing were whisperings and slitherings and rustlings, and then there was another, quite separate moment, when the sounds had coalesced into something very much more definite and something very sinister.

The scuttling of clawed feet.

Theo felt Rumour's hand tighten about hers, and then – this was extremely odd – Rumour silently passed the square, tapestry-patterned bag to Theo, and slid the strap over Theo's neck. Theo did not understand why Rumour had done this, but clearly it would not do to ask, and so she simply took the bag, which was not very heavy, and tried not to know that the clawed feet were quite close now.

They were quite near to the central hall. Theo could see the lights from the banqueting hall filtering up to them. The scuttling thing was still following them, chuckling, as if it knew they were within its reach, and as if it were relishing the knowledge. Whatever it was going to do to them when it caught them was something it would greatly enjoy . . .

To keep moving at Rumour's side with the scuttling, clawed-footed creature stalking them, was the worst thing Theo had ever had to do. She thought she was only able to do it because Rumour seemed to expect that she could.

They reached a small, galleried landing with heavy wooden balustrades and a wide, curving stair that led to the lower part of the Castle. Flaring wall-sconces and flambeaux gave out a flickering red radiance, and there were narrow leaded windows, through which thin slivers of light crept.

At the centre of the gallery was a monstrous, bulbous-eyed thing, shell-backed, but with its soft under-body somehow made up of licking, sucking tongues and gaping, toothless maws and writhing, wriggling, wormlike brain sacs.

The *Draoicht Spiaire*.

Chaos's dark and hungry Spell of Spies.

Theo and Rumour stopped at once, and Theo felt the thought slice her mind from Rumour: *it has not been following us at all, it has been* waiting *for us* . . . And knew in the same instant that the *Draoicht Spiaire* must be an immensely powerful and strongly necromantic spell.

The *Draoicht Spiaire* was formed a little like a huge crab or a lobster. Theo, who had sometimes been allowed to watch the cooks at the Porphyry Palace preparing for a banquet, had seen them cast lobsters live into vats of boiling water, or crack open the shells of the small, well-fleshed crabs that had been caught on Ireland's coasts, scooping out the soft, bright red meat beneath. She had not really liked watching, and she did not really like shell-backed creatures that scuttled and darted and waved their stalklike eyes at you.

The *Draoicht Spiaire* was exactly like a monstrous lobster or a crab. The hard shell, the carapace that covered it, was like a monstrous inverted saucer; it was shiny and veined with thin black ducts, all of them pulsating, as if black blood coursed through it, which might be true, because Great-grandfather Nechtan had always said that demons had black blood . . .

Beneath the great, black-veined shell was the creature's soft body, made up of writhing, slopping mouths and tongues for the telling of secrets, and huge, deformed ears for the hearing of them . . . And worst of all, it had dozens of tiny, wriggling, wormlike sacs that were its brains, and that would absorb the terrible secrets of its victims and store the sucked-out thoughts and the small private longings and desires and ambitions and fears and plans . . .

It had small, jointed legs – Theo thought there were four of them, although there might have been more. It was so dreadful that she could not look very closely. But as it moved, there was the hard sound of claws ringing out on the timber floors, and as it watched them, it scratched the ground as if excited. Long pincer-like arms came out from its body, jointed very nearly like elbows, but ending in huge, wickedly sharp claws that made scissor motions, snipping the air. They would scoop you up effortlessly, and they would squeeze you between the great talons until you were mangled to a pulp . . .

Theo gulped and tried to remember that they were going to defeat this thing, Rumour would defeat it, because she was strong and clever and it was impossible that she could ever be vanquished.

Stalks protruded from the *Draoicht Spiaire*'s carapace, with swivelling searching eyes like glutinous globes at the ends. There were dozens of these stalk-eyes, rearing up on bright red, gristly-looking antennae, waving and peering.

The hundred eyes of the monster that never sleeps . . .

The creature was the height of a Man; its shell was on a level with Rumour's eyes, and it was as wide as a wide-sized bed. It was crouching in front of them, the stalks that supported its eyes waving as it studied them, the lipless, toothless mouths wet and greedy, the repulsive brain sacs wriggling and squirming.

As it crouched, watching them, its body crepitating with horrid relish, there was a really terrible moment when Theo felt Rumour's courage hesitate. This was so truly remarkable that she looked up at Rumour, and saw that her face was whiter than Theo could ever remember seeing it, and that her eyes were huge with fear.

But then Rumour moved; she approached the horrid, scuttling, crablike thing, and said, quite calmly and quietly, 'You will allow us to pass, if you please.' And stood her ground, and waited.

The *Draoicht Spiaire* gave its monstrous chuckle, and its eyes swivelled on the glistening, scarlet stalks. It inspected Rumour, the eyes moving up and down her body, and smacked its repulsive lips as it did so, and reaching out with its elongated pincer-arms.

'*A tasty morsel of gossip for my Master,*' it said, and its voice was as repulsive as the rest of it: thick and gloating, so that you knew it would be able to see all your secrets and all the private thoughts and hopes and all the silly small nastinesses, and it would spread them out in the light and chuckle over them, and perhaps ponder on how it could use them to make you feel ashamed.

Rumour walked towards the *Spiaire*, holding her hands upwards, the palms turned outwards; as she neared it, it said, in its evil, clogged voice that came from not just one of its many slopping mouths but all of them, '*You are brave, Sorceress, to approach me of your own volition.*'

Rumour said, softly, 'I am curious to know more of you, for I think we have never had dealings with one another, you and I.'

The *Draoicht Spiaire* snickered. '*You employ gentler servants than you would find here, Madame Rumour,*' it said. '*Although it is true that we have sometimes had a little in common.*'

'You know my name,' said Rumour, as if she was holding a perfectly ordinary conversation with a perfectly ordinary person she had only just met.

'*Who does not know of the Amaranth sorceress, Rumour?*' said the *Draoicht Spiaire*. '*Who does not know the lady who boasts that she has had a hundred lovers.*' It moved a little closer, with its grotesque, scuttling movement, its small legs scrabbling at the ground. From where she was standing, Theo could smell its stench: rotting meat and bad fish.

Rumour appeared not to notice it. She stayed where she was, her head tilted, as if she was finding it all of immense interest, and as if she had not noticed the truly sickening stench. The creature reared up a little, waving its short forelegs as it did so, and they saw the squirming underside of the shell with monstrous clarity. It gave its fearsome chuckle.

'*You would like to see a few of my secrets?*' it said. '*You would like me to show you the things I suck from my victims and keep inside until they may be of use?*'

507

Rumour said, quite normally and politely, 'I am always interested in sorcery,' and the *Draoicht Spiaire* chuckled again.

It reared up even further, the pale flesh palpitating with evil inner life. The brain sacs were at the centre, grey lumpish organs that writhed with a life of their own. As Rumour and Theo watched, the *Draoicht Spiaire* began to retch and vomit, and several of the repulsive grey membraneous sacs opened and spewed out the most remarkable river of fluids and lights and fragments that Theo had ever seen.

Green, slimy runnels of bile, and puddles of crimson gore with tiny bony claws in them; slopping yellow creaminesses, curdled and sour-looking like milk that has turned . . . Here and there were tiny black and silver lights that winked and coruscated and half swum, half scuttled in and out of the viscous fluids . . . Theo gulped and pushed a clenched fist into her mouth.

Rumour stood her ground, and Theo understood that they must somehow get past the *Spiaire*; they could not turn back, because behind them were the chambers and the galleries and the halls of Chaos's people. They must somehow get past this creature and down to the central hall and out and away.

Rumour was looking at the grisly kaleidoscope that had spurted from the *Draoicht Spiaire*, and she said, very softly, 'The bounty of the gods . . . All there.'

'*All there, Sorceress*,' said the creature, and Theo heard that its voice was phlegmy and mucoid, exactly as it would have been if it had just been very sick in the ordinary way, from eating too much or from tainted food.

'All there,' echoed Rumour. 'The green bile of jealousy, and the scarlet gobs of lust . . .'

'*And the brittle ivory bones of ambition, and the crimson-tipped claws of hatred*,' chuckled the *Draoicht Spiaire*. '*There is the purple and black of despair – can you see that, Madame Sorceress?*'

The horrid bulbous eyes swivelled, and Rumour said softly, 'I see it, but the emotion called *despair* is not something I recognise,' and Theo looked at her because there was suddenly something wistful and something quite unbearably sad in Rumour's voice, as if she might be remembering something that somebody had once said to her, and as if the memory was infinitely precious and overwhelmingly sad.

'*There is the yellow blood of cowardice,*' said the creature. '*And the scuttering, quicksilver Goblins of treachery, for all those who turn traitor have fallen prey to the quicksilver Goblins . . .*'

Rumour said, still in the same distant tone, 'I see it all.' And still she did not move, still she stayed where she was, beneath the monstrous necromantic creature who had spewed out the secret torments and the yearnings and the thoughts of its victims.

'*Room for more of them now,*' it said at once, and Theo saw that several of the brain membranes had collapsed and were shrunken and withered. '*All the more room to suck you dry, Sorceress,*' said the *Draoicht Spiaire*, and it reared up again, its hundred eyes swivelling and moving, making sickening, glutinous sounds as they did so.

Rumour was standing directly beneath it; it was towering above her, the grinning, mumbling mouths making sucking sounds, as if they were relishing what was ahead; the squirming, collapsed brain sacs becoming agitated.

For they scent food, Sorceress, they scent the desires and the secrets and fears and the ambitions and the plots you have in your mind . . . They will eat your mind, Sorceress, and your mind will be forever stored in my brains; and I have many brains, Sorceress. I have as many brains as I have eyes to spy with and ears to hear with and lips to whisper secrets to my master with . . .

It was closing in, it was lowering its shell, and at any minute, at any minute, it would come down on Rumour who was standing limned against the grisly shape.

Rumour was not afraid; she was wary and watchful, but she was caught in the grip of an exhilaration, because she would far rather face an enemy head-on like this and try to pit her strength against it, than to creep through the dark waiting for something to pounce.

At moments of extreme danger, the mind moves with extraordinary speed and clarity, and Rumour's mind moved like a shard of quicksilver now.

Like Theo, she had seen that they must get past the *Spiaire*; there was no other way to reach the central hall and the great double doors that led outside.

All her life, Rumour had taken the reckless option. Faced with different courses of action, she had always chosen the audacious way, and sometimes it had worked and sometimes it had not, She was a gambler, a risk-taker and an adventuress.

She would not change now. She would take a huge gamble, an immense risk, and if she was lucky and if the gods were with her, she would talk and bluff and defy her way out of this danger, as she had talked her way out of others.

Because sometimes it worked . . .

But Theodora must be kept safe.

She eyed the *Draoicht Spiaire*, and saw that its slopping, gaping mouths were already dripping and dribbling with anticipation, and she shuddered inwardly.

Could the thing be traded with? An offer – some kind of bargain for their safety? And then: could we simply appear to trade with it while I distract its attention?

Trade with what?

And then she remembered how the *Spiaire* had said, 'Who does not know the lady who boasts a hundred lovers,' and how lascivious greed had clotted its voice, and she felt the gamblers' exhilaration rush through her, because she would try it; she would risk everything on this one desperate chance . . .

The *Spiaire* was edging closer, and Rumour saw that it was tensing the gristly, fibrous muscles of its legs, ready to scuttle forwards. Its wavering stalk-eyes peered and grinned, and there was a soft wet squelching sound as they opened and closed.

At any minute it would rear back, and the pincer-like arms would reach for her . . .

She stood directly in its path and said, loudly and clearly, '*Draoicht Spiaire*. I offer you the ancient Bargain of the Saturnalia,' and saw at once that she had the creature's attention.

It said in its thick mucoid voice, 'I know of the Saturnalia Revelry. But tell me of the Bargain,' and Rumour heard the question in its voice. Confidence surged into her, because she had succeeded in perplexing it and in holding its attention. She said, 'I am surprised you do not know of the custom of exchanging gifts to mark the Saturnalia.' And inched further along the corridor, pushing Theodora before her. Had Theo still the tapestry box? Yes. And the child was understanding, she was moving step by cautious step nearer the stair. Good! thought Rumour. If I can keep the *Spiaire*'s attention, Theo can get to the stair without it looking round at her. And with luck I can follow her!

She said, in a soft, coaxing voice that would have instantly raised suspicion in the minds of any one of the older Amaranths, 'Saturnalia is the ancient Winter Solstice at which revelry and unbridled licentiousness takes place.'

'I know it,' said the *Spiaire*, and its stalk-eyes swelled with horrid lust.

Rumour caught the flicker of a movement from Theo as she edged nearer to the stair. But she kept her eyes fixed on the *Spiaire*, and said, 'There are Twelve Days of Revelry, and during those Twelve Days, gifts are exchanged.' And paused, and touched, deep in her mind, the memory of Andrew telling her of how his strange beliefs had allotted the pagan Saturnalia Feasting as their Leader's birth into the world, and how they celebrated it by exchanging small gifts. Even at this moment of extreme terror she sent up a brief murmur of gratitude to Andrew and to his predecessors who had so cunningly woven the ancient feast into the new belief.

'I will exchange with you in the way of the Saturnalia now,' said Rumour.

'Well?' It had not moved, but its eyes were full of prurient greed, and Rumour shuddered inwardly. But she said:

'If you will give us both safe passage through the Castle, I will give you every sexual experience, every moment of physical delight I have ever had.' She paused. 'And there have been many of them,' said Rumour, her voice low and caressing.

The creature laughed. 'Puny creature,' it said. 'I can take them all and *devour* you, Amaranth.' It tensed its gristly legs to spring, but Rumour caught a gleam of speculation in its eyes, and thought: exactly as I guessed! It will not bargain, but I have caught its attention. She stood back and said, 'But can you take them like this, filth! Can you unroll them like a carpet before your master!' And, lifting her hands, reached for the dazzling skeins that had made up the Tapestry, her own special Spell, the Enchantment she had spun over the years, and with which she had dazzled the necromancers in the banqueting hall.

The memories poured out at once, streaming down from the creeping darknesses above their heads, lighting the shadowy gallery to brilliance, a silken, light-filled carpet that cascaded down to the bare oak floor and unfurled at their feet, perfuming the air with wine and music and passion and firelight . . . Every lover taken and enjoyed, every sweet, sensual, perfumed night, every shred of soaring delight and mischievous seduction and heady desire.

The remarkable swathes of brilliant passion and love and desire lay at their feet like a great glossy pool of shifting rainbow silk. The *Spiaire* stared down, its eyes quivering with greed. Beneath the shell, the shrunken brainsacs stirred and began to swell.

'Yours!' cried Rumour, her eyes shining with defiance and recklessness, flinging out her hands to point. 'All yours, *Spiaire*, to spread at the feet of the Lord of Chaos! To unroll for his pleasure, instead of spewing them up in a torrent of noisome filth!'

She held the creature's unblinking stare, and felt the beginnings of a great empty coldness. The memories draining, she thought. And I have yielded up so much . . . Every night of love, every afternoon of passion . . . And Andrew? said a tiny silvery voice. Have you yielded up the memories of Andrew?

No! cried Rumour in silent agony. No, let me keep that! Let me keep the sweetness and the gentle passion. And then, with an inward submissiveness: but if that is what is needed, then I will yield that also.

The *Spiaire* was staring down at the passion-threaded swathes of living colour and the rainbow pools of delight, and Rumour thought: now! Now, while it is licking its lips over the devouring of everything, and while it is dazzled and ripening with its horrid lust!

Theo was almost at the stair, and Rumour drew in a breath of thankfulness for the child who had understood what to do without being told. The *Draoicht Spiaire* was bending over the silken, pouring tapestry, its stalk-eyes quivering, its tongues sucking and lapping at the precious carpet of memories, occasionally pausing and shaking itself, as if savouring its strange feast.

If ever there was a moment to follow Theo, if ever there was a moment when the creature would be off its guard, then this surely was the moment. Now! thought Rumour, and felt the soaring exhilaration fill her up as she moved in Theo's wake.

512

She was within ten paces of the stair when she felt the fetid, bad-fish stench close about her. The *Draoicht Spiaire* caught her easily, its pincers scooping her into a gristly, repulsive embrace, the brainsacs opening like blind feeding creatures, ready to suck her mind.

The pain was far worse, much more intense than she could have believed possible. It was the worst pain there could ever be in the entire world: a great, screaming scarlet sheet of blood blinding her; a suffocating black cloud crushing her lungs. The thing's claws were fastened about her and she felt the sharp agony of bones splintering.

I have failed. I have failed because I gambled, and sometimes the gamble works, and sometimes it does not . . .

She could feel the obscene excitement from the *Draoicht Spiaire*, and there was a terrible sound, a thick, swallowing sound as the brain sacs fastened on to her.

It was important not to give way to fear. It was important to remember that this had been her own choice, her reckless gamble . . . She had tried to distract the *Spiaire* and she had failed. *Because sometimes it works and sometimes it does not . . .*

But Theo will be safe. Theo and the music . . .

The *Spiaire* gave its clotted mucoid chuckle, and pulled her closer, and she saw the slopping mouths gape again.

And then it began. The slow steady stream of her life. All of the lovely nights, all of the lovers: all of the different men . . . Some of them gentle or passionate; some of them humble, or worshipping, or arrogant . . .

All of the moonlit nights seen through a heady blur of wine and music and delight; all of the drowsy scented afternoons, when to be between silken sheets with the curtains closed against the world was the most marvellous thing in the world . . . All of the snow-crusted months of winter when you could build up a fire that would burn all the night so that you could lie entwined on the floor before it, wrapped in thick, warm rugs, drinking wine, eating exotic foods, making love until you slept, exhausted, in your lover's arms.

And Andrew. Oh, let it not take Andrew! cried her mind, and then, with sudden calm: but it can never wipe out Andrew. The knowledge and the memory of Andrew and of what he was and what they had shared gave her unexpected strength, and although her face was contorted with pain, she managed to turn her head until she was looking at Theo, and she managed to say, in a clear calm voice, 'Theo, run. Go now. Down the stairs and away . . .' The pincers closed a little more tightly, and Rumour felt the warm wetness of blood soaking her gown. She gasped and her words shut off abruptly.

Theo was huddled against the wall, her eyes huge with fear. She whispered, 'No, I can't leave you . . .' and at once Rumour said in a choked, agonised voice:

'You must. Otherwise it will all have been for nothing—' The words were bitten off again, but Theo had understood. She had understood that, so far from being a marvellous adventure, Rumour had suffered dangers and terrible perils to get into Chaos's Castle, and that if one of them did not escape, it would all have been worthless. She began cautiously to inch towards the top stair, keeping her back to the wall, her eyes never leaving the *Draoicht Spiaire*.

The horrid pulsating sacs were swelling, like water-bags filling up, and Rumour was struggling. Thin weak shards of light touched the darkness about her head, and Theo knew that Rumour was trying to call up power, something that would defeat Chaos's monstrous servant.

But it was too late. Rumour's skin was taking on a pale, waxen look, and her eyes were becoming unfocused. Theo knew that this last reckless gamble had failed. Rumour had tried to distract the *Spiaire*, she had tried to feed its horrid hungers with her own memories, and it had not worked.

And now the crablike monster was sucking Rumour of everything; all the secrets and all the innermost wishes and thoughts, and all the yearnings Rumour had ever harboured, and all the good feelings and the bad, and the nice ones and the generous ones and the cross thoughts and the impatient ones. Everything. Chaos would know everything about her when this creature spewed its filth up for him. And Rumour would die. She might already be dead. And if I do not escape, thought Theo, in silent anguish, she will have died for nothing.

The wriggling membranes of brains were bloated and distended now, and Theo felt nausea rising in her throat, because that was Rumour, it was the real true Rumour, the one who might have taken too many lovers and who might sometimes have been extravagant and reckless and improvident, but who had also been unfailingly kind and ceaselessly generous, and who had never turned her back on a friend or failed to help a victim of ill-luck.

The *Draoicht Spiaire* flung Rumour contemptuously to the floor, as if it had drained every ounce of interest from her and every shred of feeling. It was fat and greasy-looking, swollen and grotesque with the new things it had learned about its latest victim. Rumour lay on the floor, her pale gown soaked in blood, but looking so small and frail that Theo knew she was dead; she had been sucked dry of every shred of life she possessed.

She had been moving slowly, going on tiptoe, thinking that any sudden movement would alert the creature's attention. She had not quite reached the stair, but she had nearly done so when it turned away from the broken body of Rumour and fixed its wavering eyes on her.

It lumbered to its feet, and Theo saw with incredulity that it had lost some of its sly, sharp cunning. It was slow and dazed; it floundered, scrabbling at the floor, lurching across the gallery, dragging its bloated body with it, rather as an immensely fat man might move after eating a huge meal. Theo understood at once that the creature had eaten greedily of Rumour's secrets; it had gobbled them down and it had stored them in its repulsive wormy brains and for the moment it was distended and bloated.

I can outrun it! thought Theo, gulping in a huge breath and tensing her muscles. Like that it will never catch me! She grasped Rumour's tapestry box, and for the sliver of an instant, she thought something rippled from the box, and that a pure sliver of light slid from it and lay across the floor, gentle and pale and shimmering with cool beauty. The *Draoicht Spiaire* made a strange retching sound and hesitated, and in that moment, Theo tumbled down the stair, her heart pounding, her hair flying, beyond worrying about being silent, because she must reach the doors, she must get out into the night.

Her feet barely seemed to touch the floor, and she half ran, half fell into the great central hall. Just beyond it was the spill of light from the banquet, and she could hear harsh, discordant music and the screeches and the laughter of the Dark Lords. So they are still feasting! thought Theodora. Good!

There was no time to think of what was behind her; no time to wonder if the evil enchantment would be able to gather its strength to reach her. There was no time to wonder, either, if the doors to the banqueting hall would suddenly be thrown open, and Chaos and his servants would come pouring out.

But the great central hall was deserted, and Theo stood for a moment to get her breath, trying to decide if it was a trap.

Chaos would be thinking that the *Draoicht Spiaire* would have overcome Rumour – and it did! thought Theo, miserably. Would he have ordered it to take them both?

But Chaos could not know yet that Rumour had got Theo out of the *Saraigli*.

Therefore there was no time to lose. She stole silently across the darkened hall, and out through the great doors, and into the perpetual night of the necromancers' Realm.

But she had no idea of where she should go.

And then, without warning, she remembered what Rumour had said about Andrew being in Almhuin, and she remembered as well how Rumour's eyes had softened in that special *remembering* way.

That's where I'll go! thought Theo with a rush of relief.

I'll go to Andrew.

I'll go to Almhuin.

Chapter Forty-two

Andrew thought it was remarkable how he had slipped into life inside the Castle, and it was extraordinary how accustomed he had become to the twice-daily journey down to the bricked-up cell.

He had fashioned the tiny hatch through which he would pass food and water to the Crimson Lady easily enough, setting to work as soon as Rumour had gone, knowing that there would be solace in hard exhausting labour. He had tried to follow her in his mind, sending out prayers and pleas for her safety. She had thought her journey would take two or three days to complete, and in the four days after her departure, he had kept her fixed firmly in his mind and in his prayers. She would smile the slightly mocking smile at the idea of him praying for her, but she would understand.

He found logs and timber in one of the Castle stables, together with implements for sawing and honing and shaping. He thought these were not part of the Lady's torture machines, but ordinary, everyday workmen's tools, probably used for the maintenance of the Castle in the days when Almhuin must have been a huge, bustling community, a small world within itself.

And now it was empty and desolate, and the only beings who inhabited it were the evil creature who was bricked up in its bowels, and the crippled monk who must perforce limp his maimed way about its echoing halls and cavernous rooms.

He had made his living place in the stone room where he and Rumour had taken sanctuary, liking the idea of Rumour's presence which he felt still lingering there; liking the notion of sleeping each night on the pile of rugs and furskins. It would be less lonely to lie with a fire blazing in the small hearth, turning the grey stone walls to copper red, with the faint scent of

517

Rumour's extravagant, sensuous perfumes still clinging to the fur coverings. It drove back the dark desolation, for Almhuin Castle was silent and deserted now; even the villagers had been frightened away by the Fomoire, and they no longer travelled the narrow track with their tilt cart. Andrew knew he would not have been able to cope with the Almhuinians, but in the days following Rumour's departure, there were times when he stood at the Castle's great front elevations, framed in the iron-toothed portcullis, and stared down the mountain track to the lights of the strange, mountain community. He could see, quite clearly, the tiny yellow squares of light from Almhuin: the wineshop and the forge and the bakeshop. But he was grateful that the Almhuinians stayed in their homes and that they left him to his own devices in the great deserted Fortress, with only the evil, hungering thing in the dungeons for company.

She had not tried to escape during those first days, and Andrew had turned his attention to making for himself a small island of comfort in the tainted stronghold. His maimed leg still pained him, but Rumour's healing spells had caused the jagged wound to close neatly and cleanly, and he thought the pain was not as great as it would have been otherwise. He could cope with the pain.

He worked hard at becoming more dexterous, and at manipulating the stout ash stick. He would not allow himself to become prey to despair, and he would not allow the pain to quench his faith. In the dark watches of the solitary hours, he sometimes wondered whether this was the punishment for the sweet, sensual hours in Rumour's arms, and whether this was the yoke of his sin. Brief black anger surged up in him, but with the bitterness came the memory of Brother Stephen's words: 'God's wrath is not in haste to smite, nor does it linger,' and he remembered, as well, how their Leader had taught, not the harsh vengeance of eye for eye, tooth for tooth, but a gentler, more understanding creed of resisting evil.

Whoever smite thee on the right cheek, turn to him the other also ... Resist evil ...

Had he done that when he had preserved the Crimson Lady's life? He thought: I condemned her to a living death, but I did not force death on her. And I share her sentence with her, and surely there is my true punishment.

518

He had no way of telling how long the stark sentence might last but, in the accepting of it, he began to find an unlooked-for calm. Because I am offering my penance for the sin that never once seemed sinful? Because I am working my own retribution? Perhaps.

And what of the task set by Brother Stephen in that other world and in that other life? I must never lose sight of it, thought Andrew, hobbling about the great, dark Castle. But he knew he had not lost sight of it at all; he knew that when this self-imposed hermitry was over, he would go out into the world again, and he would renew his search for the Black Monk.

Curiously, he had felt himself to be closer to the Monk in Almhuin Castle than at any other time since setting out on this perilous, unexpected journey. He thought it was surely only because he knew the Monk had been here, that he had served Almhuin's Crimson Lady, but the feeling persisted, and almost without being aware of it, Andrew began to feel that the Monk was closer at hand than he realised.

He explored the Castle cautiously but unflinchingly, knowing that he could not rest comfortably until he had looked into every room and every gallery to be certain that nothing walked here, but aware beneath this that he was searching for a trace of the Monk's habitation.

But there was nothing. If the Black Monk of Torach had ever walked these halls, he had left behind no imprint. Everywhere Andrew could feel the echoes of lingering agonies, but he pushed them back determinedly. And I will try to bring light and goodness into this dark Fortress, he thought, and then was amused and scornful of so arrogant a thought. Almhuin was soaked in the evil of many centuries and countless generations; how should one man dispel all that!

The stone room was already a refuge; it had begun to feel familiar each time he entered it, and he was grateful for this small island of comfort in the midst of the immense emptiness.

He had found the kitchens – huge grim vaults – and the wine-store and the still rooms. A man must eat, no matter how much he intends to fast and pray, and Andrew, peering into deep cupboards and storerooms, found sacks of flour and wheat; crocks of various preserves, jams and fruits all labelled in a thin, clear hand. Almhuin might have been under the sway of an evil and blood-hungry mistress, but at some time – and not so long ago – it had had a provident and careful cellarer.

Andrew found sides of smoked hams and flitches of bacon, and strings of drying herbs hanging from the blackened rafters of the kitchens. In the beginning, his stomach closed with nausea at the thought of eating the Crimson Lady's food, but after a time, sanity and common sense prevailed. He thought: those were perfectly ordinary pigs, probably slaughtered in Almhuin to make smoked ham and bacon, that is normal wheat and flour which can be baked into loaves; this is fruit preserve, very similar to the apple and damson preserve we made in the monastery, and in those stone jars is plain honey. The barrels stacked beneath the settle hold nothing other than ordinary soused herrings and mackerel. And a man must eat.

There were casks of dark, sensuous wine, and of heady, fiery fluid tasting of poppies and cherries. Standing on a cool marble settle were small stoppered flagons of a beverage which Andrew had never before encountered, which tasted of apples and which he found wholly delicious.

From the stone-flagged kitchens, a tiny flight of steps led up to a small, square garden, and Andrew, manoeuvring with care, but growing nimbler by the day, saw with delight that herbs grew here: lemon thyme and sweet-scented basil and mint and parsley. A small patch of ground had been planted with vegetables: there were recognisable peas and beans, ruffled heads of kale and sturdy cabbages. God's bounty. He would survive.

After several failures, he discovered how to fire the massive iron range in the sculleries, using the logs stacked up outside, and felt absurdly pleased when he managed to make a simmering pot of soup out of a knuckle of bacon, with beans and onions and chopped cabbage. He ate it seated in his small room, and felt its normal everyday taste put new heart into him.

To begin with, the Lady was surly. When Andrew made his conscientious visits to take food and water, she was silent and withdrawn, so that he wondered at first if she had after all died. By standing on a small block of wood, using the ash crutch for support, he managed to peer into the dark oblong of the cell. For a moment he thought she was not there, and he fumbled awkwardly for a light, managing to balance his weight while he held it aloft.

As the tiny flame leapt upwards in the dry stale air, her face suddenly swam into his vision, impossibly close, no more than eighteen inches from him, so that he knew she must be standing on something just inside the cell, pressing against the newly laid bricks, perhaps hanging on to the shelf of brick made by the hatch. Her face was lit from below by the flame, giving her the look of a fiery devil, and her eyes were huge dark pits of hungry evil, staring at him. There was a dreadful moment when they both stood, their eyes locked; Andrew, appalled, felt a sudden surge of hot strong lust between his thighs. The great black eyes smiled, and one white, crimson-tipped hand came up into the light, as if the Lady was reaching for him.

Andrew gasped and fell backwards, missing his balance, crashing to the ground with a sound that was deafening and heart-stopping in the silent dungeons.

From inside the cell, he heard the deep, throaty chuckle of her laughter, and as he pulled himself upright again, it occurred to him that it had been the satisfied laughter of a creature who has laid a very careful plan, and seen the plan work.

So she is plotting against me already, and I am alone and defenceless in this evil Fortress.

Theodora had gone to the jutting, low-roofed stable block on the Castle's western side, which was taking a hugely enormous risk, but which was worth taking, because the journey to Almhuin would be much quicker and much easier if she had a horse to ride.

It was important to concentrate on being silent and stealthy. If she reached the stables she would begin to feel safer. She would play the portent game, which was not quite a game, but something she had discovered could sometimes harness a helpful power. It was something she had thought up by herself, and she had never told anyone about it, in case of being laughed at, and anyway, it did not work absolutely every time. Theo bit her lip at the memory of Rumour who had said, 'Sometimes these things work and sometimes they do not.' She would not think about Rumour yet, because she dared not.

The idea was to acquire a good omen for whatever you were

doing, and you could only acquire an omen by building up portents. The more portents you could build up, the better your chances of a good omen.

The first portent would be reaching the stone archway that led through to the stables without anyone seeing her. Once she had achieved that, the second could be getting across to the iron gateway that opened on to the stable yard, and the third had better be for the gateway to be unlocked. The fourth could be for the gate not to squeak. After that, she would see what still had to be overcome. Also, she was not very sure of the way to the stables, except that you went through the stone archway. She would be able to think up more portents as she went.

She tiptoed forward, hardly daring to breathe, and as the shadow of the stone arch fell across her, she drew a breath of relief. She had earned one portent; now she could go on to the second.

This was actually quite an easy one, nearly a cheat, because it was not very far to walk, and there were deep thick shadows to hide in. But the gate was unlocked and, as it swung silently and easily open, Theo breathed another sigh of relief. Four portents. Nearly half-way to a very good omen indeed.

Skirting the great walls of the Castle, Theo added portents as she went. You could not cheat, each portent had to be a definite step forward in your quest. Across the stable yard, dodging the light that beamed from a window unexpectedly (part of the sculleries?), gained a fifth, and managing to cross an unlit patch of cobbled yard was a sixth.

And then the stables were ahead of her, and she could have two more portents by the stable doors being unlocked and by nobody challenging her. The ninth portent would be actually getting inside.

And then she was across the yard, and she was inside the stables, and nobody had challenged her, and she had earned nine whole portents, which meant a very good omen indeed.

The stables were warm and had the friendly smell of the stables in the Porphyry Palace. Theo stood just inside the door for a moment, not making any abrupt movements, because this was something you always had to do, even when you had earned a good nine-portent omen. Horses could be alarmed by the sudden presence of a stranger. It would not do to have got this far and then cause a stampede which would bring everybody running out.

The horses were all rather big. They were much bigger than she had expected. Theo stared up at them in dismay, because she could not possibly ride any of these. She would never saddle or bridle them. Surely there were smaller horses, surely there were not just these huge, fiery-eyed stallions with their black, gleaming flanks and their ebony and jet manes and tails? A tiny voice inside her head said that, when Chaos rode out, he did so caparisoned in scarlet and armoured in black, and that he rode the NightMare Stallions. Theo looked at the black horses with fresh alarm, but these could not possibly be NightMare Stallions, because NightMare Stallions only came if somebody very powerful summoned them. They were magic and bad magic at that. Everyone knew it. These would just be ordinary marching horses.

Only, thought Theo, worried, I don't think I can ride any of them. She would have to walk. She would have to walk all the way to Almhuin, and it would be dark and difficult and it would be a very long way. She was not quite sure how long it would take. When they were packing Rumour's things in the bedchamber, Rumour had said something about several days' journey, and Theo remembered that, when Chaos brought her through the Gateway, once inside the Dark Realm, they had had to travel across the terrible, War-torn countryside, making three or four camps on the way. Chaos's night-camps had not been quite like anybody else's; they had involved pointy-roofed, silk-hung structures which the concubines had told her were called 'pavilions', and there had been elaborate meals prepared by Chaos's servants who had been waiting for him just within the dark Gateway. Theo had tried to count the days of the journey to Chaos's Castle to find out how big the Dark Realm was, but it had been difficult, because of there not being any proper night or any real dawn.

And then, quite without warning, she saw the small sleek creatures at the far end of the stables, in a little part by themselves. Delight leapt in her, because after all the portent game that was not a game had worked. Surely, oh surely she could take one of these? She approached them cautiously, seeing that they were smaller and gentler than the others; seeing that

523

they had manes of pale silk that waved gently as if a tiny wind were ruffling them, and how they had hoofs of silver and coats of ivory satin. Theo stood looking at them, and then, quite suddenly, she knew what they were.

The *Uisce*. The sleek beautiful sea-horses that the *sidh* rode, that were said to have borne Aillen mac Midha, the Elven King, into the world of the Humanish in a long-ago century. The *Uisce*, forced by Chaos into the service of the necromancers.

Theo went forward cautiously, seeing that there were four of the beautiful gentle creatures, not daring to think she could call them to her side, but thinking she must try.

They watched her approach, their cool, slanting eyes wary, and Theo understood that the *Uisce* would be held in thrall by Chaos's evil spells, and that they would almost certainly have been ridden cruelly and hard by him and his guests. Would they obey her now? How strong was the spell that Chaos had used?

Theodora, growing up in the Porphyry Palace, curled into the warm, firelit corner of Nechtan's workroom, had absorbed a remarkable amount of knowledge. Papa had said indulgently that she had a magpie mind, collecting all kinds of snippets and tag-ends of information, and probably none of it of any use.

But as Theo stood silently in the dark stables, she delved down into her mind, into the magpie assortment of spells and enchantments and bewitchments and lures, because out of all the spells she had heard Great-grandfather chant, out of all the enchantments she had listened to him recite, there had to be something that she could remember that would bring the *Uisce* to her side, and that would make it possible for her to ride them quietly and inconspicuously out of the Castle and on to Almhuin.

And then she knew exactly the right thing. A Halcyon – what was sometimes called an *Ailcin* in the old Gael tongue. A Halcyon was gentle and calming, but it also had woven into it a rather strong command of authority, which impelled its victim to obey.

She would try it. You had to say it very quietly and very softly, and you had to paint it in light, soft, cobweb colours, soft blues and greens and pinks. Theo would think about the underwater City of Tiarna, which no living Human had ever seen, but which was said to be the most beautiful place in any world ever, silver and blue and turquoise and filled with soft, pure iridescence.

She whispered the incantation of the Halcyon, enjoying the silky feel of the words, liking the way they formed fragile, spun-glass patterns on the air, grateful that the darkness of this place was not smothering it in the way the *Draoicht Spiaire* had smothered Rumour's spells.

The *Uisce* were coming towards her, their beautiful heads bowed in submission, their pale manes rippling gently. Theo thought they were the most beautiful creatures she had ever seen.

The first *Uisce* stood before her, and bowed its sleek, soft head, as if to say: you have thrown about us the compulsion of the ancient *Ailcin*, and therefore we are yours to command. Hope surged up in her for the first time, because if she could ride these lovely, gentle, light-filled creatures across the Dark Realm, she could surely reach Almhuin and Andrew.

She thought she could find Almhuin Castle quite easily. You could see the Mountains even from inside Chaos's Castle; it was a great jagged range, like jutting-up black teeth. There would surely not be more than one path leading into the Mountains and there would surely not be more than one Fortress.

She would have to take food and something to drink for the journey. You could not be knocking on people's doors inside the Dark Ireland for these things, like the gypsies and the tinkers did at home. This was the realm of the fearsome necromancers, and you did not know who might come prowling and lurching to the door in answer to your knock. But this was rather a daunting thought, and so Theo put it from her, and looked instead to see was there any kind of food out here that she could put in Rumour's tapestry box-bag.

Above the stables was a kind of loft which you climbed into by a narrow ladder. Theo remembered that there had been a similar arrangement in the Porphyry Palace and that it was where stable hands lived and slept so that they could be near to the horses. Where people lived, there was nearly always food.

She clambered up gingerly, listening all the while for the sounds that would mean Chaos had discovered her escape. It was probably being a bit foolish to linger even this long, but there was no point in setting off on a journey of several days without proper provisions. You might die of hunger and thirst on the way. And there, in a corner, was a kind of larder cupboard with a mesh covering. Inside were some wedges of rather stale bread, a crock of potted meat and a round of honey cakes. She packed as much as she could into the bag. There was a small milk churn; Theo carefully emptied out one of the small corked wine-flagons that had been in Rumour's bag, and filled it with milk.

And then she was climbing on to the *Uisce*'s back, and looping the tapestry bag around her neck again, which would be the safest way to carry it.

Theodora wound her fingers tightly in the silken strands of the *Uisce*'s mane, and they rode out through the doors of the Castle of Infinity and into the waiting night.

It was unexpectedly comfortable on the *Uisce*'s back, and it felt rather safe and friendly to be able to glance back and see the other three following. It was almost as if she was leading a tiny army of her own like this.

The *Uisce* did not quite shine in the darkness, but there was a soft, cool radiance from them. Theo thought that, wherever their hoofs touched the ground, they left a sprinkling of tiny, glinting light flecks. Lovely! she thought in delight. We are cutting a swathe through the darkness of this horrid place! And then remembered that it would be better not to attract too much attention to them, and guided the *Uisce* into the deep shadows that fringed the highroad, so that they would not be seen.

Once they were fairly clear of the Castle of Infinity, and the night had closed safely and darkly about them, Theo slipped from the *Uisce*'s back, because it might be politer not to assume they would carry her all the time. She felt quite safe walking between them.

The red boots that the concubines had given her were rather fun. When you walked, you could see your feet quite clearly, even in the horrid, swirling darkness of the Black Realm. They were a nice, clear red: a strong, vivid cherry, and you could stomp them down on the ground as you walked. Theo felt very nearly brave simply by wearing them. They would reach Andrew and Andrew would know what they ought to do. In a world that suddenly and unbearably did not contain Rumour,

Theo was clinging to the memory of Andrew. She had discovered that, if she concentrated very hard on Andrew, and on reaching him, she could very nearly shut out the terrible memory of Rumour being dead at the *Draoicht Spiaire*'s hands. She understood that Rumour had died because she had taken one last huge gamble against the *Spiaire*, and that the gamble had failed. It was precisely how anybody who knew Rumour would have expected her to die.

Because sometimes it works and sometimes it does not . . . Theo could hear Rumour saying it.

The Realm of the necromancers, Ireland's fearsome and grisly underworld, was silent and deserted. Theo had heard the whispers about the War that raged outside Chaos's Castle, and she had half expected to find herself encountering battles and terrible marching Armies, or perhaps bands of prowling sentry spells. But either Chaos's enemies and Chaos himself were mustering their forces for a fresh attack somewhere, or the War was over.

Theo, clinging to the silken floss of the *Uisce*'s mane, wondered who had won the War if it was over, and thought that the Dark Realm was exactly how you would expect a land to look after a huge War had rampaged across it. Everywhere were burned-out buildings; empty, ravaged turrets with gaping windows like eyeless sockets, great scorched fields. Here and there, the highway was pitted as if scalding liquid had been poured across it, and the trees were leafless; horrid, skeletal outlines that waved their black branches as if they were greedy hands that would reach down to pluck Theo from the *Uisce*'s back. To the east was a sinister shimmer of crimson, as if something that was the colour of blood – something that might actually *be* blood – was tainting the dark, smothery skies. It was all very grim and very terrible, but there was no means of knowing if the Dark Realm was always like this on account of being the land of the Dark Lords, or if it was on account of the War or if it was something else entirely.

When they stopped, the *Uisce* did not sleep, but simply formed a protective square about Theo so that she could rest. It was not what you would choose, to go to sleep in the open countryside of the Dark Realm, where anything at all might come prowling out at you, but it could not be helped. Theo rested when she felt tired, and ate the bread and the potted meat and drank the milk gratefully, and offered some of it to the *Uisce*, who shook their glossy heads as if politely refusing.

The Castle of Infinity was behind her; if she looked back, she could still see its spires and its towers, and the turrets, but it was fading into the distance. But it was quite a long way away now. She could no longer see the little jutting wing with the warm lights that was the *Saraigli*. It felt odd and a bit lonely to be out here and remember the time she had spent there. It had all been rather boring, but Theo would not have minded being bored just now because it was cold and dark and very scary out here.

And ahead of her was Almhuin.

She had not been entirely sure about Almhuin. She had heard the stories told by the concubines, partly giggling, partly fearful. They had clutched one another and shrieked in terrified delight, and told how the Crimson Lady sent her servants out into the mountain passes and the townships of the Dark Realm in search of prey. Theo, listening round-eyed, had thought that Almhuin must be the most terrible place of all the terrible places in the Black Ireland.

But Rumour had smiled softly and secretly at the mention of Almhuin; and she had told Theo, quite positively, that Andrew was there. Theo had guessed that Rumour had intended to return to him.

Almhuin was directly in front of her; the Black Mountains were enclosing her now, dark and silent and forbidding. Mountains were rather frightening because you did not know what might lurk and creep inside them. But at least she was hidden from view. If Chaos and his people came hurtling across the grim, burned-out countryside, they would not be able to see her.

And then they rounded a curve in the path and there, ahead of her, was the great bulk of Almhuin Castle, its huge sprawling shadow falling across the path, quenching a little of the *Uisce*'s light. Theo guided the *Uisce* carefully along the last stretch of the road and straight to the Castle's centre, because you always entered a Castle at its centre.

As she neared the portcullis, she was holding very firmly to the thought that Andrew was here. Rumour had said he was, and Rumour was somebody you could trust. Theo would trust her, she would ride up to the Castle, right up to the rather horrid-looking gap at the centre, which would be the portcullis, and she would go inside and Andrew would be there.

Even so, it took a very great amount of bravery to approach the terrible Fortress. It was important not to remember the tales about the Crimson Lady who bathed in people's blood. Probably they were not even true. It was important to remember that Andrew was going to be here and that she had trusted Rumour and she trusted Andrew, and everything would be all right.

The darkness of Almhuin closed about her the minute she rode under its portcullis. A tiny, whispery voice inside her head said: *so at last, little girl, you are inside the BeastWoman's Citadel*, which was horrid. Theo slid from the *Uisce*'s glossy back, and stood a bit uncertainly in the shadowy hall, where Andrew and Rumour, surrounded by their Almhuinian captors, had stood; she felt, as they had felt, the thick, fetid evil.

At the far end of the hall was a movement, an unexpected, rather shuffling movement, and a wavering light appeared. Theo gasped, and began to move backwards, away from the light and the person who was walking so oddly towards her.

Theo shrank back, feeling the silken warmth of the *Uisce*'s flanks and, as she did so, the light bobbed nearer, and quite suddenly, in that minute, it was filled with strength and friendship and hope.

Andrew, leaning heavily on the ash crutch, stood in the archway, and Theo sobbed and flew across the stone hall into his arms.

Chapter Forty-three

Having Theodora with him inside the Castle afforded Andrew more delight than he would have thought possible.

They had gone at once into the little, firelit stone room, and Andrew had piled logs on to the fire and drawn the child nearer to it. There was a flagon of wine which he mixed with water, and there was the remains of his noonday meal – good, strong broth he had made that morning, which could be reheated over the trivet on the fire.

Theo found these small, homely actions friendly and unexpectedly comforting. She drank the soup and sipped cautiously at the watered-down wine, and looked at Andrew who was exactly as she remembered, except that something had wounded his leg so that he had to walk leaning on a stick. She gulped in a deep breath, because here at last was something that had not changed, and something that was safe and real and that could be trusted. Andrew would know what to do.

She managed to explain about Rumour, and although her voice came out a bit wobbly, she told the tale properly and clearly, as Rumour would have wanted it told; how Rumour had taken her out of the *Saraigli* and how they had stolen through the great shadowy Castle of Infinity. How the *Draoicht Spiaire* had stalked them, and confronted them. And how Rumour had entered into that last, remarkable gamble.

Andrew listened intently, his eyes never leaving Theo's small, absorbed face. Once he said, 'So she died as she lived, in a blaze of extravagant defiance.' And turned away for a moment, pretending to mend the fire which did not need mending, because the pity of it and the loss of it and the terrible gaping wound it had inflicted on him must not show. Somehow he must endure this.

Rumour is dead. And I do not think I shall bear it.

But it had to be borne, somehow it had to be borne, because life had to go on, and there were still tasks to be undertaken. There was Theodora to be thought of now.

He took the child in his arms, feeling her small body wracked with sobs now, feeling his own tears mingle with hers. He held her to him, trying to infuse her with warmth, but knowing that he was himself cold with a deep, lonely coldness that was not physical.

Bone-cold. Heart-cold. I shall never be warm again.

As he prepared a bed for the child, and as he made his nightly vigil around the Castle, lighting the wall-torches in the great hall, building up the fire in the stone room, the cold stayed with him. And there was an ache, a deep, bruised agony that would somehow have to be faced and would have to be overcome.

Never to see her again. Never to hear her voice, never to breathe in the special skin-scent of her. Never to look up and see her watching him with that amused mockery.

My dear and only love, shall I ever forget? And then, beneath the agony: shall I ever want to forget?

With the coming of Theodora, Andrew tried to fill the days even more. There were times when he knew he must try to return her to her people; when he knew it was selfish to keep her with him.

But to have sent her to find her own way back to the Porphyry Palace was clearly out of the question, and Andrew knew himself not yet sufficiently recovered from the mutilation inflicted on him by Bailitheoir to go with her. To travel back the way he and Rumour had come – through the Black Mountains and the caves that surrounded the *sidh*'s dying City – he would have to be sure of repelling the creatures that would certainly be lying in wait.

And there is the prisoner of this Castle, said a tiny, treacherous voice in his mind. You took the task on your shoulders and you cannot leave her to die, alone and in the dark.

And so Andrew and Theodora entered into a strange half-world, where time seemed to blur, and where the pattern of their days took on a surprisingly gentle, healing rhythm. Several times Andrew tried to ask about Rumour's death: had she given Theodora anything at the last? Had there been any message? But each time he began to frame the questions the white frightened look closed down over the child's face, and Andrew understood that Rumour's death at the hands of the *Draiocht Spiaire* had been so truly appalling that Theodora was still unable to face it. And so, because it would have been cruel to have pressed her, Andrew let it go. To himself he thought that the *sidh*'s music had probably perished with Rumour.

Andrew tried to keep a count of the days, drawing a chart which they marked each night when they retired to the fire-washed stone room. He thought this would be difficult, for there was no recognisable night in the Dark Realm, and no day. But after a time, they became aware of a pattern in the hours; a time when the darkness became shot with purple, and when the brooding silence that surrounded Almhuin seemed to thicken and ferment with clotted malevolence. At that hour, with Theo safely tucked up in the small bed, Andrew would go out into the hall to where the squared pattern made by the portcullis fell sharply across the floor, and reach up to light the wall-sconces, so that light always burned here. For, if I can at least give some light to this dark fortress, I shall feel that I am fighting back the shades of the necromancers' night . . .

He did not quite frame the thought that it would have been unbearable to lie in the stone room with the smothering darkness all about them, and the terrible prisoner in the Castle's bowels.

He discovered the library early on, and experienced a delighted familiarity in the shelves of manuscripts and vellum chronicles, and in the leather-topped tables, at which a man might work and study. There was a square copper log-box, and Andrew stocked it with logs so that he could work here for as long as the mood took him, without needing to go out to the low-roofed wood-store that abutted the kitchens, in order to replenish the fire.

There was an unlooked-for joy in teaching Theodora. The child had a quick intelligence and an instinctive understanding that made the little lessons he devised a delight to them both. Andrew, with memories of his own schooling, devised small lessons for her; figuring and counting and simple exercises in logic. He set her to write accounts of incidents in her childhood inside the Porphyry Palace. He smiled a little at the vivid word-pictures she painted of the Amaranths, many of whom he recognised from his stay, and the matter-of-fact way in which she described the spinning of spells on the huge Sorcery Looms.

In turn, he recounted to her the gentler stories of the Gospel, concentrating on the promise-filled New Testament, with its messages of light and hope; omitting the dark, sometimes jealous god of Genesis and Ecclesiastes.

Theo, curled up by the fire in the little stone room, exactly as once she had curled up in Nechtan's sorcery-filled workroom, was interested in everything and fascinated by it all. When Andrew told of the rather mild revelries held in his monastery to mark the Christmas feasts, Theo was able to tell, in turn, about the Saturnalia and the Twelve Days of Revelry. And what Andrew referred to as a rebirth, which he called Easter, was very like a worshipping of one of the goddesses of Spring, whose name was Eostre, and whose festival Great-grandfather had always liked to mark. Spring was a time of rebirth everywhere, said Theo. Things you had thought dead – plants and flowers – began to grow and flower again. Birds were born in spring, and animals. She explained it seriously, careful to pronounce the unfamiliar word 'Easter' exactly as Andrew pronounced it, grasping the idea of somebody dying so that the somebody could be born again at such a time.

When Andrew touched, very carefully, on the legend of the Samildanach, Theo sat up, her eyes bright, and said, 'Then that is your Leader also? Yes of course! I see it now! The two stories are almost exactly the same!'

By now their days, far from being empty and formless, were becoming very full. For Andrew there was beginning to be comfort and healing in the steady pattern. The hours that he had identified as mornings were spent in preparation of food for that day: perhaps the baking of a loaf or the selecting of vegetables. There was an unexpected interest in trying to vary the ingredients of the soup; in using cabbage and carrots and beans one day, sliced bacon and peas and onions the next.

They ate the soup with wedges of bread baked in the vast iron range. They had several failures, but eventually they achieved crisp warm loaves which were wholly delicious. Theodora experimented with sweet loaves, because it was nice to finish your supper with something sweet. She chopped preserved fruit, standing on a chair to reach the huge, scrubbed table in the scullery, and tipped the fruit into the dough, stirring in spoonfuls of melted honey, or ginger from the large stone jars on the settle. There was ripe fruit from the small orchard behind the courtyard as well: pears and apples that scented the stone room, and the glossy blackberries that grew wild.

The chart counted off the days, and Andrew identified, as nearly as he could, Sabbath days, feast days, and days of fasting. On the days that Andrew had selected for fast days, he made sure that Theo ate properly, but for himself he took only plain vegetables, and a cup of water.

But on every seventh day, they made a small festivity of their noonday meal, and Theo was let to have a few sips of the apple wine diluted with water. They finished their meal with a bowl each of preserved fruit from the huge, shady larder, sweetened with honey. Andrew, watching Theo's small solemn face, made his libation to his God quietly and devoutly, letting the child join in or not, as she chose.

He found jobs of work to do around the Castle; mending and repairing, which he rather enjoyed. As with the modest attempts at cooking, he found it satisfying to restore life to something which had been broken, just as he found pleasure in carving wood, or tilling a patch of ground in preparation for the sewing of seeds. As he worked, he murmured prayers, remembering how the brothers had believed that continual prayer sanctified, knowing that Almhuin was so steeped in evil that there would probably be no effect, but liking the idea anyway.

There were the gentle silken *Uisce* to be groomed and fed. Andrew and Theo had housed them in the stables, and they went out each morning. They dared not exercise them on the mountain path, because of being seen by the Almhuinians in the village below, but Theo took them around the courtyard and talked to them. This was not absolutely satisfactory for anybody, but it was the best they could do.

After the midday meal, they worked in the huge library, Theo applying herself diligently to her simple lessons, Andrew sorting and reading and trying to catalogue the tumble of books and manuscripts. He liked the scent of leather that lingered here, and he felt little evil in this room, as if the Crimson Lady might not have used it much. The great library became their study place, as the stone room was their rest place.

Rumour's memory was constantly with him, and sometimes his longing for her was so fierce that it became a physical ache, and he thought he must surely look up and see her watching him. I have nothing left of her, he thought. Given that the music, the *sidh*'s enchantment that we fought to preserve, has gone.

But there was only himself and Theodora; the creature in the dungeons was quiescent and silent; nothing moved in Almhuin Castle, save the shadows, and there was no one inside the great Fortress save a monk and a child and the silent, evil creature bricked up in the Castle's bowels.

Andrew was taking what he thought of as his usual night-time vigil; each evening before supper he lit the flambeaux in the great hall, making sure that the portcullis was lowered. Now I am shut in and the Dark Powers are shut out! My house is secure and nothing can creep in while I sleep!

He never descended to the dungeons once darkness had thickened; he went to the Lady's cell twice daily, keeping to the hours he had delineated as being daylight, always making sure that Theodora was occupied either in the stone room or the library at these times. He knew it was senseless to believe that these two places were not as strongly permeated with the Lady's evil, but he did feel it. He thought of Theodora as being safe in those rooms.

It did not seem as dark tonight. Andrew stood framed in the portcullis, looking out over the mountain path, seeing the lights of Almhuin and then looking across to the east, where he could make out the ravaged skyline of the Dark Lords' Citadels, and there, arrogant and untouched above them all, the Castle of Infinity. It was as he was narrowing his eyes to sharpen the Castle's silhouette, that he became aware of a long thread of lights, strung out across the dark landscape of the Black Ireland. Moving lights. The lights of travellers.

He stood for a moment watching, seeing that they were coming towards the Castle. Fear warred with disbelief, and ice formed at the pit of his stomach. The lights were not sparse pinpoints signifying three or four travellers; Andrew had seen that on a few occasions, and although it had always been an uneasy reminder of how vulnerable he was, he had not thought that many people would venture up to the Crimson Lady's Castle.

But this was a long procession, a huge caravan, a great mass of people, moving with precision and purpose, lit by the flames of hundreds of flaring torches.

An Army.

Very faintly, so distantly that at first Andrew thought his hearing had misled him, came the sounds of cold, discordant music. He stayed where he was, straining his hearing, and presently the music formed into its own discordant, rather sinister patterns.

The music of necromancy. Andrew felt a sick fear, for the music conjured up visions and images of people marching to War, of Armies being mobilised and, behind it and beneath it all, a grim, dark purpose.

For a moment, he thought that the Army, whatever it was, whoever led it, could have nothing to do with Almhuin, for Almhuin's Lady was vanquished and caged, and Almhuin's fangs had been drawn.

And then, with sudden terrible clarity, he thought: but Chaos does not know that. Chaos believes she still rules here. And by the Lady's own admission to the strange, shadow-being called the Collector, Chaos and the Crimson Lady are most viciously at War.

This was Chaos's concerted attack. His newest, perhaps his greatest assault on the Lady who had plotted against him, and who had stolen away the Black Monk from his service.

Chaos was marching on Almhuin. The might and the power and the necromantic strengths of the Dark Lords were directed on to the Castle.

'We have to leave,' said Andrew, taking Theo's small hands in his and looking down at her as they stood in the stone room. 'We have to leave at once, and we have to go swiftly and silently.'

They stared at one another, both of them loath to forsake the tenuous security of the small world they had created; neither wanting to venture into the dark night of the Black Realm.

It had not occurred to Theo that Chaos and his people would march on Almhuin. She thought she should have thought about

536

it, but they had been so comfortable here together, and it had been so interesting to hear about Andrew's religion, and to work at the lessons and bake bread and tend the little walled garden. She asked, in a rather small voice, if Chaos was chasing her, but Andrew at once said, No, Chaos would almost certainly be wanting to take the Crimson Lady's Castle for his own – perhaps to use as some kind of base for mounting an attack on the True Ireland. He was not coming specifically for Theodora, said Andrew, he thought they could be sure about that.

This was unexpectedly comforting, because Theo would not want Chaos to count her so important that he would send out hundreds of people to capture her. It was nice if people counted you as important, but not if they were necromancers.

'But we have to escape, Theodora, and we have to somehow find our way back.'

'To the Palace.' This would be absolutely the best thing that could happen, and Theo looked hopefully at Andrew when she said it.

'Yes, to the Palace.' He could not bend down to look at her directly because of being crippled, but he still looked deeply into her eyes, as if he might be trying to speak to her with his mind. As if he might be saying *of course we shall escape and of course we can get home*. This was what Rumour would have done and thought and said, and Theo began to feel better. They would leave Almhuin at once, and they would outrun Chaos's Armies. Armies were clumsy things; they could not move very quickly because they were so many of them. They were cumbersome.

But if they took the *Uisce*, if they rode them as Theo had ridden them when she ran from the Castle of Infinity, they might get away. Theo, tumbling a few things hastily into a satchel, snatched up Rumour's tapestry box-bag, which had been thrust into the back of the cupboard and which Theo had almost forgotten about, but was exactly the right thing to take with you on a hasty journey. She dared to hope they would escape.

Andrew's mind was in a tumult. He had spared only the most fleeting of considerations for his prisoner, below in the dungeons. This was Chaos's Army that was marching on them, this was the might and the power of the Dark Lords, and they could not possibly fight it. There was no choice to make between guarding the Crimson Lady and saving Theodora from Chaos.

But to his surprise, part of him rebelled at the idea of running away. *Stay and fight the evil creatures!* said a voice inside him he had not known he possessed. *Stay and vanquish the Dark Lords!*

He thought that, if he had not been so crippled, and if Rumour had been with him, he might have listened to the voice, for the idea of beating back the necromancers was a seductive one.

For a moment, Rumour was with him; smiling the slant-eyed smile, making wild, extravagant plans that might work and might not.

For an unreal but marvellous moment, Andrew wondered whether he could do it. And then he remembered that Theodora's safety was paramount, and he remembered that Almhuin was permeated with centuries of evil, and that Chaos and his people had at their beck every dark enchantment and every evil spell ever known. And I am lame, he thought angrily. I cannot be so arrogant as to think I could oppose Chaos.

He paused only long enough to fling randomly snatched food into one of the satchels that Theo had brought from the sculleries, and to scoop up the papers he had been working on in the firelit library that day. He knew a twist of wry humour at that: am I then so much a scholar that I should count these things precious at such a moment! But he knew that the manuscripts and the diaries were infinitely precious, and that if they could be saved, they would be of immense value to the Amaranths.

The necromantic music was closer; both Andrew and Theo could hear it plainly now, a horrid raking at the senses, a dragging, jeering rhythm. As it drew nearer, there was a steady thrumming, a pulsating whirring, as if something dark and evil and immensely powerful was being spun.

When Andrew looked at Theo and said, 'Ready?' Theo at once said, 'Yes, ready,' because even like this, even thin and ravaged-faced, hobbling a bit awkwardly on a stick, Andrew was a person you would want to obey promptly.

As they went quickly through the great stone hall towards the stables, Theo looked up at Andrew, and saw that although he moved awkwardly, leaning on the ash stick, and frowning as if he might be in some pain, he was no longer the ragged, unkempt creature who had lived here, inside Almhuin, and fought Almhuin's terrible darkness. Neither was he the gentle, patient young man who had come to the Porphyry Palace, and tried to help when the Fomoire had come tumbling out of the Cadence Tower.

This was a fiery-eyed young man, strong and fearless, angry at having to run from a battle, angry because he was impatient of hypocrisy and intolerant of selfishness and because he would have liked to turn about and face Chaos and his horrid Armies. This was someone who might very well sweep aside the crowding darkness of the Black Ireland from sheer anger, purely because it was a nuisance and a petty irritation, and rather as if it was simply not worth bothering with.

It ought to have been faintly sinister, this sudden discovery that another person was looking out of Andrew's eyes, but there was nothing in the least sinister about the sudden glowing look he gave her, or the way in which he seemed taller and broader and very powerful indeed. It was a little as if there was a side to him that he thought he ought not to show to the world. It is the hidden Andrew I am seeing, she thought, and felt pleased all over again, because people only showed their hidden selves to you if they trusted you very much.

The thin pale light from the *Uisce* touched his face as they rode cautiously across the courtyard, and Theo knew that she was safe, because she was riding with someone who might very well sweep away the darkness and brush aside the creeping evil . . .

Someone who would cut a swathe of light through the Dark Realm, and force open the Gateways into the Real Ireland . . .

As the Armies of the Dark Lord of Chaos swarmed up the mountain path towards them, the *Uisce* shortened their stride and plunged forward into the deep darkness of the necromantic night.

The radiance of the *Uisce* surrounded them as they soared through the night, Chaos's terrible Armies and the Fortress of the BeastWoman still below them on the mountain path. Andrew, clinging to the silk-floss mane of his mount, Theodora at his side, and the other two *Uisce* at their heels, thought: we are breaking out of the Dark Realm. We are riding hard towards a Gateway and soon, very soon, we will be across the boundaries and on to the hinterlands, and safe.

We are cutting a swathe of light through the Dark Realm . . .

The thought was with him only for the briefest of instants, and then his breath was snatched from him by the night wind in his face, and his senses were turned upside-down by the sheer speed of the sea-horses, the creatures that Chaos had stolen from the magical underwater city and forced to carry his guests across the evil, blood-soaked NightFields of his Realm.

Andrew could feel the pouring delight of the *Uisce* as the dark thralldom lifted, and he could feel, as well, the rainbow iridescence all about them, like a cloak, like a carapace, like a shield of purest brilliance, so that it must surely force open the Gateway into the True Ireland.

The Samildanach forcing open the Gates . . .

It is not my strength, and it is not my brilliance, he thought. But it is being lent to me. I can use it.

Theodora's eyes were shining and her cheeks were flushed with delight. Her dark hair streamed out behind her, and Andrew felt again the warm surge of protectiveness that he had felt in the Cadence Tower so long ago – another life, had it been?

Behind them, Chaos's armies were rushing towards Almhuin, the torchlight from their flambeaux spiralling into the darkness, lighting it to angry red life, the cold, evil music flooding the darkness. Almhuin was becoming bathed in the eerie glow of the torches, the black rearing towers and the jagged-toothed turrets sharply limned against the skies. Andrew reined in his mount and turned its head about for a moment, looking back at the Armies with their glinting armour and their thin black spears. He could see the Lord of Chaos quite clearly, and he could see the great churning millwheels of Murder's grim chariot, blood-spattered and menacing.

Far below them, in the huddle of houses that were the Almhuinians' homes, lights were shining and people were scurrying about. Andrew and Theodora watched for a moment and, as they did so, a thin line of brave little torches appeared as the villagers started up the mountain track in defence of their Lady's Fortress. Andrew thought: so in the end they will be loyal; they will fight Chaos's people and try to save Almhuin. He spared a thought for the tiny, bricked-up cell with the single, terrible prisoner. Would Chaos find the Lady of Almhuin? And if he did not, what would happen to her?

Alone in the dark for ever, condemned to die of hunger and thirst and madness without a single creature for comfort . . .

But I had no choice.

And then they turned away, knowing that they must flee from Almhuin if they were to survive.

Theodora said, suddenly, 'The Moher Gateway!' And pointed, and there before them was the great outline of the Gateway, black and gleaming, rearing up against the black skies of the Dark Ireland.

Andrew said, 'Are you sure?'

'Yes, that is the only thing it can be.' Theo knew this was true. 'There are only three Gateways left: the Well of Segais, where Chaos brought me and where you followed. The Cruachan Cavern, deep in the Wolfwood, and the Gateway of the Moher Cliffs.' She pointed, and, as she brought her hand up, a faint shard of cool light irradiated it. 'If you look, you can see the Cliffs of Moher beyond it,' said Theo, and excitement rose in her voice.

Always look beyond. . . For a moment, Rumour's cool amused voice was with them both. Andrew thought: dear God, if only we had the *sidh*'s music! That would slice through the darkness for us!

'Can we get through?' he said.

'I think we can.' Theo pointed again. 'See? The Gateway is open.'

But Andrew paused, reining in the *Uisce*, remembering Rumour's words and the warnings of the Amaranths, remembering that it was said to be the most difficult thing in the world for Humans to force open the great, mystical Gateways. Rumour and the Amaranths had believed that the *sidh*'s music could take them down through the Well of Segais and force the Gate open – but we have nothing that will help us now, he thought.

And then he knew that, after all, they did have something. They had the soft, strong, pure radiance of the sea-horses, the gentle glowing iridescence of the sleek, beautiful creatures whom Theodora had rescued from Chaos's dark thrall, and who had poured through the Dark Realm, sprinkling light where they went. Without warning, confidence, absolute and complete, surged up in him. He felt the strange brush of the creature called the Samildánach once more; he felt the sweet breath of that other One who had promised to return and who had vowed to cut a swathe through the darkness, and to force open the Gateways into the Real Ireland.

His strength is being lent to me . . .

They could both see the dark crags and they could hear the lashing of the ocean against the wild western coast of Ireland. The skies were dark and black clouds scudded across them, but it was the darkness of ordinary night, a darkness that would presently yield to dawnlight . . . Dawnlight, thought Andrew with sudden joy. The coming of the morning after the long, evil night of the necromancers . . .

Theo, at his side, felt his sudden, soaring delight, and understood that they were nearly home; this was what she had thought about and planned for and imagined all those nights inside the *Saraigli*. This was the home-coming, and soon she would reach the Porphyry Palace, because soon they would be in Ireland again, the real True Ireland, the Ireland of blue mists and purple dusks, and deep forests where twilight slanted through the trees, and where the dawns were rose and gold, washing the tips of the Morning Mountains to such beauty that it hurt your eyes to see it . . .

Andrew turned the *Uisce*'s heads about, and together they rode straight at the Gateway.

The *Uisce* streamed joyfully forwards, and the great shadow of the Moher Gateway fell across their path, no longer forbidding and menacing, but simply and cleanly a Gateway: a door through which to pass from one place to another.

There was the sensation of swimming cleanly and swiftly through great, stagnant pools of evil and smothering clouds of malignancy; and, for the space of a heartbeat, the shadow of the Gateway was all about them. But then they were through it, the *Uisce*'s silken heads breasting a great, wine-dark sea, and the clotted evil and the darkness was falling from them, as if they were coming up from a dark, foul lake.

There was a moment – breath-taking, awe-inspiring – when

they both saw ahead of them a thin crescent arc, a ribbon of rainbow light, as if a dark sun were sinking and yielding to a rose and gold horizon.

A sunset seen from beneath, thought Andrew, and drew in a deep breath, and felt the cold night air fill his lungs. He thought: yes, this is the real world, I can smell it and hear it and I can feel it. Beautiful.

Night had fallen, true night, laden with purple mists and dusky, twilit fragrances. Ahead of them were the storm-lashed Moher Cliffs, stark and forbidding, thrusting up out of the ground, and wreathed in their own ancient magic. A little to their right, weaving slightly inland, was the cliff path, and as they turned the heads about, they both saw above them the huge, rearing bulk of the Grail Castle.

Theodora reached out to Andrew's arm, and he felt her fingers close about his wrist in fear.

'There's something lying in the shadows over there,' she said. 'And it's waiting for us.'

The exhilarating delight that Andrew had been experiencing shut off as abruptly as if a lid had been clapped down over it, and he felt the *Uisce* shiver beneath him.

Something dark and formless, something that crawled on its belly and that was held in dark and terrible bondage to whatever lived inside the Grail Castle. Something that was soaked in old dark evil and that served a malevolent, hungering master . . . I can feel that it is all of those things! thought Andrew, staring at the crawling shadow in silent apprehension.

The shape moved then, slithering and scuttling, and Andrew heard Theodora bite back a gasp of terror. He thought: but it is only an animal, some kind of beast that scuttles and crawls, perhaps a large weasel or a stoat. He thought the shape had the nearly-boneless appearance of a large snake or a huge, thick worm, and then he thought that it was exactly as if a man-sized serpent had donned a cloak and a hood, and his skin crawled with revulsion.

Quintus, helpless against the Fisher Prince's curse, obedient to the thralldom that held him, reared up in front of them and stood blocking their way. The *Uisce* whickered in fear and Andrew felt the pain and fright from them.

There was the impression of dark, swirling robes, a great

black cowl pulled down to shadow the creature's face. There was the sudden stifling miasma of old evil . . .

'Follow me, wayfarers,' said the Black Monk in a soft, beckoning voice, and in the same instant, Andrew and Theodora felt the terrible dark web of the ancient Enchantment of the Isle of Torach spin and whirl sickeningly and dizzingly above them, and then descend in a great dark cloak of unknowing.

Chapter Forty-four

The Almhuinians had not gone straightaway to the Castle when Chaos's Armies marched through the mountains and up to the great Stronghold that had dominated their lives for so long. They had not done so, because it did not do to be hasty.

They were not precisely short on courage, they said, holding a rather furtive meeting in Diarmuit's cellar. And it was not that they jibbed at facing the Lord of Chaos and his henchmen, because they would take on Chaos, yes and Murder, Misrule and Anarchy with him! they said, sinking determined draughts from the tankards of apple wine served out by Diarmuit.

But if there was going to be some kind of final decisive battle: if the simmering hatred between Chaos and Almhuin's Lady was about to erupt into a scalding explosion of necromantic savagery, the Castle was no place for any of them for the time being. Best to keep clear until it was seen which way the wind was blowing, and which wind it actually was. Best to be practical and efficient.

But caution allowed, this was precisely the time when their spying skills might be profitably utilised. There was no reason why a couple of spies could not be sent up to the Castle. There was no reason why one or two of them could not slink in the shadows and listen and watch and find out what was happening. And they all knew the Castle; they knew where you could conceal yourself, and where you could hear and see. Somebody suggested that Diarmuit's elder son and Black Aed's boy be sent. It would be good to give the younger ones a chance. And it would be the best way to discover what was going on.

Because once they knew who was holding the Castle, and who had beaten whom, they could decide where their best advantage lay.

Diarmuit's elder son and Black Aed's boy arrived back, a little out of breath but glowing with achievement. There was not hide nor hair nor whisker of the Crimson Lady, they said. She had vanished from the Castle as if she had never been there.

'Not even Chaos knows where she is,' said Black Aed's son.

'And Chaos has taken the Castle over,' said Diarmuit's son.

'The soldiers are quartered in the keep and Chaos's Lords are holding a huge banquet in the hall of the tapestries.'

And so their best advantage lay with Chaos. It was clear-cut and unequivocal. It was maybe not so very surprising when you looked at it sensibly, because most of them agreed that the Crimson Lady had been becoming something of a twice-told tale lately. She was burned out, getting beyond her best. Only look at how she had vented her rage on poor Black Aed. It was small wonder that Chaos had been able to vanquish her with such apparent ease. Diarmuit asked was there no sign of the Lady at all: were they sure she had not been flung into one of her own dungeons or maybe trussed and chained to provide entertainment for Chaos's people?

But the two sons, who had performed this very important grown-up mission seriously and thoroughly, said, No, nothing like that. Simply the Lady was nowhere to be found. Yes, they were quite sure; they had listened to the soldiers talking about it, and they had even heard Anarchy refer to the Lady's absence: 'The bird has flown,' he had said, and he had sounded very regretful as if he had been looking forward to a confrontation.

Whatever had happened to Almhuin's Lady, everyone was agreed that the thing to do now was to swear allegiance to the Lord of Chaos, and that as quickly as possible. Any creature found still loyal to the Lady would be very summarily dealt with! they said, nodding wisely. No one wanted to find himself at the wrong end of Chaos's wrath, and no one wanted to find himself being crushed to death beneath the millwheels of Murder's chariot. Everyone in Almhuin knew the tales of the entertainments that Misrule devised for his Lord, and no one wanted to end up roasting on one of Misrule's spikes (with, or without his mouth sewn up) simply to give extra light to the revels inside the Castle of Infinity!

And so, when Diarmuit said they would just go along and offer their services to Chaos and his people, everyone thought this a splendid idea.

Even so, it felt odd and a bit uncomfortable to make their way along the steep mountain path, just as they had done so many times in the past. Ahead of them, the great mountain stronghold of Almhuin looked exactly as it had always looked; it was rather disconcerting to know that it was no longer the dwelling of the Lady whom they had served for so long.

They were admitted to the Castle by the strange, silent servants, and they were received with apparent courtesy by Chaos himself, who was seated in the great central hall, with the remains of a banquet on the massive oak table, exactly as the two boys had reported. Candles burned in the tarnished holders, shedding soft light on the decaying tapestries, the rotting velvet drapes, crumbling panelling and the stonework. The immense depiction of the famous Dark Passing Over hung directly behind his chair, and for a brief space the Almhuinians had the eerie impression that the tapestry had come to life and that they were seeing a living enactment of the historic night when the necromancers had gathered about Medoc to sup with him before his death and defeat.

Chaos's people were seated at the table, with Murder and Anarchy on each side of him. They would be the foremost necromantic Lords, of course, which Chaos would have brought with him to vanquish the Lady. They would not be as powerful as Chaos, but they would have to be reckoned with. The silent servants stood in the shadows, blending rather sinisterly with the Twelve Tapestries that hung around the hall, and had come to be known as the Twelve Stories of the Lady of Pain. The Almhuinians paid the tapestries scant attention, because they had seen them innumerable times, but they glanced uneasily at the servants, because didn't everyone know the kind of people who served Chaos? Unnaturally bred creatures they were, raised from strong necromancy, born from the *Draoicht Roghnacht*. You could admire and revere a Dark Lord capable of such things; the Almhuinians did admire and revere him, and they were perfectly prepared to offer their allegiance to him. But they did not much like the results of the *Roghnacht*.

Chaos greeted them courteously, and asked, in his soft, cultured voice, the purpose of their visit.

The Almhuinians had sorted this out before leaving the village. You could not have upwards of a dozen people all talking at once, and so two of them had been selected by the drawing of the ivory sticks. The two were, in fact, Diarmuit himself, who had long since discovered a way of rigging the stick-drawing ritual, and Black Aed's wife, who had naturally been very upset at Aed's death, but who was very pleased to forget her grief for a while and join in such an important event. And so it was these two who moved to stand before Chaos, leaving the others grouped worriedly by the door.

Chaos watched their approach, his narrow, dark eyes unreadable, his long slender fingers curled about the stem of his wine chalice. He was accoutred for a battle, in the gleaming black armour of his House, with a scarlet velvet cloak thrown negligently about his shoulders, and the Silver Star of Medoc glinting on his breast. Diarmuit and Aed's wife thought he must have arrayed himself for a battle against the Crimson Lady. But there were no signs that a battle had been fought, let alone won, which was puzzling. Had Chaos, then, been victorious so easily and so swiftly? What had happened to the Lady?

But it would not do to ask, and so they stood respectfully before him, seeing that on his left, Murder sat silent and fearsome in the swirling black cloak, his face and his eyes in shadow. Anarchy sprawled in the chair at his right, a look of determined alertness on his slightly immature face, rather as if he was hoping people were watching him and seeing how intelligent and how deeply involved in everything he was. Diarmuit and Aed's wife had never seen Anarchy, and they were surprised at how extremely young he was.

But when Chaos asked their business, Diarmuit, who had prepared a bit of a speech, spoke out firmly, explaining how they'd come to offer their services and their fealty to the Lord of Chaos and his people. They hadn't the necromantic powers, said Diarmuit (it had been felt as well to emphasise this from the beginning), but they had other skills which could be of use. They had the knowledge of fighting, and the experience of spying, and the inherited skills of creeping up on enemies in the dark and infiltrating their castles. All good, useful skills in a

548

battle. And they'd be honoured, said Diarmuit, they'd be honoured and proud if Chaos would take them into his Armies and allow them to fight on his side.

There was a moment of profound silence, and the other Almhuinians looked furtively at one another, because although Diarmuit's speech had sounded very good indeed (the use of the word 'fealty' had been a master-stroke), no one had moved or spoken all through it, and no one was moving or speaking now. Chaos remained seated, resting his chin lightly on one hand, his entire pose gracefully relaxed, his face pale, his eyes deep, burning pits. The burning gaze of those eyes was a bit uncomfortable, truth to tell.

And then Chaos said, in his soft, gentlemanly voice, 'So, you are prepared to desert your Lady are you? Now that I find immensely interesting,' and the Almhuinians thought that, put like that, it sounded a bit unpleasant.

But Black Aed's wife said, 'She was never our Lady, sir. And we prefer to be on the winning side,' and the Almhuinians glanced at one another, because Chaos would be pleased at such a grand bit of flattery.

And it seemed that he was, because he was smiling, although one or two of them could not help thinking it was actually a rather cold, malice-filled smile. But he said, softly, 'I am honoured by the allegiance and the fealty of your people,' and the Almhuinians were pleased that he'd picked that one up, because didn't it show Chaos that he wouldn't be dealing with unschooled peasants but creatures of some learning and refinement.

'Your willingness to follow whichever Master will give you the most does you credit,' said Chaos, and at his feet Anarchy let out a hoot of rude mirth. The Dark Lords smiled in a slightly sinister fashion, as if they found the Almhuinians amusing, but for all the wrong reasons.

'I believe,' said Chaos slowly, 'that I could make use of you.' He studied them in turn, and the thin, cold smile touched his lips again. Anarchy gave vent to another raucous laugh, as if he were trying to indicate that he knew something that nobody else did.

Diarmuit made bold to ask whether there was a battle ahead, and Chaos said, 'Since I hold Almhuin Castle, there is nothing left within this Realm for me to conquer. The entire Dark Ireland is mine.'

'And with the timely removal of Almhuin's Lady,' said Anarchy, jeeringly, 'the way is *apparently* clear. If, that is, we were so foolish as to trust to it.' He made a rude gesture at the Almhuinians with the glinting curved knife he wore at his belt, which was shaped like a huge phallus, but which had a very sharp tip.

'The disappearance of the Lady,' said Chaos in his soft voice, which Diarmuit had suddenly realised was sounding very menacing indeed, 'is the most interesting thing of all. You knew that she was no longer here?' said Chaos. 'Yes, I see that you did know.'

'And we should all like to know *how* the snivelling rats knew,' said Anarchy.

There was an awkward pause, and then Diarmuit said, 'We did know she had gone, sir,' because wasn't it as well to let Chaos think they had their own sources for information. 'But we don't know how,' he added firmly.

'Of course they know,' said Anarchy, impatiently. 'Sire, I told you. There is only one way she could have escaped, and that is if she was smuggled out.' He glared at the Almhuinians. 'I would not trust those turncoats an inch,' he said. 'They've got the Crimson Lady away into hiding somewhere, and just as they think you've been fooled into relaxing your guard, she'll be at your throat! And they'll be at her side! Rats!' said Anarchy in a voice of loathing, and bounded out of his chair towards Diarmuit and Aed's wife. But Murder was there in a silent slither of darkness, one dark, gloved hand hooking about Anarchy's neck, pushing him into his chair again. Anarchy subsided with a bad grace, and when Murder released him, refilled his wine chalice and sat glowering at them over its rim.

Chaos had ignored Anarchy and Murder's quelling of him, rather in the way of ignoring a rude child who has been subdued. He leaned forward, and said in his soft voice, 'Let us return to how I intend to use you,' and the Almhuinians looked uneasily at one another, because they had not liked the way that Chaos had said 'use'.

'You will perhaps know of my work?' said Chaos, his eyes dark and unfathomable, and the Almhuinians glanced uneasily at one another, because didn't the whole of the Dark Realm know of Chaos's manipulations and tamperings, and the blending of warring peoples and of alien strains. They hoped they were sufficiently open-minded about these things, but didn't it give you a shuddering grue to think of Goblins breeding from Giants, or Humans breeding from snakes. Say what you liked, it was unnatural.

But it was politic to appear interested, and so Diarmuit said, 'Indeed we do know . . .' and, uncertain as to how Chaos ought to be addressed, added, 'sir', which, as Aed's wife had said, was pretty much a general term of courtesy and should be acceptable. 'And have always found them of interest,' added Diarmuit for good measure.

Chaos appeared amused. He said, 'That is very gratifying. And since you have come to offer your fealty to me, and in such a courteous and *prompt* fashion, I have no doubt that you will not object to returning with me to my Castle, to assist in the – ah – *furtherance* of my work.' He paused and, at his feet, Anarchy laughed again, with an immature, unbroken, boy's laugh.

'I believe I shall need only the females,' said Chaos, apparently considering the matter carefully. He looked up and something harsh and cruel shone from his eyes. 'Although we shall take you all.'

'Take us?' said Diarmuit. 'As prisoners?'

'Oh, my prisoners can be made very comfortable,' said Chaos, in an amused voice, but there was a red gleam in his eyes that made Diarmuit and Aed's wife glance uneasily at one another. 'And your females will enjoy helping in my work.'

He stood up. 'But prisoners you will be,' he said, and his lips were suddenly thinned into a cruel, cold line. 'You will work in my service until I have satisfied myself as to your *true* allegiance.' He nodded to the darkly accoutred Captains, and instantly a dozen of them sprang forward, surrounding the Almhuinians, their swords drawn and poised to strike.

Diarmuit was by now very worried indeed, but he said with as much courage as he could muster, 'And could we know, sir, what might be required of us? Within your service?'

Chaos studied Diarmuit, and now it was the icy appraisal of a superior species studying an infinitely lower one. At length he said, 'Within the Beyond Ireland, somewhere inside the Realm of the High Kings and the Amaranth sorcerers, has been born a creature who poses a great threat to me. He is the only creature who can hinder my march to absolute power, and he is the only one who can truly challenge my complete possession of both Irelands.' He paused, and his eyes blurred, as if he were looking beyond the candlelit hall and the long banqueting table. He said, in a soft voice filled with hatred, 'The Fisher Prince. Coelacanth's spawn.'

There was a sudden silence and, despite the menacing guards, the Almhuinians looked at one another, because this was the first any of them had heard of Coelacanth having a son.

Chaos said, half to himself, 'He should never have been born. If I had known in time, I would have murdered the creature before it drew breath.' He paused, frowning, and then said, 'But somehow he has clawed his way into the world. Somehow he was begotten on to an Amaranth Lady, and somehow he was gestated and given his warped and grotesque birth. It was Coelacanth's final and greatest revenge. His son to enter the world . . .' A red gleam shone from his eyes, and his fists curled into predator's claws. At his side, Murder made an abrupt movement, and Chaos seemed to recall himself.

He said, 'As yet I know little about the creature, other than that he was taken from the birth chamber to a place of concealment. That much my people have been able to discover.' Anger flared in his eyes, but it was normal impatience now. 'They have not been able to find out where he is hidden,' said Chaos, and his eyes fell coldly upon Anarchy.

'I have searched and I have sent out spells, sire,' said Anarchy in a whining, it-isn't-my-fault voice. 'But there are so many ancient fortresses and so many isolated strongholds: Ireland is thick with them,' he said sulkily.

'You failed,' said Chaos, coldly. 'There will be one more chance for you, and if you fail that time, you will be fed to the WarMongers.' Anarchy slumped sullenly in his chair, hunching his shoulders pettishly, although he sent a nervous glance to Chaos and hot, embarrassed colour stained his cheeks. Chaos turned back to the Almhuinians. 'And since my people have been unsuccessful in finding the Prince,' he said, 'I must look for better methods and better servants.'

'You must find spies,' said Diarmuit, staring.

'I must find spies.' He studied Diarmuit with interest. 'That is astute of you,' he said, and stood up, seeming to tower over the great hall. At once the Rodent Captains snapped to attention, thrusting the huddled Almhuinians forward. Murder was on his feet also, and Anarchy sprang up, his sulk forgotten.

'The spies I send into the Beyond Ireland to find the Prince must not be recognisable as creatures from this Realm,' said Chaos. 'I could use you . . .' Again there was the appraising look, as if the Almhuinians were insects to be dissected. 'Oh yes, I can use you,' he said. 'But I cannot use you as you are now. Once beyond the Gateway you would be instantly recognised for Almhuinians, and you would be taken and imprisoned. Perhaps you would be executed. Any value you had as spies would be ended.' A frown touched his eyes. 'I do not make the mistake of underestimating the Beyond Ireland,' he said. 'The High King is very strong, and he has for advisers and sorcerers the Amaranths. And the Amaranths are the strongest and the finest sorcerers in all Ireland.' A thin, secret amusement touched his lips suddenly. 'But I am stronger,' he said, and he was no longer courteously explaining a battle plan to underlings; he was suddenly the unchallenged Overlord of his Domain; the greatest necromancer throughout the entire Black Ireland.

'And so I must perforce create a new species for the work.' He looked very straightly at them. 'As Almhuinians, you have in your veins the blood of spies. Yes?'

Diarmuit spoke up again, saying how they'd always been known for their skill in spying, in creeping into castles and strongholds and houses, listening at keyholes, peering through chinks in windows. 'We have centuries of spying in our blood,' he said, proudly. 'It is our trade.'

'Ah,' said Chaos, as if this pleased him. 'That is precisely what I understood. Generations of spies. Then I have a good foundation to work from.'

'A – foundation?' said Diarmuit, and everyone looked worried.

Chaos smiled at Diarmuit, but his eyes flickered over the female Almhuinians. 'Necromantic race breeding,' he said softly, and a shudder went through the Almhuinians. If Chaos saw it or felt it, he gave no indication. He said, 'Any enchantment must be created on a firm foundation. A strong base that will stand up to assault. It is precisely the same principle as building a castle or even a cottage. If the foundation is not firm and suitable, then the castle or the cottage will become unsafe.' He paused, appearing to arrange his thoughts.

'In my Castle,' he said, after a moment, 'deep within the Castle of Infinity, dwells one of the most fearsome and one of the cleverest enchantments I have ever spun.' He paused, and no one moved or spoke. 'It took many years and much study, and many of my enemies have tried to steal it away from me.'

There was a pause, and the Almhuinians, guessing what was coming, shifted their feet uneasily.

'But it remains in my possession,' said Chaos, softly. 'It roams my Castle whilst my people are sleeping, and it hears their secrets and it listens to their intrigues, and it spies out their plots. And then it brings them to me.' He looked round the hall, and a ripple of disquiet went through the Almhuinians, because everyone knew that Chaos was referring to the *Draoicht Spiaire*, the hungering thing that swallowed and then regurgitated its victims' thoughts and secrets and memories.

'The *Draoicht Spiaire* is one of my most valuable enchantments,' said Chaos. 'But because of its extreme ferocity, it cannot be unchained during the normal hours of working and feasting and living.' The frown twisted his face again. 'It is the creature's only weakness,' he said. 'Its bloodlust. Its hunger not only for the minds and the secrets and the intrigues of its victims, but for their bodies.

'And so because of that, I cannot send the *Draoicht Spiaire* into the Beyond Ireland to spy for me as I would wish. It would assuredly find the Prince, but it would serve its own greeds as well. It would slaughter and mutilate as the need took it, and since it has not the slyness to resist capture, it would become useless to me.

'It needs – we will say – tempering,' he said. 'It needs a little Humanish or perhaps Rodent blood in with its essence. It needs to be blended with creatures who have the slyness to remain unseen and unheard, and the cunning to creep into castles and strongholds and listen unheard and pry unseen.' The smile became very faintly malicious. 'I believe I have quoted you more or less accurately, sir,' he said to Diarmuit.

'I – yes.'

554

'The results of a blending of the *Spiaire* with – let us say, an Almhuinian – would be very interesting,' said Chaos. 'The issue of such a mingling would be unparalleled for spying and cunning and stealth.' He appeared to consider. 'So far, I have blended the blood of Goblins with Giants, and the blood of Rodent creatures with Humans,' said Chaos. 'And there have been several other mutant strains that I have created. All immensely interesting. But for the purpose of discovering the Prince's whereabouts, I shall create a new race,' he said. 'A race born of a necromantically controlled mating between Almhuinian females and the *Draoicht Spiaire* who lies muzzled and chained in my dungeons.' He smiled at them. 'That is how I shall use you,' he said. 'I am going to feed you to the *Spiaire*. You are going to breed from it.

'It may take some time,' he said. 'For there will be the conception and the birthing. There will be the growing up of the spawn. Also, there may need to be several attempts before the blending of the two bloods is balanced correctly.

'But however long it takes,' said Chaos, 'Coelacanth's son will still be waiting for me. If it takes ten years to produce the race I require, I shall wait ten years.

'Several lifetimes would not be too long for me to wait to find the Prince and kill him. For only then can I realise my dream. Only then can I ride unchallenged into Ireland and take it for my own.'

And so they set out for the Castle of Infinity, the Almhuinians unsure of what they had talked themselves into, but telling one another that you could not lightly ignore the wishes of the Overlord of the whole Dark Realm. You could not ignore, either, the fact that the Rodent Armies, under the direction of two of the Captains, had surrounded the Almhuinians and brandished their swords, and had really made it rather awkward for the Almhuinians to refuse to go in procession to Chaos's Castle of Infinity, there to await his bidding.

Prisoners, said several of them crossly. They were no more than Chaos's prisoners.

But in the end, everyone had fallen into line with as good a grace as possible, and had told one another that anyway wasn't this what they had intended?

They made their preparations for the journey swiftly, scurrying about the Castle to gather up things that might be needed: swords from the Castle armoury, spurs and chainmail cloaks and helmets.

Several times they felt the Lady's presence with them, and so strong was it that they looked around, half expecting to see her standing in the shadows. They even began to hear her voice, raised in one of the frantic rages that they knew so well, and the sounds seemed so real, that they found themselves stopping their tasks and listening.

But there was only the scrabbling of something from the dungeons – a rat or a weasel probably. Although just for a few minutes it had sounded eerily like the scratching of Human nails against bricks.

The Almhuinians paid it no attention. The Castle had ever had its share of ghosts, and it had always been overrun with rats. A few more made little difference. In any case, they were leaving it all behind them.

They were leaving the Castle to the ghosts and the rats and weasels and to the dark memories . . .

And to the single living creature bricked up in the dungeons and left to die in the dark . . .

Chapter Forty-five

The people of Moher always knew when the Prince was hungering for new victims, and when he was planning one of his grisly revels. There was a feeling, a scent, an essence. A dark brooding that seeped through the thick stones of the Grail Castle, and was borne on the wind into the farmhouses and the spinners' workshops and the butteries and the crofters' cottages.

There was no longer any pleasure in farming the rather sparse land around the Castle, and there was no longer the innocent delight in making your living out of the little cottage crafts: wool-spinning and weaving and wood-carving. There was no longer any tranquillity or any pride in living in the shadow of Ireland's ancient, myth-drenched Fortress.

When twilight stole over the cliffs, and the great oceans that lashed the shores turned black and cold, the people of Moher double-locked their doors and huddled round their firesides. You did not, if you valued your life, venture out after dark any longer; you stayed by your own hearth, and you listened for the shuffling of the creature Quintus coming along the narrow street, oozing the poison of the sores inflicted by the Prince all those years ago. You heard him and you smelt him and you prayed to whatever god you held dearest that he would not sniff at your keyhole and peer through the chink in the curtain and demand your daughter or your wife or your sister for the Fisher Prince.

But that did not happen so very often and, in the main, Moher itself had remained safe. The Prince had not often fouled his own doorstep, it was said, with one of the uneasy laughs that were all the Moher farmers could allow themselves these days.

The tales spread with the years, of course, and there were

many gallant young men who came to Moher; reckless, eager-eyed adventurers who had pledged themselves to discover the Grail Castle of legend. There were many boastful boys who wanted the glory of having slain the Moher Monster. It hurt to hear the terrible expression; it hurt the people who had been proud of their small community, and who had enjoyed their work and taken love and care over it, whether it had been tilling the sparse land or farming the sheep, or simply spinning the rugs and the cloaks out of the fine, soft wool that the Moher sheep grew against the creeping sea mists. They had enjoyed their happy, uneventful lives, they had helped one another when times were hard, and they had enjoyed welcoming travellers and hearing the tales of their journeyings.

They welcomed travellers and pilgrims no longer, for travellers were grist to the Prince's sinister appetites; they were caught by the prowling Quintus, they were smothered by the terrible Enchantment of Torach, and thrown into the Castle dungeons, there to await the Prince's pleasure, or even, of latter years, the Fomoire's. It had been a terrible day when the Prince had enslaved the Fomoire.

Sometimes the prisoners would be brought up to the great hall, where the Prince would hold sinister revelries and dark, gruesome banquets with the Fomoire in attendance, and where the light would be provided by the burning of the prisoners themselves, impaled on spikes and set afire. At one time it had been one of the Prince's pleasures to hold races between his prisoners, to decide which should be burned and which should be given to the Fomoire.

But the banquets were less frequent now, the Fomoire's Hunting Songs were not so often heard echoing eerily down the dark cliff paths. The Prince had taken to creeping down to the dungeons by himself, rutting and killing and mutilating the poor chained wretches with his own hands, bellowing like a bull in lust as he did so, using the victims' bodies in a dozen terrible ways, until finally his evil lusts were satiated.

His dark appetites had grown and his powers had increased with the years. The people of Moher were unsure as to how many years the Prince had been in their midst, because you did not count the years or the months of an oppression, you simply lived through them. But they could remember the day when Quintus had caught the child who had come through the Moher Gateway, because it had been the night when the strange, icily beautiful music had shivered briefly on the air, and the Prince had howled with such rage that the villagers had trembled in their cottages, and had not dared venture out for several days. He had rampaged about the countryside, the cringing Quintus at his heels, roaring with unbridled fury and lust and then falling on such unwary travellers as Quintus had been able to snare for him.

That had been the last time any living thing had come through the Gateway, although there were occasionally whispers of chinks of dark, smeary light showing, and there had even been murmurs lately of strange, slinking creatures being glimpsed: ugly things that walked upright like Humans, but that had an odd, scuttling gait, and eyes that protruded from their heads on stalks. But these were the kind of rumours that always echoed about Ireland's dark Gateways.

No one knew what the Prince had finally done to the child, although the young man who had been with her was still at the Castle, toiling rather taciturnly in the gardens alongside the strange, silent Maelduin, who had been with the Prince ever since anyone could remember. The people of Moher guessed that the Prince took a cruel delight in being served by these two, for both were mutilated: the thin dark-haired Andrew was crippled and walked everywhere leaning heavily on a stout ash crutch, and Maelduin was known to be a mute.

But no one knew what the Prince had done with the child.

Deep within the Castle of Infinity, the Lord of Chaos eyed Murder and Anarchy, and pushed towards them the plans drawn up for the final great battle: the storming of the Grail Castle and the taking of the Beyond Ireland.

Murder studied the plans, his eyes in shadow, no trace of emotion showing on his face. He did not speak, but there was immense concentration in his expression.

Anarchy read them noisily, flipping pages over with a rustling sound, turning back to verify a point, showily making notes, frowning and then grinning, poring over a plan of Tara's interior, counting up the number of fighting forces listed. At length he looked up at Chaos, who sat quietly in his chair at the head of the table, and grinned.

'At last, sir,' he said, in his light, undeveloped voice. 'At last we are ready to take the Beyond Ireland.' He drained his tankard of wine, belched, and reached again for the flagon that stood at the table's centre.

Chaos said, with immaculate courtesy, 'I am glad that my plans find favour with you. You will be expected to play a leading part.' And so you had better be properly prepared, said his tone.

'I'll be there,' said Anarchy, grinning. 'Villages to burn and towns to raze! Humans for the slaying and females for the taking! I'll dance on their dying carcasses and cause the streets to run with their blood!'

Chaos regarded Anarchy coldly. 'You do not improve with the years,' he said. 'You are as selfish and egocentric as ever you were. You do not change.'

'I do not wish to change,' said Anarchy, sprawling back in his chair. 'Nor do you wish me to. By being selfish and egocentric, I serve your needs very well.'

Murder said, in his cold, passionless voice, 'You are confident that the plans will succeed, sir? And that you can slay Coelacanth's spawn?'

'I cannot slay him,' said Chaos, and a tiny frown appeared in his eyes. 'Only the Samildanach can slay those who issue from the line of the *nimfeach*.' He reached for his own wine, which had been poured by one of the silent servants into a ruby-encrusted chalice. 'You know it as I know it. That is why I have hesitated so long. That is why this plan has been so many years in the birthing.'

'I thought it was all a legend,' said Anarchy, a bit sulkily. 'The Samildanach. Who believes that old legend now?'

'It is very far from being disbelieved,' said Chaos, sternly. 'The Samildanach once walked abroad, preaching his accursed doctrines. It is certain that he lived.'

'And may live again,' put in Murder, softly.

'The *Draoicht Spiaireachts*, the sons of the *Spiaire* that we sent through the Moher Gateway, believe that he does live again. Within the Grail Castle, under a Veil of Unknowing, is a young man who may very well wear the Samildanach's mantle.' The dark eyes rested on Murder. 'He does not know it, but the marks were upon him. And we all know that the mark of the Samildanach cannot be mistaken.'

'The Man of Each and Every Art,' said Murder, half to himself.

'Yes. And if it is true – if we find that the Samildanach does indeed walk the world again – it will be your task to kill him.'

Murder inclined his head, and Chaos said, rather sharply, 'Do not waste time on bloody battles, if you please. There is to be no feeding of individual appetites and no sating of individual lusts. The time for that will come later.'

'You are generous, sire,' said Murder in a remote voice.

'We have waited long enough for this,' said Anarchy, petulantly.

'You may have – you may both have all the blood and all the slaughter you want. But first this creature – if in truth he is the Samildanach reborn – must be killed. There must be no opportunity for him to fight us. There must be no mistake.'

'But,' said Anarchy, pleased to have found a flaw, 'if we dispose of the Samildanach, we shall not be able to deal with Coelacanth's son. We cannot kill Coelacanth's line. Only the Samildanach himself can do that. You said so.' He sent Chaos an impudent grin, rather in the manner of a rude child who has scored a point.

'The Samildanach will not be killed until he, in turn, has slain the Fisher Prince,' said Murder coldly and contemptuously. 'We shall permit him to live until he has done that, and then we shall kill him.' Really, you are very stupid, said his tone. He turned away from Anarchy and said to Chaos, 'What of the Princess, sir? It is almost ten years. If she lives, she will be a beauty by this time.'

Chaos looked back at Murder. 'Whoever weds the Princess of the Amaranths will hold very strong power in Ireland,' he said. 'If the Prince still has her, then I should expect him to take her into his bed. It is what Coelacanth would have done.' His lips curved in a sudden smile. 'It will be interesting to see if the son resembles the father,' he said. 'I fought Coelacanth and won. I banished him to the Pit. But I shall enjoy fighting his spawn.'

Murder said, 'If the Princess is inside the Grail Castle, what will you do?'

'She will be brought back here,' said Chaos. 'After we have forced the Samildanach to kill the Fisher Prince, and after Murder has slain the Samildanach.'

'If the Amaranth Princess still lives, she will lie in my bed on the night we take Ireland.' The thin, cold smile touched his lips. 'As I always intended her to,' said the Lord of Chaos.

The concubines hung as far as they dared over the ledge of the *Saraigli* to watch the procession set out. They did not normally like Wars and battles – horrid dull things! – but Meirdreach had said they must know what was going on, because if Chaos was to invade the Beyond Ireland it might affect them all.

They had understood this, and they thought that after all they might like to watch a procession, which would be something out of the ordinary. And then AnCine had told them that they could all please themselves, she was going to sit on the window-ledge and cheer the Army on its way. She was a vulgar, loud creature, and growing coarser with the years, but if she was going to drape herself on the window-ledge and cheer the Army, the other concubines were going to do so as well.

They spent the entire morning getting ready, running anxiously to the window at intervals to be sure that the procession was not already assembling, and then scurrying back to the looking-glass or the bathhouse, selecting gowns that would compete with AnCine's scarlet, trying out the effect of threads of silver gilt. It was a time when you wanted to look your best. There had been a fashion some years earlier for very short hair, tipped with silver and gold; several of the older concubines still wore their hair in this way, in imitation of some long-ago sorceress who had visited the Castle and made the *Saraigli* the now-famous present of the Enchantment of Seduction. The concubines still giggled over this, and told one another that Chaos would *not* know what had happened when they were summoned to his bedchamber with the Seduction Enchantment draped about them! It had been used a number of times, and Chaos had never suspected. The younger, newly arrived concubines listened to tales about the Seduction Enchantment enviously, because it was interesting to hear about things that had happened so long ago. But they tossed their long flowing locks with self-admiration, and looked disparagingly on the ugly, short hair of their elders, and wondered how anyone could wear her hair in such an unbecoming style, never mind if fifty famous sorceresses had set a fashion.

The procession was assembling at last, and the concubines squealed in excitement, pushing one another aside to get a prominent place at the two large windows, glaring at AnCine – who had been there for quite half the morning, and very vulgar it had looked too – but telling each other that you had to be charitable, because it must be *years* since she had been summoned to Chaos's bed!

'Better to have been summoned in the past than never to be summoned at all,' said AnCine, who thought the younger concubines pert and showy.

At the head of the procession rode Anarchy, very splendid in a new suit of glinting gold armour, astride a pure white stallion. The concubines nudged one another and said wouldn't the armour be splashed and muddied before the day was out, and would you look at the huge gold phallus Anarchy had strung about his middle and arranged to hang over his genitals, the big show-off!

But Anarchy was to lead the procession through the Moher Gateway, riding at the head of the Rodent Captains.

They were there, of course, their black armour glinting, their visors lowered so that all you could see of them was their narrow red eyes. Nasty things, Rodent people! said the concubines, and giggled all over again, because they'd smuggled a Rodent Captain into the *Saraigli* one night, and hadn't the vain, boastful creature vowed to take a turn with every one of them, but hadn't his strength run out at the seventh, weakling that he'd been! It was to be hoped the Rodents fought better than they attended a lady! said the concubines daringly, and screeched with mirth at their own wit.

The Rodent Armies were massing behind the Captains, and a remarkable and very splendid display they all made. The poor, pale creatures of the Beyond Ireland would be sent running and tumbling into hiding at the very sight of them! The Almhuinians, brought out of the Crimson Lady's domain all those years ago, marched with the Army. You could not precisely admire them; they were sly, furtive-looking creatures, but they were believed to be expert in all kinds of Warfare. They had not mixed much with Chaos's people; the women had been thrust into the *Saraigli* when they first came, and several of the older concubines could remember how they had all sulked for days over it. The Almhuinian women had been sly and miserly with their possessions, and had thought themselves above the concubines on account of the mating with the *Draoicht Spiaire*, which had gone on for several months, and which the concubines had shuddered daintily over. But the *Saraigli* had been an unhappy place for a time, and Meirdreach had had her work cut out to keep them all from falling into scratching, biting, hair-pulling fights.

The WarMongers were on the edges of the procession, their fearsome chariots behind them. You could never quite make out which was which, but the concubines shivered and remembered that the WarMongers had names like Agony and Torment and Mutilation and Despair, and that they were cruel, pitiless fighters.

There had been a time when the Fomoire would have been there, of course, dancing and leaping in glee, screeching their Hunting Songs; but the Fomoire had long since gone from Chaos's service, and there had been a rumour – five years ago had it been? – that they had been seen within the Grail Castle itself.

At the centre of the procession were the nine *Draoicht Spiaireacht*, the strange creatures spawned on the long-ago night when Chaos had invoked the now nearly legendary spell that had been woven into the Dark Realm's myths and lore. The blending of a spell; actually a living creation of pure necromancy and strong black sorcery with the Humanish, it had been. Tales were still being told around firesides of Chaos's supreme temerity and his remarkable powers at actually breeding between the *Draoicht Spiaire* and nine of the Almhuinian females. Those concubines who were sufficiently old enough to have been in the *Saraigli* on the night it had happened, and then later, when the screams of the Almhuinians in their birth agonies had rent the Palace asunder, pointed them out. The *Spiaireacht* were sinister, ugly creatures; they were so nearly Humanish, so nearly Almhuinian, that they might almost pass unnoticed in an ill-lit room, or on a shadowy road. They had arms, legs, a torso, a head with rather fibrous hair sprouting. They each had a normal face, with eyes and a nose.

But the eyes protruded on stalks, and swivelled and peered, and the lips were fleshless and mumbling and evil, and there was not only one mouth, but several, some of them gaping and grinning from the creatures' rather thick necks, all arranged one atop the other, some of them opening from the creatures' chests. And although the pale, fibrous hair looked reasonably normal, beneath it there was no hard, bony skull, no rounded bone to protect the brain.

The brain. . .

Beneath the thatches of strong, coarse hair, were dozens of tiny writhing brain sacs, normally a greyish, nearly colourless hue, but reddening and swelling when the creatures had sucked out a secret or an intrigue or a plot. The concubines, suddenly silent, stared at the *Spiaireachts*, and remembered the tales of how they had come slinking back to report to Chaos after scouring the Beyond Ireland, and how those very brain sacs had been so swollen with knowledge and so throbbing with gleaned secrets and plans and intrigues, that they had bulged out of the *Spiaireachts'* heads, and spilled over on to their foreheads like slopping bags of warm fluid. Horrid! said the concubines, daintily repelled by such nastiness, and turned with thankfulness to where Chaos himself, with the most powerful necromancers of the Realm at his heels, was walking out of the Castle to take his place at the centre of his armies.

There was a burst of necromantic music – grand, stirring stuff – from the musicians who would march with the Armies, and Chaos sprang astride the gleaming black stallion that had been held for him. There was a moment when the Captains and Murder and Anarchy waited for the signal, and there was a moment when the scarlet and black pennants of the Rodent Armies fluttered in the breeze. A good moment, a moment to anticipate the victory that lay ahead. The concubines would look forward to Chaos's return after his victory, because everyone knew that winning a good, strong victory gave the victor an arousal that might last for days. They giggled and told one another to look out for a lively time when Chaos returned!

The music poured out, stirring and strong, and the Lord of Chaos, from his position on the black stallion high above the rest, surveyed his Armies. And then he raised his hand to Anarchy and the Captains, and the Army marched forth.

To kill the Samildanach and possess Ireland.

Chapter Forty-six

The first thing to penetrate Theodora's mind was the music. It was not really very loud, but it was an irritant; something you would want to brush away, blot out. It impinged on your mind when you were preparing for the banquet to be held in the great firelit hall, and it was dark and disturbing. Theo, trying not to hear it, was nevertheless aware that within its core dwelt pain and evil darkness and obscene lusts. It was not in the least like the other music that was occasionally heard inside the Castle – perhaps when the Prince held one of his grisly revels, when the doors of the immense banqueting hall would be firmly shut by the silent young man who shared the scullery tasks with Theodora.

At those times Theodora tried to shut her ears, because the music would mingle with the screams of pain and the pleas for mercy from the Prince's victims. The sounds would drift into the sculleries where Theodora worked for most of the time, and even out to the small, ill-lit room where she slept, and which she had tried to make comfortable by dragging in a pallet bed and filling it with fresh straw, and by arranging jars of field flowers, and the sharply scented herbs that grew in the Castle herb gardens. During the warm weather, the little room would be scented with lemon verbena and rosemary and sometimes with night stocks if any could be found. Theodora would lie, trying to sleep, enjoying the scents but trying to shut out the sly, rollicking music of the feasting, because the prisoners brought up from the dungeons by Quintus would all die slowly and dreadfully; they would die there in the great stone hall as she listened; and it was unbearable and terrible and there was nothing any of them could do about it, because the Prince was too powerful. Theodora had once seen a couple of prisoners – travellers they had been – try to overpower him, but they had been felled instantly; the Prince had only to look at them and they had simply shrivelled where they stood; their skins had dried and wizened until they were tiny, mummified old men.

The music tonight was not anything like that played at the banquets. Nor was it anything like the strange, elusive ripples that very occasionally sent shards of cool beauty into the dark Castle and that made the silent Maelduin look up, flashes of turquoise iridescence glinting in his eyes. At those times, the Prince would fly into slavering rage, and hurl himself through the Castle, Quintus at his heels, ransacking the great empty rooms and the echoing galleries, as if he must find the music's source and destroy it.

But the music always faded of its own accord, as lightly and as regretfully as the insubstantial will o' the wisps that danced maddeningly across the marshes, and the Prince would shut himself away in his own part of the Castle – sometimes not emerging for weeks – and Quintus would return to the stables where he lived.

The music Theodora heard now was quite different. It was hurtful and intrusive and it was harsh and ugly. And I believe I have heard it before somewhere, she thought, and with the thought came a stirring, something deep within her mind lifting its head and pulling at her memory; and although she tried to remember, although she thought she almost caught the skirts of whisking, vanishing memories, in the end there was nothing.

Because I have only ever lived here, and there was never anything else before that . . .

The other servants had been disturbed by the music as well. Andrew, who worked in the gardens and mended the Castle's fabric when it needed it, and acted as scribe and librarian to the Prince, looked up suddenly as it trickled into the stone-flagged scullery. For a remarkable moment, something flared in his eyes that might have been recognition, and this was so interesting that Theo turned round to watch him. After a moment, he said, very softly, 'Something is approaching.' And looked across at Theo. 'You hear it?'

'Yes. I believe I have heard it before.' She thought: why have I said that? I cannot have heard it.

Andrew said, 'I cannot remember . .' and for the first time ever there was anger and impatience in his tone. He looked across to where Maelduin was standing in the stone archway, his hands full of the fruit he had gathered for the night's banquet, but light shining in his eyes. For a breath-snatching second he was not the pale withdrawn young man who went about his work silently and self-sufficiently, but something slender and shining and eerily beautiful. Theo stared at him.

'The Dark Realm,' said Andrew, at her side, and Theo looked back, because although the words meant nothing to her, she had the feeling that they ought to mean something very fearsome indeed. Andrew was frowning, but after a moment the light died from his eyes, and he shook his head impatiently and turned abruptly back to his task of setting out wine-flagons for the banquet. Maelduin stood for a moment longer, and then he too turned back to his work. A veil has come down, thought Theo, watching him. For a few seconds there was something brilliant and strong within both of them, but it has vanished. It is behind a veil again. She shivered and wrapped her arms about her for warmth, which was something you frequently had to do here; the Prince did not care for his Castle to be warm. 'Fishblood!' Andrew had once said, smiling his rather sad sweet smile.

But there was no time for any of them to be listening to the strange, hurting music. There was a banquet to be prepared; fires must flare and the lights must burn. Quintus had been sent out into the cliff paths and the crags to bring back prisoners.

Tonight the Prince was entertaining the Fomoire.

The opening of the Gateway concerned the people of Moher deeply. No one could deny it any more; everyone had heard it, creaking softly in the half-light of dusk, which was called in parts of Ireland the Purple Hour, and which was believed by many to be a time of magical stirrings and prowling enchantments.

But at Moher, the Purple Hour was a time when evil woke and walked; when the black powers of the Dark Realm seeped through the cracks in the Moher Gateway: the strange, not-quite-Human shapes with stalk-eyes and gobbling, greedy mouths that had been seen these last months, and that stole through the Gateway and slunk down the cliff path before vanishing into the night.

They'd all heard it happen tonight, and they'd heard, for the first time, the distant, terrible music. It was music to make a man want to gather up his loved ones and protect them. And yet there was an unexpectedly rallying quality to it, so that you felt a slow anger kindle, and so that you questioned your loyalties and your courage, and asked yourself, did you really intend to spend your life in hiding and in fear of the Moher Monster?

But it was music heard through a closed door, it was distant and muffled. If the Dark Lords were holding revelry on the other side of the Moher Gateway, it was no concern of anybody's.

Even so, they found themselves gathering almost without thinking in one of the larger houses, because a man could feel stronger and braver in the company of his friends. There was home-brewed poteen handed round and cider; somebody's wife had baked brack and somebody else's wife set a dish of brawn on the table. One or two of them essayed a mild joke, and as the poteen jar went round again, their spirits lifted a little.

And then there was a moment – and no one quite knew how this came about – when the men sprang to their feet, their eyes suddenly alight, and the women hustled the children to their side, and everyone stared at the barred windows and the shuttered, locked doors of the farmhouse kitchen.

Because this time there were more than scuttlings and furtive scurryings coming through the Gateway. This time the music was no longer coming to them through a closed door, because the door was unmistakably opening.

And there could be do doubt about what they were hearing, and there could be no ignoring it either.

Thudding hoofs and clashing armour and pounding marching.

The sound of a fearsome Army pouring through the Moher Gateway.

The door was yawning wide and the Dark Lords were storming into Ireland.

Theodora could feel the dark stirring and the harsh, intrusive music seeping through the Castle walls, but she tried not to notice it. She had tried to overlay it with the singing of the Fomoire which echoed all about the banqueting hall.

They had prepared the banquet between them, carrying the

food into the hall as they always did; Maelduin and Theo taking the great sides of beef and ham, Andrew bringing the wine. It always seemed to afford the Prince some malicious inner amusement to see that. Occasionally he taunted the crippled Andrew, asking if he had been sampling the wine in secret, and whether it had not fired his ardours. Theodora had noticed that Andrew was never roused to anger or impatience at this; he simply placed the wine before the Prince and retreated to the small, austere room which he had made his own, as Theo had made the brick room off the sculleries hers. He did not say very much at all, other than occasionally to bid Theodora and Maelduin a good morning, or, very rarely, to ask for help with carrying something that was awkward. Theo did not know him very well, but then she did not know either of them very well. Maelduin was courteous and he shared in the work, but he did so rather in the manner of a machine or a puppet, and his inability to speak made him withdrawn. None of them spoke much, now that Theo thought about it.

And the repulsive Quintus was never permitted inside the Castle, other than to take prisoners to the dungeons. Theo had seen the Prince lash out at Quintus once when he had crept into the scullery for warmth one bitter winter night. She had seen Quintus cringe and try to throw up his hands to shield himself, and she had felt, not pity exactly, because no one could feel pity for Quintus. But the way he had cowered had somehow stayed with her, and once or twice she had stolen out to the pitiful place where he slept, taking an extra blanket or a bale of fresh straw; now and then a mug of soup or stew. The sunken eyes in the loathsome face had flickered with something that might have been gratitude, and the cowled head had bowed in acknowledgement of the small kindness. Theo had tried not to think too much about the way that Quintus had bowed his head and been grateful.

When she and Maelduin entered the hall, carrying the dishes of ham and beef and the casks of warm, spiced wine, the Fomoire were singing one of their sly Hunting songs and several of them were trying out some new steps to their creeping, ugly dance, occasionally stopping to leap up on to the long oaken tables, which had already been set with dishes of crystallised fruits and flagons of the sticky sickly wine that the Prince always gave his guests before a banquet, and which Theo thought extremely unpleasant.

The Prince was seated before the long table, watching the Fomoire, resting his chin on one hand, and Theo repressed a shudder at the sight of him. He was wearing a suit of soft black velvet with the emblem of some ancient House about his shapeless neck, and the gills in his neck were opening and closing. Like this, richly garbed, he was far more sinister, far more menacing and repulsive than in the plain dark breeches and jerkin he normally wore.

'*You are in a haste to leave us tonight, my dear,*' said the Prince in his repellent, glottal voice, his eyes resting on Theodora as she set the dishes down and stood back. He reached out, and a webbed hand curled about Theo's wrist, pulling her closer. Behind her, Andrew and Maelduin made as if to move, but although it was no more than a hesitant, fearful twitch, the Prince sent out a lashing, glinting spear that knocked them to the floor.

'*Do not meddle, paltry Humanish,*' he said, his eyes suffused with hatred. '*You know what happens when you meddle. Or must I remind you?*' The flat, pale eyes in their cushions of swollen-looking flesh gleamed with anticipation, and Andrew and Maelduin flinched. Beneath the banqueting table, the Prince's gristly fin stirred slightly, as if the sudden brief violence had excited him, and Theo bit back a shudder. He looked back at Theo, and as he did so, the Fomoire danced across the floor and stood in a grinning circle about her.

'Tonight, Master?' they cried. 'Tonight? You promised us it would be tonight!' they cried, and the Prince smiled the terrible flat smile.

'Tonight,' he said nodding, and the Fomoire whirled into a delighted Goblin-dance, four of them snatching Theo from her feet and carrying her across the hall and flinging her into the great carven chair at the Prince's side. Theo felt the breath knocked from her at the unexpectedness of it, but she fought them, because it was quite unspeakably dreadful to be carried along like this. She could feel their little wizened hands digging into her flesh, and she could smell the warm, greasy, meaty stench of them. She struggled again and the Fomoire screeched with mirth.

'A pretty pigeon,' they cried, leaping into the air, the cloaks of Human skin flying outwards. 'See how she wriggles! A lively little one! Let *us* have her for an hour, Master!'

'Let us take her skin and wear it, Master!'

'Such a fair skin.'

'Such a *pale* skin.'

'There never was such a pale, fair, Humanish skin!' they cried, and linked hands at the centre of the hall, dancing and gibbering with evil glee.

The Prince was still watching Theodora. '*All these years,*' he said, softly. '*All these years of watching you and anticipating you...*'

'*I have kept you safe, princess,*' he said. '*You have been safe and secret here, and none has searched for you.*' The wide, lipless mouth stretched in a terrible smile. '*And now, the time has come for me to have you at my side,*' he said softly. '*The time has come for us to return to the Porphyry Palace.*' He broke off, watching her closely. '*You recognise that?*'

'I am ... not sure.' With the words 'Porphyry Palace', there had been a brief flare of something: warmth and comfort; brilliant shining creatures and colourfully garbed people. Laughter and music ... 'I am not sure,' said Theo again, and the Prince smiled.

'*You will see it soon,*' he said, and his pale, swollen-eyed face swam closer. Theo shrank back in the chair. '*White-skinned,*' said the Prince, and there was a lick of wet anticipation in his voice. '*White-skinned and dark haired, and with the Royal Amaranth blood.*'

His eyes raked her body and he moved closer. Theo shuddered, and struggled to free her hands from his grasp. There was a dry, rustling sound as the membraneous fin began to unfurl, and the Prince shifted slightly in his seat. Theo, caught between fear and panic, saw the fin distend a little more.

'*Perhaps the Fomoire will help to change your opinion of me,*' said the Prince in a guttural whisper, the gills in his neck opening and closing like dreadful, sucking mouths. '*Perhaps I shall allow them to tie you down before I ravish you, Princess.*'

At once the Fomoire leapt high with glee.

'Tie her down!'

'Ravish the Princess!'

And then:

> 'Anoint the maiden, skin the bride
> Peel the skin and keep the hide.
> Hair and teeth and bones and fur.
> Amaranth skin and Amaranth hair.'

The Prince smiled, as if he found this faintly amusing, as if precocious children had tried to entertain him.

'*For ten years I have kept the Amaranth Princess, the heiress to the great Royal Sorcery House of Ireland,*' he said, in a soft, gloating voice. '*I have kept you safe, and none has challenged me.*

'*And now the waiting is over. Now we shall celebrate the culmination of ten years. Now, here, with the Fomoire who have served me so well.*' The smile lifted his lips again. '*And if I find you pleasing,*' he said, '*then perhaps I shall allow the Fomoire to sample you also.*'

At once the Fomoire screeched and whirled excitedly about the hall, their claws scrabbling on the stone flags, the skin-cloaks flying wildly.

'*And tomorrow,*' said the Prince '*tomorrow we march on the Porphyry Palace.*' His eyes narrowed.

'*But tonight is our wedding night,*' he said.

The Fomoire leapt and screamed into delighted dancing again, and the two who had borne Theo to the carven chair, pounced on her again, carrying her to the centre of the hall. They laid her down, and two more leapt forward, taking her wrists and ankles. Theo, fighting and clawing, her mind tumbling, felt them stretch her feet apart, and as she sobbed and struggled to get free, she felt their little hard claws ripping the thin gown from her.

Deep within her mind she was aware of Andrew and Maelduin standing at the far end, and she was aware of a flare of something brilliantly blue-green and icily powerful from Maelduin. Would they save her? Could they save her?

But the Fomoire were dancing and jeering all round the hall, their grotesque shadows silhouetted against the dark Castle walls, and the Prince was moving across the floor towards her.

And he is taking his time, thought Theo, staring at him.

He moved slowly, unhurriedly, as if he were savouring the moment, and his expression was flat and calm.

But behind him, the pale, monstrous fin was unfurled; it was distended and erect in obscene lust, framing the squat, black-clad figure.

The Fomoire had been singing as they danced, screeching their grisly Hunting Song, their skin-clad claws ringing out on the huge stone flags of the hall. It seemed to Theodora, that the ancient hall was filled with horrid sly singing and with scrabbling clawed dancing, and with the meaty, grease-soaked odours of the Fomoire.

And then the Prince was standing over her, and there was no doubt about his excitement now: it was blazing from his eyes and it was pulsating from him in thick, grotesque waves. The membraneous fin framed him and, as he looked down at her, Theo felt the cold ancient sea-magic of his terrible House enfold her; his breath, tainted with the stench of rotting fish, gusting sickeningly into her face.

As he reached down, the Fomoire ceased their singing and dancing as suddenly as if an order had been given, and came to stand in a circle about her.

Into the abrupt silence came the swelling sound of the cold, painful music that had trickled out of the Gateway and down the cliff path earlier on.

Theo saw the Prince lift his head, listening, and his eyes narrowed in cold anger. The Fomoire turned, their Goblin-faces wary and frowning, and in the same instant Theo saw Andrew and Maelduin half turn.

The doors to the banqueting hall were flung open, and light and heat and noise poured in.

Through the great arched entrance – glinting evilly, armoured in black, caparisoned in scarlet and gold, steeped in ancient evil – came the Armies of the Lord of Chaos.

575

Chapter Forty-seven

They came streaming in, black and gleaming, the chariot wheels of Murder's grisly carriage scudding across the ground, the Rodent Armies swarming forward, with the Almhuinians close behind them. Beyond them the WarMongers were massing, sinister and shadowy, but emanating the fearsome powers they possessed: Mutilation, Agony, Torment, Terror . . .

The Fisher Prince sprang back from Theodora, his grotesque features contorted with rage, and the sly, red-eyed Rodent Captains surrounded him at once, their thin rat-tails twitching with horrid delight, their narrow, mean faces grinning.

The Fomoire released Theodora at once, and she half ran, half fell across the hall to where Andrew was standing.

Behind the Rodent Armies and the Almhuinians were the repulsive stalk-eyed *Spiaireachts*, the creatures born of the *Draoicht Spiaire*, warped, mutant things born of black necromancy. They scuttled into the hall, their brain sacs bulging and quivering, spilling out of their skulls with eagerness. At the sight of them, something raked cruel claws across the surface of Theodora's mind, stirring at something dark and hurting . . . I have faced these creatures or something akin to them once before . . . And I escaped then and I shall escape now, she thought.

In the face of every one of Chaos's creatures was greed and blood-lust and animal hunger. They came swarming and pouring into the Grail Castle to the sound of the raging, discordant music, and as the music increased, the air became thick and fetid, clotted with old, evil magic and with strong necromancy.

As the music fell about them, Theo stared and, quite suddenly, in a single, glorious blaze of understanding, felt lights explode inside her head and memories start to open up. She thought, with surging delight: *I remember*. So overpowering, so breath-taking was the knowledge and the emotion, that for a moment she could not move; she stayed where she was, staring at the rushing Armies, and thought: of course! Memory uncurled further, its edges sharp and fragrant and fresh, and Theodora thought: these are the evil creatures I ran from, through the darkness of Chaos's Realm, on the *Uisce*, with Andrew.

Andrew . . .

As she turned, he was with her, his arms coming about her, the warmth and the immediate feeling of safety he always gave her instantly there.

'You remember—'

'I remember,' he said softly. 'But there is no time to think of it now, Theodora.'

Theodora . . . The gentle, courteously careful pronunciation of her name enfolded Theo with the old love and protection, as sweet as the flurry of a summer's breeze stirring a scented night-forest.

'No time to think of it,' repeated Andrew. 'For these are Chaos's Armies.' And even though he was horrified and appalled at the might and the force of the Dark Armies, his own mind was singing and the memories and the understanding was pouring into him, as if he was being filled to overflowing with sweet, precious life once more.

Theo was dizzy, her mind was tumbling as layer after layer of memory rolled back, but Andrew was right; there was no time for remembering, there was no time for questioning . . . Chaos's Armies were in the Castle, the might of the Dark Ireland was before them and they must fight for their lives. She glanced across the hall, and saw the strange, silent Maelduin watching, the light blazing from his eyes, as if he, also, were remembering, as if he, also, had been dragged out of an enchantment by the crashing music and the pounding hoofs of the Armies. As if he, in turn, were seeing the memories and the images unravelling, and as if he, also, were emerging from the half-light of the years in the Grail Castle.

A Veil is tearing, thought Theodora. That is exactly how it feels. A thick misty Veil has been shrouding us, but now it is being blown away, and we are seeing and we are hearing and we are remembering; not all at once, not in a bewildering, dazzling cascade, but a little at a time. Snatches, glimpses, like a flaring torch illuminating first one and then another chapter of our lives. Despite the danger, and despite the rampaging creatures in the Castle, she wanted to hold on to the moment, because it was so surgingly marvellous and so tremendously beautiful to see and to feel everything – your whole life – come tumbling back to you.

The Prince was on his feet, the Fomoire running to his side. The Fomoire were leaping and jeering, their cloaks flying outwards, screeching imprecations at the Dark Armies, but the Prince barely moved, and hardly seemed to look at the creatures invading his lair.

And then he raised one of his webbed hands, and something spun outwards and scissored through the air. There was a sudden, sizzling, slicing sound, and the heads of every single one of the Rodent Captains were scythed from their bodies in a single clean sweep, as if a giant invisible scimitar had sliced straight across them. Blood and gore spouted from the neck-stumps and gushed over the floor, and the ranks of Rodent soldiers hesitated and glanced at one another, disconcerted by such remarkable power.

But the Almhuinians and the *Spiaireachts* were before them, jeering at such squeamishness, wading through the squelching, slopping blood, raising their spears, encircling the pale, squat figure of the Prince. The *Spiaireachts* scurried forward, and Theodora saw that their armour was not ordinary silver or iron or metal, but hard shell, thick, crusted bone, that grew over their backs. Lights exploded in her mind, and the memories came tumbling and flooding all over again – painful, hurting, but marvellously, blessedly familiar. She thought: the creature in Chaos's Castle! The horrid Enchantment of Spies that killed Rumour! These are its creatures! And even in the midst of such fear and such tumult, knew a sudden, terrible pain for Rumour who had died – and I had forgotten! thought Theo with agony.

The Fomoire leapt for the Almhuinians, linking hands and dancing, pointing with their bony fingers, producing the razors and the slicing tools they used for their grisly skinning work.

'Humanish skins, lads,' they shouted.

'Cloaks for the peeling and fat for the roasting!'

'Heat the fires, lads, warm the cages!'

'To work, lads, to work!'

The Almhuinians struck out, wounding a couple of them, but the rest closed in, whirling and dancing, jabbing at the Almhuinians' legs with their tiny, wicked knives, here and there drawing blood.

Andrew had stood with Theodora, holding her to him, feeling, as she had felt, the gentle, marvellous tumbling of memories, understanding as the light flickered on the lost years of his life, what had happened. *We were the victims of an enchantment . . . A long, terrible spell that blanked our minds and our memories . . .* He stared at the turmoil and the fighting in the hall, but for a breathspace of time he did not think: we are at the centre of one of the greatest and bloodiest battles in Ireland's history, but: *how long has this creature held us in bondage!* Anger flared, a deep, slow-burning anger that threatened to engulf him. He glanced to where the Prince was standing, a little removed, the flat, pale eyes watchful and unblinking, and cold rage filled his mind.

That is the evil creature whose sire hurt Rumour, who has kept Theodora chained in this Castle, so that she was unaware even of who she is . . . He has made her work like a scullion, he has taunted her and jibed as he taunted and jibed me, and he has taken pleasure from it . . .

He felt the fingers of both hands curl as he watched the Prince, and he began to calculate how he could be across the hall, dodging a path through the fighting and the seething, boiling mass, and be at the creature's throat.

For, man of peace that I am, I should like to tear the creature's throat out and gouge out its eyes and stamp on them . . .

And then, as he tensed his muscles to move, he became aware that the music had faded, and that a silence had descended on the hall. Every head turned to the open doorway; in every face now was eagerness, avidity, a strange, dark adoration tinged with terror.

The doors were still open to their widest extent, so that it was possible to see the night sky with the scudding black clouds, and to see quite clearly the crags and the cliffs of the Moher coastline. Andrew caught, very faintly, the sound of the ocean

579

hurling itself against the cliffs, and quite suddenly this was a clean, strong sound; something natural and good, something that was a part of the real world. Something that had no part to play in evil Dark Lords, and in grisly, repulsive sea-kings who came from strange, tainted worlds and stole people's minds and their memories.

And then, without the least sound, he was standing framed in the great doorway, a slender, almost slight figure, wrapped in the scarlet velvet cloak, the Silver Star of his sinister profession on his breast.

The evil Dark Lord who claimed descent from the House of Medoc. The arrogant, beautiful Lord of Chaos, surveying his new Domain . . . The greatest necromancer ever known, ready to enter and claim Ireland.

A power so tremendous radiated from him that Andrew and Theodora both flinched. Andrew felt a tremor go through Theo's slight form, and she made a quick movement, as if she would have liked to shield her eyes. The anger that had surged up earlier swirled and flowed, and with it came the whisper, the flurry of that other presence, that strange, alien strength and fury that had been there once before, many years ago, when Andrew had faced Coelacanth . . .

The mantle of the Samildanach descending once again . . .

The Lord of Chaos stood motionless for a moment, only his eyes alive, scouring the hall, finally coming to rest on the grotesque, evil figure of the Prince. Light showed in Chaos's eyes, and with it recognition, rather as if he had entered the hall at the invitation of an unknown host, and now sought that host to make him his compliments. He walked forward, slowly, unhurriedly, as graceful and as fastidious as a cat, and the Dark Lords moved into the hall behind him, standing grouped together near the door.

As Chaos came to a stop before the Prince, Andrew thought it was as if two immense protagonists were facing one another. He thought: this is surely one of the most momentous occasions in all of Ireland's history. And through the fear and the tumultuous array of emotions, through the still-churning memories and the bitterness of what had been done to him, even beyond the agony he was feeling for Theodora and her safety, a strange thought formed itself: *it would be a pity if this was never*

580

properly set down for all Ireland to know of it . . .

Chaos was studying the Prince. He said in his soft, cultured voice, 'I make you my obeisance, Son of Coelacanth,' and the Prince said, in his harsh, warped tones, 'And I, yours, Lord of Chaos.'

But Andrew, listening very intently, thought that there was a faint uneasiness in the Prince's voice, rather as if he had encountered something he had not expected to encounter, or as if he might have underestimated the strength of this particular adversary.

Chaos felt it as well. When he spoke again, it was in a stronger, much more amused voice. 'You did not expect me?' he said, and glanced about him. 'I see you did not. I see you were too engrossed in your own affairs to hear my approach. The marriage with the Amaranth Princess? How fortunate for me.'

'You do not need the caprices of fortune to lend you strength,' said the Prince coldly.

'I do not disdain Fortune's favours, however,' said Chaos, and the amused note was more noticeable now. Andrew heard it with something that was very nearly relief, because people do not allow amusement into their voices unless they are feeling very sure of themselves. And if we have to choose, I believe I would rather by far be at the mercy of Chaos than the Prince, he thought. For Chaos is at least some sort of gentleman . . .

The Fisher Prince said, 'So you know my ancestry, Lord of Chaos?'

'Certainly.' Chaos was regarding the other with the slightly indulgent, very nearly fatherly mien of one who is meeting the very young son of an old friend. Andrew thought it was almost as if Chaos were saying, Ah, so this is Coelacanth's boy, is it? How very interesting. Let us see how he has turned out and if he has his sire's looks or his sire's intelligence. Against the elegant and sophisticated Chaos, the Fisher Prince suddenly seemed gauche and unlicked.

Sent into the world scarce half made-up . . .

'I knew Coelacanth rather well,' said Chaos, walking round the hall as if he might be planning on how he would arrange it when he had taken it. He turned round sharply, and the scarlet velvet cloak billowed with a whisper of sound. 'It was I who condemned him to the Tanning Pit,' he said.

'I am aware of that,' said the Prince, the flat fish-eyes never leaving Chaos's dark, slender figure.

'And . . . have sworn to be avenged on me as a consequence?' Andrew thought there was no doubt about the amusement now. Chaos said, softly, and quite courteously, 'Then perhaps you would care to try your strength against mine, Prince? Perhaps you would like to fling your half-formed powers against the breeding and the generations and the centuries of scholarship I have inherited.' He paused, his eyes resting on the other with indulgence and pity. 'I am an aristocrat, you know,' said Chaos. 'I have studied and read and learned for more years, more centuries, than you will ever count.' His voice held a purring tolerance, as if he might be saying: and as an aristocratic I am in honour bound to treat you with a degree of courtesy, no matter what I may secretly feel. I am a Lord of my Realm, while you are a monster, a mongrel-thing, bred on to a part-Human, spawned out of a brutal rape. And I can deflect anything you care to summon . . .

The Prince did not summon anything, he seemed almost to shrink before Chaos's dark force. Andrew caught the flicker of movement on the edges of his vision, and turned to see the Fomoire creeping backwards. He thought: they see it. They see that their Prince is being defeated and that Chaos is the stronger. Will they change sides and give their allegiance back to Chaos?

And then the Prince whirled about. He seemed to tower to thrice his former size, and the monstrous fin that had curled about his webbed feet erected in a single, repulsive movement and enclosed him; and in the same moment, malignant power streamed outwards from him: a cold, pouring vapour that hit Chaos full on.

Chaos half fell, the streaming cold light all about him. A white rim formed on his armour, and ice outlined his head.

The Prince gave his glottal laugh. 'You condemned my sire to the heat of the Tanning Pit, charlatan!' he screeched. 'But I condemn you to the cold and the frozen ice of the Petrified Forests!' He moved closer to Chaos, and stood looking down at the necromancer, his flat, ugly face stretched in a lipless smile. 'How does it feel, Chaos,' said the Fisher Prince in a hissing whisper, 'how does it feel to have the blood in your body becoming solid, and your heart encased in ice? To know that you are hardening into brittleness.' He leaned nearer. 'Presently, your bones will be so brittle that they will splinter even as you breathe,' he said. 'You will be a Man of Ice. And very soon now your eyes will solidify. How will you feel when that happens? And how does it feel to experience *this*!' cried the Prince, and with the flick of one hand, sent a second blast of icy vapour at Chaos's face.

At once the air surrounding Chaos became blue-tinged, and the Almhuinians and the Rodent soldiers, who had been unsheathing their swords, backed away.

Chaos was fighting the ice sheets, but Andrew could see that they were too strong for him. Twice he lifted a hand to slice away the ice with fire spears and with cascades of pouring flames, and both times the Fisher Prince's ice doused it instantly.

The Dark Lords had not moved, but Andrew saw that, at the centre of their small group, twisting fire columns were forming, and knew that they were preparing to fight the Prince for their Lord's freedom.

The Prince glanced contemptuously in their direction and, raising a hand in a negligent gesture, caused the ice to pour forward again, encasing them. The Dark Lords shrieked and fell back, scrabbling at the thick, cold air, screaming in fear and pain.

Chaos's face was pure white, and his eyes were glazed. Andrew, struggling to free his hands from the cords, saw that the necromancer's eyes had suddenly taken on a hard look, a glazed, fixed look. He remembered the Prince's words, and understood that the liquid part of Chaos's eyes was freezing into solid globes. Chaos's eyes were turning into two spheres of ice in his head, and in another moment, in another moment . . .

The Prince sent out his evil, bubbling laugh again, the gaping fins at the side of his neck opening and closing. Bending down, he struck Chaos hard across his eyes, and at once there was a dreadful, cracking, shattering sound.

Chaos fell writhing on the ground, terrible agony in his movements, both hands flung upwards to shield his eyes. As he did so, there was the sound of his bones splintering and shattering, and he curled in agony on the ground.

But there had been a split second when his eyes had been uncovered, and in that second, Andrew had seen that they had cracked; they had smashed and crazed into a hundred tiny shards, exactly as thin pottery would craze, or as fragile glass might shatter.

The Fisher Prince had left Chaos sightless and in unremitting agony . . .

The Dark Lords were screaming and trying to reach the door, tumbling over one another in their haste to escape the fate that had befallen their Master. But Andrew could see that each of them now had the staring white orbs, the immovable solid eyeballs. The Prince struck at them again, and Andrew heard once more the grisly shattering of their eyes, and as they fell, moaning in agony, he heard their bones smash like thin glass.

Chaos's armies had retreated, the Almhuinians slightly wounded from the Fomoire, the Rodent soldiers looking nervous. Cowardly at heart! thought Andrew. Is this the moment when I can somehow break free? On the other side of the hall, the Fomoire crouched low on the ground, rather like children making a circle to play some secret game. In the shadows, he saw the silent, strange Maelduin, who had shared their long captivity, move forward, his eyes glinting. But I cannot be sure of that one, thought Andrew. He was never in my memory and he was never in my life. I have no knowledge of his allegiances or of who he is. It is up to me.

And sure, there would never be a better moment. Chaos and his Lords were blinded and dying; the Rodent Captains were dead. If I can but get across the hall, he thought, and with the thought, reached for and felt the strength of that other one, that unknown creature who was not unknown at all, and felt the strength uncoil a little.

As he did so, lights exploded at the far end of the hall, and the doors of the Grail Castle were once more flung wide.

The people of Moher, brandishing home-made weapons, their faces set and determined, erupted into the hall and fell on the Almhuinians and the Rodent soldiers.

Now Andrew did not hesitate. The power was pouring through him, light-filled, ancient, but so brimful of beauty and strength and dawn magic that for a moment his vision blurred and wavered.

The people of the Moher Cliffs were laying about the Rodent

creatures and the Almhuinians, spearing them with their rather makeshift weapons, but inflicting a good deal of damage. Andrew saw them kill several Rodent soldiers, and there were certainly six or seven Almhuinians bleeding and badly wounded on the floor.

But the Fomoire had recovered themselves, and they were advancing on the Moher army. They were tiptoeing forward in their horrid, exaggerated parody of naughty children trying not to be seen. Andrew looked across the hall, and saw that the Prince was standing watching the furore, sinister amusement on his face. Chaos lay at his feet – Dead? thought Andrew, and knew at once that Chaos was not dead. He was maimed, he was sightless, his bones were shattered, but he was not dead. And which of them do I attack? thought Andrew in sudden agony. Which of them should be disabled first?

And instantly came the answer: the Prince, for the Prince is far and away the more powerful of the two.

The strength was filling him up, exactly as it had done in Tiarna when he faced Coelacanth. Now, facing Coelacanth's son, he could almost see the power and the force of the legendary Samildanach, he could feel it: pouring blue light forming the shape of a cloak, enclosing him with its ancient strength and its long-ago power.

It is not my strength and it is not my power, as it was not when I killed this creature's sire. But it is vouchsafed to me and it is somehow filled with light and love and hope and I must use it . . .

For a moment the famous beautiful words of the One he served were all about him: *I am the light of the world . . . And so walk while ye have the light, lest the darkness come upon ye . . .*

I have the light, thought Andrew. For a breathspace of time I have the light: *the light of the world . . . Take it and grasp it firmly, for there will never be such another moment as this one . . .*

The Samildanach, the Man of Each and Every Art who will cut a swathe of light through the darkness and drive back the Black Realm for ever . . .

I don't understand it, thought Andrew wildly, and at once came the answer as it had come before: *You do not need to . . .*

He did not need to understand. He needed only to turn it outwards, this soaring, pouring light, this immense, marvellous force.

The light of the world . . .

He moved forward, using the ash stick that was always with him, but moving swiftly to stand before the monstrous spawn of the Fisher King, Coelacanth's son, the light-filled essence all about him. He was briefly aware that Theodora was nearby, and there was a sudden warm, pouring comfort from her, but there was a strength from another also . . . Andrew caught, on the edges of his vision, a blur of blue and green, the sudden, almost-blinding flash of a creature who had been enclosed in a Humanish carapace, but who was somehow composed not of Human skin and bones and hair, but of soaring, silken sleekness and mischievous, brilliant eyes, and the cool sea-magic of a close, secret race . . .

Slay the Prince, Humanish Monk, and I will deal with the other one . . .

Maelduin shot across the hall, a pouring, darting silhouette, and although Andrew was not conscious of having moved, he was standing before the Prince, and the evil, ugly thing was regarding him with contempt and amusement.

'*So you think to challenge me, Humanish Monk,*' said the glottal voice, softly. '*You think to pit your puny strength and your paltry powers against me.*'

Andrew regarded him for a moment, and when at last he spoke, his voice was stronger and sharper; it was filled with pouring golden light and soaring anger and with every strong emotion ever felt or dreamed or imagined. It was a voice unmistakably and beautifully Irish, the pure, lovely Irish of long-dead peoples: of the Cruithin who had spoken the untainted golden speech that had been in Ireland before Tara was raised from the rock; of the silver-tongued druids who had understood about harnessing light in everything they did, and had carried that light into their own, jealously guarded language; of the Celtae and the ancient race of Pretani and Qreteni who had traded with the East and been known as tribes of a misty blue and green northern isle; of the Lagin of the south and the Veneti of the north, and every other forgotten lost race of Ireland . . .

He stood before the Fisher Prince, and said, in the soft, ancient language, 'Regard once more the Samildanach, Coelacanth,' and saw fear, pure and undiluted, leap into the

Prince's eyes. 'You remember the vow I once took to slay you and your House?' he said. 'I am here to make live that vow, Coelacanth.' And with the words, leapt at the creature's throat, exactly as he had done with its sire in Tiarna.

The Prince fell back, throwing up his hands, and the two of them crashed to the floor. Andrew's hands were digging into the Prince's thick, scaled neck, his thumbs were gouging deep inside the gills, choking the monstrous thing, shutting off its air, throttling the evil, tainted life out of it . . .

Light filled the great hall of the Grail Castle, and with it a silver, scaldingly beautiful music, gentle and pure and so lovely you would gladly die if only it would never stop, and so unearthly that you would be afraid to see it take shape . . .

Maelduin stopped in his tracks and half turned his head, and an expression of the purest joy shone from his eyes. He seized a Rodent Captain's sword, and shot arrow-straight across the hall in a whirl of turquoise and silver and with the brief, blurred impression of a wingless dragonfly.

He fell on the blinded and dying Lord of Chaos and, lifting the sword aloft, buried it deep in the necromancer's heart.

Chapter Forty-eight

Andrew moved slowly and warily through the silent Grail Castle, and felt the weight of its age and the heaviness of its memories descend about him. He thought it was not absurd to think that the Veil of Unknowing had smothered the Castle as well as its prisoners, and that with the slaying of the Monster who had for ten years dwelled within it, the memories and the legends were tumbling back through the vast halls and the immense galleries.

And I have completed my task, he thought. I have completed both my tasks: for Theodora will be safe, and I have slain the Monster of the Grail Castle, and ended the tainted House of Coelacanth, the Fisher King. I killed the creature, thought Andrew, exactly as I killed his sire.

And with the memory of that other killing, for a sudden, sweet moment, Rumour was with him again, and he could feel the cool ruffle of mockery and the soft, amused irony. Remembering me with sadness, Andrew? Remembering me as a part of the battles and the struggles and the deprivations?

And of course it was not how she would have wanted to be remembered. She would have wanted to be remembered with happiness. Music and wine and firelight and laughter . . . All the good things . . . Andrew paused in his slow search of the great, dark Fortress, and felt the beginnings of a smile lift his lips. She was gone, of course, that wilful, extravagant creature, and he would never see her this side of eternity . . .

But perhaps she was not completely gone from him. Perhaps he would hear the echo of her laughter, and perhaps he would remember her reckless bravery and her dauntless humour. Perhaps he would be able to remember her with happiness in time.

It is how I should wish you to remember, Andrew . . .

It was how anyone you had loved would wish you to remember.

The Samildanach's mantle had left him as swiftly as it had come, and Andrew had fallen back from the Prince's threshing, dying body, covered in the sour black blood that had spurted from its gills and its mouth. Andrew had staggered away from it, choking and shuddering. But Maelduin had not hesitated. He had plunged the sword into the helpless body of Chaos, again and again, before whipping round and setting about the Dark Lords. The eerily lit hall had become a place of gore and terror and dying agonies; it had echoed to the screams of the Rodent soldiers and the Almhuinians, and the eldritch squealing of the escaping Fomoire.

And then Maelduin had stood up and Andrew had seen that a brilliant, mischievous light shone in his eyes, so that they were glowing, slanting pools of colour, turquoise-blue jewels that gave his face such eerie beauty that Andrew wondered how he could ever have believed the boy to be Human.

Maelduin said, very softly, 'We will fling the carcass of this evil one into the ocean, and it will return to its people if that is the gods' wish.' And there had been such radiance pouring outwards from him that Andrew and Theodora had both blinked, and Theodora had stared at Maelduin with sudden understanding, and the light had fallen about her small, heart-shaped face, making it so purely lovely that Andrew had felt a deep, secret pain twist his heart. He thought: she is dazzled by him. And in the same moment, had understood completely; for he too was dazzled by Maelduin.

And my task is ended, he had thought again. Theodora will be safe, the Dark Ones are dead, and I have found Quintus.

Quintus.

He had gone then, leaving the two of them together, seeking out Quintus, finally coming upon him in a kind of outhouse, perhaps a part of an old stable block.

'You have lived – here?' said Andrew, pausing in the doorway, seeing the dirt that was ingrained into the floor and the walls, seeing the bed of straw, the mean, sparse furniture: a straight-backed chair and a small deal table. It was cold and draughty, and what little light there was filtered uneasily through a thickly grimed window high up in the outer wall. So

Quintus had lived here, thought Andrew, he had lived here for all these years, the Fisher Prince's dreadful curse eating his flesh, helpless beneath it, seeing himself become a thing of such loathing that people could hardly bear to look at him, feeling himself grow into the repulsive, vile creature that had terrorised the surrounding countryside.

'You have lived here?' said Andrew again, and this time did not try to keep the horror and the disgust from his voice.

Quintus was seated quietly on the straw, the dark cowl folded about him, but his eyes calm and steady. Andrew saw that, although the Monk's skin was still raw and in patches still seeping blood, the Fisher Prince's fearsome curse had receded a little. This was no longer the foul, suppurating creature that had crawled at the behest of the Prince and cast the black net of Torach about its prey. Andrew understood now that Quintus had lived alongside the Prince's servants with full knowledge, and with complete understanding. Had it been easier for Quintus to know and understand what was being done to him? Or worse? Quintus had been spoken of as an outstanding Brother in the Order; he had possessed intelligence and sensitivity and he had had a deep appreciation of beautiful things. Was that one of the reasons he had fallen prey to the dark allure of the necromancers? He remembered the adage that the devil chooses the best when he scours the world for prey, and he understood that the devil, the Dark Lords, the necromancers of the Black Ireland had done just that when they had lured Quintus to this terrible thralldom.

Andrew was torn between compassion and anger against one who had succumbed to so much evil and who had sinned so deeply and caused such terror and such bloodshed. But even as the thought formed, a tiny voice inside him said, very quietly: but you too have sinned, Andrew. You too broke the vows you made and fell victim to temptation.

You too put another before your god. It is not for you to pronounce sentence or make judgement. And Quintus has surely made reparation.

Andrew stared at the quiet figure before him, and thought: but can I be sure that the evil has gone? Can I believe that Quintus has finally and for all time routed the black core, that the evil centre is gone? *Dare I trust him?*

Quintus said in a quiet voice, an exhausted, drained voice, 'I do not know if you can trust me, Andrew, because I do not yet know if I can trust myself.' He looked around the dim, dirt-encrusted room, and a deep and bitter agony filled his eyes. 'I have tried to tear out the black evil that Chaos recognised in me, and that the Fisher Prince harnessed. I struggled to pluck it out in the depths of the Dark Lords' Pit! I thought I had succeeded!' cried Quintus in anguish, and torment flared in his eyes again. 'I thought I was paying the debt, serving my penance. I have tried, Andrew,' said Quintus very quietly. 'May God forgive me, I have tried.'

Andrew, hardly daring to breathe, said, very gently, 'But – you feel that you may not have succeeded?' And waited, and presently Quintus said, 'I feel I may not have succeeded.' He lifted his head and looked directly at Andrew. 'Help me,' he said.

There was no other course of action open to him, of course. There was nothing to do but accept the weight of this new responsibility. Could he do it? Could he bring this tormented, tortured creature back to the ways of the Order? Could he snatch Quintus from the brink of the dark abyss on which he still – Andrew could feel it – hesitated?

He stood in the ancient quadrangle, bounded on all sides by the great Stronghold, and looked about him. A place of immense sadness and of brooding secrecy. But, for all that, a place where happiness had once flourished and, God willing, could flourish again.

He felt, as if it were a tangible thing, the sufferings and the torments and the despairing lonelinesses of the place, but he felt, as well, a hidden joy here. There had been happiness and contentment inside these walls; there had been years of scholarship and study, times when the Castle had been revered and sought-out, times when pilgrims and searchers after truth had travelled to it with eagerness and delight.

His mind went to the immense, book-lined room at the Castle's western side, where surely a man – several men – could work and study and be at one with God. With sudden, startled delight, Andrew saw how the Castle was a place where a community, a small cloister, a whole Order could grow and flourish; where devout men could work and learn and imbue the

591

old stones and the ancient bricks with tranquillity and prayer and calm.

And spread God's word and Christ's way of life into Ireland.

Just as Andrew had always intended.

Theodora sat curled into a deep, velvet-covered chair in the warm, firelit bookroom of the Castle, her eyes fixed on the slender, graceful figure of Maelduin, her cheeks flushed with delight and with the fire's heat.

Maelduin regarded her thoughtfully, his head on one side. He was seated cross-legged on the floor before the fire, and the firelight was cascading over his slight, slender form, washing him with its soft radiance. Theodora thought she had never seen anything so utterly beautiful and so entirely inHuman as this creature of firelight and strange, subtle nuances and glinting, turquoise eyes.

But she only said, 'Your world of Tiarna is spun into so many of our stories and so many of our legends, and yet no one from my world has ever seen it.'

'And yet we have been together, working alongside each other, for ten years,' said Maelduin.

'Yes. The Veil of Unknowing.' It still made Theo shudder when she thought how they had all lived unknowingly and unseeingly for so long under the Prince's evil. But it did not do any good to look back. All you could do was look forward, and so she said, 'Tell me about your world.' And sipped the wine they were sharing, and watched the firelight play on his slender form, and felt the shadows of the Fisher Prince roll back a little further.

'We guard our world,' said Maelduin. 'Particularly we guard it from the Humanish.' He smiled at her, and Theo thought: his voice is like molten silver, or the pouring, sweet-scented fire rivers of the Morne Mountains . . .

Maelduin leaned forward, so that the light fell across the planes of his face, making it mysterious and unearthly. He said, very softly, 'Tiarna is a place of soft, gentle radiance and rippling, silver water-light. But you would recognise it instantly, Princess.'

'I – would I?'

'Yes. For Tiarna is Tara's heart-image, it is the Bright

Citadel, the Shining Palace of the *nimfeach* who stole the sorcerer-architects' designs for Tara and copied them.' There was the glint of cool amusement again. 'While it lived,' said Maelduin, 'before Coelacanth stole the music, Tiarna was filled with the elegant magic of my people and with the flowing, beckoning music created from Men's souls and their senses.'

While it lived . . .

Theodora said, carefully, 'You make it sound so beautiful.'

'It is beautiful,' said Maelduin, and Theo thought: and he will return to it all. Yes, of course he will. He will find a way to restore his people to life and he will return to it. Perhaps I could help him, or perhaps the Amaranths could. But I can have no part in his world, she thought. I can have no part in his world nor he in mine. He is a *sidh*, a cool, elvish creature of mischievous enchantments and gentle, fey music, and he is Tiarna's Crown Prince . . .

And the ancient faery *sidh*blood could never mingle with the Amaranth Flame . . .

Maelduin said, very softly, 'Will you come with me to Tiarna, Princess?' and Theo looked up, because there had been something so intimate in his voice, and something so – what had he called his music? – so *beckoning*, that it was impossible not to feel its allure.

She stared at him and felt an entirely different delight, and knew that it would happen, he would take her there, and she would see for herself the shining, secret world, the heart-image of Tara, stolen all those centuries ago, the Tiarnan Palace that lay through the ancient water tunnels and beyond the Silver Caves where the only light was the rippling water-light of the oceans . . .

When your people and mine are restored . . .

Maelduin thought: this remarkable creature is the most extraordinarily beautiful Humanish I shall ever know. She is fragile and slender, but beneath it all she is stronger than any Humanish I have ever seen. And her hair is like a raven's wing, and when she laughs, her eyes glow, so that I can see the dark flame of the Amaranth power. I believe she has the power essence of the entire sorcerous House of Amaranths all rolled up into one . . .

He stood up and held out his hands, and Theodora stood up

with him and felt the coolness of his skin against hers as his hands enfolded her own.

'Come with me now,' said Maelduin, his eyes glowing. 'Come with me to find the lost music.'

The music . . .

As they went hand in hand through the Castle, Maelduin was listening and feeling and reaching out for that flurry of cool, elvish singing that had thrummed on the air just before he had killed the Lord of Chaos. He was strongly aware of Theodora at his side, and he was aware, as well, of the warmth and the strength of the ancient Amaranth Flame glowing within her. Sudden delight surged up in him, and he thought: together we would be invincible, she and I . . . The sea-magic of the *sidh* and the Sacred Flame of the Dawn Sorcerers . . .

Could it be done? Could I find a way?

But he thrust the thought from him, and turned his entire concentration towards the light, silvery thread that he could feel somewhere at the heart of this dark, Humanish stronghold. For *it is somewhere here. I know it and I sense it and I feel it. And I will not leave this place until I have found it* . . .

The Grail Castle must have hidden and harboured many secrets in its time, but Maelduin thought there could never have been so strange a secret kept here as the *sidh*'s music, stolen all those years ago by Coelacanth, searched for by Coelacanth's son – yes of course! thought Maelduin, remembering, as Theodora was remembering, how sometimes at dusk the music had sung quietly to itself, and how the Fisher Prince at those times had rampaged through the Castle, tearing down hangings and ripping aside panelling. He heard it and he felt it and he feared it. But he never managed to find it, thought Maelduin. It hid from him throughout all those years. But it will not hide from me now.

For I am the Crown Prince of Tiarna and it will answer my summons . . .

The old imperiousness was still with him, and as he stood at the Castle's centre, he felt the ruffle of cool beauty brush his mind.

Yes, it is here and it is safe!

There was a moment when it was all about him, swooping

joyously everywhere, assaulting his senses and drenching him in its soft, seductive bewitchment. He could feel it breaking out of the Veil cast over the Castle by the Prince, just as the Prince's servants had broken out. He could feel it thrusting upwards out of the smothering evil, its beauty unquenched, its power no longer trammelled.

Theodora, standing at Maelduin's side, her senses spinning with delight at the music's allure, looked about her, and knew, quite suddenly, where the music was . . .

Because I brought it out of the Dark Realm when I broke through the Moher Gateway with Andrew and the *Uisce*. And then, with painful understanding: it was the *sidh*'s music that Rumour gave to me! she thought. Rumour knew . . . And for a brief space, Rumour was with her, the amused mockery that had been Rumour's stock-in-trade, the faint disdain that had characterised her, but also the warmth and the generosity that had run like a rich river beneath.

Rumour had saved the music for the *sidh*.

Theodora turned to Maelduin, her face glowing, and said, 'I know where the music is.'

They stood together on the Castle steps, the *Uisce* waiting obediently for them, their few possessions packed, and there was nothing more to be said to the two who would remain, except, 'Farewell.'

Can I say it? thought Theo, staring at Andrew. Can I do it? Can I truly ride away with Maelduin, and bid farewell to this strange, thin-faced monk with haunted eyes and a sweet, sudden smile?

And who has within him the living seeds of an old, old legend, and who slaughtered Coelacanth and Coelacanth's terrible son?

The Samildanach who would come into Ireland when Ireland least expected it, and who would come modestly and quietly, but who would cut a swathe of light through the Dark Lands . . .

And then, quite suddenly, it did not matter about making correct speeches, or about pretending to be brave, or struggling not to cry, or even about saying they would remember one another. It did not matter, because it would not be farewell. They would be together again in the future – not once, but many times. And so it was simply, 'Until the next time we are

595

together.' Wasn't there a phrase for it, something in ancient Gael, or Qretani or Cruithin?

And then Andrew, the golden strength of the Samildanach shining in his eyes, said, the unfamiliar lilt in his voice again, '*Beannacht leat go bhfeicfidh me aris thu.*' And smiled.

Theo said softly, 'Until we meet again.'

'Yes.' He held out his arms and Theo went into them.

'When you come back, Princess, I shall be here.'

That said it all, thought Theo. *Goodbye until we meet again. And when you come back, I shall be here . . .*

Yes, he would be here in this dark old Castle, which might not be dark any more, because Andrew would fill it with gentle, scholarly learning, and with his strange, rather beautiful prayers and rituals, and with the soft rhythmic singing of his Order. He would work with Quintus – a quiet, pale, shadow of a man now – and they would both mingle with the people of Moher, the shy, courageous farmers and hillside people who had so bravely stormed the Castle and helped to slay Chaos and the Fisher Prince. And in time, perhaps others of their beliefs would join them. Moher with its stark, awe-inspiring beauty could once more become a place of pilgrimage, as it had been in Ireland's Golden Age.

It would happen. And I can leave him knowing it will happen, thought Theodora, and as Maelduin helped her to mount the *Uisce*, despite the pain of leaving Andrew, there was a sudden spiral of excitement, because all Ireland was stretching out before them, and the light was shining from the *Uisce*, and Theodora felt the joy well up all over again. Because we are going home, we are going home, and although I do not know what may have happened during the dark years of my enslavement, I am returning to the Porphyry Palace of the Amaranths.

As they rode out of the Grail Castle, she could see the faint light irradiating from Maelduin, so that it was as if he was sprinkling cool, elvish light across the countryside. She thought: I should never forget that he is not in the least Humanish, and I shall never forget that he is from the strange sea world of the *sidh* . . .

Because, although he walks with ordinary Humanish tread, and although he wears the plain garb of a Humanish traveller, in reality he is a creature that once had a silken, iridescent shape that darted like a will o' the wisp through the Wolfwood and hunted the Humanish for sport. And once he was so shiningly beautiful that it would have been certain madness and sure death to look on him . . .

And the cool *sidh* could never mingle with the Dawn Flame of the Amaranths.

At her side, Maelduin, watching her covertly, understanding her feelings, thought: within her eyes is the thin bright flame of the ancient Amaranth power, and at her beck are the spells and the enchantments, and all the inherited learning and force of Ireland's Royal Sorcerers; the magical, mystical enchantments from the far-away days when Tara was created by the sorcerer-architects who poured magic into the land as easily as if they were pouring water from one jug to another. And she is the hereditary ruler of her House . . . A smile curved his lips, and the light that shone in his slanting eyes was not entirely cool any longer.

She will brook no interference; she will have her own ideas and she will have her own ways, and she will be strong and she will depend on no one.

But I believe that, between us, we could rule both worlds, he thought. *Between us, we could do it . . .*

Could I do it? he thought suddenly. *Could I really abandon Tiarna and my people? Embrace the world of the Humanish, not just for a time, but for ever?*

It had never been done. But that did not mean it could not be done.

The grin touched his lips again. *Because if I can do it,* he thought, *if I can but restore my people and return to them the stolen music, if I can find a way to wear the Humanish Enchantment for ever, then together Theodora and I could blend two magical peoples and make Ireland far stronger and far greater than ever in her history . . .*

The grin deepened, and together they rode into the sunlight, the Crown Prince of the ancient underwater empire of Tiarna, shining with the gentle sea magic of his people; and, at his side, the Amaranth sorceress, the exiled heiress, the captive Princess, returning to Ireland's Royal House.

Both of them going home.

Epilogue

The legendary Tapestry Enchantment, later called the Unfinished Spell, and later still called, quite inaccurately, Amaranthian Nights, was not added to until several years after the sorceress Rumour's death.

They had all been so busy, said the Amaranths firmly, emerging blinking into the world again. When you had been under the *Draoicht Suan* for so many years, never mind how planned it might have been, there was a great deal to be done when you came out of it. There were stray enemies still to be dealt with, and there was the re-Sealing of all the Gateways. Neit and Manannan mac Lir had taught them a useful spell or two for that, they said, and might, perhaps, be pardoned for allowing a note of pride to creep into their voices when they referred to this camaraderie with a brace of gods. And then, of course, there had to be a proper ceremony for Theodora to take her Solemn Vows. All these things took time and energy. They also took money, although Cerball did not say this, or at least not more than once a week.

And so the Tapestry Enchantment lay, for many years, not entirely forgotten, but ignored, until the Amaranth, Theodora, studying the Cadence with delight, rediscovered it and ordered it to be spun for the occasion of her wedding, and the entertainment of the wedding guests.

And so the Silver Looms of Theodora's great-grandfather, Nechtan, were powered, so that Theodora might add her own story to her cousin's marvellous, mystical spell.

The Enchantment had lost nothing in the keeping, for Rumour, the most extravagant, certainly the most brilliant of all the brilliant Amaranths, had spun it thoroughly and well, and it had been protected by the silver-tipped pages of the Cadence. It had not lost any of its power to charm; when it was unrolled by

Theodora in the banqueting hall of the Porphyry Palace before the assembled guests, it was as dazzlingly beautiful and as enthralling as it had been on the long-ago night that Rumour had summoned it for the Lord of Chaos's dark banquet.

Theodora came to stand at the Enchantment's pouring centre, and in front of them all, spun effortlessly and immaculately her own chapter to add to her aunt's magical Tapestry.

It was a chapter that told of how she and the *sidh* Prince had ridden into the heart of the slumbering Porphyry Palace, and how they had had to break through the thickthorn hedges and the wild briars that had grown up around it. It told of how they had walked together, hand in hand through the silent Palace, Maelduin sprinkling the cool, elvish light of his people, Theodora chanting the awakening spell that would dissolve the gossamer cords of the *Draoicht Suan*.

It told of Theodora's own sojourn inside the Dark Realm and, later, the strange, Veiled years in the legendary Grail Castle . . .

It told of the intricate, intensely powerful enchantment finally spun by the *sidh*: the pure, beautiful Cloak of Humanish that Maelduin had donned and that had enabled him to live in the Humanish world as easily and as naturally as he also lived in Tiarna, under the Elven King's strong, but occasionally tolerant rule.

But best of all, it told, in whirling blue and green, in silver-threaded, light-filled beauty, of how Theodora had travelled to Tiarna, the first Amaranth ever to be permitted entry. And of how she and the Prince had gone to the Silver Cavern, the precious beautiful music of the *sidh* held between them, and had laid it before the Elven King.

And for a moment, for a spell-binding, breath-taking moment, within the great silver and gold and crimson pageantry of the Tapestry, the entire chiaroscuro vision unfolded.

The soaringly beautiful Silver Cavern, with the immense glacier rocks, and the smudges of blue and green, and the occasional glimpse of huge, iridescent wings . . .

And then the change: the colours seeping gradually, imperceptibly into the pale rock walls as the *sidh* were drawn back, the threads of turquoise veining the pale air, the silver and ivory and pearl becoming bathed in pure jewel colours . . .

And then, on the edges of hearing, on the outermost rim of perception, the tiniest stir of sound, the merest thread of something moving, something ruffling the still surface... Music, fragile and brittle and achingly sweet, creeping into the Cavern, lying on the air in soft, cobweb strands.

And then the final and scaldingly beautiful awakening of the *sidh*; the joyful sound of wings, hundreds of them beating on the air, until the Silver Cavern was a whirling kaleidoscopic maelstrom: blues and greens and purples and turquoises and indigos; the cool sea-colours of the ancient magical *sidh*; Maelduin's people, the strange creatures who hunted the Humanish for sport and stole away their senses, but who were also bound by fierce ties to Ireland's Royal Houses, and would never fail to answer a summons for help...

And Theodora at the centre of it, Maelduin at her side, in the midst of the shining, joyful whirlpool; while, on the great Silver Throne of the *nimfeach*, at last, after the years of his own dark bondage, the Elven King opened his eyes and looked straight at them.

And if, in the end, Maelduin never became quite entirely Humanish, there were very few people in Ireland who would have wanted him to. And if Theodora never quite lost the habit of laughing during solemn ceremonies, there were very few people who would have wanted her to be any different either.

As Rumour had once said, 'If you cannot be remembered with a smile, then it is better not to be remembered at all.'

ROGER TAYLOR

Author of the epic fantasy FARNOR

VALDEREN

Chilled and cowed by the violent fate of Garren and Katrin Yarrance and the mysterious disappearance of Farnor, the villagers can only stand by helpless as Rannick, increasingly unstable, and with his terrifying powers growing daily, turns his ambitions towards the land beyond the valley.

But in the wake of the plunder and the captives brought in triumph to the castle by Nilsson and his men, confident and arrogant again, comes a shadow from their past...

Meanwhile, in the Great Forest, Farnor has survived his flight from Rannick's ancient and unholy companion with the help of the Valderen. But his soul is consumed with anger and hatred, and an overwhelming lust for vengeance darkens all future paths. Despite their care, the Valderen fear him.

As do they to whom the Great Forest truly belongs. For they sense the power that he unknowingly possesses.

FICTION/FANTASY   0 7472 4149 X

A selection of bestsellers
from Headline

THE WINGED MAN	Moyra Caldecott	£5.99 ☐
COLD PRINT	Ramsey Campbell	£5.99 ☐
THE DOLL WHO ATE HIS MOTHER	Ramsey Campbell	£4.50 ☐
SIGN FOR THE SACRED	Storm Constantine	£5.99 ☐
ANGELS	Steve Harris	£5.99 ☐
THE FUNHOUSE	Dean Koontz	£4.99 ☐
OUT ARE THE LIGHTS	Richard Laymon	£4.99 ☐
SAVAGE	Richard Laymon	£4.99 ☐
ELEPHANTASM	Tanith Lee	£4.99 ☐
THE REVELATION	Bentley Little	£4.99 ☐
THE HOLLOW MAN	Dan Simmons	£4.99 ☐
VALDEREN	Roger Taylor	£4.99 ☐

All Headline books are available at your local bookshop or newsagent, or can be ordered direct from the publisher. Just tick the titles you want and fill in the form below. Prices and availability subject to change without notice.

Headline Book Publishing PLC, Cash Sales Department, Bookpoint, 39 Milton Park, Abingdon, OXON, OX14 4TD, UK. If you have a credit card you may order by telephone – 0235 831700.

Please enclose a cheque or postal order made payable to Bookpoint Ltd to the value of the cover price and allow the following for postage and packing:
UK & BFPO: £1.00 for the first book, 50p for the second book and 30p for each additional book ordered up to a maximum charge of £3.00.
OVERSEAS & EIRE: £2.00 for the first book, £1.00 for the second book and 50p for each additional book.

Name ....

Address ....

....

....

If you would prefer to pay by credit card, please complete:
Please debit my Visa/Access/Diner's Card/American Express (delete as applicable) card no:

Signature .... Expiry Date ....